Chro...

Tren Steggell

Kydrëa

Fissures of Auk

Kac'Lunc
Wolfenaven
Kr'Ra

Cryos

Nayu
Duulin

Haakviid Ocean

Shjävalk
Sverlta
Thyre
Faldin
Xagar Mountains
Fenn
Cape Auda
Cyos Run
In'Gor River
Zòl Kyden
Dawngôr
Raulek

Gai'Lagon

Miles
0   250   500   750

This is a work of fiction. Names, characters, places, and incidents either are the products of the author's imagination or are used fictitiously. Any resemblance to actual persons, living or dead, businesses, companies, events, or locales is entirely coincidental.

Text copyright © 2024 Tren Steggell
Jacket art copyright © 2024 Tren Steggell
Illustrations copyright © 2024 Tren Steggell

All rights reserved. No part of this publication may be reproduced, distributed, or transmitted in any form or by any means, including photocopying, recording, or other electronic or mechanical methods, without the prior written permission of the author, except in the case of brief quotations embodied in critical reviews and certain other noncommercial uses permitted by copyright law.

kyneofkydrea.wixsite.com/mysite
Instagram: @thelegendofkyne
Facebook: The Legend of Kyne

SUMMARY: Kyne is cast through time and events are undone while old and new enemies emerge.

ISBN-9798325444418

Printed in the United States of America
2024

Chronocide is set in the world of Kydrëa in which elements of war, fighting, occasional adult language, murder, blood, imprisonment, dismemberment, burning, and other forms of intense action and violence are portrayed throughout this story

---

For my wife Rachal, the Auriel to my Kyne

Pronunciation guidelines
ah is a soft a sound such as in the word tall
eh is a soft e sound such as in the word epic
ih is a soft i sound such as in the word ill
uh is a soft u sound such as in the word luck
oo is a soft o sound such as in the word food
au is a hard o sound such as in the word ouch
ay is a hard a sound such as in the word say
ee is a hard e sound such as in the word see
ai is a hard i sound such as in the word time
oh is a hard o sound such as in the word go
zhj is a strange one, like a sh sound but deep, almost making a j sound simultaneously, French j sound

Pronunciation Guide: Names

Alamere – ahl-uh-meer
Aaldra – ahl-druh
Aera – ee-ruh
Aeris – ehr-ihs
Aidon – ay-duhn
Akami – uh-cah-mee
Alai – uh-lai
Alderiun – ahl-dehr-ee-uhn
Aria – ahr-ee-uh
Ariov – ehr-ee-ahv
Armon – ahr-mun
Arpri – ahr-pree
Auriel – ah-ree-ehl
Aute – ah-oo-tay
Aya – ai-uh
Breyanne – bray-an

Eldunaga – ehl-doo-nah-guh
Elucia – eh-loo-see-uh
Emrys – ehm-rihss
Enotach – ee-noh-tahk
Enyk – ee-nihk
Findel – fihn-dehl
Garet – ger-eht
Hayame – hai-yah-may
Heitrite – heet-rite
Ilana – ih-lah-nuh
Inaba – ih-nuh-buh
Iterasu – ih-ter-ah-soo
Jaren – jehr-ehn
Jcobe – j-kohb
Jezzi – jeh-zee
Jurnen – jur-nehn

Kioni – kee-oh-nee
Kitsune – kiht-soo-nay
Kyne – kine
Liam – lee-uhm
Lioné – lee-oh-nay
Marok – mah-rahk
Mizu – mee-zoo
Lily – lih-lee
Lycas – lai-cuhs
Lurdoc – ler-dahk
Nahonian – nah-hohn-ee-uhn
Ni'Bara – nai-bar-uh
Nyloc – nai-lahk
Orichite – or-ih-kite
Pretarch of Avalk – pree-tark of uh-vahlk
Roco – roh-coh
Rosé – roh-zay
Saathe – sah-th

Seri – seh-ree
Shjilo – zhjai-loh
Soriah – sor-ai-uh
Suka soo-kuh
Tayvel – tay-vehl
Theo – thee-oh
Thirak – thai-rack
Thraepos – thray-pohs
Tiernyn – teer-nehn
Tira – tih-ruh
Umbra – uhm-bruh
Vira – vai-ruh
Voira – voy-ruh
Voron – vor-ehn
Voara – voh-ahr-uh
Windra – wihn-druh
Yu – yoo
Zawiet – zah-weet

Pronunciation Guide: Locations

Agar – ay-gar
Ak Dorme – ack dorm
Ak Runor – ack roon-or
Althaz – ahl-thaz
Alakyne – al-uh-kine
Asmathen – az-math-ehn
Auk – ah-ook
Cape Auda – cape ah-oo-duh
Cryos – cree-ohs
Cynor – sai-nor
Dawngôr – dahn-gore
Delük – dehl-ook
Duulin – doo-lihn
Faldîn – fahl-deen
Feout – fee-oht
Gaeil – gah-eel
Gai'Lagon – gai-luh-gahn
Guelok Lokóna – gway-lock loh-koh-nuh
Haakviid – hahk-veed
Hohen – hoh-hehn
Ilora – ih-lor-uh
Iterasu – ih-tehr-ah-soo
Izal – ai-zahl
Kae'Lum – kay loom
Kaerav – kay-rahv
Karstead – car-stehd
Ki'Rai – kee-rai

Kol Faldîn – cohl fahl-deen
Kunok – koo-nock
Kydrëa – kai-dray-uh
Linala – lihn-ahl-uh
Loke' Ynen – lohk een-ehn
Narok – nar-ahk
Neuiron – nee-yur-ahn
Otoruh – oh-tor-oo
Raulok – rou-lock
Riigar – ree-gar
Riigona – ree-goh-nuh
Sickalth – si-kahlth
Shjavalk – zhjuh-vahlk
Svertha – sverth-uh
Ta'Ak – tah-ack
Ta'Gor – tah-gore
Tor'Kar – tor-cahr
Tsora – sor-uh
Thyre – thair
U'Res – oo-rehz
Velik – veh-lihk
Venïk – vuh-neek
Wolfehaven – wohlf-hayvehn
Xagar – zay-gar
Xinwei – zihn-way
Ysaroc – ee-suh-rahk
Zol Kyden – zohl kai-dehn

Pronunciation Guide: Spells

Aerysil — ehr-ih-sihl
Aira tar – ah-ee-rah tar
Altyne kin fel – al-tine keen fehl
Altyne ulkin – al-tine ool-keen
Asira – ah-see-ruh
Aven igni – ay-vehn ihg-nee
Avenseiose – ay-vehn-say-ohs
Cligen – clai-jehn
Cri'oar – cree-or
Destikon – deh-stai-cuhn
Dohvav – doh-vahv
Eitala nuname –ee-tah-luh noo-nuh-may
Erodath – ehr-oh-dahth
Etoch – ee-tahk
Gihta – gee-tah
Igathion – ih-gay-thee-ahn
Ilumace– ih-loo-mahs
Ilumace beor – ih-loo-mahs bee-or
Ilumace bial– ih-loo-mahs bee-ahl
Ilumace lho– ih-loo-mahs loh
Kaiodin – kai-oh-deen
Kitala – kee-tahl-uh
Linguas – ling-oo-ahs
Mar'bi tan – mar-bee tahn
Mar'bi fos – mar-bee fahs
Novuk – noh-vook
Oo'nar – oo-nahr
Oo'nar ek ato – oo-nar ek ah-toh
Orus – oh-roos
Otri – oh-tree
Raicun - rai-coon
Rik'tar – rihk-tahr

Aural Strike
Ball lightning
Be seen and heard
Be unseen
Heal
Warp
Warp the summoned
Calm
Form ice
Swallow light
Crush
Retrieve what was hidden
Force
Shield
Straighten
Ignite
Light
Bright light
Flashing light
Following light
Stop
Retrieve
Understand
Disintegrate earth
Flowing earth
Explode
Move air
Swirl air
Rise
Enter
Shatter
Bend lightning

Roe'gar – roh-gahr	Create fire
Roke – rohk	Break
Seioin - say-oh-ihn	Summon and see
Seiose – say-ohs	Summon trail
Sei'var – say-var	Control water
Sekri – seh-cree	Cut
Sen sytori – sen sih-tor-ee	Lance
Simdath – sihm-dahth	Force wave
Sital – sih-tahl	Down
Thu'mar – thoo-mahr	Shape earth
Thu'mar deor – dee-or	Liquify earth
Tor kinala – tor kee-nah-luh	Camouflage
Uantum – oo-an-tum	Gateway
Vae dynori – vay dihn-or-ee	Raise and sustain
Varme – vahr-may	Warm
Vertai – vehr-tai	Divert
Vly – vlai	Focus
Y'vinu – ee-vih-noo	Pull

Weapons

Arrow – A small piece of wood with a sharp metal tip. Used as a projectile.
Ballista – massive artillery weapon, giant crossbow.
Bow – A piece of wood bent with a string. Used to launch projectiles such as an arrow.
Caestus – leather hand wraps with iron studs that rest against the users knuckles. Causes severe damage with standard punches.
Crossbow – a mechanical bow like weapon, used to fire bolts with a trigger.
Dagger – A small piece of sharpened steel. Used for quick stabs and cuts.
Dao – wide and curved short sword.
Escrima – short wooden sticks used for blunt damage. As long as a short sword. Usually in pairs.
Glaive – A curved sword at the end of a long staff. Used as a very efficient long-range weapon.
Kama – A sickle shaped blade mounted into a handle a little over one foot long with broadheads on the pommel. Usually in pairs.
Katana – slightly curved single edged sword.
Kunai – small dagger like blade with a ring on its end. Used for close combat as well as being thrown.
Sword – A double edged piece of sharpened steel. Used as a standard weapon for soldiers.
Spear – A long pole with a sharp iron tip. Used for long range thrusting attacks.
Stave – a staff made usually of wood adorned with a sorcerer's catalyst.

Species and peoples in The Legend of Kyne

Human
Dwarf
Kydrëan
Gaeilian
Iterasun
Windra
Otoruhn
Riel
Dragon
Eldercobra
Roc
Leviathan
Ethereal

Faori
Nyloc
Reaper
Wraith
Faldîn carniverous birds
Ryucus
Golem
Sea creature of the Aera ocean
Wyvern
Lurdoc
Seraph

Part 1: DISPARITY

1. THE TIPPING OF THE SCALE — 1
2. WHEN AM I? — 12
3. TEMPEST — 22
4. THE HUNTING OF A SHADE — 35
5. THE KING'S ARCHIVE — 46
6. TO POKE A SLEEPING DRAGON — 61
7. AKAMI — 74
8. PRETARCH OF AVALK — 87
9. TOWARD KYDRËA'S CROWN — 95
10. THE RELIC OF YSAROC — 99
11. SEEKING OUT A MYTH — 112
12. THE WIND AND THE ROSE — 126
13. MANGROVES AND GUELOKS — 132
14. THE WILTED FLOWER — 144
15. FRIENDS OF AN OLD WAR — 156
16. ASTRAY AMONG THE MALEFIC — 164
17. WHAT HAS BEEN HIDDEN BENEATH — 177
18. EMBODIMENT OF DEATH — 181

Part: 2 UNWIND

19. UNWARRANTED KINDNESS — 193
20. SPEED OF THE INABA — 203
21. FROM THE EAST — 209
22. HERESY — 212
23. FLAME OF THE SETTING SUN — 217
24. MIRRORS — 221
25. THE PATH TO HELL IS PAVED WITH GOOD INTENTIONS — 235
26. WOULD YOU LIKE YOUR TEA WITH VENOM OR HONEY — 242
27. FACADES — 247
28. AN UNEXPECTED ALLY — 251
29. BOUND AND DIVIDED — 263
30. RECKLESS TEENS — 279
31. THE CENTER OF EVERYTHING — 284
32. THE LORD OF THE DOMINION — 290
33. A FATAL DISCOVERY — 301
34. SHATTER — 308

Part 3: FRACTURE

- 35. STRANDED — 317
- 36. SLUDGE — 324
- 37. THE HOST OF WINDRA — 335
- 38. LOOKING OVER THE PRECIPICE — 345
- 39. WELCOME TO THE NEW WORLD — 351
- 40. LET US SEE IF YOU REMEMBER WHO YOU ARE — 356
- 41. CAST TO THE EDGE OF DESPAIR — 362
- 42. A LEAD — 367
- 43. THE CHILDREN OF THE PAST — 383
- 44. BITTER COLD — 389
- 45. DWINDLING AURA — 393
- 46. RUINS OF ALAKYNE — 399
- 47. DRACONIC — 402
- 48. THE CURSE OF THE CHILD — 415
- 49. THOSE WHO WANDER THE ROADS OF KYDRËA — 420
- 50. THE LEGEND — 428
- 51. THE SORCERESS OF TSORA — 433
- 52. A COLD NIGHT — 449
- 53. POTATOES — 460
- 54. FLASH — 472
- 55. A FRIEND OR A FOE — 477
- 56. A DEAL — 483
- 57. AN ILLUSION OF ALLIANCE — 494
- 58. A LITTLE FRIEND — 504
- 59. TIERNYN OF TSORA — 508
- 60. FEAST AND SUSPICIONS — 517
- 61. TRIALS AND TEMPTATIONS — 521
- 62. A CHANCE OF ESCAPE — 530
- 63. THE LAST NIGHT — 538
- 64. TO FINALLY SPEAK — 549
- 65. SEARCHING FOR THE DAWN — 559
- 66. THE FOURTH — 571
- 67. THE SWEETNESS OF A PASTRY — 575
- 68. MR. TADPOLE — 582
- 69. PESTILENCE — 591
- 70. UNDER THE VEIL OF BEAUTY — 597
- 71. REMOVING THORNS — 603
- 72. TO RISK EVERYTHING FOR A CHILD — 611
- 73. DIVINE CONNECTIONS — 619
- 74. MIST AND SEAFOAM — 623

75. AUTE — 632
76. XEONO — 641
77. TO BLOOM IN THE WIND — 653
78. OUT OF SIGHT BUT NOT OUT OF MIND — 661
79. A BOY OR A GOD — 671
80. A HARROWING REVELATION — 676
81. BACK TO WHERE HE STARTED — 680
82. ETHEREAL FLAME — 685
83. FAMILY — 691
84. ONE FINAL STEP — 696
85. A SORCERER'S SYMPHONY — 710
86. DRAGONSOUL — 724
87. THE CARETAKER — 733

"Then today a god falls!" snarled Ni'Bara and flames appeared between his fangs.

Part 1: Disparity

The Legend of Kyne: Chronocide

1. The Tipping of the Scale

A flash of light caught Kyne's eye and he ducked out of the way just as a blast of aura ripped through the air. The tingle of energy crept across his skin like fire across water and he could feel the hairs on his arms singe away. Twisting hard, he drove his foot into the ground, regaining his balance before launching his own attack back.

Shining bright, even in the glow of the setting sun, the energy hurtled through the air leaving a trail of sparkling energy like that of a comet. Approaching the attacker, the aura cast its bright light all around creating long distorted shadows as it rocketed towards its destination. Moments before his aura connected, a loud crack sounded and it redirected, launching far to the side in a violent flash of light.

"Too slow," panted a deep raspy voice nearby and Kyne just narrowly dodged a swing of a man's fist as it sailed through the air.

"Not quite," he replied and dropping down low, he swung the back of his leg around and into the attacker's own, knocking him over in a sweeping motion.

The man grunted loudly as the wind was knocked out of him, but Kyne paid it no attention. Swinging his own gaze back, he was just able to recognize another incoming attack moments before it struck.

"Kaiodin!" he yelled and suddenly the attack froze midflight. Orange in color, but radiating almost like an ember from a flame, the attack pulsated as he tried to hold it back. Incredibly powerful, he could feel his hold on it star to slip. He couldn't hold it forever! The power was too intense and quickly draining his aura! Stepping to the side, he released his hold and the attack continued on its trajectory, flying past him a few dozen yards before slamming into the trunk of a tree.

"That was close," he panted as he scanned around the area. Two others were nearby, seemingly paying them no attention while a

The Legend of Kyne: Chronocide

short man rose to his feet coughing and trying to catch his breath.

Kyne took a quick inhalation as his mind ran through all the possibilities. He was fighting on the defensive but now it was his time to act!

Dashing low, he rapidly approached the shorter man at a quick speed, but moments before they collided, he felt the ground give underneath him and panic raced through his mind. It was hard to move and with each step he could feel the ground giving away underneath him as if he were walking upon the softest cotton. As his momentum slowed, he realized what was happening! He could feel the hum of energy in the air and just as he turned to look, a blast of aura struck him hard in the chest, knocking him off his feet.

He crashed hard upon the ground, laying there for a long moment dazed and out of breath. His mind was foggy and his vision dark around its edges as he tried to gather himself. Rolling over onto his hands and knees he took a shuddering breath and felt the frustration and anger wash over his being. *This fight isn't over yet!* roared his mind as he stood up to his full height.

"Roe'gar," he whispered under his breath and as the pull of aura left his body, he dropped down low and swept his foot through the air. A jet of flame erupted from his sole, spreading like a disk of fire and causing cries of shock to erupt from the short man.

Kyne grinned, he knew the fire wouldn't burn him, it was but a mere distraction.

Leaping forward just as the flames died down, he watched as his target came into view an arm's length away. With his arm drawn back, he sailed his fist through the air, eyes drilled upon the edge of the man's jaw.

"Erodath!"

A massive force struck into Kyne, and he was thrown to the ground, coughing and gasping for breath. Dirt and twigs littered his hair and arms, staining his skin dark and red from countless scrapes. He tumbled to a stop, panic racing through his mind as his abdomen quivered, unable to draw in the oxygen his body craved.

"I ca... I... I can't breathe..." he gasped while he crawled to his hands and knees. His mind was racing as he tried to catch his breath. The panic of suffocating taking a hold and clenching down upon his mind. Nausea was setting in deep in his gut and before he could stop

The Legend of Kyne: Chronocide

himself, he threw up, the rotten acidic taste burning his throat as he quivered for breath.

A hand was felt on his shoulder and a voice spoke, "Breathe Kyne, slow deep breaths. Your diaphragm is spasming. You have to calm it down if you wish to breathe."

"I... I'm trying," he panted out and his head dropped low as he stared at his chest quivering.

The hand moved down and touched his abdomen right under his ribs and the voice spoke again. "Feel it right here."

Kyne concentrated and felt the presence of the hand on his abdomen. He could feel the quivering slow and his breathing grew easier. A few long moments passed, and he gasped a deep breath of relief.

"What was that for Voron?" he glared as he looked up at the older man who was kneeling beside him.

"You let your guard down Kyne. By switching to a more ambitious role as attacker, you forgot there was more than one opponent. You seemed hellbent on attacking Thirak when you should have been engaging all parties in the fight. Your attack left you wide open for my own."

"Ai," said Thirak as he reached his hand out and helped Kyne to his feet. "I agree with Voron. Switching to the offensive is just as important as defending, but you need to be more observant of everything that is going on. As for myself," the dwarf chuckled. "I am quite glad you made that mistake. I was not in the mood to get punched by you."

Thirak's words made Kyne smile slightly as he was helped up to his feet. They all went back over to the campfire and took a seat next to the other two figures who had been nearby. Goliath and Queidn were discussing plans for when they reached Guelok Lokóna in a few days and what was to be expected.

The sky was the red of rust and streaks of golden pink raked through the clouds above in tassels of color. The hum of the night insects was starting to begin, and Kyne coughed as he tenderly touched his chest. He knew it was bruised but not too bad. His ego was bruised more than anything else.

"Finished with your training for the evening?" asked Selim as he and Meko approached from the tree line. Across their backs they

The Legend of Kyne: Chronocide

had a few small animals and fish connected to a thin rope. Their dark skin was glistening with the sweat of their labors and their jet-black hair was beginning to fall out of their braids.

"Training him is getting harder and harder Voron," laughed Thirak. "I don't know how much more I can take of being pummeled day in and day out."

"Impressive," said Meko as he sat down, his hands already prying off the first of his two muddy boots. "Maybe Selim and I will have to have a go against him one of these days."

"Bring it on," laughed Kyne lightly before he clutched his bruised chest. Every breath caused a dull aching pain to flow through his ribs.

"He is making leaps in his progress," Voron said turning towards Kyne. "But just like today, you failed to see the bigger picture. Every action that you take has a consequence. Some minor and some much larger than you might even realize at the time. You must strive to take a moment to think. Even the quickest of moments during a battle can change a defeat into a victory. Take these moments and try to imagine the consequences of your actions."

"The consequences of your actions," Kyne murmured to himself as he opened his eyes, the memory drifting back into his mind where he locked it up tight. He sighed as he ran his hand through his hair. "How am I to always look for the consequences?"

The light from around was bright, but as his eyes quickly adjusted, he rose to his feet. Dressed in a white shirt and shorts that matched, the archmage of Tsora looked just like any other common Kydrëan. His golden hair and eyes reflecting the ancient common trait of his people made that obvious, but what would have caught people's attention would have been his left arm.

Covered from up on his shoulder all the way down to each fingertip were grey dragon scales, each sharp and flat against one another like the shingles of a house. Upon his fingertips were pearly white claws nearly an inch long.

The strange catalyst that he had received when his aura combined with Ni'Bara's own. In a powerful reaction, he was transformed. Gifted the aura of a dragon, as it melded with his own it

The Legend of Kyne: Chronocide

created something far more powerful than the sum of its parts. Something unique and full of mystery.

Kyne stared at his open palm before clenching it, the scales on his forearm rippling as the powerful muscle beneath contracted and relaxed. Reaching with his human hand, he ran a single finger with the scales for a moment, feeling the warm steel like hardness before changing directions. As it ran against the scales, he felt the very outer surface of his skin scrape off as if he were rubbing the roughest sandpaper.

He still didn't have all the answers as to why his catalyst had taken this form, but he did have a few ideas. Ever since he traveled to the world of the Riel and Dragon and learned of the history of all the races, he had finally had some light shed upon it. For some reason, the fusing of two different races aura had created something very unique and powerful.

He lowered his hands down and looked out of the room he was in towards a large balcony. Beyond, he could see a hazy blue light accompanied by fog like clouds high above. As he walked out of the room onto the ledge and took a deep breath, he looked upon a magnificent sight for below, lay the city of Voara, named after the seraph of humanity.

The beautiful city was built straight into the ancient everlasting tree that lay hidden within the Sea of Cinder. Thousands of feet above him were branches wider than city streets and adorned with millions of verdant leaves.

Looking over the ledge, he followed the trail of buildings as they arced down the side of the tree. The city growing denser the further down it went as it made its way towards the sea below. Everything from the buildings to the roads themselves had been etched out of the stone like wood that was the trunk of the great tree.

Hundreds of people were seen, dotting the city streets below and he smiled as his vision continued on. The further down towards the large cavern that had been carved into the tree, the more people he could see. Down nearly two thousand feet the city stretched until it reached the dark sea. Small ships dotted the water nearby and a few had set sail, traveling out into the great expanse of the Sea of Cinder.

So much had changed since he had returned to his own world. Great things were happening, and he couldn't be prouder of them. The

5

The Legend of Kyne: Chronocide

city of Voara had been abandoned longer than any records or stories have lasted. The city of some of the first people to walk the earth was a priceless gem that had just been rediscovered. He understood the necessity of keeping Tsora the pristine sorcerer school of the country, but he also knew that aura was knowledge that could be easily lost if people forgot its teachings and practices.

Auriel had shown him that to her own people, aural manipulation was like walking and talking. It was a necessity that kept their culture going. When they had returned after nearly a year of being gone, Kyne had finally decided that many things needed to change.

He approached King Theo with that very motive. Everyone in the country that is not of a criminal background should be allowed to learn aura. Everyone who wanted to were urged to travel to certain checkpoints and make their way to this city under the land. Here, some of Tsora's top sorcerers would help teach basics to the people and they would start to implicate aural manipulation into their day to day lives.

At first it seemed like it might not work. People were hesitant on leaving their lives behind, but loners, people who had no family after the Dominion's occupation, or Kydrëans who wanted to accept the challenge began to make their way. Surprisingly, thousands seemed to flock to the city in search of knowledge and it quickly started to boom.

Kyne looked down over the city towards the docks and could just make out some boats were arriving presumably with supplies. They were able to farm most of their crops within the Sea of Cinder. Its warm mineral rich water was perfect for the plants and after finding a few small islands, they started to farm. With the warm climate and the consistent light, the plants erupted and quickly made their way onto the Kydrëan's tables where they would be crafted into lovely meals. What few things they still needed were shipped in from the outside. The city of Voara was nearly self-sustaining and Kyne couldn't be much happier.

"It is getting late," he muttered to himself as he left the edge of the balcony. Making his way into his room, he grabbed a small black knapsack with a silver ouroboros and his scabbard where the blade Aurora lay, and he approached a small painting of a dragon scale.

Running his hand over the surface, he could feel the pull of something hidden there and with a deep breath, forced his own aura

The Legend of Kyne: Chronocide

into it. A ring of energy swelled into existence and beyond he could see his room in Tsora. It was empty but the sun outside was casting an orange glow through the window.

He smiled at the sight and the ease in which traveling had become. So much knowledge had been shared from Auriel and he had only just begun.

With a little leap, he dashed through the ring before releasing his aura and it snapped back closed leaving Voara behind.

Kyne placed his things down neatly on his bed before leaving his room and heading down through the building and finally out onto the grassy field of Tsora. All the classes seemed to have come to a close, but the field was not bare. Dozens of students lay spread out talking or studying together. Some were dueling with wooden weapons while others were playing some game with unique items. Towards the edge of the field a flash of pink and grey caught his eye.

"Auriel," called Kyne as he jogged over to the beautiful Riel woman. Her silvery blonde hair lay over her shoulders in thick waves as she smiled at him. Dressed in her usual orichite laced shirt, it formed tight to her body and hung over a pair of black pants. She turned towards him and flashed a brilliant smile as his golden eyes met her blue.

"You are back!" called a squeaky feminine voice and a blur of pink leapt through the air and crashed into his chest knocking him to the ground.

"Rosé get off him," chuckled Auriel and the small rose gold dragon reluctantly clambered off him allowing him to sit up. "You are nearly as big as him. One of these days you might hurt him."

Kyne laughed as he rose to his feet.

"If she ever starts growing," rumbled Ni'Bara's voice as the dragon swung his head toward them all. "It's as if she just wants to stay small."

"That's mean Ni'Bara," cried Rosé in a fit and the grey dragon chuckled.

Looking at Rosé, Kyne was surprised at how fast she really had grown. They had only been back a little over year and she was already bigger than a large dog. She quite easily outweighed him, and he knew from his experience with Ni'Bara that she would continue to grow at an

The Legend of Kyne: Chronocide

exponential rate until she hit full size around her fourth year.

Everything well with Voara? spoke the grey dragon as he touched minds with Kyne.

Yeah, nothing really to say. Every time I go, I am needed less and less. Maybe one day I won't even need to go at all.

You could never do that, replied Ni'Bara and Kyne nodded his head as he took Auriel's hand in his own.

"How has Tsora been in my incredibly long absence?"

"Nearly burned down in the whole four hours you have been gone," she replied with a small sly smile.

"Probably these two rough housing again," laughed Kyne as he eyed Rosé and Ni'Bara.

"I am really good at my fire now look," said Rosé enthusiastically and a small jet of pink flame flew from her lips out over the grass, singeing the tops and leaving a smoldering line.

"Really good indeed," remarked Ni'Bara sarcastically and the pink dragon bumped his head with her tail.

They all laughed for a moment before Kyne said to Auriel, "Have you eaten yet?"

"Not yet but I bet there is some stuff in the dining hall for us. Let's go take a look."

As night enveloped the small island of mountains in the sea of trees, Kyne eventually found himself back up in his room getting ready for bed. Ni'Bara and Rosé were nearby in the dragon roost and Auriel was lying on the sheets in a beautiful silk nightgown.

Silvery white, the gown crept down from her shoulders before traipsing across her body to the tops of her thighs where it delicately rested. Her skin was smooth, silky and tan, and she pulled one leg up upon the other as she watched Kyne.

As he finished writing down a few notes on a parchment of paper, he sighed before stretching and turning to look at her. She beckoned for him to join her, and he smiled. Her beauty was unlike anything he had ever seen and every single day he grew more infatuated with her. The woman he had so recently married and vowed to spend the rest of his life with. His partner and love.

Climbing in bed, he slid next to her and ran his hand across her smooth thigh. Tracing it up, feeling her smooth skin, he brought it

The Legend of Kyne: Chronocide

underneath her gown where it rested upon the top of her hip against her waist. They met eyes for a long moment before his lips touched hers and with a wave of her hand the torchlight cast them in darkness.

    Kyne rolled over in bed and stretched his hand to find Auriel was not there. Shock flew through his mind temporarily as every conceivable bad thing flashed before him. Jolting, he sat up quickly and looked out the window. The stars had visibly changed their positions and he guessed he had been asleep for a few hours.

    He got up and looked in the bathroom and then out on the balcony but couldn't see her anywhere. Finally, he said, "Seiose," and a light aural haze appeared leading out of the room and downstairs.

    He followed Auriel's aural trail quietly throughout the building, through twists and turns and the further he went, the more certain he knew where she was. Located deep in the older sections of Tsora, where the old school resided lay a large black double door with aural symbols scrawled over its surface. He could feel his pulse quicken as he stared at the door. He knew exactly where it led and knew for certain Auriel was within.

    Pushing the door open, he stepped inside to be greeted by foggy figures forming around him. He could see the red bark of the trees near the Riel capital and could make out two children running around an outdoor table. The king and queen sat quietly watching with smiles and Auriel hovered behind them watching intently.

    "Try and catch me Auriel," cried a little boy's voice and he dashed out of the way of the other child's outstretched hand, up onto the table and over the food to his parent's dismay.

    "Sephriel get down," shouted the queen but the little boy paid no attention and he continued to play chase with his sister.

    Kyne made his way towards the real Auriel and placed his hand in her own. At his contact, she clamped her fingers tightly around his and embraced him with the images around fading away into the fog from which they came.

    "I miss them so much," she cried softly as tears streamed down her cheeks.

    Kyne placed his cheek on the top of her head and held her tightly. He knew how heartbroken she was about it. She had chosen to go with him and the two dragons and to leave her old life behind. She was happy at first, but he knew that it pained her every day that she couldn't see her family anymore.

He had tried so hard to make a way to get to her planet. He studied and perfected the portal spell but there was just no possible way to create one that could cover that distance. He hadn't found anything that could, but he would never stop trying. He wanted to do everything in his power to make her happy.

He had spoken to her before about the Room of Recollection, showed her what it was so that she could see her family sometimes, but more and more often he was finding her there reliving old memories. He could feel the danger that the room possessed. It was almost addicting to relive happy memories and he personally had to cut himself off completely from it or he could've fallen victim as well.

I will speak to her more about it in the morning, he thought to himself as he led her back towards their room. The air was soft and still as he sat on the edge of the bed, watching the steady breathing of Auriel as she slept. *I don't know what else to do Ni'Bara,* he said as he left the room and headed down out onto the grass field. *I am running out of options to research.*

As am I, the dragon replied. *I have studied the texts that I was given from the other dragons and have found nothing. I am not even sure if all the humans in Kydrëa united aura that it would be enough to link our worlds. She is, as far as I can tell, trapped here forever.*

Please don't say trapped, said Kyne softly. *I don't want to think of her as trapped here.*

Well... She isn't really trapped, Ni'Bara started, *she did volunteer to come here with us. More like she just isn't able to go back.*

The more you try to justify it, the more it sounds like trapped, said Kyne with irritation. *She is trapped here and there is nothing we can do to get her home.*

But is this not her home?

You know what I mean, Kyne started. *I just don't...*

His thoughts were suddenly interrupted by an incredible headache. The feeling of a spear pressing in upon all sides of his brain caused him to drop to his knees with a small cry.

Kyne? asked Ni'Bara and he flashed thoughts towards the dragon.

The Legend of Kyne: Chronocide

It's happening again!

Kyne forced his eyes open and looked at his arm in panic. He could see silhouettes of his arm, visually echoing behind like a trail of them. He took a stumbling step forward as he tried to stand up. The whole world around him seemed to be distorting as it shifted into different versions of itself.

His hands were no longer alone, hundreds of them identical in every way trailed his movements as he tried to stand but he fell again.

I can't stop it... Kyne's thoughts faded and then he was gone.

2. When am I?

The smell of summer hung in the air and Kyne could feel warm sunlight upon his back. The tickle of grass was felt across his face as he began to move. Groaning, he opened his eyes to see he was in Tsora, but not his Tsora. It was the Tsora of old, much smaller, and far less people. A small stone wall, more for decoration than anything, surrounded the area with a building situated against the steep mountainside beyond. Divided into three sections, the building contained all the sorcerers and their knowledge.

His head was still pounding but it was fading quite quickly. Throwing a glance around the area, he could see two unfamiliar sorcerers meditating nearby. No one had seen him yet and with a slight sigh of relief, he dashed out of the open area and dove headfirst over the wall that stood higher than a man's head. Sailing into the shadows of the nearby vegetation, he rolled over his shoulder and leapt to his feet in a sprint. Every footstep took him further away from Tsora as he pounded down the mountain slope before finally coming to a stop near a large bush. Crouching low, he pushed his way into its depths, the heat radiating off the leaves in waves.

Lying low, Kyne punched the ground in frustration and grit his teeth hard.

Why does this keep happening! roared his thoughts throughout his mind. He was scared. He hated to admit it, but he was. He knew where he was, but the true terror is, he didn't know *when* he was!

Ni'Bara! Kyne screamed with his mind as hard as he could, but all that replied was emptiness. He was alone in some long-lost time.

He could feel his breath quicken as adrenaline flooded his veins and he rubbed his hands onto his pants to try and dry his sweaty palms. He could feel it, all throughout his arms. The trembling that accompanied the adrenaline, the trembling that accompanied the fear

The Legend of Kyne: Chronocide

he was experiencing.

Taking a deep breath, he closed his eyes and tried to calm himself as much as he could.

"This has happened before. You will get back," he whispered, and he clasped his arms around his knees pulling them tight to his chest as he hid within the branches of the woodland bush.

Just as he went to say another thing to calm himself, he heard voices and clamped his mouth tight. He couldn't make out anything, just that it was two and they seemed to be growing nearer.

Do they know I am here?

He wasn't afraid of them in a fight, he knew that he could fend them off and could escape. The confidence in that area he attributed to his dragon aura. More specifically he attributed it to Ni'Bara's own confidence. Within certain situations he was grateful for it, but it did have its drawbacks and he didn't want his confidence to turn into arrogance. Arrogance could lead to recklessness, and recklessness often leads to mistakes.

The voices drew even louder and soon they were nearby. Straining, he could make out a few words. "Here... Training... Apprentice."

He shuffled through the branches, as slowly and quietly as he could, adjusting himself so that he could peer out and see where the voices were coming from. Through the gaps in the branches where sunlight was shining from above, he could make out two figures a few dozen feet away. Behind them lay a small waist high stone wall that marked the old trail to Tsora. Packs had been placed against it and Kyne could see a wooden staff leaning nearby.

The figures had their backs to him, making it hard for Kyne to see who they were so he sat and watched, hoping that they would turn and show their faces. It was hard for him to hear them, and he was worried about the use of aura. They would be able to sense it if he did anything to amplify their voices so he strained his ears as hard as he could.

One figure was small, a young boy around the age of fourteen Kyne guessed. He was certain it was a boy by the shape of his shoulders and how he walked, as well as his voice when Kyne caught glimpses of it.

The Legend of Kyne: Chronocide

The other figure was taller, but Kyne guessed not much older, probably near his own age. His hair was dark, and Kyne could see the sides of his jaw were covered with a thick trimmed beard.

He said something to the apprentice and the apprentice ran to one of the bags before returning with a large chunk of useless glass. When Kyne saw the boy's face, he could feel a slight familiarity but not very enlightening.

He looks familiar but it could just be one of those faces. I am not sure who he even looks like.

The person that Kyne assumed was the master held out his hand for the glass shard before using his aura to levitate it above his palm. It hung there, lightly drifting through the air in place casting shards of light throughout the area. Kyne shielded his eyes as the sunlight reflected towards him for a few seconds before it was gone.

More words were shared, and the boy aimed both palms at the shard and furrowed his brow in concentration. Kyne could see his mouth moving but he couldn't read his lips to figure out the spell.

Suddenly the shard of glass warped and shifted, spiraling into a double helix shape. As if made from moving water, the glass rippled and twirled around above the master's outstretched hand, glimmering brilliantly from the sun's light. As its shifting slowed and stopped, the master lowered it back into his palm and exclaimed to Kyne's complete and utter horror,

"Aaldra that was amazing! No one has mastered that skill so fast! It took me many months to do what you did in just a few moments!"

Kyne watched the young man's face and saw for a second a flash of bashfulness at the master's praise. Then it hit him. Aaldra was incredibly talented, but he was not initially wicked as a young boy. He seemed to be almost embarrassed by the pride and was incredibly humble. Kyne knew something eventually would change within him though. Obsession and lust for power would consume him and he would grow up to become a corrupt monster.

Kyne strained his ears as hard as he could while holding his breath trying to hear any words shared between the two of them.

"It is all because of your teaching," spoke the boy and the man chuckled.

The Legend of Kyne: Chronocide

"Do not be modest Aaldra. You have a gift. I just want to help you hone your skills and morph them into something that will help all the people of Kydrëa. Greatness is in your future. People will speak your name for decades after we are all gone."

"Indeed, they will," Kyne muttered to himself. "Just not in praise."

Straining hard to hear the apprentice's response, Kyne nearly gasped at what he heard as it all seemed to click.

"Thank you, Master Voron," replied Aaldra and the master chuckled before tossing the glass spiral to the ground and embracing the young man in a playful hug.

"What are we to do for the rest of our lesson today," said the young boy as he broke away from Voron.

"Well, I was expecting that to take you a little longer than two minutes, so I don't have anything else really in mind."

The young Aaldra laughed and took a few steps towards Kyne's bush before turning around. "How about you try and catch me?" In a flash, the boy took off in a sprint heading straight towards Kyne before arcing around him and continuing down the mountainside.

"Always with the running," grumbled Voron but Kyne could tell he was happy and enjoying himself as the young master ran after the boy.

Kyne had never seen Voron acting like this before, he seemed happy. Kyne felt a tug in his chest for a moment at the thought and he felt a little bit of jealousy towards Aaldra. Kyne had searched through Voron's memories that had been gifted to him and knew that at one point he trained Aaldra. He had discovered Aaldra was orphaned as a young boy and was trained by a few masters including Voron, but he avoided those memories as much as he could. He had moved past the trauma the man had caused him in Zol Kyden, but it was still a touchy area for him, and he tried to avoid it as much as possible.

Aaldra was the perfect student to Voron and watching them play brought sorrow to Kyne. He had never gotten to experience things like this with Voron. Most of the time was spent training towards the goal of freeing his people. They did have good times and Voron was like a father figure to Kyne, but from the looks of it, Voron was pretty much an actual father to the young and orphaned Aaldra.

The Legend of Kyne: Chronocide

The two of them were soon gone, running far down the path and Kyne could see them just as they crested a hill before being lost to his view. Another sorcerer and student, both unfamiliar walked down the path towards that way at a much calmer pace. Once they were out of sight, Kyne removed himself from the vegetation and stood up to his full height.

He knew that he was physically there in the past and he ran his hand along the bark of a tree. It wasn't just a memory like he had experienced before. It was too vivid and real.

But if I am truly here in the past, can my actions affect the future? Or is the future untouchable and already written? he thought to himself as he stooped down and picked up a small uneven stone. He had never really been able to test it and he thought maybe this would be the time to do it.

Using his aura, he inscribed a series of dots and lines on one edge of the stone. To anyone else, these markings would look natural, and no one would pay them any attention, but to him, he would be able to recognize them.

He placed the stone at the base of a nearby tree that he was certain still stood and then returned to the vegetation he had hidden in. Not a soul was around and he wasn't sure how much longer he would be in this time. Every time he was warped lasted longer and it was growing more and more difficult to get back.

Curiosity eventually got the best of him as he eyed the packs leaning against the waist high trail wall and he soon ventured over to them. Looking down the trail in both directions to make sure he would not be seen, he paused for a nervous moment before finally caving and turning towards the packs. He had suspected it and when he saw it he smiled, for there next to Aaldra's pack lay the Ouroboros Bag just as it looked in his day. Smiling, he knelt down and reached out his finger to trace the silver serpent.

As his finger connected with it, he felt the raging headache viciously return. It tore through him like a raging storm, and he could feel time warping around him again. Turning his head, he looked down the trail and saw it stretch away into oblivion with dozens and hundreds of his own body dotted along its length. He turned to look the other way and watched as hundreds more followed suit in a rippling

The Legend of Kyne: Chronocide

fashion as the sun in the sky flashed in and out of existence.

The headache intensified and he dropped to his knees and then suddenly it was gone. The sunlight had vanished, and the sky above was littered with twinkling stars. The trail that he had been standing on had been overgrown with plant life and webs of ivy dug deep into the crumbling stone wall. As he rose to his feet, he took a long sigh of relief.

Opening his eyes, he observed his surroundings. To his right, up the old trail he could see the three towers of Tsora silhouette against the star covered sky. He was back in his own time.

Auriel leaned against the side of a wall with her hands rubbing first her forehead and then her cheeks. Across her face were many emotions, but most prevalent were anger and fear. Kyne could see it in her eyes as he finished explaining what had happened to him and where he had disappeared to.

"So that's why your aural trail just vanished," she muttered to herself as she walked over to a chair and took a seat. "You were not even there anymore, literally in a different time. Why Kyne? Why didn't you tell me about this before?"

"I... I..." stammered Kyne as he racked his brain for the right words. It was so incredibly important now to think about everything he said before it was spoken. This could turn into a much bigger ordeal than it needed to be.

"You what?" she cried in frustration. "You have been leaping through time without telling your own wife?"

"It's just..." started Kyne but Auriel immediately interrupted.

"You told Ni'Bara though!" she raged.

"He didn't really tell me," rumbled Ni'Bara as he placed his eye in the doorway to their alcove. "We are connected Auriel and when it happened, I was already..." Ni'Bara's voice died away as Auriel threw the dragon a death glare.

"Auriel," Kyne said reaching out a hand and touching her arm. She immediately pulled away and turned her back towards him.

"I thought we were supposed to trust each other," she whispered. "I thought you could trust me with everything."

17

The Legend of Kyne: Chronocide

"I do trust you my love," he replied reaching his hand out again. "I wanted to see if I could get it under control but..."

"But what?"

"It is getting worse. I am not sure how much longer I will remain stable."

Those words erased all the anger from Auriel immediately and what was replaced was a look of true terror. "What do you mean? You're going to eventually leave our time and not be able to return?"

"I am not sure," said Kyne and he rose to his feet. "Honestly, I don't even know what is going on, why this is even happening. I don't even know if what I do in the past effects the future."

"How many leaps does this make Kyne," said Rosé as the dragon slipped around Ni'Bara and into their room.

"This was the third."

"Have you tested anything to see if it effects our time?" asked Auriel.

"It's a lot more complicated than that. Even a slight change could alter history in which I never find Ni'Bara, or worse, make it so that I am never born."

"That is true," the Riel princess murmured to herself as she furrowed her brow. "It may be best if you don't try and test it at this time. Maybe we can plan something that will keep the timeline intact."

The air was silent for a moment.

"About that," chuckled Kyne weakly. "I kind of already tested it."

Ni'Bara snorted in amusement and Auriel was struck with an appalled expression before relaxing and chuckling herself.

"Well, "she started, "What's done is done, I guess. What did you alter?"

"Nothing too serious," he smiled weakly. "Just your name Ni'Bara."

"What?" Roared the dragon in shock. "What was my name before?"

"Bi'Nara..." muttered Kyne and he looked at the ground for a moment trying as hard as he could to not smile.

"You can't be serious?" gasped Ni'Bara again.

"No, I'm not serious!" laughed Kyne and he smirked at

The Legend of Kyne: Chronocide

Ni'Bara. "But I did have you going for a little bit."

"Not funny," snarled the dragon and Auriel joined in on Kyne's laughter.

"I scrawled some markings onto a small stone, nothing that could be thought of as unnatural. I placed it at the base of a tree that I believe still stands outside of Tsora."

"Then let us go look for this stone. If we find it, then Kyne is indeed altering the timeline. If we do not, then..." Auriel's voice stopped.

"Something else may be happening that we don't have an answer for yet," said Kyne. "The sun should be rising soon. Let us go look for this stone and get closer to solving this problem."

They all left the room and were soon out on the grassy field of Tsora heading towards the main entryway. No students were awake yet and only a few sorcerers stood guard around the school, their dark robes keeping most of them hidden from sight. Exiting the gateway, they followed the path as it led down and out around a black glassy reflection of a lake. Halfway around it, Kyne turned off the trail and started to lead them down the mountain slope until they arrived at some old stone rubble.

The further they went, the more they started to notice that it was an old trail, grown over by vegetation and wildlife but a trail nonetheless. The waist high stone wall was to their right and the further they traveled, the more Kyne started to recognize where they were.

Most of the plants were different but the trees were almost identical in location, and most were larger than before. They soon found the spot where Voron and Aaldra had placed their packs down and all four of them ventured off the trail heading into a scattered group of trees.

Rosé was leaping around, bounding onto every tree base looking for a rock with energetic enthusiasm while the adults trudged on, each step giving them more and more anxiety. Ni'Bara was quite large, but the trees were far enough apart that he managed to make it through the gaps with little difficulty. Vegetation was crushed under his mass as he cautiously stepped around the largest of them. His tail flattened everything as it slid behind. Soon they were all staring at the tree Kyne was pointing at.

"It was here," he said, and he knelt down and ran his hand along a clump of moss that clung to the lower bark. The velvety softness was nice under his skin and as he traced the moss all the way down to the ground, he felt a lump underneath it.

A pit formed in his throat and slowly he dug his fingers through the moss and withdrew a small familiar stone. Holding it up to his eye, just as the sun started to peak up over the horizon casting its morning pink glow, he saw the marks. The same exact marks he had made all those years ago were there, upon the stone.

"What does it mean," he whispered as he met Auriel's eyes.

"I don't know Kyne. The things you do in the past do affect the future. One simple change could theoretically erase us all."

"Why is this happening to me," he murmured in despair as the stone fell from his hand and landed upon the forest floor, burying itself into the undergrowth.

"It's as if the world is no longer in balance," rumbled Ni'Bara. "With the death of the Darkness, maybe it is causing time to unwind and rip into fragments."

"That would explain why the Relics of Aute seem to help," said Kyne with realization. "When I touched the ouroboros bag in the past it helped send me back here."

"That must be it then," gasped Auriel. "We need to find more of them. Maybe having you come into contact can stabilize you."

"But where do we even find them? They are legendary items lost to the ages."

"You have two in your possession," said Ni'Bara. "And I know where a third lies."

"Xeono is staying right where it is," said Kyne fiercely. "It is too powerful for anyone to handle. I will be damned if I rely upon it like Aaldra did."

"We are not saying to use Xeono, just to have it in your possession," said Auriel. "No one would even know you had it except us."

"No!" said Kyne intensely. "I don't want it. I will find other relics then but not that one. Not the one he used!"

"You stubborn man," muttered Auriel with irritation. "Then

The Legend of Kyne: Chronocide

where are we to find these items?"

"I am not sure," said Kyne and he started to walk back up towards Tsora not waiting for the others to follow. "They could be anywhere, even on a different continent. Why would there be any more in Kydrëa."

They took off after him. "Alakyne had one and the sorcerers of Tsora had one. Maybe more are in Kydrëa just hidden. Where did Alakyne find Xeono?"

Auriel's words stopped Kyne in his tracks, and he thought for a moment as the morning sun shined through the trees onto his skin.

"I don't know where Alakyne found Xeono, but I do know of a place that might hold the answers. The King's Archive in the capital."

"The Dominion didn't burn it down?"

"Aaldra wouldn't let them. I am certain nearly all of it survives. If there are any texts about where Alakyne found Xeono they would be there."

"Then what are we waiting for," squeaked Rosé and the small dragon bounded up past Kyne before turning around to face them. "We should hurry!"

* * *

3. Tempest

Kioni's breath was soft and still as he clung like a gargoyle to the edge of a building roof. His shoes gripping the old, rugged shingles, he leaned his weight back to sit more comfortably, a cool night breeze rustling his cloak. It was a dark night, no moons and no stars shined above, completely obscured by a layer of clouds. The shadows of the night kept him concealed, hidden from sight.

He took another calm and steady breath as he surveyed the area around him. From building to building, he traced their silhouettes slowly with his vision, looking for anything that looked suspicious.

There he is, he thought to himself with satisfaction as he saw the slightest twitch of movement on a nearby roof. He didn't risk saying it out loud, for fear of someone hearing, but he did let loose a slight grin from underneath his mask.

Slow as he could, he shifted his balance away from the edge of the building and leaned out over the roof, looking for his target, but pinched his mouth tight when he didn't see them down below.

He had been waiting there for hours, ticking away every single second by waiting for their target to appear. He would probably be there a few more hours, if they showed at all. Their intel had specifically told them they pass by this location every third night.

Kioni shifted his weight back and scanned the edge of the buildings again, trying to make out any of the others around. He knew there were four others, all scattered along the roofs of the buildings surrounding the target zone. He had found one, but he didn't know where they all were.

He treated it almost like a game, watching and waiting for anything that could give them away. He felt he was pretty good at it, patience and consistency with his gaze allowed him to spot the subtlest

The Legend of Kyne: Chronocide

of movements from them.

Some of them were better than others at holding still and it still shocked him at it. A few never seemed to be uncomfortable in any position that they sat. He didn't understand how they did it, if it was just incredible self-discipline or something more, but either way it was still impressive.

A slight woosh of air was heard to his right and silently, he ripped his kamas out from their sheaths at his waist and took a defensive stance. A moment later a shadow, barely noticeable against the dark background beyond appeared and the quietest whisper of a voice spoke.

"Tempest, I fear our intel was off," said a man's voice, muffled as if something were upon his face. "I am not sure as to why they have not arrived, but it could be due to many things. I do not believe they are aware of us, or we surely would've known by now."

"I agree Umbra," replied Kioni with his breath light in his voice. He hadn't spoken in hours and hearing his own voice out loud was slightly odd. Reaching up, he adjusted the mask upon his face and felt the cool metal against his fingers.

"We will regroup in fifteen minutes there," and the figure pointed a dark shaded finger further through the city. The shadowy buildings were difficult to make out, but Kioni could see where he was pointing at.

The city they were in was enormous, comparable to that of Alakyne, but not out in an open plain. It was instead situated up next to the edge of a steep mountain going up its slope. The mountain massif formed a half bowl shape, protecting the city on three of its four sides.

The building that the figure was pointing to was decorated with an ornate roof and lay further within the city up towards the pinnacle with only the royal palace beyond. Many ledges and barriers were dotted along its slanted surface, and he understood why that spot would have been selected. It would be easy for them to speak with their voices carrying up and away from prying ears. They also would remain hidden from sight as they crouched low behind its many barriers.

A woosh sounded from a cloak as the figure swept away, dashing along the edge of the roof before leaping beyond his line of

The Legend of Kyne: Chronocide

sight.

Time flew by as Kioni looked out over the city. He could see the movement of guards patrolling the streets below with their lanterns casting small bubbles of orange light. How oblivious they were to what was going on. Kioni almost pitied them and their job.

He had traveled far to the east, to one of the lands who had fought against Kydrëa a few decades prior. The land of Iterasu, the people of the sun. Their culture was strange to him and quickly he understood why he had been sent there.

Kydrëa had been watching them for years now, especially since the war with Gaeil. The family line who had been ruling the country since then had ended. It ended in a coup to seize power by the king's own sister. She had invaded their home and with her task force killed them all, even their youngest son who was still but a boy. With their deaths, they took over the country and began militarizing, returning to a style of government that they had before the Eastern Wars.

'Conquer and pillage all who are not of our blood' The new axiom of their people had been imprinted all over the city and the towns that dotted the foreign country. Kioni could not read the language, but he had come to familiarize himself with those specific markings.

Not of our blood, those words hung in his mind a little longer than the rest. Such a wicked thing to say and by saying it, she is corrupting her people into a thought of supremacy. If they think that they are superior, then every neighboring people will be in danger, especially Kydrëa.

Kydrëa was regaining strength since the Dominion occupation but was in no shape to fight a war. Even being an aural superpower, there were not enough sorcerers to make a significant impact in a full out war. Maybe Ni'Bara could do some major damage, however he is but one huge target and they will surely try to take him out.

Kioni knew that Kydrëa would win in a war with them, but at what cost? How many lives would be lost fighting in a war that shouldn't even be happening? That was why he was there. To take out this new totalitarian leader and hopefully cause enough uproar that reform will be their only option.

"Kydrëa cannot be suspected as the one who started this," rang

The Legend of Kyne: Chronocide

King Theo's voice from his briefing. "If they do, then the new leader's death will be nothing more than a martyr to fuel their vengeance."

That is why the king of Kydrëa sent his Shades in for this mission. The Shades were the only trained people that he trusted with this task; he didn't even trust Kyne with it. The archmage was talented but he was also excessive. A stealth mission would quite possibly result in half the city getting destroyed and very few people could do that. He would be recognized, and it would lead to a catastrophe.

As Kioni's mind rested on Kyne, he felt an anger boiling within him. He had grown to hate him. Had let it fester into a mutilated wretch that tore at his very being. He was the reason that his only sister, the sister he had just gotten back into his life, was now dead, buried on the mountainside near her school. He was so angry, and he hated Kyne for it.

Deep down, masked beneath the rage, he knew that it was not truly his friend's fault. He was his best friend and had been for years, but Kyne had promised her safety and now she was gone, and he didn't know who else to blame.

Kyne had tried to contact him, talk about what happened but Kioni had refused. He remembered the day that the sorcerers came to tell him. He had returned to Alakyne and had been living there for a short time, the small-town life not suiting him. He was greeted one day by a dull knocking upon his door.

It wasn't even Kyne who told him of it, but someone else that he couldn't remember their face, let alone their name. His friend had left after she died, supposedly trying to get revenge, but then he was gone.

So many months passed with no word on where he was. Tsora was struggling to regain its balance and Kioni was alone again. He had stayed in Alakyne for a few weeks, barely speaking to anyone and hardly eating anything. He lost a lot of weight and had nearly ended everything.

But that all changed one day when he was walking near the palace. One of the generals had been passing by and recognized Kioni. To his shock it was Aidon and the two spoke for a short time before the old leader of the Sword invited him to speak to Theo.

Theo had been impressed with Kioni during the war and

The Legend of Kyne: Chronocide

presented him with a position on his royal guard. After a few months of proving himself, eventually Theo met with Kioni privately and awarded him with a position as one of his Shades. His most elite task force, the Shades, were trained in the art of deception and espionage. Tasked with missions that others would dismiss as impossible, they did it with quick and ruthless efficiency.

It was time and Kioni dashed off the roof, heading up towards the main building as he saw the other Shades ahead of him. The wind rushed in his ears, and he slid down a slanted roof before leaping across a large gap to the next. Within a minute, he was crouched on a small ledge hidden on all sides and surrounded by four others.

Each and every one of the Shades wore a dark mask that concealed their face. All were very similar, but each was slightly different allowing them to recognize each other. Kioni's was engraved with symmetrical lines and swirls that accented his face shape to give it an almost feline appearance. Adorned at the top were two cupped triangles that resembled large ears to further enforce the resemblance of a cat.

Kioni didn't even know what anyone looked like beneath their masks, and no one knew what he looked like. It was standard for the Shades to keep their identities as shrouded in secrecy as possible. No one other than King Theo and his top advisors were aware of the Shades' identities. It was safer that way, for everyone.

"Umbra, what is the meaning of this?" said a female's voice, her face hidden behind a mask. "Have we been discovered?"

"As I already stated Fox, we have not. However, I believe that this night will not remain uneventful for long. Our target is no longer suspected to walk along this path tonight. I am not sure exactly what is going on, but I do not suspect treachery is a foot."

"It could be anything," added another female voice. "She could be feeling sick or could have had any sort of issue arise. We should not allow our travels to have been wasted. It is highly unlikely that anyone knows of us. Only a few do and they are trusted."

"I agree Owl," spoke Umbra. "If any of you, however, feel like this is not a task you wish to proceed with, then you may leave. I will not persecute you for treason and I will speak to our king about the matter."

26

The Legend of Kyne: Chronocide

A long silence stretched on before the fourth and final Shade spoke. He was much taller than the others, easily a head over Kioni and his voice was distinct, raspy but confident and calm.

"I believe none of us will be leaving tonight until the mission has been completed."

Another long silence followed with a few nods of agreement from the others before Umbra spoke.

"Thank you for your input, Raptor. We will go then, in the cover of darkness and find our target. By bringing him down, we can prevent thousands of our people from dying!"

Kioni's breath was quick as he dashed across the edge of the roof. His hair was pulled back tight beneath his mask and his hood was drawn up with only the metallic ears protruding.

With a quick and powerful jump, he leapt over an alleyway and down a few feet to a balcony below. His thighs tightened on the impact, but he didn't roll, there was not enough room. A few other light thuds sounded and soon the other four were next to him, all crouched down low.

Kioni eyed them each individually, wondering who they all were but he had no idea. Each mask covered their features and when they spoke, they tried to alter their voices to remain as hidden as possible.

They continued on, creeping around the balcony with the royal palace looming beyond. Its many levels decorated with hundreds of windows and balconies were mostly hollow of light with the occasional orange glow passing between as some inside guards continued their patrol.

They were right next to the edge of the palace, near the third floor with a nearly thirty-foot fall to the ground below. In quick succession, each and every one of them dove headfirst over the edge and sailed through the air before landing on their hands in a silent dive roll upon the palace's lower roof.

As Kioni brought up the rear and dove over the balcony's railing, he spotted the edge of the roof through the eye slits in his mask. He held his breath as he sailed for what seemed like a few seconds before his hands connected with the rounded stone shingles.

The Legend of Kyne: Chronocide

Immediately he tucked his shoulder down into a roll, slowing his momentum down and taking nearly all of the pressure from the landing.

The others were already moving on and Kioni dashed after them as they ran up a wall, each footstep propelling themselves further up. Just as their momentum came to a stop on their third step, they pushed off in quick succession, leaping up and backwards while grabbing the lip of an overhang.

Kioni followed suit and soon all five were dangling, still as bats with their fingers clamped around the edge of the lip. A long moment passed as they hung there, the stone lip firm under Kioni's weight. Glancing at the others, He could just make out the silhouette of Umbra as the leader nodded, signaling they had not been spotted and to continue on. Heaving themselves up onto the walkway they drew their weapons and scanned the area for prying eyes.

Each Shade was trained in the art of a weapon unique to themselves. Twin hook swords were gripped in Raptor's tight grip, each blade dropped low as the tall man leaned over the edge, nodding to confirm that they remained unseen.

Fox had smaller weapons as each hand was decorated with a tight wrapping of cloth and leather. Resembling Kyne's caestus, the wraps adorned her knuckles and had been laced with thick metallic spines. A very brutish weapon, the strikes that she landed on any opponent were lethal.

The other female shade, Owl carried two escrima. Short stick like weapons that had been adorned with a broadhead upon their ends. More reminiscent of small spears, the escrima were armor piercing weapons that could easily take out anyone that was unsuspecting.

Wielding his two kamas, he clenched them tightly in his hands and felt the cool steel underneath his gloved grip. The sickle blades were adorned with a straight dagger like protrusion upon the pommel, providing another dangerous and useful weapon.

Finally, the leader Umbra carried a thin curved sword. It was still sheathed against his waist, but Kioni could see the dark outline of the scabbard before they all took off running up the slanted roof towards the railing that lined its top.

They dashed over the railing and into the palace hallway, quick

The Legend of Kyne: Chronocide

on their feet and quiet to the ear. Each footstep seemingly matching Kioni's heartbeat as he tried to control his breathing. The dark shadowed shapes of artwork and furniture flew past them as they delved deep within the palace when suddenly Umbra swept his arm up in a signal. An orange light was approaching down an adjoining hall, and they all dashed to the sides. They positioned themselves behind what few items were there to block as much of their figure before remaining inhumanly still

"Huy, et ali?" asked some voice in a language unfamiliar to Kioni. Another voice was heard and then a second orange glow appeared with both coming into view.

There were two guards, dressed in red decorative armor holding pole-arm weapons against their forearms. In their other hand each clutched a metallic lantern with a small orange flame flickering in its depths. As they walked around the corner and out into the open area of the hallway intersection, the two slowed their patrol.

To Kioni's horror, both of the guards suddenly stopped their movement and began quickly discussing something with each other, seemingly oblivious to their presence. One of them smacked the other on the shoulder with a slight chuckle before they both nodded and separated. One continued on the way they had been going while the other paused for a moment before turning down the hallway that they were hidden within.

He held his breath and felt a bead of sweat drip down his forehead as he watched the guard walk past Umbra and then the rest of them. As the guard passed Kioni, he took a few steps forward before pausing and making a noise that sounded like a mutter of confusion. The guard turned back towards them as if he saw something, but it was too late.

In a flash, Owl had leapt forward, driving the two small blades of her escrima under the guard's chin. She pushed him against the wall next to Kioni in rough jerking motion while the others all surrounded him, covering his mouth and holding him still. The guard sputtered and tried to thrash around, each movement growing weaker and weaker as the blood and life leaked out of him.

Kioni threw his vision towards the other guard, but he was long gone, having not noticed anything with the orange light of his

The Legend of Kyne: Chronocide

lantern out of sight.

As the guard's movements grew slower and finally stopped, he helped the others lower the body quietly to the floor and they slid it behind a nearby decorative shelving table. There, no one would notice the guard until the morning when they would be long gone.

I hesitated! roared Kioni's thoughts in frustration at what had occurred. It was a fragment of a moment, but he had hesitated. He should've been the one to take out the guard, not Owl.

"That was too close," muttered Umbra quietly. "It is difficult to stay hidden with so many of us. We will separate and go..."

"But shouldn't we stay together for better odds of remaining unnoticed?" interrupted Fox. "More parties within their palace gives more opportunities to get spotted."

"Fox mind your tongue," hissed Owl and the two stared hard at each other with the flame of the lantern casting their shadows upon the walls of the hallway. Kioni could feel a great tension in the air as the two faced one another, their dark eyes burning with hate.

"Knock it off you too," hissed Umbra. "I am sick and tired of you always fighting. If we cannot be civil and work together then one of you will need to leave."

Owl turned her head away from Fox and a small defiant grunt was heard under her mask.

"Splitting up will increase our chance of success," continued Umbra. "Fox, you are with me. Owl and Raptor, you will be with Tempest. Find him and get out. Once you have fled the building, alert the others with a flash bead." He withdrew a small group of white spheres, each no bigger than a pea. "Release it outside and it will alert us to escape. If something happens, use a red flash bead."

Umbra's voice grew dark. "Do not let anything happen." He paused for a long moment. "Good luck and may the shadow be your ally in the dark of night."

All of them nodded and crossed their arms over their chests with their palms facing out. They sat there for a brief moment in respect to the shadow before separating with Umbra and Fox heading the way that the guards had originally come from.

"Come and let us end this night," spoke Raptor as he extinguished the guard's lantern, and he took off with the other two

The Legend of Kyne: Chronocide

hot on his heels.

They continued on down the hall they were in, avoiding any orange glowing lights that approached and managing to not alert any guards of their presence.

There are a lot more night guards than I initially was expecting, thought Kioni as he rounded a corner and ran quietly up a set of stairs. *It must be due to the coup that occurred a few months ago. They are wary of intruders; we will have to stay vigilant in our tasks.*

They were once again on the edge of the palace, the long roof reaching out beyond a railing and the dark city further on. They were much higher now, near the top of the palace as Kioni peered out over the city. He could see the dim orange glow of patrolling guards slowly moving as they continued their patrols while the rest of the people slept in their homes or out on the streets as beggars.

The sky was still dark, obscured by cloud cover with the scent of rain in the air. No moonlight spilled its silver light upon those who dwelt below, and no twinkling stars sparkled. The night was shadow just as they were.

The three followed the railing that lined the top of the roof as their path angled up at a slight degree. Moments before Kioni ran around another corner, Raptor stopped immediately and clamped hard on Kioni's collar bringing him to a rapid stop.

Kioni ripped around towards him in a moment of rage but saw the tall figure with his finger upon the lips of his mask signaling them to be silent. Owl came to a quiet stop, and they all listened intently.

A hushed set of voices were heard around the corner, but no lights were seen. The only thing allowing any of the Shades to see was the ambient light from throughout the palace and from down in the city below.

Raptor withdrew a small, silver mirror and crept along the edge of the wall, stealthily easing it around the corner allowing him to get an idea of what was hidden down the hall.

He suddenly motioned for the other two to look and when Kioni did, he caught his breath in his throat. A small lantern lay towards the end of the hall, shielded so as to prevent most of the light from alerting anyone to their presence. It did, however, allow him to see what was hidden. A full ballista with three guards seated nearby.

The Legend of Kyne: Chronocide

Kioni scanned the ballista and saw a large wooden drop chute loaded with dozens of arrows allowing for rapid firing against enemy invaders.

"Why do they have that there?" breathed out Owl as she withdrew from the small mirror.

"It looks to me that they have something or someone of importance within there. It might be in our best interest if we were to get inside," replied Raptor and he rose back up to his full height and withdrew from the wall.

Kioni and the others quickly scanned the area but saw nothing that could help them. There was no easy way to scale the walls outside to get onto a higher floor and even after they did that, they wouldn't be able to get back down into that room. They were going to have to go straight through the ballista and guards.

The sound of footsteps echoed down the hall and all three of them leapt over the railing before ducking low and hiding behind a pillar. Kioni fumbled for a moment on the rounded shingles as he fixed his footing, and he leaned low over Owl and Raptor's shoulders. The three of them were still as stone as they hid behind it but any moment they could be spotted and their quest over instantly.

Kioni breathed out slowly and steadily as the sound of footsteps echoed closer and closer. His breath was hot under his metallic mask and the humidity was felt upon his cheek as his skin grew a familiar sticky feeling. The shallow breathing of the other two grew into rhythm with his own as the three crouched down low, remaining as still as possible for any movement would surely be noticed.

"Here is our chance," muttered Raptor and Kioni quickly realized the Shade's plan. A brief nod from Owl stated that she understood as well, and they waited as the footsteps grew louder.

Just as the light came into view, they saw two guards with a single lantern clutched in one of their hands. Leaping out from behind the pillar, Owl and Raptor quickly slew the first guard and Kioni felt his kamas sink through the second guard's flesh right where his neck connected to his shoulders. Just as the guard went to utter a cry, Kioni ripped out one of the kamas and spun over his shoulder before lodging the pommel blade through the man's trachea.

A few coughs came from the guard as his hands grabbed at

The Legend of Kyne: Chronocide

Kioni's, but they were minor, and Kioni knew he had mere moments before death. Lowering the man to the floor, he felt his arms go weak and then the man was gone.

Owl, Raptor, and Kioni all heaved and threw the two bodies over the balcony's railing where they slid along the short roof before falling to a dull thud in the vegetation below that lined the edge of the palace.

Drawing up the lantern and twisting a metallic nob, Raptor made the flame dim considerably to shield their masks. They were ready!

Rounding the corner, all three of them walked slowly, mimicking the patrolling guard's gait as they approached the guards and the ballista. Upon seeing them, all three guards leapt to their feet and one dashed to the ballista.

"Huy, huy hi?" spoke one of them with a firm and assertive voice. Kioni could feel the adrenaline coursing through him, causing his hands to start to sweat and tremble. Raptor reached into his cloak and withdrew a piece of paper to Kioni's disbelief.

"Ayi," said Raptor as he waved the paper at them. "Ayi," he said again, and they continued their approach.

The guards had clear confusion on their faces and Kioni could tell they were struggling to see them as one lifted the lantern up and squinted his eyes.

Raptor held the paper up blocking his mask from view as he reached the man, and the guard took it before looking first at one side and then the other side in confusion.

"It's blank," muttered Raptor and with a swift kick, blew out the man's knee before ripping his hooked blade across the man's upper chest.

Kioni and Owl quickly dashed around him just as his body slumped to the floor. The guard seated on the ballista cried out in shock as he released a flurry of arrows, but he was too slow, as Kioni dashed around the weapon and leapt up towards him. A few strikes from his kamas and the guard was dead.

Throwing his vision towards the last guard, Kioni watched as Owl stepped away and their body fell to the floor. The final guard was no more, and the three Shades quietly approached the door.

The Legend of Kyne: Chronocide

The door, to no one's shock was locked, and they began to search around for a way to open it.

"This should help," chuckled Owl as she withdrew a large keyring from one of the guard's corpse and she inserted it quietly into the lock.

A light click sounded and the door swung inward, allowing them to step inside the dark room. No lanterns lit it up but the ambient light from the hallway gave them a rough idea on its layout. A table stood in the corner dotted with parchments and books, while a massive bed lay at the back of the room with the shape of something laying in the sheets.

"I'll take care of it," muttered Owl and she ran over to the figure. Withdrawing the sheets, Kioni heard her gasp in shock. "There's no one here, it's... It's just a pillow!"

"That's odd," whispered Raptor as he scanned the room. Kioni followed his example as adrenaline made its way throughout his body. They were alone but something didn't feel right. This entire mission was not going how it should.

Owl left the bedside and approached them.

A woosh, like the sound of a bird's wings was heard and suddenly a powerful force struck him in the leg, sending him sprawling to the floor. Another thump sounded and Kioni heard the muffled grunt as Raptor too was knocked down.

"Who the hell..." started Owl as Kioni raised his eyes up towards her.

The air rippled behind her, and a figure materialized, their face hidden within darkness.

"Behind you!" cried Kioni and as Owl turned to see the figure, a blinding flash of blue light struck her in the face. The brightness intensified for a second before fading away and Owl slumped over the ground. Her body thrashing around uncontrollably as she screamed.

The Legend of Kyne: Chronocide

4. The Hunting of a Shade

Before Kioni could even register, Raptor was upon his feet, and rushing the figure, his hooked blades drawn. Leaping forward, he brought them down towards the figure, but they twisted out of the way. A flurry of strikes flew from the Shade, but the figure managed to dodge every single one of them, their body twisting and turning as if they could sense the very strikes before they were even made.

Kioni's mind snapped back to himself, and he swung his kamas blindly around him, hoping to strike whoever had knocked them down but there was no one there.

Panic flew through his mind as he turned back to face the duel. Raptor was impressive but this figure, this sorcerer, Kioni assumed was merely toying with him.

"Raptor! They are a sorcerer! We need to get out of here!"

"Obviously," roared the Shade and he ducked as the figure blasted a wave of blue light. The very air seemed to buzz with power and Kioni felt a warmth radiate around.

Two more strikes flew from the Shade before he feigned an attack and leapt backwards, a kunai flying out from his sleeve and striking the figure.

Dashing towards Kioni, the Shade cried, "Go!"

The two flew towards the doorway and out past the ballista. Kioni's boot kicked the lantern and in moments the hallways were ablaze with flaming oil. He felt the heat spread around behind him, and he hoped it would hold the figure back at least long enough for them to escape.

Glancing back, he could see Raptor right behind him and beyond that, within the room the shadowy figure appeared in the doorway.

The Legend of Kyne: Chronocide

Ripping around the corner, Kioni watched as Raptor came into view right behind him when suddenly a blast of the blue light tore through the hall, enveloping the Shade in its heavenly glow.

A cry of pain flew from the man as Kioni shielded his eyes, the light tingling the skin upon his arms. It itched and then burned like he had sat too close to the flames of a fire and the radiant heat was scorching his skin.

As the light faded away and Kioni watched his companion's running slow to a stumbled walk. Raptor turned his head around as if he were confused about what was going on.

Kioni grabbed a hold of his wrist and yanked him towards the railing. Guiding the disoriented man over the railing, the two made their way along the edge until they came to a spot they could leap down to another roof. Kioni looked back, expecting to see the figure pursuing them but there was no one.

Urging Raptor to jump, they fell a short distance and landed hard on the lower roof, Raptor sprawling to the ground and Kioni dropping to his knees. His leg where he had been struck hurt badly and as he climbed to his feet his knee buckled under the strain. Gritting his teeth, he pulled Raptor up and they continued on.

Further down the roof, Kioni found a small alcove that was blocked on three sides by the palace wall. It was small, just large enough for them to fit next to one another. It could potentially house them for a brief time to catch their breath and as Kioni guided Raptor to sit, the man started to thrash around.

"I'm burning up. I'm burning up!" he said, each time growing louder. Kioni clamped his hand upon the mouth slit of his mask. Raptor struggled against him for a moment before dropping his arms weakly to his sides and shuddering as his breathing grew ragged.

"Temp...Tempest," mutter Raptor as he coughed, his whole body trembling as if he were freezing to death. "Remove my mask."

"But the code," started Kioni but Raptor shook his head.

"Forget the code, I want to die with my eyes free of this mask."

Die? Kioni's mind went numb at those words. He knew that Raptor was injured but for the man to die. Kioni hadn't known him for long, a few months as they had only completed one other mission before this one, but he had grown accustomed to the tall man's

The Legend of Kyne: Chronocide

presence and the authority that he seemed to command. He was not the leader of their group, but they all knew that he was the most dangerous of them all.

Kioni stared at the man's mask for a long moment, the hooked beak reminiscent of a bird of prey lay upon the mouth with angled eye slits above it. He could just make out the glimmer of his eyes behind it in the dim light. The mask glimmered and as Kioni's vision changed focus it allowed him to make out his own reflection.

Die? Raptor is going to die? Kioni thought again and he placed his hands upon the man's mask. Slowly withdrawing it, he was not surprised to see what he looked like underneath. A younger man, not much older than himself with darker skin. A thick black beard covered his mouth and his eyes seemed to be fading away, a glaze materializing over them.

"Tempest, I... I want to give you something," and Raptor raised a trembling hand up to his mouth.

"No, no," Kioni started. "Save your strength. We need you to complete this mission," he said even though he knew it to be a lie.

"Don't lie to me Tempest," Raptor said suddenly with a bit more strength.

"I..." started Kioni but Raptor interrupted.

"I don't want my last moments to be littered with lies about me surviving and returning home. I know that I am done. Whatever they did to me is fatal as witnessed by our other companion. You need to escape Tempest. These people have powers that I have never even heard of and can seemingly kill someone with light. Escape with your life my friend and live to fight another day. Use my gift to save you and return back home to Kydrëa."

Suddenly, the man's figure started to ripple and change as he grasped something unseen upon his mouth. As he pulled it away, Raptor's size suddenly shrunk to a little bit smaller than Kioni and his skin lightened. Most surprisingly, his face changed into that of an old man clutching a silvery metallic kerchief.

"Here," and he shoved it into Kioni's hand. "Keep it hidden and secret. Allow no one to know other than those you trust with your life. Many would kill for this sort of item in an instant."

Kioni opened his palm and stared at the cloth. Its image

37

seemed to shimmer as he twisted it in his hand, and he could see that it had been wrinkled in two opposite corners signaling it had been tied around Raptor's face many times.

Just as he lowered his hand, his eyes lingered on a small silvery white serpent biting its own tail in a ring. He had almost not seen it and was puzzled by the image.

"Farewell," murmured Raptor as his eyes glazed over and his head fell weakly forward signaling his death and leaving Kioni alone upon the roof of the palace.

A low rumble sounded down from in the city and then the falling of rain swept over the palace, its icy cold drops soaking Kioni's clothes in an instant. It was as if the sky was mourning the loss of Raptor.

A burning in Kioni's chest appeared as he lowered the Shade to the roof and crossed his limp arms upon his chest. There he sat for a long moment as he mourned the loss of his friend.

He knew what had to be done but he didn't want to. To him it was almost barbaric, but it had to be done. He placed the silvery cloth inside a small pocket in his cloak and then reached into Raptor's own cloak pocket.

Removing a small black pebble, he placed it upon Raptor's forehead and felt the pull of aura leave his body as he activated the talisman.

Raptor's body began to disintegrate, starting from the point where the stone touched and rippling throughout him in waves. Kioni rose up and stepped away, watching in pity as the former Shade turned to a pile of pale grey dust. His body was no more and even his clothing had been destroyed. Just as the destruction was ending, Kioni leaned over and tossed Raptor's mask into the pile, it too turning to dust.

He shook his head in frustration at what had just happened. It was unfortunate that he couldn't receive a traditional burial, but they all knew the consequences in their line of work. They couldn't let anyone know anything about them.

"I have to get out of here," he muttered to himself as he stood up, wincing from the pain in his leg. His adrenaline had worn off and the pain was starting to set in. It wasn't broken, that much he knew, but it was badly bruised and would pose many problems if he were to get

The Legend of Kyne: Chronocide

caught.

Making his way along the edge of the roof, he came to the railing and peered around the corner. The rainfall echoing down the empty corridor, but no other sounds were heard. He wondered where the others were when a thought suddenly popped into his head as he remembered the beads he had been given.

I need to alert the others! he thought with shock. He had been so preoccupied with everything that was happening that it hadn't crossed his mind.

As he reached into his robes and searched for a bead, a brilliant flash of scarlet light lit up the night sky for a brief moment. The source of the light was blocked by the edge of the palace, but Kioni could tell roughly where it was. Someone had beat him to it and the color signaled trouble.

The others were in danger, but he wasn't sure exactly who had used it, either Umbra or Fox. The red light was eerie as it faded away in the pouring rain, each drop reminiscent of blood as if the sky had a gaping wound that was dripping all over the land below.

He needed to escape; he knew that was the thing to do. That was what they had been ordered to do, escape at all costs. If any of them were to be captured, they were to commit suicide immediately for fear of the enemy gaining any intel on them. Kioni knew that each and every single one of them would leave him to die, most without a second thought, but as he climbed over the railing and crept along its length like a silent cat, he struggled within himself.

He couldn't leave them. If there was even a minute chance of them surviving because of him then he had to take it, no matter the cost. Life was sacred and his companions, whoever they were, were part of his company, his new family.

The outside of his leg ached as he propelled himself down the corridor. Turning a few times and dashing down several flights of stairs, he encountered no one on his journey. The patter of the downpour outside echoed around whenever he came into view of it as he ventured lower within the palace towards the source of the light. Staying on the outside would allow him an escape opportunity if it came to that and soon, he was dashing along a hallway with one wall to his left and to his right, the open air of the city beyond.

The Legend of Kyne: Chronocide

A flash of light caught the edge of his eye, and he watched as an arc of lightning crept across the sky before vanishing between the clouds. Its jagged figure lit up the dark walkway and Kioni watched as a figure a few dozen feet away came into view. It was hard to make anything out, but it looked as if they were crouched low.

Drawing his kamas, Kioni stopped his run and approached the figure as quietly as possible. The darkness seeming to lighten up as his eyes adjusted after the bright flash and he could just make out the figure, still crouching down. They hadn't moved at all since he had spotted them, and it puzzled him greatly. If he had been spotted, surely, they would've moved to intercept him.

The figure was growing clearer as Kioni neared and another flash of lightning brought into view a sight that made Kioni's stomach churn.

It was Umbra, his silver mask dripping with blood as a sword pierced diagonally through the eye slit and out of the mouth. Thick sticky globs of blood fell from the blade as the fresh corpse knelt down as if praying to some unknown god. A single spear had been thrust through his back and out his abdomen so forcefully that it had wedged itself partway into the stone ground, holding him up in his sickening kneel. Kioni's arms dropped limply to his sides as he stared at the leader of the Shades, brutally murdered and set up as if on display. Display for the others who would come to find him.

Footsteps sounded from behind him, and he whipped around, his kamas lusting for vengeance but to his shock, he saw Fox running quickly towards him.

"Get away!" he whispered with the loudest sound he dared to call out. "It's a trap!" Fox stopped her run and Kioni started to approach her. "We need to get out of here! Owl, Umbra, and Raptor are all dead. We are all that remains."

A chuckling sounded from Fox. "We... No, you mean you are all that remain."

Suddenly Kioni's jaw clamped down tight and his arms slammed to his sides as Fox brought both of her hands together in a clap. Rigid as a board, Kioni struggled against the indomitable force that held him together. Each muscle quivered intensely as they fought it but no matter what he did, he couldn't beat it.

The Legend of Kyne: Chronocide

Movement caught his eye and a blur of steel, a flash of red, and a burning across his neck all simultaneously happened. The world seemed to grow slow as he felt the sting and warm trickle of blood drip down his neck to his shoulder where it pooled in the pocket of his clavicle.

He was going to die!

Whispers were heard and then a figure walked around from behind him revealing a lightly tanned woman with fire red hair and a devilish smile. She spoke a few words to Fox and the Shade took off her mask revealing an average looking Kydrëan woman.

Kioni's vision darkened around the edge, and he felt his eyelids grow heavy.

"You aren't going to die yet, Kioni of Thyre," said Fox as her face rippled and contorted into a new face similar to the other female. Light tan in color, with the hair color of a red fox, the woman barred a striking resemblance to his companions many years ago, the brothers Meko and Selim from the sword of Kydrëa. This woman who he had thought was Kydrëan was actually of the eastern people!

As his vision sharpened from the anger and adrenaline rush that followed. He wasn't sure if it was from the blood loss or from the fear itself that had caused his lethargy, but it was gone now, replaced by disgust and rage. He tried to speak, to call out vulgar things at the traitor that stood before him, but he couldn't. His jaw remained tightly clamped and his arms bound at his sides.

"He looks quite angry sister," said the other with a chuckle and Fox smiled.

"I would think he would be angry after finding my trophy. Such a beautiful piece of artwork. Maybe I shall give it to Theo himself. Make him stare at it as my people tear down Alakyne's walls and butcher every single living person within."

Kioni grunted in rage as he tried to thrash in her grip, the veins in his head and neck bulging as if they were going to burst.

"We can't have you acting like that now can we," she suddenly said and jerking her arms up, launched Kioni sky high were he slammed his back into the ceiling, knocking the wind out of him and sending a sharp pain through his back.

There he remained pinned for a few moments as he gasped for

The Legend of Kyne: Chronocide

breath, the two staring up at him with gleeful smiles before Fox dropped her arms, releasing her hold and sending him falling to the ground.

Kioni twisted around as he tried to right himself but to no avail and he crashed hard on his already injured leg. Cries of pain erupted from him, and he curled up, grasping it as he rocked from the pain.

Fox stooped down and pried his feline mask off his face before tossing the metallic object away where it clattered loudly. "Such a pretty man," she giggled as the other woman knelt down and lightly touched his cheek with her palm.

"Pretty but dumb," said the other before swiftly slapping him hard.

The sting lit up across his face and he grit his teeth in pain, both from his leg, and from the strike. His leg wasn't broken, but his muscles were torn or injured somehow. Rolling over, he tried to stand up, but Fox swiftly kicked him in the ribs, sending him rolling into the outer railing where he coughed and heaved for air.

His gasping, accompanied by their laughing and the pattering of rain outside was an eerie and wicked combination as the two began to talk to one another in a foreign tongue.

Kioni recognized none of it as he lay there gasping for breath before he managed to get out a single word.

"Why?"

Their talking stopped immediately, and Fox eyed him with a much different gaze. A gaze of superiority lit across her face. Its arrogance and pride displayed it all.

"Why what? Why did we kill all of you? Why did we interfere with your plan? Or maybe why did we infiltrate your company?"

"Why haven't you killed me yet," coughed Kioni. "You killed the others without a second thought, yet you toy with me like a cat and her prey."

She was silent for a moment, intrigued by his question and she ran a finger across her bangs, brushing the long red hair out of her eyes.

"Exactly that reason Kioni of Thyre, brother of Ilana and friend of Archmage Kyne. To toy with one's food and tear out all the juicy pieces that we desire before we devour you whole is such a

The Legend of Kyne: Chronocide

beautiful thing, is it not sister."

"Indeed, it is."

Their words made Kioni's blood run cold and he struggled to rise up but fell hard against the stone ground. Out beyond the railing, he could see the glow of lanterns had begun to appear as people from beneath the palace gathered around outside as if looking at something.

"Who are you?"

"We are the Kitsune, the spirits of the east that will tear apart Kydrëa and leave it to rot. Your Shades and Tsorans will each fall to our power as we slaughter them all. We will pillage their knowledge and burn everything leaving the last memory of them a smoldering piece of ash. You Kioni will be long gone, a speck in the grand time that will be the everlasting of our kingdom. Your life will be of one purpose, to be shifted and molded into a pawn of ours. One that will infiltrate Tsora's sorcerers and assassinate that friend of yours along with his beast. He is the only threat to our plan and with him out of the picture then we will have no one to stop us."

"That damned fool," Kioni muttered to himself. "He always seems to make enemies everywhere he goes."

"What was that?" asked the other Kitsune as she approached and kicked Kioni again in the ribs. He coughed hard for a moment before looking up and meeting her eyes.

"You don't stand a chance against him. No matter what you do, he will stop you. Your magic might hold me, but it is nothing compared to what he possesses."

Rage flew across both of their faces and as Fox approached, ready to strike him hard, Kioni smiled briefly, satisfied that they had fallen for it.

Touching a small hidden gem in his coat, he felt a massive rush of aura flow into him, and he said, "Simdath."

A wave of power flew from him, colliding into the two Kitsunes and sending them flying back down the hall where they tumbled to a stop.

Kioni was not gifted in aura by any means but what little he knew could be amplified with the aural stone he had been storing aura into the last three months. Daily before he would go to bed, he would pour as much of his aura into the small gemstone as he could, just for a

The Legend of Kyne: Chronocide

time like this. It was a pity though as he had used every single drop of the aura in that one spell.

Quickly climbing to his feet, he pulled himself over the railing and onto the slanted roof where he took one step on his injured leg before collapsing and tumbling down its slope. His body jerked around and then was momentarily weightless before he crashed into a pile of crates down in the city below.

Dust and debris littered the ground, and he groaned as he pulled himself up, his shoulder screaming in pain. Clutching it weakly, he was startled to see hundreds of people all around him. Many of them were watching him while the others continued to stare up at the palace. Swinging his vision, he saw through the thinning rain the orange glow of flames as the upper portion of the palace was lit ablaze. As if the eastern people were cursed, the rain seemed to diminish even more and the palace continued to burn, the flames licking the wood as they continued to migrate up its tall spires.

Guards were seen running along the walkways and residents of the palace were seen fleeing. Movement suddenly caught his eye, and he watched as both of the Kitsune came into view, their dark eyes scanning the crowd for a moment before landing on him. The second pointed at him and as Fox's gaze rested upon Kioni, he felt the air vibrate and tremble with an incredible power.

Dashing away, Kioni watched as the area he had been standing suddenly imploded in upon itself, sending a shockwave that threw everyone nearby to the ground.

The crowd was thickening the further Kioni went and after a few moments of pushing deeper, he looked back to see the two leap down from the roof and run into the crowd after him.

They are going to catch me! he thought as he limped on, each step agonizing and his shoulder aching. He was certain he had dislocated it from his fall. He wouldn't last a second against these two as he tried to lift his arm up to no avail. He couldn't fight and he could barely walk.

He really was going to die! He had to make a choice, get captured, tortured, and then brainwashed to help them kill his people. Or he could end it all right now, before they got a hold of him.

He had never truly thought about the pebble that would end

The Legend of Kyne: Chronocide

his life, the small seemingly innocent stone that sat in the breast pocket of his cloak. When it was given to him, he felt invincible. He thought he would never get captured and have to use it. The thought seemed foreign to him, but it was now his only logical option. Reaching into his cloak, he searched for the pebble but just as his finger touched it, he felt the silky touch of a cloth.

Raptor's cloth!

He had a chance, a slim one, but something that might work. He had no idea how to use it but as quickly as he could, he pulled it out and wrapped it tightly over his mouth and nose. Thinking of a crippled old man he had just passed a few moments ago, he felt the mask seemingly vanish and his spine started to hunch forward as if he was aging rapidly.

Just as his transformation finished, a hand was felt upon his shoulder, and he was forcefully jerked around to be met by Fox's piercing eyes.

Panic raced through his body as he stared at her for a long moment, sure that she knew it was him. Confusion suddenly flitted across her face as she eyed him for a moment before she muttered something, and the tingle of aura was felt in the air.

She's trying to see if I'm masking my appearance with aura!

A moment later the tingling stopped, frustration appeared across her face and then she jerked him out of her way before dashing further into the crowd.

He stumbled to the ground and gasped in shock at what had happened.

I'm alive?

*   *   *

5. The King's Archive

Kyne took a deep breath and sighed as he noticed, far on the horizon, the shadow of a large city. Triangular in shape and situated upon a large sloping hill, he could just make out the outline of the spear-like spires that dotted the citadels roofing. Arcing nearby was the Ta'Ak river with its silvery sheen reflecting brightly against the verdant grassy plains. Further away, he could just see the faint forking of a small river lake, splitting the river into two different paths. Small buildings were scattered along the river, trailing its path like travelers along a winding silver trail. Each was accompanied by fields for farming and pastures that were dotted with the shapes of livestock.

The steady slow beats of Ni'Bara's massive wings were a constant and everlasting reminder of their progress through the sky. The ground straight below moved, but looking further out seemed to cause their journey to draw on as if they were going slower and slower. Every few minutes the small dragon whined about their progress and Kyne had to consistently tell Rosé that, "Yes we are indeed still moving very quickly," and, "Ni'Bara is going as fast as he can."

The small dragon had grown up very quickly, being similar in size to a large dog with her long tail lazily drifting off of Ni'Bara's back and flailing in the rush of wind. Her wings were tucked tight against her sides and as she lowered her head down onto the saddle, she snorted a long and whining sigh.

"We will be there soon Rosé," added Auriel as she placed a hand on the young dragon's head. She leaned forward and whispered in Kyne's ear, "It's like we already have our own child."

Kyne chuckled at her words and looked sneakily back at the dragon. He was very fond of Rosé, but she did indeed act like a young child. Whiny and always wanting things right at that moment. He never really had that problem when Ni'Bara was young. The grey dragon was

The Legend of Kyne: Chronocide

forced into work almost immediately and grew up with determination and a drive. Kyne didn't feel that all the time from Rosé. However, at some moments, she shocked him with her endeavor but then at other times, she was more playful and just wanted to have fun.

As her dragonfire within grew though, Kyne knew without a doubt that she would be a fierce dragon in her prime, able to confront anything that crossed her path. Until that time however, he and the others had to teach her how to act and help her mature into a young proud dragon.

A quarter of an hour later, they were soaring over the great river that skirted around Alakyne and could see the city's outer wall. Dozens of feet high above the city below, it separated the outer city and its farmlands from the inner city and its hundreds of buildings.

The battlements still contained siege weapons of war. Ballistae and other projectile weapons hid behind the stone battlements, peeking out from their shielded positions and their steel tips glinting in the sun. They remained in case of an attack, but they had aged in their unuse. Wood rot was beginning to set in and the iron brackets that held them together were beginning to show signs of corrosion.

No longer did he see Dominion sentinels patrolling the wall in their bronze-colored armor decorated with its right shoulder spike. Instead, he saw the Kydrëan guard armor upon those who patrolled the wall. He saw dozens of them all marching around and a flashback to the Siege of Alakyne reminded him of how quickly things can change.

The massive shadow of Ni'Bara passed over two guards and Kyne leaned over and watched as they curiously looked up, only to be shocked by Ni'Bara's descending mass. The dragon was a celebrity to nearly everyone in the country, but they all still had that fear. He was a predator of incomprehensible prowess. Alone he could quite possibly destroy every single thing in the country if no aural users were present.

Ni'Bara snorted as Kyne's thoughts drifted into his mind and Kyne grinned as well.

You would never do that right Ni'Bara? chuckled Kyne.

I make no promises, laughed the dragon as he glided lower into the city, still dozens of feet over their roofs.

A single aimed flap could rip the buildings up from their foundations, so Ni'Bara merely glided through the triangular shaped

The Legend of Kyne: Chronocide

city, heading towards the top of the hill where the great citadel stood upon its apex.

Enormous in scale, the towering castle was surrounded by a second smaller wall with a few large towers scattered around. Huge multi-level buildings all seemingly connected together to form the largest building in the country. Spires of unparalleled magnitude dotted its silhouette coming to dangerous points in a show of deadly aesthetics.

Rosé raised her head up as if finally interested. She yawned and stretched her arms out before unfurling her wings. Suddenly leaping off of Ni'Bara's back, the young hatchling joined his glide. Occasionally flapping to maintain his pace, the small pink dragon was doing astoundingly well.

Ni'Bara and Rosé suddenly dropped in altitude and soon they all felt the absorbed impact as the dragons landed in the central courtyard of the citadel. A few citizens ducked out of view, hiding within the walls of the citadel resulting in the courtyard bare of all life. At the center, Kyne could see the statue of Alakyne, with his arm reaching up and the chiseled form of Xeono carved into his wrist.

The clamber of footsteps echoed from across the courtyard and then he heard voices join them. Moments later and they all dismounted as a group of royal guards entered the courtyard followed by a man dressed in fancy elegant robes and a thin circlet upon his brow.

"Your majesty," Kyne and Ni'Bara said simultaneously, and they bowed their heads with Rosé following quickly after. As the king approached, Kyne watched as Auriel was the last to bow, very slowly and not very low.

They had spoken about it the first time that she had met Theo, and it was still hard for her to show the man respect. She did not like him and did not think that his title of king meant anything. She herself was of royalty but she was not one to express that upon her people. To her, Theo was just a man who was slowly being corrupted by his power.

"He did help free all of Kydrëa," muttered Kyne low under his breath. "Without him nothing would've happened."

Auriel snickered but said no reply to his words.

Theo approached and they all lifted their heads up to greet him.

The Legend of Kyne: Chronocide

"Archmage," said Theo and he grasped forearms with Kyne in the typical Kydrëan fashion. "Ni'Bara, Rosé," he nodded quickly to each individual before turning his attention towards the Riel. "Auriel."

The princess was unmoving as the two met eyes for a lingering moment. A heat of dislike was felt all around and after an unbearably long moment, the king turned his attention back towards Kyne. "What brings you here to my city? It's rare for you to show up without any prior word of your approach. I hope nothing of ill fortune has befallen you or your school."

Kyne shook his head, quickly hiding the facts about what was going on. He trusted Theo but not with everything. He knew that the man once loved Kydrëa more than anything but as the years tolled on, Kyne had started to notice that he had changed. Strange things had started taking place in the last few years. People of power going missing, neighboring countries falling into anarchy. Even aural skills that were not supposed to be known by the common folk were seeming to pop up in odd locations, as if someone was stealing information from Tsora. The most disturbing thing to Kyne about the whole thing though was that he now believed Theo would sooner save himself than his country if it came down to it. He couldn't trust him with what was going on, not yet at least.

"Oh," the king retorted with a puzzled expression. "Then what has brought you to Alakyne?"

"A simple history lesson," Kyne said cheerfully, masking the dread he felt in his heart. "I wanted to teach Auriel and Rosé about our history, especially about Alakyne and I knew that you had the greatest collection of works quite possibly in the world on the subject. I was hoping that you would allow us to immerse ourselves in your books and manuscripts."

"Absolutely," replied the king. "I can have one of my guards take you now if you would like. Ni'Bara however will not likely fit unfortunately. I hope that is not going to be a problem."

"It always is," rumbled the dragon with irritation in his voice. "I will manage though like I always do."

"Perfect then," exclaimed King Theo and he clapped his hands together while turning on his heel. "I can have some chambers arranged for you. I have a very large one that I had shaped specifically so that

The Legend of Kyne: Chronocide

Ni'Bara can room with you, I hope it will be to your liking."

"It sounds great," Kyne replied cheerfully. "Thank you, sir."

"Of course," he replied before he stroked his beard with one hand. "I had almost forgotten as your presence caught me off guard. There is someone here that you should meet with if you get the chance. He is an old friend of Voron's."

"Friend?" Kyne asked puzzled before he glanced at Ni'Bara.

"Who is he?" the dragon chimed in.

"Surprisingly one of the old aurals, Enotach."

"Enotach!" gasped Kyne as the name flashed in his mind. He had heard it many times from his lessons from Voron. A powerful and wise sorcerer, Voron was certain he had been killed with the others in the Tsoran Genocide. "He is alive?"

"Surprisingly so," he replied with a chuckle. "Been hiding in the south beyond Otoruh for the last decade. He returned a few months ago and has been staying in the palace."

"Were you going to tell Kyne about this?" asked Auriel with a hint of irritation in her voice. She had her eyes drilled upon him and her arms folded.

"In due time," he replied coolly. Now, I have duties to perform if you might excuse me. Good day to you then," and the king started to walk away.

"Theo?" asked Kyne quickly stopping him in his tracks.

As the king turned to face him, there was a brief flash of anger on his face for a moment before quickly being masked.

"Yes, Kyne?" he said deliberately, enunciating his name specifically without his title.

"Kioni works here in the palace last time that I heard. Where may I find him?"

The king paused for a moment, "He is not here and won't be back for some time."

"Is he doing well?" asked Kyne. "He hasn't returned any of my letters and I haven't heard anything concerning him in months. Last I heard he was working in the palace but that is all. What is he doing?"

"I cannot speak on the matter as of now," spoke the king slowly. "Archmage or not, you do not have the luxury of information concerning the Kydrëan government."

The Legend of Kyne: Chronocide

"Archmage or not?" snarled Ni'Bara darkly, the deep rumbling vibrating their bones. "His title of Archmage qualifies him of any information he wants."

Eyeing Ni'Bara for a long moment, Theo turned back to Kyne, his affect visually quite irritated. "All I can say is Kioni is fine. I will not speak on the matter again!"

Turning his back to Kyne and the others, the king took two steps before pausing. "And Kyne, do not forget who I am. I am your king, and you will acknowledge that, understood?"

"Yes, your majesty," said Kyne quickly as he bowed his head to mask the shock on his face at Theo's words.

As the small party left the courtyard, one of the guards remained behind but Auriel was already addressing him with visible irritation in her voice. "We do not need your escort, we can find it on our own," and the princess of the Riel waved her hand dismissing him.

As they were left in the courtyard, the three looked at each other with eyes wide opened in disbelief at Theo's words.

"His ego has grown larger these past few years," growled Ni'Bara lowly. "I am with Auriel on this one Kyne. His title of King means nothing to us, and it should mean nothing to you. If anything, he should be bowing his head to you not the other way around. The war was only won because of you, and it seems he has forgotten that. I bit my tongue this time, but I cannot do that forever. His arrogance and pride have grown too large for comfort. If he is not kept in check then he very well could become an enemy one day."

"Absolute power absolutely corrupts," muttered Kyne as he remembered the old proverb. A glance at the statue of Alakyne and then images of Aaldra appeared in his mind. "It happened to Aaldra. It could surely happen to Theo."

"We will keep an eye on him, watch and make sure that it doesn't get out of hand," started Auriel. "If it does then we will address it."

"Agreed," said both Kyne and Ni'Bara simultaneously.

"I am so confused," said Rosé as she raised her head up to their level. "What do you guys mean about that king guy?"

"We will explain later, for now if you encounter him show the utmost respect," said Auriel in a low voice.

The Legend of Kyne: Chronocide

"Alright," said Rosé.

She could tell it was serious and would treat it as such. She was a child, but she was actually a lot more observant and mature than the others realized. She liked it that way. By playing the naïve child she was able to keep up on events while not being limited to boring adult stuff.

"What do you think is going on with your friend Kyne," asked Auriel as they began a slow walk towards the edge of the courtyard. "Theo got really defensive about the subject."

"He is hiding something that is for sure. I am not sure what Kioni has gotten himself into. but it can't be good. I just pray he is using his head and not doing anything stupid."

"Do you think it might have something to do with this Enotach?"

Kyne pursed his lips at the thought. "Enotach being here does prove to be an anomaly. Very strange indeed that Theo would keep that hidden from me."

"You mean *King* Theo," Ni'Bara snorted.

"*King* Theo, I'm sorry you're right," he said with a slight grin. "Yeah, it's all just highly suspicious but currently that's the least of our problems."

"Indeed, it is," Auriel said, and she interlaced her fingers with his own. "One problem at a time."

As they neared the edge of the courtyard, they came to a stop and Kyne turned towards Ni'Bara. No words had to be spoken between them. Ni'Bara knew he couldn't continue on and would have to await their return outside.

"Goodbye Ni'Bara," said Auriel as they ventured into the citadel. "We will keep you updated on what we find. Wish us luck."

"Good luck," rumbled the dragon in a sassy tone as the three others were lost from view.

"I am not finding anything!" exploded Auriel suddenly as she slammed an old dusty book on table sending up a cloud of fine powder. Orange sunlight from outside streamed through the dust in beams as it drifted back down all around them. "I only am finding very vague stuff surrounding Alakyne. Are you sure he was even real?"

"I am quite certain that he existed," said Kyne as he placed a

The Legend of Kyne: Chronocide

book softly onto the table. A golden glow of light had been coming out of the book into his eyes, but it quickly faded as he ended the spell.

"He could literally be a myth; someone who never existed and some of these feats could've been multiple people. How do we know that he was indeed the one who last had Xeono?"

"Because the Priloc says so," muttered Kyne as he grabbed another book "The Priloc is the most well trusted piece of history that we have to date. I trust that Alakyne existed." He said a quick spell and a golden light erupted from the book and struck his eyes, flooding his brain with all the knowledge held within its pages.

"We have been at it for hours Kyne with no luck. I am tired, Rosé is running through the aisles bored out of her mind. Can we pick this up tomorrow?"

As Kyne finished the book and sat it down, he sighed. He too was exhausted, both physically and mentally from the strain of knowledge that he had been rapidly infusing into his head.

"Yes, we can be done for the day," he said with a weak smile.

"Thank you," said Auriel with clear joy on her face as she embraced him. A quick kiss was shared and then she continued. "I believe you about the Priloc. If you trust its knowledge, then I do as well. We will keep searching and find out all we can."

They gathered all the books they had gone through which were nearing the hundreds and placed them in a neat stack near the table they had been using. They were in the center of a massive semicircular room adorned with animal mounts from all areas of the world. Sunlight streamed in through the flat wall that was more glass than wood allowing them to look out over the back wall of Alakyne and to the grasslands beyond.

The bookshelves were incredibly tall, reaching nearly two dozen feet in some parts and they had to climb up and down a ladder to retrieve the books. Thousands and thousands of books filled the library, but luckily, they had been sorted quite thoroughly and the section that discussed Alakyne was nearly a fourth of the way read by them. It would take a few days to get through them all but at least they didn't need to read all the books in the library.

Kyne sighed in relief at that thought and he rubbed the palms of his hands hard upon his closed eyes, massaging all the skin on his

The Legend of Kyne: Chronocide

face. His cheeks felt heavy from fatigue, and he yawned wide before rising to his feet. As they walked down one of the long aisles toward the exit, he gazed up at the works the library contained. To read all the books in there, even enhanced by a hundredfold with aural speed reading would take years to complete and by then he wasn't even sure if his mind could take it all.

As they came to the entrance of the library, not a single guard in sight, Kyne sighed as he realized that in his hand, he still clutched one of the books from the pile. A slight flash of frustration at his mistake as he lifted the book up to his eyes.

'Alakyne and His Centurions'

The book contained stories and parables that Kyne had just recently read but none of which gave him any insight into Xeono or anything that they were looking for. Most of the stories were mere children's tales, many of which he felt were more and likely not true as some were quite outlandish.

"Seven feet tall he stood with the strength of ten men, Alakyne wielded the sun and blade that could cut down his enemies in a single strike."

A flicker of doubt entered his mind as he thought back to Auriel's words about Alakyne. *Could he really not be real? No*, and he shook his head. T*he Priloc says that he was and everyone in all of Kydrëa follows its teachings. I mustn't have doubts about it as it could impact my studies.*

Looking at the bookshelves and spotting an area where he could stick it, he hesitated for a moment before deciding against it. It was a lazy thing to do and was disrespectful to those who had sorted the library years ago.

"Auriel," said Kyne gaining her attention as he showed her the book. "I will be right back. I have to put this back and then we can go."

She nodded and continued with Rosé out of the library, lost from Kyne's view. Turning around, he walked back down the aisle heading towards their study area. A few moments and he was there, placing it neatly upon the other books.

Kyne sighed again as he stared at the pile of books they had gone through. It was going to be a long few days and he was worried that they wouldn't find anything on Xeono or any of the other relics. If

The Legend of Kyne: Chronocide

they didn't get a lead soon, something dreadful would be bound to happen.

A shadow moved past his peripheral vision just out of focus but just as Kyne looked, it was already gone. A strange sense came over Kyne, as if he was being watched. Someone or something was there observing him.

More and likely some guard or even just a child, Kyne thought to himself as he turned around and left the area. Walking down the aisle, he felt the hairs on the back of his neck rise up slightly as that feeling came over him once again.

Not turning his head only his eyes, Kyne scanned the bookshelves to his sides, peeking through the gaps into the other aisles looking for any sign of his follower.

There! roared his thoughts as a shadow of movement was seen on the aisle to the right. Whoever was spying on him was about to be caught.

As he came to an intersection in the aisles, Kyne rapidly turned right and dashed into the aisle only to be startled to find it completely empty. No sign of the spy was found he ran to the next aisle and then another. All signs of the shadow were gone, and he felt his skin crawl. He and an eerie feeling and was incredibly uncomfortable. As Kyne exited the library, the feeling did not reappear. Whoever, or whatever was watching him was gone.

Very odd, he thought to himself. *I was sure someone was there but then...* his thought trailed off as he threw one more glance behind him to see an empty aisle lined with dusty old books. *No, someone or something was there, I am certain.* Whether they be friend or foe, he was unsure but either way he would be wary while he was in Alakyne.

Taking another step forward, a thought came into his mind, and he muttered, "Seiose."

A few trails of aura appeared and after a moment he found what he assumed to be the culprit. It was different than a normal trail, wispy and faint, more like a shadow of a trail he could sense no malice coming from it. Kyne trailed it with his gaze before it suddenly went straight up the bookshelf as if the owner could levitate. It trailed down the top before jumping across to the next aisle and then the next. It was right up against the wall, curving up its face a dozen more feet to a

The Legend of Kyne: Chronocide

balcony overlooking the library.

The owner of the trail was gone, Kyne was certain of that. He could follow the trail but for now they were fine. He would place some aural wards the next time they were there that would alert him of any other presence.

As he stepped out onto the stone patio that lined the edge of the courtyard, he saw that Auriel and Rosé had been waiting for him with Ni'Bara. The grey dragon's massive tail was straight out across the courtyard, nearly a hundred feet long and causing a lot of problems as the guards and other nobles had to skirt around it.

Kyne could feel the humor come from Ni'Bara as his eyes drifted down its length and he shook his head. The dragon loved to bother people; it gave him great joy to be a nuisance. Just as he approached, he noticed Ni'Bara shift his arm and his mind closed off from his own as a figure was revealed.

An older man, in his apparent late fifties with longer dark black hair that swirled in light waves. His mouth was covered with a greying beard and mustache that was laced with dark streaks of the fading black.

"And you must be Alakyne," he said with a cheerful smile, his cheeks pinching up against the edges of his bright blue eyes.

"It's just Kyne," he replied. "And you are?"

"Enotach," he replied but Kyne had already assumed. "His majesty had alerted me of your presence in the city and I thought it best to come and meet with you. I would've joined you in the library, but I got talking with Ni'Bara. His stories concerning the war are just fascinating."

Kyne eyed the dragon with a raised eyebrow and the dragon snorted in response. "It's nice to meet a friend of Voron's," Kyne said, and he reached an arm out. The aural took his grip and upon his touch Kyne could feel the power emanating from him.

It was familiar, almost reminiscent of Voron's own and sensing it made Kyne smile at the fond memories.

"You are quite powerful just like the stories say," Enotach laughed as they released their grip. "I am impressed."

"You are quite impressive yourself," Kyne replied. "Your aura actually reminds me of Voron's. Its similar in an odd way."

The Legend of Kyne: Chronocide

He laughed out loud. "I was wondering if you would notice it. Voron and I have a very similar aural mark, we are brothers after all."

"Brothers!" Kyne and Ni'Bara gasped. "Voron never told me he had a brother. I never even saw anything about it in the memories he gave me."

"Those memories were probably selected ones he chose for you to see," he sighed. "My older brother always thought two steps ahead of everyone else. I am glad that he was the one to have trained you. It is fitting that his last apprentice was able to defeat his prior."

The words were followed by silence as dark thoughts enveloped Kyne and Ni'Bara's mind. Thoughts of a mad king bathed in a golden glow.

"I apologize," Enotach said quickly after noticing the shocked look upon Kyne's face upon hearing his words. "I should think before I speak. Trauma should be acknowledged but not at times where happiness is the focus. I hope that I haven't offended you."

"It's alright," Kyne muttered, trying hard to push the thoughts out. "You didn't mean anything by it."

"He doesn't like to bring it up," Auriel added. "Would you like us to bring up horrific things that you had to deal with?"

"As I said before, I should think before I speak. I am sorry to have offended you and your family Archmage Kyne."

Kyne looked at Auriel and could see that she herself had seemed to accept the apology and he nodded his head. This man hadn't meant disrespect so he would forgive him as well.

"May I introduce my wife."

"Auriel," he said before Kyne finished. "The gem that you brought from beyond our world. I have heard the stories." He smiled at her, and Kyne saw the resemblance of Voron, especially in his eyes.

"And this must be the young one Rosé," he said, and he knelt down towards the pink dragon who eyed him curiously. She didn't say anything but just stared at him.

"Anyways," he sighed as he stood back up. "I have been staying in the city for some time, getting back into the Kydrëan custom as I haven't been home in a long while. I have been meaning to visit Tsora and I have heard you have done wonders with it?"

"I would like to think so," Kyne laughed. "I am trying

The Legend of Kyne: Chronocide

anyways."

"He's not trying, he is doing phenomenally," Auriel interjected. "Don't be modest Kyne. Brag about it. Tsora is stronger than ever and it's all because of him."

Kyne beamed at her praise and Enotach had a look of shock on his face for a moment before he smiled again. "I am glad to hear that. I should make my way to the school here soon so that you can show me around if you don't mind."

"I wouldn't mind at all," Kyne replied.

"Well with that note, I think I best be letting you young ones enjoy your night. I need to get back to my quarters. Maybe I will see you around the citadel. If I don't then it'll have to be in Tsora."

Kyne nodded and watched as the older man walked away vanishing into the citadel leaving them alone.

"He seems pleasant," Auriel said.

"Asked a lot of questions about the war," Ni'Bara added.

"I think he was spying on me in the library," replied Kyne causing the others to drop their mouths open.

"Spying on you?" Auriel gasped.

"Yeah, I felt some presence watching me when I was leaving, and I am pretty confident it was him."

"He was out here with me for quite some time," Ni'Bara said. I don't know if it was an apparition or what but..." his voice trailed off.

"Is he dangerous?" asked Ni'Bara lowly.

"I don't think so," he replied. "I didn't feel any sort of malice from him. If it indeed was him, it was probably curiosity. I think we should be cautious but not withdrawn from him. He is Voron's family; I can tell by his features alone. That I think gives him some credit."

It was growing dark as the sun had just recently set. They had been in the library for hours and Kyne felt his own stomach rumble as the last sliver of sunlight set far on the western horizon.

"Where are we to eat," asked Auriel as she laughed at its rumbling. Slightly embarrassed, she had heard that, he shook his head. He wasn't sure where to get food in the palace, nor did he want to. He was tired of it and wanted to roam the city down below and get some authentic Kydrëan food.

The Legend of Kyne: Chronocide

"I kind of want to venture into the city and leave this palace. I don't feel like we are welcome here anyways," he said as he recalled their interaction with King Theo.

"I am fine with that," she grinned, and she climbed up onto Ni'Bara. "Let's go find something to eat."

Kyne and Rosé joined her up on Ni'Bara's saddle and then they were off flying down into the darkening city. Lanterns were beginning to light up the streets and he could see many people shuffling in and out of specific buildings which he assumed were the taverns.

Finding an open area, Ni'Bara landed softly, straining his body in an awkward position to avoid crushing anyone or breaking anything. Cries of shock from the few onlookers were heard but he paid them no mind. It was just a normal occurrence.

Rosé was the first one off of his back, gliding quickly to the ground before bounding up and down the cobblestone street. Kyne slid down the dragon's leg, making sure to go with the scales to not tear up his clothing and skin. Auriel followed him and even though she didn't need it, he provided support with his hand as he helped lower her softly to the ground.

She was the strongest woman he knew but he could tell that she loved it when he treated her like his own little princess. As her feet touched the ground, he brought his hand down her waist to her hip before taking a step back and allowing her to step away from the dragon. Her shirt was soft under his hands as his touch was removed, tracing her curve for just a moment before she was out of his grasp.

He stared at her for a long moment, just in awe of her physical beauty. Her hair was long, brushing the back of her thighs in its large wavy curls. Silvery blonde, the light cast from nearby made her hair shine an almost fiery platinum. Tracing his eyes down, he followed her muscular arms down to her tiny waist before returning back to her face. His favorite part of her, the part that would remain the most constant as the sands of time weathered her down to an old woman.

She smiled as she noticed his lingering gaze before shyly averting her eyes.

"I am going to go on a hunt," said the dragon suddenly, breaking the tension between the two like a dry twig under a boot. "I

The Legend of Kyne: Chronocide

am in need of food as well and I doubt wherever you go that they will have enough for me. I will be back later this evening. Keep him in line Auriel, don't let him do anything reckless."

    The Riel laughed at that and Ni'Bara nodded his head in amusement before taking off and leaving the three alone in the city streets.

6. To Poke a Sleeping Dragon

The orange glow of street lanterns cast eerie shadows upon the cobblestone road as Kyne, Auriel, and Rosé made their way down the street. The city of Alakyne was filled with thousands of people but Kyne hadn't been down within its streets in years and was in disbelief at the condition.

The further they traveled down the road and deeper into the city, the less sophisticated it seemed to get. Kyne could only imagine what the areas against the walls would resemble. Shaggy hulking masses of buildings in extreme disrepair with the Kydrëan people living within struggling every day for food.

A bitter taste was left in Kyne's mouth as he walked past a vagrant lying against a building. He was missing a leg and looked to be in pain, wincing as he shifted positions constantly, never truly comfortable.

Kyne had not had much experience with vagrants, seeing only a few and never really interacting with them much. He was aware of some people taking advantage of others good will, taking handouts, and returning to their home to live off their daily earnings. To Kyne, it was not right and incredibly dishonest, but this man was different, and as Kyne watched him draw the grey faded blanket up over his shoulders, he decided to act.

"Hello sir," said Kyne and he knelt down near the man, startling him.

"Wh... What... Oh, hello young man. What may I help you with toda..." the man coughed hard, interrupting his sentence.

"I actually had a question for you," Kyne replied with a smile

The Legend of Kyne: Chronocide

as Auriel walked up next to him and Rosé approached on his other side.

"A dragon! Wait!" and the man pointed at Kyne's uncovered left arm, the dark grey scales reflecting the orange light cast from nearby. "You are him!"

"Indeed I am. May I ask how you came by the injury to your leg?"

"The archmage!" the man shuddered. "I... Why would you speak to a lowly parasite like me? Please leave me be, I am not worth your time."

"Just answer my one question," Kyne said cheerfully as he watched the man shift under his gaze, visibly uncomfortable with Kyne's presence.

"Oh this," and the man gestured to his stump. "Dominion sentinel took my child from me. I tried to stop him, and he struck me with his blade."

"I am so sorry for your loss," murmured Auriel as she bowed her head down in respect.

"They took my boy," he whispered quietly with a shuddering breath. "Took him right from me and left me there to die. I haven't seen him since that... Since that damned day!" and he struck the ground with the edge of his hand.

"To tear children from their parents is horrific in the highest degree," Auriel said. "It saddens me of your sufferings."

"Thank you young lady," said the man politely. "I feel beyond honored to have you here in my presence. Even though I know I deserve none of it."

"The honor is all mine," Kyne chuckled. "To be in the presence of someone with enough valor to lose their own leg fighting for those they love. I see that it still pains you?"

The man nodded.

"Probably nerve damage," muttered Kyne and he leaned in, placing his hands lightly upon the stump while muttering the healing spell, "Asira."

Concentrating on the energy within the man, Kyne could feel the rivers and signals flaring through his leg. Each and every sensation traveling through the man's nerves to and from his brain. He searched

The Legend of Kyne: Chronocide

for a moment, weaving through the tangled mess of energy webs and then he finally noticed it, a cluster of nerves damaged and continuously sending out signals that Kyne could understand as pain.

He took a deep breath and intensified the spell upon those specific nerves, mending them together as best as he could. A few moments later he ended the spell and removed his hands with the man gasping in shock.

"It... It doesn't hurt anymore!"

"I fixed the nerve damage as best as I could," said Kyne as he rose to his feet. "Unfortunately, there is nothing I can do about the missing leg itself or I would have."

"Do not be sorry at all," the man laughed with pure happiness in his voice. "You do not understand what this means for me."

"Hopefully it can undo even the slightest amount of your suffering sir." Kyne smiled and left the man alone with the other two flanking his sides as they walked away.

"That was a very kind thing to do Kyne," said Auriel as she grasped his hand in hers. "I know that spell was a draining one."

Kyne chuckled. "Not too bad. I just want to do whatever I can to help those that deserve it."

They continued down the street for another minute stopping to laugh as two dogs played roughly in the street. One was large, rust red with long thick fur and her child, obvious by his head was a mixed breed. His jet-black fur flapped wildly as he dove face first biting at his mother's scruff.

They didn't stop again, traveling a few more buildings down into an entrance to a brightly lit tavern. Its wooden walls were old but looked to be in good condition, as if the owner took great pride and care in their business. Inside they could hear the cacophony of people talking and laughing with the occasional clink of glass as a toast was given or a drink shared. It was here that Kyne could feel the true representation of Kydrëa. Here within these walls people of all ages, races, gender, and type were like family sharing meals and having a merry time. A small flicker of light within such a dark and bleak city.

Kyne gestured at it and both Auriel and Rosé nodded, agreeing on the decision. They walked inside the tavern and were instantly met with an uproar of noise and the smell of cooking meat. Kyne felt his mouth water at the aroma, and they started to make their way through the crowd to a table positioned next to the back wall.

As they passed, they noticed people's voices gradually change from loud conversations to whispers and muttering. Soon nearly everyone in the tavern was staring first at Rosé and then at the other two as they drew upon the table. Auriel sat first followed by Kyne while Rosé sat upon the floor, her long neck rising up high so she could see the others across the table.

It seemed that someone who was working knew who they were for mere moments after Kyne and Auriel had sat down someone was there placing two glasses of amber liquid upon the table for them. Another person quickly followed with a large bowl full of the same liquid and placed it on the table where Rosé lifted her head up and drank a large gulp.

"What is this?" Auriel asked as she eyed it suspiciously.

"Azani. A berry nectar derived from some local Kydrëan fruit. It's a good healthy drink. Keeps the mind sharp and helps replenish the bodies energy."

"Like a riproot?"

"Not even close to as potent though," laughed Kyne and he downed the glass quickly. "I have always enjoyed it though."

Auriel nodded and took a small sip before nodding and taking a larger gulp. A few minutes passed and the workers had returned with a large drumstick from a fowl bird for all three of them and some Kydrëan mashed potatoes.

The three of them ate in silence, enjoying their food and watching as the throng of people in the tavern returned to their normal loud drone. People still looked at them curiously, but no one seemed to have enough courage to approach them and that made Kyne happy. It was easier this way, to remain secluded and not interrupted during his meal.

As he was nearing the end of his food, with a few spoonfuls of potato left upon his plate, a cloaked figure suddenly walked up and took a seat across the table from them to all three of their shock. Rosé barred her teeth as he withdrew his hood revealing pale skin adorned with dozens of piercing all over his face and his neck tattooed straight black giving the illusion that he was but a floating head within his

The Legend of Kyne: Chronocide

cloak. Dark powder had been applied around his eyes giving them a hollowed appearance and when he smiled, they saw his teeth were yellowed and rotten.

Kyne knew who he was as he clenched his napkin tightly, his knuckles white. His stomach began to turn following the rush of adrenaline as his anxiety began to ebb into his mind.

"Ashaki Priest," he muttered under his breath. *Why would he dare approach us here out in the open like this? That's not like them at all.*

"Can we help you?" Auriel stated sharply as she dropped her metallic fork onto her plate with a loud ring.

"I think we can help each other," he said with a raspy voice and a wicked grin. "I believe I have some information that you may be seeking."

"Not interested," said Auriel flatly and she waved the man away. "Nothing that you may know is of any concern to us."

"Agreed," Kyne remarked as he felt a disturbing feeling coming from the man. "Leave us at once Ashaki Priest. We do not wish to partake of your cult."

"It is concerning your search for knowledge about Alakyne and Xeono."

The man's words caused both of their eyes to widen, and Rosé looked at them in shock.

"How do you know of that," breathed Kyne dangerously as his eyes met the man's own.

"I have my ways," he smirked as he looked first at Kyne and then towards Auriel, his eyes drifting down as if tracing her figure.

"What do you want for this information," said Kyne regaining the man's attention. Kyne pressed his lips together as his nose twitched in anger at the man. He was a disgusting piece of filth that Kyne wanted nothing to do with.

"You want gold?" asked Auriel.

"I did at first but... But I think I have found something else that I fancy more. My information is worth heaps of gold so this shouldn't be too much trouble."

"What is it," said Kyne darkly.

The man rolled his shoulders and interlaced his fingers momentarily as he flexed them tightly together. The hairs on Kyne's

The Legend of Kyne: Chronocide

neck rose as the man's vision turned over towards Auriel and then slowly drifted down tracing her body once again.

A swift crunch sounded as Kyne's fist struck the man square in the face breaking his nose under the force. Before the man could even utter a sound of pain, Kyne gripped the back of his head and slammed him hard onto the table with a deep thud causing the wood to shudder from the impact.

"You're not going to even look at her!" Kyne breathed in his ear as he pressed the man's cheek down upon the table. "If you do, you won't be seeing anything ever again, is that clear enough for you to understand! The disrespect you show my wife is unbelievable! Do you even understand who I am? The things I have done. I have killed a master sorcerer and defeated the god of darkness. You are but a vile and repulsive cultist! I could crush your mind and body in an instant, leaving you nothing but a broken and empty shell, a fate so much worse than death that I pity those who would endure it!"

The man groaned as Kyne pressed harder upon him with his superhuman strength feeling the table underneath bow from the pressure. Auriel was speechless and Rosé was staring with intrigue.

"Take this opportunity to think before you speak. Plan the right actions that follow, for one false move, one wrong word and I swear upon the spirit of my fallen master I will end you!"

Kyne's roar silenced the room, and everyone stared in shock as they watched him hold the man face down against the table. A few moments passed and Kyne jerked him up and shoved him back into his chair where he tipped back and fell to the floor with a crash.

Kyne rose to his feet and approached, not touching him anymore but drawing his face within inches of the man's, able to smell his putrid breath. The man shivered in fear as he felt the power radiating off of Kyne's body; shivered in fear as he stared in the golden eyes, the pupils replaced by jagged slits.

"Altyne kin fel," roared Kyne as he cast a spell over everyone else in the room, muffling their voices and blurring their shapes so that no one would be able to overhear their conversation. "Tell me!"

"There is an old crypt..." stammered the man. "Very old to the north. Inside there are tomes and scrolls long lost to the outside world. Tomes carrying knowledge specifically about Xeono and supposed

The Legend of Kyne: Chronocide

other items of power."

"North of what? North of Alakyne?"

"Farther, much farther north. North of Asmathen," he coughed.

Kyne rose up and clenched his jaw in anger. "North of Asmathen you say? So, what you're telling me is that there is an old crypt north of the great lake, that houses information about Xeono?"

"Y...Yes I..."

"You waste my time you filthy piece of trash. You are just spouting out information concerning Ysaroc and the location where I found Xeono! Everyone in Kydrëa knows the stories of our quest to find Xeono. Don't you dare tell me that this information you are providing is anything special. Orus!" he shouted, and the Ashaki Priest lifted up off the ground, bound tight under Kyne's force.

Leaning in, Kyne barred his teeth and said with venom in his words, "Every part of my being says that I should kill you now. I can you know, with literally no repercussions to me. I could tear you apart right here or burn you alive. You have angered me, you rot! You have angered me in such a way that I find it difficult to calm myself. Anyone who speaks ill of my family or threatens them in anyway should be met with my full fury, my full wrath!"

With flames on the edge of his mouth, Kyne pursed his lips and blew a small jet of flame just long enough to lightly touch the man's cheek. Immediately the flesh began to bubble but just as the man could utter out a single cry of pain, Kyne roared, "Erodath!" and the man was blasted across the room and through the window out into the street.

Kyne ended his illusion spell on the patrons and was greeted by concerned stares. The room was still as stone, and he could almost feel their eyes piercing through him.

"Return to your conversations. This is nothing of your concern," he said and with a glance at the other two, the three of them stood and gathered their things. Sweeping out of the tavern, He tossed a few gold pieces to the waitress and nodded towards the shattered window, and then he was back into the cool dark of night.

He took a few deep breaths as he looked around for the figure, but the man was gone, vanished into the shadows. He tried to calm the

The Legend of Kyne: Chronocide

incredible dragonrage running through his body. His hands were trembling, and he looked up in the sky to see the shimmer of stars and the crescent shape of the moon Thraepos, the planet of the dragons.

"Kyne, are you ok?"

He lowered his gaze to see Auriel facing him with a concerned expression on her face. Without saying anything, he embraced her, pulling her tight to his chest.

No words needed to be said, she understood everything that he was feeling. She admired him for it and was still pleased with what he had done. A slight smile, concealed by Kyne's shoulder appeared on the edge of her lips as she remembered the man's face the moment Kyne had struck him.

"That was awesome!" cried Rosé bounding up and down around them. "I can't believe you did that!"

The couple withdrew from one another and watched as the pink dragon leapt around them in excitement.

"Kyne, I have never seen you do anything like that. It was so cool. That guy didn't even know what hit him."

The two looked first at the young dragon and then at each other before erupting in laughter. Their laughs echoed down the dark and empty street as the excitement of the night hit them all. The rest of the day had been so boring and slow, so the change of pace was a dramatic change.

"So did you just make a literal cult your enemy now?" asked Auriel as the laughter began to die down.

"Just add it to the list," he muttered. "Ni'Bara is not to know a word." Auriel mimicked a key locking her lips tight. The Riel smiled.

Kyne turned to Rosé and watched as her tail waved back and forth rhythmically. She nodded briskly but he knew Ni'Bara would find out, either by the youngling or by his own thoughts. Kyne knew that the dragon would actually be proud of him, it's something that Ni'Bara would have done, and Kyne smiled at that. They were so similar and connected, truly brothers.

Kyne's thoughts returned to the man and the odd feeling that he was being watched in the King's Archive. Something just didn't sit right in his gut. He felt confident that it had been Enotach watching him, but strange things were afoot in this city. Things that he didn't

The Legend of Kyne: Chronocide

like one bit.

"Seiose," he said quietly so as to not alert the others. Trails of aura left by the lifeforms who wandered the street flickered into his view and he gazed around for a moment before he saw the trail coming out of the building's broken window.

Every single life form left its mark upon the earth just like an odor that would fade with time. And every trail looked different from one another, like a fingerprint. It was hard for Kyne to describe. They were all different colors and shapes, with some light and wispy and others thick like smoke.

This mans was a dark sludgy greenish brown and odd as it hung in the air abnormally still. The trail curved down the road before suddenly rocketing straight up the side of a building and vanishing beyond the edge of the roof.

It was different from the other trail that was following him in the library. That one was faint, more like a shadowy wisp. This one was ugly and seemed to emanate deceit and treachery. *How did they know I was looking for info about Xeono then if it wasn't him in the archive?* Someone or a group of people knew what they were up to, and he glanced at his family with a flit of fear.

If anything happened to them, he thought before he shook his head and smiled at Auriel hiding his concern.

Nothing will happen to them; I won't let it!

Ni'Bara returned just as they had made it back to the palace gates and within seconds, Rosé was already speaking about what had happened in the tavern to Kyne and Auriel's dismay.

"Ni'Bara it was so cool!" the dragon cried in excitement. "Kyne even burned his face just to leave a reminder."

The dragon gave Kyne a long stare and he could just make out the twitch of the dragon's lip as he fought hard against a smile. His thoughts were being tightly held back but Kyne knew he was right about what Ni'Bara would do.

As they made their way to their chambers Kyne quickly told Ni'Bara about his suspicions concerning the prying eyes in the King's Archive and the altercation at the tavern. The dragon was silent for a long moment before nodding his head and the simple act spoke

The Legend of Kyne: Chronocide

volumes.

After the dragon and Rosé separated from them gliding up and around the citadel towards their chambers, he explained it to Auriel.

"I think using wards would be wise," she said as she undid the braids in her hair and shook her head releasing them. "I am not sure how they know what we are looking for other than possibly overhearing us in the library."

"We were pretty open with what we were looking for," Kyne started as he thought back. "I am not sure if these two are working together or not. Whether it be just them or possibly others I am not sure, but we will be vigilant in our time here."

"We won't be here for much longer anyways," replied Auriel. "What are your thoughts on visiting Ysaroc?"

"Not very convinced," he said. "I highly doubt that was a legitimate lead. It was too obvious that it was false anyways."

Day two of their search for information about Alakyne began in the late morning. Kyne and Auriel lined the area with wards that would alert them of any motion. With stacks of books lining the tables, the two sorcerers began speed reading everything they could. It was draining work and as Kyne opened up another volume, this titled 'Alakyne's Last Meal' he sighed as he would bet a lot that it had nothing that would be beneficial.

"Kyne," said Auriel, drawing his attention away from his book. "What is it?"

"I think I am noticing something odd about all of these texts," she continued as she shut the book she had just finished and placed it down. "Every one of these books were written well after Alakyne had died. I have checked many of them and the Priloc itself was written nearly two hundred years after Alakyne's death."

Kyne's eyes widened with shock, and he scrambled through his stack of books, searching for the date that they were written.

Year 409.

Year 456.

Year 335.

Every single one of the books was far after the time of Alakyne. The Kydrëan calendar was roughly based upon Alakyne's unification of

The Legend of Kyne: Chronocide

Kydrëa, making the year they were currently in 1373.

He continued through the books, no longer reading anything but the date that the manuscripts were written and placed into the collection. Page after page he turned and each volume causing him more and more anxiety at what he was starting to think.

Could Alakyne really be a myth?

Resting his forehead softly onto the table, he sighed and closed his eyes. He mustn't lose hope. Hope not of Alakyne but of finding anything that could help him. Even if Alakyne wasn't real someone used Xeono. It was real and the info in the Priloc proves that someone witnessed its power and documented it.

Opening his eyes and turning his head to the side, his vision rested upon a small book, leather bound and stamped with a P upon its spine.

Kyne reached out and took it. Across its cover, it said, 'Of his Vision and Will, Alakyne - Kydrëa's Hero'.

Opening it slowly, Kyne scanned down the first few pages looking for a year before flipping to the last page where he saw a small script at its base.

Written by Pretarch of Avalk. Last living descendant of Alakyne Year 167.

"Pretarch of Avalk?" muttered Auriel as she read the line again as Kyne held the book out for her. "Who do you think that is?"

"Somebody claiming to be Alakyne's descendant. I know many people to this day still claim to be part of his bloodline, but this seems different. This seems like a lead."

"Kitala Pretarch of Avalk."

A jostling was heard down one of the bookshelf aisles and then suddenly a single book hurtled towards them before stopping right directly in front of Kyne.

Reaching out and grasping it, he saw that it read, "Family of Avalk, Founders and Friends."

Reading through it in a few minutes, Kyne eventually sat it down and said, "It describes the family that founded the town of Shjavalk. It talks about many things throughout their founding and history but if you put Alakyne as an ancestor it does seem to make sense based upon a few things it says. It does state that Pretarch was the

The Legend of Kyne: Chronocide

last of his line and never had any children. It also says that he was buried in Shjavalk's graveyard."

"We should go check it out Kyne," said Auriel suddenly. "If he had anything to do with Alakyne it might be connected with Xeono."

Kyne was silent for a long moment, hesitating as he contemplated her words. He could go there, following some far-off lead about someone who was related to Alakyne. He also could remain here and search through the other books.

"I'm not sure about that," he said slowly as he flooded all of the current events towards Ni'Bara's mind, allowing him to catch up on what was going on.

"But what if it leads somewhere?"

"What if it doesn't though?" Kyne responded. "It's a single thought. Some random descendant of Alakyne. It doesn't necessarily mean that he is connected to Xeono in any way."

"But why is his book the oldest one that we have found out of the hundreds we have searched through? There must be a connection with that."

I agree with her on that point, added Ni'Bara.

Kyne furrowed his brow and looked down at the old book, the cover nearly falling off of the old worn-down binding. Something about it did intrigue Kyne, however. He found it odd that this Pretarch of Avalk would specify that he was the last descendant of Alakyne.

He sighed in frustration. He didn't know what to do. If both of them were thinking this could be a lead, then maybe he should go with it. It did have some merit anyway.

"Alright, we can go," he finally said as he rested the book down on the desk. Suddenly a pounding headache appeared, and Kyne felt his whole being contorted in pain.

"Auriel," he grunted as he hunched over in his chair. "It's happening!"

"Touch your sword," she said suddenly.

Of course! I had nearly forgotten.

Reaching down towards his scabbard, he wrapped his hand around the hilt and immediately felt his headache fade away.

He held his hand there for a long moment before cautiously withdrawing it. No distortion was felt, and he breathed out in relief.

The Legend of Kyne: Chronocide

"It worked!"

"I really seems the Relics are connected with what's happening to you Kyne. I don't know why but it must be connected with the Light."

"And with the Darkness," he replied. "Maybe destroying it somehow really did put our timeline off balance like Ni'Bara said."

Auriel was silent for a long moment, a look of realization spreading across her face. "That's it, I'm sure of it. The seraph Voara mentioned that the Darkness had been defeated before, but they locked it away. He said that the Light didn't want to destroy his family but maybe the Light was worried that the universe would be off balance."

"Without the Darkness existing..." Kyne paused. "How do we stop it?"

"Somehow the items that were touched by the Light seem to be stopping it. Maybe like we said earlier, gathering more of them could help. Maybe getting enough of them together would draw the Light to meet with us?"

"I don't think that is going to happen Auriel. The Light said to me that he would be watching us, but we would never see him again. I am sure he is aware of what is going on and either is not interested or knows that we can figure it out on our own."

"But," Auriel started and then stopped. She had a feeling that was the case, and she wouldn't argue it further.

"At least we have more hope that this can be stopped. Let's try the lead in Shjavalk. If it turns out a dead end, then we can always return here."

* * *

7. Akami

Screams of rage echoed around the room as Akami sat upon the edge of her bed, a servant braiding her long black hair. Her sister was stomping around the room, flinging furniture in a fit before saying some word and a blast of energy ripped the dresser from the wall before crushing it and flinging the debris out the window where it fell in a large crash.

"We had him!" she screamed in a foreign tongue as she clenched her red hair firmly in her hands pulling it tightly. "That damned bastard escaped us! He didn't even know aura and yet somehow, he escaped me!"

Akami just stared at her older sister, grimacing slightly as the servant pulled her hair tight up into a braid before grabbing another strand of her black hair.

"That strange man that I encountered right as he escaped still haunts me," she hissed through bared teeth before throwing a vase against the wall shattering it into hundreds of jagged pieces. "I could've sworn it was him and then suddenly it wasn't. Even his presence seemed different."

Akami was silent for a moment as she watched her sister take a few more heavy breaths before she spoke.

"How is it that you were around him for weeks and you didn't just kill him while he slept? You could've killed them all right? You even took the name Fox when you infiltrated their stupid little group and yet you were bested by him?"

She whipped her head towards Akami with malice in her eyes.

"Bite your tongue little sister," she snarled. "Don't you even try messing with me right now."

"Or what," said Akami calmly and the servant stopped for a

The Legend of Kyne: Chronocide

moment and stared at her sister. "Continue," Akami said darkly to the servant before turning her gaze back. "You act like a child Hayame. Throwing a tantrum because you and your little blood oath friends couldn't capture some stupid Kydrëan. It is your own fault that you failed, your cockiness and arrogance know no bounds."

"Why you little bitch!" Hayame hissed before taking a step towards her, a dagger already in her hand.

Suddenly three sharp strikes rapped across the door and Akami smiled as Hayame froze, the dagger aimed at her face. For a moment they stared at each other before she slowly lowered the dagger. Three more strikes against the door.

"What do you want!" she screamed. "I am busy!"

The door swung open slowly and to her horror the empress stepped into the room. Dressed in a brilliant jade dress that brushed the floor, her black hair was done up in an elegant braid and bun. From her ears hung sparkling gold and jade earrings that dazzled as she stepped slowly into the room. Her beauty was immaculate but across her face was a look of complete displeasure.

"Mother!" gasped Hayame in shock and she dropped to both of her knees sheathing her dagger quickly in one motion before bowing her head and placing her forehead to the floor.

The servant dropped immediately to the floor and bowed down, mimicking Hayame.

"Mother," said Akami calmly as she nodded her head shortly, her unfinished braid bouncing softly.

The empress said nothing as she eyed the room, seeing the destruction that her eldest daughter had caused before resting her eyes upon her scarlet head. A slow shaking of her head signaled her disappointment before a quick glance at Akami and then she said one word.

"Pathetic!" before she turned sharply on her heel. As she left the room, two royal guards stepped into view, flanking her on either side as the door was slowly shut behind them.

The servant stayed bowed for a moment before a short tap was felt upon her shoulder and she could see Akami looking down upon her with a sweet smile.

"You can continue."

The Legend of Kyne: Chronocide

Hayame rose to her feet, brushing her pant legs off and snorting in annoyance. She glanced at her younger sister for a moment before she started to say a word and then stopped. Then Hayame was gone.

"She acts like a child," Akami said to her servant as her braid was pulled out and connected to the top of her bun. "Acts like she's the center of the entire universe. Her failure didn't just hurt her ego. The man she let escape burned down half of my home. It's their fault, her and those Kitsune that she associates with."

The servant was silent and Akami gave her a glance that caused her to stiffen, and her voice trembled as she spoke.

"Yes, my lady."

"Speak freely," said Akami flatly. "I don't have many others who I can talk to, Mother is preoccupied lately and obviously Hayame, and I don't really get along."

"Yes, my lady," the servant said again. "My room and all of my belongings were burned away because of that Kydrëan. I lost everything and I..." Her voice quivered as she fought back tears.

"Alright, no more," Akami said flatly as she stood up, the final braid falling down upon the side of her face. Turning towards the mirror, she turned her head side to side, eyeing the immaculate bun and braids that adorned the top of her head. A large metal clasp lay right at the base that was studded with jade and gemstones. Raising her hand up, she wrapped a finger in the lone braid before smiling and turning towards the servant.

"I like the way this looks. You can be done for the day," and she flicked her hand signaling for the servant to leave immediately. Scrambling, the servant gathered her things and dashed towards the door. Just as the door was opened, Akami called out, "If you cry next time, then you might be done for more than just the day."

The dark words made the servant nearly run as she dashed through the doorway, leaving her alone in the disheveled room.

Twirling around, Akami stared at her reflection, eyeing the dark green dress that was reminiscent of her mother's. Gold trimming lay upon its edge as she twirled again. Long in the back, the fabric just delicately touched the floor as it shortened up to above her thigh in the front. Her smooth tanned skin was flawless, and she ran her hand across her thin abdomen.

Turning on the ball of her foot, her feet bare of shoes, she waved her hand and the bed behind her imploded in a splintered mess. Puffs of feathers flew in the air as the blanket and pillows were shredded to pieces and she laughed a pleasant laugh that would make a normal person's skin crawl.

Stepping through the door and out of the room, she eyed two servants, one older man and another young child scrubbing the floor down the hall. The commotion had gotten their attention and when they saw her look towards them, they panicked and returned to vigorously scrubbing the floor.

"Fix it before I return," she called out and then she was gone, gracefully stepping down the halls.

She passed by a few other servants on her journey and after each of them saw her they ferociously returned to whatever they were doing. She had been raised with servants her whole life and gave them little attention. She didn't really care what happened to them either way, they were almost like furniture to her. If it got damaged or you wanted to switch the design of the room, then you would get rid of it.

She had a feeling she knew why her mother had really come to her room and as she rounded a corner to see the bright morning sunlight streaming in through the window, she was face to face with some of the upper officials in her mother's court.

"My lady," they all said as they bowed their heads briefly. "We were just coming to get you."

"As I guessed," she sighed while twirling her lone braid. "What is it?"

"Your mother wishes for you to be present for her speech to address what happened this past night."

"And," she sighed as she looked out the window over the beautiful city that lay tucked up against the mountains.

"And..." stammered the older man. "And what? She wants you there. I don't understand why you don't understand that."

"When is this speech," Akami yawned, and she tilted her head to the side as she eyed the three old men.

"The runners have been spreading word throughout the whole city all morning. It is to be in nearly twenty minutes. Please hurry."

The Legend of Kyne: Chronocide

They turned around and scuttled off leaving her alone.

"Twenty minutes?" she remarked with irritation. "I literally just got my hair done and haven't even had my first meal."

Her stomach growled and she grit her teeth in annoyance. Puffing out a breath, she stepped quickly through the hallway, her bare feet making little sound and her dress flowing up. Swinging into the dining area, she snapped her fingers at some servants and took a kneel next to a food mat. Rolling her eyes as they scrambled to prepare her a meal.

"If I'm late then..." her voice trailed off as she smiled watching the servants panic.

Moments later she had a ceramic bowl placed in front of her with a clear broth as well as two steaming white buns. Delicately, she took her time, sipping the broth from her spoon and once it was gone, grabbed one of the steamed buns. Tearing it in half, she revealed the shredded juicy meat that lay inside, and she felt her mouth water. Placing it gingerly in her mouth, she took a few bites eating the half before standing up from the mat, she watched as a servant came up to her with a confused look upon his face.

"My lady, you haven't finished your meal. You need to eat to remain strong."

She eyed the short ugly man and placed both hands upon her small waist, rubbing it around its circumference before placing a finger in her braid and tilting her head.

"I would like to keep my figure the way it is. Bite your tongue or I'll have it removed," and she swung around, purposefully clipping the edge of her bare foot upon the plate and flipping it over where it spilled the remains of her breakfast all over the mat.

Leaving the dining area, she sighed in annoyance and made her way towards the platform her mother was going to speak from that overlooked the city. Approaching the steps, on either side were a dozen guards, Pole-arm weapons clutched in their hands and intricate armor upon their breasts. Without looking at them, she started up the steps, coming to the summit and stepping out into the bright sun of the morning.

A great amphitheater lay upon the edge of the mountainside in a large half bowl shape with dozens of high-ranking nobles and officials

The Legend of Kyne: Chronocide

scattered upon its seats. At the base of the amphitheater where the speech would take place, she could see a few servants scrambling with an elegant carpet on which her mother would step. She rolled her eyes at that; she knew she was prissy, but her mother was on a whole different level.

Sitting down, near the top of the amphitheater, she watched as hundreds to tens of thousands of people down in the city below gathered and looked up waiting for the empress to appear and just as if on cue, a loud gong sounded, and the chorus of people stopped immediately.

Everyone in the high seats stood up and watched as the empress came into view, flanked on either side by her guards. A few stares were shot at Akami from the other nobles as they noticed she was still seated, and she just grinned playfully at them.

As the empress walked down the carpet and centered herself upon the podium, she turned first towards the nobles, meeting her daughter's eye before turning towards the crowd and raising her hands up, each curved in a crescent shape and her wrists twisted so that the back of her hands were touching mimicking the symbol of their people. Everyone except Akami mimicked her and a great roar of applause erupted from the crowd below. The empress held her arms up for a long moment before she dropped them, and the applause ceased immediately.

The nobles all sat down in their seats and awaited her speech.

"Late last night, my family was attacked by foreign conquerors, the Kydrëan's far to our west! They infiltrated my home, killed my guards, and tried to assassinate me!" Screams of uproar erupted from the crowd and she waited a long moment before raising her hand in silence.

"I fortunately have been aware of this attempt for weeks now and we managed to kill the invaders before I was harmed!"

Again, screams erupted from below and Akami watched as five figures stepped out of the hallway heading towards the empress. Each had the same matching red hair and three were clutching a bag in their hands. At their lead was her sister Hayame.

Stepping up onto the podium, she and the others fanned out and she removed something from the bag that Akami couldn't see. The

The Legend of Kyne: Chronocide

other two followed suit and simultaneously they raised them up.

Gripping the severed head by the hair, the three raised them up, the silver masks they bore shining upon the crowd below.

"The legendary Kydrëan Shades have been slaughtered!" cried the empress and as if on cue the Kitsune reached their other hand up removing the silver masks. The faces of two men and one female were revealed with their eyes torn out and their mouths open in a voiceless scream. Their skin was ashen from death and patches of purple signaled the pooling of blood.

Cries of happiness came from below and shouting that Akami could just make out showed the crowd was very pleased. The three Kitsune suddenly dropped their heads where they rolled off the podium and down far below into the crowd with their cries of happiness replaced by screams of disgust and shock.

"But yet one remains!" continued the empress and the Kitsune all simultaneously dropped their heads in shame. "A single Kydrëan male with no aural knowledge seemingly bested my Kitsune and escaped! Even escaped my daughter. My displeasure and disappointment knows no bounds!"

Boos erupted from the crowd and Akami watched Hayame's face, just making out the baring of teeth and rage. She smiled at the humiliation her sister was facing. She didn't like her, or her attitude and she deserved every bit of this.

"I should have them all executed," cried the empress. "Their skin flayed from their bodies and them paraded around the streets before beheading them for their failure. Their shame brings dishonor to themselves and dishonor to me for are they not the ones who are supposed to protect my family? But what am I to do," she said before resting her gaze upon each of them individually.

"They let the Kydrëan escape, the one who set fire to my home and killed many of my guards," she continued. "I fear that he may return and attempt to kill me once again. The dishonor may be too much, and they may be unredeemable." The crowd continued booing down below and a few pieces of trash were thrown up, striking one of the Kitsune.

"Alas, I can't have all of my Kitsune executed, for who would protect me, even though their protection would be not much more

The Legend of Kyne: Chronocide

than not. These five were those tasked with guarding me and my home so shouldn't they all be punished? I have others as you all know. Many more whose prowess makes these failures look like children. But..." she sighed, her voice trailing off for a long moment before she continued. "I will allow this, one will die today in place of the others, allowing their honor to possibly be redeemed. But who should it be? Should it be my daughter? Or her Kitsune sister who both allowed this Kydrëan named Kioni to escape and best them?"

Akami bit her lip as anxiety entered her mind. Her stomach began turning into a tight knot as she listened to her mother. She didn't like her sister, but she didn't want her dead. Not like this.

"I know," gasped the empress and she clapped her hands together. "We will play a game. But what game you all may be asking. A simple game. The first of the two of you to get this bracelet and bring it back to me will live," and she removed her bracelet. The dark green jewelry laced with gold trimming dazzled in the light as she held it up for all to see. Turning it over, time seemed to slow as everyone focused their gaze upon it before she suddenly threw it out into the crowd.

Immediately the two Kitsune dove after it headfirst and Akami watched her sister vanish past the edge of the roof.

Dashing down the steps, her bare feet light upon the stone, Akami got ahead of most of the nobles as they all pressed forward, eagerly wanting to see the battle that was taking place. A massive flash of light and screams erupted from down below just as Akami reached its edge. A few unfortunate common folk lay dead, their bodies smoking as the two Kitsune launched aural attacks at each other. A crash and a flash of fire and the crowd surged away, trampling anyone who fell as they all evacuated the area.

Akami scanned her eyes around the area and then she saw it, the gleam of jade and gold clutched in some scorched hand from the soul who caught the bracelet.

"He had the worst of luck," she muttered when suddenly her mother's voice was heard nearby.

"So interesting how quickly sisters will turn upon one another. The rest of you Kitsune are spared today. Don't make it a second time."

Suddenly the bracelet flew out of the charred fingers snapping them before being caught in Hayame's hand. An aural attack erupted

The Legend of Kyne: Chronocide

and then a flash of light as the ground quaked. Akami watched as her sister nearly died from the blast, launching back against the wall the bracelet dropping out of hand with a metallic clink as it hit the stone.

Immediately, it rocketed towards the outstretched hand of the other Kitsune but just before it reached her it stopped.

Coughing Hayame rose to her feet with her one hand outstretched, blood dripping from a cut across her face and that familiar rage in her eyes. She called out a nasty curse towards the other Kitsune before running towards her, a blade drawn and the tip ready. Clashing, the two met blades as the bracelet dropped to the floor. A flash of blood and then Hayame was down, the blade sliced across her abdomen.

Akami's gut wrenched as the other Kitsune made her way toward the stairs and slowly climbed up towards them.

Get up! thought Akami fiercely. *Get up!*

The Kitsune was close now and as she took her final step off of the stairs, the empress held her hand out for the bracelet, her face blank of emotion.

Akami could see the Kitsune smiling with glee as she stumbled towards the empress, her leg injured from the battle. The happiness at her success was all over her face and then suddenly she was gone, knocked over roughly to the side where she struck a noble and knocked the woman down hard.

Hayame was their panting as she staggered to keep her balance. The bracelet had been dropped to the ground and with a spell, it flew into her hand.

"No!" screamed the other Kitsune as she leapt to her feet, but it was too late, and the empress was handed the bracelet.

"We have a winner," she said flatly and raised it up, apparently annoyed her daughter had won. "Which means we have a loser," and she turned around. In moments, royal guards had bound the Kitsune and gagged her so that she couldn't speak and use her aura.

There she was dragged across the amphitheater base before she was forced into a kneel in front of the empress.

"One Kitsune must die to save the honor of the others. You should be grateful," and with a wave of her hand, one of the guards said some spell and sickeningly her skin was ripped completely from

The Legend of Kyne: Chronocide

her body.

Muffled screams of pain erupted from the Kitsune as her flesh was revealed, the striations of her muscles clearly visible without the protection of her skin. Her clothes had been torn off, revealing a naked and skinless human screaming in pain.

There the entire city stared for a long moment as the empress looked down upon the poor woman who thrashed upon the ground. Her screams were terrible and Akami fought the urge to puke. Every part of her wanted to look away but she couldn't, she had to watch.

"Death before dishonor," muttered the empress as she placed the sole of her shoe against the Kitsune and pushed her off the platform. She fell a few dozen feet to the stone with a crack and was still.

"Redeem your honor," said the empress. "Bring me Kioni the Kydrëan!"

The Kitsune were gone, dashing away and not looking back at their fallen sister.

"This meeting is over! We are to prepare for war!" and the crowd below erupted in screams and chanting began. Gongs rang about and trumpets sounded echoing over the city bathing it in their noise. The nobles all left, venturing back into the protection of the palace with the crowd below disbanding. A few minutes later Akami was left alone with her mother and her personal guards.

"I am sending you after him," said the empress suddenly. "You who are my prodigy child, the one I know can complete this task. I expect your sister to fail me once again. I need him so that we can use him to extinguish that damned archmage that they have. He is the only thing that truly proves a threat to us."

Akami was silent for a long moment as she looked out over her city before returning her gaze towards her mother.

"But why me?"

"Because you are my daughter, and I am telling you so. Prove to me that you are the heir that I need for Hayame is not."

Akami sighed and she reached up to grab the lone braid. She had grown so accustomed to the lavish life of royalty these last few years and she was frustrated to let it go. She had just turned twenty and her whole life seemed to always be planned for her, never allowing her to

The Legend of Kyne: Chronocide

truly make her own decisions.

"I will go, but when I return, I don't want to be burdened with anything again. I want to have the spoils of royalty and be waited on for the rest of my life until I am a decrepit old thing like grandmother was."

The empress was silent for a long moment in thought.

"I have always wished for you to join the Kitsune with your sister, ever since you turned the offer down when you were only fourteen it has been one thing, I have wanted more than most. But," she paused again. "I will make you no promises. We shall see when you return."

Akami sighed before tilting her head and looking back over the city, the crowd scattered away, people running to gather supplies, children crying and other forms of chaos.

"Ok," was all she said and then she was off, her bare feet making little sound as her dress trailed behind her. Walking slowly down the steps, she traced her route back towards her room and cries of shock erupted from the servant in her doorway as they continued trying to remove the crushed bed.

Paying them no mind, she slipped the straps off her shoulders and allowed the dress to fall to the floor.

"Out!" she commanded and a moment later she was alone in the room.

She was beyond annoyed about this turn of events, but she would succeed, she wasn't a failure like her sister. Stepping over to her closet, she removed a tight pair of pants and a shirt in which she tucked into the waistband. Leaving her hair braided, she grabbed onto a pack and loaded it with a few items of clothes, some strange glowing marbles, and other things. before sealing it up and swinging it over her shoulder.

Grabbing a scabbard from her closet, she removed the blade and stared at it for a long moment. A katana, the single edged blade was thinner than average and short, perfect for her small stature. The blade curved in a nice bend allowing for the perfect cuts to be made in battle. She hadn't seen the blade in over a year and with a sigh, sheathed it before placing the scabbard against her hip.

A final look in the long mirror at herself and she chuckled

lightly.

"At least I still look good," and then she was gone walking out of her room with small tight black shoes upon her feet and a silk cloth wrapped partway up her ankle.

She passed by a few guards and servants but ignored any words that were said as she made her way to the stables. Her sister and the others were most likely quite a distance away from her but that was fine. She could give them a head start.

Entering the stables, she passed by some horses and even a few camels before coming to exactly what she wanted. From the badlands to the southwest, they had obtained it and she had become quite fond of it.

In front of her stood a single hare, a rabbit-like creature that was nearly six feet at the shoulder. Slightly larger than an average horse, the hare wielded long powerful legs that rippled as it shifted its balance. Upon seeing her it snorted and thumped its massive hind leg shaking the ground from the force.

Akami grabbed a bridle from a hook as well as a saddle and approached the hare. The inaba as it was called sat completely still, its black eyes staring straight at her as she laid the bridle across its face.

Tucking its ears in so that it could be placed correctly, she felt the thick cartilage upon her fingers as the ear shot straight up. As long as her arm, and blazing hot, the ears were eerie as the animal held deathly still. Once she finished placing it, she attached the saddle upon its back and then opened the stable guiding it out.

Each little hop guided it forward as she led it down the row and outside to the outer stables. The sun was hot, and it shined across the desert-colored hare as it hopped out.

Sitting as a hare does, the inaba held still while Akami reached into her pack and removed a torn piece of cloth. It was a piece of Kioni's cloak that they had found earlier that morning. Lifting it up to the inaba, the creature smelled it, and a twitch ruffled its fur as a few of the people in the area started to stare. It jerked its head a few different directions as its nose twitched madly before it suddenly grew rigid.

It had found the scent.

Climbing up onto the saddle and hooking her feet into the stirrups, she leaned dangerously back from the angle. Akami struggled

The Legend of Kyne: Chronocide

to not yank upon the reigns for fear or toppling the inaba over and managed to balance herself by grabbing onto the front of the saddle. She said a command and the creature slowly rose up to its full height.

There they stood for a moment as the sun beat down upon them, sweat already forming on her brow before she guided the inaba down the street towards the opening in the wall to the farmland beyond. The common folk parted allowing her passageway and all stopped and stared at her as the large creature continued its tiny hops carrying her forward.

Coming upon the central field that contained the archway outside, she stopped the creature and looked back up at the palace high up on the mountainside. Her home she was leaving and might not be back for some time. Her life was ruined by a single night.

A sound was uttered from her mouth and the inaba rocketed forward at a blinding speed, dashing down the large field in two hops before jetting to the side and out into the open farmland that lay beyond the wall.

The inaba was faster than any horse and Akami struggled to situate herself upon its back as each hop propelled them faster and faster causing the grass next to them to blur.

I am coming for you, Kioni! and then she was gone, bounding to the west.

* * *

8. Pretarch of Avalk

Shjavalk, the port city far to the northwest of Alakyne. During the Dominion's occupation of Kydrëa, the city had lost a lot of its economy in both tradeable goods and people fleeing to different areas of the country. Shjavalk was not in the most ideal part of the country with the harsh rapids of the Tor'Kar river just a few dozen miles inland from the sea making it nearly impossible to effectively transport goods into Kydrëa.

Other cities, specifically Dawngôr, were able to keep much more of their economy stable with the few goods that were still traded. Dawngôr had the much gentler Ta'Gor river which was much more navigable and thus allowed the city to trade with other major cities such as Gôrvon and Alakyne.

Kydrëa was split in nearly two halves by the jagged Riigar Mountains. The vast majority of economy and trade remained located in the country's southern half. More ports and rivers to sail, along with roads that traveled east along the edge of Kol Faldîn and into the eastern countries.

Most other countries had slowed their trading with Kydrëa once the Dominion had taken over. They all seemed to turn a blind eye to the occupation, either in denial of the danger it could pose to their own country, or to spite Kydrëa itself.

Kydrëa was a powerful country with very few nations rivaling its military might. Throughout its past it conquered a few smaller nations, integrating their cultures into its own and had gained a reputation throughout the world that it was not the friendliest to its neighbors.

In more recent years, only a few generations in length, the expansion had all but stopped as Kydrëa turned to a more peaceful approach with its neighbors. This sparked the war with the Eastern peoples as they perceived the lack of Kydrëan expansion as weakness that could be conquered.

    Shjavalk was slowly returning to a major port city though in the recent years with the rebuilding of the city of Faldîn as well as other towns further into the Kol Faldîn forest were being made. The city was still struggling but had seemed to rise back up to its feet from the steady crawl it had been doing over the last decade and a half.

    Ni'Bara flew down lower towards the ground as the buildings below grew denser, the small wall that wrapped around the city crumbling in parts rushed past them as they entered the air above Shjavalk. Hundreds of people dashed out of their homes and other buildings to watch the massive dragon fly above, silhouetted black against the azure sky.

    Kyne had no idea where the city's cemetery was but with all three of them, they eventually found it. Sloping down a gradual hill that connected to the city's palace. The cemetery was littered with thousands of flat stones all etched with names of the deceased.

    Near the center of it lay a building surrounded by an iron fence. Thick rods adorned with metallic broadheads, rusted from the years sat in a still and eerie silence around Shjavalk's mausoleum where only the wealthiest, those of nobility were buried above ground. It was uncommon for normal people to be buried in the ground nowadays as land was expensive. Most common folk resorted to cremation as their burial choice.

    As Ni'Bara landed softly in an open patch of grass, they watched as a single person quickly approached. The afternoon sun baked against Ni'Bara's scales and Auriel brushed a drop of sweat from her forehead. Kyne slid down the edge of Ni'Bara's leg, his feet connecting with the ground in a large thump which was soon followed by another much lighter sound as Auriel floated down from the dragon's back. Rosé was already wandering around through the graveyard reading off the names of the deceased and trying to find the oldest grave as she listed off the years they had died.

    The figure was quickly upon them, dressed in light grey robes with his hands connected together hidden within the sleeves and his hood raised up, the man was of an older age. Kyne could tell from the

The Legend of Kyne: Chronocide

wrinkles upon the edges of his eyes he was probably in his early sixties.

Deep wrinkles and scars lined his cheeks from sun damage and most likely horrid acne as an adolescent. He was not a pretty man which saddened Kyne because in this world, features like that would lead to a life like this man led, tending a graveyard in the company of oneself with few visitors and almost fear from the community.

Grave wardens were not a respected profession, similar to executioners. People feared them and avoided them at all costs. It was even rumored that they were not even real people, but ghouls who feasted upon the dead bodies in which they watched over.

Kyne chuckled at that thought just as the man dropped his hood before he came to a stop. The rumors were false, he was certain of it, and he would be as respectful as possible to this poor man.

"Archmage," he stammered. "Archmage Kyne, and the beautiful Riel princess Auriel" he bowed his head quickly. "And," turning towards Ni'Bara, Kyne watched as the man swallowed a lump in his throat and a bead of sweat formed on his brow. "The embodiment of a storm, the dragon Ni'Bara."

Ni'Bara puffed out a jet of hot air that blew the robes of the grave warden around in a brisk wind, nearly causing the man to jump out of his own skin.

"What brings you here?" he stammered.

"We are looking for the grave of someone," Auriel said. "He was known as Pretarch of Avalk."

"Pretarch of Avalk," the man mumbled as he looked towards the ground and bit his fingernail in deep thought. "I know of the Avalks, the founders of this city but Pretarch is a name I am not recalling. Are you certain this is his name, and he didn't go by anything else?"

"As far as we know it to be," said Kyne. "He claims to be the last living descendant of Alakyne."

"Well, what a claim," chuckled the man. "I know of nearly a dozen graves who have that same claim. The last descendant of Alakyne, Alakyne's great grandson, Alakyne's last blood. Royal blood of Alakyne, yadda yadda. Every single one of them I believe to be completely fabricated, but Pretarch of Avalk. I am intrigued by someone with this name as I have never heard of it. I also have never

The Legend of Kyne: Chronocide

heard of someone pretending to be of the Avalk family line as it ended centuries ago. They were a very wealthy family but very secluded and not much is known about them."

"Do you know where the family graves are?" asked Ni'Bara as his tail repositioned itself, narrowly avoiding striking a gravestone as its length stretched in between them like a massive grey serpent.

"Most of the wealthiest families have their resting places in mausoleums like the one behind me. This one houses a more recent family that ruled after the Avalks I'm afraid. The Avalks were actually buried not in this graveyard at all but in the catacombs beneath the city's palace. I am warden over those graves as well and have not ventured into their depths in quite some time, but I can lead you there if you wish."

"That would be great," said Auriel. "But before that, we haven't learned your name."

"Oh," he said. "You may call me Jcobe."

Jcobe took off in a brisk walk across the cemetery, with Auriel and Kyne following along. Ni'Bara laid down in an open patch and told Kyne that he wanted to rest and to let him know if they found anything. Rosé was still wandering around the headstones and by the time she realized what was happening, Kyne and Auriel were nearly on the other end, so she decided to remain with Ni'Bara.

The cemetery lay just along the border of the city's palace with the raised earthen platform that the building stood on making a stone wall that bordered it. An archway with an old wooden door was where they were heading and as Kyne approached, he noticed an ornate keystone at its top decorated with ancient Kydrëan. He could read a little and was pretty sure it read "Solemn be the dead."

Withdrawing and old rusted key ring from his robes, Jcobe fit it into the lock and a moment later a deep thud sounded as the wooden door swung inward on its hinges. The door surprised Kyne at its thickness as Jcobe pushed it all the way open revealing stairs into a dark void.

"Are there torches for us to see," asked Auriel as Jcobe took his first step down the stairs.

"Oh yes, they are just a bit further in. I can light it before you come down, wouldn't want you two to slip and fall."

The Legend of Kyne: Chronocide

"I can take care of it," she said and aiming her hand down it to focus the spell, she lightly spoke the word, "Igathion."

A tiny flash of light flew out of her hand and to Kyne it almost seemed like a little fairy as it zipped down the dark path before darting back and forth. Within less than a second, torches began to light up the darkness revealing a short flight of stairs going down and then a long hallway.

"Incredible," breathed out Jcobe, stunned as he looked first down the hall and then back to Auriel and Kyne. "Breathtaking would be a better word," he chuckled and then turning back he started down the stairs.

He was an odd man, but Kyne had a liking to him and felt that he actually was a genuine and good person. Grabbing Auriel's hand just for a moment, he met her eyes and gave her a light smile, which she returned before leading the way after Jcobe.

The floor was not stone to his shock as they stepped off the final step and continued on, but a very fine grey sand that left footprints in it. Kyne scanned around and could see the markings of rats in it as well, their little, tiny tracks darting off in random directions.

As if reading his mind Jcobe said, "Looks like those damned rats are back. I get rid of them and then they just seem to appear out of nowhere. We don't want them making their way up into the palace above. The kitchen itself is actually one of the closest rooms that they could reach."

A grumble of frustration sounded from him as he reached into his robe and withdrew what looked to be pieces of food. Throwing them towards the ground, he nodded as if in satisfaction.

"Wouldn't want to eat that food that's for sure," Jcobe muttered to himself devilishly.

They continued on for half a minute before coming to an intersection and the first set of tombs. Each had been engraved with the deceased's name, any titles they had received in life, as well as their family crest.

"The Avalks have their own section," he said as they turned down one set of tombs.

Long stone rectangles, Kyne imagined the bodies that had laid

The Legend of Kyne: Chronocide

inside, lining the hallway with their corpses. Jcobe pointed to one in particular and Kyne saw the name Avalk, faded upon its surface. Looking over the faded stone he could just make out that it read the year 165.

Looking down the line, Kyne saw that the tombs were three high and went down in a long line as the hall curved forming a dead-end bowl shape. At the very end of the hall the tombs ended and carved into the stone was a large upside-down tree with names decorating its branches.

They continued on, stepping lightly through the fine sand at their feet as they passed the remaining tombs before coming to the carved mural. Without saying anything, the three of them scanned the names starting at the trunk and running down each branch until finally Auriel found it, "Pretarch" inscribed on a twig of a branch nearly forgotten at the very bottom of the wall.

"Well according to this he is the last of his line," muttered Jcobe and turning to the side, he briskly started searching through the graves as if he knew where his should be. A few moments later he said, "Here."

The grave was quite bare save for his name, family crest, and the title of storykeeper. No year was seen on the stone leaving the date of his death unknown.

"This is what you have been looking for," started Jcobe. "Now what are you going to do?"

"We don't know," said Kyne as he read over the script again. "We weren't really sure what we would find."

Reading it one more time, he noticed something very faint as if it had been nearly rubbed off. Squinting at it, he couldn't make it out, but he had an idea. Touching the stone, he said, "Eitala nuname."

Suddenly a golden light washed over the stone, pooling in the parts where the stone had been carved. Waving his hand, the light peeled away revealing a light marking of words that had once been hidden.

"Scholar of Alakyne of Ysaroc, ancestor and hero of Kydrëa"

"Alakyne of Ysaroc," muttered Kyne. He had never heard it worded like that before. He had always thought of Ysaroc as the name of a tomb, and in Kydrëan culture, he had never heard of someone

92

The Legend of Kyne: Chronocide

being named as coming from their tomb. It was custom to state where they are from with either being the city or the country itself.

Could Ysaroc be something more than just a tomb? he thought to himself. *If it is, then what secrets could it have?*

"Thank you Jcobe," said Auriel. "You have been so helpful. If I may ask one more question, was it normal to bury the deceased with any personal belongings?"

Jcobe furrowed his brow for a long moment as he pondered the idea.

"Not particularly common here no. Any of the deceased's belongings were given away as they wouldn't be needed in the next life. Are you wondering if Pretarch had something buried with him?"

"I was yes," she said, and she placed a hand on the stone grave. "I assume you are right, but I still want to be sure."

Saying an inaudible spell, Auriel sent a shock wave of aura through the stone. Bouncing off of anything within, it formed an image in her mind revealing that indeed Pretarch had been buried with nothing. Nothing remained in the tomb, it was empty but a pile of dust as all of his flesh and bones had degraded over the thousand years it had been locked up.

"It's empty," she said with a bit of frustration hidden in her voice.

"Of course, it is," muttered Kyne with irritation. He was hoping something would be there. Some special book that he never published that shed some more secrets into Alakyne or even a Relic.

As Jcobe led them back out to the surface, Kyne knew Auriel was thinking the same thing that he was. Once they were left alone, with the bright sunlight blinding as they shielded their eyes, they started at the same time.

"'I think we should go to Ysaroc."

"You do," gasped Auriel immediately after. "I thought you said that it was a bad lead."

"That was until I heard Alakyne of Ysaroc. That's a very strange title and my gut is screaming at me that it's a legitimate lead. I have never heard that title before and it's just so odd sounding. Something might be there. I just hope that it's worth the trek."

Ysaroc was incredibly far, on the other side of the country. He had traveled there before with a company covering the distance in a few months but with it being just them and Ni'Bara they should be able to make it there much faster.

"What do you think," he asked Ni'Bara as the four of them gathered together.

"It is quite a journey for a hunch," he rumbled. "A hunch that just the other day you said was completely false and not a true lead. I agree with you that Alakyne of Ysaroc is a weird thing, and it might be something to look into but..." his voice trailed off for a moment.

"If it's not then we will be chasing ghosts and getting nowhere," Kyne finished. "I am aware."

"If you are willing to take the risk then I will agree with you and I will carry you there."

Kyne thought for a long moment as he swung his gaze first over the four them. His eyes lingered on his family as he struggled with the turmoil within him. It was a long journey and Ysaroc was dangerous. He had no idea what other dangers lay within its dark depths, but something was screaming in his gut to go there.

Lifting his gaze up towards the sky, he squinted from the bright sun as he watched the rolling white clouds slowly drifting across the azure sea. The early summer sky was beautiful, and the land was warm and full of life. A life that he wanted to spend with his family, and he had to do everything it took to stay with them.

"I am willing," Kyne said as he lowered his gaze towards Auriel. "Will you take the risk with me?"

She nodded without saying a word. She would follow him to the depths of hell if he asked her to. She trusted him with her whole being.

9. Toward Kydrëa's Crown

Withdrawing from the Ouroboros Bag, Kyne grasped a parcel full of dried fruit and meat. Clutched under his other arm, he held a container full of water for them all to share. His footing was solid as he balanced upon Ni'Bara's saddle, thousands of feet of open air beneath him down to the verdant green forest below.

The wind was warm against his skin as he sat down and opened up his items for the other two to partake, which Auriel did happily. Rosé disliked the fruit but snapped up a few pieces of meat eagerly, not even chewing it before it slid down her throat.

They had left Shjavalk a few hours ago and had already made it to Kol Faldîn, the enormous forest that lay in the center of the country. From this high up, he couldn't make out the individual trees but occasionally could see the reflections of small lakes and rivers that split the green sea.

He had mapped out their path before they had left, planning as straight of a flight as possible so that they could reach the tomb in the fastest time. Their trajectory led them across the forest and into the Riigar Mountains where they would camp overnight.

They estimated that with Ni'Bara's speed and his flight stamina they should be able to reach the tomb in three to four days depending on weather and other factors. Much faster than traveling on foot, Kyne thought back to his trek through the forest down below.

He had learned so much on his journey, continuing his training with Voron and the others. He and Ni'Bara could've made it there much faster, but he wouldn't have had time to master the aural spells he would need to fight the manticore. He would've never crafted his catalyst and as he thought about it, the choice to send them all on their journey traveling by foot was what saved their country from

The Legend of Kyne: Chronocide

Aaldra's rule.

The horizon was a dark line revealing a seemingly endless forest with no end, as if the edge of the world would be found before the Riigar mountains. They still had a few more hours before they would even come into sight and swinging his gaze up and around, he traced the arc that the sun had made since they started and nodded his head in satisfaction. Ni'Bara had not drifted a single degree from his trajectory. His internal compass kept him directed at where they needed to go.

The sun cast streaking red beams of light that were cut with sharp shadows of stone peaks as Ni'Bara curved across the face of a mountain. Snow and stone were all that lie this high above their bases and Kyne suspected few animals ventured up onto their chilling summits.

White walls of ice lay carving down their surface as glaciers littered the mountains. Their blue ice piercing the shadows of the setting sun. Surging rivers exited their bases as they roared down the gorges they had carved through the stone before resting in teal-colored lakes at their bases. There were dozens of them, and as Kyne looked down below them his eyes wide with wonder.

He had not grown up in the mountains, but the mountains were where he felt at home, that is why he loved Tsora so much. These massive, jagged peaks were home to the hardiest of creatures, those that could scale their slopes and tread the grassy meadows in the valleys below.

He knew golems called these mountains home as well, but they meant little to him now. A golem would be child's play to him as well as the others. Rosé would be his only concern, but that concern would only last a few more years.

To a human, a golem was death. Their massive earthen figures would crush and dismember anything they could get their hands on whether that be human or animal. He could remember the beady red eyes when he had encountered it all that time ago. They had stumbled into its trap like a fly in the web of a spider.

Drifting slowly down, Kyne touched his companion's mind and noticed that he had spotted an area that they could make camp.

The Legend of Kyne: Chronocide

Situated in a small glade part way up the mountain, it would be relatively flat and large enough for all of them.

An updraft caught Ni'Bara's wings, and he stopped flapping, gliding strongly against it for a moment before it dissipated, and he continued on gliding down. The tops of the trees grew nearer and in less than a minute, Kyne felt they were close enough he could reach out and touch them. A powerful flap dramatically stopped their momentum and with a dull thud, Ni'Bara alighted upon the grass covered area crushing the wildflowers and other plants beneath his feet and claws.

A brush of his tail struck a tree with a loud crack and Kyne turned his head just in time to see it slouch over slowly, the fibers struggling to resist as they broke apart. With a crash the tree slammed into the ground and Kyne shot the dragon a thought of disappointment to which the dragon dismissed it.

They made camp with Auriel starting a fire and Kyne using his aura to raise the earth into a domed shelter. As he debated on leaving the roof bare, he glanced around the darkening sky and noticed the absence of moons and stars. It was overcast and in the mountains the weather can change in an instant. He decided not to risk it and filled in the center of the dome leaving a doorway for them to enter.

Do you want a shelter?
I'll be fine, I don't sense rain so I will take that risk.

Kyne nodded his head at Ni'Bara's response and grabbed the bedrolls from his pack. Auriel had heated up some of the fruit and vegetables that he had acquired some time ago. As they were finished, they sat down and ate, the yellow squash melting in their mouths and as their teeth sank into the peppers and onions Kyne fought back a gag. He really disliked them but knew that Auriel loved them.

The night came and went and when they awoke, Kyne stepped outside to see the ground slightly moist and raindrops still clinging to the grass. He threw Ni'Bara a look and the dragon snorted out a jet of hot air whether in embarrassment or annoyance Kyne couldn't tell.

They flew through the mountains the whole day, stopping that evening in the northern foothills just beyond their reach. Kyne traced the landscape with his eyes as he sat next to the fire, the rolling hills all around with snowcapped peaks faded far away in a blue haze.

The Legend of Kyne: Chronocide

Two more days passed with endless flying, and they were all very uncomfortable. They had each taken turns in the ouroboros bag to stretch their legs, but it didn't really help and resulted in the journey seeming even longer. The air had grown much drier as the landscape below began to lose the green grassy plains, replaced by sagebrush and the red of desert.

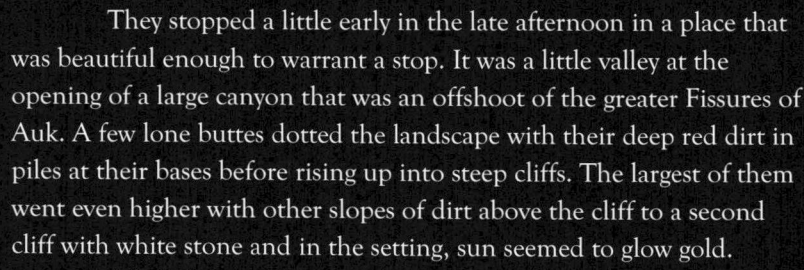

They stopped a little early in the late afternoon in a place that was beautiful enough to warrant a stop. It was a little valley at the opening of a large canyon that was an offshoot of the greater Fissures of Auk. A few lone buttes dotted the landscape with their deep red dirt in piles at their bases before rising up into steep cliffs. The largest of them went even higher with other slopes of dirt above the cliff to a second cliff with white stone and in the setting, sun seemed to glow gold.

A light breeze blew across the landscape, and they all sat and watched as the twinkling of stars appeared and the moons came up from the horizon. Glancing at his wife he saw her staring up at them intently, as if trying to see some sign of her people there so far away.

The Legend of Kyne: Chronocide

10. The Relic of Ysaroc

There it is, Kyne thought as the bitter chill of the wind swept across his cheek blowing his hair up briefly. The gaping hole of Ysaroc lay in front of him flanked on either side by three stone columns. The crunch of snow signaled Auriel had dismounted and he followed suit, his feet sinking knee deep into the snow ridden ground. The chill touched his ankle followed by moisture as the snow that had been captured by his pant leg was swiftly melting from his body heat.

"Vae dynori," They both said in unison and stepped out of their foot holes onto the surface of the snow. It pushed in nearly an inch but held from the significantly reduced weight.

The heavy fog around them hid most things except for their immediate vicinity. No mountain peaks lay scattered all around them and no azure sky above their summits, only the dark depths of Ysaroc and the mysteries that it hid.

"Kyne," said Auriel, drawing him back to reality. "Shall we enter?"

He nodded and took a few steps before turning around to look at the two dragons.

"Before you even start Rosé," he said, eyeing the dragon. "You aren't coming and that's final. Ni'Bara," and the dragon swung his long neck around so that he was staring at the small metallic pink dragon who lay perched on his back.

"Do you understand?" rumbled the grey dragon.

A long whine erupted from her as she swung her head back and forth in frustration.

"It's not fair. Why do you always get to have fun? Why can't I..." Her voice was cut short as she was quickly launched off of Ni'Bara's back and landed face first into the deep snow. The grey dragon snorted

The Legend of Kyne: Chronocide

in satisfaction before nodding that the other two could venture into Ysaroc. A quick farewell was shared between Kyne and him and then they were gone, lost into the mountain's depths.

Drip...Drip...Drip...
Every few seconds the dripping of water was heard as they stepped lightly through the stone cave. Shoulder to shoulder, the two of them continue on, avoiding small puddles of stagnant water and fallen stone. Dull white light cast their shadows forward from the hovering lights that trailed behind them and after a few times of kicking stones that were hidden by the shadows, Kyne waved his hand guiding the light in front of them.

"Much better," he muttered to himself, and he could just make out the breath of a laugh from his wife.

He wasn't sure why, but his trip seemed much shorter than the first time he had come here whether it was from the stress before or the familiarity now. Coming to a stop, they each stood in front of an intricately carved archway with ancient Kydrëan aural script.

"Can you read it?" asked Auriel as she eyed it. "It's a different language than you Kydrëans write in."

"Death awaits all," he said slowly remembering when Voron had said those exact words.

"Well, that's ominous," she said as she eyed the markings one last time. "Shall we continue?"

Kyne nodded and took a step forward with thoughts running through his head. Thoughts and memories of an ancient aural dampening spell upon the area. With all of his teaching, he still hadn't found anything more to explain it, but he felt immediate relief as they both passed through the archway and their aural light did not extinguish.

Continuing on, the stone path below their feet ended, replaced by silt and fallen stone. stalagmites and stalactites stretched towards each other from the ceiling and floor as the two wove their way between them. Their slick wet surfaces reflected the light from the aural companion and as Kyne reached his hand out to touch its surface he paused before deciding against it. Its earthly beauty was impressive, and he didn't want to taint it with his skin in fear of dirtying it or even

The Legend of Kyne: Chronocide

breaking the fragile looking stone.

Separating around a long and skinny column, the two of them regrouped before entering into a small cavern. The trickle of water pouring off its edge drew their attention, and they peered over to see a long drop down to a subterranean lake.

Its surface was black as the darkest night reflecting the glowing white orb from above, their reflection was distorted from the ripples caused from the falling water. Ever-present, the trickle echoed in the cavern as they looked down for a long moment. The lake was small, only thirty feet to the other side, so more of a pond but Kyne still wondered how deep it could be. a couple inches or hundreds of feet.

They skirted around the lake and continued deeper into the mountain; the earthy air caught in his throat. It stunk down here, like an ancient decay and being here gave him horrific memories; memories of his master fallen in a bloody puddle.

He shook his head trying to push the thoughts out and resorted to focusing on his steps, each one guiding him closer to his destination. The shadows danced along the stone walls, stretching and distorting as the two of them continued and a few more minutes passed when they were nearing their destination.

"Remember to be on your guard. The manticore was quite formidable and I don't know what else could be down here."

Auriel nodded as she recalled the stories, he had told her of the strange winged and venomous lion. She had creatures and monsters in her world but this one seemed stranger than most.

"Igathion," Kyne said as they entered the massive area, igniting dozens of torches all around to survey the scene.

The underground tomb was brightened revealing its many walkways and stone buildings. All of them stemming from the crumbling remains of a circular stone platform. Rubble lay strewn across its surface from the chunk of earth Kyne had dropped onto it many years ago. Beneath its mass, Kyne could just make out the jagged fractured bones of a beast. Every other part of it that had been uncovered was gone, scavenged by the treasure hunters who had come to explore the mysteries just as they were. Even the crystal obelisk that once bore Xeono had been shattered into pieces and taken away leaving only a rough and jagged base.

The Legend of Kyne: Chronocide

"So disappointing that people have to take and destroy things," Auriel muttered to herself as she made her way down towards the central platform.

"It saddens me," Kyne replied, signaling he had overheard her. "Treasure hunters and grave robbers, those are the kind of people who visit these types of places. The few who had found this before the manticore was killed were in turn killed by it preventing any thievery from occurring. Now that it is gone it seems it is all up for grabs."

"It's a pretty good chance that nothing else of danger resides in this cave," she said, and Kyne nodded as the thought entered his mind. If people had ventured here and taken things, then she was probably right. No more monsters were here. People though were monsters in a whole different aspect, and he still needed to be wary of anyone else here.

"Seiose," he said, suddenly revealing the trails of aura all around. To his satisfaction not one of them looked fresh with nearly all of them so faint he could barely see them. No one had been here in months if not years.

"So, what are we looking for specifically," said Auriel as she stooped down and touched the broken base of the crystal obelisk.

"I was thinking of trying to find Alakyne's tomb specifically. When we first came here, I assumed it was right underneath the platform and honestly got distracted with Xeono *and* the manticore *and* even Saathe, so I didn't think much of it. It doesn't look like that is where he is buried however, and I want to see if there is anything within it that might help us."

Placing his hand on the ground, he said a quick spell and nodded his head signaling he was right. There was no tomb underneath the obelisk like he had previously thought.

"So, if Alakyne wasn't buried here then where would he be?" he muttered to himself, a shadow of doubt creeping into his mind of what Auriel had said about Alakyne never existing.

Auriel had wandered off, venturing up a walkway and around some of the old buildings leaving Kyne alone on the platform. He scanned his vision around the tomb before peering over the edge of the platform into the deep darkness. Casting his light, he could see nearly a hundred feet down lay its base, a pile of boulders and rocks. Following the edge of the platform, Kyne dropped his light down into the abyss and guided it down its length revealing the whole bottom looked to be covered in rocks. As he came to the edge, he noticed that the rocks here began to pile up in odd and peculiar ways as they balanced upon themselves.

Watching his footing, he leapt the gap to the other side where he continued up a ramping walkway towards the wall of the cavern all the while peering occasionally at his light as it continued on, following the sloping wall of rubble as it climbed up towards him. Just as he reached the wall, the white glow of his light came into view and a look of disbelief lit up across his face as he saw that the edge of the cavern was actually the continuing pile of rocks from down below. Brightening his light, he shot it up its length and it continued on until it reached high above him when he saw that the ceiling too was made in a conglomerate of stone.

Anxiety began to enter his mind at the thought of an earthquake bringing the entire mountain down upon their heads but that was soon snuffed as he thought how long the tomb had already lasted. The chance of it coming down the moment they were there was so unlikely.

Scanning around, he could see Auriel up in the higher buildings, her light momentarily lost behind them as she trudged on. He turned his head back to the stone wall and placed a hand on it. Using his aura, he scanned the inside and was shocked to see it was incredibly thin, only a couple feet before the outside.

They were right up against the edge of the mountain!

Thoughts flew through his mind, tempting him and he scanned the wall again before scanning the ground, analyzing everything to make sure it was as strong as he needed.

Eventually, he used his aura to raise the earth around him, reinforcing the wall in a few spots before he strategically broke pieces of it.

"Roke," he said, and a large crack appeared in the stone in from of him. "Roke," he said again cracking it in a different spot.

A few more spells were said and then he could just make out a tiny glint of light from within the crack. Before he finished, he called out to Auriel and as she came up next to him, he quickly explained

The Legend of Kyne: Chronocide

what he was doing.

"Are you sure this is a smart thing?" she said, eyeing the cracks he had already caused. "This seems pretty stupid."

"I am confident," he replied. "And if it falls upon us, we can protect ourselves with aura. As I said before, the stone is not very thick so it shouldn't be a danger to us with our aura."

She remained still, refusing to agree with him. She thought it was dumb but didn't want to disagree. He had made a good point and she trusted his judgement.

Seeing that she wasn't going to stop him, he turned back to the wall, causing more cracks to appear before a massive circle of dim light was visible from the outside.

"Erodath!" he said, forcing a massive amount of aura into his spell. The force slammed into the wall, and it felt like the whole mountain was trembling as the stone fell apart, fragmenting outside onto the snow-covered mountainside.

The light from outside was bright to Kyne and he shielded his eyes for a moment as he listened to the avalanche of stone tumble down the mountainside, the deep echoes and crashes reverberating around for a long moment before silence. The only sound that followed was the wind as it met the edge of the opening.

Kyne threw Auriel a devilish smile before eyeing the wall that still remained. It held firm and after a few more moments he nodded his head and chuckled to himself. Not to his or her surprise at all but a few moments later both Ni'Bara and Rosé had appeared, hovering near the opening, dumbfounded at what they saw.

Flooding Ni'Bara with updates about what was going on, they all ventured back into Ysaroc to look for the tomb of Alakyne. Kyne decided to follow the edge of the wall that rounded it while Auriel ventured back up into the buildings with Rosé bounding along after her.

As he gazed up at the dozens that hadn't had light shined upon their surface for many years, he started to acknowledge something he had been thinking about. The tomb was more and likely an ancient city, alluding to the title he had read back in Shjavalk. A hidden city beneath the earth.

I wonder why they buried it, he thought.

The Legend of Kyne: Chronocide

Probably an effort to keep people away and to trap the manticore within, replied Ni'Bara. *Alakyne was an important figure, and I am certain that people would try to seek out his tomb.*

The city was small, with only a few dozen buildings, most of which seemed to be ancient dwellings carved out of stone and brick. The rough edges of mortar that held them together was not pretty by any means but would have been sufficient in their time.

A tomb that is also a city? he thought. *Did people use to live here after he died? or was it before?*

Suddenly he heard his name called by Auriel.

The Riel had climbed quite far into the city with her silvery tattoos shining from her own aural light. She was standing next to some building that almost looked like an old one room house. Situated at the end of a walking path with a steep hill reaching down upon the other side, the building was one of the last on the line. Down below it he could see the rooftops of the other buildings as they covered what he presumed to be the actual mountainside.

A few moments later he was soon standing next to her, and he followed her outstretched finger to the ground where there lay a small unremarkable stone with some carving across its surface.

The stone had been placed next to the building at a slight slant from the hill in what could've been a garden or front area. It was small and rectangular, grey in color with a visible layer of dirt and grime across its surface. He could just make out very eroded carvings of ancient Kydrëan.

"I can't read it, but I used my aura, and someone was buried here. That's how I found the stone so quickly in the first place."

Kyne knelt down and brushed his finger along the carvings. Ancient Kydrëan was not his strong suit as most of the scrolls he read were in the modern tongue. A few words though he recognized, and one stood out more than the rest.

It was a longer version of his own name that he believed he knew what it said.

"Alakyne," he breathed as he traced the symbols.

"The body is long gone," Auriel said as she knelt down next to him. "The way the stone is shaped underneath however is the form of a person as if someone crafted a cast of their body out of the stone."

The Legend of Kyne: Chronocide

"Is there anything inside?"

"It's hard to tell. It almost looks like sand or dirt but I'm not getting a good image from my aura. Kyne, are we really going to dig him up?"

The question was the one Kyne had been dreading for a long time. He knew that it was a terrible thing to dig up a grave, but he had tried to justify it. Tried to think of anything that made it ok for him to do it.

The body is gone, just like she said, and it has been so long. If it was more recent then I wouldn't but...

"I think we should," Auriel said as she could tell Kyne was lost in thought. "His body isn't even there so it's not like we are digging up a corpse."

Kyne nodded his head as the heavy weight was lifted off of his chest.

"We need to be as respectful as possible."

"Of course," she replied and with focused aura, the two cracked the stone and lifted it off revealing the indentation of a person below.

Kyne could make out the round shape of what would have surrounded his head and shoulders tapering down to what would've been his feet as he laid there. At the base of the cast, he could see a fine layer of dust that was probably his remains. He gasped in shock as nestled upon the dust on what would've been his chest lay a few tattered and torn pieces of parchment, the writing upon its surface faded to near nothing.

Stooping down, he gently grabbed at it and cursed as the paper fell apart immediately once he touched it. The bundle of pages was too fragile, and he wasn't sure what to do.

"The fact that it lasted this long in that condition is quite impressive," said Auriel as she knelt next to him. Reaching out her hand, Kyne called her name in shock and disbelief that she would try and touch it but the moment before she did, she said a spell and the pages suddenly began to glow with aura.

As her finger touched it, the glow began to brighten, and the paper changed from a dusky grey to a more tan version of the parchment it once was. Removing it from the pile of dust, she clutched

106

The Legend of Kyne: Chronocide

a few pieces of parchment, bound by an old rotten string. She stretched out her hand and placed it in Kyne's own with a brilliant smile.

"It looks like most of it was beyond repair," she said as she pointed at the missing front of the book and most of the pages. "But I saved what I could."

Kyne bit the inside of his cheek in a happy frustration. Happy they had something but also terrified it might not be what they needed. Eyeing down at the pages, he gingerly pinched one and flipped it over. The writing was incredibly faint but had been reinforced by Auriel's magic and he was just able to read it.

"But wait," he cried in shock. "It's in actual Kydrëan, not the old writing. How is this possible?"

"Really?" said Auriel and she looked at the manuscript before also gasping in shock. "No, it's not! It's written in Riel! But how is that even possible?"

"What?" said Kyne dumbfounded as he eyed the writing that was clearly Kydrëan. *How could she be seeing it in Riel though unless...*

"Could it be that Alakyne placed some spell upon its pages to allow anyone to read it in their own tongue?" he muttered. "I wouldn't say it to be impossible but still."

"If he really is the legendary figure that your people seemingly worship then I think it to be very possible."

He nodded before calling out to Ni'Bara and Rosé. Once they had gathered around the tomb, he lifted it up and began reading from its ancient pages.

Day 5909

16 years I have searched for these damn items to bring her back and I have found only 6. The Relics of Aute as I have come to learn they are called are powerful, as if crafted by the gods themselves but alas, I do not believe in such gods. Such gods would not have let us suffer and burn under the rule of those corrupted monstrosities. But I can seemingly hear you tell me, you whoever is reading these notes that if the gods were real would they have not

The Legend of Kyne: Chronocide

blessed us with these artifacts to stop their reign? And with that I have no comment. As far as I am aware, no one has seen or heard from these supposed gods in thousands of years with the only texts I could find speaking about some war in which they fought along our side.

    Gods fighting with mortals, ha, I laugh at that thought. Gods do not associate with mortals. Mortals were created to serve the gods, not be their equals, right? Anyways, I have gone off on a tangent as my old age is getting the best of me. As I sit upon the steps of my home, hidden from the world and writing this by the flame of a candle I struggle to weep but I cannot. My tears have long since dried up at her death. I used to sob daily at the thought of her gone lost to the afterlife and me trapped here but I must continue on. If these so-called relics are really crafted by these gods, and even if they are not, they still might provide answers. Maybe if I am to gather enough of them then I would be able to bring her back.

    Just maybe.

Day 5910

    I dreamt about her last night; how young she was. I still can't believe that today marks my 67th birthday. Nearly 55 years without her. I tried to forget, I tried to move on but in the back of my mind she haunts me. That is why I pursue them. Supposedly there are 12 and I have come across 5 so far. 5 of these relics in such a long time. I fear that I will not be able to find them all before my time is over and then it would have all been for naught. Alas, the writings of an old man mean little to those in the future who might find these

The Legend of Kyne: Chronocide

notes. I do not know why I continue but I do.

Day 5911

Today was uneventful and as I sit here still upon the steps to my home. I have rested my old bones for the last few days as I crafted a housing for the Relics, and I am nearing completion. 12 relics that I have come to learn about. I know what they all are, or what they are supposed to be, but I can't seem to find the last of them. They could be anywhere across this large land. I fear that some of them might even be more powerful than the one that lies upon my wrist. Its power is unlike anything else I have seen.

It scares me.

If it were to fall into the wrong hands, then the world could fall. But I am a king you say, a king who freed his people from those monsters. I deserve this power that I have been given. It was not of my own doing for if the others wouldn't have been there then I surely would have fallen. I wonder how they are and if they made it back to their home.

Day 5912

This is my final day here before I am to venture on. I don't know if I will ever be back, but I have ordered my subjects that if I am to pass on to the next life during my journey then I would like to be buried here, at my home. I hope she would be proud of me as I lay a decrepit old king who despises this crown upon my brow. My subjects are strict as they never leave me alone, even here as I am quite capable of defending myself, I have three guards I can see.

I grow weary of this life, and I might stop these entries. If I

The Legend of Kyne: Chronocide

do, then whosoever reads this know that these relics are not to be trifled with. Even one alone is too much for a normal person to wield. Power gets loved ones killed; I should know.

Day 7256

Alakyne has passed in his sleep, I, his scribe, was ordered to write this down as his last and final wish. I was told to be honest in the hopes to dispel the myths that Alakyne was a god. He was not, he was just a man with an unnatural talent at attracting the unwanteds. He did not die a heroic death and died at an old age of 72. He contracted an illness when we were in the southern jungles that brought yellow to his eyes and a terrible fever. He fought it hard but, in the end, it took his life. He was not able to complete his quest, only able to obtain 6 of these Relics that he was looking for. 2 more were nearly in our grasp but to take them from their current home could have caused a war with the desert people upon our southern border.

He is to be buried in the tomb known as Ysaroc, the home of his childhood. It will be sealed up and protected by a creature that the sorcerers of Tsora are obtaining. Their Aurals have all decided that the relics will be separated between their highest ranks with one remaining here to be protected from use. Xeono was condemned by Alakyne himself as a weapon of both gods and devils. He feared that it could be used for evil but also says it could be used by a hero in a time of need.

This journal will be placed in his tomb and protected from age as much as possible. In all honesty I don't believe it will ever be read and Alakyne will go on, worshiped as a god. He was no god

The Legend of Kyne: Chronocide

but a strong and brave man who did everything in his power to protect the ones he loved. He was my king, and we lost a hero today.

11. Seeking Out a Myth

Kyne placed the tattered and torn pages down upon Alakyne's remains as he met Auriel's blue eyes in shock. The two of them couldn't even speak as Kyne's last words echoed around the underground city. Even Ni'Bara was silent as he contemplated what he had just heard.

"He found six of them," Kyne breathed out slowly, his mind racing. "And five of them were given to the Tsoran sorcerers!"

"That would explain why you were given the Ouroboros Bag from Voron. It had probably been passed down for dozens of generations," said Ni'Bara.

"That leaves four more that were given," Auriel started. "If they had four more then where would they be?"

Kyne had no idea. He hadn't really thought about where they could've went, only that they were gone. Nothing he had encountered truly stood out to him that could be a Relic.

"I don't know," he said. "If there indeed were others, Aaldra might've taken them, or the other dark princes could have as they were once Aurals themselves, but I don't believe that they even knew what they were. When I was given the bag from Voron, he only said it was a bag imbued by magic. I don't think he had any idea what it truly was. Everyone was so fixated on the item they couldn't have, the power of Xeono that the others were cast out of thought."

"If the Relics did go with the sorcerers though, it could explain some of the strange forms of magic we have encountered before, specifically that dampening effect that you were talking about earlier," said Auriel. "I have never heard of anything like that before and it seems like a clear contender to me."

Kyne nodded slowly as his mind raced through all of the texts and scrolls he had read. Maybe if he could think harder, something would stick out.

I just can't remember, he thought frustratingly as he kept drawing up blanks. His memories were not detailed enough to recall every item he had encountered in his travels. No one's memory was that good. Then it hit him! He had a room in which he could look through his memories exactly and could pinpoint what he was looking for.

"I just came up with an i..." His voice trailed off as his mind exploded with another thought that drowned out all the rest. He had found one and he had used it himself on a few occasions! He was certain of it! The Room of Recollection was among the strangest aural oddities he had ever come across, but he had never put two and two together until now!

It must be a Relic! That explains so much!

"What did you come up with?" said Auriel confused. He suddenly grabbed her hand with a massive grin on his face.

"The Room of Recollection is a Relic of Aute!"

A big pause as both her's and Ni'Bara's eyes widened in disbelief.

"Are you certain," said the dragon. "That is quite a journey to go back home."

"I would bet a lot on it," he replied as he knelt back down and grabbed the tattered remains of Alakyne's journal. "Wouldn't you?"

The dragon paused before nodding his head in agreement. It did seem incredibly likely that it could be a Relic and he was mildly frustrated with himself for not recognizing it first. He expected Kyne and the others to not notice that it could be a Relic with there being so many different aural objects in the world but from his perspective that one always stood out as strange. Either way he was glad that they at least had a lead.

Kyne's smile widened and as he placed the journal into the ouroboros bag he turned to Auriel.

"Coming here wasn't a complete waste of time!"

"It seems so," she started as her eyes dropped low for a moment. her somber expression confusing Kyne.

"What's wrong my love?"

The Legend of Kyne: Chronocide

"I fear that looking for these Relics might become an obsession like it did for Alakyne. He spent so much of his life pursuing them to prove what? To bring back some love he once had? I don't know what getting all of them will do but I am worried it might be a futile quest."

Her words stung him, and he turned away frustrated. He wasn't obsessed, just excited. *It was the only thing that seemed to prevent the temporal distortions and even the Light had mentioned looking for others. Maybe he expected this to happen, and this was his hint to help.*

"It is not an obsession if it is a way to keep me with my family. Do you wish for me to just vanish from this time, cast to some distant past or future unable to return? Away from you and any children we could have, away from my friends and students and fellow sorcerers. You aren't being fair Auriel!"

She met his eyes and his anger vanished as she saw them glistening with tears.

"Of course, I don't want you to leave, I just don't want this to consume you and our last moments together to be corrupted by this ineffable quest."

"But I have to try," he whispered as he pulled her into an embrace.

"I know," she whispered back as she rubbed her eyes. "I know," she repeated again.

"Then let's continue on, maybe I only need one more Relic. Maybe that will be enough to stop it for a few years or maybe indefinitely. I don't know, all I know is I need to try and do something, and this is the best lead that we have."

They separated and she took a few steps away wiping her eyes before leaning against Ni'Bara's shoulder.

"So, there's another one that we know for sure. That leaves the mysterious shadow Relic and the other two," she said.

"And the other one that we know exactly where it is," rumbled Ni'Bara.

"We talked about this," started Kyne. "Xeono should stay put."

"And I disagree with you Kyne," replied Ni'Bara as he swung his head around to face him. The dragon's mind disconnected from Kyne's and the two stared at each other for a long moment.

"You can disagree with me all you want but I don't want

The Legend of Kyne: Chronocide

anything to do with it."

"You speak of all of your efforts to stay with your family and travel across the land to find these items, but you won't even try to get Xeono? What if you need all of the relics to stop it? Would you get it then or would you still be a baby and cry about how it's too scary. Grow up and be a man!" Ni'Bara snarled and his eyes flashed with dragonfire.

Those words sent anger flying through Kyne's brain.

A baby? A baby!

"Don't you ever say that!" he snarled with cyan flames upon the edges of his mouth. "Don't you ever say I am too afraid or scared of it!"

"I'm calling it how I see it boy!" roared Ni'Bara with his voice causing the very ground to quake. rearing his head up, he snarled revealing his fangs and his own dragonfire upon his maw.

"You are being a baby and I am tired of it! I flew you here so you could do all of this, and you whine about the quest getting a little harder. Don't you even start with me there!"

Kyne was silent as he fought against the dragonrage boiling in his veins. He was pissed off! Pissed at Ni'Bara, pissed at the world, and more importantly pissed at himself. He knew the dragon was right, but he didn't want to admit it.

"So what if I am afraid of Xeono!" he screamed back. "The power it has could destroy cities and topple nations! Could kill thousands if not millions of people if wielded in the wrong hands!"

"But isn't that what you could already do right now with the power that you wield in your arm?" replied Ni'Bara more calmly and he lowered his head down. "*You* could destroy cities and topple nations; *you* already have done those things. The power you have right now stopped Xeono and killed Aaldra. I do not understand why you are so afraid of it. Wield it and let us end this folly."

Utter silence save for the increasing howl of the wind from outside the city whistling distantly away. Kyne could feel his heart thumping in his chest hard and he dropped his gaze down to look at the scales that covered his arm. Each fingertip adorned with a pearly white claw and grey scales that crawled up his flesh to match his companions.

"As always you are right Ni'Bara," he sighed as he raised his head back up to meet the dragon's and their minds reconnected once more.

You act much older than you actually are you know, said Kyne. *You are much wiser than a human would be of your age.*

I just listen and observe. I have an outside perspective that lets me see things with a special eye.

"Kyne," said Auriel softly and he felt her hand wrap against his upper arm. "What do you want to do?"

Kyne took a long pause as he eyed each of his family members. First Ni'Bara as the dragon clung to the edge of the mountainside, his long serpentine tail flicking around dangerously close to the roofs of the buildings below. Each of his hands was adorned with white claws and thin membranes that stretched to the wings that were tucked at his sides.

Turning his gaze to Auriel, he traced her silvery hair, wavy and full that stretched to below her waist and her aspen leaf shaped ears laying nearly hidden behind her hair. Her silvery tattoo that traced down her arm in elegant swirls seemed to shimmer with every movement and he looked down at his human wrist revealing a small silver swirl not much larger than a fingernail, his bond in marriage with her.

Finally raising his eyes back up, he rested them upon the small hatchling dragon who was still but a child. Her metallic scales shimmered with a beauty that even outshone Ni'Bara's and her young eyes burned with a passion and innocence that couldn't help but cause him to smile.

"You all win. I will retrieve Xeono."

The grey dragon snorted with satisfaction and Kyne felt Auriel's hand release from his arm and her fingers interlock with his own.

"Thank you," she whispered in his ear before letting go and separating from him.

Rosé bumped him with her snout, and he smiled down at her.

"Your fight with Ni'Bara really got you worked up. I am glad he could knock some sense into you."

They all chuckled lightly at that before he turned back to his friend. "How are we to retrieve Xeono and the room's Relic? That is going to be an incredibly long journey."

"If we have too then so be it. I can fly you to either one first and then we could backtrack to the other. I really would be very annoyed though if we are to leave Tsora only to realize another Relic is there."

"Any thoughts on where the shadow Relic could be," he asked the dragon. "I really don't think it's at Tsora and I can't think of anything else there that could be a Relic. Nothing in the old wings scream anything to me and I have seen basically everything that is there."

"I've been trying to come up with anything that makes sense but no. If that is really a Relic and not some unknown spell, then I agree. I don't believe it lies with the sorcerers of Tsora."

"Could it be here?" asked Rosé suddenly. "You keep talking about the shadow thing that you felt here but it's gone now? I don't understand that."

"It could've been here at one time. Could've even been here the last time I was, and we just didn't notice but I guarantee if it was it is long gone, taken by some grave robber. I don't think that's the case though. The journal spoke of it going with the sorcerers, I don't think they would've brought it back."

"Oh," was all Rosé said and she looked away over the city out towards the open hole to the outside. snow had begun to accumulate around the edges, forming small drifts of the powdery white flakes.

"It might still be in our country, but I am not sure who would know," started Ni'Bara. "Is there anyone who might know anything that would be of use?"

"I think I know someone who might," said Kyne with a grin. "He seems to know a little about a lot of things. Maybe he has heard something about some mysterious items."

"Who is it," asked Rosé as she bounded around the grey dragon's arm.

"My friend Thirak."

"Oh, the small hairy man," she said with a puff of smoke out her nose. "He always seems to smell funny, like sweaty guy and some weird plant smell."

All three of them laughed at that as the last encounter they had, Thirak was trying to teach them about some medicinal plants he had been rubbing on his shoulders to help with some pain.

"That's a good idea," said Auriel. "He does seem to know a lot of stuff. Can you scry him?"

"I could but he doesn't know aura so he wouldn't be able to speak to us, we can just see where he is."

"I thought you said he used aura when he made your sword," she said confused. She had only met him on a few occasions and had never really thought about it.

"Well yeah, he used aura but it's what his people call ukcha. It's not like verbal aura, just forces his energy and spirit into his craft. He doesn't know any spells and the rest of his people don't really either."

"Ok, well where is he so that we can make a plan on where we are going," yawned Ni'Bara. "I want a plan before we just up and leave."

"I would assume he is in the Duulin. The new dwarven high city where the Riigar Mountains meet the ocean."

"I don't like assumptions," muttered Ni'Bara under his breath as he swung his head around before climbing away, making his way up above the houses to an open spot in which he could lay. "Figure it out!" he called down before dropping his head down and closing his eyes.

"Why don't you just scry him then, figure out where he is and then we can make a plan?" suggested Rosé before she dashed away up the mountain heading towards her older brother.

"Would that be weird?" he asked Auriel. "To scry him without his knowledge?"

"I feel like anyone would know something was off if they were to be scryed. It gives a feeling of unease as if you are being watched. Well because you are," she laughed. "I don't see it being a bad thing if its quick and you are able to discern if he's in Duulin. But it's up to you, my love. It is however, getting late and the others are exhausted as well as I. Please come up with a plan."

"Yes, my love," he said quietly and then she was gone, joining the others up on the slope. The large, covered area they were in was cold but much warmer than the snowy outside beyond and with a quick glance at the snowdrift that was rapidly growing by the opening

The Legend of Kyne: Chronocide

he guessed it was more of a blizzard.

"I guess I'll scry him," he muttered to himself, and he used his aura to carve a depression out of the stone near the house. Withdrawing some water from his pack, he filled it nearly to the rim and waited for it to become still. Focusing on Thirak's image in his head, Kyne said the spell and looked down at the surface of the water. Momentarily seeing his own reflection, he saw his golden hair looked pretty ragged and messy before it vanished revealing a dark room.

The orange glow of a small candle flame lit up the edge of the bed and Kyne could just make out two figures. Focusing harder, he watched as one stood up revealing the bare back of a topless figure. By the shape of their shoulders, he could guess it was a woman, but it was too dark to see anything else.

He could hear voices and straining his ears, he couldn't make anything out. Another figure entered into the image briefly, merely a shadow before stepping back out and Kyne couldn't see any discerning features. The woman said something before moving across the frame and another candle came into being casting her shadow around as she was silhouetted.

"I have an uneasy feeling," spoke a deep raspy voice and Kyne recognized it as Thirak's as he hid just outside the images frame. "Like I am being watched."

"What was that dear?" said the woman and the other figure stepped into the frame turned to reveal completely nude Thirak."

"Ahh!" cried Kyne in shock and he quickly rubbed his hand through the water smearing the image and ending the spell.

"That is why I didn't want to scry him in the first place," he mumbled, gritting his teeth in frustration. "I'll figure out where he is in the morning. I will just tell the others that he was sleeping in a dark room."

I don't think he'll be doing much sleeping, chuckled Ni'Bara's thoughts in Kyne's mind and the archmage slammed him out.

"Damn it!" he said out loud. "Damn everything! I didn't want to do that in the first place, and I don't want Xeono. I don't know why it scares me so much, but it does."

Kyne continued mumbling to himself as he trudged past Alakyne's home and made his way up the slope towards the others. He

The Legend of Kyne: Chronocide

was trying hard to make an argument, but Ni'Bara's was very valid. He would have to get Xeono and would have to figure out how to use it. In the meantime, however, he would need to figure out the plan for the other Relics.

He would scry the dwarf in the morning, but he was pretty confident that he would be in Duulin.

"Kitala map," he muttered as he approached the others and a scroll popped out of his backpack, landing in his hands.

Sitting down next to Auriel, he told her he couldn't find Thirak's location and she sighed before turning over and going to sleep.

Unrolling the scroll, he sat down on the barren mountain slope that had been hidden for over a thousand years. No vegetation was there, and the ground was hard and bare of anything but dirt and rocks. Reaching out, he grabbed four small stones and placed them upon the corners of the map of Kydrëa and Otoruh that lay in front of him.

Its northern edge was covered with small triangles representing the Agar mountains with the bottom edge barren except for a single river and the Otoruhn cities that lined it. The left side had the ocean and at its edge lay the outline of the large island that held the remains of Zol Kyden, the massive port city that Aaldra had converted to the Dominion's capital. It was being rebuilt slowly after the lava flow that burned most of it away, but it was making good progress and the Kydrëans were happy to be back home.

Placing a couple more rocks upon the parchment, he arranged them so that one was where they were, just north of the Sea of Asmathen in the Agar mountains with another placed upon the mountains in the eastern half of the forest Kol Faldîn.

"The Room of Recollection," he whispered as he placed the stone where Tsora was. "Thirak," he said as he placed one where Duulin was. "And Xeono," as he placed the third rock upon the island of Zol Kyden.

The island that once used to be a massive port city converted to the capital of the Dominion's occupation of Kydrëa. *Aaldra really wanted to stay out of most of the conflict; use the foreigners that he persuaded to join him to do the grunt work. I bet if they had won the war that he would've moved back to Alakyne.*

The Legend of Kyne: Chronocide

Kyne's eyes rested upon the small black symbol that marked Alakyne's location. He wasn't sure where Kioni was, but he was worried for him. A thought entered his mind of scrying him, but he quenched it just as soon as it was thought.

He would know, I am sure of it. He would know it was me and it would just make the situation worse. I will let it be for now.

Turning his eyes back to the paper, he focused upon the pages when a massive headache ripped through his head. Scrambling, he grabbed a hold of the pommel of his sword and felt the headache subside temporarily before returning slowly.

Damn it! he thought, panicked as he fumbled over to his pack. His head was raging as it was stretched and contorted, dampening his thoughts and focus. He barely made it and placed a hand upon the pack. The distortion ceased immediately, and he sat down panting, his head still swimming. The others were asleep but as his eye rested upon Ni'Bara's he saw that the dragon had one eye open and was staring at him.

Their minds were still not connected but Kyne could tell everything the dragon wanted to say just from the look.

It's getting worse and you need more items, but it might not be enough. Each Relic might just be a bandage trying to stop a hemorrhage. It will soak up as much blood as it can, but you will soon need another, and then another until suddenly you're out and...

He looked away from the dragon back down to the map and he tried to come up with a plan to get to all of the places as fast as possible. Ni'Bara was the fastest thing they had but it would still be weeks to do all of the things and he feared that might not be enough time.

They could separate, with Auriel and the two dragons going to get the Relic in Tsora while he traveled to Duulin.

No, he thought, shaking his head. He didn't want to separate and even if he did, by the time he made it to Duulin they would probably be arriving shortly after. Even aided by aura he still was just a human and traveling on foot would be slow.

Drawing lines with his eyes between Tsora, Duulin, and his present location, he clenched his jaw in frustration at the triangle it made. Tsora was closest but not by much. They were nearly the same in all directions, making the most inconvenient travel plan possible.

"We will go to Tsora first," he mumbled quietly. "Then we can head to Duulin if that is where Thirak is before heading over to Zol Kyden. If Thirak knows something, then we might be able to postpone our trip for Xeono a bit longer."

Kyne liked that plan as he glanced over the map again, eyeing the massive forest and mountains that split his country in half. He wasn't sure where any of the other items would be. Could they be in some tomb like Xeono? Or buried deep in the earth at the base of the Fissures of Auk?

He sighed as he scanned over the map at least a dozen times, eyeing the cities that were marked upon its surface with nearly all of them situated next to one of the great rivers that dotted the landscape. Clenching his jaw at the journey that lay ahead of him, he slowly removed the rocks and began rolling the scroll up. Placing it in his pack, he gathered his own bedding before closing his eyes and resting.

But sleep never came and as he lay there in the deep darkness with the constant slow breathing of Ni'Bara next to him, his mind continued to race with thoughts of flashes of light and pain.

He laid there for what seemed like hours with the constant whistling of the wind outside being his only companion before he decided to get up. Without using a light, he amplified his night sight with his aura and quietly crept away from the others, traveling down the inside mountain slope heading towards the large hole he had made.

The howling grew louder, and the icy touch of snow brushed his cheek as he stepped out into the dark blizzard. No stars were seen, and he could barely make out objects only a few dozen feet away. The cold was brisk, but he was comfortable in his clothes and was energized enough to use aura if necessary.

Taking a deep breath, he ventured out into the snowstorm, skirting around the hole he had made before beginning the journey up the outer mountain slope. Each footstep pressed deep into the snow and after a moment of trekking knee deep, he used his aura to lift himself up and continued upon the snow's surface.

The mountainside was steep and littered with the bare cliff faces of stone that the snow struggled to cling to. Planting his foot firmly upon a flat outcropping, he launched himself up a few feet to

The Legend of Kyne: Chronocide

another before launching himself even further to the top of the rock. More lay before him and after a few more powerful jumps, he left them behind, continuing on up the side of the mountain.

The air was wickedly cold, and the snow was fluffy and dry, with each step causing a squeaking sound as his boot pressed onto its surface. Ysaroc was high up upon the mountainside, but he still had a ways to go before he would reach the summit. It was growing harder to see as the wind intensified, blowing his hair around as icy snow blew from the cliffs striking his cheeks. It burned slightly as the ice tried to cut his skin, but he was fine, still comfortable with the temperature and the more he traveled on, the warmer he seemed as his legs burned, and his breathing grew heavier.

His breath rolled out of his mouth in a thick fog as he trudged on, placing his hands upon the stone wall that stood before him. Hooking his fingers around a natural lip, he pulled himself up, firmly planting his foot before stretching his other hand up to another spot he could grab.

Scaling the wall, eventually he glanced down and was startled that he could no longer see where he had begun his climb, obscured by the blizzard and at least thirty feet below him. He couldn't tell how far it really was, so he returned his gaze and began climbing once again.

The air was thin this high, the Agar Mountains themselves were large, not as large looking as even the mountains of Tsora but large enough that they scraped the sky. The entire northern half of Kydrëa sloped up to a high plateau making this entire mountain range the highest on the continent, so high that most people wouldn't be able to breathe easily upon the summits.

Kyne was accustomed to the elevation however as his school towered two miles above the forest of Kol Faldîn and he regularly flew the skies with Ni'Bara. He took a deep breath trying to maintain a steady rhythm as he pulled himself upon the top of the cliff. He brushed the snow off of his pants and continued on.

After another quarter of an hour, he noticed that the blizzard seemed to be lightening up and to his relief, another fifteen minutes and it was gone, left behind him upon the lower mountain slope.

Up above, no moons shined but thousands of stars twinkled in the bitter night sky. The outline of the adjacent mountains were seen and he could just make out their peaks, jutting out of the dark layer of clouds like little islands.

His destination was up ahead, only a short distance away and as he neared the summit of the mountain, he saw a familiar mound of snow. Frozen in a long oval shape, Kyne knew what lay there and sitting down next to it, he sighed as he looked out over the world.

"I wish you were here Voron," he said. "You always seemed to know the right thing to do. You would guide me and help me with what needed to be done."

The air was still and utterly silent as Kyne's voice drifted away. There was no response as he sat upon the high mountain summit towering over the world. Alone and away from nearly everyone, Kyne sat there for a long time, trying to meditate and grow the courage to do what needed to be done.

"I know Xeono can help me, but it caused me so much trauma. I don't even think the others remember how Aaldra humiliated me before crushing my hand and prying it off my wrist. I'm lucky they were able to fix it so well," and Kyne rubbed his right palm, a familiar faint ache coming from it that he had learned to deal with.

"Xeono is safe where it lies, locked in the stone. If I am to remove it, I am bringing it back into the world. A world in which real monsters lie, people who would do anything for the power. A power that could start wars and ravage my country. I understand why Alakyne locked it away and I wish to do the same, but it seems that I am going to be forced to release it."

There was once again no reply and Kyne sat there a moment longer, the thick storm clouds below him thinning out revealing the snow strewn mountainside. Far away he could just make out the general area in which his family lay hidden in the mountainside.

His family believed in him, and he suddenly felt a large flow of calmness through his body as he gave in. A part of him deep down wanted Xeono, its power would be incredibly useful if he needed it and that part of him was what scared him the most, but the more he thought about it, he came to the realization of the fact that because it scared him meant he truly respected the power it held. He slowly climbed to his feet and looked first at the snow mound that held his master's body before looking up at the star strewn sky.

The Legend of Kyne: Chronocide

"I will retrieve Xeono and find a way to stop this curse in which I have had placed upon me. Whether it be caused by slaying a god or by some other means, it needs to be stopped."

*   *   *

The Legend of Kyne: Chronocide

12. The Wind and the Rose

The wind blew Kioni's hair back roughly as he guided the horse forward in a fast canter. This was the third horse he had stolen since he had fled the eastern capital of Xinwei, and he could tell it was beginning to fatigue. It was late in the evening and itching his nose, he strangely didn't feel the silvery cloth upon his face.

It was there though, camouflaging him as some eastern person as he continued changing faces and stealing horses. He had ridden the rest of the night and the following day, trying to get back to Kydrëa as fast as he could. He knew that they might still be after him and he needed to get away.

His own horse had been dropped off nearly a week's ride away, at a site that stabled horses for travelers. He hated doing it more than anything for fear of something would happen to it, but he always did. He never kept his own steed close to his quest. If something were to happen such as this, it wouldn't be able to get him away fast enough and would have to be left behind or he could be captured.

He felt it again, the strange feeling that he was being watched but concentrating hard, he blocked it out. Someone was scrying him and he would resist with all his might.

He continued on, guiding the horse forward as the sun continued its descent, first casting the grass into a golden color and then transitioning into an orange. He slowed the horse down to a trot and continued on. He would travel partway through the night before stopping to get some rest. It stressed him out stopping but he knew the horse couldn't go for much longer.

As the sun faded away and the sky darkened, to his surprise, thousands of yellow green light began to blink in and out of existence. He was near a small grove of trees and as he guided his horse to a stop, he could hear the trickle of a stream. Kioni dismounted and began to

The Legend of Kyne: Chronocide

set up camp. A few moments later the sound of the horse drinking was heard.

The night was warm and with the glow of the fireflies he was able to see most of the things around him. The stars were bright, and the moons were low in the sky, thin crescent shapes.

He had no sleeping pad or blanket, just the clothes that he had stolen from the current person's face he wore. Each time he changed, he switched his clothes, keeping only two things. a small bag full of aural items including his suicide stone, and his kamas.

As he lay upon the ground, he watched the periodic glow of the fireflies blink in and out of existence. It was peaceful there and he could feel fatigue setting in. He was hidden, off the road he had been following a far distance and was confident no one would be able to find him, so he closed his eyes and allowed sleep to overtake him.

Deep thumping shook the ground jarring him awake and he fumbled in the dark, trying to see what was coming. His heart was beating hard in his chest, and he grabbed onto his kamas tightly as a great dark shape burst through the trees before coming to a stop. His horse whinnied in shock and flailed its head as a dark figure leapt from the creature's back.

The glow of the fireflies revealed their silhouettes and to Kioni's surprise he thought that the creature almost looked like a massive rabbit.

"Kioni!" spoke a female's voice and suddenly an aural power grabbed a hold of him binding his arms at his sides. He dropped his kamas as a silvery orb of light appeared revealing a beautiful eastern woman as she leapt to the ground in front of him. She was small and petite but had power behind her eyes. As his face was illuminated, a look of confusion spread across her face. She turned sharply and grabbed the reigns of the giant rabbit creature. Guiding it forward, each hop brought it closer until suddenly Kioni felt its hot breath upon his face. A few snorts and its nose twitched before it swung its head away from him.

"What the hell!" screamed the woman in frustration. Her eastern language unknown to him. "You're not Kioni then why would the inaba bring me to you? Who are you?"

The Legend of Kyne: Chronocide

Kioni understood only one word of that whole ordeal and it was his name. She was after him, but his disguise had kept him alive, at least for this long. He was still groggy from sleeping and confused about who this woman was. She wasn't Fox but she did have a slight resemblance to her but far more beautiful as he stared at her tight bun upon her head adorned with braids. A single braid must have come undone as it lay against the side of her face.

"I don't speak your language," he said as his mind tried to scramble for a plan. "I speak Kydrëan."

"Why do you speak Kydrëan?" she asked in his own language to his shock. Her accent was surprisingly light from what seemed like years of practice.

"I live near the border and grew up speaking their language as that's most of the travelers we encountered. My parents didn't teach me my native tongue."

"That still doesn't explain why my Inaba brought me to you. It was supposed to be searching for some Kydrëan not this," and she gestured to his figure whom he resembled a middle-aged peasant man. "Why could that be," and she began to draw her blade for her hip.

Kioni's mind was racing, and he just blurted out, "Maybe it was the man that gave me this horse," he said gesturing towards it. "He was a Kydrëan like you said. Seemed to be in a rush and really wanted my other horse. Wanted to trade for some reason. Little did he know that my horse was old and this one looked much better," he laughed as he tried to sprinkle in some fabricated details.

She looked first at him and then at the horse.

"Where?"

"Where what?"

"Where did you trade him and where was he going?"

Kioni's mind worked quickly, and he thought of his options. If he said the other direction then it could take her away from him, but if she forced him to come with her, then she would drag him back towards the people he was fleeing. Maybe he could use it to his advantage then.

"West, down the road about a day's ride," he lied.

"A days ride?" she gasped. "How in the... How the hell did he get there so fast? Maybe he used an inaba? No, they are not the

The Legend of Kyne: Chronocide

direction he would be fleeing."

"Can you release me," said Kioni as he watched the lady muttering to herself.

"Suddenly he was jerked up and dragged towards the Inaba. She withdrew some rope and bound him up to his dismay before hooking him on the saddle.

"Looks like you're going to take me to him," and she jumped into the saddle and the inaba was off, dashing through the trees heading west and leaving the horse alone in the grove with the fireflies.

"My horse," Kioni cried out in shock as the wind from accelerating blew him in the face. This creature was incredibly fast and soon the grove was gone, lost to the darkness of the night.

Kioni squirmed in his bindings for a long while, unsuccessfully freeing himself and unable to say much over the roar of the wind. They traveled for about an hour before the woman guided the creature to a stop and tossed Kioni to the ground where he lay, still bound up.

"Who are you," he said as she said something, and a pile of logs caught flame.

She ignored him and sat down, meticulously trying to fix her hair as she tucked in a few loose braids but left one out.

"You kidnapped me and made me lose my horse, the least you owe me is a name."

She was silent for a moment before laying down and turning away from him. "It doesn't matter, you won't need to be knowing it where you're going."

Kioni was frustrated but didn't ask again. Instead, he looked around, noticing that she herself was looking in her pack. Just as he thought about trying to escape, he heard her say five words.

"If you try you die."

And there they slept, Kioni with his hands bound behind his back laying awkwardly upon the ground, face first with insects periodically climbing across his cheek. He got a little rest but just as the sun's light became visible, he was yanked up by aura and perched upon the saddle once again.

They were quickly off, traveling at a blinding speed down the road. They passed no one on their journey but Kioni was still thinking of a plan. Listening, he had memorized some of the commands she had given her steed and after nearly an hour of fumbling, managed to rub his bindings against the pommel blade to one of his kamas.

Slowly he rubbed back and forth timing each one with the hops of the inaba. But what was he going to do once he was free? She knew aura and could beat him in a moment. He suddenly felt the rope around his wrist give and carefully, he released it, dropping to the dusty road and vanishing far behind them.

One more rope.

The last one bound his arms to his sides but now that his wrists were free it would be much easier. Wiggling carefully to readjust, he couldn't help but stare at the back of his captor's head. Her jet-black hair was still neatly in its bun, but he could tell it was beginning to fall out and no matter how hard she tried it would soon give. She was small, he knew physically he could overpower her, but her aura seemed adept, and he wouldn't win there.

He could kill her, stab her in the throat with one of his kamas so she couldn't talk, but that thought didn't seem right with him. He wasn't sure if it was because she was a girl, or especially because she was a pretty girl, but he didn't want to kill her, even though he knew she would probably kill him without thinking.

He had to stop her from speaking and get her thrown off the steed. If he could do that, he could steal it and maybe get away.

He had to do something; he had no other choice.

Cocking his arm back, he saw her start to turn her head as if she felt something but before she could finish, he jabbed out, striking her in her lower flank as hard as he could. She cried out in pain and quickly, he clamped his hand around her mouth as she struggled against him.

The inaba jerked and then they were on the ground, tumbling through the dirt in a heap of limbs before coming to a stop. The inaba continued for a few hops and then stopped a short distance away.

A sharp pain erupted in his hands as she bit down, but Kioni was fast and struck her hard in the shoulder. She gasped out in pain as she struggled and with his bleeding hand, he grabbed a hand full of dirt from the road and tried to force it into her mouth. She clamped her mouth shut as she fought against him, and he felt her sharp elbow ram into his abdomen knocking the breath out of him.

The Legend of Kyne: Chronocide

If she gets away, I'm dead!

Reaching up, he grabbed onto her perfect bun, tearing it apart and jerking her head back. She screamed in pain and at that moment, he rammed the handful of dirt into her mouth choking her and causing a coughing fit.

This is it, it's all or nothing!

Two swift punches struck her in the abdomen, and she doubled over, gasping and coughing up dirt as he scrambled to his feet. Dashing as fast as he could he felt the cloth across his face come down and his clothes suddenly grew very tight as his body returned to normal. Leaping upon the inaba's saddle, he said the command and the beast took off leaving her behind. A flash of energy flew through the air, but it narrowly missed him and as he looked back at her, he saw a look of utter confusion across her face as she saw him for who he really was.

There, Kioni left the once pristine eastern captor in a disheveled mess. Her hair was ruined, undone in wavy rags and her face smeared with blood and dirt.

*   *   *

13. Mangroves and Gueloks

"There's that strange feeling again, like I'm being watched," Thirak said as he rubbed the back of his neck, his thick fingers catching in his red and wavy hair. "It makes me uneasy."

"I bet it does," muttered Kyne as he stared over the small puddle of water, the glow of his aural light casting upon its surface. He watched for a moment as Thirak swung his head back and forth searching his room. No other figures were seen in the room and Kyne rolled his eyes as he thanked God for that.

I don't think that is the Light's doing, rang Ni'Bara's thoughts but Kyne dismissed them as he looked back down at Thirak.

Sunlight was streaming through the window, landing upon an ornate rug at the base of the bed. Against the wall was a dresser and a mirror in which Thirak stared at for a moment. A couple shadows lay upon his cheeks and Kyne caught a gasp in his throat. The shadows were dark bruises that lined his cheeks, and he could make out a few deep red scratches across them as well. Dried blood sat against their edges in little clumps as the dwarf picked at it for a minute before he got most of it removed.

Concern racked through Kyne's mind as he stared at his friend who looked like he had been in a fight but after thinking about it for a moment he tried to push it out. Thirak was a grown man, older than himself by nearly ten years. He could take care of himself, and Kyne chuckled as images of the other guy entered his mind. A faceless figure beaten and bloodied.

Thirak was no pushover that was for sure. Shorter than most Kydrëans, the dwarf, whom Kyne had realized not long ago was actually just a different race of Human, was just under five feet tall. Thick and stocky, he carried a lot of muscle on his small frame and the calluses across his palms and knuckles showed he knew how to fight.

Suddenly, he licked his hands before running his fingers through his hair, clumping it together in thick red waves. He said something before looking over his shoulder towards Kyne's direction before shaking his head and muttering some more. A moment later he turned towards the window and walked towards it and to Kyne's delight onto a balcony. The moment the sunlight hit the dwarf's face Kyne reached up and placed his hand across his mouth in a puzzled look of thought.

Before him lay Thirak standing upon a balcony overlooking the upper district of Kydrëa's capital Alakyne. The citadel lay to his right, a few blocks away with most of it cast in shadow from the morning sun.

Kyne ended the spell immediately with the last thing he saw being Thirak looking back at him, a look of unease upon his face. As the image faded away, Kyne looked up at the others to see his wife sitting next to an orange fire a little ways away. A pot had been suspended with some intricate tying of branches and Kyne could make out the steam of whatever was inside beginning to boil.

If he is in Alakyne then that changes things, he said to Ni'Bara. *Tsora is still our best bet but at least we don't have to travel all the way to Duulin.*

I do enjoy the thought of not having to go all the way there. That will save days of constant flying.

"So, Thirak is *actually* in Alakyne," announced Kyne as he approached the Riel and smaller dragon.

"Oh, that's great," she said as she stirred a spoon into the pot. Withdrawing the spoon, Kyne watched as thick dark brown liquid glopped off of it. "So, what's the plan then? Are we going to Alakyne first or Tsora?"

"I was thinking Tsora would probably be better. It could give us a little bit of a boost to get a Relic before heading towards Alakyne and then getting Xeono."

The Riel nodded as she stirred the pot, her hair drawn up into a tight ponytail. "I wonder if traveling to Alakyne might be better though." Suddenly, she removed the spoon. "Breakfast is done," and Rosé squealed in excitement before bounding around.

The Legend of Kyne: Chronocide

Removing the pot from the fire, she took three bowls that had been set out and filled each of them up with the stew before sitting down next to Kyne.

"What makes you say we should go to Alakyne?" he asked, in between a mouthful of the warm stew.

"Because of Thirak. If he is really there, how long do you think he will stay? It could be a few weeks or months or just days. We might miss him and then we are back to square one trying to find where he is. If he starts heading back to Duulin then it will just make our journey longer."

Kyne sipped some of the stew from his spoon and then nodded his head. He hadn't thought of that.

"I think she might be right," rumbled Ni'Bara. "We have no idea why he is in Alakyne. We should take advantage of it."

Kyne nodded his head again and took a few more mouthfuls of his stew. Soon he was finished, and he quickly cleaned the bowl before tossing it into his pack. Gathering the others as they finished, he packed them and extinguished the fire.

Summoning a few more aural lights to combat the darkness, he sighed.

"Ok, Alakyne it is then. If we are going that way at least the first leg of our journey won't be much different. I wish to visit Guelok Lokona as I haven't been there since I was captured. I have heard that the city has had quite the dramatic shift since the Dominion was removed and I would like to see it."

"Fine with me," said Auriel as she rose to her feet. "Are we finished here though? Is there anything else you wish to do in Ysaroc?"

"Well," Kyne said slowly as he contemplated the idea. He hated leaving the place without having searched every square inch of it, but he felt in his gut there more and likely wasn't anything else that he would need.

Then a thought struck him.

"Actually, there is one thing I would like to do," he said. "I want to make a gate to Tsora as I did with Voara."

Auriel smiled as she liked that idea but then her brow furrowed.

"But it's so far," piped in Rosé. "Last time you did it you were

The Legend of Kyne: Chronocide

super tired. Won't this one be harder?"

"It shouldn't really be any different. It's making the gateway itself that drains me. After it's made, I will just take the other end to Tsora."

He hated draining so much of his energy so early in the day; he knew it would be a long travel but hopefully he could possibly just sleep. It also worried him to use so much aura for if something bad were to happen he wouldn't be able to contribute much.

We will be fine, said Ni'Bara. *Auriel and I are quite capable.*

Kyne nodded his head and scanned the area in which he wanted to place the gateway. He eventually rested his eyes upon Alakyne's grave and decided inside the ancient home seemed like a great place.

Walking down the slope of the mountainside, he stepped onto the ancient stone road and continued on, passing a few of the out skirting homes before he came to Alakyne's. To anyone else the home looked average but to Kyne and the others they knew that hidden within the stone lay the remains of the most legendary figure in all of human history. Even other countries spoke about him for he didn't just liberate Kydrëa but the whole world.

Stepping past the empty doorway where the wood had long since rotted away, he found himself in a small room. A single window opened to the outside and he watched the dancing of light as Auriel's figure walked past it, her light trailing behind her.

Concentrating on the source of his aura, Kyne said, "Uantum."

As the portal spell began to form, Kyne forced more aura into it, splitting it into two halves and as they separated, he felt a massive pull leave his body. His vision darkened dramatically, and he took a few breaths to bring it back, focusing upon the spell. He had to not just make a portal but create a version of it in combination with everlasting magic that he had learned from Auriel. Drawing power from the surrounding area, the portal could be sustained indefinitely, forced open only when it was needed.

He felt his legs begin to buckle and his arms grow heavy as he struggled to finish the spell. The swirling rippling surfaces of the two swelled for a moment before shrinking into pinpricks where they

The Legend of Kyne: Chronocide

hovered still as stone.

Kyne sighed with relief and leaned up against the wall of the room as his vision began to darken for a moment. Complete fatigue as if he had run the entire day set in and he took another deep breath. It was done and now he just needed to transport it.

"Kitala vial," he muttered and a small vial that once held a seraph flew out of his pack. Forming a small bit of aura around one of the gateways, he moved it from its position and placed it into the vial.

"Otri," he said softly and threw it towards the pack on his back where it vanished into its depths.

"Let's go," and he hobbled out of the room and began the excruciatingly long journey towards the hole in the wall. His breathing was heavy, and his legs buckled with each step as he followed the others down the sloping trail into the city's center.

A few minutes later they stood out in the bright morning sun as it reflected off of the snow. The air was cold but not as bad as the night before and not a single cloud dotted the azure sky. Stepping into the deep snow, Ni'Bara swept his tail through it scoring a great furrow to allow the others to approach him as he dropped his shoulders low. They all climbed up into the saddle but before they took off Kyne lightly touched Auriel's hand.

"Can you close it up? I don't want others to get here easily as it might ruin it. I would do it myself but…"

"Of course," she interrupted, and she leapt down immediately and approached the opening. Using her aura, she pulled earth from all around and piled it lightly around the hole blocking Ysaroc from the outside world.

Their journey took them off of the mountainside out into an open canyon. The rough craggy surface of a blue glacier lay below them, snaking like an icy serpent as it carved its way down. Upon all sides of their view all they could see was stone and icy peaks of the Agar Mountains, bare of all vegetation except for near their bases where thin grass had grown. Even in the summer this far north and as high as they were still remained bitter cold with only the hardiest of animals living here.

Kyne felt his eyes grow droopy and swinging his Ouroboros Bag around, he attached it to the saddle and leaned forward resting his head upon its black leather surface. in moments he was asleep, drained from his use of aura.

Kyne pried his eyes open, the grime that crusted between his eyelids fighting with every bit of its strength until it gave allowing bright light to enter his pupils. He squinted as he waited for his eyes to adjust and slowly, he saw the blue of the sky.

Or is that water, he thought as he raised his head up while rubbing his eyes. It *was* water, as he looked again. As far as the eye could see was the dark blue water of Asmathen. The massive lake that resembled the ocean stretched all across the horizon where it met the azure of the sky in a hazy line.

"You're awake," said Auriel's voice and he turned to see her back with her head turned just so he could see her eye. In front of her was Rosé and they were playing some game she had sprawled upon the saddle.

"How long was I asleep for?"

"Not that long, a couple hours. We left the mountains some time ago and have just had the boring blue of water all around to keep us entertained."

"Thats why we are playing a game," said the hatchling as she raised her head up to look more at him. "It's hard though for me to move the pieces so Auriel is doing it for me."

Auriel laughed lightly as turned back to the board and moved a piece.

"Ha exactly what I wanted you to do!" roared Rosé in triumph and she guided Auriel in moving her piece. "I think I have won now!"

"Or," said Auriel calmly as she moved one of her pieces to the side. "You did what I was planning."

Rosé stared at the board dumbfounded for a few seconds before whining out a long cry.

"Not fair!"

Auriel laughed as she gathered the pieces back and was starting to reset the board.

"Would you like another shot?"

"You always win, it's no fun."

"I'll go easier on you this time," said the Riel and she

The Legend of Kyne: Chronocide

continued arranging the board.

"That's what you said last time though," whined the dragon and Kyne turned back in his seat as the two started another round.

Are you doing alright?

I'm fine, replied Ni'Bara. *We have a good tailwind, so it has been easy flying for the most part.*

Kyne liked that very much. He felt like he always took Ni'Bara for granted just as anyone else took a horse. They did all the traveling and the human just wanted to be there faster, not realizing the work that was being put into it. He had been trying hard to show his gratitude to the dragon and was trying to make it as easy on him as possible.

Kyne stretched his arms up and yawned as he looked over the world below. The waves were too small to recognize with their height and he zoned out. The sun finished its ascent and started on its journey down when far off he noticed the hazy blue line had revealed land.

"Finally," he muttered, and he showed the others who basically said the same thing he did.

As the land drew closer, Ni'Bara began to descend lower towards the surface. Tracing its edge, Kyne could see the thick dark line of a river appearing and some hazy figures near to it that he assumed was Guelok Lokona.

The city was quite large, the largest city in Kydrëa's northern half with hundreds of wooden buildings right next to where the river met the lake. As they approached, he noticed dozens of large fishing boats docked at the port and dotted across the shallower parts of the lake. Small dark figures of the people that inhabited the city were seen.

He watched as a few of them began running and then more began to join, all fleeing the port and heading into the city where they dove into their buildings. Ni'Bara and himself hadn't been here in years and the people were not accustomed to seeing a massive grey dragon.

His head alone was the size of a horse and with his long snakelike neck and tail that stretched twice as long as the rest of his body he was easily over a hundred feet long. His silvery wings would blot out the sky and each of his claws were the size of human swords. Ni'Bara glided down lower and nearly brushed the buildings

The Legend of Kyne: Chronocide

sending humans screaming in fear as he banked around before landing just outside the city gates. No area within the city was truly large enough for him and the only place that could possibly work was filled with what people had remained and small shops.

The three dismounted and as they began walking into the city Ni'Bara took flight, heading out across the sea to hunt. To Kyne Guelok Lokóna looked much different than before. The earth was firm and new stone bricks had been laid down replacing the muddy disaster that once lay there. The buildings themselves seemed to be doing better as well. Drying fish dangled from strings connected to their roofs and verdant houseplants littered their windowsills.

Upon seeing them, a few of the citizens ran to him and bowed down upon the dirt, praising Kyne and Ni'Bara with some even comparing him to Alakyne.

"No no, please stop," he said, genuinely uncomfortable. "Just stop please."

The three of them skirted around the cheering people heading towards a shop to purchase some supplies. Pulling out a coin purse, Kyne heard exclamations about Rosé and then suddenly the dragon yelped in shock as someone had grabbed a hold of her tail. Tucking it to her body she dashed between Auriel and Kyne who both had whipped their heads around with fire in their eyes.

"You lay a hand upon our daughter, and you die," snarled the princess and the woman who had grabbed her cowered in fear. The others surrounding them grew quiet and Auriel swung her gaze over all of them. "That goes for the lot of you. Leave us alone please. Stop gawking and do not lay a hand upon Rosé."

They continued on and the crowd began to disband with a few people hanging around just out of their personal space but still hovering as they stared at the three strangers.

"How can I help you," stammered a young girl in her mid-teens as they approached her shop. The smell of stinky fish hung in the air, and they could see fillets hanging nearby drying in the mid-afternoon sun.

"We would like to purchase some supplies," Kyne said as he lifted up his coin purse. "Would you be able to help us?"

"Oh, of course," she stammered as she looked briefly at Kyne

The Legend of Kyne: Chronocide

before resting her eyes upon the silver haired Auriel.

"You... You must be Auriel the person from the other place." She nodded her head.

"I don't mean to stare but your beauty is just how it has been described. I... I apologize," she said suddenly dropping her eyes and continuing cutting up more fillets. "I don't mean to act like the others, it's just."

"It's alright," said Auriel cheerfully. "I don't take offense from you; you seem very polite."

The young girl smiled and looked over the counter down at the rose gold dragon.

"And your name is Rosé?" she asked to whom the little dragon met her gaze and nodded. "Beautiful name."

"Thank you," she replied, and she bowed her head, her tail stretching back out to normal and waving mimicking a happy cat.

"What can I get you?" said the shop keep back to the adults.

"All of the fish you have as well as some fishing supplies."

The girl's jaw dropped for a moment in shock and then she realized he wasn't joking.

"Uh..." she stammered as she placed her knife down and rubbed the fish blood upon her apron. "Let me get my brother, one moment," and she dashed inside.

Murmuring was heard and then she came back out accompanied by an older man similar in age to himself.

"My sister says you wish to purchase some fish?"

"Indeed sir," Kyne said dropping the coin purse down. "This should suffice."

The man eyed him suspiciously and his sister reached her hand out to untie the knot bundling it up. out spilled a few dozen gold coins to which they both gasped in shock.

"This is far too much," he stammered and then suddenly began to take down all of the fillets as well as removing some that had been salted and aged from within the shop.

"I think it will suffice," Kyne said with a smile and the girl stared at him for a moment before a call from her brother and she began scrambling through their things trying to pack all of the fish.

"Why are you overpaying?" leaned Auriel as she whispered in

140

The Legend of Kyne: Chronocide

his ear.

"Because they seem like good people, and I like helping out. I have more money than I could ever need from my status as archmage and most of the time I never spend it. I just want to help out good people.

As the fish were all wrapped up and bagged, Kyne was pleasantly surprised to see there was actually quite a hefty amount in front of him. Even if he and the other two gorged themselves on fish it could probably last a few weeks.

"And my sister said you wanted fishing supplies?" asked the man as he placed down the last package.

"Just two rods and some bait."

"May I ask why? You just purchased a large number of fish."

"Just wanted to enjoy my evening," he chuckled, and he began sending the packaged fish into the Ouroboros Bag. The man stared at him for a long moment, mouth slightly open in confusion as his bag kept accepting more and more fish, holding far more than it should before he shook his head and dashed over to the side where he removed to long stick with thin thread attached to the end. His sister arrived just as he sat them down and placed a small container of very stinky chum that they could use for bait.

Kyne thanked them and then they left them walking deeper into the city. Most of the shops were boring but they were able to find a few pieces of clothing for each of them and Rosé got a sweet treat. The sun was about two hours from setting and Kyne had seen enough of the city to be satisfied. It was beautiful and seemed to be thriving and as they left, they noticed Ni'Bara hadn't returned.

Skirting around the city, they traveled a few hundred feet towards the lake shore and then continued, walking along its edge heading for a far-off cluster of mangrove trees whose roots stretched up out of the water. Their branches thick and covered with moss, Kyne placed a hand upon the wet velvet before hoisting himself over a root and continuing deeper into the trees. He wasn't sure if they would catch anything, but he just wanted to have a nice relaxing evening, and this seemed like the perfect place.

Auriel followed him and Rosé dashed up ahead, leaping quickly up and over roots before vanishing into the thick vegetation.

The Legend of Kyne: Chronocide

Moments later they saw the top of her snout stick up and they watched her push through until she managed to leap out onto another root.

They continued on for a moment more before coming to a good opening and positioning themselves upon the roots. The water was fairly deep and clear enough for them to see the silvery outlines of fish as they darted in and out of view. He withdrew the two rods and after attaching some stinky bait to the hook at their ends, they each lowered them down into the water on opposite sides of the root.

It took only a few moments before Kyne felt the first tug but just as he went grab it, it was gone. Sighing, he raised the hook revealing the chum had been strategically removed.

A *lucky fish*, he thought.

Auriel cried out in shock, and he whipped around to see her hoisting a fish the size of her forearm out of the water. Its silvery scales reflected the light in a rainbow sheen, and he watched as his wife smiled in delight.

They removed the fish from the hook and killed it before it was placed in the pack with the others. They continued to fish, each catching a few when eventually Rosé called out that she saw Ni'Bara. Kyne shot a light orb up into the evening sky and soon he felt the dragon's mind touch his. After sharing updates, Ni'Bara landed near the trees on dry flat ground while they finished their fishing.

The sun finally set and as it began to darken, they gathered their things and began to head out of the trees. Climbing over the mossy roots, Kyne felt the furry velvet with his hands. It was soft and pleasant to the touch. Rosé was up ahead and suddenly she cried out in shock, leaping back off a root and baring her fangs as something stirred upon the tree.

Kyne reached for his sword as did Auriel but before anything could be done, a large creature the size of Rosé leapt from the tree onto another root before adjusting itself and giving them a better picture of what it was. It was a massive frog, its skin rough and patched with different shades of green that blended in perfectly with the moss upon the roots. The frog blinked its eyes as it looked upon them for a moment, each eye shining like an emerald before it leapt away onto another tree and scurried up into its branches.

"What was that?" gasped Auriel in shock as she sheathed her

The Legend of Kyne: Chronocide

weapon. "It was so pretty."

"It's a guelok," chuckled Kyne. "I have never actually seen one, but it looks just how I have been told."

Suddenly a single call echoed through the trees, soft and pleasant reminiscent of a single drop of water striking a still pond. Again, it repeated and as they made their way through the trees more calls began to appear all around.

It was growing darker but silhouetted against the darkening sky Kyne stopped the other two and pointed revealing the outline of a guelok as it called the pleasant sound.

As they exited the trees, they listened as the calls continued and to their delight found Ni'Bara close enough so that they could listen through the night as they slept. Small insects began to land upon their skin, but a quick spell was said, and an invisible aural shield was placed upon them killing any insect that landed upon them.

Setting up their sleeping pads, all of them stared up at the stars as they drifted off to sleep, the periodic calls of the gueloks giving them pleasant dreams.

*   *   *

14. The Wilted Flower

Each footstep was followed with a sickening slurp as Akami's delicate shoes were covered in grime. The mud was deep as its surface was pattered with a constant light sprinkle of rain that had begun early in the morning. The repeated clomping of her horse accompanied her as she led it down the path.

She cursed as she lost her footing, staggering forward in a few steps with her shoe nearly being ripped off of her foot, her muddy ankle wraps the only thing keeping it in place. She pulled hard on the horse's reigns, yanking its head forward as she struggled to remain upright, the animal whinnied in shock, puffs of steam blowing from its nostrils as it whipped its head up nearly taking Akami off her feet. She cursed again as she righted herself in the mud, the tops of her shoes caked in the grime as she stood there for a long while breathing hard before finally continuing on.

It was Kioni, she was certain of it as she remembered the olive-skinned man as his face was temporarily revealed before he was gone, bounding into the dark of night upon her inaba. She had tried to pursue him immediately, taking the horse he had left behind, but the beast was fatigued and after nearly an hour of a brisk trot she had to dismount. She couldn't stop, she had to keep moving as she imagined the seeming boundless energy of the hare each second taking him further and further away.

She had been humiliated, biting her lip in fury as she brushed her soaking wet hair from her face, her bun completely undone. Her clothes were water resistant, but the rain was persistent, and she had been thoroughly soaked.

She was sick and tired of the rain. She felt disgusting and dirty and wanted nothing more than to sit next to a warm fire. She knew

The Legend of Kyne: Chronocide

that a small town should be nearby along this road. She had been trained the majority of her life in all aspects concerning her country and had memorized a lot of their map.

Returning to the image of Kioni, his face fixated in her brain, she summoned his aural trail making sure that she was still on the right path. To her shock it was different than before, just as fresh but changed to a different person. She was confused and angry and she swung her head back towards where they had come, the road vanished behind the veil of falling water. The trail continued on far out of view but right beneath it she could see the trail of the inaba.

He must have some strange spell that shrouds him somehow, she thought with frustration as she guided her horse on relieved that she was still on the right trail. She had never heard of such a spell, and it frustrated her even more. She was not one who lost, at anything. A prodigy, she had grown up the youngest of her siblings, two brothers who were killed in the eastern wars with Kydrëa and her older sister.

The youngest was nothing of a handicap to her and she seemed to have a natural talent for everything that she did. Aura was her favorite as it allowed her to do nearly limitless things and to be beaten by someone, someone who couldn't even match her was beyond irritating.

She could imagine the disappointment upon her mother's face if she found out what had happened. How he had not beaten one but two of her daughters and escaped. She had to catch him; her own honor was on the line now! This wasn't just to defeat her sister once again.

It was personal!

Far along the road through the haze of the rain she could make out the orange glow of lights. She was nearly there, and she felt her mouth water as she imagined eating a warm meal and getting out of the soggy rain. She passed a few homes; great fields lay spread out around each littered with crop and the leafy stalks of grain just barely visible in the faint light.

"This town must have a tavern or something," she muttered as she gritted her teeth. Her wet hair dripping down her face and she brushed it back behind her ears.

The horse whinnied again, trying to guide her to the fields so

The Legend of Kyne: Chronocide

that it could eat but she jerked the reigns hard keeping it on the road.

"You don't eat until I have," she hissed in rage. "I am royalty and to have to trudge down a road like this... like a damn peasant is beyond humiliating!"

A longer building came into view and she could just make out the silhouettes of a few horses tied up and left out in the rain.

She increased her speed, her stomach growling and her mouthwatering again. Each footstep was followed by the sucking sound of mud as she trudged on. Her feet were soaked, and she could feel in a few places the beginnings of blisters forming. She needed to get out of this.

A few minutes later she had arrived, throwing the rope over the wooden stake near the other horses. She tucked herself underneath a small overhang just as a young boy ran out from underneath an outside covering waving his arms trying to get her attention.

"What do you want," she snapped, using her aura to dry her hair as best as she could before eyeing the young boy with disgust.

"Two coppers and I'll feed and clean your horse."

"Clean it, with it raining?" she asked incredulously as she waved her arms around. "You can't be serious?"

The young boy, dressed in clothes that were way too small and littered with frayed holes just looked at her and held out his hand for payment.

"You're a foolish disgusting little boy," she scoffed, and she took a step up towards the tavern door. Suddenly she whipped her hand out, a single copper piece pinched between her fingers. "You get one. Feed it."

As the boy reached up for the copper, a gleam in his eye, she flicked her wrist sending the metallic coin flying into the mud. She smiled wickedly before continuing on and pushing the door open to the tavern.

Flicking her damp hair nonchalantly, she expected everyone in the tavern to turn and gawk at her beauty but all she got was a few looks before they all turned back to what they were doing.

Confusion, followed by embarrassment, followed then by rage flew through her mind. She had always been constantly adored by everyone she had met. The beautiful daughter of the empress, talented

The Legend of Kyne: Chronocide

in everything. A flower hidden among the driest desert.

She stepped into the tavern, her muddy shoes leaving a great glob on the wooden floor.

"Aye you miss," snapped the bartender from across the room. "Watch your filth or you can get out."

His tone caught her off guard and she glanced down at her shoes before meeting his eyes, a fury rising in her chest. She wanted so badly to rip them off and hurl them right at his bald ugly face.

"Thu'mar," she said, and all the mud peeled off her shoes forming a nice and neat pile which she placed delicately next to the door with a wicked grin. The bartender shook his head, clearly not pleased but didn't say a word, instead turning around to get a patron something. "Sei'var," she said quietly, and she felt the moisture from her shoes and all of her clothing fade away as the water was drawn from it.

Tilting her head around, she eyed all of the nearby tables before spotting an empty glass. The guests were in a heated discussion and seemed to not notice as she waved her hand guiding the dirty water into it.

Grinning for a moment, she waited for her smile to attract any stares to which it didn't. Finally, after an agonizing length of time, she stepped into the tavern, making her way to the bar. She met a few eyes, all of which seemed uninterested and frustrated, she sat down, waiting for her order to be taken.

Every time the bartender walked past, however, he refused to look at her and after a few times, she tried to speak up in an attempt to get his attention. He still seemed to not care or did not hear; she wasn't sure and when he finally came in front of her she slammed her hand down on the wood. Turning his head, he eyed the small girl for a long moment.

"Are you ever going to take my order?"

"Are you ever going to act like an adult. You walk into my tavern and act like some damn princess. Mind yourself and maybe you'll have people actually interact with you."

His words stung and he didn't look away as she averted her eyes for a moment. She had never been spoken to like that before. Maybe by her mother, but that was different. Her mother talked to everyone like that and half the time Akami didn't even pay attention.

As she raised her eyes back up to gaze, she noticed him furrow his brow and purse his lips while nodding his head as if waiting.

Order, he wants my order! her mind gasped.

"Sake," she said. "And some rice balls."

Grunting, the man turned away from her and began working on her order.

"You don't seem to be from around here," said a voice nearby catching her attention. A large man had spoken to her, a dark cloak draped over his head and shoulders concealing most of his features. From what she could see he was ugly and ugly peasants meant less than dirt to her.

She snorted and turned away from him, clearly not interested, which seemed to gain his attention even more. Lowering his hood, he revealed himself to be a dark-haired man, a large coarse beard covering most of his face and his hair long and rough.

The more she looked at him, however, the more intrigued she grew. He was actually sort of attractive in a scruffy kind of way as Akami eyed him up and down. By his constant staring, she could tell that he was into her.

"Have you seen a Kydrëan recently?" she asked as the bartender brought her drink which she took a big swing.

"A Kydrëan?" he chuckled before sipping at his own drink. "That would be pretty uncommon, especially being so close to the capital. Not of *our* blood, right? Our new motto? If you ask me, I don't know why we can't just mind our own business."

"I didn't ask your opinion," she said flatly. "I asked if you have seen a Kydrëan. If you keep spouting off your political view to strangers it might get you executed."

He nodded his head with a smirk. "So, what if I have seen a Kydrëan?"

"So, you have then," she said turning towards him and flashing a smile. He knew something, she could tell and maybe she could use her looks to get something of use. His aural trail shows that he had stopped at this tavern just like she had but not for long. His trail didn't seem to linger so he probably had been getting supplies or maybe looking for a different route. If she could figure out where he was heading, she might be able to possibly keep up with him.

The man grinned through his beard before turning to face her completely.

"You're quite the inquisitive one aren't you. Yes, if you must know I did see a Kydrëan."

"And?"

"And that's about it. Saw him, then he left."

"What was he doing?"

The man smiled and took the final sip from his drink. Just as he opened his mouth to say something, a loud sound was heard outside of multiple horses arriving. It seemed to gain the attention of most of those inside and the room grew quiet as they listened.

Akami soon heard the riders dismounting and the muffled voice of the boy before a thud slammed against the door, bursting it open with the boy falling to his back.

Inside stepped four women wrapped in orange and white cloaks, seemingly untouched by the rain.

"Aye what the hell do you think your..." The bartender's words were cut off as one of the women flicked her wrist up, launching his body up to the ceiling where it was pinned tight.

Gasps erupted from everyone in the tavern and as she lowered her hand, the bartender crashed to the ground.

"Who are you," he coughed, clutching his chest. "Why have you come here."

"It doesn't matter who we are. There was a Kydrëan seen here, we know. We want all the information you have. Don't try to protect him or you will die."

The bartender hunched over the counter for a moment, his breathing heavy before he spoke.

"I saw a Kydrëan here. Didn't order anything. Just got food for that weird rabbit thing and asked for some directions. I never spoke to him."

"And who did," said one of them as she walked quickly towards him, seeming to glide over the floor. Akami turned more away from her and to her horror, she stepped right in between her and her new talking buddy. "Who might've talked to him then?" she hissed darkly.

The Legend of Kyne: Chronocide

"I know the boy did," he said pointing at the unconscious young child who laid sprawled out across the floor. Other than that, I couldn't tell you."

The Kitsune seemed to growl in frustration before slapping the counter, the force sending a large crack through the wood.

"Four sakes and a wild fowl for my sisters and I," she snapped and all four of them walked over to a table near the wall that was already occupied. The four of them hovered for a moment before the one in the lead flicked her hand signaling, they should vacate their seats at once.

They didn't hesitate after what had already transpired and getting up, they chucked a few coins towards the bartender before nearly running out of the tavern.

They all sat down and removed their hoods revealing their fox red hair. Akami glanced out of the corner of her eye and quickly recognized her sister sitting with the others.

Damn it! she thought fiercely. *If they find me, they might suspect what I am doing and that might make them angry enough to act. Any once of them I could take easily but I can't take all four at once.*

Akami cursed under her breath and turned quickly away, grabbing hold of a rice ball and quickly eating it.

"Interesting," muttered the man in her ear. "First you come here looking for some Kydrëan, and then these four show up almost at the same time seemingly looking for the same man. He must be quite lucky."

"That's not how I would put it," remarked Akami through a mouthful of rice. Dipping it in the dark sauce that accompanied them, she finished one and moved on to the other.

"I know where he was heading," he whispered in her ear, making the hair on the back of her neck prickle at his breath.

"I am listening," she responded, swallowing her mouthful of rice.

"Not in here," he mumbled. "I don't want to draw attention to them. They seem a lot more hostile than you," and his words made her smile slightly.

"Come he said, rising up from his seat. Placing a silver coin on the table, Akami was impressed with herself for working this man so

The Legend of Kyne: Chronocide

well. That was enough to pay for his drink as well as all of her things.

Turning to leave, Akami accompanied the man, flanking low on his side away from the Kitsune who seemed preoccupied with the drinks they had just been given.

They stepped over the kid's body, who was beginning to groan signaling he was waking up and then they were outside in the wet drizzle that had not ceased. She could make out her horse feeding on moist hay that had been laid out for it but instead of going towards it, the man guided her around the corner of the tavern and towards a clump of trees.

Akami felt an uneasiness creep in her as she slowed her steps letting him gain some distance on her.

The man stopped right as he entered and turned around for her and seemed to be waiting. As she approached him, she noticed another horse tied up under the trees, protecting it from most of the rain and the uneasiness lifted some. As she withdrew her hood from her hair, she brushed it away from her face.

"So, what do you know," she said as he stooped down towards the ground and seemed to be playing with something in the mud.

"He seemed to want to know the fastest way to get to some horse station near our western border. I overheard them give some directions about what road to take. I can show you if you want," he said as he rose up to his feet. Turning towards her he walked towards her slowly, causing her to back up until she felt the bark of a tree as her back was pressed up against it.

"I think that it might cost you though," he breathed at her, and she looked up at him as he towered over her. She suddenly felt his hand placed against her waist and just as his fingers curled around the edge of her shirt, she decided she had had enough.

"Erodath!"

The man was jerked roughly back away from her before slamming hard into a tree, the crack of his head against the bark making her twitch.

"How about you just tell me and your payment could be staying alive," she said with a wicked smile as the dazed man looked up at her. Blood seemed to be dripping from the back of his head. His eyes were glazed over, and he fumbled for words for a moment before sagging over limply in the mud.

She stooped down and put her finger near his nose, just brushing the dark hairs above his lip.

"He's still breathing," she muttered, rising to her feet. "But he's not going to be any help now." Swinging her gaze around, she noticed his pack and after searching through it, to her surprise found a few interesting items before tossing it to the wet ground.

"Actually," she said suddenly as she eyed the horse that was tied up who seemed to be very conditioned. "Maybe he will be."

Climbing up into the saddle, she flicked her hood back up over her head and guided the horse out of the woods.

Approaching the front of the tavern, she noticed the boy had made his way back out onto the steps and was sitting down holding the back of his head. She shook her head as she approached the front of the building, the road only a few dozen feet away when suddenly the door swung open and to her shock her sister walked out.

The boy cried in fear and dashed away, hiding between the horses that were tied up nearby, but she didn't seem to even notice him. Swinging her head around as if looking for something, her eyes rested on Akami and then Akami felt her body jerk through the air as it was ripped from the horse's back.

As she flew through the air, she said a spell and twirling like a cat, landed upon her feet, a blade drawn, and her teeth bared. Her hood dropped to her shoulders and at the sight of her Hayame began to laugh ecstatically.

"Oh my god look at you," she said as she stepped down from the steps. "My gorgeous little sister, pristine and privy turned into a slob lower than even most peasants."

Akami was silent as she stared at Hayame who was still laughing uncontrollably.

"Why the hell are you all the way out here? Let me guess, mother sent you here to mess up my quest. Of course, she would," she said, and her laughing ceased. "Greatest mother ever right. Seems like she just wants me dead."

"It would seem so," said Akami lowly.

"And it looks like you might as well," she responded, and her eyes darkened in anger.

The Legend of Kyne: Chronocide

"I wouldn't say that," Akami said, not taking an eye off her and keeping her thin katana ready. "Just wanted to beat you once again."

Her words caused Hayame to frown and then her face evolved into rage.

"How dare you!"

"How dare I? How dare you, you are the one who messed up. Don't blame your mess ups on me. Mother hates you for a reason."

"She's hated me since the day I was born. I could never be good enough. Her two sons, children lost in the war were all she could seem to think about and when I was born, I could never replace them."

Akami paused for a moment as she listened to her sister as if for the first time. Their mother really seemed to have always hated her and she never really gave it a second thought as to why.

"Mother has always been nasty to everyone, even dad. Don't think you are the only one she's mean to."

"This coming from her perfect little princess who can do whatever she wants. Are you seriously telling me that you don't see it?"

Akami was silent.

"I had a thought that I could see her do something like this but to actually send my little sister to basically try and kill me is just beyond disbelief."

"I didn't want to have you killed," Akami started but she was interrupted.

"Then what did you think would happen? You saw what she did. Basically, filleted my Kitsune sister in front of my eyes as she would've done to me if I hadn't won. If I fail this quest, then I will be executed for sure!"

Her words struck Akami hard, and she lowered her katana, the tip nearly touching the surface of the mud. The never-ending sprinkle of rain began to intensify the sound changing to a low drone.

"To send my own sister," she repeated. "I never thought she would but when I saw your aural trail melding with the one we were following, I couldn't believe myself. I knew it had to be you Akami. Your aural trail is unique, all pretty and sparkly. It really is disgusting."

Akami didn't respond to her and standing straighter up, she sheathed her katana.

The Legend of Kyne: Chronocide

"But what was interesting is, how after a short time your aural trails separated with his going off with the one that was following you. I once again couldn't believe my eyes, but I am pretty sure I know what happened. He beat you and took your hare thing. Took it right from you and left you in the mud. Would explain this," and she gestured towards Akami's disheveled self. "Did it hurt your ego being defeated by a common Kydrëan? Have him knock you off your seat with the gods so that you may tumble down the mountain to interact with other mortals?"

Akami bit her lip. She didn't have a counter to her words.

"You know if you return home without him then mother might be so upset even you might not escape her wrath. It is an interesting thought though, two sisters vying for the same prize. I wonder who will get him first," and as if on cue the other three Kitsune phased into existence behind her as if they had been watching the whole time. Their hair was wet, but their faces bore sly grins.

"I..." stammered Akami. "I didn't know."

"Consequences little sister," said Hayame and she spun slowly in a circle as she eyed the other Kitsune. "Everything you do always has a consequence, and it seems yours has finally caught up to you. Caught up and overran the pretty little princess, trampling her into the mud."

She grew silent as the rain continued to intensify, filling all sound with it as it struck the muddy ground. Akami's new stolen horse had walked off a short distance but seemed to be content standing where it was.

"I am not like you however," Hayame started. "I hate you with every fiber of my being, but you still are my own flesh and blood. I don't know if you remember but when you were so very little you and I were nearly inseparable. It saddens me that this is what we have become.

I don't wish you to die, I have thought this since I first came across your trail and have decided I will offer something to you just this once. If you wish, join us on this quest and we can bring him home together. Mother will be upset, that is beyond obvious, *but* it will allow both of us to continue on with our skin still upon our bodies."

"Hayame!" gasped one of the Kitsune, the one who had spoken to the barkeeper. "You do not have the authority to offer that

The Legend of Kyne: Chronocide

to anyone let alone her. She is the one who has mocked us, said we were beneath her skills, and you offer her a place among us?"

"I did not say she could join our sisterhood," snapped Hayame. "And who says I don't have the authority. Who is going to stop me, you? I would like to see you try."

The two Kitsune stared at each other with fire in their eyes. Akami wouldn't have been shocked in the slightest if the rain had begun to steam.

The Kitsune eventually broke eye contact ceding control to Hayame who smiled briefly before turning towards her sister.

"So, what will it be?"

Akami paused for a long time as she stared at the Kitsune. She hated working with them, they all annoyed her so much with their weird cultish club, but Hayame was right. If they didn't work together then one of them would die and she was on the lower ground in that fight.

"I'll join you."

* * *

15. Friends of an Old War

Traveling south, it took them nearly a week to make it to Alakyne. The Riigar Mountains were passed with their jagged peaks seeming to call to Kyne as he stared at their beauty. Spending only one night upon their slopes, the group eventually left the mountains behind and were soaring over the dark green forest of Kol Faldîn.

Kyne looked one final time back at the mountains they had left, sad and torn for he wanted badly to stay and explore them more.

Maybe one day I could build a home there where I could raise my family, away from the chaos of the world.

Kol Faldîn was large and for the most part a continuous sea of green save for occasional small grassy meadows. Like little islands, they were scattered amongst the trees and littered with colors of wildflowers. Small streams cut through them, splitting the fields and trees like sparkling cracks upon glass.

Two nights were spent in the forest and then they were gone, leaving it for the grassy prairie upon which most of the Kydrëan cities lie. Alakyne was soon on the horizon, and as they descended down, Kyne hoped that their arrival would catch Thirak's attention.

Eyeing the city, Kyne scanned the buildings in the area he believed Thirak had been but to his dismay saw no red-haired dwarf. They circled a few more times, trying to gain as much attention as possible before banking around and landing in the courtyard that contained the statue of Alakyne.

Kyne expected King Theo to come out, just as he did before but to his surprise he never did. Instead, a herald appeared telling them of King Theo's preoccupation and asking if they needed any of his assistance. He dismissed him saying they were fine and met Auriel's eyes just as she rolled them showing her disapproval of him.

The Legend of Kyne: Chronocide

"Lazy lazy man," she muttered as they sat and waited.

It was only about five minutes that they waited before a figure stepped through the archway huffing and puffing. He bent over for a second, his hands placed upon his knees, but Kyne knew who it was and smiled.

As Thirak caught his breath, he took off in a light jog towards Kyne who met him in a warm embrace.

"My little man!" chuckled the dwarf as they separated, and Kyne eyed him mischievously.

"Little," Kyne laughed as he placed the palm of his hand on top of his head before extending it over Thirak's, nearly a foot above it.

"Still little," he laughed back before smacking Kyne on the back. "What brings you all here?" he said, turning towards Auriel and bowing his head. "My lady," he said respectfully before kneeling down towards the small dragon. "My you've grown so much," he bellowed.

"And you don't stink anymore," sassed Rosé to which Kyne and Auriel gasped in shock.

The dwarf laughed hard at that and smacked his knee. "Nope, I don't. Turns out those plants don't actually heal shoulders wouldn't you know," and he reached forward and rubbed Rosé's head to which she smiled and closed her eyes.

"It's good to see you my friend," he said as he met Ni'Bara's gaze, and he lightly punched the dragon's scaly hide.

"Looks like you've had a rough past few days," replied the dragon as he eyed Thirak's yellowing bruises upon his face.

"Well," Thirak blushed as he turned towards the others. "I might've met a lady and dwarven culture is a bit eccentric."

Ni'Bara snorted. "We are aware."

Thirak's eyes widened in shock and as he met Kyne's he saw the archmage awkwardly avoid his gaze.

"It was you!" cried the dwarf. "I thought someone was spying on me and had a feeling it might be you."

"Thirak I..." started Kyne.

"You're a sick sick man Kyne," laughed the dwarf. "I know I am quite attractive, and me and her are quite the sight, but that is my private time. You wouldn't want me spying on you."

"I didn't mean it," pleaded Kyne to which Thirak smirked.

The Legend of Kyne: Chronocide

"Whatever you say."

"I told him to, so we would know where to find you," said Auriel clearly not enjoying the current conversation which brought Thirak out of his taunting as he understood.

"Oh, why did you need to find me? Is everything all right?"

"We are looking for some things and we think you might know where to find them," chimed in Rosé as she bumped him roughly with her head.

"Things?" he said puzzled as he eyed the others.

"Keep your voice down," Kyne started. "We don't want unwanted ears."

"Altine fel," he said, and he cast the sound spell around blocking out any unwanted listeners. "There, now we can talk more candidly. We are looking for the Relics of Aute. I told you about them once before."

"I remember," said Thirak, his cheerfulness gone. "Why are you looking for them Kyne?"

"I hesitate to tell you, but I trust you with my life Thirak. I am leaping through time and it's getting out of control. It seems like the Relics are the only thing that can keep me bound to our time."

"Leaping through time," gasped Thirak. "You are kidding right? You can't be serious?" and as the dwarf saw the grave look upon all of their faces, he knew it to be true. "What's causing it?"

"We are not sure," said Auriel. "We think it might have something to do with killing the Darkness. With it gone, Kyne seems to be temporally unstable."

Thirak paused for a minute as he was lost in thought. The muffled sounds of some patrolling guards walked past but Kyne waved them away.

"So, the Relics help you so you don't go through time?"

"Yes, for now. I'm not sure if it's a permanent solution, but for the time being it's working. We want more of them so that they might be able to stop it completely. We have a few leads on what some could be but no idea where they could be. You know a little bit about a lot of things, and I thought if anyone has heard of something then you might."

Thirak shook his head slowly. "I'm sorry lad but no. I haven't heard of any magical items come into interest since people started talking about Xeono all those years ago. I don't think I'll be of much help."

"As I feared," muttered Kyne. "Anyways, if you hear anything please let me know."

The dwarf nodded. "If that is the only reason you came, I am sorry to have been such a letdown. Let me buy you a meal and we can talk about updates in our lives."

"That would be great," said Kyne trying to mask his disappointment.

"Kyne, why don't you ask him about the suspected one anyways just to make sure," said Auriel.

"Oh yeah, I totally forgot! Do you remember when we were in Ysaroc and the whole place was dark, with Voron and I unable to perform Aura?"

"Yes, I do. Right before we fought the winged cat."

"We think that might be caused by a Relic. There is no spell that either of us have heard of that could do it and it seems to be a likely contender."

Thirak furrowed his brow in thought. He had actually heard of something, but he couldn't remember exactly what it was.

Then it hit him!

"I actually know something about it," said the dwarf and they all lit up with excitement. "I don't know much but I do know that there have been a few different sightings of dark aura blocking power seen in Kydrëa. Its old, but I think I recall actually something saying a place in Alakyne used to have it."

"Alakyne? Like here?" and Kyne gestured all around.

"From what I can recall yes, but I personally think it highly unlikely that it still remains. The most populated city in the country. I doubt there are any secret places that haven't been found."

"I disagree with that," chimed Ni'Bara. "I think it highly likely there are places here that are hidden from most. I would bet the citadel is littered with them."

Thirak was silent for a moment in thought and then said, "I redact my previous statement. I agree with Ni'Bara. I think it highly likely there are secrets here worth looking for."

The Legend of Kyne: Chronocide

"Where should we look first?" said Auriel. "We can use our aura to look through most walls so that should help."

Kyne nodded his head as he looked out towards the citadel. Taking a few steps, he ended the spell and with the sounds of the others behind him he continued, and they all journeyed into the citadel. They were to spread out and sonar everything, starting from the lowest floor all the way up until they reached the restricted section. Thirak accompanied them and after searching for only ten minutes they found their first hidden room but to their disappointment it contained nothing except old wine crates and bottles and spiderwebs.

They continued on, floor by floor as the afternoon waned on until eventually, they stepped out into the courtyard just as the sun set.

"I think we should pick this up tomorrow," said Thirak. "I promised you all dinner anyways."

Kyne felt his stomach rumble and he noticed Auriel give him a look that she thought the same. He nodded his head, and they began walking across the courtyard. The large statue of Alakyne drawing nearer.

It was old and faded but it was eerie for Kyne to put a face to who's journal he had previously read. Thinking that made him feel more connected and it gave him a little peace.

They continued on, following Thirak to a high class Kydrëan restaurant and were seated on a great patio overlooking the lower part of the city. The food was delicious, but the dwarf refused to let Kyne buy and paid for the whole thing, even the massive barrel of mead that Ni'Bara had downed as he lay stretched out near the edge of the building.

Alcohol didn't work well on the dragon, but Kyne could tell by their connection that he was quite dizzy and nearly fading away.

There they all sat, chatting about old times and retelling past stories. Auriel laughed at jokes the dwarf told and Kyne sipped his mead. A bard eventually came into view, withdrawing a beautiful lute. He sang merry tunes, most of the sound drowned out by the chorus of talking patrons and Ni'Bara's constant rumbling, but when the notes changed to a darker tone, the sounds slowly vanished as he continued plucking the strings and then his voice sang a dark song that drew all of their attention.

The Legend of Kyne: Chronocide

They came one day with a smile so fair,
Two children came alone.
For deception was within the air,
Their hearts as cold as stone

Gifts were given and bread was shared,
Two children sold their souls.
The demons of three who took the pair,
Would burn all those as coal.

Demon of the wind, demon of the sea,
Two children death did follow.
Demon of the flame, the last of three,
The people that it would swallow.

Cities fell and the ground stained red,
Two children would atone.
For selling their souls would be the end,
Their coming would be foretold.

They traveled alone with a smile so fair,
Two children met the shore.
Deception was there but everyone was aware,
And the children were no more.

Kyne leaned back; his skin covered in goosebumps. An eerie feeling hovered in the air and the bard left without a word.

"What a creepy song," Auriel muttered.

"It is very old." Kyne replied. "When my brother and I were young my mother would sing it to us. I had nearly forgotten it."

"I haven't heard it in a long time either," mumbled Thirak as he stroked his beard in a deep thought.

"Were they real?" she asked before she finished the last of her own drink.

"I don't think so, probably just an old fable," Kyne replied. "Just a lesson to not mess with demons."

The Legend of Kyne: Chronocide

They left the restaurant and after saying their farewells to Thirak, separated from the dwarf as he went to his current lodging. They didn't have a place planned out, but Kyne was certain they could stay in the palace just as they had before.

Ni'Bara lazily took flight and leapt over the walls of citadel, climbing up into the air and vanishing into the darkness.

"It's hitting him hard," laughed Kyne as they climbed the steps, passing the guards and entering the courtyard.

As all three of them walked inside, he felt fatigue stretch across his eyes as he spoke to a few guards. Moments later they were told their chambers were ready and as they opened the door, they were startled to see Ni'Bara already there, the bed slid a few feet to the side and a vase shattered on the floor. The grey dragon snored loudly signally he was asleep, and Kyne shook his head. Walking over to the other pieces of furniture he slid them over closer to the door and away from Ni'Bara's tail in an effort to preserve them.

The light from outside cast a silvery glow through the window as they laid down upon the large bed. Kyne and Auriel side by side with Rosé at the foot, still able to enjoy the soft mattress with her size. Ni'Bara groaned and moved, his body curling up tight like a cat, but his neck stretched out and his great head lay next to the bed, nearly as large as it was.

Goodnight my friend, said Kyne and he placed a hand upon the dragon's snout.

But sleep never came. Hours crept by slowly, but the fatigue that Kyne had been feeling had faded away. Every ounce of his mind was scrambling for potential leads to a Relic. Anything that he could think of in the city that stood out to him.

He rolled again in his bed trying to find any comfort and allow the drowsy feeling of sleep to settle but alas it did not. Finally, he sat up straight in bed and stared out the window. He took a deep breath and silent as a cat, left the room behind, stepping through the halls quietly. Very few souls stirred that late in the night and he encountered only a few startled guards.

Making his way down without even realizing it, he was soon face to face with the statue of Alakyne. One of the king's arms clutched the hilt of a blade as if he had just drawn it from its scabbard. The

The Legend of Kyne: Chronocide

other lay reaching, fingers outstretched as if gesturing towards something far off in the distance.

The carved shape of Xeono lay upon his wrist, eroded nearly all away and only noticeable by those who knew of it or had truly studied the statue.

Kyne ran his hand along the cool stone base as he walked slowly around it, staring intently at Xeono. He was shocked no one had really ever known what it was. A statute that was seen by millions of people and Xeono had been lying right under their nose.

Kyne furrowed his brow at that thought and then an idea crept into his mind. As he finished his circling of the statue, he was soon face to face with him, his namesake. Kneeling down, not sure if he had hope or just curiosity, he sent a sonar through the ground under the statue.

Dozens of passageways deep below lit up in his mind as the wave continued on for a few hundred feet before fading away.

He had found something!

16. Astray Among the Malefic

"Can't sleep?" said Auriel startling him as he rushed into the room.

Kyne shook his head as he saw her sit up and he took a deep shuddering breath trying to calm himself.

"Neither can I," she murmured.

"Me either," spoke Rosé from down near their feet. A low rumble sounded to the side, and they all knew Ni'Bara was awake as well.

"I found something," Kyne blurted out to everyone's shock. "I found something underneath the statue outside."

"You what?" she gasped as she threw the covers off of her legs. "Are you serious?"

"Dead serious."

Placing his scabbard onto his side, he looked at the glowing light within the glass pommel of Aurora and felt confidence flow through him. A last second thought and he grabbed the Ouroboros Bag off of Ni'Bara. He wasn't sure how much stuff they would find and how hard it would be to carry it all out. Ni'Bara wasn't going to fit so he would take it himself.

Auriel had gotten dressed and the three of them climbed upon Ni'Bara's back as he stepped out onto the small ledge that peeked out from their room. Kyne could sense his friend's dizziness from the alcohol was gone, replaced by concern and determination and a flap took them airborne. Gliding softly through the air the dragon took them down into the courtyard where the statue of Alakyne lay waiting for them.

The Legend of Kyne: Chronocide

Kyne stared at the statue again for a long moment as Auriel used her aura to see through the ground.

"It's vast, dozens of tunnels going in all directions all under the city."

"How was this not discovered before?" asked Ni'Bara and his tail swept over the stone ground behind him. The rubbing of the scales on stone echoed dully around them as he swept it back, bringing it around all of them in a long arc.

"The tunnels all reach their apex here, at this statue," Auriel said. "They dive deep into the earth steep enough that not much lie near the surface. It is quite plausible that the vast majority of people simply walked over this spot without truly knowing what was beneath them."

"Thu'mar," muttered Kyne and he swept his arm to the side. Immediately the statue of Alakyne groaned and where it connected to the ground cracked as it separated. The statue slid over a few feet revealing a deep and black hole underneath, just large enough for a single person to drop down into.

"Wow," gawked Rosé as she bounded up next to the hole and peered inside. "It's so dark I can't see a thing."

"So, this is it," Kyne muttered as he adjusted the Ouroboros Bag on his shoulders and he and Auriel approached the hole. "Rosé, you are not coming this time."

"Wait what!" the little dragon gasped in shock. Kyne could see the hurt flash in her eyes and then it was replaced by a fire like anger. "That's not fair. I want to come and see what's in there."

"Not this time," said Auriel softly and she knelt down next to her and placed a hand on the back of her neck. "It is far too dangerous. We do not know what is down there and if anything happened to you."

"We would never forgive ourselves," Kyne finished, and he felt the agreement come from Ni'Bara.

The dragon's long tail swept around and slid Rosé slowly away from the hole pulling her close to his mass. The entire time she remained rigid with irritation all over her face.

"I'm sorry," said Kyne.

"As am I," Auriel added and then they turned back to the hole.

The Legend of Kyne: Chronocide

"Ni'Bara, I do not think our link will last long. If anything happens to us, I will try my best to make it known. Auriel, if we encounter something that we cannot handle, warp up through the earth back to the surface and shoot an aural flare so Ni'Bara can find us. Ni'Bara when we are down there, reseal this hole. No one should know about this place yet."

Auriel nodded and looked down into the dark hole. Kyne followed her gaze and felt an uneasiness settle in his stomach.

"So, you're going first right," muttered Auriel and Kyne felt the pressure hit him hard. He normally wasn't nervous about things like this, but this place felt different; ancient and unknown.

Reluctantly, he said, "Ilumace lho," and a small orb of light appeared next to him following his movement. He guided it into the hole so he could see how deep it went. The drop was far for a normal person, but he could manage and with a quick hop, fell into the hole nearly a dozen feet where he landed with a deep thud.

Another lighter thud sounded next to him signaling Auriel had landed and he smiled. So impressed by how she still used her aura consistently to make herself lighter. The drain it caused was ever so constant and he could handle it but had to constantly remind himself about it. To her, the spell was second nature, having used it nearly her whole life.

Above the hole the sky shined dimly with the flicker of stars, the rest of their vision down below utter black except for the faint aural light. The tunnel was deathly quiet, each one of their breaths amplified by its echoes. It was roughly seven feet tall and rounded on all sides forming a steep circular shaft as it continued on deep into the earth. The walls were bare of any sign of human life but there were old spiderwebs signaling these did live in these caves.

Auriel breathed out and her breath became visible as the aural light shined through the fog. A shiver went down her spine and she pulled her arms tighter to her body.

"It's cold in here," she said quickly drawing a cloak from her own pack and placing it over her shoulders. "Why is it so cold?"

Kyne looked at her puzzled for a moment before he noticed her breath. The cold hadn't even seemed noticeable to him but the more he concentrated, the more he could tell that it was cooler in here

The Legend of Kyne: Chronocide

than the outside.

"Something is off about this place," Kyne spoke quietly. "This place hides something that is vile and wicked. An ancient air, a miasma hangs in the air that makes me feel uneasy."

"I feel it too. I don't know where it is coming from though. It is making me uneasy; we really need to be careful down here."

They started walking down, Auriel adding a second light that drifted behind them whilst Kyne's own led them on deeper into the tunnels. A low groan came from behind them as the statue was slid back over the entrance to the tunnels.

They came to an area where the tunnel split into three others. Not knowing which to take, they decided upon the middle one and continued on. They encountered many tunnels taking them deeper into the labyrinth, but they could tell they were getting further into its bowels from the pressure they were feeling.

A few minutes later, they came around a bend to be greeted by an old archway made of stone brick and mortar, two unlit torches hung in iron holders on either sides of the archway but beyond was utter darkness. As they neared, Kyne felt a familiarity as their aural light was unable to pass beyond the barrier.

"What is this?" Auriel murmured, as she forced her light through the arch only to have it immediately extinguished.

"It's what we were searching for," replied Kyne. "This is the shroud that was encased over Alakyne's tomb preventing the use of aura. If it really is a Relic, it resembles a forged copy of the old barrier between our worlds. It was used to scare intruders that wanted to loot the tomb of its treasure. If that failed, then the manticore would finish them off. Here it might be similar, designed to put fear in our hearts and make us turn back."

"It only makes me more certain that something of value lies hidden within," breathed Auriel as she grabbed one of the torches and lit it with her aura.

"I feel the same," said Kyne and he followed suit. "It might wear off, or it could go the rest of the way so we will need to be even more cautious than before. Without our aura we are much more vulnerable."

Kyne passed the glowing torch through the archway and to his

The Legend of Kyne: Chronocide

satisfaction saw it did not go out. These torches were left here for a reason, and they were granted permission to cast their light.

As they stepped through the old brick archway, they were greeted by an intense feeling of dread and icy cold as if the air itself was trying to sap them of all their heat.

Beyond the archway, the tunnel was no longer natural, but man made, decorated with cracked stone along the floor and stone bricks lining the walls. Each piece of stone carved perfectly to fit into place beside the others, with no mortar seen in between. Above their heads, hundreds of old cobwebs lined the curved ceiling and Kyne felt a few brush his hair. He quickly rubbed them away as he felt shivers run down his back.

He was not afraid of spiders, he actually respected the creatures but here, in this place with a constant feeling of dread looming around them, anything could startle him, even simple abandoned cobwebs.

The tunnel continuously sloped down but at a lesser decline and soon they entered into a larger room with alcoves along all of the edges. Stone platforms lay within, and more cobwebs hid what lay upon them. Human skulls lay situated in small shrines between each alcove, three steps each centered with a single skull. The bones had been fractured with pieces missing as the sands of time ate away at them.

Auriel approached the nearest alcove and using her torch, burned away the old webs. The Riel gasped in shock and Kyne ran over to her to see what she had uncovered. It was a human corpse, well preserved as it lay with its arms crossed over its chest and its eyes closed.

Its skin was shriveled and dried, resembling old left out jerky and its hair had nearly all fallen out. No clothes were placed upon the body, but Kyne could not tell the gender. It was well preserved, but still had rotted away leaving only a type of mummified shell of whoever they once were.

They both backed away and looked upon the alcoves with new eyes. There were twelve of them and within each held a mummified body of someone of importance. A few items of value were decorating each alcove, signaling that no grave robbers had made it there, but Kyne had no idea how long they had remained hidden.

At the end of the room, they could see the corridor continued on. They passed the last alcove and Kyne peered inside to see this

The Legend of Kyne: Chronocide

mummy had their mouth open. To his horror, he saw that their canine teeth had been filed to a sharp inhuman point and he shuddered again.

Something wicked happened in this crypt.

Kyne muttered a spell under his breath and felt the slight pull of aura for a moment before it failed. The blanket of ancient energy was still blocking their power. It had lessened but was still there and Kyne doubted he could fight it as he momentarily tried to as a test.

They walked along the tunnel, more and more shrines adorned with skulls appearing on either sides, but they paid them no mind as they delved deeper into the darkness.

A few minutes later, they entered into another identical circular room as the first with twelve alcoves each adorned with body.

"Another one?" asked Auriel. "It's like we are going in circles down here."

"I feel the same way," Kyne replied, and they pushed on through the room and into the hallway beyond, all the while going at a descent. A few more minutes later, they stepped out into a third circular room with alcoves and Auriel stopped in her tracks gasping in frustration.

"We are getting nowhere!" her voice echoed around.

"Auriel," whispered Kyne. "We are not sure if anything is down here, please be a little more quiet."

"I'm serious Kyne," she continued, this time a little quieter. "I don't like it here; it doesn't feel right."

"I know, I feel the same way. This place is designed to instill fear and paranoia upon any intruders. We must push on."

Auriel paused for a moment before nodding her head.

"Alright let's keep..." her voice trailed off as her hand reached up. A slight gasp came from her mouth and Kyne followed her finger to see an alcove with an unmoving body within.

"What is it Auriel," he said.

"Look at the spider webs. They've been burned!"

"What!" gasped Kyne and he dashed over towards them to look closer. Indeed, the webs had been burned, identical to the way Auriel had cleared them before. "How is that possible? We have been traveling deeper every time!"

"Let's get out of this area, regroup outside where we can use our aura. Maybe we can have some of Theo's soldiers come with us."

"I hate it, but I am absolutely fine with that," nodded Kyne as he rose to his full height. "Let's go," and both of them took off in a sprint through the tunnel they had come from.

The path went flat for a moment before to both of their horror, it started to slope down. A few seconds later, they ran out into the same circular room with the burned webs."

"What is this place?" breathed Kyne as terror began to fill his very being.

"How are we going to get out?" she hissed.

"I have no idea," he said, taking a few steps forward before turning back. "Let's try to head back up again, see if it works this time."

Auriel nodded and they ran back the way they came. The path went straight for a time but then it slowly began to slope downward and the two ended their run to a slow walk.

"Kyne," whispered Auriel. "I don't like this."

They came into the same circular room adorned with alcoves but before Kyne could respond, however, he noticed something different about the room. It was identical in every way except all twelve bodies were gone, no longer in their alcoves. A light chilling breeze filled the room and both of them drew their blades.

Auriel's single edged orichite blade shined brilliantly in the orange glow and as Aurora was withdrawn, Kyne felt an incredible calm fill him for a moment. The feather blade, gifted from the Light, was the most beautiful and deadly weapon ever crafted. Able to kill anything and always protect its true owner, Kyne.

The icy zephyr ended, and Kyne took a few steps until both he and Auriel were in the center of the room, scanning their vision all around them to prevent anything from sneaking up on them.

The air was quiet for a long moment when a single low groan echoed from the path they had come from. A groan that made Kyne grit his teeth and the hairs on their necks stand up on end. An inhuman groan of something long thought dead.

As it neared, they both watched as one of the corpses staggered into the room, a massive claymore held up against its shoulder. The creature paused for a moment as its shriveled black eyes rested upon them and then another groan erupted from its mouth, and it rushed

The Legend of Kyne: Chronocide

forward at a blinding speed.

They both separated just as a blur of steel covered their vision and the massive crash as the claymore struck into where they had just been standing, cracking the stone floor into fragments. The creature groaned as it lifted its sword up and eyed the two who were now on separate sides of the room.

"Watch out!" cried Auriel as the creature leapt towards Kyne, sweeping the five-foot-long blade in an arc towards his chest. As the blade sailed through the air, Kyne dropped low and swung his own hard, where it met nearly no resistance as it passed through the creature's legs.

It dropped to the floor and the claymore rang off the stone bouncing a few feet away.

"What is that thing," cried Auriel as it flailed on the ground trying to reach for its weapon.

"I am not sure," said Kyne as he placed the sole of his boot and pressed the creature hard into the ground. "I encountered something similar in the Whispering Swamp, however," and he thrust the blade through the undead corpse and embedded it nearly a foot into the stone beyond. "Those hollows were different, slower and weaponless, using the water to drown their victims with their vast numbers."

He withdrew the blade and lifted his foot off of the creature while approaching Auriel. "That was the first so there will be eleven more. We should be able to take them, especially if they are alone but be wary. We never know what..."

"Kyne!"

Auriel's cry made his blood run cold and he ripped around to see the hollow running at them with its claymore held high, ready to strike.

With a loud high pitch ring, the two blades collided, shaking Kyne's arms from the impact. The creature withdrew and slammed the blade down, but Kyne was not taken by surprise this time and instead, parried to blade to the floor and ducked down just as Auriel's orichite blade sailed through the hollow's chest, shoulder to shoulder, rending it in two.

"What the hell!", yelled Kyne in frustration and he sliced

The Legend of Kyne: Chronocide

Aurora through the corpse nearly a dozen times, leaving it a pile of dried pieces. "Reanimate this time," he muttered, and he kicked the long claymore across the room where it ricocheted off the stone wall and slid to a stop a few feet from the dark tunnel beyond.

A low groan came from behind them, and they both stood ready as two more of the creatures stepped into the room, each holding a claymore of their own.

"Auriel!" screamed Kyne and they both defended as the monsters leapt towards them. A few moments later, with the ringing of metal echoing down the halls, the two hollows had been dismembered, limbs scattered around the room.

A bead of sweat dripped down Kyne's cheek and he wiped it with his shoulder. He watched the bodies for a moment before movement nearby caught his attention. To his horror, he watched the first corpse shudder as its many pieces came together returning it to its original form. As it stood up to its height, both he and Auriel felt their mouth go dry and they backed up towards the deeper tunnel entrance.

"I think they are revenants," murmured Kyne as he watched the other two begin to form together.

"What's a revenant?"

"It's like a hollow, but more pure, much more potent. All of these revenants have had their souls corrupted beyond recognition. Something incredibly dark lies in this crypt and I think it's controlling them, giving them some of its power. See, watch how they come together, it's almost as if something is piecing them back together like a grotesque puzzle."

The first revenant was fully formed but without its weapon, not much of a problem as both Kyne and Auriel slashed it down. The other two, however, quickly followed after it, nearly stabbing Kyne only to be severed in two by Auriel.

They could handle these revenants for now but how long would they last? He could already feel the fleeting effects of fatigue as he held his sword up in a defensive position.

Another low groan sounded, and two more revenants staggered into the room, each of them wielding a claymore making their total five.

"What do we do?" whispered Kyne as the five revenants began

to encircle them, trapping them against the dark behind them. Their torches lay scattered at the edges of the room, casting their flickering orange light all around.

"I don't know," replied Auriel and she raised her sword up as she waited for them to attack. The revenants continued their slow approach and were nearly upon them.

I refuse to die here, like this! roared Kyne's thoughts through his mind as he searched for any idea that could help them. His eyes rested on Aurora in his hand and felt the frustration at not being able to kill them. *This must not be their true form, that's why we cannot defeat them!*

The thought roared through Kyne's mind, and he clutched tight onto the blade in his hands. He didn't know how they could find it though. They were close, only a dozen feet away and Kyne, in a desperate thought, tried to see if his aura would work.

The pull left his body, and he watched as his blade levitated just a tiny bit out of his hands. A grin appeared on his face and just as all five revenants dashed forward, he cried, "Erodath!"

An incredible force tore through the room, launching all of them far to the back where they crashed and slumped to the ground.

"How?" gasped Auriel as she stared at him.

"Whatever is controlling the revenants has to use aura, so the aural suppressor has been broken. Let's get out of here!" and they took off, running to the edge of the room before Kyne turned back and held out his arms. "Kitala torches!"

The flaming rods flew through the air and landed in his hand. He handed one to Auriel and they took off down the deeper corridor, which to their delight did not continue down but came to a simple split going in two directions.

Behind them, they could hear the low groan as a dozen revenants started after them, but they had the lead. Each footstep echoed dully around them as they continued on, orange firelight lighting up the bleak tunnel.

No longer were the stone walls decorated by empty alcoves, but each one held a body as they dashed through more rooms. Kyne felt as if someone was watching them as they darted past. These corpses did not stir, at least for now, but he would not throw out the possibility. Suddenly they came to an intersection with two other hallways.

The Legend of Kyne: Chronocide

"Which way?" asked Auriel as she looked back quickly, expecting to see the sprinting hoard that was after them.

"I... I don't know," stammered Kyne as he looked down first the left, and then the right. Returning to the left, he shot an aural light down its length, only to have it curve out of view nearly a hundred feet away.

He did the same with the path on the right and found this one traveled straight but not as long before flickering momentarily and then it was gone, lost to the dark. Kyne shot another and this time watched it intently, using his aura to amplify his sight. As it flew down the dark path, suddenly, it looked as if it passed through something that was falling and then through a barrier of some sort.

"What is it?" breathed Auriel as she watched the light vanish.

"I'm not sure, it could be anything."

"Which way Kyne?"

He had no idea and darted his head back and forth as he looked at the two pathways. The air was still and old, reeking of an ancient time and he could feel its icy chill just as Auriel shivered and drew her cloak tighter around her.

He closed his eyes and reached out with his mind, stretching it around, looking for that foreboding darkness. He didn't want to go closer to it, every part of his body resisted, but he knew that was where they would find answers.

"That way," Kyne muttered as he pointed to the right where the two lights had vanished. "That is where the cold is seeping from."

"That's where you want to go? To where it is?"

"That is more and likely where we will find answers," he mumbled regretfully as he took a step down the hallway. He paused for a second, straining his ears trying to hear anything.

It was deathly quiet, even their breathing seemed to be muffled, but just as he went to continue on, he heard something that made his blood run cold. The sound of many footsteps approaching from behind them.

"Auriel, they are coming!" He exclaimed and they both took off in a sprint. Each footstep propelling them rapidly down the tunnel at a blinding speed and soon he understood why the light had vanished.

The Legend of Kyne: Chronocide

Before them water was starting to drip from the ceiling and the further on they went, the louder they could hear the rumble of a waterfall. Coming to a black wall of falling water, they stopped. Its water was dark and chilling to the touch as both peered through its glass-like surface.

"Sei'var," they both said in unison and the water split straight down the middle allowing them past. It was a wide waterfall, nearly four feet and covering the entire hallway, but not too thick with beyond it being utter darkness. They could see the water flowing down a steep slope and out of view.

The moment their feet touched the slope, their spell holding back the water ceased and they slipped hard, falling onto their backs and beginning a rapidly increasing slide towards something unknown.

Auriel cried out in shock as she screamed spells trying to stop their descent. No aura was working, and panic shot through Kyne's mind as he flailed around looking for something to grab onto.

Suddenly Auriel's torch went out as it was dowsed in the inch deep water as it dragged them down the steep slope.

Kyne lifted his torch high as he reached out and grabbed onto Auriel with his hard, clamping down to keep them connected. But how long would this slope last? What was at its end?

Kyne heard Auriel shout but couldn't make anything out until he saw what she was pointing at.

She was yelling cliff!

His heart jumped in his chest as he rolled prone, dropping his torch and slamming his dragon claws as hard as he could into the stone. They slid another few feet and Kyne felt Auriel's weight increase and then his own legs cleared the edge. With satisfaction he felt his claws wedge into the stone and hold fast. They came to a halting stop with just inches of stone left as they dangled above the dark abyss, Kyne's torch sizzling as it drifted on past them and out over the edge. Kyne couldn't watch it as he struggled to breathe against the onslaught of water striking them from above.

"Kyne! I'm slipping!" screamed Auriel as her other hand reached up and tried to grab his wrist. The water was making everything lose its grip and he could feel her sliding out. He grabbed harder, but she was still slipping!

The Legend of Kyne: Chronocide

"Kaiodin!" he roared, trying to stop everything around them, but nothing happened, and his voice echoed away. He tried again with another spell, and then another, each one failing and Auriel slipping further out of his hand. She had only a few seconds left when suddenly, to his horror, the edge of the stone cliff broke away under his claws and they both tumbled far below in utter darkness.

17. What Has Been Hidden Beneath

Icy cold water erupted around Kyne as he struck the water's surface with his back, a massive pain racking his body as he was thrown beneath its surface. Everything around him was black as the darkest night as his vision strained trying to see his wife, the pain upon his back overtaken by fear for her safety.

He erupted out of the water with a massive breath of air, immediately calling out Auriel's name as he treaded the icy water. No response sounded for a moment before nearby to his right he heard the splash of water as something surfaced.

"Auriel!" he called again, hearing the coughs from her as she tried to catch her breath.

He swam over, making his way cautiously through the black abyss and using his hearing to guide him to her. Eventually he felt her chilled skin touch his fingers and he grabbed onto her tightly, helping her the best he could while they treaded water.

She was shivering hard, and he could hear her teeth chattering together.

"Auriel, we have to find someplace to stand," he tried to say calmly, but he felt his jaw quiver as he too began to shiver. "We can't stay here for much longer."

"I can't see a thing," she called out, her voice echoing around them. "We have no idea how big this lake is."

"Wait Auriel," said Kyne. "Yell again and listen to the echo."

Auriel was silent for a moment as she understood what he meant and then she called out with just a loud sound, no specific wordage. It hit Kyne's ears, and then he waited for a split second before

The Legend of Kyne: Chronocide

it returned as it bounced off some nearby wall.

"That way!" they both exclaimed and took off, paddling hard through the cold water. The movement made his skin colder, but he could feel his core warming up as his muscles started to burn from the strain. Each push of their hands and kick with their feet propelled their bodies further through the water until suddenly Kyne's hand slammed deep into the sandy bottom of the lake.

They had found the shore!

With grunts and coughs, they both pulled themselves up onto the cool dry sand and laid upon their backs as they tried to catch their breath. He could feel Auriel shivering nearby and he sat up and went to remove his Ouroboros Bag when suddenly, dim lights shined from above casting the area in a grey light.

The lights seemed to be coming from nowhere and everywhere at the same time, illuminating everything. They were in a large cave with the waterfall directly across from where they lay upon the shore. All around, Kyne could see the walls of the cave decorated with round broken pieces of stalagmites and stalactites, forming strange archaic walls and columns all around. The cave stretched back from the shore nearly a hundred feet as it sloped slightly up and came to a strange altar.

"This is it," breathed Auriel as she rose to her feet, shivering uncontrollably.

"Auriel, I think our aura is back," said Kyne as he tested the pull. Something was controlling the aural suppressor, and he didn't like it one bit.

"Varme," the Riel spoke, and a great warmth surrounded her as her clothes dried quickly. Kyne followed suit and once they both were dry, they approached the altar.

Each footstep sank into the fine sand as they made their way up the sloping hill. No shells or larger rocks dotted the beach, just a uniform pale colored sand with occasional pillars poking out. As they neared one of the pillars, its length stretching high up to the ceiling a few hundred feet up, Kyne could see that pieces of the stone had crumbled around its base.

"How old is this place for the stone to erode so much," he muttered as he drew closer. With the grey light above dimly lighting the

The Legend of Kyne: Chronocide

area, it was hard to make out details but eventually Kyne could see the pillar for what it really was. It was not made out of stone like he had initially thought but made of skulls. Hundreds of skulls all pressed together in some ungodly object. Looking around the cavern, he understood what he hadn't seen before. Thousands and thousands of skulls lined the walls and decorated the pillars all around them.

"Bones," he gasped to Auriel drawing her to a stop as she looked where he was gesturing. "They are all bones. Thousands of people lay hidden deep in here, blocked from the sun and cast in eternal darkness."

Auriel shuddered as she looked around them before returning her gaze to the shrine they were nearing. It was a large black stone reminiscent of an obelisk with sharper edges and a curved top. Dozens of books and other strange objects had been placed at its base near a bowl with pieces of mummified flesh nestled within it.

A large symbol had been placed in front of the altar surrounded by a perfect circle with splattered old blood stains covering the stone. Three curved lines, connecting together with each half as long as the one previous. The shape was incredibly familiar to Kyne and as he stood upon the circle, he spun around trying to see it from all its angles.

He couldn't quite grasp it however and soon joined Auriel where she was kneeling next to the books and withdrawing a large red leather one. It had been bound up by a metallic clasp, but no key was needed and as she opened it up, he could hear the pages groaning from their age. The pages were littered with inscriptions and drawings of things they had never seen before.

"Let's just take them all and get out of here," Kyne muttered, and he took off his pack and began to stuff the books deep inside. Once they were all taken, he grabbed a few of the items and then watched as Auriel picked up a strange shaped object with each side a flattened pentagon.

She turned it momentarily in her hand before handing it to Kyne. Just as he took it, a low groan sounded from the water, and they whipped around to see a dark shadowy figure rising out of the depths.

Suddenly a massive headache ripped through Kyne, and he watched as his body began to trail in afterimages around him as his

The Legend of Kyne: Chronocide

time distorted. He fought it as hard as he could, focusing on pulling his body together against the strain but it was too much.

"Auriel!" he cried with his voice chorusing as if spoken by a hundred Kyne's. He fumbled, grabbing onto the pommel of his sword and felt the distortion slow but it did not stop. His pack was nearby, within an arm's reach, but a massive rumble erupted behind them, distracting him into turning and seeing the thing step onto the land.

The distortion intensified and inches from touching his pack, Kyne vanished from sight leaving Auriel alone.

18. Embodiment of Death

Kyne's vision swam, flashing all around him and his head roared in pain but as quickly as it started, it ceased and he was kneeling on all fours in the same chamber, lit with the orange light of flame.

He had no idea how much time had changed, how far back he had traveled. The columns looked identical to what they had been before and nothing else had really changed. He groaned as he rose to his feet, scanning the area further and he almost shouted with shock.

Two hooded figures lay seated with their legs crossed facing each other upon the strange symbol on the ground. Their faces were dark, covered by their hooded cloaks but he could see their pale white skin as their hands stirred.

"How did you get here!" hissed one of them as they rose to their feet. Kyne could tell that the voice was feminine but was unable to see what she truly looked like.

"You trespass upon sacred ground,"

Kyne took a step back as the second cloaked figure rose to their feet. They withdrew their hood and looked at the female while saying, "Shall I dispose of him master?"

As the female nodded and spoke, the other turned to face Kyne and he gasped in shock, as he saw his face.

"Drain his life Saathe."

* * *

Auriel watched as the shadowy figure glided over the beach towards her. It was not humanoid, nearly resembling a dark cloud with billowy tendrils stretching over the ground grabbing onto broken skulls. Lifting them up, the creature was almost like an octopus with each tentacle adorned with a skull and its dark center shifting and flowing as if it had been a contained thunderstorm.

Auriel drew her sword as it took a few steps forward.

Kyne, where are you?

He was gone, lost to the ages away from her and unable to help. She was alone and would have to defeat this creature or die trying.

She watched as it tore through one of the pillars, sending bones falling all around as it made its way slowly towards her. She needed to figure out how to destroy it, but she wasn't sure what it was.

She leapt to the side, dodging a flying skull as it crashed into the shrine behind her shattering a glass item. Another skull flew through the air at a blinding speed, but Auriel managed to parry it to the side with her blade.

"Kyne said those other things were revenants, so could this be the wight? Could this be the thing that was controlling them?"

A third skull rocketed at her and as she twisted over her shoulder to dodge, she unleashed an aural attack of her own in the form of a bolt of lightning. A bright flash lit up the cavern completely as it passed through the creature followed by a deafening thunderclap, amplified by the echoing cavern.

The creature shifted for a moment, as if in discomfort before a deep roar sounded and one of the tendrils shot towards Auriel with the hollow eyes of the skull meeting her own.

* * *

Kyne realized what the symbol was now as he faced them down. It was a scythe, and they were reapers. He understood now where they were and why this place was so dark and wicked. These bodies, these humans who lay here deep under Alakyne were sacrifices from the reapers as they performed their corrupted rituals.

A wave of bright blue fire roared to the side of Kyne as he leapt out of the way, the heat upon his skin nearly unbearable. Another fierce attack flew from Saathe, shooting fast and straight in a jet of flame.

"Vertai!" Kyne cried as he waved his arm in front of him,

The Legend of Kyne: Chronocide

altering the course of the fire around him and shooting out over the dark lake.

"Do not humiliate me!" seethed the other reaper as she walked behind Saathe, snaking her head from one ear to another. "Kill him now!"

Saathe screamed in rage as he swept his hand across the area bathing the entire land in a raging icy blue firestorm. The blast flew towards Kyne like a flaming tsunami, and he barely had enough time to take a breath and utter a single word before it overtook him, bathing him in a bright light.

Kyne could feel the heat seeping through his shield as he fought hard against the reaper's attack. Saathe was indeed an incredible sorcerer, Kyne could feel the power radiating from him.

The flames pressed on, growing more intense for long moment before finally giving way. As the flames subsided, a few of the bones around them caught a weak flame, splitting and cracking with loud popping noises.

Kneeling down, Kyne ended his spell, pushing the remaining flames away from him before he rose to his feet. He could feel the rage inside him burning hotter than these reaper flames. He had dragonfire within him, and nothing burned hotter!

With a roar of his own, he opened his mouth and let out a blast of his own cyan dragonfire, engulfing both reapers in its blaze. Deepening his stance, Kyne pulled his head back, before intensifying the attack. He didn't want them burned, he wanted them scorched to ash!

A flash of movement was seen out of the corner of his eye, and he ended the blast while twisting his torso just as a sickle shaped blade ripped through the air narrowly missing him.

As the fire subsided, he saw the panting figure of Saathe, kneeling on one knee with a hand weakly raised. The other reaper, the master was standing up in front of him with one hand as if she had thrown something and the other clutching a small sickle weapon.

"What is he?" she growled as Saathe rose to his feet and the two harbingers of death faced the dragonkind.

"His aura is strange, not fully human," hissed Saathe as he drew his own scythe, grasping it in both of his pale hands.

The Legend of Kyne: Chronocide

Kyne knew that he shouldn't interfere, lest the timeline be altered but right now, it was survival. He would deal with the consequences later and he drew his own blade out of its sheath.

The barbs of the feather shimmered in the blue light, each sharp as a razor. He felt the cool metal under his hands and brought it in front of him with his arms low and straight in a traditional stance.

Light on his toes, he focused his breath, listening and watching as the two reapers separated and began a slow approach.

At once, both reapers dashed forward, the nameless master going low as Saathe struck high in opposite directions. The scissoring of the blades prevented Kyne from blocking both, instead he ducked under Saathe's scythe and took the full impact of the smaller sickle blade close to his cross-guard.

Quick as a snake, she ripped her sickle from the clash and spun over her shoulder, sailing the blade in the air right for Kyne's neck.

Startled, he raised the hilt of his blade high, catching her attack on his cross-guard again where they clanged together in a loud ring.

A flash of icy fire flew at him, and he leapt back, knocked off balance as he tried to dodge the onslaught of attacks, but the female was upon him in an instant. Kyne struggled to find his footing, she struck three times, each strike getting closer and close to meeting its target.

As the third strike landed, Kyne felt his foot catch something and then he was falling back, the gleam of murder in his attacker's eyes.

Time seemed to slow as he fell towards his back, Aurora's tip drifting up in the air.

I can't die here! roared Kyne's thoughts as he remembered the last thing he saw with Auriel. The dark creature rising out of the water. *I can't leave her by herself!*

The hiss of sharpened steel was in the air as she dove at him with her mouth in a wicked smile. Kyne could see her face now, middle aged but looking much older and paler with the same nearly white iris that Saathe had.

Dipping the tip of Aurora down as he fell, Kyne crossed his body and connected with the sickle's curved blade. As he felt it slide

The Legend of Kyne: Chronocide

together, he guided it to the side as he rolled back. With his feet planted against her chest, He pushed as hard as he could, launching her over his head in shock where she sailed into the edge of the dark water with a splash.

A shriek of rage came from Saathe as he dove at Kyne, but he was too slow and the archmage managed to get up and knock him back over his head where he landed in the water next to his master.

The icy water dripped from her hair as she withdrew her hood, revealing demonic tattoos upon her scalp and her head shaved into a long mohawk. Her eyes screamed murder and she raised her sickle up preparing to throw it.

A flick of her wrist and it zipped through the air at Kyne.

He leaned to the side and to his shock felt the sickle catch the edge of his robe, tearing a long slice through the fabric as the weapon came to a crash nearby.

Kyne looked first at his robe in shock before turning back to the reapers. In disbelief, he watched the sickle materialize in her hand and she took aim again.

"No more!" roared Kyne and with a swipe of his arm, unleashed a full powered dragonrend towards them.

The sickle flew through the air but disintegrated as it touched the attack and with a loud crash it smashed into the water. Mist rained down all around as Kyne saw Saathe rise up from a low crouch with a look of shock on his face as he stared at his master who was frozen in place, a look of confusion upon her own face.

A long silent moment passed as the water droplets finished raining down when suddenly, a long streak of blood appeared diagonally across her chest. With a cough, her eyes glazed over and her torso from her armpit to her hip slid apart from the rest of her body and both pieces fell into the water with a low splash.

A massive headache erupted through Kyne's mind, and he staggered as he tried to remain standing. He focused hard upon Saathe as he watched the apprentice turn to face him with utter rage across his face. He grunted in pain as the headache increased and his voice echoed as if it had been said simultaneously by a dozen others. Dropping to his knees he fought hard against the pain. He didn't resist the pull but embraced it, every thought focused on getting back to his

The Legend of Kyne: Chronocide

wife.

"I will kill you," roared Saathe as the reaper splashed through the water, running at full speed with his scythe raised up high.

"You will try," panted Kyne and then he flashed in place for a moment before vanishing, leaving the reaper alone in the empty cavern.

*   *   *

Auriel ran along the edge of the wall, using her aura to keep her balance as she ran around the cavern heading up towards the waterfall. Long black tendrils chased after her and she launched an aural attack, momentarily stunning the wight.

The waterfall was nearly within reach and just as she pushed off the wall and sailed out into open space, something struck her hard and she flew down a few dozen feet to the water with a crash. The impact knocked the breath out of her, and she choked for air under the water.

A gasp erupted from her just as she surfaced, only to be ended quickly as something clutched hard onto her ankle and ripped her down under the surface of the dark water, snuffing out all the light to see.

She struggled hard, trying to pry it off of her but it was impossible.

Her lungs burned for air, but she had to use some of it. "Ilumace!" she screamed underwater, and a massive burst of light erupted all around allowing her to see what was beneath her.

The wight was much larger than she had truly understood and was a large distance below her with all of its massive tentacle like appendages drifting up through the water. At its center, Auriel could just make out the shape of something white before it was covered by the dark veil of the wight.

"Sekri," she yelled, sacrificing more of her air but with satisfaction, she watched the ethereal tentacle around her leg sever and dissipate in a black fog. The creature below flailed in pain for a moment and then all the tentacles around darted towards her.

It was now or never.

"Y'vinu," and she used her aura to pull her at a breathtaking

The Legend of Kyne: Chronocide

speed deeper in the water away from the incoming tentacles and towards the white figure at the center of the wight.

I don't know if this will work but it's all I have, and she dodged the rolling central mass of dark smoke that was concealing the figure.

It was a human body, paper white and naked with its hair long and flowing around it in the water. Its mouth was ajar in an eternal scream and its eyes were glazed over and milky white. Clutched in its hand lay a small metallic object, reminiscent of a torch.

Stretching out her hand, she flew through the water, dodging tendrils and hurtling as fast as she could. Her ears screamed from the pressure change and her lungs burned. It was there, right in front of her and with a swipe of her sword, she struck it hard in the side where it held fast as if striking stone.

The wight turned, its hollow eyes burning deep into her soul as its open mouth contorted in a horrific smile. Auriel tried to swing her blade pulling upon it with no avail. The creature had clamped its hand upon it and was holding fast.

Auriel's lungs were screaming for relief, crying out for a single breath!

She could feel her mind growing foggy, her vision darkening upon the edges. Thoughts of Kyne flew throughout her mind, and she pulled upon the sword again with no success. Reaching out, she swung her fist through the water, sluggish and slow towards the wight with no other thought of options. It dodged her blow with a leaning motion, just managing to stay out of reach.

She swung again and it avoided her attack, releasing its grip upon her sword. Her vision continued to shrink, tunneling in so all of her focus was on the wight. She had to; it was her last chance!

Kicking forward, aided with her aura, she dove forward, striking the creature with her fist directly in the chest where it held fast and grew rigid. Instantly a shriek erupted from all around, so loud that she had to cover her ears. She could see the wight in front of her, flailing madly before starting to gain color of normal human skin.

The shadow around its body began to fade and then the wights body dissolved away, the metallic object dropping from its grip and falling deep out of sight.

Her lungs screamed in pain and her vision grew totally black as her consciousness faded. With the last bit of will, she used her aura to pull her up and in moments she erupted at the surface gasping for relief.

Her bright light below the water ended and trying to catch her breath, she turned toward the shore to see a column shudder as skulls began to fall off of it, damaged from the wights attacks. It seemed to hold, at least for now and then to her shock she watched Kyne's figure phase into being. He was kneeling near the edge of the water, but something was off.

"Kyne!" she yelled, but he didn't respond, and panic raced through her as she used her aura to lift her up and she dashed across the surface of the water in a great sprint. As her last stride brought her to him, she saw him raise his eyes up to her own and the panic in them made her blood run cold.

"What's wrong?"

"I... I couldn't help it," he stammered as he rose to his feet. His whole body distorted for a moment, trailing in dozens of versions. "I had to!"

"Had to what?"

"I altered the timeline!" he cried out.

"We have to get out of here!" screamed Auriel and she grabbed onto him. Using her aura, she raised the earth below them pushing them high up in the cavern. She could feel him shudder and felt her own being tremble as it began to overtake her as well. They neared the ceiling, and she waved her hand, the earth parting around and allowing them to continue their ascent.

A flash of bright light blinded both of them as they flew up onto the surface and Auriel felt a massive headache rage through her own mind and Kyne collapsed again. Staring at him, she saw her own arm phasing as he was.

The sun had just risen over the city of Alakyne, and dozens of people had stopped and were staring at them as they erupted in the middle of a street intersection. They were only a few hundred feet from the citadel wall and guards were beginning to rush down towards them.

Ni'Bara! roared Kyne's mind in desperation and within moments, the grey dragon burst up over the wall followed by Rosé's glimmering pink figure.

The Legend of Kyne: Chronocide

The two flew quickly towards them and Kyne flooded the dragon with what transpired.

Kyne, what's going to happen?

"I don't know!" he replied out loud in a scream as his body shook uncontrollably. It felt as if every atom in his body was tearing itself apart and he screamed in pain again as his head felt like it was going to burst.

Auriel, Rosé. and Ni'Bara all clustered close to Kyne and stared as he shook violently with a strange glowing halo forming around his body. It grew brighter and brighter, making it hard to look at him.

Just as Auriel screamed his name, Kyne unleashed a deafening roar and there was a massive flash of light.

The explosion ripped through Alakyne, tearing shingles off roofs and knocking people over as it swept over the countryside. The air cracked and split, stemming from the central explosion like a fragmented tree and racing outwards far over the land making the very sky resemble a broken window.

Then there was utter silence.

*   *   *

The Legend of Kyne: Chronocide

Part 2 Unwind

The Legend of Kyne: Chronocide

19. Unwarranted Kindness

The steady sound of rain filled the air accompanying the slow suction as the horse's hooves walked down the muddy road. Overcast was the sky, a bleak grey, but lightning had not shown itself yet.

Kioni glanced up at the sky as he shielded his eyes from the falling water. He could tell that it was daytime but could not pinpoint where the sun was. He had been traveling for a few hours since he woke up this morning to the storm and guessed it should be around midday.

A loud splash sounded nearby as the inaba that was tied to his horse's saddle stepped into a large puddle sending muddy rainwater all over its tan fur. Looking down, Kioni could see the brown mud clinging to the pale hair as the creature continued its steady hopping with occasional pieces flicking off back down to the ground.

Kioni ran his hand across the horse's white mane near the saddle before patting it softly. The horse seemed to take no notice of it, but Kioni did it again anyways.

"You're a very loyal horse Variel. Thank you," he whispered before patting her softly again.

This horse many years ago was Kyne's, given to him by the sorcerer Voron during their quest for Xeono. After the quest had been completed and the war finished, Kyne was no longer in need of a horse.

Kioni thought back to the day when Kyne had approached him and given him the reins.

"She is a great horse, Kioni. I am no longer in need of her services, but I care deeply for her. I trust very few people would treat her how I would approve, and you are one of them."

Kyne's voice echoed in his mind for a moment and Kioni grinned slightly at the memory before he ended his smile. He clenched his jaw tight as the anger towards Kyne flashed into his mind and he

The Legend of Kyne: Chronocide

grabbed tight on the reigns until his knuckles were white.

A small black bird, neither a raven nor a crow swooped down low past Kioni's head and landed upon the edge of the road a few dozen feet away. He watched it as it hopped quickly around before jamming its beak deep into the mud. A moment later, it withdrew a worm and jerked its head back and forth quickly as it eyed the area for predators. A moment later it threw its head back and swallowed the wriggling thing whole before taking a few hops and leaping into flight.

Kioni furrowed his brow as he watched, noticing the oozing mucus on the edge of the bird's beak moments before it flew away. He knew to a bird a worm was delicious, but it was quite appalling to himself.

The falling rain intensified around them, and Kioni drew his cloak tighter around him. The rain was warm, an early summer rain that smelled of petrichor and forest. Kioni took a deep breath, enjoying the crisp scent.

The road continued on straight for a long while until it became but a pinprick, hidden from the falling rain as if it were a veil of a new bride. There were very few trees, each clumped with a couple others with great spaces in between. The trail edged along the middle of a large hill, more of a wrinkle in the earth with his left sloping downwards at a mild angle. He couldn't see very far with the rain but at the valley's base he thought he could see the silhouettes of more trees and possibly a river.

Kioni continued on for a long while, an hour, possibly two with the rain never ceasing. At times it would slow and others it would intensify but it never truly ended. The rain just constantly fell, soaking everything it touched with its water.

The more time that went by, the cooler the rain felt upon the skin on his wrists. His cloak was dotted with beads of silvery water, but none pierced through the fabric to the fibers underneath. An oily coat had been placed over it making it nearly waterproof.

Something far up the road caught his eye and he squinted hard trying to make it out. The closer he got, the more he could see until he understood what it was.

It was a wooden caravan, drawn by two black stallions with lanterns lit on all four of its corners. The caravan was not large, long

The Legend of Kyne: Chronocide

enough for an average person to lay flat and wide enough for three at the shoulder. Its driver was seated on a bench at the front with the reins clutched tight in their hands and as Kioni neared, he noticed the smolder of embers from a pipe in their mouth.

Kioni ducked his head down for a moment as he realized something that he could do to remain hidden. Reaching up, he grabbed at the silvery kerchief that was tied around his neck and pulled it up covering his mouth. As it crossed over the bridge of his nose, he felt the material seemingly vanish and he concentrated on a new face.

Looking at his wrists, he could see that his skin was no longer its light tanned, olive complexion but dark, the color of walnut. He grunted and noticed that his voice had changed as well, much deeper, making his throat vibrate with the sound.

"Greetings traveler," said the old man as the caravan came to a stop next to Kioni. Kioni pulled back on Variel's reins causing her to stop and he nodded at the man. "Not much of a talker, are you?" chuckled the man as he stretched both arms out to the side and yawned largely.

"I speak when I feel the need to," boomed Kioni's voice accompanied by the constant patter of the rain.

"Well," said the man with a puzzled expression as he pursed his lips to the side. "Interesting fellow aren't you, traveling all alone through the rain."

"That must make you interesting as well," replied Kioni.

The man laughed at his words. "You got me there. Why are you heading into Kydrëa?"

"No reason in particular," Kioni lied. "I wander here and there. I have traveled all over the continent and now seemed to have made my way to this land."

"Well, I am not Kydrëan myself, not really any nation actually. I travel back and forth between a few different areas. I always am sad when I leave Kydrëa though. Its people are quite unique, and I find them in good company."

A flash of light blinked over the hill on the side of the road and Kioni whipped his head around just to barely see the bright white of lightning as it zigzagged through the sky before it was lost back up in the clouds.

The Legend of Kyne: Chronocide

He held his breath while counting slowly in his head. Just as he said five, a sharp thunderclap rolled over them causing all three horses to stomp their feet and throw their head around in fear.

Kioni patted Variel as he tried to calm her and a few moments later she relaxed.

"I think that is the sign that we should part ways," said the man as he started his horses off in a trot. The wooden wheels of his caravan bounced hard upon every rock and Kioni could hear it loudly. Kioni guided Variel on and just as they passed each other, the man called back to Kioni, "I forgot to get your name. Mine is Alai. You are?"

Kioni did not look back and acknowledge the man. He honestly did not care one bit about his name or any of the things he said. Kioni would never see him again and the man especially didn't need to know anything about him, let alone a fake name.

He shook the reigns, guiding the white horse into a nice steady gallop. The quadruple slapping of her hooves in the mud was rhythmic along with her bouncing as she continued along the trail, the man long lost to the rain behind them. Without much effort the inaba stayed right at her side, its pattern of hops much different than hers as it traveled.

He would continue bringing the inaba with him, intrigued by its speed. He loved Variel, she was a great horse but the inaba was just so much faster and had a greater endurance. Never in his life had he traveled so fast across the land and for such a long time. His plan, as of current was to bring his horse back to Alakyne and then use the inaba more frequently. Thoughts of the eastern woman flew through his mind, her ravishing beauty reduced to a disheveled mess as he left her behind. He felt a chill go down his spine at the vengeful gaze she had given him just as he escaped.

A gust of wind flew down the hill catching Kioni off guard. Nearly falling off the side of his horse he was able to just barely keep his balance as he leaned into the gale. His cloak blew madly, and he felt his eyes begin to tear up as he ducked his head down. Variel slowed to a trot as she leaned against the wind hard, fighting against its push as it relentlessly fought to push them over.

"Come on Variel," Kioni said as he gritted his teeth. "We need to keep moving!" and he urged her back into a gallop.

The Legend of Kyne: Chronocide

We need to find shelter, thought Kioni as he glanced up at the darkening sky. The rolling underside of the storm clouds were lit up by brief flashes of lightning deep within. The storm was going to be large and dangerous for them to be out in it.

The massive storm cloud stretched far along the horizon creating a great rotating shelf as it crept along its path of destruction. The wind intensified but Variel did not slow, she instead accelerated a bit as if she could understand the danger that they were both in.

An arc of lightning erupted out from deep within the storm and broke into dozens of zig zagging strikes as they raced for the ground. The instant one finally made it, all the others vanished, and the sky lit up with a massive surge of light.

The thunderclap shook inside Kioni's chest mere moments after it was seen, and panic filled him. The trail was so hard to see now, veiled by a wall of falling water and Kioni could only see roughly a hundred feet into the distance. What he saw was faded and blurred from the rain, but he could just see the edge of a tree line and a dim glow of orange beyond it.

"Hiyah!" he cried guiding Variel into a full speed gallop. Each hoof beat splashed mud high into the air as she thundered down the road with the orange lights coming into better view. The rain roared around them, drenching everything with its torrent, even managing to saturate his oil ridden cloak so that each second it grew heavier.

Kioni first saw the rectangular shape of the windows followed by building walls. With a surge of hope, they pushed on as they rushed into the middle of a small town. Kioni quickly scanned around, looking for anything but he couldn't see much of a place where they could shelter.

"There!" he muttered to himself, guiding the muddied white horse and giant hare to the edge of a house. There they found a stable with other horses and a few stalls that were empty. Dismounting, he felt his boots sink deep in the mud and he struggled with each step as he moved her into the space before locking it tight. Untying the hare from her saddle, he guided it into another stall where it awkwardly squeezed its large body in before tucking down, its massive ears still straight up.

Another few struggle induced steps lead him around the beast to the back of the stall where the stable roof and the home's roof met with a few inch gap in between. He found a few sacks filled with sand and after fiddling with them, was able to make them into somewhat of a seat with the walls raised up high enough to block him from most of the wind as long as he hunched over.

His back lay pressed firmly against the wall with Variel to his left and the hare straight in front beyond his sandbag shelter. Around the stable, where the roof met the walls lay a few openings to where the outside storm was seen. Another flash of lightning and thunder hit nearby and the animals in their pens bucked and whinnied in fright. The animals had no real higher level of thinking. To them this storm and lightning was utter terror.

The wind rose up and Kioni crouched tight in his makeshift shelter. Water rushed from one side into the stable, a small river cutting straight in front of him. The ground was unable to accept any more water as it pooled and flowed through the stable soaking the hare's fur. He watched the large creature shift its position, moving out of the way of the stream and it snorted in annoyance before dropping its head back down.

This storm could very well flood the town, he thought as he looked to his left out into the street where a few inches of water flowed through the town. Along its surface were millions of ripples as raindrops pounded from the sky, the storm cell straight above them.

It was dark, similar to evening and the constant rainfall chilled the air to the point that Kioni withdrew another cloak from his pack. He wrapped it tight around his legs and soon felt the relief of warmth as he hunched down and endured the storm.

"Hey, what are you doing out here?" asked a voice startling Kioni awake. Still groggy from his sleep, he looked around to see that the storm was gone, revealing the orange gold of sunset. A few lone stars decorated the indigo sky near the horizon, their silvery gleam emerging in the newborn night.

"Hey boy?" asked the voice again, catching his attention. It was an older lady, standing nearby with a shaky hand pointing at him.

"My apologies," Kioni said quickly as he gathered his things. "I was just waiting out the storm."

"You were out here the whole time?" she asked incredulously.

The Legend of Kyne: Chronocide

"If I would've known I would've let you inside where it is warm. If you're in no rush you could join me now. My grandson and I have just finished our supper, but I believe there might be some leftovers."

"Oh no, thank you. I really must be on my way."

"I insist," she said cheerfully and turned her back as if she had already won the discussion.

Kioni watched her vanish beyond the corner of the house before he picked up his pack. A gurgle sounded in his stomach and the nauseating pain of hunger edged into his mind. He had food in his pack, but it was dry travel food, much less enjoyable than a home cooked meal. He didn't even really care what it was, just that it was food.

He looked over and met Variel's eyes. "What should I do," he mouthed to her as if expecting a response. Her long stare said everything that he was thinking, and he went over to pat her quickly before walking towards the front of the house.

He could see the town now that the storm was gone and was pleasantly surprised. In no way was it a city. More of a cluster of two dozen buildings, most homes with a few others that sported a tavern and possibly some assembly building. He glanced around and noticed that additional homes dotted the landscape around them with farmland nearby. Their crop was still growing, many months from harvest but it was green and thriving especially from the water it just received.

The wind had torn up a few fence posts that lined the street, but most things seemed to have survived. A single tree, not much bigger than his arm around had snapped in two and the top lay covered in the muddy silt left from the storm caused river.

He could see a few other people around, picking up the pieces of broken wood that they found and assessing the damage to their homes, but it was very few, most still hidden within their homes.

Kioni pushed open the front door and was greeted by a nice warm current of air adorned with the scent of food. His hostess was nowhere to be found and he stepped inside, closing the door softly behind him. A pile of worn-out shoes decorated with holes stood by the door and understanding the house rules, he removed his own boots and placed them neatly nearby.

The Legend of Kyne: Chronocide

The home was quaint and small, looking like only a few rooms with a low roof but it was well cared for and he felt a sense of security being inside. On the wall he could see a few paintings with the look as if a child had drawn them and a portrait, sketched to the resemblance of the older lady with a man and child in her arms.

"I fixed you up some supper," said the woman's voice startling him. He turned to see her holding a small plate adorned with vegetables. "You look like a meat eater but unfortunately meat is a luxury that I cannot always afford. I hope this will suffice."

"It is more than enough," Kioni said bowing his head. "I am very grateful for your hospitality."

"It's no trouble at all. You are also welcome to stay the night if you wish. It's just me and my grandson here so you could set up your pack right in this room."

"Thank you again," said Kioni as he accepted the offer and the plate from her. He hadn't been planning on staying the night but the homey atmosphere he was feeling was so pleasant to him that he couldn't resist. He hadn't experienced anything remotely like this since before the Dominion's invasion so many years ago.

He sat on the floor with the plate on his lap, eating slowly and enjoying the food. Most of it was long green beans with a side of chopped potatoes and another root he wasn't familiar with. The final part was a lump of bread like food that was soft and moist.

As he finished his meal, he glanced out the window to see the sun had set, casting the world in deep shadow. It had been nearly a week since his mission had been completed, or rather failed and he just wanted to be home and sleep in his own bed.

Laying his head down on his pack, he made himself comfortable on the floor and closed his eyes waiting for sleep to take him.

"Who are you?" asked a young boy's voice. Kioni opened his eyes to see the boy staring at him from only a few inches away.

"Who are you?" Kioni retorted as he sat back up.

"I asked you first mister," said the boy as he brushed his long sandy blond hair behind his ears. The boy was young, ten years old Kioni guessed with long hair and tan skin showing that he was outside a lot.

The Legend of Kyne: Chronocide

"I am just a traveler heading home."

"I haven't seen you here before, do you live nearby?"

"No, I live very far away. It will take many days to get home," Kioni replied discretely.

"Oh," said the kid puzzled by his answer. "Is that why you have the dirty horse in our stable?"

"Indeed, it would be. To go on foot for that long of a journey would be much, much worse," said Kioni slightly annoyed. "She is only dirty from the storm. She is quite a beautiful horse."

"Whatever you say mister," said the kid. "What's with the giant bunny?"

"It's a hare," he replied flatly.

The kid shrugged his shoulders as if not very interested before he walked over to Kioni's pack and picked it up. "Do you have a sword?"

"No!" said Kioni frustratingly and he snatched the bag out of the kid's hand, but the child seemed to not care. He instead had walked over to Kioni's other side and looked at his clothes.

"What do you need?" said Kioni.

"I'm just looking at you. You're the first traveler that I have not recognized before. The very few that we see are always the same people traveling to and from places, passing through our town."

"What is this town called," asked Kioni as the question popped in his head.

"Hohen," said the woman's voice drawing both of their eyes.

"I didn't even know this town existed. It's not on any maps of Kydrëa I have ever seen."

"Most don't bother adding it. Being far to the east between the Loke Ynen Desert and the Riigar Mountains, we don't get many visitors from the main population. Most are travelers like yourself going to and from other places, just passing through."

Kioni nodded and looked at the boy.

"It's time for bed. Stop bothering this man," she said sharply, and the boy stood up and left the room.

"Thank you again," Kioni said, and the woman smiled briefly.

"My pleasure to help wherever I can."

She left the room and Kioni doused the small lantern that had

The Legend of Kyne: Chronocide

lit it up casting him in darkness. His cheeks underneath his eyes felt tight and his eyelids felt heavy as he laid his head down. It had been a long day and even with his terrible nap, all he wanted was some rest.

20. Speed of the Inaba

Kioni opened his eyes, slowly adjusting to the beams of sunlight streaming in through the window. Outside he could hear the chorus of birds chirping with their little tweets, a cacophony of sounds.

Gathering his things, he quietly exited the home, stepping out onto the stone porch. The clouds of the storm were completely gone, with not a single white speck across the azure sky. Mud still covered the ground and a furrow had been carved into the road from the river the previous night but already the surface had dried and was beginning to crack as the moisture evaporated. Soon the ground would return to it once was.

He rounded the corner and came to the small stable to see Variel inside, her tail flicking away a few flies. The hare still had its head tucked down as it lay bundled up, but a twitch of its long ears told him it knew he was there. He opened the pen, noticing that someone had loaded it with hay as he could see a few scraps around signaling the animals had fed.

Kioni shook his head as he smiled slightly while guiding Variel out. These people were so polite and kind. They knew nothing of him or what he could be. It was almost dangerous and foolish for them to do it.

Kioni attached his packs to her saddle and hopped up onto it, situating himself comfortably on its hard leather. Swinging the hare's rope, he looped it over and secured it to them.

A sound was heard, and he turned around to see the old woman standing in the doorway, her hands folded tight to her body. Kioni smiled at her and waved to which she mirrored. A mutter of a command and the horse trotted out from underneath the shade of the stable roof and into the early morning sunshine. A few other people

The Legend of Kyne: Chronocide

were already out as Kioni scanned the different buildings in the town. Small moving dots near the houses that dotted the landscape showed the farmers were already out, preparing their crop.

A quick bump from his heel against her sides and Variel took off in a gallop out of the town.

As the town faded away behind them, the horse slowed to a more manageable trot and Kioni withdrew some of the travel food he had in his pack and scarfed it down. It was dry, much less enjoyable than the meal he had enjoyed last night but it would suffice.

The terrain slowly changed as they traveled for nearly an hour, the rolling hills flattening out revealing the Riigar mountains on the right horizon. Their snowcapped peaks a faded blue from the distance and only slightly visible.

To his left, the land spread out far and flat. He could just make out the fading color of the grassland as it neared the unseen desert, hidden by the curve of the planet.

Suddenly, a massive arc of white light shot up high into the sky, fading away as it left the atmosphere far to the west. A sudden rush of energy blasted over the landscape almost faster than Kioni could register and it nearly knocked Variel over from the pressure.

"What the hell was that?" gasped Kioni as he righted himself and stared towards the dimming light. The source was far away, so far that he had a feeling he knew where it could be from the direction.

Another pressure wave rushed across the landscape, but they were ready and took it much better than the first. A giant crack erupted from the source of the light, rushing out in a jagged pattern across the sky above him. More cracks followed and then, with a third pulse of power, hundreds more broke off from the main cracks.

Above, the sky resembled a piece of broken glass as far as he could see all stemming from the source, an enormous glowing beam of light.

"Its Alakyne!" shouted Kioni as he reached for his pack. "Something is happening there, something terrible! We are still hundreds of miles away, and at the rate we travel it could be weeks before we reach the source. Variel is not fast enough," he said solemnly. Looking over, he saw the hare standing still as stone, staring out towards the cracking sky.

The Legend of Kyne: Chronocide

It could get me there, but she can't keep up. He looked at the back of her white mane and stroked her head softly. "I'm going to have to part ways with you my lady," he said and with a spur of his heels, they turned around and took off, heading back towards the small town.

They were there in 15 minutes as he surged the horse at her top speed, each hoof beat accompanied by the thump from the hare's powerful hind limbs.

Dashing into the town, He spotted the home and wasn't surprised to see the old woman and young boy both outside staring at the sky. Everyone seemed to be fixated on the cracks, stemming from the beam like the roots of an enormous upside-down tree.

When they saw him approaching, the woman started walking towards him, confusion and concern spread across her face. She met him on the edge of their land just as he brought his steed to a halt.

"You're back," called the boy from the porch.

"Why have you returned?" she asked.

"I want to ask of favor of you," he said. "I trust you; I truly believe that you are good people. I have to get to the source of that," and he pointed to the west. "I think it's in Alakyne."

"Why do you need to go there?" She questioned. "Why does it concern you?"

"I can't explain but it does. I have to travel fast and she," he said directing towards Variel. "She's not fast enough. Would you take her, keep her safe while I am away? I can pay you."

The old woman held her palm out stopping his speaking. "No payment is necessary. We will treat her as our own. Come back when you can."

Kioni felt his heart skip in his chest, and he dismounted his white horse, transferring his packs to the hare's saddle. A few words were said to her and then he handed her reigns to the woman.

Mounting the inaba, he looked back one last time at his horse before saying a command. The force from the takeoff nearly took him off the seat as they dashed down the road out of the city, the cries of shock echoing behind him.

The hours passed but the hare never once slowed its pace. It's speed was incredible as it quickly traveled over the grassland, each thump of its dashing thundering upon the road. He wasn't sure how

The Legend of Kyne: Chronocide

long the hare could last but he pushed it forward, traveling well into the night before finally stopping. They rested for only a few hours, Kioni getting a short power nap as he stared at the sparkling cracks in the sky before boarding the hare and taking off again.

With a verdant forest soon flanking their right, he knew they were getting closer. The night faded away into early morning, but he pushed on. The sky above was littered with cracks, each pulsating with a white cosmic energy. It was as if all of reality was breaking down and Kioni started to notice that the cracks not only covered the sky but spiked up into the reaches of space and beyond. A few miles away, he watched as another crack branched off from above and pierced through the ground, disintegrating everything that it touched.

Every ounce of his being willed the hare towards Alakyne. The animal's endurance seemed to be unmatched, but he could tell that it was taking its toll. The day wore on and Kioni saw no other people as they traveled rapidly down the old road. They were making great time and should be arriving in Alakyne later that day.

Kioni steered the hare around a cart that had been blown across the road and watched as a few other people stared as he passed them. Up ahead, the later afternoon sun cast its light upon the city of Alakyne's great wall. The outer city was littered with debris from the increasing shockwaves that seemed to roll from the epicenter every so often and some people had started barricading their homes on one side to help against the pressure.

Dashing up the road, Kioni eventually slowed it down to a steady pace and they traveled through the archway into Alakyne. A glowing haze radiating from a street near the citadel. Great cracks spread from it, branching from the ever-present beam and signaling it was exactly where Kioni was wanting to be.

The guards seemingly paid him no mind as they fiddled with disassembling things. To Kioni, it looked as if most of the city was fleeing the area, afraid of what was happening. He saw abandoned homes, carts wrecked and pillaged upon the sides of the streets, and other terrifying things that made his stomach lurch.

The capital city was dying.

After they passed through the wall, Kioni commanded the hare into a much brisker pace and they dashed up through the city streets,

The Legend of Kyne: Chronocide

avoiding anyone who got in their way. The closer they got; the more Kioni felt drawn to head to the citadel instead. Speak with King Theo directly about what was going on. The king would have more answers than he had.

With reluctance, he veered up a road that took him away from the center and passed into the citadel wall. No guards blocked his path, which was strange, and he was shocked to see the grounds nearly empty. A few guards looked to be carrying items of value in packs and Kioni rode over to them.

"Hey, you there," he called as he dismounted. "Where might I find the king."

Both of the guards looked first at him, and then at the hare before looking at each other for a long moment. Suddenly they both burst out laughing.

"You want the king?" one laughed.

"Like King Theo?" chuckled the other.

"Indeed," said Kioni, slightly confused. "I have been gone for a while on an assignment straight from him. I have the clearance to speak with him. Where might I find him."

The laughter died down immediately, and they glanced at each other before one said, "He must not know what's going on."

"We should tell him."

"What do you mean," demanded Kioni with anger rising in his voice. "Where is King Theo?"

"He's gone lad. Fled the city pretty much immediately once this all went down," and he gestured towards the sky. "Such a great king of ours."

"Thought to be a war hero who would give anything for his people," said the second.

"Bah, like that was ever really true!" replied the other guard. "He only cares about himself, and his cowardice proves that! Screw him, screw his royal guard, screw the Shades, screw it all!" he roared in anger. "We were never anything but pawns in his own power grab from Aaldra."

"Destined to rule because his father was once the king. I heard they aren't even descended from Alakyne and that it's all a myth."

"I heard that too!" gasped the other guard as the two seemingly forgot about Kioni.

"Gentleman!" shouted Kioni, gaining both of their attention. He was so angry at the king and everything that was going on, but he knew it wasn't the time. "What happened then?"

"We don't know. Rumors are something about the archmage guy and his lady friend came up from underground. He was screaming about something and then poof."

"Poof?" asked Kioni.

"Well, more like boom!" said the other guard, emphasizing the final word. "Both of them as well as the two dragons that were accompanying them exploded in that flash of light."

"It looks like it might be the end of the world," muttered the other guard. "Things are changing. People vanishing, memories fading. It's as if existence itself is unraveling and it all is seeming to stem from that damned distortion at the center of it all."

Kioni nodded and mounted the hare. "Thank you, gentleman," he called and with a command they dashed out of the citadel gates and back into the city, heading for the epicenter.

* * *

21. From the East

The other Kitsune were aghast at those words.

"I'll join you."

Akami could hear the muttering and mumbling coming from them.

"You can't be serious Hayame!"

"I agree with Suka," said another. "We can't trust her."

"We can trust her, and she will trust us," Hayame said flatly. Akami felt a chill down her spine. She wanted to trust her sister, trust that she would hold her word but deep down she knew that she couldn't be. *The moment that they have Kioni and I let my guard down they will either kill me or something else to prevent me for receiving credit. I'll be killed and she will be rid of me.*

Akami watched as Hayame turned to face the other Kitsune and was it her imagination or did she seem to be smiling?

They left the tavern shortly after, the Kitsune upon paper white horses while she rode her stolen horse. They traveled for days, each time setting up wards before going to sleep and she remained upon the outskirts of camp with her own wards up to alert her of any danger she may be in. As the days passed, she grew slightly more at ease, traveling in the back of the group most of the day at a fast trot before they would set up camp. If they wanted to kill her it was logical to think it wouldn't be at this time, but she still set her wards up inconspicuously every night before sleep.

Kioni's trail was beginning to lighten up as he gained distance on them but they were able to keep it for the time being. The summer was hot as they traveled on and Akami tried her best to keep her appearance up. Using her aura she would clean her clothes daily,

The Legend of Kyne: Chronocide

stripping down and bathing in rivers while using her aura to scrape the grime from her skin.

Her hair still hung down, not in a bun and no braids as she didn't know how to do them, every time it had been done by a servant. She wished that she knew how now, she liked her braids.

Brushing a bead of sweat from her brow, she looked down, recognizing that her arms had grown quite tan in her travels. Her skin was naturally a tan color but now it was way darker, lines of untanned skin hidden under her sleeves as she peeked at them. She hadn't noticed before and she cringed. Her flawless skin was tainted with the strange pattern of her clothing imprinted there by the sun.

More days passed and eventually they came to small building with dozens of horses out among the fields. They spoke to the owner, one of the Kitsune breaking his nose in the process before he told them of Kioni's horse and how he left with both it and the inaba.

Using their aura, they saw that the two paths they were following had been joined by a third and as they continued on noticed that it didn't seem to grow fainter with time.

"He is traveling slower now," said one of the Kitsune. "His trail maintains the same consistency. He must be upon his horse with the hare accompanying them."

"That is good news sister," said another. "Our horses are trained in endurance and with time, we should begin to catch up."

And as they went, they noticed that day by day the trail began to grow stronger. Not by much but Akami knew that they were correct. They were slowly catching up, but she knew he was still days ahead of them.

He is going to make it back to his country before we will catch him, she thought that night as she lay out on her bedroll beneath the stars. Her hair was laid out above her head after being freshly brushed and her silky clothes felt nice upon her skin.

If we can't catch him then we will need to switch up tactics. The Kitsune are especially brutish, even to their own people and they have gained quite the reputation. If the Kydrëans catch word that they have entered their land, then we will be confronted quickly. Kydrëa has lots of aural users and we would be outnumbered. I know that I should stay with Hayame, at least for the time being with hopes that she is being genuine. With that said, however, if the

The Legend of Kyne: Chronocide

moment arises then I will need to separate from them.

A few more days passed when they awoke in the early morning hours just as they had done before. They gathered there things swiftly before starting off on the road, the Riigar Mountains that separated their country just barely visible on the horizon. The early morning blue was beginning to lighten, casting the earth's shadow away as an hour passed before the brilliant sun lit up the grassland behind them. The warmth was welcomed but she knew it would be hated in due time as it beat upon them.

Suddenly a massive blast of energy rapidly approached before overtaking them, nearly knocking them all from their horses. Cries of disbelief and shock were shared before it suddenly rushed at them again.

"Are we under attack!" screamed one of the Kitsune, dismounting and drawing a strange item that was her catalyst. The others followed suit and as the third wave rushed at them, they noticed that it was coming from very far away to the west, rushing over the entire landscape.

"What is it," Hayame said under her breath before suddenly massive, jagged cracks split the sky, spreading out from whatever seemed to be causing the pulses. The cracks split again and again, fracturing into dozens of smaller pieces. Nearly a mile away, a piece split down before piercing the ground, anything it touched disintegrating immediately.

"It's the Kydrëans," said Akami as she stared at where it seemed to be coming from. She couldn't see it, but she just had a feeling. Something really bad was happening.

"A command and all of them took off faster than before, using their aura to urge their horses at a much faster pace. It was a sacrifice that they needed. Their curiosity peaked as they aimed for the source of the fracturing world.

* * *

22. Heresy

A blinding light radiated all around and then Kyne felt the breath leave his lungs as he landed hard upon the stone ground. His eyes slowly adjusted revealing the stone streets of Alakyne, but things were different. The sky was hazy, laced with smoke from some unknown source and the buildings looked to be much more ravaged than before.

A grunt nearby signaled Auriel and he scrambled over to her, embracing her as she crawled to her knees.

"What's going on," she coughed as she scanned the area. "What happened?"

"I have no idea," said Kyne. "The last thing I remember was feeling like I was being ripped apart and then a bright flash of light."

"I remember that too. When I touched you, I could feel the distortions that you told me about. What happened down there?" and she pointed at the ground.

Images of Saathe flooded his mind, the horror of seeing his disgusting face and the memories it recalled, the memories of Voron's murder.

"I think I altered the timeline somehow," he whispered. "Something terrible has happened."

Auriel remained silent, his words making her skin crawl.

"How?"

He explained it quickly, everything that occurred in the catacombs. As he finished, she was silent, and she looked around slowly for a moment before jumping to her feet in shock.

"Where's Rosé! And for that matter where's Ni'Bara!"

Panic raced through Kyne as he reached out with his mind trying to find his companion to no success.

The Legend of Kyne: Chronocide

"Do you think that..." Auriel started.

"They were right near us when this all happened," and he gestured around at everything. "I don't know what could've been different for them."

"What are you doing?" shouted a whispered voice from a nearby building. "Get inside before they see you."

"What?" they both said in unison as they turned to the building. "Before who sees us."

The voice did not respond and suddenly shouts of alarm came from further up the road.

"Transgressors! Halt under His authority!"

Kyne and Auriel turned to look at the people now quickly approaching them.

"What the hell?" stammered Kyne and he took a step back in shock. "It can't be."

"What's wrong?" asked Auriel as she looked towards them. "Kyne tell me!"

The approaching men clanged down the road with their bronze armor contrasting against the mulled-out colors behind. Each clutched a drawn sword as they approached and upon their breastplate was a familiar triangular symbol.

"They are Dominion sentinels!"

"What?" gasped Auriel in horror as the names from the countless stories Kyne had told her finally took form in front of her. She could see them with their right shoulder plate spiking sharply up creating an asymmetrical appearance. "It can't be!"

As the sentinels rapidly approached, Kyne reached down towards the hilt of his sword, thoughts raging in his head. He would tear them apart, use his dragon aura to rip their armor to pieces and pry the bones from their flesh! Just as he contacted the sword, he felt his mind ease, the dragonrage retreating allowing him to think more clearly. Looking down at his arm, he sighed before unrolling the sleeves of his shirt, covering his dragon arm and he withdrew a pair of black leather gloves.

"They don't know about this, and I can use it for an advantage if the opportunity arises," he muttered quickly as Auriel noticed what he was doing. She nodded her head in agreement before turning back.

The Legend of Kyne: Chronocide

The sentinels drew upon them and fanned out in a semicircle. Seven in all, their swords were aimed at their chests and Kyne could just make out the foreign green eyes under their helms.

"You have transgressed. By setting foot out into the streets, unaccompanied by a sentinel or other official you have gone against His will, and His will is law! All transgressors are set to death by mutilation and torture. You will not resist or those of your kin will seek the same fate."

"I have no kin here," retorted Auriel with a flick of her head. "I do not plan to die, nor do I plan on having you lay a finger on me."

Her words seemed to startle the sentinel for a moment before he regained his composure.

"Take her and the Kydr. They will get the full treatment to wash away their crimes."

Two guards on either side stepped in to apprehend each of them but in a quick blur, all four lay in a bloody puddle upon the ground, their swords clanging dully upon the stone.

A cry of rage swept through the remaining three sentinels, and they attacked them with a furious whirlwind. Sword met sword and there was a flash of blood as two more sentinels fell. The remaining took a staggering step back and dropped to his knees looking at the sky.

"Protect me oh Lord!" he screamed and before they knew what was happening, he withdrew a small spherical device and lit a protruding string on fire.

"Auriel get away!" roared Kyne and they both leapt back just as the sparking string vanished into the sphere. A small explosion of red ripped from the sphere, blasting the sentinel to pieces and sending a mighty cloud of red powder up into the air.

Auriel's ears were ringing as she staggered to remain standing, the red smoke blocking all of her field of view. The explosion had torn through the city, creating a small crater and pieces of debris fell to the ground. Screams from the homes nearby were heard but she ignored them.

She stumbled around, looking for Kyne. He had been behind her and much closer to the blast. Movement through the dusty fog caught her attention and she dashed over to see him coughing hard and laying upon his back. Blood dripped from his ears and small cuts

The Legend of Kyne: Chronocide

littered his face.

"Kyne... Kyne!" she shouted, shaking him hard and he groaned. "Get up! More are coming, we have to get out of here!"

His ears were a buzzing hum as he was shook violently. He could just make out the muffled sound of Auriel's voice and he struggled to open his eyes. She was standing over him, her silvery blonde hair matted with dirt and debris and a few streaks of blood upon her arms.

"Auriel?" he asked shakily as he struggled to his feet. With her help, he managed to stand up and his auditory sense was starting to return. "What happened?"

"More are coming Kyne. We need to leave now!"

Shouting sounded up and down the street and as the red dust fell to the ground, clearing out the air, they found themselves blocked upon either side with dozens of sentinels. No command was heard but their unified shouting seemed to drown out all other thoughts as they rushed the two.

"Vae dynori," the Riel muttered, and, in a blur, she dashed out with her blade drawn, slicing massive cuts through their armor. Her orichite blade made quick work of a few of them but more were still coming.

"I grow tired of this!" roared Kyne. "Aira tar!"

A bright ball of lightning arced towards one sentinel. Passing through them, it exploded, spreading out and striking another, and then another all in the blink of an eye. A great thunderclap shook the earth and nearly ten sentinels all crumpled to the ground with smoking wounds in their flesh.

"Heretics!" screamed one sentinel and they backed away.

"Heresy of no other higher transgression!"

"Summon them!" screamed another. "Summon them to wipe away their sins!"

The sentinels all simultaneously beat hard on their shields, echoing the loud clangs through the city. Over and over, they beat them, unified in sound it was deafening.

A blur of movement flew past Kyne and before he could even react something struck his hand, covering the glove and forcing its way up his sleeve. He glanced down and was startled to see the silver aural

The Legend of Kyne: Chronocide

tar that he had once used himself. Another blur and more struck his other hand where he clutched Aurora.

A scream of pain rang nearby, and he turned to see Auriel had been struck a few times as well and was now kneeling on all fours, the silver tar rippling and swelling.

A massive shocking pain ripped through Kyne, and he staggered, trying hard to remain standing and each second getting weaker and weaker.

He knew how to get rid of this stuff but just before he uttered the spell, a glob of tar struck him directly in the face, blinding him and choking him.

The world seemed to be spinning and suddenly he felt the hard hit of the ground as he toppled over. Muffled voices were heard and then as his mind grew cloudy, he lost consciousness.

*   *   *

23. Flame of the Setting Sun

Ni'Bara groaned as a raging pain was felt through his head. He could feel water running over his cheek and as he gradually opened his eyes, he could see that he was lying at the edge of a wide river. A large gouge had been carved out of the bank, cut through deep into the river where he lay. It had been from him crashing into the river like a meteor.

The great dragon lifted his head shakily and stared around, looking for any sign of his companions but none were seen. A panic raced through him as his muddied mind tried to focus. *If they had landed in the river,* he thought. *Then...* and his vision darkened as his head swayed around. *I have to find them!*

The dragon staggered up to all fours, scanning his vision all around. It was midday, that he was certain of as he could feel the warmth of the sun above. A dozen miles or so he could see a black haze hanging over the silhouette of Alakyne. Billowing plumes of smoke rose from all around the city, even beyond the wall in the burning or construction of something unseen.

The grey dragon groaned again, and he took a single step before his arm buckled and he crashed back into the shallow water with a splash. Gasping for breath, he managed to turn his head so that his nostrils peaked above the surface before he lost consciousness.

Ni'Bara awoke with a jolt and scrambled to his feet, barring his teeth in anger. His mind was much clearer and as he looked around, he was startled to find that the sun had trailed through the sky and was now near the horizon with roughly an hour of sunlight left!

Kyne! roared the dragon's thoughts all around as he cast them out into the void.

The Legend of Kyne: Chronocide

"Kyne! Auriel! Rosé!" he roared, this time out loud as his voice carried far.

As it died down, no one responded, and the dragon felt something very rare for him. Fear and despair! Looking through the riverbed, he saw no sign of anything signaling his friends had been there. No footprints, no floating items, nothing.

He roared their names again and again for a time with no response. If they were still alive, they weren't anywhere nearby. He swung his head around, looking down the river before his gaze lingered on the hazy silhouette of Alakyne a few miles away.

He leapt up into the air and unfurled his long silvery wings, stretching them out and casting a large portion of the river in shadow. A few flaps and he was off, gliding at a rapid pace down the river looking for anything that would tell him where his friends were.

As he continued on, he glanced over towards Alakyne and saw the sooty haze hanging over the city once more. Nearly the entire citadel was blocked from view with only a few of its higher turrets visible. Smoke and other pollution rose steadily from different parts all over the city with more billowing clouds from outside the wall.

Further down the river, the dragon could see some sort of fortification had been built directly upon the bank with another large column of smoke rising from it up into the once azure sky. The wide river was littered with dozens, if not hundreds of ships and as the dragon neared, he could see they were ships of war. Large boats adorned with weapons and other items for battle all moored along the shore with dozens more under construction.

What is going on? he thought as he turned away from the river. His friends were not here, and the more he thought about it, the more he convinced himself that they were cast to a different area than he was. Both Kyne and Auriel had been touching and Rosé was nearly upon them but he was a few feet away when whatever happened, happened.

Following the road up to the city a few miles away, Ni'Bara could make out hundreds of carts guided by soldiers as they carried copious amounts of coal and metal ore.

The dragon coughed a bit as the air transitioned to the sooty polluted atmosphere over the city. The wall had been adorned with ballistae and barrels of oil to burn enemies who attacked the city.

The Legend of Kyne: Chronocide

Soldiers patrolled the walkways, and the streets below were bare of almost everyone. The glimmer of the golden metal heitrite decorated the tips of the ballista bolts threatening to tear even a dragon out of the sky.

Down below the streets were fairly empty, the few groups of humans that he saw always being led by at least one soldier, no one was ever seen alone.

Ni'Bara glided down into the city where the explosion had happened and was startled to find it stained with dark red splotches upon the stone. A few nearby soldiers darted away upon seeing the dragon and he puzzled at their fear.

Normally people avoided him or praised him from afar. It was very rare for people to cower in fear.

As the soldiers clambered away, Ni'Bara caught a glimpse of something that made even his dragonfire fade down to nearly a smolder. The symbol of the Dominion emblazoned upon their breastplate and shield. As if gifted sight for the first time, the dragon looked upon the city with new eyes seeing flags carrying the symbols, ragged and worn in their posts. Upon every door, the symbol had been burned into the wood leaving its black scar visible for all to see.

Suddenly a roar sounded above, and he glanced up in shock to see the silhouette of a massive dragon gliding down towards him. With a crash, the beast landed upon the stone street, cracking the stone into massive fragments.

Its copper scales glimmered in the hazy light and with a roar it bathed the nearby street in dragonfire, burning everything and leaving the fronts of the building smoldering.

"You are back!" roared a male voice but Ni'Bara already knew exactly who it was. Something truly dreadful had happened.

"Indeed, I am," he replied slowly, unsure of how to act around this creature.

"The Otoruhns were no match for you I presume. Their cities were laid waste and their people burned?"

"To ash," replied Ni'Bara, masking his shock at the horror of what he had just said.

"I would be impressed but they really weren't that much of a threat to begin with. I just wish I, Ky'Ren, The Flame of the Setting

The Legend of Kyne: Chronocide

Sun would have been the one to decimate their people. Their filth has roamed along our borders for far too long, plaguing our waters with their ships and confusing our people with their rebellion. It was only a matter of time before He would have grown tired of their annoyance."

Ni'Bara nodded his head with a snort.

It's as if we are friends or something, he thought to himself as the copper dragon gestured towards the citadel.

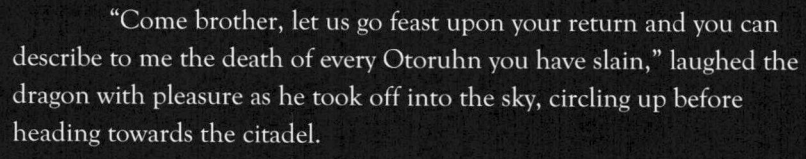

"Come brother, let us go feast upon your return and you can describe to me the death of every Otoruhn you have slain," laughed the dragon with pleasure as he took off into the sky, circling up before heading towards the citadel.

* * *

The Legend of Kyne: Chronocide

24. Mirrors

A blinding light erupted in front of Kyne bringing him back to consciousness as he squinted against it. At first, he couldn't make out anything except that single white glare directly in front of him. He tried to move his body but quickly understood that he was bound, both of his hands locked together in some device and his legs connected by a short chain. He was seated on a chair, but he couldn't really see anything else.

As his eyes tried to adjust to the glaring light, he could just make out a dark shape move behind it but nothing else.

"Where am I?" he asked glancing around trying to make out anything else. Auriel was not with him, he was alone.

The dark shape from behind the light stepped towards him revealing a humanoid figure, silhouetted black. A swift strike ripped across Kyne's cheek as he was struck hard with the back of someone's hand and then there was the sound of someone spitting upon the ground.

Anger poured through him but as he tried to form the spell to break him out, he was shocked to find that he could not. No matter how hard he tried he could not formulate the words of power in his mind so that they could be spoken and free him from his bindings.

The light in front of him suddenly dimmed, allowing him to see where he was. The grey of stone bricks surrounded him on all sides. Behind the figure he could see the iron of cell bars locked and guarded by two sentinels beyond.

The figure turned to face him, and he was startled to see a pale woman with fire red hair and piercing green eyes meet his gaze. Quickly raising her hand, she whipped it across his cheek again, smacking the back of her fist against his flesh and launching his head to the side.

The Legend of Kyne: Chronocide

"Do not lay eyes upon me Kydr!" she hissed. "I know not of what sorcery you have done to change your appearance," and she gestured at his figure. "To mock this form perhaps? Or to commit espionage?" she added thoughtfully. "I personally want you dead. We want all of you dead, but He says that you will all serve your purpose in his great ambition. That the Kydrëans are of use to him."

"Change my appearance?" muttered Kyne confused. "What do you mean change my appearance? Who is He? Where is Aur..." A swift punch into his abdomen silenced him immediately and he doubled over gasping for breath. Intense nausea radiated from his stomach, and he cried out in pain as he felt his hair pulled, ripping his face up, the female drawing only an inch away.

"Speak again Kydr," taunted the Gaeilian. "I dare you."

"You touch me again I kill you!" spat Kyne startling her. In a flash he swung the lock binding his hands up towards her face.

She reared back, doing exactly what he had planned. Hooking his feet behind her ankles, the moment she lost balance he rammed forward sending them both crashing to the ground. Scrambling for a hold, both he and the female struggled for a moment before he elbowed her hard in the ribs, sending her sprawling upon her back.

Kyne felt his dragonrage flowing through him and tried to draw upon his aura, but it was hidden behind a veil, impeding his access to it. In a rage, he drew his iron lock up and slammed it down, aiming straight for her face.

"Erodath!" screamed a voice and before Kyne could even recount what she had said, he was launched back across the room where he slammed into the chair breaking it into fragments. His breath burst from his lungs as he landed upon the ground and before he could react, she had dashed out of the cell, slamming it closed behind her.

Kyne met her eyes one last time as he watched the blood from his attack drip down the side of her head and her chest heaving as she tried to catch her breath.

After a long moment as she calmed down slightly, she slowly rose back up proud with her chin high and turned on her heel with a flick of her red hair. The sentinels outside his cell remained nearly motionless as they stared straight forward, seemingly unaware or uncaring of what happened.

The Legend of Kyne: Chronocide

Kyne sat up and slid back to the wall where he rested his back against the smooth stone surface. His mind was searching, grasping at the foreign word she had said. He knew it lay somewhere in his mind, but he couldn't remember it and every moment that passed caused it to be hidden even more. After a long while of digging through the depths of his mind, he finally gave up and slouched back.

"Where are you?" he muttered quietly to himself as he thought of his three companions.

* * *

Auriel groaned as she opened her eyes trying hard to focus on her surroundings. She was in a large circular room adorned with tall skinny windows casting in the faint light from outside and a single wooden chair near the wall. Directly in front of her across the room was a large metallic door.

Her arms were bound together and hung above her head where they connected to a long iron chain. She hung with only the tips of her toes brushing the floor and as she realized it, she felt the strain on her shoulders ache in pain.

Her mind was cloudy and as she stared down at her feet, her mind seemed to stray, drifting away in a slight confusion. She consistently had to focus her mind back to the now, where she was and what was going on.

"Kyne," she mumbled, and she jerked in her suspension, rapidly jarring to a stop as an unseen chain that bound her legs grew in tension. She was trapped and unable to get out.

"Auriel, you need to focus!" she said with ferocity. "Focus on a spell to get you out of here!" But no matter how hard she tried, she was unable to formulate the words of power.

She scanned the room once again, her mind clearing just enough for her to understand exactly what was going on. She had been stripped down to almost nothing, a single tight piece of cloth was wrapped around her chest and another tight piece covered her hips. Her tattoo was nearly fully exposed, its silvery swirls wrapping around her skin upon her arm and curling up over her shoulder and chest.

She screamed in frustration and thrashed around in her chains

The Legend of Kyne: Chronocide

for a long while, enraged by what was going on but after a time, she grew fatigued and ceased. There she hung limply and nearly exposed for a long while before voices were heard outside.

The low whine of ungreased metal upon metal signaled the door was opening and she could see two people speaking quickly to one another beyond it. The first was a younger man with very short jet-black hair. The second was a woman with brilliant red hair who seemed to be flustered from something.

Straining her ears, she only heard the very end of what was said.

"I don't know what to do with him. He attacked me!"

"It seems to me that you provoked him, Sister. Heretic or not, he has shown dangerous power and needs to be treated with the utmost caution."

"I don't need to be lectured. Leave me with her! I would like a word."

The younger man nodded and left down the hallway flanked on either side by a Dominion sentinel. The woman paused for a moment before turning to look at Auriel. They stared at each other for a long moment before she finally stepped inside and shut the door behind her.

As she drew near her, she grabbed the wooden chair and dragged it over directly in front of the Riel and sat down. Crossing her leg, the redheaded young woman stared at her with her fingers all placed together tip to tip. There she sat in silence for a long time before Auriel finally broke the silence.

"What do you want with me," she said slowly. "What have you done with my husband?"

Raising her eyebrows in intrigue, the woman stood up and walked directly over to Auriel. The Riel could see a fresh bruise appearing on the side of her head with a hastily cleaned line of dry blood.

"You are quite interesting aren't you," said the woman and she looked up and down her. "Clearly not Kydrëan that is for sure. Your beauty shows that," and she lifted her hand up and pushed Auriel's silver hair back revealing her aspen shaped ear.

"Not Kydrëan at all," she continued, and her hand dropped to

The Legend of Kyne: Chronocide

her shoulder softly. With a single finger, she ran it along the lines of her tattoos causing Auriel to shudder from the cool touch. Trailing all the way down her chest and side, the fingers crossed abdomen and then continued down her leg.

"Get your hand off me," snarled the Riel as she thrashed slightly in her bindings.

"Fiery, I like it," said the woman as she bit her lip and withdrew her hand. "He would like to speak to you," she said. As she turned on her heel and walked towards the door. "Do get dressed though, modesty is a virtue," and she waved her hand.

The lock holding Auriel suspended opened and she crumpled to the ground in a heap. Another click signaled her leg shackles had opened and then the sound of the door shutting echoed through the chamber.

Staggering to her feet, her shoulders aching in pain, she looked around and noticed a pile of clothes lying on the ground by the shut door. Walking towards them slowly, her gait uneven and shaky, the Riel bent over and picked up the clothes. It was a plain dress, white in color and a pair of thin shoes.

*   *   *

Hours passed in the small cell, or at least that is what it felt like to Kyne. He had no concept of time. The only things he could see other than iron and stone were the two guards outside his cell who hadn't moved a single bit and the orange flickering light of the torch further down the hallway.

The sound of a creaking door echoed down the hall, its metallic whine causing the hairs to rise on the back of his neck. Rising up to his feet using the wall against his back for balance, he watched as two people came into view. Both of them stopped outside his cell in between the guards.

The first he could tell was the female he had attacked, the second, a young man with dark black hair and a smooth hairless face.

The man nodded to the sentinels and both of them turned to face Kyne while the man opened the cell. Both of the sentinels accompanied the man into the cell with the female waiting outside.

The Legend of Kyne: Chronocide

"Don't do anything stupid," he said to Kyne. "Come with us now. He wants to speak to you."

"Where is Auriel!" spat Kyne as he dashed forward towards him in a single jump. His movement was much faster than any of them realized and before the sentinels had even moved, he was an inch from the man's face. They were roughly the same height but Kyne easily had fifty pounds on him of muscle from years of training. This man, more of a boy was frail and weak.

A look of shock was upon the man's face as the archmage stared him down for a long moment before the sentinels reacted and grabbed a hold of him, throwing him back towards the wall. His chains binding his feet together clanged as he lost balance, crashing his back into the stone with a thump.

"All in due time," spoke the man clearing his throat and trying to regain his composure. "She will be joining you soon. Come and let us get moving." Spinning on his heel, the man turned and walked out of the cell with Kyne standing there facing the two sentinels.

He took a short step forward and felt the chain tense up from its short length. Another step followed and soon he had made it out of the cell, painstakingly slow. Each footstep less than half a normal walking gait.

Rounding the corner, he saw a steel door blocking the way and watched it slowly creak open as the man lead the rest of the group through it and up a flight of stairs. The glowing light of torches lining the walls was the only thing allowing them to see.

At the summit of the steps was another door which they passed through and then began a long journey throughout the hallways, periodically heading up more flights of stairs. Kyne focused as hard as he could through his clouded mind, mapping his path through the dungeon. He had never seen any part of it before, making him uncertain of his exact location.

Another minute passed and light from outside was seen down another hallway. It was a faded light, cast through the outside pollution but it was so welcoming to him. He was finally on the surface!

Traveling through the corridors, he started to see familiarity of it. He knew this place as the lower levels of the citadel of Alakyne. The further they went, the more certain he knew where they were going.

The Legend of Kyne: Chronocide

It was the King's Chambers, a second type of throne room where only the highest-level people would be allowed. Kyne was certain of it.

It would still be a bit before they arrived and with his chains binding him, he held the group up. The sentinels trailed behind him with the two others in the front. The man didn't look at him once and kept a slow and steady pace. The red-haired young woman however continuously glanced back at him and scowled, as if she was irritated about his speed.

"If you undid these chains I could walk faster," Kyne sassed when she looked back one particular time.

"Not going to happen heretic," she spat. "Do not speak to me!"

Kyne chuckled for a moment before his foot caught the edge of a stair step and he fell forward hard onto the stone, slamming his forearms against the corner.

The burning pain was intense through his bones and rapidly he was jerked back up to his feet by the sentinel who then followed it with a quick shove, sending Kyne staggering for balance.

Eventually they drew upon a set of large wooden doors, the faces of each decorated with ancient Kydrëan script and symbols. Two golden rings stood nearly touching each other in the middle of doors and with an elegant motion, the man grabbed one and rang it three times.

The solid thud of each strike resonated briefly and for a long moment there was silence.

"Enter!"

The thick rich voice contained power and upon hearing it, Kyne's blood ran cold. The door swung open and as he was led inside, he felt his eyes widen as he stared at the smiling face of Lord Aaldra.

"Interesting, interesting indeed," chuckled Aaldra as he rose and took a few steps towards Kyne. "The spitting image of him yet, slightly different."

Kyne's mind raced as he scanned the room. Two other sentinels stood nearby and to his delight and also terror, he saw Auriel standing in between them, her silvery eyes meeting his own.

"So similar," muttered Lord Aaldra as he approached Kyne.

The Legend of Kyne: Chronocide

The old archmage of Tsora placed his hand underneath Kyne's chin and lifted it up so that they were eye to eye, each a deep golden reflecting their Kydrëan heritage.

"What are you talking about!" snarled Kyne and he thrashed his head out of Aaldra's grip who chuckled and took a step back while dropping his hand.

"Son!" called Aaldra and he turned towards the back of the room to see a previously unnoticed door swing open.

Three figures stepped out, each one causing more mental stress to surge through Kyne's mind. The first was a seemingly transparent man, ethereal as if he was not truly there. Kyne had heard stories of the man who was not quite dead, Diahl. The second was the familiar dark robed figure, Saathe the reaper. The third figure walked in with pale robes and thin wispy grey hair upon his head. His eyes were completely glassed over. It was the necromancer Alderiun!

All three of the dark princes led a fourth smaller figure who walked in with their back hunched over and their head low. Short blond hair was visible, but Kyne couldn't make out a face as the young man walked over to Aaldra.

As they stood side by side, the young man raised his head and both Kyne and Auriel gasped in shock.

"I would like you to meet my son," called Aaldra with his voice booming. "Kyne son of Aaldra!"

Auriel cried out in shock and Kyne caught his own breath.

"What is this," screamed the Riel. "What games do you play, toying with us like this!" she flailed around in her grip trying to get loose, but it was futile. The two sentinels clamped hard upon her bindings holding her firmly in place.

"How?" muttered Kyne as he stared at the alternate version of himself. This Kyne was different, much more frail and timid than he himself was. The way he stood with his shoulders hunched forward and his eyes constantly looking upon the ground.

The different Kyne shifted his weight and raised his eyes towards them. First, he stared at Auriel and then as his eyes drifted towards Kyne's, their eyes met, and a look of shock spread across his face.

"What is this father?" he asked with his voice quivering. "Why

The Legend of Kyne: Chronocide

does he look like me?"

"Don't call him Father!" roared Kyne. "He is not our father; he is a traitor and a murderer! Our father Zawiet was a great man! Do not sully his honor with those words!"

His words seemed to shock the son of Aaldra, and his eyes leapt towards the ground. His shoulders seemed to quiver as if he were fighting the urge to sob.

"Hold your tongue!" snapped Aaldra and he placed his hand onto his son's shoulder. "He is my son, maybe not by blood but by spirit. He has disowned all of his previous dealings years ago. Who are you and why do you mock his face?"

Kyne clenched his jaw in rage as he looked around the room staring at all of the familiar terrible faces. His greatest enemies had all returned as if the universe was spiting him. As his eyes drifted to the alternate version of himself, they met and for a long moment each stared at the others' golden eyes.

Kyne focused his gaze as if trying to communicate through the look but after a moment, his counterpart broke their gaze and turned his back to them. Taking a few steps, he said with a low quivering voice, "They frighten me father."

And then he was gone, led out of the room by the three dark princes. Aaldra stared at the door as it closed for a long moment before turning around and returning to his throne.

"Explain why you are here," he said darkly while placing his hands together pressing the opposite fingertips upon each other.

"We will do no such thing!" hissed Auriel and she thrashed hard in her bindings. "You do not control us!"

The lord of the Dominion chuckled deeply.

"Oh, but I do. I control everything within my Dominion and soon will have control of the entire continent. Tell me why you are here, or I will be forced to kill you where you stand."

"Why don't you make me!"

A quick nod to the sentinel came from Aaldra and a steel sword was drawn and placed against the front of her neck. The sharp edge pressed hard into her skin and the slightest lateral movement would result in rapid death.

"Wait!" screamed Kyne. "I'll tell you!"

The Legend of Kyne: Chronocide

Aaldra rose from his throne and approached them rapidly. "Not who I was speaking to. I would like her to explain it to me," and he directed his gaze to Auriel.

Auriel remained silent and stoic as she stared down Aaldra. Her lips pursed together tightly and then she raised her upper lip in a scowl.

"Auriel don't be foolish!" cried Kyne in a panic. "Don't risk your life for this!"

"I would listen to the boy," said Aaldra much more darkly. "I am growing tiresome of your insolence."

Auriel shook her shoulders roughly fighting against the grip of the sentinels. Her mind was much clearer now but try as she might, she could not formulate the words to manipulate her aura. She glanced to her right and met Kyne's pleading eyes as he struggled against the sentinel's grip.

Deep inside she knew what she should do, and the more she decided it the more she felt humiliation.

"Fine, I will tell you," she muttered causing Aaldra to break out in a wicked smile.

"Delightful. First tell me your true names, both of you."

Auriel met Aaldra's gaze with the fire of defiance burning within her silvery eyes.

"I am Auriel, princess of the Riel and wife to the archmage Kyne son of Zawiet."

Her words startled Aaldra for a long moment as he looked back and forth between them. A long moment passed, and the red-haired woman and her brother began whispering behind them, but no words were made out.

"What the hell is a Riel?" muttered Aaldra and with a puzzled expression he looked her up and down.

"If I may my lord," said the red-haired woman and she stepped up behind Auriel and roughly pulled her hair back revealing the Riel's aspen leaves.

"Ah interesting," he said. "She's not human. That would explain why her features are foreign to any people I have seen before. She is still irritating however, no matter how beautiful she is." Aaldra jerked his head towards Kyne and smiled. "So, you are Kyne? That is

The Legend of Kyne: Chronocide

odd because I thought my son was Kyne."

"We are from another timeline," said Auriel softly.

"A timeline where I killed you and Kydrëa defeated the Dominion of Gaeil!" said Kyne with a smile of his own.

Aaldra's eyes darted to him and judging by the look on his face, he seemed to believe their words.

"Get them out of my sight!" he spat before sitting back on his throne. "I will contemplate what I want done with them."

"Yes, my lord," said all four sentinels simultaneously and the two prisoners were jerked back out of the room. Stumbling down the hallway, Kyne tried hard to see Auriel and could just make out glimpses between their escort.

They came to a branching hallway and to his shock, Auriel's sentinels guided her the opposite way he was taken.

"Auriel!" he screamed as he thrashed in his grip trying to get towards her.

"Kyne!" Auriel replied as she struggled briefly. "It will be alright!"

Kyne felt his rage increase as the sentinels tried to pull him back and with his full strength, he slammed his knee into one of their thighs. The sentinel cried out in pain and dropped to one knee but before Kyne could strike the other, two quick blows struck him across the face, and he was seeing stars.

As he crashed to the floor, his mind muddy and dazed, he could just make out the shape of Auriel struggling in her grip as they dragged her away, her voice muffled and fading.

The taste of blood was filling his mouth as he was jerked back up to his feet, he watched the sentinel he had attacked stand up slowly.

"You'll pay for that heretic!" the sentinel said, and he thrust his fist up into Kyne's abdomen knocking the wind out of him.

He doubled over, gasping for breath and saw his vision fade in and out for a moment again. A glob of bright red blood dripped from his face and fell to the ground in a sticky splat. He focused hard on it, trying his best to remain conscious. If he lost consciousness now, he might not remember the path that led him to his cell. It could be a completely different one from before.

An agonizing moment passed as he gasped for breath. Each

inhalation was one of the hardest things he could do as his diaphragm spasmed from the strike.

"Move!" shouted the sentinel and he was jerked into a forced walk. Panic flew through his mind as he tried to breathe, each breath bringing little relief to his burning lungs. Focusing hard, he managed to inhale and exhale every other step, using the rhythmic walking to calm him down and help regain his breath.

They led him down the identical path as before, following turns and corridors until the outside sun was blocked by the grey of stone. Orange torchlight guided their journey and eventually they came face to face with his cell, the wooden chair still left in splinters.

"Get that out of there," ordered one sentinel to another. "We wouldn't want him to try anything with it."

The other sentinel ran quickly inside and tossed the broken chair pieces outside of the cell. As he exited, Kyne was thrown roughly inside where he tripped and fell forward, sprawling onto his chest.

"We will be back in an hour for your next dose," chuckled a sentinel as the door clanged shut behind him and they left. He was once again alone in the dimly lit cell.

Seconds melded into minutes which turned to hours as Kyne sat upon the stone ground, his back leaning up against the wall. His joints ached and his stomach rumbled as the time wore on. The two sentinels eventually returning and after a futile struggle, they blew some powder into his face.

Immediately his mind clouded intensely and the aural words that he was so close to grasping were ripped out of his reach. Slumping down to the floor, he lay curled up in a fetal position, his thoughts fogged as the drug seeped throughout his body.

Kyne awoke to the sound of metal on stone. A tray with a small portion of slop very few would call food slid next to him. He struggled to rise, his vision swimming before him and he placed his hands upon the ground for support.

As his vision slowly focused, he saw that he had also been given a moldy piece of bread that went with the glop of food. He wasn't even sure what was in it and reluctantly he placed the tray on his lap and began to eat it.

The bread was like a rock with small patches of sour that he

The Legend of Kyne: Chronocide

was certain was the green mold that had burrowed throughout it. The slop was bland and had chunks of something that he thought once might have resembled meat.

As it slid down his throat, he shuddered as a chill ran up his back. It was so disgusting and humiliating to eat this garbage. He hoped far in his mind that Auriel was faring much better.

* * *

Auriel was in the same cell as before but had been allowed to keep her clothes and remain unbound. The red-haired female spent hours within the cell, staring at her completely unmoving.

Auriel felt much more exposed than she ever felt as she slowly ate the food that had been given to her. When the tray first arrived, the red-haired woman whom she had found out was called Voira ripped into the servant, ordering much better quality of food for her. Auriel had been taken aback by this as she watched him scuttle away closing the door behind him.

"I won't have you eating that sort of filth," Voira whispered quietly to herself as she rose up to her feet. Approaching Auriel, she traced a finger across her bare shoulder before running her hand through her hair.

"Would you like me to brush it for you?" Voira said, as she continued to play with Auriel's long silver hair.

"I would like you to stop touching my hair," she spat, and she whipped around to face her. They stared at each other for an entire second before movement flew through the air and Voira slapped Auriel straight across the face.

Standing up abruptly, she marched over to the door where she was suddenly greeted by the previous servant bringing a better tray of food.

She grabbed it from him and threw it into the room where it landed with a metallic clang followed by the slam of the door.

Auriel rubbed her cheek from the blow and rose up, slowly making her way to the spilled tray. A wedge of cheese along with a piece of bread and some cooked vegetables lay scattered upon the stone floor. A few moments later, she had gathered them all up and returned to

The Legend of Kyne: Chronocide

where she had been seated.

      Her stomach rumbled and she scarfed the food down quickly, enjoying it temporarily before images of Voira came into her mind and she shuddered intensely.

      The young woman made her skin crawl every time she laid her eyes upon her. There was something within that Auriel couldn't quite understand whether it be fascination or jealousy, or much worse in lust and envy.

      The light from outside her window slanted as the hours waned on and then it shined a deep red, the sun's light cast through the pollution like the light of an eclipse. Eventually it turned to night and after a long time of thinking as she tried to clear her mind from the drug, she gave up and laid upon the small uncomfortable bed. Closing her eyes, the last thoughts she had were of Kyne and of the other two who they had seen no sign of.

*   *   *

25. The Path to Hell is Paved With Good Intentions

Rosé peered out into the street from her hiding place high up on a roof. The two soaring figures of Ni'Bara and another copper dragon were seen flying away up towards the citadel.

She had been so close to him. Nearly there when Ky'Ren had landed and interrupted her. She had heard his name before a long time ago but couldn't exactly remember what it was.

She eavesdropped on the two of them as they spoke briefly before they flew away. She heard it all and shuddered at the wickedness that emanated from the dragon.

Ni'Bara was acting very strangely, and she wasn't exactly sure why.

He is hiding something, she thought as they vanished around the edge of the citadel. *Something is very wrong.*

Down below, she could just make out the movement of a few groups of people led by soldiers in bronze armor. The city was much more different than it had been before they had arrived, and she had no idea what was going on.

Shouting caught her attention, and she watched as a man was struck to the ground by one of the soldiers. Others in his party screamed and pleaded with the soldier but he seemed to not care as he struck the man over and over again. Each strike landing with such force that within moments the man's face was bloodied and hardly recognizable. Eventually the soldier stopped with one final kick to his ribs before he spat upon him and walked away.

The Legend of Kyne: Chronocide

The party rushed over to their fallen and tried to help him quickly to his feet.

"Shouldn't they help him? Why are they trying to get him up?" murmured Rosé.

"Hurry, hurry," she heard one of them say, a young man. "Get father up so that we don't get left behind. If we are out in the open alone then…"

"We all know what happens," said another man nearly the same age as they hoisted the limp body of their father over both of their shoulders. The other two members of their group, an early teen girl and who Rosé assumed to be their mother cried in grief as they all ran after the sentinel who was laughing as he continued up the street.

"Wicked people should burn!" snarled Rosé as she felt her rage flow through her. She dashed along the edge of the roof, keeping low so as to remain hidden. She leapt into a quick glide out over an alleyway to another roof as she pursued the family and the soldier.

The sun was setting with its orange glow all around casting long shadows. Lanterns were being lit along the road below by other soldiers but very few people walked the city, and everyone was always accompanied by at least one of them.

The family rounded a corner and entered a short alleyway following the soldier.

Perfect! thought Rosé savagely as she dashed across the roof to the other end of the alley. No one was on the other road and hunching low, she looked down into the alleyway where the family was following the soldier. Their father moaned and dripped blood behind the two brothers as they painstakingly carried him after.

Anticipating her fall, Rosé bared her teeth and dove off of the roof. Pulling all four limbs in tight, she watched as the soldier came directly beneath her and with a growl, she drew his eyes up towards her. In a crash, the small pink dragon slammed hard into the soldier sending him toppling to the ground, his metallic armor muffled with pieces of straw and wood that lay scattered throughout the alleyway.

Cries of shock erupted from the family but Rosé paid them no mind as she turned to face the soldier who was stumbling to his feet. His face was lit up with shock and his hand was placed upon his hilt.

In a blur, Rosé leapt toward him, her claws outstretched and ready for blood, but he was fast. Twisting around, he avoided her attack as she sailed past him. His sword was drawn but instead of attacking, he opened his mouth.

He is going to call for help! Panic raced through her mind and just as he took a deep breath to call out, she shot a jet of flame directly at his mouth. His chest momentarily swelled, and his eyes screamed out in pain before he staggered back. Slumping against the alley wall, he started to shudder and thrash. The dragon looked him dead in the eye as he tried to breathe, his lungs burned beyond repair.

As the man's life faded, she turned to face the trembling family who stared at her with open mouths.

"It's alright I am a friend," she said quickly as her snarl faded from her face.

"It's a..." stammered the mother.

"It's a dragon," finished one of the sons and he staggered back nearly toppling the other brother and their father over.

"Are we to die this day?" cried the mother in fear as she dropped to her knees.

"No, you are not," said Rosé quickly and she took a step towards them. "I do not wish you any harm. I couldn't just sit back and watch you get beaten and humiliated by that soldier."

They were all silent for a moment as they eyed first her and then the dead man.

"If that is true then your act of heroism has killed us all," said one of the two brothers.

"What do you mean?" gasped Rosé. "No one saw what happened."

"But that sentinel was our escort. If he goes missing, then we are to be the primary suspects."

As his words touched Rosé, she felt her stomach drop. She had made a grave mistake.

"What are we to do Roco," said the young girl. "Are we going to die?"

"I will do everything in my power to not let that happen Seri. Lioné let's set father down for a minute so that we may take care of this sentinel."

As the two brothers sat him down, Rosé watched them quickly

walk over to the man and check to make sure he was truly dead.

"Good riddance," said Lioné and he kicked the sentinel's boot lightly. "The world will be better with you gone."

"We can't leave him here, there is nowhere to hide him," said Roco as he looked around the alleyway. "Home is close, let's get him there and then we can figure out what to do with him."

"We can't get him and your father home without being noticed," wailed the mother as she sobbed on her knees. "We will be seen."

"I can scout out ahead and give you the clear when no one's around," piped Rosé. "I can help."

They all stared at her for a long moment before a look of anger flew across the mother's face.

"This is all your fault," she hissed, and she rose to her feet. "All of our deaths are on your head."

"Mother stop," said Lioné and he grabbed onto her arm. "She was trying to help us. Can't you see she is just a child?"

The mother's scowl did not fade but she stopped fighting against his grip and instead turned and knelt next to her husband where she began to sob once more. The little girl seemed to agree with her brothers, and they discussed what to do.

"Our home is across this street and the next," said Lioné. "We can't carry both of them at the same time and I don't think either of us will fit in the sentinel's armor."

Roco eyed the sentinel for a moment and nodded. Both of them were larger than he was, and it was highly unlikely that they would fit. Lioné was the taller of the two but even Roco was large. All of them were dressed in old clothing and they all carried the golden hair of the Kydrëans with the father nearly bald, his scalp covered like a horseshoe.

"I'll watch out for the sentinels while you cross with your father and then him," Rosé said. "We can do this."

"We need to go now then while there is no suspicion of foul play. We should've been home a long time ago," added Seri. "It's getting late."

"I agree," said Lioné and both he and Roco walked back over to their father. Hoisting him up, the two of them as well as the two girls

The Legend of Kyne: Chronocide

followed Rosé to the edge of the alleyway. A few flaps and the pink dragon shot up into the air and landed out of view on the roof.

After a moments her head appeared over the edge, and she called down to them.

"Two groups are down the street to your right a few hundred feet. They should be out of view in just a moment. Now!" she said and on cue, all four of them ran quickly out into the street. The street was wide and took them nearly ten seconds to make it across, the whole time Rosé scanned up and down the street looking for any sentinels.

She watched as they placed their father down lightly and looked back at her.

Another glance and her heart nearly skipped a beat. Approaching from the other side of the street were two sentinels, their heads facing forward. The pink dragon nudged her snout towards them signaling the approach and to her relief it seemed that they all got the cue, crouching low against the same side wall while making themselves as small as possible.

The world seemed to stop as the sentinels walked past the alleyway, their heads never moving and within a few seconds they had passed, continuing on down the street. Rosé breathed out a sigh of relief and as the sentinels disappeared from view the two brothers dashed across the street as fast as they could.

Hoisting the sentinel's corpse up, they approached the edge of the street. A quick signal from Rosé and they crossed quickly once again hidden in the shadows of the other alleyway. The red orange light shined over the city of Alakyne as Rosé looked up at the sun. Its normally beautiful light was blocked out by the smoke and pollution that covered the city, turning it a deep red.

Rosé flew over the street quickly and was soon on the roof of another building. This roof was different, more of a home with slanted shingles and a smaller lip to hide than the first. Stepping as slow as possible, she quietly crawled across it so that she could peer out into the street beyond. Immediately her heart sank as she saw sentinels standing on the edges of the street in groups of two. There were six in all, looking out across the street on either side.

Rosé leapt from the roof and landed softly next to the family, startling them.

The Legend of Kyne: Chronocide

"The street is covered with sentinels," she spoke rapidly. "What are we going to do?"

"It's sundown," said Lioné solemnly. "Sentinels patrol the streets all night long looking for anyone out alone."

"What are we to do then?" gasped the mother. "We can't stay here all night; they will find us."

"We won't stay here," said Seri. "I have an idea that involves you," and she pointed at Rosé.

"What would you have me do," said the pink dragon.

"Start a fire, something large enough that the sentinels will have to act. Roco, do you know any abandoned buildings?"

"I know of a few on our street, but I have a better idea. There is a sentinel gathering spot at the end of the street. A lot of them like to hang out there. You should burn it down."

Rosé nodded and after Roco showed her the exact building, she flew back up on the roof and started to make her way towards it. It was three buildings down, identical to the others but not as raggedy. Two sentinels sat in chairs out front of the building and lights inside signaled dozens of others inside.

Perfect! she thought as she stealthily approached the building. Crossing the open street, she soon was in the alley next to it.

Looking for a good spot, she eventually found it and took a deep breath. She blasted out a wave of her pink dragonfire, engulfing the lower edge of the building in flames. She continued swinging her head from side to side as she lit the whole bottom ablaze. As she ended her blast and saw the flame continuing to eat at the wood she was satisfied and she flew up and headed back towards the others.

Just as she landed and peered down into the alley, she heard the cry and shock from sentinels followed by the clanging of their armor as they ran. Swinging her head, she turned to see the building ablaze with one side completely covered by orange flame. Billows of smoke rose high into the sky where it melded in with the pollution.

Rosé scanned for any others before signaling the family to cross. All four ran fast to a small door that she assumed was their home. Other doors lined the building on either side showing her how small of a space they must live in. Movement of a door opening and then they were all gone inside, vanishing from view.

The Legend of Kyne: Chronocide

Rosé sat hidden on the roof for a long moment, her eyes pinned upon the door when suddenly it opened and after a quick look from side to side from Roco, the two brothers dashed back across the street.

"Almost there little brother," Rosé heard Lioné say as they heaved the sentinel up.

"Tell us when," called Roco's voice from below her. A flick of her wing out in the alleyway signaled she understood, and she scanned the street. Sentinels were flocking towards the building with more running down the street. They were going to have to cross with the sentinels looking the other way.

"Now!" she called out and they ran as fast as they could. Just as they neared the middle of the street, Rosé watched in horror as the nearest sentinel stopped running and started to turn around as if he heard them.

Rosé ripped one of the stone shingles off with her claws and as fast as she could, hurled it down the street where it shattered with a loud crack.

The sentinel turned towards it quickly and stared at it, allowing just enough time for Roco and Lioné to get into their home.

As the door shut, Rosé felt her heart sink slightly. She wasn't expecting to join them but it still was strange sensation being left alone once again. Turning to look down the street, she watched as the sentinels fought against the fire, the flames slowly dying down as buckets of water were thrown.

"A pity," she said, and she gave the house one more look. Her eyes widened with shock as she saw Seri leaning out of the door gesturing for her to come.

A brief flash of joy erupted in Rosé and after quickly scanning the street for the prying eyes of sentinels, she flew over and entered their small home.

26. Would you like your Tea With Venom or Honey

Two swift strikes crashed against the door, the wooden paneling shuddering from the blows and then silence as Rosé felt her stomach drop. It was early morning the following day. She was laying down, curled up near the foot of the bed that filled the main room, her tail tucked around one of the posts.

Two knocks struck the door again and muffled voices were heard. Nearby Rosé watched as the mother, whose name she still didn't know, placed her hands over her mouth in a silent wail. Roco and Lioné had both approached the door, flanking either side and were quietly bickering back and forth between each other as they thought of what to do. Shadows moved across the curtains that covered the window and Rose shuddered, wrapping her tail even tighter around the post.

Suddenly Roco turned to Rosé and flicked his hand gesturing for her to hide. She nodded as she realized and wiggling backwards like a worm, she slid fully under the bed, all the way to its head where she curled up tight, her tail wrapped against her side. She could only see the ankles of the two men as the door suddenly swung open. Beyond, standing in the entryway were two sentinels, their golden colored boots glimmering in the sunlight as it streamed through the doorway. Studying them, she realized she could just make out the distorted reflection of the men from the mirror-like sheen off their boots. Their gruff voices were shared, and she strained her ears trying to make any of it out.

"Where is he?" Roared a guard as he rammed his finger into Lioné's chest. "He was last seen with you lot last night. Heard he kicked

The Legend of Kyne: Chronocide

the snot out of one of yous."

"I don't know where he is," Rosé heard Lioné speak slowly. "He brought us home and then left. I assumed he went to your little gathering place for a drink."

"He didn't!" snapped the sentinel. "No one saw him after you!"

A low groan sounded, and the back door opened revealing the hobbling figure of the beaten father as he gradually walked towards the sentinels.

"Oh ho ho," laughed one of them loudly. "What do we have here? Damn I'm jealous! I would love to just beat the piss out the Kydrëan trash that we have to deal with! Would make our jobs so much more *entertaining*."

The father stopped his walking and Rosé couldn't make out anything that was happening, the images obscured upon the boots. She guessed he was probably just staring at them.

"What the hell do you want piss breath?" the other sentinel muttered.

"I think he might want another beating," said the first and he took a single step into the home, the wooden floor creaking under his weight.

"Maybe I'll have a go," said the other. "I just might not be able to stop."

"That's the trick my friend," said the first as he turned to face him. "It's called moderation. Beat them occasionally so that they survive to endure another beating."

"That's some wise words there," he chuckled back and then Lioné was upon his father guiding him back into the room and setting him in a chair.

The mother stood still as stone, her ankles the only thing Rosé could see, close enough she could reach out and touch them.

"What about this one?" asked the sentinel pointing at Roco. "He hasn't been much help has he."

"Not much at all, let's ask him again. I know you had something to do with it, where is he."

"I. Don't. Know."

"Last chance."

The Legend of Kyne: Chronocide

"I told you; I don't know!"

Rosé heard a dull thud and then Roco dropped to his knees, his face coming into her line of sight. His mother let out a shrill scream, the tone ringing her ears.

"Shut her up or you'll be next!" barked the sentinel and Roco lifted one hand up as if pleading with her to stop.

"Do you want more?"

"No sir," coughed Roco

The sentinel drew his head back and spit on Roco, a hot sticky glob splattering against his cheek.

"We will be back and if we haven't found him, you can expect far worse!"

The door slammed shut.

Another muffled scream came from the mother, and she dashed into the back room. From under the mattress, Rosé stared for a long time, terrified about what she had done. She had tried so hard to help save a family and, in the end, had doomed them. They would be back, and they would find her or the corpse that lay hidden beneath the floorboards in the kitchen. He was already beginning to stink, and it wouldn't be long before the putrid scent of death spread through their home.

There wasn't much else they could do.

What would Ni'Bara do if he were in this situation?

Burn them all, she thought for a moment, imagining his voice before dismissing it.

No, he wouldn't say that. He would think all of the possibilities through.

I could just run away, but she shook her head. Even if she could abandon this family to their fate, she would surely be caught by the other dragons or worse, shot out of the sky with one of the war machines that covered the city wall. *If we burned the body then maybe that would buy some time,* but then her inner voice chimed in.

But they would surely see the smoke.

Maybe in the night, she thought. *If we last that long.*

"You can come out Rose," said the voice of the young girl Seri startling the dragon out of the debate going on in her head.

Slowly, she crawled out from beneath the bed and made her

The Legend of Kyne: Chronocide

way over to the wall where she leaned against it.

"It's not your fault little one," said Roco as he walked up to her, his cheek already swelling from the blow. "You were just trying to help."

"And I messed everything up."

"That you did!" hissed the mother as she revealed herself in the doorway. "I should have given you up to the sentinels when I had the chance! Maybe that could've been enough to save my family from the hell you have brought upon us!"

"Mother stop!" Snapped Roco. "She is but a child, mind yourself!"

"You would talk to your own mother like that?" she said aghast. "How dare you!"

"How dare you Mother!" Added Lioné. "You would seriously sacrifice a child to those monsters?"

"A child? Don't talk about her like she is a person! She is not! She is a dragon, more of a beast than anything!"

Rosé felt her heart sag at the woman's words and then the door slammed signaling the mother was gone, back into the depths of the house.

"I apologize for her," said Roco as he placed a hand upon her head.

"It's alright," she said fighting the warm feeling in her chest that signaled tears were imminent.

"Oh, young one," he said, and he pulled her in to an awkward embrace.

She fought tears and the comfort helped.

"Mother can be mean," added Seri. "Really mean."

"I just don't know how I can help fix this," said Rosé shakily.

"I think I am going to sneak out tonight," said Roco suddenly.

"Outside the house? You'll get killed," gasped Rosé.

"Only if I get caught," he laughed with his voice carrying fear. "I'll figure out where we can dump the body and then hopefully, we can survive the punishment when they come looking for vengeance."

"But what about Rosé," said Seri suddenly. "If they come looking for us, they'll find her."

"Then I guess I will have to leave," sniffed the dragon. "I can't

The Legend of Kyne: Chronocide

stay here much longer anyways. I need to find my family."

"Where are they?" Seri said as she sat down next to the young dragon. In her hand she had a small bowl filled with what smelled like tea. She offered it to Rosé, placing it on the ground and the dragon took a sip, the warm liquid bland, but nice. "Sorry we don't have any honey," Seri added softly.

Rosé shook her head, grateful for the drink anyways and took another sip, hiding the initial reaction at the bland taste.

"I think they were captured but I am not sure," she said, answering Seri's question. "I saw my brother flying away with some other dragon, but I don't really know what to do.

"Brother?" gasped Lioné. "Which one, Sunset Death or the Murderous Grey?"

"What?" asked Rosé confused.

"Ky'Ren or Ni'Bara?"

"My brother is Ni'Bara."

"The storm that destroys everything it touches. How could you even associate with that monster?" murmured Seri.

"What do you mean?" she asked, shocked and then offended. "My brother is a great dragon. He saved all of Kydrëa from the Dominion and everything!"

"Saved us?" they all gasped before laughing.

Roco's voice grew dark. "He *is* the Dominion Rosé. What are you even talking about?"

"I'm serious! My brother is not like you guys say."

"Even if that is the case then why would he burn people alive just for sport?" Lioné added. "Why would he carve the land with his flame destroying crops and causing death? So much death and senseless killing. The other one is bad but he is just vile."

"This place is just wrong," she said. "Everything seems so strange ever since that big flash of light."

"I'm so confused," said Seri. "I'll believe you for now, but you just wait. If either of them gets bored, then you can witness firsthand what His dragons like to do!"

* * *

27. Facades

Ky'Ren landed upon the large platform, his copper scales glimmering in the light from the setting sun. The citadel seemed to shake under the weight, but it held strong. With a flick of his tail, he crawled out of the way, allowing Ni'Bara to land. The platform was massive, easily holding both of them as it hung out over the citadel before reaching within its walls.

Ni'Bara did not recognize this area of the citadel before and after looking at its design realized it had to have been created within the last few years. Built into the back side of the citadel high up, it was three walls and a great balcony allowing them to peer out over the wall and beyond across the grassy fields. Their brilliant green was long gone, replaced by yellow corpses as what little sunlight pierced through the atmosphere was not enough to sustain them.

Beyond that lay the edge of Kol Faldîn, large swaths having been cut down leaving only stumps. Thousands of acres had been destroyed, consumed by the Dominion's glutinous war machine. Ni'Bara watched as the last carts of the day traveled from the forest's edge, laden with dozens of logs.

Following the path, he saw that it curved along the edge of the forest heading straight for one of the facilities near the river where the war ships were being created. Massive craters littered the fields near to the river from stone quarries and metal mines.

The Dominion was destroying Kydrëa and everything that it contained.

"Bring me food!" roared Ky'Ren drawing Ni'Bara's attention back into the large alcove.

He could see the dragon had pushed open a human sized door with his snout near the back of the room and was roaring throughout the castle causing the stone under foot to vibrate. Ni'Bara sized up the dragon, eyeing him from tail tip to snout.

He was identical to when he had last seen him, save for a few small scars along his tail. The scars looked as if another dragon had bitten him.

More and likely the alternate version of myself, he thought as he fought the urge to attack Ky'Ren right there. *It would be so easy to take him out, his neck is wide open*, he thought before he shook his head. *He would sense it before it even happened. I know I would. I have killed him before and I could do it again, however, I don't know where any of the others are. He might though, so for now he serves a purpose.*

"Ah finally," Ky'Ren rumbled darkly as he withdrew his head and two servants cautiously stepped inside. Within their hands they each held a rope leading three cattle linked together.

Upon seeing the dragons, the six cattle bellowed in fear, pulling hard towards the door but it was immediately shut behind them. The servants let them go and like a snake, Ky'Ren snapped his head towards them. Ni'Bara watched him relish in their fear as the first one was torn in two and the pieces gobbled up. The rest of the cattle ran away, trying to find escape but he took them out, one by one leaving three left.

It was disgusting to Ni'Bara as he watched it unfold before him. He was a hunter and to do this to prey was wicked and evil. Their deaths should be as quick and painless as possible.

Ky'Ren turned towards Ni'Bara and licked the blood off of his lips with a smile.

"Their fear makes it so much more delicious."

Ni'Bara was silent and turned to see the remaining cattle had all clambered into the corner, their rumps pressed up against each other in the middle of its angle.

"Are you to feast brother? Or shall I," hissed Ky'Ren as he feigned attacking them. They cried in fear and cowered even tighter, their hooves scrapping against the stone.

Ni'Bara looked at them all, their quivering bulbous figures and felt a huge surge of pity. He didn't want to eat them, but he knew they would die no matter what.

Stepping forward, he lowered his head towards them and felt the own pull of his dragon aura. It was so much different than anything

The Legend of Kyne: Chronocide

the humans did, but he had been training and had learned this one.

As the cows met his gaze, they seemed to stop shifting in place, growing still as if caught in a trance. Mesmerized, the cattle seemed to lose interest in everything and quick as a blur, the grey dragon took all three out as quickly and mercifully as he could.

He couldn't help but enjoy the taste however as he swallowed the last piece, and he turned back towards Ky'Ren. Cattle were among his favorite pieces of food.

"What did you do to them?" asked Ky'Ren in shock.

"What do you mean," Ni'Bara said gruffly as he ignored the question. Crawling over to one side of the alcove, he lay down sweeping his tail close to his side.

"It's like you put them under a trance or something," Ky'Ren continued. "They just stopped fearing you."

"That's not what I saw," said Ni'Bara calmly. "I saw them cowering so badly they nearly died from fear itself. I think they just gave up after what you did to the others."

Ky'Ren was silent for a long moment. "Maybe... But that was really odd."

"Anything else I can do for you Master Ky'Ren?" spoke a quivering voice. "Or you master Ni'Bara?" Ni'Bara looked over to see that both of the servants who led the cattle in were still there, quivering as they looked upon the two dragons.

"Get out of my sight!" he snarled and shot a jet of flame towards them. The servants leapt to the side just narrowly avoiding it before running out of the door, the metallic clang as it shut echoing behind them.

Ky'Ren laughed darkly. "Pathetic things, these humans are. Very few of them are even worth speaking to. One of these days I might just eat one of them along with the cattle they bring. Do you not agree Brother?"

Ni'Bara remained silent as he stared at the shut door. This world was so wrong. So many things changed, undone, and corrupted as if everything they had worked for was just gone.

"You are acting very strange Ni'Bara. What happened to you in your visit to Otoruh?"

"What?" asked Ni'Bara, distracted by his thoughts.

The Legend of Kyne: Chronocide

"Just like that. You are acting really strange. Before you left you would've been the one tormenting the stupid servants. Are you... Are you growing soft?" Ni'Bara's focus drew back towards Ky'Ren as the dragon continued. "You wouldn't be growing soft like that female dragon you killed those few years ago? Siding with those weak northern tribes was... Distasteful." His voice dragged out in a hiss. It should've been me to streak her white scales with red! I wish I could've tasted her blood, the *urge* it gives me with just the thought..." he shuddered.

Ni'Bara tried hard to remain in control as the words from Ky'Ren tore through him.

She lives? How is this possible?

"You bore me," Ky'Ren muttered as he clambered away to the other side of the alcove. "Even like that, those words should have drawn a rise out of you but nothing."

The sound of scales upon stone signaled the dragon had laid down.

"Oh, one other thing," Ky'Ren sighed. "I have a feeling you won't care much as you are so *distracted*, but I was told to tell you by Him, that some people of interest have been apprehended down in the city. One is a female who isn't *human*, and the other well," his voice trailed on. "His resemblance would shock you."

As the copper dragon laid down and turned away from Ni'Bara, the grey dragon's mind began to race.

Kyne!

But no reply came.

I know that is you and Auriel that he speaks of, he called out with his mind into the empty darkness. *I know you can't hear me, but I am here, and I will do everything in my power to get you out of here, even if I have to carve this city with dragonfire!*

* * *

28. An Unexpected Ally

Kyne awoke to the sound of a metallic door opening and then shutting, its familiar groan becoming a sign that he hated and dreaded at the same time. As if on cue, a sentinel stepped into view with a tray of slop food.

They feed me morning and night, he thought to himself as the sentinel threw the tray in where it crashed to the floor sending food everywhere. *Why am I so lucky?*

Walking slowly over to the food, waiting for the sentinel to leave, he stooped down and managed to scrape up most of the slop, leaving the part that touched the ground out of the pile. The ground was covered in rat feces and other vile stains that he didn't want to know what they came from. He surely wasn't going to put it in his mouth.

As he ate, he stretched his mind out, looking for Ni'Bara but was once again met with the emptiness that he had grown to know. Whether it be distance or the drug blocking him, he didn't know. He had no idea where his friend was. He might not have even come to this timeline. He could be back home having a much better experience. *If there even was a home left,* he thought. He wasn't quite sure he knew the answer and part of him didn't want to even think about it.

The first thing I need to do is get out of this place. Once that's completed, Auriel and I will be able to start searching for a way to cause the time distortions. If I can get back to the correct time, then I can prevent all of this from occurring. Hopefully that will undo all of this.

He had little hope though, his mind constantly lingering on the fact that he was still here and hadn't gone back to his original time yet. Additionally, his thoughts focused on Auriel and how she was doing and all of the strange things they had witnessed.

The Legend of Kyne: Chronocide

A few minutes passed when suddenly the whine of the door down the hall sounded.

Kyne stumbled to his feet, his mind still hazy and he swayed a bit, his sight threatening black.

He would be ready for them this time. Certainty filled his mind that it would be the sentinels, ready to drug him again dragging the aural thoughts far away but he was shocked to see the alternate Kyne peering around the corner into his cell cautiously.

"What do you want," Kyne called out.

The other Kyne cowered out of view for a moment before peeking back around the corner.

"Who are you," he stammered quietly.

"I am you, at least a version of you," said Kyne and he took a step forward.

The alternate Kyne inched away from him, sliding down the bars to where they met the stone wall. Kyne raised his hands quickly in a gesture, hoping to stop him from leaving.

"It's ok, I won't hurt you," he said softly.

His words seemed to intrigue his twin and he stepped more into view.

"How do I know you are really me and not some skin changer?"

"Ask me something only we would know."

The question hung in the air for a long moment. The alternate Kyne furrowed his brow and looked first at the ground and then down the hall before returning his gaze towards Kyne, never making eye contact.

"What was our brother's favorite food?"

"That's the question you came up with? Aeris's favorite food? Wow... Well obviously, you're probably wanting me to say mom's chicken stew but it's actually,"

"Trout," they both said simultaneously.

"Believe me yet?"

"What did our parents give us on our tenth birthday?"

Kyne smiled and held out his hand showing the silver ring with the small green emerald.

"I haven't seen that in so many years," muttered the other

252

The Legend of Kyne: Chronocide

Kyne. "I haven't been back since..."

"Since the Dominion attacked and killed our family."

"Father says that I mustn't talk about the time before him. He says that era is over and..."

"And nothing!" roared Kyne. "How can you call that man your father? It's dishonoring our family and is honestly quite disturbing!"

The other Kyne pulled away from the bars and took a step back.

"He warned me that you would try to corrupt me. He told me I should stay away from you."

"Corrupt you? You are already far more corrupted than I could possibly do myself. Aaldra has tricked you, convinced you that he is your father and that all of this is *right*," and he gestured around him. "Look at what he has done to our country! Look at what he has done to our people!"

"I... I..." stammered the mirror Kyne. "I don't..." and then he took off running out of the dungeon, slamming the door shut behind him.

As the metallic echo faded away, Kyne was left once again alone. A nearby squeak of a large brown rat caught his attention, and he watched it crawl through the cell bars. The small rodent looked up at Kyne for a moment before continuing on, its small nose vibrating as it smelled the floor. The rat did not seem to fear Kyne and he watched it as it crawled in a zig zag, all the while its sense of smell leading it to the pile of slop that Kyne had left on the floor.

His own tray lay nearby with a little bit of the food still remaining. Stooping down, he picked it up before the rat made it to it and he returned to the back of his cell. Eating the food quickly, he managed to gulp down the final bite and hold it back as he nearly retched.

The rat gorged itself in the slop as it found it, its whiskers hanging low as it stuck to the fine hairs. After a few minutes two more rats appeared out in the hallway and crawled through the cage, joining the first.

Kyne's mind was beginning to clear, the feeling of his aura returning. He still couldn't quite focus the words of power and even with all of his effort, his dragon aura still did not work.

The Legend of Kyne: Chronocide

They will be returning soon to drug me once again. I do not know how long I will even last here. Aaldra could have me killed at any time. I don't think that me being his prisoner is going to be a long ordeal.

There were two sentinels before when they last came, he thought. *I wasn't even expecting it. They just walked in and blew it right into my face. It must take effect when I breathe it in.*

As that realization struck him, he formulated a plan that he thought could work but also could prove quite disastrous if caught. Until then however, he would sit and meditate, trying to clear his mind so he could use aura. If he could use aura, then everything else would be significantly easier.

Eventually the sound of the door opening caught his attention and he nearly leapt to his feet. His stomach was turning in anticipation, and he watched as two sentinels walked into view. One was holding a small cloth bag and had his hand pressed inside it.

"Against the wall!" ordered the other sentinel to which Kyne ignored. "I said against the wall heretic, or I have orders that I may act accordingly. I can't kill you, He would not like that as He has plans for you. I could however remove one of your arms!"

"Would you like that?" added the first sentinel sarcastically.

Backing up, Kyne soon felt the cool stone upon his back. His tray was nearby, and he almost stepped on it, ruining everything. His plan could work. Would work, and he kept telling himself that as he watched the two sentinels unlock the cage and step inside. The one with the pouch removed his hand and Kyne could see the dust of white powder trailing from it as he approached. The second sentinel had drawn his sword and was standing with his back to the shut cage, blocking any sort of exit.

The approaching sentinel lifted his arm up as if presenting it as a gift to Kyne before he took a deep breath to blow it at him.

Now! roared Kyne's mind and with a flick of his foot he slid the tray towards the sentinel. The movement was smooth, and he seemed to nearly not notice it but just as he placed his foot down, it slid underneath his sole.

Immediately as the sentinel's weight was pushed down, the tray shot out from underneath him knocking him off balance where he flailed his arms in an attempt to stay upright.

The Legend of Kyne: Chronocide

Kyne dashed forward and in one clean motion, rammed his bound hands up into the sentinel's own, smashing it and the powder it held directly into his face.

A short cry came from the man and then he went limp as he rapidly lost consciousness. Cries of alarm erupted from the other sentinel, and he ran forward, his sword aimed low at Kyne.

A swift and precise kick from the archmage directly to the open pouch that contained the powder launched it in the air where it spread out in a thin fog.

The sentinel stopped abruptly as he covered his mouth and nose with his palm trying to not breathe it in.

Too easy!

Kyne leapt forward and jammed his bound arms hard through the gap in the sentinel's armor and right up into his abdomen. The force caused him to gasp for breath and a moment later, he crumpled to the ground. Kyne's own lungs were burning as he scanned around the cell. The dust was nearly over every part, and he wouldn't be able to breathe until it settled, which could take minutes.

Quickly walking to the cell door, he pushed the bars open, relieved at the stupidity of his guards for leaving it unlocked. A few steps down the hall and he finally took a deep breath. He sat there for a moment as he watched his cell clear up before he ventured inside and took the guard's keyring, forcing each iron key into the locks that bound him as he looked for the match. With only a few left, he finally found them, and a light click followed by the bang as the device that bound his hands fell to the ground. Forcing the same key into his leg shackles, they too unlocked and he swung his leg up in front of him, relieved that his motion was back.

"Now to find Auriel!"

He ran down the corridor, coming to the metallic door. Opening it quietly, the familiar groan absent, he saw that a single sentinel stood a few feet away with his back to him. Thoughts flew through Kyne's mind as he tried to think of what to do.

Slowly returning the door shut, he raced back to the unconscious sentinels and fumbled through their belongings. He needed a weapon, at least until he found his own. Each sentinel carried a sword and a small dagger upon their waist. He clipped the belt with

The Legend of Kyne: Chronocide

the sword scabbard to himself and held the dagger in his right hand.

The metal weapon was of average craftsmanship. Not terrible nor impressive. It was a standard soldier weapon, but it would work for what he needed to do. He was not fond of killing people but was very familiar with it. It was an eerie feeling to him but as he thought more about it, he lost his sympathy for them quite quickly. He would do what needed to be done.

"They shouldn't even exist, and even though they do, they are evil," he muttered.

Kyne cautiously opened the door and spotted the sentinel once again in the same position he had been in. He had one chance to make this work. If it was not a smooth killing, then their scuffle could alert others. Stepping through the doorway, he shut the door behind him as quietly as possible and approached, the dagger gripped tight in his hands.

Eyeing the sentinel's armor, memories of his hours and hours of training flew through his mind. He had studied their armor, knew its weak points and its openings. The one he wanted was right at the bottom of his helm, just below the jaw.

As he stepped towards the right of the soldier, he tapped the man lightly on his left shoulder. Puzzled the man turned but Kyne stepped around him. Just as the sentinel turned back, quick as a snake, Kyne drove the blade straight through the opening, piercing up through bottom of his mouth and embedding it into the soldier's brain.

The green eyes went wide and then dark as his body went limp, his life fading. Kyne grabbed hold of him and lowered him slowly to the floor. Little blood oozed from the embedded dagger and grabbing this sentinel's own dagger, Kyne decided to leave the first in its new sheath.

Opening the door again, he dragged the body back through it before he shut it one final time and then he was off, dashing through the dark corridors of the underkeep.

He retraced his steps exactly as he remembered them. Following each turn and staircase, he wound his way up through the citadel. He had no idea where she was being held but he knew where he had last seen her and that was where he would look first.

The Legend of Kyne: Chronocide

He tried to form a spell and almost had it but not quite and he growled in frustration. His aura would be of great use right now, but he wasn't sure how long it could take. By that time the sentinels might know something was wrong when three of their comrades had gone missing.

Leaping low against the wall, he crouched next to a small wooden piece of furniture that decorated the hallway. Two sentinels suddenly came into view up ahead and began briskly walking down towards him. They hadn't noticed him yet but eventually they would, he couldn't sit here forever.

Sunlight came in from a window nearby as Kyne watched them approach through a narrow opening in the wooden furniture. They were both average in all aspects. He could more or less take them, but he didn't want to, it was too dangerous.

As they neared, he could just make out their words as they spoke to one another.

"It just caught ablaze last night. Nearly the whole thing left to ruin."

"Those damned Kydrëans will pay for that," growled the second and to Kyne's shock they both stopped and looked out the window overlooking the city. "I loved that place."

"As did I," said the first. "We will find out who did it. It's only a matter of time."

As Kyne shifted his balance, he leaned against the furniture and noticed it slid slightly from his weight. To his shock he placed his hand over a knob and opened a small door.

Perfect, he thought, and he sent a silent prayer to any gods of any religion that were helping him right now. He crouched low by the open door. *If they aren't paying full attention, they shouldn't recognize it for what it is.*

The voices grew louder, and Kyne ducked low, pulling the small door slightly around him to block him as best as it could. The clank of their boots sounded right next to him, and he watched as they walked on right past him without seeming to notice.

As they continued on for a dozen more feet, Kyne quietly rose up and stole down the hall as fast as he could. Just as he rounded the corner, he saw another sentinel walking away from him. He turned to

The Legend of Kyne: Chronocide

run back but the first two had stopped once again, continuing their conversation. He was out in the open and would be spotted in moments!

A nearby door was his only place of escape and without hesitation, he quickly entered it, closing it quietly behind him.

His breathing was heavy, and he took a shuddering breath, his eyes still on the door as he half expected shouting to come from the hallway. Only silence and as he turned around breathing a sigh of relief, he nearly jumped out of his skin. In front of him in a large open room was a nyloc.

The great ugly cat creature was unaware of his presence for now, and he watched its twin tails flick around in the air as it shifted its position. Two of its horns were cracked, one completely broken off at the base, adding to the creature's haggard appearance.

Kyne's heart began to race as he quickly scanned the room, looking for any sort of cover as the nylocs ears twitched, its yellow eyes still hidden behind its eyelids for now. Suddenly out from behind the door he could hear the sounds of voices. He knew it had to be the sentinels and to his frustration, he continued to hear their voices muffled through the wood.

They must be sitting outside the door for some reason, he thought to himself as he crouched low to the ground. *I can't make any of it out but by their tone it sounds like they haven't noticed my absence. I can't stay here forever though; this thing will spot me sooner or later.*

Sooner came much more quickly than he had suspected. A low groan sounded from the nyloc, and he turned and met its yellow eyes. There they stared at each other for a long moment before another rumble came from the creature. A much darker and hostile sound. The sound of a deep guttural growl within its throat.

Kyne fumbled for his sword, momentarily trying to touch the pommel for comfort and was instantly disappointed when he realized it was not his real sword. Taking a step back, he reached for the doorknob. It was the only way that he could see out of this room, and he was running out of time. The sentinels or the nyloc, either would easily kill him.

The nyloc continued a slow walk towards him, each step nearly silent from the massive pads. It was large, easily the size of a horse at shoulder height with short coarse grey fur all across its body except for its twin tails.

A hiss came from the beast as it bared its fangs, drool dripping down in thin spider silk like strands.

"Kai... Kai..." fumbled Kyne as he struggled to formulate the spell that could save his life. It was so close! just right there on the tip of his tongue!

The nyloc snarled and leapt towards Kyne, its claws spread wide and its teeth bare.

Whether it was the adrenaline, or the imminent danger itself Kyne didn't know. All he could think of was one word.

"Kaiodin!"

The memory of the spell seemed to solidify in his brain the moment the words left his mouth and a massive smile spread cheek to cheek. Immediately, the creature froze still as stone only a few feet away. Every muscle of the creature trembled and strained as it fought the spell. Reaching out a hand, Kyne touched the nyloc for the first time in his life.

The fur was not as coarse as he had once thought, almost soft and its skin was thick like a normal cat. He glanced at its face for a moment and saw its yellow eyes pinned on him at all times.

"Cligen," he muttered, and a soft light stretched from his hand and flowed over the creature. The nyloc's body almost immediately seemed to loosen up. No longer was it flexing every muscle trying to break free from the spell.

Taking a risk, he ended the spell and cautiously stepped away from the nyloc keeping both eyes trained on it. For a moment it eyed him, and then it sat down and stared as if waiting for a command.

"Fascinating," Kyne muttered to himself. Throughout his life he had been warned of certain darker creatures who embodied malice and destruction, from the golems of the Riigar Mountains to the nylocs of Gaeil. "Maybe they aren't inherently bad like we were led to believe. Maybe the acts of others change them into what they are."

The nyloc shuddered and then turned to Kyne, the hairs upon its back rising in an aggressive mohawk. He used the calming spell again but knew that it was time.

"Let's see how the Dominion sentinels like you shall we," he said with a slight laugh to the nyloc, and he walked towards the door gesturing for the nyloc to come. The large cat creature rose up and walked after him where they both paused next to it.

Kyne pressed his ear up against the wood for a moment, voices could be heard but they were more distant than before. He grinned and cautiously opened the door and peered outside.

A group of sentinels stood a few dozen feet away all talking to one another. A second larger group of sentinels were approaching them from the other side.

Kyne stepped back and guided the nyloc quietly through the doorway. With a quick point of his hands at the sentinels, he unleashed the full power of his aura into the beast.

"Ator."

The rage spell shrouded the nyloc in a slight reddish haze as all of its hair went completely rigid. Throwing its head back in a frenzied state, it snarled and dashed down the hall towards the exclaiming sentinels.

"Altyne ulkin," Kyne muttered casting the invisibility spell upon himself and he ran out of the hallway. Behind him the screams of sentinels and the clatter of their metallic armor rang.

He couldn't see his body, it was a very strange sensation as he rounded a corner, slamming his shoulder into the wall. He grunted in brief pain before continuing on, much more aware of where his body was even though he couldn't see it.

Up ahead, two sentinels were running right at him. Without stopping, he dashed right in between both of them without them even noticing and they continued on their way running towards the rogue nyloc.

A minute later he found himself looking down the hallway in which Auriel had been taken from him. The sunlight from outside lit the hallway dimly and he paused for a moment to overlook the city.

The sky hung in a grey haze, causing faraway objects to fade out of sight. Down below he couldn't see the streets themselves, the citadel wall blocked it from sight. He could, however, see the rooftops of most of the buildings. The city was so familiar but also so different. It reminded him of the time when it was under Commander Shjilo's rule. Kydrëan's living in poverty and filth, starving and unable to drink

The Legend of Kyne: Chronocide

clean water.

Voices caught his attention, drawing it away from the city. Approaching him was a sentinel and to his shock the alternate Kyne. His twin was agitated and seemed to be arguing with the sentinel about something. After another few words, the sentinel scoffed at him and marched away leaving him alone with the invisible Kyne nearby.

The mirror Kyne paused for a moment as if thinking about something before stepping over to the window that Kyne had been looking out previously. They were nearly touching, and he watched as his strange twin stared out over the city, face hidden from view.

What should I do? Kyne thought to himself as he watched his twin. *He's so fragile and strange. I know deep down inside he knows Aaldra is evil, but I think he is just too afraid. Maybe if I give him the opportunity to escape with us then we can help one another.*

"Kyne," he said softly as he ended the spell.

His twin yelped in shock and jumped back, eyes wide open. He snapped his head down the hall towards Aaldra's room before returning it back to Kyne's eyes.

"How... How did you get out?"

"Never mind how I did it. I am escaping and you are completely welcome to join me, if you want to."

"I can't, Father would never forgive me," he stammered.

"So what about what Aaldra thinks. He is not our real father. He has tricked you in some perverted fantasy of his. Are you coming or not?"

His twin was silent.

"I need an answer now!"

"I am not sure," he started. "What if we are caught?"

"We won't be," grinned Kyne. "Where are they keeping Auriel?"

"The girl? Oh, she's up in one of the royal cells, in the northwest tower."

Kyne reached out his dragon arm, The leather glove and his shirt sleeve still concealing it from everyone.

"Are you coming?"

His twin stared for a moment before reaching out and they grabbed forearms.

The Legend of Kyne: Chronocide

"Let's get moving!" and he took off in a sprint with his twin following closely behind. They ran down the hall before turning sharply and scaling a spiral set of stairs. A few minutes later and they were standing in front of the wooden door with his twin motioning that this was where Auriel was.

Pushing it open, he stepped inside and raised his hand to block his vision from the light coming in the windows. He could see a wooden chair situated near a small bed but to his shock, Auriel wasn't there.

"Where is she?" he said as he turned around. The moment he laid eyes upon his twin, his heart nearly stopped. His palm was held out and a small pile of fine powder lay upon it. A quick puff struck him in the face.

His mind swirled and swam as he struggled to remain standing. He tried to summon his aura, to rid himself of the powder but felt it slipping through his grasp. Falling to the floor, his mind started to fade in and out.

"I am sorry," he heard his twin whisper in his ear. "They knew you were going to get out that's why they have relocated Auriel. I don't even know where she is. You would've been caught and killed before you escaped. At least this way you may stay alive for a little while long…" his voice trailed off as Kyne lost consciousness.

The Legend of Kyne: Chronocide

29. Bound and Divided

The cool touch of stone was felt across Kyne's cheek as he shifted. A low groan left his throat and he felt drool had slathered the side of his cheek. His head was swimming and as he struggled to sit up, he felt the glob of drool slide down the side of his face before hanging on his chin, not enough to fully drip off.

Squinting, it was brighter than he remembered, much different that the dimly lit cell from before and as his eyes adjusted, he tried to understand where he was. He was in a much different cell from before, a round room similar to the cell in which he had searched for Auriel's surrounded him. A small bed near one side. A tray of slop food lay nearby upon a table.

Stumbling to his feet, he swayed before losing his balance and he crashed to the ground with a thud, the breath forcing itself from his lungs. He coughed for a moment before the sound of slow clapping caught his attention.

Near the door, previously unnoticed was the young man with black hair, the brother to the redhead. He was seated in a small chair with one leg crossed tightly over the other. A black cape embroidered with the Dominion crest was draped over one shoulder and an amusing smirk was across his face.

"I wouldn't try getting up," he chuckled. "We gave you a much higher dose than before. After your little escape, we thought it best."

Kyne clenched his jaw as he glared at the man. He was of similar age but much more dainty, a rabbit left in a room with a wolverine. Oh, how he would like to clamp his hands around his neck and force the life out of him. The dragonrage was flowing through him, flooding his veins and he tried once again to rise to his feet.

"Oh, come on," laughed the man and he rose out of his chair. Slowly approaching the swaying Kyne, he lightly kicked his leg. The tap

The Legend of Kyne: Chronocide

was all it took, and Kyne lost his balance, falling back to the floor with a crash.

"You now have my full attention after that little stunt you pulled," he hissed as he leaned in close to Kyne's ear. "If the Lord's son had not been the one to find you then you surely would've been killed. If it were up to me, I would get rid of you quickly before something else happens."

"Well, it isn't up to you is it," growled Kyne. "You have no say in the matter."

The man pulled away and rose back up to his full height. Looking down upon Kyne, his grin had faded away to a cold gaze.

"True, it isn't up to me," and he swiftly kicked Kyne hard in the ribs. The pain ripped through his side, and he hunched over gasping for breath. "However, I have some jurisdiction over you, and I can make your life much more painful."

Turning away, he marched out of the cell and slammed it shut behind him, leaving Kyne alone as he gasped in pain.

* * *

Auriel sat on the edge of her bed, a puzzled look upon her face. Just moments before she thought she heard her door shut but it hadn't even been opened. Looking around her room, she furrowed her brow in frustration. She was certain it had come from her room, the sound much too noticeable, too loud to be caused by another door down the hall.

She had tried to escape a few different times but was always overpowered and that powder was always blown into her face. No matter what she did, they always seemed to best her, either from sheer physical power or by taking advantage of her in her dazed state.

The last few times they had come had been much more often than before, making it harder for her to even focus as the drug was never given an opportunity to wear off much.

Something must've happened with Kyne, she thought to herself as she tried to make a justification for their frequency changing. *Maybe he tried escaping like I did and had better luck. Maybe he found the others and was able to get out of the city.*

The Legend of Kyne: Chronocide

Happiness mixed with sorrow filled her head at the thought and she tried to push it out. He wouldn't leave her even if he escaped. *He would come back I know it.*

Time ticked by and the obscured sun outside slowly reached its peak before it started its afternoon descent. The hazy air smothering its outline creating more of a glowing presence than an actual sun.

Two more times the sentinels burst into her room and drugged her, each time her resistance being not nearly enough. A few hours passed and then, suddenly, a light knock sounded upon her door, rousing her from her daze.

Confusion shot through her and she stared intently at it, expecting someone to burst through any second. Another quick succession of knocks sounded and after a moment, she decided to answer them.

"Enter."

The door creaked open and to her shock she watched as Aaldra entered followed close behind by the mirror Kyne. A long, beautiful cloak was draped over his shoulders and upon his waist she could see the glimmer of a large crystal set into the pommel of his sword.

"How are you today my beautiful young lady," he said as he walked towards her and grabbed the chair. Dragging it over, he placed it a few feet away and sat down in it, his eyes trained upon her.

"What do you want," she spoke flatly. "Your presence is not welcome."

"So hostile," he said mocking as if slightly offended. "Even after all of the things I do for you, you decide to repay me like this?"

"Do for me? Like keep me your prisoner, drugged and unable to leave? If that's what you think deserves repayment, then you are sorely mistaken."

"I am referring to not killing that copy of my son. He tried to escape you know. Got right up to your door, even opened it," and he laughed darkly. "My son was able to subdue him before anything got out of hand."

Auriel's eyes opened wide, and she looked upon the mirrored version who had his eyes drilled upon the floor.

"I... I am sorry," he stammered but Aaldra raised his hand up quickly.

"Do not apologize," he said. "You did your country a favor and you are a hero. His words of corruption and deceit have plagued your mind."

The alternate Kyne tightened his mouth and continued to look down almost with a look of shame upon his face.

"When I heard what had happened my first reaction was to kill him, actually to force you to do it in fact," and a wicked grin came across Aaldra. "My son was able to calm me enough and get me thinking straight, however. I do need him. I want to break his mind and show me all of his knowledge so that it may help my cause. You could help my dear. Well help *him* I mean. If he were to willingly give me what I wanted, then I wouldn't have to pry it out of him now would I."

"He will never help you!" she spat. "He would rather die."

"Well then," and Aaldra rose to his feet. "Honestly, it's what I expected you to say. I just thought that I would give you the option to help him out before his mind is turned to goo."

Turning around, he walked towards the door and opened it, waiting for his son to follow. The alternate Kyne hesitated for a moment, then without looking at her once, turned around and followed Aaldra out of the cell.

As they left, Auriel's mind raced as she remembered everything they had said. *Kyne doesn't have much time. They could be heading to his cell right now! I just don't know how to escape. Every time I try and fight them, they overpower... Wait! That's it!* her thoughts roared in her head. *I will make them think that they overpowered me. I'll give them a show that they will never forget.*

The Riel princess grinned slyly as she formulated her plan. She had a few worries about what could go wrong but it should work. It had to work, for her and more importantly, for Kyne.

As she sat there Aaldra's words kept coming back to her and the more she thought about them the more confused she got. *Got right up to your door, even opened it. Is he toying with me or was he serious? Kyne never opened my door. I have been here the whole time.*

* * *

The Legend of Kyne: Chronocide

A loud ring sounded throughout Kyne's cell and then another as he slammed the metallic device that pinned his hands together. Over and over, he struck his bindings into the stone ground as hard as he could, every strike jarring all the way up into his shoulders.

The slight squeak of his leather glove was heard as he adjusted his grip. Once again, his captors had left him in his own clothes, not revealing his secret, at least as of yet. Kyne struck the metallic device again as hard as he could, his frustration fueling the strike.

The loud echo reverberated around the room over and over again as it progressively faded away. He was so angry and enraged by what had happened.

I was right there! I was so close and yet I was betrayed.

A distant clang echoed through his room and his eyes opened up in shock. Scanning the room, he furrowed his brow. There was nowhere that it seemed to come from.

Suddenly another distant sound happened, and as it too faded away, he scrambled across the ground. Over and over again, the sound came and went, Kyne dragging himself around the room as he tried to find the source.

It seemed to be coming from the bed, but how? he thought as he pulled himself up onto it. Sitting on the hard mattress, he ran his binding against the metal railing and then struck it firmly.

A high-pitched ring erupted from the metal and almost immediately after, another much more distant sound followed it from nearly the same position.

"What the hell?" he muttered to himself, and he struck it again, this time with two hits. A moment later, two more strikes followed, much more spaced out than his own.

"Could it be?" he thought to himself. "Maybe it is! Auriel!" he screamed as loud as he could, his voice nearly giving out and his throat aching in pain.

No response.

"Auriel!" he screamed again.

Puzzled and disappointed, he tapped lightly on the bed making a series of rings. A few moments later a similar set followed.

"I wish I had a code I could send," he muttered to himself.

The Legend of Kyne: Chronocide

Sitting there for a few moments, his mind searching for a solution, he finally gasped and sat up. "She should know the order of the Kydrëan alphabet, at least I hope she does. Maybe if I tap and count out the letters, she can decipher it."

Kyne started tapping, not too fast but each tap saying the letters of the alphabet. "A. B. C," he counted until finally he hit the first letter, K. He paused for a long moment before he started again counting all the way to Y. Continuing on painstakingly slow, he managed to spell out his name. After the ringing stopped, he sat and waited for a long while.

Distant rings soon started, and he began counting them. After the first three letters were known he started to wail upon the metallic bed in excitement. "It's Auriel!" he gasped. "But how? It's as if she is here but not quite here."

There they sat and communicated for a long while, Auriel explaining her plan to him as briefly as possible. To get out even a sentence took minutes and they both were frustrated beyond belief.

As Kyne was tapping his bed, spelling out a personal message to her, his door suddenly opened, and he stopped immediately. As the person stepped inside, Kyne felt a brief flash of anger rise in him.

"How could you!" he yelled to his alternate twin. "You betrayed me!"

The mirror Kyne hung his head low for a long moment before he muttered, "I had to, they would've found you eventually and would've killed us both."

"No, they wouldn't of!" Kyne roared. "I could've overpowered anyone in my way. I killed nearly all of them in my own world. I would do it again!"

Those words took the alternate Kyne by surprise, and he looked up in shock, his eyes wide.

"You're not serious?" he gasped. "All of them, even Father?"

"I wasn't lying when I said it to him during our meeting. If you hadn't stopped me, we could be long gone now."

"I... I am sorry," he said softly. "I had no idea you were so powerful."

"I am, but I am also you," he replied. "You could have just as much power as I do but you chose to forgo all of your previous attachments. You betrayed everyone; did you betray Voron too?"

"Voron?" he said confused. "Who is Voron?"

"My master. The one who taught me everything I know."

"I never met him before. No one uses aura here other than my father, the Dark Princes, and a handful of other officials. Anyone else caught is committed of high treason and deemed a heretic. They're executed."

"Voron was the one who rescued me from Saathe," Kyne said. "Does that sound familiar?"

"Oh..." he replied as if understanding coming across his face. "I remember him, the old man who tried to ambush Saathe. When Saathe captured me, he didn't kill me for some reason. Just said that I would be of use to him. Voron as you say never got a chance to ambush Saathe. He was overpowered and killed that same night."

His words struck Kyne hard, and he steadied himself, his mind swimming.

"Then that is how the timeline changed," he muttered. "Saathe must have recognized me, I mean *you*, from our previous encounter. That's why Voron never got the upper hand on him."

"What do you mean timeline changed? You keep talking about how this isn't the proper timeline, but I don't understand what that means."

"It's a long story. Events led up to me flying through time and encountering Saathe back when he was still an apprentice himself. We fought and then I escaped. After I returned to my timeline, everything started to break down and I wound up here in your timeline."

"So, you used your aura to change events?"

"Not on purpose. Something is causing me to do it and I don't understand why."

"I understand now," he said. "What are you to do?"

"I want to escape here and figure a way to distort back to when I altered the timeline. If I could prevent that then..."

"Then I will never exist," he replied solemnly as he realized it. "If you are successful then my entire timeline will be erased."

"If you help me escape, I might be able to take you with me, back to my time. There you will be able to live in peace, free of these monsters around you now."

The Legend of Kyne: Chronocide

"I... I don't know," he muttered softly, and he began too slowly back up. "I don't know if that would work. What if when you change it back, I get erased?"

"If that were to happen then I wouldn't be here right now," Kyne replied immediately. He felt pity for this version of him. He was almost still a child unable to fend for himself, or even think for himself. "I will take you back to my time where you can do whatever you want. I can even teach you aura if you would want."

The mirror Kyne chuckled lowly. "If only. I will have to think about it," and in one quick movement he opened the door and vanished down the hallway leaving Kyne once again alone.

He sat there for a long time, staring at the sun a hand width away from the horizon. Eventually, he tapped out a message to Auriel, explaining what had transpired. By the time he had finished, the sun was turning a dark red.

A low knock sounded, and a few sentinels stepped into the room accompanied by the young man with dark hair.

Kyne tried to resist but was subdued almost immediately by the man's aura, the dust flowing into his lungs and his eyes glazing over as he lost consciousness.

* * *

Auriel heard the door to her cell slam distantly away and she waited for her own turn. She thought she had a good idea what was going on. Somehow the cells Kyne and herself were in were overlapping one another, seemingly occupying the same space. *Something must change it from one to the other, that is why Kyne couldn't find me before*, she thought as her door opened up. Three sentinels accompanied by the young man stepped in and she sat still upon the edge of her bed.

I have to make this believable, she thought as her heart began to race. It was beating so loudly she was fearful that they could hear it. If they knew what was going on, then she would never have another chance.

When they were right by her, she leapt out of her seated position and charged the guard. Moments before she reached him, her body was bound by aura and a cloud of dust was blown into her face.

The Legend of Kyne: Chronocide

She swayed before falling over onto her side, her eyes closed.

"They never seem to give up," said the man and a few moments later the cell shut leaving her alone.

Auriel's eyes opened up and she gasped a big gulp of air, satisfying her burning lungs of their hunger. *It had worked! She was one step closer to getting out.*

There she laid upon the cold stone ground for a long time, not wanting to get up too fast for if the sentinels returned, they might think something was going on. The day waned on and as the sentinels never returned, she finally got up and made her way over to her bed.

Tapping her fingernail lightly against the metal, she created a short ting that faded quickly away. She tapped a few more times and waited, seeing if Kyne was going to reply. After a few minutes with no response, she grumbled in frustration and leaned against the wall her bed was against, half of her lower legs hanging over the edge.

Slouching there for a long time, she focused her mind trying to unlock her aura and as time went by, she could feel it getting closer to her.

They will surely come back to drug me again before my power has returned. I will have to fool them a second time.

More time passed and then, as if far far away, a light tapping sounded from her bed.

"Kyne!" she gasped out loud and she quickly began to tap out a message. It was so painstakingly slow that she cut out as much as she could.

You ok?

"Drugged," she muttered as she deciphered the last letter he sent. Tapping back, she sent a message that he would love to hear.

"Tricked them," she said as she finished tapping. The final ring faded away and there was a long pause of silence before taps started to come back, much quicker than before.

"E," she said as she found the first letter. "S," as the second letter was finished. Just as the third set of taps started, the door to her cell sounded and it swung open. Furiously tapping upon her bed as she turned to face who had entered, she hoped that he would understand and stop his message.

To her disbelief, the alternate Kyne stepped into her room

carrying a tray of food.

"I brought this for you," he stammered as he approached. "I hope it is to your liking."

"Why are you here?" she retorted with a hint of anger in her voice. She knew that she couldn't say anything Kyne had told her that happened. He might suspect something.

"I wanted to see you," he stammered again. "I wanted to tell you what happened, so you understand fully."

"Is that why the sentinels return much more often and use higher doses of that drug?"

"Aurabane," he muttered. "Yeah, that drug from Gaeil is quite potent. In small doses some of the nobles use it as a sedative. It helps them sleep at night, probably so they forget about the atrocities that they have committed."

"What happened?" Auriel said trying to get information from him without sounding too desperate. "Is my Kyne alright?"

"He escaped, got right up to your cell door and was captured before he could rescue you."

Auriel dropped her head low, acting as if the news had shocked her. "So Aaldra wasn't lying."

"He is still alive."

"Where is he?" she said, her eyes rising up to meet his. Once they connected, he quickly looked away.

"I am not supposed to say."

"Please tell me!"

"Well, he is... Well, he is here in this room, but not quite this room," he started. "It's hard to explain.

"Like the cell next to mine?" she asked knowing full well it wasn't what he meant. This Kyne was weak, and she was going to manipulate him as much as she could.

"No, the same cell as yours."

"I don't see him in here. If you don't know where he is, then stop lying to me. It's not funny anymore."

"Both of your cells occupy the same area of space, overlapping like two sheets of paper in one book. He is here but you cannot interact with him, and he cannot interact with you."

Auriel furrowed her brow. "That doesn't seem possible."

The Legend of Kyne: Chronocide

"It is possible, Alderiun was able to learn the art when we attacked the people south of Otoruh. They contained many powerful mages with sorcery and skills never heard of here."

"How do I get to him?"

"You can't. Only those who know the design of the cell are able to open it. Very few know it though."

"Do you?"

He laughed a sad laugh. "No one tells me anything. I am more of a pet than a son. I had to sneak out to even come here."

"Then who would be able to tell me how to open it?"

"The only people I know are my father, his Dark Princes, and the twins."

"Twins?" asked Auriel confused. "I'm not familiar with them."

"Voira and her brother Ariov. They led both of you when you met with my father."

Auriel knew exactly who they were but was startled at what he had said.

"Twins? I knew they were siblings but not twins."

"Not identical no but born on the same day from the same mother. Both of them know the cell design. Good luck convincing them to tell it to you though. Both of them are strange ruthless cold-hearted people. I think that is why my father lets them lead the sentinels."

"Thank you," Auriel said and to her surprise, the alternate Kyne smiled back at her.

He looked so similar that it was almost disturbing, and she felt herself smile back at him.

"I better get going," he said, and he turned before pausing. "I haven't really introduced myself to you. I am Kyne, but… I guess not quite your Kyne," and he laughed as he stretched out his hand towards her.

"I am Auriel, princess to the Riel," and grasped his hand in her own in a quick handshake. His hand was thin and so awfully cold that she had to resist the urge to rip it out of his grip to not offend him.

"Nice to meet you your highness," he said with a slight bow. "Maybe one day you will be able to tell me of your people." As they let go of one another and he started to walk towards the door, Auriel

273

called out to him.

"What's going to happen to us?"

"I am not sure; Father hasn't told me. If I find out I will tell you," and then he was gone leaving her once again alone.

Auriel, as soon as the door shut, began to tap frantically upon her bed. She needed to tell Kyne everything she had learned. As she finished her first few clusters of words, a sound caught her off guard and she stopped tapping against the bed as three sentinels stepped inside.

"Stop that damned tapping!" one roared as he stepped forward. "It's so annoying! I feel like my head is going to explode!"

Have they been outside the cell the whole time? she panicked as they quickly approached. In the doorway, she could see the redheaded Voira leaning against the door frame. Her eyes were pinned upon Auriel, and she was biting her bottom lip as if in anticipation.

Jumping at the sentinels, Auriel managed to kick one of them hard right under the chin before another one took her to the ground. A quick scuffle and then a puff of dust struck her in the face. She held her breath tightly and faked her body going weak in their grip. A few moments later they stood up, releasing their hold upon her and motioned to leave the cell.

Auriel's eyes were closed but opening them ever so slightly, she could see a figure approaching through the fuzziness of her eyelashes. Trying hard to breathe calmly, half expecting the drug to still be airborne, she was grateful as her mind stayed clear.

Each breath was hard to breathe in calmly, her diaphragm nearly shaking from the strain, but she managed to maintain a calm steady breath as if she was unconscious.

"Such a beautiful thing," muttered Voira right near her head. The feeling of her breath upon her cheek made her nearly shudder in disgust as she fought the urge. Voira grabbed her snarled silvery hair and brought it to her nose with a deep inhale.

"A shame you won't be around much longer."

The rhythmic clunk of her steps signaled she was leaving and just as the door shut, Auriel's eyes slowly opened up. She hated that woman with nearly every ounce of her being. She would get the information from her. Even if Kyne wouldn't approve of her *methods*.

The Legend of Kyne: Chronocide

The sun outside eventually set, signaling the second day was over since they had arrived. Her aura was beginning to return and once it did, she was going to use every bit of her power and knowledge to get out. She was not spending another day as a prisoner.

As the sky darkened, night falling, her aura returned. Slowly at first but after a short time of warming up, she was back to full strength. She wouldn't sleep. She couldn't chance them sneaking into her room and drugging her while she slept. It would ruin everything she had worked for.

Time dragged on so slowly and her eyes began to sag but she fought the urge to close them. Her cheeks felt tight from fatigue, but she couldn't and wouldn't sleep.

"I'll sleep when I'm dead," she muttered to herself moments before she slapped her face lightly. The brief flash of pain helped a bit but not as much as she would like, and the drowsiness returned with a vengeance.

Her vision seemed to tunnel as her eyelids sagged. Waves of dizziness swept over her, but she fought them fiercely. At times she jumped to her feet and did pushups or squats, anything to get her moving and awake. Sitting still hurt more than helping her.

As she finished an old series of strikes she hadn't done in years, she heard the sound of a key in a lock.

Panic rushed through her and she dashed to her bed lying down as still as stone. The room was extremely dark but as they walked in, she could see the orange glow of a lantern.

It was two sentinels and to her relief, Voira was coming up the rear. The woman stayed near the back of the room as if blocking the door.

Like she stands a chance, chuckled Auriel in her head. *This ends tonight!*

"Y'vinu," she muttered under her breath as she directed it over the red-haired woman.

Suddenly she yelped in shock as she launched forward rapidly and smashed into the sentinel's backs taking them all to the ground in a disheveled heap. Auriel leapt to her feet and in one fluid motion jumped over their heads in a twisting flip while using her aura to pull both of the sentinels' blades to her hands.

The Legend of Kyne: Chronocide

As her feet landed lightly upon the stone she swung the swords straight across the sentinels' necks, decapitating them in a bright red flash.

The lantern tumbled to the ground where the glass shattered, and oil spread across the ground. Catching fire, it crawled rapidly around lighting the room up in a wicked orange glow. Voira was screaming in shock at what had just happened, seemingly rooted to her spot in between her dead guards.

"Orus kaiodin!" cried Auriel as she tossed the blades to the ground in a loud clatter. Voira, bound by her aura rose up and hovered a few inches off of the ground. Auriel twirled her hand and her captor slowly rotated so that they were face to face.

Blood was oozing all over the floor, sizzling where it touched the burning oil and the smell of iron hung in the air. Voira's mouth was tight with rage and shock, but she was bound, unable to speak or move from Auriel.

"Tell me how to reach Kyne," said Auriel lowly.

Auriel released her hold on Voira's mouth and waited for her answer.

"Rik'tar!" Voira screamed immediately and a flash of lightning flew towards Auriel.

"Vertai!" Auriel said at a blinding speed as she swept her hand. The bolt ripped to the side where it struck into the wall with a deafening roar.

"Bad decision!" Auriel replied and she tightened her aura across Voira. Squeezing her fist in rage, she watched as the Gaeilian squirmed in pain, her body struggling under Auriel's grip as she was crushed tighter and tighter. "No second chances you creep," she muttered and without hesitation forced her mind out where it collided with Voira's own.

It was as if she were battling a raging storm, Voira's mind strange and alien to her own. Auriel had trained in mind manipulation with Kyne and was confident that she could overcome Voira, but it was still going to be hard work.

Smashing her mind into Voira's own, she was met with a wall like that of a tsunami, powerful and forcing back upon her. Auriel attacked again and again, trying to throw her off her focus.

The Legend of Kyne: Chronocide

She thrust forward, prying at her thoughts and with satisfaction felt the wall crack and a few fleeting memories flew past. Auriel brushed them to the side, she had no use of them. She only wanted one thing and that was the key to the cell!

Picking at the crack in her defenses, Auriel pulled out more and more of Voira's thoughts. Flashes of happiness and rage flew past followed by more and more thoughts of power and control. The more Auriel dug the more the thoughts started to confuse and worry her. Her thoughts were not seamless, there were gaps and holes as if someone had tampered with them.

Finally she found what she wanted and with a fierce tear, she unleashed the memories of the cells design. Images of a spell, weaved into the very stone came into her mind and the more it showed her, the more she understood. The spell was overlapping the room just like she had thought, creating two separate but nearly identical rooms, offset by just a nudge. It was as if Kyne's room was at a slightly different wavelength than her own and all she had to do was push them back together.

Voira cried out in pain and rage as Auriel freed herself from her mind duel. The redheaded woman collapsed upon her hands and knees panting hard and visibly shaken by what had occurred.

"You violated me!" she screamed in rage with tears running down her face. "How could you!"

"You left me no choice," Auriel muttered flatly. "It was your own doing, just be lucky I left you in one piece."

Voira screamed in anger and leapt towards Auriel, reaching for her throat.

"Erodath," and with a swipe of her hand, Auriel launched Voira to the side where she slammed into the wall with a large crack. Falling limply to the floor, a visible streak of blood appeared upon her brow dripping down to the floor in hot scarlet drops.

"Now to undo this spell," she said, and she concentrated hard. With a quick incantation, she held out her hands and forced a great amount of aura into the whole room causing it to visibly vibrate and shift in and out. To her satisfaction she watched as Kyne seemingly materialized in front of her, laying upon the bed, his eyes glazed over.

The Legend of Kyne: Chronocide

* * *

30. Reckless Teens

"You are far too quiet," Ky'Ren hissed as he snaked his head, eyeing Ni'Bara. The copper dragon flexed his wings, the light streaming in scattering around in dazzling gleams decorating the room with his beauty. "I really wonder if the desert rats did something to you." Ni'Bara opened one eye and stared at the dragon. He knew he needed to keep the charade going, at least for a bit longer, but he hated it. Every inch of his being wanted to destroy Ky'Ren right there. It pained him at the same time he felt his dragonrage spark. This monster at one point was like a brother to him, so long ago he could barely even remember.

And her! he thought as he recalled what Ky'Ren had said the previous day. *They had killed her somehow, the other egg that was taken from the Serati, his eggmate.*

He felt his dragonrage boil more and he raised his body up, eyeing Ky'Ren and swelling his chest.

"Oh, the big boy wants to fight aye," sneered Ky'Ren and he stood up taller, matching the grey dragon's height. "Did I hit a nerve? Or are you really just soft."

The rage intensified and through the burning flames, he saw Kyne and the others flash into his mind, and it quickly diminished. He had to find them and getting information from this snake was his best bet. Lowering his puffed-out chest, he continued leaving his eyes piercing Ky'Ren's.

"The desert rats burned in their sand homes as I swallowed their cattle and plucked their children from their mothers. The king's flesh bubbled off as he screamed, meeting my eyes in his final moment. Do not question my savagery Ky'Ren," Ni'Bara snarled.

"Delicious," the dragon replied, his words seeming to draw pleasure from the beast. "I was so irritated that I could not accompany you but alas, I was returning from Gaeil and couldn't make it in time. I get the next carnage! I want those who we conquer to feel my flame as I partake in their young. To watch as their fathers see me burn their families alive brings me such joy!"

The dragon roared a laugh that shook the palace, and he swung his head around. "I grow bored. Let us tour the countryside. Let's see the progress He has made," and the dragon approached the opening, beckoning for Ni'Bara to follow.

This was it, he thought. This is my chance to try and get some info on where they could be and what has happened to this world.

Following Ky'Ren, the two drakes leapt from the dragon keep's edge and glided over the back wall of the city toward one of the smoky pillars that dotted the edge of the forest.

It was too hard to speak while they were flying, so Ni'Bara just followed along, trailing slightly behind the other dragon and scanning the landscape for any sign or scent of his family.

The edge of the forest was further than usual and as they approached, he was devastated to see the stumps of thousands of trees dotting the landscape. The forest was being executed; the trees viciously cut like a head being severed by a guillotine to fuel the war machine that the Dominion had made. They had conquered Kydrëa and were pillaging its resources and everything it had.

Miles of tree stumps flew by underneath them as they approached the column of smoke. Up ahead, they could see small dots of people and work animals as they slowly progressed deeper into the forest, chopping tree after tree down.

Ky'Ren's abdomen started to glow and then as they ripped over the heads of the workers, Ni'Bara heard them scream in fright at their sight before a jet of dragonfire erupted from his maw igniting dozens of trees in an orange blaze.

Horrified, Ni'Bara watched as a huge swathe of trees was ignited, the heavy black smoke rising as they burned away.

Ky'Ren swung wide as he ended his flame and smiled wickedly at Ni'Bara before nodding his head as if gesturing to participate. A pit formed in his stomach as Ni'Bara hovered where he was. Down below he could he screams as humans tried to flee the spreading wildfire as it began to spread and grow.

The Legend of Kyne: Chronocide

He had to, he had to keep his identity secret.

With his own abdomen beginning to glow, he opened his mouth and let forth a torrent of flame. Spewing out in a fan shape, it struck dozens of innocent trees, burning them to charred silhouettes. He continued, sweeping his head across burning dozens more and he couldn't help but feel a slight hint of satisfaction. The satisfaction of destroying something that everyone seemed to have, but to a dragon, was so much more.

To give into that temptation, he thought as he ended his dragonfire and turned to see Ky'Ren flying off towards the next soot streak in the sky. *Is to turn into something like that. A monster with no morality, only narcissism and rage.*

They hopped from site to site, burning trees, eating some of the work animals. Ky'Ren even crushed some of the Dominion workers and one he snatched up before climbing high into the sky and releasing him. Gliding down next to the man, Ni'Bara could hear the dragon taunting him before the loud splat as he struck the ground, dead instantly.

As they finally returned to the dragon keep, Ni'Bara heard Ky'Ren swear under his breath. "Looks like we might've pissed someone off."

As Ni'Bara looked closer, he saw a figure standing in the center of the keep. Fear ripped through his mind at his sight, and he clenched his jaw. He knew he was here; he had a feeling but as they landed, he watched as Aaldra frowned at the two of them.

"You have got to be kidding me," he raged and suddenly a force struck both Ky'Ren and him across the face hard. "Burning my lumber yards!" Another force struck them in the face again, launching their heads to the side.

"I thought..." Ky'Ren started and before he could finish a force struck him first in the abdomen. He gasped as the breath burst from his lungs, and Aaldra flicked his hand down. Ky'Ren's head jerked down, slamming into the stone ground with a crash.

"You thought nothing. You thought only of your own amusement. I should show you just how angry I am!" and a golden glow began to emanate from his wrist. Ni'Bara watched in horror as Xeono formed a golden bolt of lightning which the king of the Dominion grasped lightly in his hand.

"I should punish you, leave my own mark! On the both of you!" and he swung his gaze towards Ni'Bara. "When the hell did you get back from your job? Awfully fast if you ask me, awfully suspicious with the situation I am dealing with. Why did you not report to me immediately?"

Ni'Bara's head swam as he tried to formulate a response to the king.

Situation? he thought. *Could he mean the others? If so, then somehow, he might know they aren't from this time and that means he could suspect me!*

"It's my fault sir," gasped Ky'Ren. "I intercepted him right as he arrived."

Aaldra turned his dark gaze towards the copper dragon.

"Indeed," Ni'Bara said tentatively. "I sort of forgot."

"Forgot?" Aaldra gasped incredulously. "You forgot?"

The dragon snorted, trying to act arrogant as he assumed that how this versions Ni'Bara acted. "Didn't seem important."

Aaldra's face lit up with rage and a bolt flew from his hand, narrowly missing Ni'Bara. Suddenly another force slammed into his head and both he and Ky'Ren struck the ground hard completely pinned as Aaldra approached them.

"You two conceited dragons act like children. Like the entire world revolves around you! Well sorry," he hissed as he walked right up to Ni'Bara's eye. "The world doesn't revolve around you. It revolves around me. You only exist to do my bidding, don't forget that. You may be powerful but I. Control. You."

He turned on his heel and the moment he left the doorway, the hold on the dragons lifted and they were able to move again.

"That could've gone worse," chuckled Ky'Ren darkly as he swung his neck around as if stretching it.

"Why did you defend me?"

"Because I owed you, don't you remember? For that time in Gaeil that you always seem to rub in my face. And now you forget? Maybe something did happen to you in Otoruh," and the copper dragon snaked his head away and laying down.

Outside the sun was getting low, casting long shadows over the landscape. It shocked Ni'Bara how long they had been gone, what felt like a few hours had been nearly the entire day.

* * *

31. The Center of Everything

Kioni sighed in disbelief as he strode next to the beam of light that centered the city intersection. The source of all this chaos, finally here in front of him. A swirling white haze of light nearly twenty feet in diameter climbed high into the sky rising out of a pulsating sphere of energy. All around the area few people were seen. Most seemed to be looters with a few elderly people trying to gather their belongings.

He took a few cautious steps towards the core of the distortion. Its white swirling light pulsating. He could feel a strange feeling emanating from it. He couldn't describe it really, more of a full body déjà vu. Momentarily the beam brightened, before dimming and then a massive crack split from it, ripping through the city block.

The pulse of power nearly took Kioni off of his feet and he ducked low, staring in shock as the severed buildings groaned before half broke away, falling to the ground in a cloud of dust. The crack through space time went straight through the city block, zigzagging away where it tore through everything it touched.

"It's the end of the world!" cried an old man nearby and he dropped to his knees. "We all have sinned, and the gods have deemed it fit to punish us!"

"Punish you maybe," said a gruff voice from across the street. "I sure as hell don't plan on dying. I am taking full advantage of the situation."

A large man, slightly overweight but half a head taller than Kioni walked down the street straight towards the man. On each side of him was another thug, one a skinnier man and the second a very heavyset woman with half of her head shaved bald.

The Legend of Kyne: Chronocide

"If you plan on dying then you don't mind if I take this," said the leader as he tore a satchel away from the elderly man. "Surely you sinners don't need items of value where you're going!"

His chuckle rang out loud around the area and as he turned his back, his two companions leapt upon the old man, tearing away his clothes and everything he had on his person until he was literally bare-naked weeping upon his knees.

The scene before disgusted Kioni and he clenched his jaw tightly. He knew that he shouldn't intervene. That this one person's situation was not any of his business, but he couldn't. It was a terrible thing what these people were doing to him and to everyone else they came across.

"Hey how about you give all that stuff back. A bunch of thieves have no place here." he called out. The group all froze in shock before they turned to look at him in surprise.

"And who might you be?" hissed the thin man.

"A damned fool!" roared the woman.

"Or a hero," Kioni sassed as he rolled his shoulders with a few quick warm up swings of his arms.

"Words like that could get yourself killed *Hero*," chuckled the leader of the trio. "Now we wouldn't want that now, would we?"

"I *would* prefer to stay alive," said Kioni sarcastically.

"I would like that as well you see," started the man. "However, you insulted me, you insulted my people. I am not sure if I can let any of that slide."

Kioni shrugged his shoulders, "Are you sure there's nothing that I can do to change your mind?"

"He is pissing me off," muttered the heavy woman. "It's as if he is mocking us."

"I am one hundred percent mocking you," called out Kioni with a much darker tone. "Give that man his belongings or you will have to deal with me."

The leader clicked his tongue a few times and shook his head. "Such a dumb thing to say." He drew his sword from its sheath. "Why don't we teach him a lesson, eh?"

"Gladly," replied the woman and she approached, drawing a large dao from her waist. The wide single edged sword was short, only two feet long, but the weight of the whole weapon was enough to severely damage any armor it struck. Kioni, dressed in nothing but his light tunic and pants was completely unprotected.

Every single action matters, he thought to himself as he drew his two kamas and rolled his wrists briefly. Scanning his vision at each of the three bandits, he noticed the other two had separated and were slowly flanking him as the woman approached in the center.

She was tall, taller than he was and probably weighed nearly double as well. Dressed in clothes that looked as if they hadn't been washed in weeks, she bore a resemblance more of a mountain troll than a woman. Thick gages had been bored through her ears leaving large sagging holes where flesh once was and across her breasts lay a twine necklace lopped through a bird skull.

Kioni rolled his wrists again and started to lightly bounce on his toes. She was nearly upon him, only a few feet away and he was going to need every bit of speed for the fight that was going to take place.

"Ahh!" she screamed as she suddenly ran forward, ripping her blade through the air at a blinding speed and nearly taking Kioni's head off as he ducked out of the way. Spinning around a second thrust of her blade, out of the corner of his eye, he saw the thin man running at him for the ambush.

"Not today," he muttered as he twirled out of the way of his attack. Dropping low, he slashed his kamas through part of the man's cloak with a hiss as the fabric was sliced.

Growling in frustration at his missed strike, he leapt back out of the way of another attack, crashing them together in a tumble leaving both of them slightly disoriented. Their leader had edged closer but cleverly stayed out of the main fray, looking for Kioni to be off guard.

Kioni ripped his kamas through the air in a deadly dance as he defended against the attacking swords. Each strike ringing around as he redirected their momentum continuously knocking them off balance. As they both swung towards him in the motion of a scissor, he delicately caught one blade against his own curved sickle and with a hopping step, brought it around and down in front of him just inches from his own leg.

The Legend of Kyne: Chronocide

A great clatter erupted as it struck into the other blade, the momentum knocking them into one another and sending the man toppling forward. A swift kick to his chest from Kioni launched him back and in one motion the two collided and fell to the ground in a gasping heap.

A flash of light was seen out of the edge of his vision and as quickly as he could, Kioni dropped his arm low, catching a sword blade with his weapon before it collided with his leg. The force slammed the back of his kama into his thigh causing a massive muscle spasm dropping him to one knee as he cried out in pain.

He was face to face with the leader of the group, his rancid breath breathing onto his face. Behind him, Kioni could see the other two staggering to their feet, rage visible across both of their faces.

"Much more of a pest than I thought you would be," muttered the large man and whipping his sword out of the kamas grip, he pulled his arms back and thrust forward aiming for Kioni's abdomen.

With a cry of pain as he put weight upon his still spasming leg, Kioni twisted to the side causing the sword to sail out in front of him in open air.

A thought came across Kioni and as the man tried to regain his control over his blade, Kioni round house kicked him as hard he could directly into the man's shins. A great bellow erupted out of the man as he fell forward, dropping his blade and grabbing feebly for Kioni. Kioni's own shin barely felt anything at all as he stepped back, but the man managed to grab a hold of the pack across his back, tearing the fabric and sending Kioni's belongings all over the road.

Staggering back, his leg nearly collapsing as the spasming diminished, Kioni distanced himself from the howling man as he faced the other two. They were distracted as they stared at the items that had been tossed all around.

He rubbed the outside of his thigh hard as he tried to loosen up the tight muscle. It seemed to be helping and he used their distraction to every part of his own advantage. He needed his leg to work properly.

The howling diminished as the man pulled up his pant leg revealing a dark black bruise and a slight indentation on the bone. He was gritting his teeth tight together in malice as he brought them towards Kioni.

"You're going to pay for that you little bastard!" he screamed as he tried to stand. A brief grunt of pain burst from his lips, but he managed to rise to his feet. "You will pay!"

"He... He is a Shade!" gasped the woman behind him.

"What did you say?" he asked as if he had not quite heard her. Turning to face her, the man followed her finger as she pointed at a silver mask lying upon the stone.

"Well well well," he said as he turned back to Kioni, a massive grin had spread across his face. "What do we have here then? A little Shade performing who knows what kind of rituals. Were you going to sacrifice people to that light behind you?"

Kioni bit his cheek in frustration. The one simple thing that could not happen. His identity had become known.

"Everyone surely sees that this man is a Shade!" he roared as loud as he could, his voice echoing all over the section of the city. "A Shade who probably had something to do with this calamity that has befallen our very own city!"

To Kioni's shock, people started to appear on the corners of nearby streets and peering through windows towards them. Their muttering voices attracted to what this man was now preaching.

"Are you all to sit around and watch as this man, this Shade as he tries to kill me and my companions for trying to find answers to this apocalypse! He is trying to silence us!"

Horror spread throughout the growing crowd of nearly a dozen Kydrëans. Their muttering grew and grew, changing to a roar and they started to circle and push in, approaching them. Kioni tried to look for the man that had been robbed, to have one voice to help against their lies but he was gone. Kioni was trapped with his back against the pillar of distortion and a mob of angry people.

A shock wave erupted behind him, and he turned to see another crack tear through the building nearby, spreading out far beyond the city. The force nearly took Kioni off his feet, and he staggered forward trying to remain upright.

The groan of the building caught his attention and to his horror, he saw small pieces of stone fall away as it teetered towards him. The building was three stories tall and when it fell would cover nearly

The Legend of Kyne: Chronocide

the half of the open area.

"You're not getting away!" screamed the leader as he saw Kioni looking for an escape. Suddenly he took off running towards him.

There! his mind roared as he spotted an alley just beyond the glowing light. When the building fell, it should miss that section preventing him from being crushed to death.

He took off in a limping sprint, the building to his side teetering beyond the edge of balance and then it started to fall, fall towards him! Suddenly something tackled him to the ground, and he whipped around to see the man, his eyes full of rage. The light from the sun above was suddenly blocked out as the building shaded them. Small pieces of stone raining from above.

He wouldn't make it! The alley was too far!

I have no other option! At least with this I might have a chance!

A swift kick straight to the man's nose loosened his grip and Kioni pulled himself up to his feet. Just as the building toppled over, he dove headfirst into the epicenter of the distortion leaving the man screaming in rage just before he was flattened in a heap of dust.

* * *

The Legend of Kyne: Chronocide

32. The Lord of the Dominion

"Kyne!" called a faraway voice. It was just barely audible, and he struggled to focus upon it.

"Kyne!" it called again, and he groaned, trying to see where it was coming from. His vision was a swirling mess of shapes and sounds before him, nauseating and confusing. He could barely focus on his own breathing let alone see what was saying his name.

"Kitala Aurabane."

Kyne started to cough violently as air was pulled out of his lungs. A flash of panic at the thought of suffocating flew through his mind and he started to thrash around. His vision was clearing up and a figure was standing in front of him, their hand held out towards him.

Who is that? he thought as his mind began to clear from the fuzz. His vision focused more, and he saw a trail of white power flying out of his mouth, nose and eyes. It swirled into a small sphere that was growing upon the figure's outstretched palm.

"Auriel?" he muttered as he started to make out her features. Her silver hair was the first thing he saw, snarled and knotted from her time locked up. Then her beautiful smile was visible, and he smiled back at her.

His mind fully cleared, and he took a gasping breath before he leapt up from the bed, embracing her. He had never been more happy to see her in his life. She was everything to him!

"It worked!" he said with enthusiasm as they withdrew, and the Riel nodded her head.

"They really upped the dosage and frequency. You were so drugged it almost looked like you were dead."

"It felt like I was dead," he muttered as he clenched his fists.

The Legend of Kyne: Chronocide

"That drug is very dangerous. I think it's the same thing they gave me when I was trapped in Guelok Lokona."

"Probably the same one. The other Kyne told me about it. It's from Gaeil."

"You spoke to that little bastard!" Kyne fumed. "Did he tell you how he betrayed me?"

"Yes, he did. Kyne, I think he was just afraid. He genuinely seems to care about us. He was the one who helped tell me about the cell."

Kyne furrowed his brow in frustration and turned to look outside. "I still don't like it. Being betrayed is not something I enjoy. If Ni'Bara were here he would have some choice words to say on the matter."

"Have you seen anything of him or Rosé?" asked Auriel. "I still don't know what happened to them. I didn't say anything about them to anyone. I wasn't sure if they had been seen or not."

Kyne nodded his head, grateful that she had thought the same thing as him. "No, I haven't. I tried reaching out to him when I escaped but I couldn't find him. I'll try right now."

Ni'Bara! roared Kyne's thoughts as far as he could reach. He waited for a long moment before suddenly he felt his companion connect minds.

You're alright! rumbled Ni'Bara with happiness emanating from him. *Where have you been? Why haven't you contacted me?*

They captured both me and Auriel and had us drugged so we couldn't use our aura. I tried but I couldn't reach you.

I had heard some things about prisoners that were captured and was quite sure it was you. I have been trying to find out where you were, but it has been hard.

Where are you at?

In the dragons keep on the back of the citadel. Kyne, Ky'Ren is here and there is another Ni'Bara. I haven't seen him yet, but he will be returning soon.

I was wondering if we would see that wyrm again. Aaldra is back as well.

I am aware. It's as if all of the things we did were just wiped clean. What happened?

The Legend of Kyne: Chronocide

Kyne paused for a while, ashamed and not wanting to tell him. *It was my fault. I altered the timeline.*

You what? How?

It couldn't be helped. I distorted when we were in the catacombs, and I encountered a younger Saathe. I fought him and then warped back. That's when all of this happened.

Kyne flooded Ni'Bara with all of the memories that had taken place. All the horrors of their capture and his attempt at escape. As it ended, Ni'Bara rumbled in thought.

So that is what they meant when one of you resembled Aaldra's son. Very strange.

Indeed. Auriel is with me now and we are escaping. Do you know where Rosé is?

No, I do not, he replied solemnly. *The last time I saw her was right when everything happened. She was near you two.*

So, she must be somewhere nearby or never came to this timeline in the first place. If she did, maybe she escaped outside the city. I haven't heard anything about a small pink dragon.

Nor have I. Ky'Ren would've been upon her in a heartbeat if he knew. Hopefully we are able to find her. You two escape. I'll take out Ky'Ren and then meet you in the central courtyard. Keep in contact with me at all times. If something happens then I will burn the entire city down!

I will. Beware the Dark Princes and Aaldra. He has Xeono and is an incredibly skilled sorcerer rivaling both me and Auriel. I don't want anything to happen to you.

The dragon snickered at the comment and Kyne nearly laughed himself. He knew Ni'Bara could take care of himself.

Kyne explained the situation quickly to Auriel and after he finished, they both knew it was time to leave. Voira was still unconscious leaning limply against the wall and Kyne almost felt pity for the poor woman.

As they came to the door, Auriel used her aura to send out a pulse through the wall searching for any objects beyond it like a cetacean and their sonar.

"There are two people standing outside, one on each side of the doorway," she said as she withdrew her hand from the wall. "They shouldn't be too difficult."

The Legend of Kyne: Chronocide

Kyne nodded and with a quick signal from Auriel, he ripped the door open, and they both dashed out into the hallway facing opposite directions. In a blur, Kyne and Auriel quickly dispatched of the sentinels, killing them and placing their bodies within the cell.

The door slowly clicked shut and with a wave of her hand, Auriel locked it, but Kyne shook his head.

"We should make it a little harder for them," and he grabbed onto the metal knob. Using the full strength of his dragonaura, he brought forth his inner flame through his palm, liquefying the metal and pushing it flat against the door.

The metal glowed a dim red as it became loose putty, easily manipulable and as Kyne withdrew his hand, he nodded with satisfaction. The knob and lock had been fused together and pressed flat up against the door. No one was getting in easily.

Running down the hall, Kyne consistently conveyed their location with Ni'Bara who was planning on ways of dispatching Ky'Ren.

We will find you and take him out together, Kyne said as he slid low under a sword swipe from a sentinel. Auriel dove headfirst over the same swipe and with the sound of grinding armor, thrust her blade directly through the man's chest plate.

"Where are our belongings?" muttered Kyne as he climbed to his feet. "We cannot leave them behind."

"I will scry them."

Pulling the sentinel out of view, she muttered, "Sei'var," and his body seemed to shrivel as water rose out of it to form a small hovering sphere. "Seioin."

Images flashed into view within the sphere and suddenly it stopped. They could see a large wooden door and the throne of Aaldra.

"Of course, that's where it is," Kyne growled in frustration. "Anywhere else would be too easy."

"That *is* nearby," said Auriel optimistically as she studied the sphere. "It looks like no one is there at the moment."

"Let us hurry then," and they both took off at inhuman speed with their aura. They encountered no more sentinels on their quick journey and soon they were face to face with the set of doors, their things hopefully beyond it.

The Legend of Kyne: Chronocide

Auriel sent another sonar pulse to search for anyone inside and nodded they were clear. Pushing the door open, they slipped inside and began looking for their belongings. It didn't take them long, they were all on one side of the room, decorating a wooden shelf. The Ouroboros Bag, as well as Aurora and all of their clothes seemed to be set up as trophies.

Kyne entered the bag and quickly checked to make sure nothing had been tampered with and was relieved to see everything in order. As he exited the bag, he summoned his and Auriel's armor from its depths and within moments they were dressed, ready for war.

Wearing their light armor, Kyne's heitrite, crafted by Thirak, and Auriel's of orichite gave them almost instant relief. Now they wouldn't be taken out in a single hit as easily as before. They needed all the luck they could get.

"Well well well," said a deep voice accompanied by a set of slow clapping. "I honestly did not expect this."

Turning quickly around, they both drew their blades, the green of the orichite and the silvery white feather of Light. Standing across the room, they could see the Lord of the Dominion, Aaldra with a furious smile upon his face.

"More of a nuisance than you are worth!" and the golden flash of electricity erupted from his palm forming a long spear. "I grow tired of this!"

The spear of lightning ripped through the air straight towards Kyne. It was so fast that they barely had time to leap out of the way just as it struck the wall sending a shower of sparks all around.

Kyne rolled over his shoulder and leapt to his feet just as another spear was hurled towards him. He twisted over his shoulder and the world seemed to slow as the bolt missed by mere inches.

"Kyne!" screamed Auriel and he looked to see her running fast towards Aaldra, her blade low and ready.

He understood the signal and propelling himself forward with aura, he flanked on Aaldra's other side. Xeono was incredibly powerful, but it still was a long-ranged weapon.

A flash of lighting shot straight up and collided with the ceiling bathing the room in a shower of golden sparks. In one sweeping motion, the tyrant king withdrew his own longsword and it collided

The Legend of Kyne: Chronocide

with Auriel's.

Fueled with rage, he withdrew and swept towards her horizontally but the Riel was much faster than he was and dropping low, she brought her sword up across his inner thigh. A long strip of cloth was sliced through and to both Kyne and Auriel's shock he remained unharmed, narrowly dodging her swipe.

A fierce glow erupted from the crystal on his pommel and just as Kyne dove in for an attack of his own, a massive force of energy erupted from Aaldra, spreading out in a furious sphere. Furniture and decorations as well as the two prisoners were launched across the room where they collided hard with the wall.

Kyne's vision flashed in and out of focus as he slumped down. He could hear to his left the sounds of Auriel gasping as she tried to catch her breath from the blow. In front of them, the golden flash of lightning appeared in Aaldra's hand as Xeono formed another spear. Aaldra looked first at Auriel and then at Kyne before a wicked smile appeared on his face.

"You are first!" he spat and ripping his arm forward, he launched the bolt towards Kyne at a blinding speed.

Vertai!

The word never even left his mouth, just barely formed in his head and Kyne's arm suddenly rose up, the bolt ricocheting to the side and slamming into the wall in a bright golden flash. His vision tunneled as aura fled his body but it slowly returned and he saw Aaldra with a look of bewilderment.

It happened again! roared his thoughts and he struggled to stand. *Words not spoken should have no power!*

Another bolt flew towards him and closing his eyes, he let control of himself go to whatever was guiding him. Twisting to the side out of instinct, the bolt flew right past his chest and with a swipe of his arm he unleashed a dragonrend toward the king.

A scream of shock erupted from Aaldra, and he dropped his sword and raised both palms up forming an aural shield. The two forces collided and for a moment, they froze as they waited for one to give.

A crack flew through Aaldra's shield and then a blue flash of light filled the room!

The Legend of Kyne: Chronocide

Aaldra was lying face down on the ground, dust falling upon his back as the room shuddered from the force. A massive gaping hole in the back wall revealed the outside air, and the dark city of Alakyne beyond. Kyne scrambled over to Auriel and helped her to her feet, and they turned back to face Aaldra.

Lord Aaldra coughed hard and climbed to his knees, his chest quivering as he gasped for breath. A look of terror flew from his eyes only for a moment before it was replaced by a hellish rage.

"What are you!" he screamed at them. "What is this witchcraft?"

Kyne reached down and removed his glove and in one motion, tore his sleeve off revealing the dragon scales beneath. Raising it towards him, he spoke slowly.

"You mess with things that you do not understand Aaldra. You think that you own this world, but you are wrong. I defeated you once and I will do it again!"

The glow of cyan fire appeared on his mouth and with a roar, Kyne unleashed a wave of dragonfire upon Aaldra.

A sudden tempest erupted, and the blaze was forced to the side where it engulfed the wall in flame. Shock flew through Kyne's mind and as he ended his attack, with the glow of liquid fire as small puddles covered the ground, he saw the misty figure of Diahl hunched near Aaldra.

The apparition seemed to make the air grow chilly and heavy, a deep despair filling his chest and he could tell Auriel was feeling the same as she looked first at him and then towards them. Auriel suddenly sent an aural attack towards the two of them.

Diahl shot his own in one motion and just as it collided, the figure faded away.

"Auriel behind you!" screamed Kyne and Auriel whipped around with her blade low just as Diahl struck towards her. The ghostly man's sword collided with her own and as fast as she could, she rebounded her blade off his and swept it through his body where it passed straight through him.

"What is he?" she gasped in shock, and she leapt back as he faded away. Using her aura to amplify her senses, Auriel constantly defended against Diahl as he repeatedly phased in and out of sight.

The Legend of Kyne: Chronocide

Every time she struck him, her blade passed straight through as if he wasn't even really there.

Aaldra had stumbled towards the gaping door and to Kyne's horror, he watched as the hooded figure of Saathe glided in, an icy blue fire trail left behind him.

"Auriel use his own blade! That is how Kioni defeated him! I'll take the other two!"

Inhaling a deep breath, Kyne unleashed another blast of dragonfire upon the Lord and his reaper. The pair were engulfed in the bright blaze before they could attack and out of the corner of his eye, he could see Auriel dancing away from Diahl.

Two more times, he phased in and out as she waited for the precise moment. Just as their swords finally collided, she jabbed out her hand and grabbed onto his hilt.

"Erodath!" she screamed, and a force collided with the ghostly man, prying the faded blade from his cold grip. As he staggered to regain his footing, Auriel leapt forward and thrust the tip of the blade straight through his chest.

Auriel felt the resistance as the blade pierced his flesh and with a look of disbelief, the Pale One dropped to his knees before falling forward to the ground.

Auriel turned and watched as Kyne dueled against Aaldra and Saathe. The reapers scythe tore through the air at Kyne, but he managed to block every strike with his own blade. Aaldra was still attacking, the golden bolts of lightning flying towards Kyne but they were smaller and less frequent than before.

He was feeling his fatigue!

Kyne blocked another attack from the reaper as the dark cloaked figure pressed in on him aggressively. No matter what Kyne did though, the reaper consistently continued his assault not allowing Kyne time to breathe.

"We meet again!" he hissed as Kyne guided the scythe into a large piece of wood where it hung fast.

"I should've killed you when I had the chance," He replied through gritted teeth as he backhanded Saathe with his dragon arm. The force knocked the reaper back and he crashed to the floor, his scythe still embedded into the wood.

The Legend of Kyne: Chronocide

A flash of light filled his vision and fueled by his dragonrage, Kyne raised his scale covered palm up and caught it. A massive golden glow lit up through the destroyed room and as it dimmed, Kyne was there, holding back the force of Xeono with his hand. He could feel his feet sliding back as the bolt fought hard against him.

He could do it, he had to!

Snarling, Kyne forced his aura into the spear and with a flash of hope, watched as the tip changed from gold to cyan. Spreading through the spear, the blue glow of Kyne's aura replaced the golden light of Xeono.

Cries of anger erupted from Aaldra, and another bolt flew towards Kyne.

"Erodath!" screamed Auriel and the bolt curved out of the way, flying through gaping hole in the wall and out over the city where it exploded lighting up the dark night.

"Alderiun!" screamed Aaldra and to their shock, the grey necromancer stepped into view as if he had been waiting, both hands outstretched. A blast of dark aura flew towards Kyne and Auriel deflected it once more as the archmage slowly gained control over the cyan spear of lightning.

Saathe had risen to his feet and joined his brother in darkness, sending his own attacks towards them. The three were pressed up against one another, separately launching attacks at Kyne as Auriel deflected them.

"Her! Take out her!" screamed Aaldra and just as Alderiun turned towards the Riel, Kyne threw the bolt at them.

All three launched their own aura towards it where it collided, and everything seemed to freeze. Kyne could feel his hair rising up and he reached out a hand towards Auriel as she ran towards him. All around, stones and other fragments of debris began to float dangerously in the air as the colliding forces pulsated.

Swirling into a black sphere, the collision seemed to start drawing them in. Kyne watched as the hovering dust and rocks flew into the sphere, vanishing into the depths of its power.

"Do. Not. Stop!" screamed Aaldra and he raised his other hand, another jet of his aura flying into the sphere. "Do not stop!"

A pulse of energy flashed from the sphere and Kyne grabbed

The Legend of Kyne: Chronocide

on tight to Auriel with his hand. Turning his back to the blast, he placed her right in front of him and screamed the shield spell, "Etoch!"

Suddenly the colliding attacks collapsed, and a massive explosion tore the room to pieces.

* * *

Ni'Bara felt the citadel underfoot shake violently as a massive explosion burst from above him. Ky'Ren raised his head up in disbelief and Ni'Bara took the opportunity.

Lunging forward, his fangs aimed straight for the copper dragon's throat, Ni'Bara attacked!

Ducking out of the way, Ky'Ren slammed the top of his head up under Ni'Bara's chin slamming the grey dragon's mouth shut with a loud clash.

"I knew it!" snarled Ky'Ren as he snaked away from Ni'Bara. "You are not him!"

Ni'Bara remained silent and the glow of fire appeared between the scales on his chest. Ky'Ren retaliated and with a roar, the two dragons unleashed their dragonfire where they collided with one another.

The flames fanned out in a disc, bathing everything in fire but the two did not cease. Instead, they both inched closer and closer to one another. Ky'Ren had fought other dragons before in the past but so had Ni'Bara. Ni'Bara had trained against some of the greatest dragon fighters in history and Ky'Ren did not expect what was to come.

Ending his fire suddenly, Ni'Bara ducked down as Ky'Ren's copper colored flame erupted from the disc and slammed into the wall behind him. Ky'Ren's eyes widened with shock, but it was too late, as the glowing outline of dragonaura laced Ni'Bara's tail.

Flicking it towards Ky'Ren, the instant it touched the dragon's chest, an unimaginable force crashed into him, slamming him back where he collided with the wall. The citadel shuddered from the impact and Ni'Bara roared in triumph as he turned to face him.

Ky'Ren struggled to raise his head as he looked at Ni'Bara with shock across his face. In his eyes burned a hatred only caused by the death of his own ego. Ky'Ren truly believed he was unstoppable. He had been sorely mistaken!

Taking a step forward, Ni'Bara's silhouette started to glow with a hazy light as he approached Ky'Ren.

"Do you fear death?" he said darkly.

"I fear nothing!" hissed Ky'Ren. "Let alone you!"

Raising his claws up, Ni'Bara lunged forward for the death blow.

A force suddenly slammed into him, and he stumbled to the side in shock, his tail flailing as tried to remain upright. With a look of shock, Ni'Bara saw the dark-haired man known as Ariov panting heavily in the doorway. He looked to be completely exhausted as if he had used every ounce of his aura to attack Ni'Bara.

A blur of copper flew past Ni'Bara and with dragonrage spreading through him, he watched as Ky'Ren fled the dragon alcove.

"You will not escape!" roared Ni'Bara and he leapt towards the edge, spreading his wings and launching up into the sky. Above him a couple hundred feet near the pinnacle of the citadel was Ky'Ren continuing his rapid ascent.

Ni'Bara was rapidly gaining on him but just as he soared higher than the citadel, a dark shape flew at him from the other side. He twisted out of the way with disbelief at what he was seeing.

Another grey dragon was turning in a great arc, its silvery wings spread out wide in the banking turn. As the two made eye contact, Ni'Bara understood exactly who he was. It was the alternate version of himself, and he knew immediately the danger he was in.

* * *

33. A Fatal Discovery

The young dragon watched as Lioné laced up his boots, the mud peeling off of the fraying strings as it was threaded through the holes before being tied up tight in a knot. He drew a dark cloak around his shoulders and after throwing the hood up, turned to look over at his family once more. His eyes lingered upon his young sister Seri for a minute, and he smiled weakly, his mouth nearly the only thing visible on his face.

Outside the window was obscured by the drawn curtains but no light shined through the cracks. It was late in the night, the Kydrëans who lived in the city forced back into their homes as if they were dogs being locked into a kennel. No sentinels had returned to their home looking for the one they had killed but they knew they would be back, probably in the morning so they had to act now. It was do or die and Lioné was risking everything with what he was about to do.

Roco was fuming, beyond angry at Lioné for taking over. He was supposed to take the body, he was the one who volunteered but Lioné wasn't having it. He was the eldest and with that he said it was *his* responsibility.

The sliding sound of canvas upon stone drew Rosé's attention and she tuned to see Roco walk into the room pulling a rope over his shoulder. Behind him a long shape was being dragged and Rosé could smell it immediately, the smell of putrid death as the rotting corpse was drawn past her. She watched as Seri gagged and turned away and then her eyes met the mother's whose bore into her one like a hot knife into fresh butter. They were piercing eyes full of hatred and loathing.

"So, what's the plan then Lioné?" asked Roco as he drew the wrapped-up body near the front door and dropped the rope. "Where are you putting it?"

The Legend of Kyne: Chronocide

"I was thinking our best option would be down into the sewers below the city. I know of a drain grate a short distance away. If I can get him there then maybe he won't be found for a long time."

The rest of the family murmured to themselves as they contemplated the thought.

"I don't know why you are doing this Lioné," hissed their mother. "It's her fault that we are even in this mess. Make her get rid of the body, if that happens then we win no matter what. Either she disposes of the body which is great or if she gets caught then also great. It'll be completely off of us."

"You disappoint me mother," he said lowly. "A mother who raised her own children should know the value in a child's life. It sickens me that you would treat her so poorly."

Turning his gaze towards Roco, the two brothers grasped forearms for a moment before Lioné stooped down and threw the bound corpse over his shoulder. Roco pulled the door open slowly and peaked outside. The entire home seemed to freeze as they waited, waited for the signal to show that he was in the clear.

A few long moments passed and then Roco slid to the side, swinging the door open widely and Lioné rushed through as quickly as he could, vanishing into the shroud of night.

A click and then silence as the whole family held their breath for a long moment, Rosé's heart thumping loudly in her chest. Roco was the first to speak and he did so very quietly, almost inaudible.

"Be swift and hidden brother."

A few minutes passed as they waited, and Rosé quickly grew impatient. Rising up, the young dragon started to pace around the room, her tail swinging back and forth across the ground, grinding her scales upon the wooden floor. Turning around, she continued to walk back and forth a few times before a malicious glance from the mother screamed "Stop!" She averted her eyes and took another step before hesitating. The anticipation was killing her and moving was the only thing really helping.

Swinging around, she ventured back deeper into the home, leaving the shabby front room full of humans. The doorway led to a small cooking area with a bed in the corner and two small closet sized rooms beyond, each just large enough to hold a small bed.

The Legend of Kyne: Chronocide

The dragon started her pacing again, circling the table that stood in the center of the room. Over and over, she walked, trying to push out the horrendous smell of death that lingered. It masked everything in a heavy blanket of odor making it hard to even breathe as she struggled not to gag.

The body had seemed to be cooking as it sat in the back of the room for over a day, waiting as they tried to find out what to do with it and it was enough time to leave its mark upon the home.

She circled the table again and a flicker of the sentinel's smell hit her nose, not the putrid odor of death but the powerful oily smell that she had noticed when she killed him. As if he had been rolling around in a bush, the smell was strong but even now she was shocked it had still lingered for so long.

She circled again.

There it is! The smell hit her nose again. More noticeable than before as her nose was growing numb to the odor of decay. The strange smell that didn't seem to belong. She looked around the room, expecting to see some plants or something to signal the smell and she nodded as she saw them. Two bundles of dried clusters, each tied up and hanging above an empty stone basin faint sunlight streaming in a thin rectangular window high up on the wall.

She circled again, her anxiety nearly driving her mad and as she made it to the plants, stretched her neck up. Rising up on her hind legs she just managed to nearly touch her nose to them when her mind was immediately filled with confusion. They stunk, that was for sure. Reeked of very powerful smelling plants, but the scent was different. It wasn't the scent that the sentinel had but something completely distinct.

She lowered herself back down and looked back and forth around the room for any other plants, but there were none.

Her stomach started to feel uneasy, as if it were telling her something was wrong and she ventured first to each room, inhaling deeply as she searched for the source of the scent. The first room was empty and coming to the second she found it to be occupied with their father, his sleeping mass lying on the bed, but the room was bare of the scent.

Then she smelled it as its odor drifted into her nose. Dropping low, she inhaled deeply and started moving around the room, sniffing the ground like a dog as she nearly brushed the wooden planks.

Her sense of smell was keen and following the trail, she came to a section of the floor with the smell strongly emanating from it. It was odd though as she looked around the area, expecting this to be where the body had been hidden, but the scents she could smell told her he had been concealed nearly on the other side of the small room.

Placing one of her hands onto the wooden plank, her wing tucked tight to her body and her claws just barely touching its surface, she felt the board wiggle as if it were just a little looser than the others.

She withdrew her hand and hooking a single white claw in between the boards, she felt it wiggle again and forced the sharp tip underneath it. A slow motion raised it up and beneath it made a pit form in her stomach.

The sentinel's helm lay under the board, removed and hidden away. It was hidden in such a place that if the home was searched it would surely be found.

Who could do this? she thought in a panic as she swept her tail into the hole and pulled the helm out.

Balancing it on the tip of her tail, the young rose gold dragon crawled across the room and ventured into the room with the Kydrëans. Her movement caught Roco's attention, and he smiled weakly at her for only a moment before her tail came into view and it was replaced with a wide-eyed gasp.

"What is that?" he nearly shouted, his voice cracking. "Why do you have that?"

"I...I found it, under a board," she stammered, and she dropped it to the floor where it clanged in a dull ring.

"Under a board? What board? Why was it there in the first place? It should've been on the sentinel when Lioné took him. If that were to be found, then..." he paused for a long moment and then his eyes widened in even more disbelief. Turning to his mother he gasped. "How could you? You would threaten to get us all killed for what?"

She was silent for a long moment, her affect flat as she slowly turned to face him.

"How could you mother!"

"It is her," she said slowly, turning towards Rosé. "She is the problem. It was all supposed to happen tomorrow when we had hidden her. The helm was to be discovered and then I was going to give her away, saying she threatened to burn us alive if we didn't hide her."

"Mother!" gasped Seri and she leapt from her seat and stood in between Rosé and her. "What is wrong with you?"

"What is wrong with me?" she sneered as she stood up from her chair. "What is wrong with a mother trying to protect her own family? I found a solution to rid us of this vermin and I am to be shamed for it?"

"Get away from us!" roared Roco and he approached her, but she was quick and leapt towards the empty doorway to the back of the home. "Do not threaten your own mother!" she hissed. "I brought you into this world, don't think that I couldn't take you out of it."

"Go to bed," he said darkly, his voice carrying venom. "I can't deal with you now. I have to focus on this," and he stooped down and grabbed the helm.

She scoffed and spun on her heel running face to face with her beaten husband, his face littered with bruises as he looked at her with such disappointment.

"What happened to the sweet woman who tried to defend the neighbor's daughter from that sentinel?" he whispered.

"She was beaten and broken," she responded and pushed past him, vanishing into the small closet with a bed. The door slammed shut and they were left in silence, the dire situation heavy in their thoughts.

"The helm needs to be dealt with," said the father softly and he started to turn away before he looked back at Rosé. "I haven't been able to thank you for what you did," and he smiled weakly before leaving them and joining his wife.

"I might be able to catch Lioné," Roco said, and he ventured toward the door.

"Stop," said Rosé quickly and she dashed forward, snatching the helm from his hand. Clutched in her mouth, the young dragon eyed the two friends she had grown fond of in the short time. "It's my fault. I'll find him," she said, her voice muffled from the helm clutched in her mouth. Turning towards the door, she waited and Roco stared for a log moment before reluctantly opening it knowing full well there was no way in talking her out of it.

The Legend of Kyne: Chronocide

Peaking his head out, they waited for a minute and then the signal was given, and she dashed out into the cool night air.

Ripping down the street, the dragon took two large bounds before leaping high and spreading her wings, gliding up onto the rooftop where she ducked low and searched for Lioné's scent.

There!

Dashing off the roof, she glided down, flying through the street rapidly, her eyes peeled for any sign of sentinels. A dark figure was noticed on the edge of her vision and dropping down at a steep angle, she alighted in front a panting Lioné who nearly jumped out of his skin at her sight.

What are you doing out here!" he gasped, beckoning for her to move to a better location. They slid into a small gap between two buildings that would hide them for the moment and then he saw the helm!

"Wait! Where did that come from?"

"We will explain when we get back. Did you already hide him?"

"Well... Well yes, I did," he said, and his brow furrowed. "But it seems now I have to head back there?"

She nodded. "I am sorry."

He grinded his teeth and scanned down the street before leaning tight against the wall as voices suddenly became audible and drew nearer.

Two sentinels passed and after they were a good ways away, they continued their conversation.

"I can take it. You head back home."

"No!" she said fiercely. "Either I take it, or I come with you."

His mouth was open, aghast at her words for a moment but looking at her stern face, he saw the glimmer of pink flame in her iris. He wasn't winning this argument.

"You can accompany me then," and a few glances were shot down either end of the street before he took off sprinting as fast as he could while keeping his footsteps quiet.

Rosé leapt after him, bounding like a cat as she easily kept up with him, right to his flank with the bronze helm clutched in her maw.

The Legend of Kyne: Chronocide

The air flew past her cheeks, whistling off the scales in her ears as they rounded a corner. Up ahead, Lioné pointed at something on the road near a building and they slowed down. It was an iron grate at an angle and the odor coming from it was wretched. Feces and urine and any other waste that could be thought of emanated from that hole. It nearly made her gag from the stench. She handed Lioné the helm, he slid it through the grate and with a light toss, it flew down a few feet in the darkness where it landed with a thick viscous sounding splash.

Shouting was heard down the street, and they tucked in tight against the wall as nearly a dozen sentinels dashed in and out view, running through an intersection, their lanterns swinging dangerously as they traveled. More commotion was heard and to their other side a large group of sentinels were seen heading the same way.

"What's going on?" whispered Rosé. "Do they know we are here?"

"I don't think so," responded Lioné. "But we should get back quickly. Go! Go!" and he nudged her before they took off running away from where the sentinels were heading. They rounded a corner and made it partway up the street when suddenly the ground trembled and a flash of light lit up the sky behind them.

Swinging her head around, Rosé watched as another flash of light lit up the silhouette of the citadel, a massive explosion of energy bursting from it. Hundreds of orange lights covering the top of the wall and in the city were all running towards it. The ground trembled again and then a familiar roar caught her attention.

Coming to a dead stop she listened as another roar shook the city and then a dark shape circled around the back of the citadel before a wave of cyan flame filled the sky.

"Ni'Bara!" she screamed, and she took off in a few bounds, Lioné calling out for her to stop. "I can't! It's Ni'Bara! I have to get to him!" and leaping up, she spread her wings out and darted off into the night sky heading towards the citadel.

* * *

34. Shatter

      Kyne's ears were ringing as he struggled to open his eyes. The haze of dust covered his entire vision, and he clenched his hands, searching for anything. To his surprise and relief, he felt Auriel's own hand still in his and a cough next to him signaled she was still alive.

      "Kyne," said a distant voice and he tried to sit up.

      "I'm alright," he gasped as he collapsed onto his back. The throne room was completely decimated. Most of the upper ceiling had been blown to bits and the back wall was gone. As the dust settled, he could start to make out things. Far on the other side of the room were the three shapes of the Dark Princes and Aaldra, whether they were dead or just unconscious, he wasn't sure. He and Auriel were lying on the floor, it being slanted at a slight angle with a massive space a few feet away revealing the rooms below them.

      Kyne tried to rise to his feet and felt a little sturdier after a few moments, so he sat up. Something nearby caught his eye and to his disbelief he saw the hunched figure of his alternate self running quickly towards them. He had never been more happy to see him before.

      "Are you two alright?" exclaimed the mirror Kyne as he reached them.

      "I am. I am not sure about Auriel."

      The mirror Kyne reached out and touched her shoulder. Auriel groaned and her eyes flickered open.

      "Kyne?" she mumbled.

      "I'm here," he said, and she turned first from his mirrored version to her own version with understanding.

      "What happened," she groaned as she sat up shakily, letting go of Kyne's hand and rubbing her face briskly.

      "Your aural attacks exploded," said the mirrored Kyne. "We

The Legend of Kyne: Chronocide

need to get up."

Reaching out his hand towards Kyne, the mirrored version smiled weakly.

"Thank y..." the instant Kyne's hand touched his alternate version, his eyes glazed over, and a rush of memories flooded his mind.

The first was of Saathe killing Voron and taking him to Zol Kyden. As it shifted, he watched as he was beaten and tortured for weeks before he finally was allowed to leave. He was given to Aaldra, and he witnessed the destruction of Kydrëa from his side.

The memories suddenly shifted to him sitting in a room, muttering spells from an old book and making a figure levitate.

Kyne was finding it hard to focus on anything but the memories as they continued to flow, forcing into his mind and threatening to consume him. His alternate self-trained in the art of aura and he watched as years passed. Eventually, to Kyne's horror he witnessed the most brutal thing possible.

The mirrored version of Kyne walked into Aaldra's personal bedchambers, the flicker of candlelight licking the walls. Aaldra was seated at a desk scribbling at some paperwork when he turned to see him enter.

"You do not have permission to be in here." snarled the leader of the Dominion as he rose from his chair. "You are lucky that Saathe convinced me to let you out of your cell. Leave now or you will return to it for much longer than before."

"How about you sit down Aaldra," said Kyne calmly and with a wave of his hand and a muttered spell, Aaldra grew rigid and slowly sat back down.

"W... What have you..."

"Done?" said Kyne finishing his sentence. "It's not what I have done. It is what you and all of the users of aura have done. You have been corrupted by its... Its *power* and failed to resist the temptations. Aura is a wicked thing; a cardinal sin and I will rid the world of all of it."

"You... You can't be serious!" gasped Aaldra and he cried out as if he were in pain. "How will you..."

"Do it?" he finished. "First, I will use your forces to kill as many users of aura as we can find. It will take many years, but I will not stop until everything is how it should be. With that in mind however, I will need you and your influence." Stepping forward, the alternate Kyne smiled wickedly and placed a hand upon Aaldra's brow. "You are mine now!"

To Kyne's horror, he watched the mirrored version of himself crush Aaldra's mind leaving nothing but a hollow shell. The images flashed and more and more people lost their minds to his power as he took control of the Dominion.

As the memories faded away, Kyne returned to his present situation, the room coming into view, and he was still grabbing a hold of his twin's hand.

A wicked smile spread across his twin's face as his eyes turned dark, a deep blackness appearing along the outer ring of his iris. He stood up straighter and taller than before, much more confident and disturbing.

"It seems as though my facade has come to an end," he laughed. "As you have seen my past, so have I seen yours," he hissed and with a flick of his hand, sent Kyne and Auriel tumbling across the room where they stopped dangerously close to the edge. "Such power you have obtained my near twin. Very interesting indeed. I am very fond of this Light and Dark that you have encountered. They might be the answers to the end I seek!"

"What is going on?" gasped Auriel. "What is he talking about?"

"It's him! It's always been him!" screamed Kyne. "He is the leader of the Dominion Auriel! He has been playing us this whole time in some sort of sick and twisted game!"

"But how?" she stammered as she glanced at Aaldra's unmoving figure. "I thought..."

"He crushed their minds, he crushed all of their minds!" screamed Kyne in anger. Climbing to his feet, he felt the boiling power of his dragonrage beginning to erupt. "The single most evil thing one person could do to another!"

The mirror Kyne smiled as he began to walk along the edge of the missing floor towards them.

"Evil is a strong word. I prefer useful and righteous. I am the savior of this world. I am its salvation and its cleansing. With your power though, I now truly believe my goal to be possible!"

A flash of energy flew toward Kyne, and he managed to deflect it down where it collided with the ground beneath their feet in an explosion. A great crack split around them and then it collapsed dropping both Kyne and Auriel down to the next floor in a heap of rubble.

Coughing and gagging on dust, the two looked up to see the dark Kyne staring down upon them with a big smile.

"Thank you for being the gateway to the new world," he laughed. "I truly appreciate it!"

Another attack flew at them, but Auriel deflected it this time, launching it back up towards him.

"Kyne, we have to go! Where is Ni'Bara?"

Kyne looked up and high above them he could see the three shapes of the dueling dragons as the sky was bathed in fire.

Ni'Bara! We need you!

I'm coming, snarled the dragon and they watched as one of the dark shapes peeled away from the other two, diving swiftly down towards them.

Above, the dark Kyne was out of view for the moment and without a second thought, the two of them ran and jumped off the broken flooring, falling a hundred feet to the ground below. The whistle of the wind in their ears drowned out nearly everything except for a distant roar.

Using their aura to slow them down, they alighted with a stumbling run and took off heading as far away as they could. Up ahead was the inner wall with the courtyard underfoot as they approached it. Sentinels were running towards them in shock, the glow of their torches casting upon them in glowing puddles of light, but they paid them no mind as they intensified their speed, each step powered by their aura.

Kyne was exhausted and he was certain Auriel was as well. He understood the power this other Kyne presented and knew it full heartedly in the state they were in that they stood no chance. They had to escape!

A great dark shape suddenly crashed in front of them with a furious roar.

It was Ni'Bara!

They leapt onto his back and with a massive flap, launched into the air just as the ground was bathed in cyan and copper dragonfire. Behind them, they watched as the two dragons scrambled apart, avoiding the building walls before curving back up towards them. A small dark shape, nearly a dot from the distance flew from the citadel and landed upon Ky'Ren's back.

"He's coming!" screamed Kyne as he flooded what had happened into Ni'Bara's mind.

Auriel looked back and launched a weak aural attack towards them that was easily avoided.

"Don't waste your energy!" roared Ni'Bara. "I can outrun them!" and his flapping increased as they continued their ascent. The entire city of Alakyne was growing smaller as the distance increased but behind them the two dragons seemed to be keeping up.

"Ni'Bara faster!" screamed Kyne and the dragon snarled in response.

"Watch out!" screamed Auriel but before Ni'Bara could move, a dark shape flew up right next to them and grabbed onto Kyne's shoulder. Pulling himself onto the saddle, the mirrored Kyne used his aura to freeze Auriel in place and he touched Kyne on the forehead forcing his mind into his.

The force was the most intense thing he had ever felt as their two minds collided. This alternate version of himself put to shame all of the mental duels he had trained with against Ni'Bara and Auriel.

He could feel his mind flaking away as the ravenous beast clawed its way deeper and deeper into his mind. The longer they fought the more he couldn't seem to recognize his own thoughts.

Kyne was fading, being dragged around by the mental giant that was his twin as he thrashed in his clutch looking for any way out. Suddenly another joined in, and Kyne felt Ni'Bara's mind flood into him, driving into the invader.

They pressed on in their mental battle, time seeming to slow down. A glowing light started to emanate from the point where they were touching and as Ni'Bara rolled hard trying to get him off his back, he finally released his grip.

The Legend of Kyne: Chronocide

Kyne gasped for breath as the mirrored version stared at him in shock. Kyne looked down and to his horror saw the echoing ripple of a time distortion coming.

"Erodath!" screamed Auriel and the mirrored Kyne was launched off of Ni'Bara's back where he fell down out of view.

"I can't stop it!" cried Kyne as he fumbled, touching his blade and the pack upon his back. "It's much different this time!" and his entire being seemed to shudder. Reaching out, he grabbed the pommel of Aurora tighter, but no relief came.

He shuddered again as his very being seemed to phase in and out of existence.

Screaming in pain, Kyne twisted in his seat just as Ni'Bara twirled to the side as an aural attack sailed past them from below. He was violently launched from the saddle and stretching his arm out towards Auriel's own outstretched fingers, less than an inch away.

A blinding flash of light swirled around them and then they vanished, all three completely gone.

* * *

The Legend of Kyne: Chronocide

The Legend of Kyne: Chronocide

Part 3 Fracture

The Legend of Kyne: Chronocide

The Legend of Kyne: Chronocide

35. Stranded

Kioni's chest struck hard against the stone slabs of the road knocking the breath violently out of him. His mind was racing at the realization he was still alive. All he could remember was a flash of light and then it had seemed to vanish.

A piercing thought of the falling building ripped through his mind, and he scrambled to his feet leaping out of the way just as a massive cylinder seemingly appeared out of nowhere, stretching out from some point before colliding with the ground in a large crash.

It was the building, as if someone had drilled a hole straight through the side of it and tossed it to the ground. Kioni could just make out the edge of a wall, the wooden grain visible as it had been cleanly cut through and some of the furniture items that use to be inside, or at least part of them.

Shouting was heard, gruff voices calling out in alarm. Kioni climbed to his feet, surveying the scene as he gripped the kamas in his hands. It was Alakyne but something was different. The sky was hazy, as if a sickening miasma hung over it, and the sun seemed to glow a deep red as its light pushed through the smog. He could hear the quick footsteps of armor and more shouting before his heart nearly leapt out of his chest.

Dominion sentinels were rapidly approaching him, their crest emblazoned upon their breastplate.

Dominion sentinels? But how? What the... and he raised his kamas for a moment before hesitating and lowering them back down, the veins in his forearms throbbing as he tightened his grip in frustration. He was a Shade, a master of deception and espionage. He needed to get away and quickly before anyone else saw him. Something was terribly wrong, and he needed to find answers.

The Legend of Kyne: Chronocide

Turning on the balls of his feet, he glanced down another street seeing more sentinels approaching and then his eyes rested on an empty alleyway. Fast as a snake, he dashed towards it with uproar erupting behind him. Into the shadow of the alley, he ran around some old crates and trash before seeing a small stone wall and a door. Eyeing the trajectory, he leapt up, planting one foot upon its surface before propelling his body up. He still wasn't high enough and a single footstep was made upon the wall as his momentum rapidly slowed.

With a final push, he rocketed over to the other side of the alley where the roof was a few feet lower and stretching his hands up, managed to catch the edge of its lip. He hoisted himself up as fast as he could and was soon sprinting across the slanted roof of some unknown person's home.

More sentinels were coming into view down in the street to his left and making his way up over the triangular shape of the roof, he was soon on the other side, out of range of their crossbows, at least for now. A leap brought him to another home and a few steps later he was leaping again. The sentinels were falling behind, but their shouting was drawing more attention and as he jumped again, he noticed a family of Kydrëans nearby being led by a sentinel, the two children pointing at him with their mouths open in shock.

He had to get out of the open, hide somewhere he couldn't be found! But where? The chain of roofs he was running upon was ending in a few more buildings with a crossing street that he wouldn't be able to leap across.

He knew where he was. He was in the upper district of the city, where the wealthy lived in their large estates. He had walked these streets hundreds of times before when he worked in the citadel, but he couldn't think of where he could hide.

Then a thought popped into his mind and dashing up the slanting roof, he was soon on the other side once again, shouting from the sentinels made him smile at their frustration as they tried to switch sides, temporarily losing sight of him.

His old home was nearby, only a few streets over and he knew that there was a small crack in the wall of the attic. If someone knew of it, they could potentially sneak inside. It was a long shot and part of him was worried that it wouldn't even be there, but he had to risk it.

The Legend of Kyne: Chronocide

Running full speed down the roof, his ankles pointed awkwardly from the slanted angle, he jumped as far as he could, sailing through the air as he dropped before his feet connected with the hard ground. Absorbing the impact, he tucked into a fast roll over his shoulder and leapt up to his feet keeping most of his momentum and he accelerated, his head down as he pushed each step fast and faster. The edges of two building ripped past him as he flew into an alleyway and then out into another open street. Two glances, first left and then right showed him only two sentinels on his right side. Sharply turning left, he ran down a few buildings before turning down another alleyway in hopes of shaking some of his pursuers.

The home was coming up and as he saw it come into view, he noticed it looked to be in rough shape, not the same home he once resided in.

Where am I?

Flying across the street in a blur, he leapt off the porch in one step and pulled himself up onto the roof. A quick sweep of his vision showed him no sentinels in his immediate vicinity.

It was now or never!

Scaling the slanted shingles, he was soon on the other side, and he dropped down onto a little flat spot in the roof that overlooked the alleyway between homes. Ducking low, he wrapped his fingers upon an old wall board and pulling with fleeting hope in his mind, he grinned with satisfaction as the resounding pop of the nail coming loose was heard. Pulling it down, the board bent forward just enough that he could just barely squeeze into the crack. With a gasp, he slid it back and the deformed board snapped into place, casting him into darkness.

His breath was heavy as he tried to slow it, the air smelling of old musty attic. He wasn't sure if anyone lived there but he hoped and prayed to any god that existed that they didn't hear him. Crouching low, he focused on his breathing and strained his ears, listening for any shouting outside or movement below his feet.

Minutes passed but no sound was heard and after another quarter of an hour had gone, he finally relaxed a little. His eyes struggled to adjust to the small cracks of light that shined through gaps in the wood. It was way too dark. He couldn't even see his own hand.

The Legend of Kyne: Chronocide

The attic was scorching hot as it had been baking in the sun all day and he was quickly drenched in sweat, his clothes clinging to his body. Eventually he stripped down into just his underwear, keeping his clothes and his kamas nearby when his hand brushed the cloth around his neck, and he sighed in exacerbated frustration.

I could've used the cloth! he raged at the thought as he remembered his exhausting escape. *But wait,* as he continued to think about it. *If I would've changed faces, I would've still been wearing these clothes. It wouldn't have worked anyways.*

That thought made him feel better as he hadn't missed out on some great opportunity. But he could use the cloth to his advantage. If he could take out a sentinel maybe he could replace them temporarily, allowing him to gain intel on what was going on.

Hours ticked by and the light outside began to dim, eventually fading into a deep dark. He waited a little longer, in hopes for anyone else to go to sleep, lessening his chance to get caught and then he began to creep across the attic floor, slowing placing each step down upon the wood to minimize the sound. Feeling around, eventually he found the board and with a jerk and a thud that made his skin crawl in anxiety, he pushed his way out, clenching his jaw in anticipation of sounds to erupt from beneath him. A few seconds passed and there was nothing.

Sliding it back into place, he sighed as the cool night air touched his sweaty skin and he brushed his hair back, still wet. The city was dark with most of the stars outside obscured by the smog filled sky. Near the horizon, he could just make out the silvery crescent shape of a moon. It was blurry from the haze but after a moment of looking at it, a pit of realization formed in his stomach. It was back to the silver lifeless moon he had grown up with, not the blue and green planet that mimicked his own it had transformed into.

"Where am I?" he muttered to himself; the thought being spoken aloud again. "This is not my world, that is for sure, but where?"

Swinging his head around, he could see the glow of lanterns lighting up sections of the streets from where he assumed patrols walked. One came into view, and he watched the sentinels, knowing he was cast in the dark and hidden from sight.

"They patrol in twos it looks like," he whispered. "That may be a problem though. Taking out two shouldn't be that hard especially in

The Legend of Kyne: Chronocide

an ambush but masking myself afterwards would be hard to explain the missing partner."

He sat there for another long time, eyeing the patrols and every time one came into view, he grew more and more discouraged. The moon had risen up high enough that it signaled he needed to start moving so dropping down, he landed softly on the ground. His kamas were sheathed at his sides and with a quick thought, he pulled the mask up, changing his features and eyes to that of a Gaeilian.

It might prove useful, he thought and then after eyeing the street, dashed out and began making his way through the city. He wanted to get back to where he had appeared, see if there was any indication of where he was. It took him a long while, having to stop frequently to avoid guards, leaping in and out of shadows and holding his breath as he waited for shouts to signal he had been seen. None were heard and eventually, he was there, still hidden and up ahead the cracked cylinder of building in the center of the intersection.

From the looks of it the sentinels had already boarded the area off with wooden fencing surrounding the structure and signs ordering them to stay away. Two guards patrolled around it, each walking around in the opposite direction as the other, passing each other every minute or so. They walked slowly, their lanterns swinging at their hips casting dancing shadows around. He watched them for a time, analyzing them. They both looked to be bored or tired, he couldn't tell but their pace reflected it, slow and monotonous.

There seemed to be no sign of the distortion at all, the beam of light completely absent. Swinging his gaze around the dark shadowy silhouettes of buildings, his eyes rested upon the building that had toppled over, standing once more perfectly unscathed like a strange copy. He slowly circled the scene, remaining hidden as he kept to the shadows. He frowned at the strange piece of building. The distortion was gone, nothing there reflected it. No strange power was felt. To anyone else that area was mundane, a simple street intersection.

Tucking next to a building as the approaching sentinel came into view, he watched as they passed, their footsteps slow and heavy as they trudged on to what he assumed would be a long night of walking. Then an idea came into his mind, and he studied the sentinels as they continued on their march. Dashing to another location, he made it to a spot where directly to his right, in the circular path they were marching the two sentinels passed by one another.

Kioni crouched low against the building, his calves screaming in objection, and he watched as one approached right in front of him just as the other one vanished beyond the far side of the cylinder. As they marched around, he counted in his head as they walked their somber march.

Twenty-five, he counted just as the sentinel came into view. *Twenty-five seconds for me to kill a sentinel, take his armor off his corpse, put it on myself, and hide his body. There is no possible way that could happen!*

He watched as they circled around again, eyeing each one and looking for a weak spot in any of their armor. Suddenly a massive flash of light erupted from the citadel and the ground shook as part of the building was blasted apart. Deafening roars sounded and two dark shapes flew out of the palace. A blast of flame from one and Kioni knew it to be a dragon.

It must be Kyne! roared Kioni's thoughts and he took off running up the street, the sentinels too distracted with the commotion to notice him. He was far away and as another blast of energy erupted from the palace he watched as a dragon glided down toward the ground.

That must be Ni'Bara, as a blast of cyan flame flew from the dark shape. Another roar and then the dragon took off into the air. Kioni was still too far away, and some nearby sentinels had just noticed him as he dashed past them.

"I am not going to catch them!" he panted fiercely in a panic, and he dashed up onto the roof once again. He was fast but he still had a few hundred yards to go, and his worst fear happened as the two dragons rocketed high up into the air. Slowing his run, he watched upon the roof as one pursued the other in the dark sky, their silhouettes illuminated by the moon.

A flash of blinding light erupted from what he assumed to be Ni'Bara and then silence as they vanished from sight.

Kioni was stricken with fear and anxiety as he lowered his gaze back to the shadowed roofs of the unfamiliar Alakyne. His one hope to figure out what was going on was gone. Poof.

Movement out of the corner of his eye drew his attention and

The Legend of Kyne: Chronocide

he watched as a dark figure leapt across a roof about a hundred feet away. For a moment he thought it was a cat and then he saw the silhouette of wings as the figure glided between the buildings out of sight.

Was that a... Was that another dragon?

Climbing over the roof towards it, Kioni stopped suddenly as a massive scream ripped through the air, shaking his very being with immense power.

"Find her! Find the hatchling that they brought with them!"

Down below, he watched as the sentinels grew rigid in a trance like state as the voice repeated once again, shaking Kioni's very bones with its power.

Kioni was confused as he looked back towards where the dragon had vanished. *It couldn't be... His voice... It almost sounded like Kyne.*

* * *

36. Sludge

Rosé dashed through the slightly ajar door into the Kydrëan's home just as a massive scream was heard outside. It shook everything in the building, glass vases trembling and crashing to the floor in loud shattering clangs. She tucked her head down under her wing, trying hard to block out the sound but it continued to eat into her very mind.

As the echoes of the scream faded away, she felt something touch her on her shoulder. Looking out from underneath, she saw Lioné was kneeling next to her, a look of fear emblazoned upon his face. His eyes were wide and his mouth hanging open for a moment as if he were going to speak before he pressed his lips tightly together forming a thin line.

"What did you do?" trembled Seri's voice and the dragon turned to see her cowering behind her brother Roco. His face matched his brother's, and he guided her tighter behind his back.

"It wasn't... I didn't..." she started but Roco lifted up his hand signaling for her to stop. "Young one, I know you mean well, and I don't believe you want to endanger us but the longer you have been here the more it seems you are. I don't even want to know what was just calling out for you. The sound..." and he shook his head. "That voice shakes me to my very core. I don't know who or what it was, but it wasn't Lord Aaldra and part of me actually wishes it had been."

His voice faded off and she felt Lioné's hand lift off her shoulder. "I am sorry Rosé," he said softly, and he rose up to his feet. "I think it might be time for us to part ways. Whatever you have done, whoever you have interested in you is more than we can handle," and he gestured around. "I wish you the best, but you must leave. If you hurry, you might be able to still use the cover of night before the sentinels search for you."

The Legend of Kyne: Chronocide

Rosé felt her eyes watering and she looked down at the ground. Her chest heaved but she wouldn't cry. She took a deep shuddering breath before she said, "Thank you for all..."

The door right behind her started thumping vigorously, each strike making her wince. She turned around, leaping back out of the way just as Lioné and Roco skirted on either side of it. Clutched in their hands they each had a small wooden club, but they were nothing that would stand up to a sword.

The banging continued, more ferociously than before, for a few more seconds and then it stopped completely. The silence was nearly worse than the actual noise as they all held their breath. Seri had migrated to the kitchen doorway, cowering behind its frame with just a single eye peaking around. Behind her Rosé could see the parents had joined, silently observing with somber expressions from their father and manic fear from their mother. They did not say anything but stood in silence as three more strikes followed before a voice spoke.

"I know you are in there dragon. Let me in!"

Silence.

"Rosé, I know it's you! Let me in!"

Silence.

The pounding returned in three hard strikes.

"What do we do?" Roco whispered to his brother. "They are going to get in no matter what."

"It looks like we go down swinging," he replied just as the door exploded inward under the force of a powerful kick bending the metal hinges from the strain.

A dark shadow stepped in and the next thing that happened was over in four seconds.

Roco leapt forward, his club swinging for the intruder's head but with a quick duck and a twist over his shoulder, the figure roundhouse kicked him hard in the ribs dropping him to the ground instantly. Lioné hesitated as he watched his brother fall and just as he regained his composure and started to swing, it was too late.

Like a snake, the figure dashed right at him, two swift jabs striking him in the nose before a third punch hit him in the abdomen. Lioné sputtered out a gasp, managing to keep a hold of his club but before anything else could be done, a hook punch crunched across his

The Legend of Kyne: Chronocide

jaw knocking his vision dark and he tumbled to the floor.

Rosé watched as the two men fell before the figure turned towards her, his dark short hair messy and sweat dripping down his face. He bore no sword and she could see his fist dripping blood as the skin had been torn from the knuckles splattering upon the wooden floor in dark drops.

Seri screamed and vanished into the other room as cries of outrage erupted from their father as he took off running towards the figure, all signs of injury vanished from the rush of adrenaline filled rage.

Standing up straighter and taking a deep calming breath, the man stepped forward, meeting the father's strike with his own guiding hands as he parried them away, knocking him off balance before a swift kick sent his knee buckling and he crashed to the floor.

He cried out in pain, grasping his knee in his hands as the two brothers hunched upon the floor, beaten and broken. The man turned to face Rosé, and the small dragon could see the glimmer of steel underneath his cloak.

The hooked blades made her stomach turn and she watched as he shifted his stance, the cloak obscuring them back beneath its dark shadow. He turned and awkwardly shut the door behind him, a quick jerk wedging it shut.

She was terrified as she stared at the broken door and the men beaten at his feet. The friends she had made so easily defeated made her jaw clench and she could feel a deep heat rising in her belly as she looked upon the man. She hated him with everything she could feel, and she wanted nothing more than to reduce him to a pile of ash.

"Woah woah," he suddenly said, waving his hands at her, his hardened expression replaced by a look of concern. "Don't get hasty Rosé. I am not here to hurt you."

"Funny thing to say right after you beat the crap out of them!" she snarled, snaking her head up, the glimmer of pink flame upon the edge of her mouth. She could feel the warmth pressing in upon her mind, like the heat of a raging wildfire as her anger increased.

"They attacked me first," he stammered but she kept her focus drilled upon him. Making him step backwards, she followed his motion, approaching with a slow step, her fangs barred.

The Legend of Kyne: Chronocide

"Rosé don't do this," the man said shaking his hands. "I come as a friend!"

"No friend of mine!" she hissed, taking another step forward, pressing him towards the corner of the home.

"I am a friend; my name is Kioni!"

Kioni? Her mind questioned, the anger evaporating immediately. *I have heard his name before, from Kyne but how could he...*

"I am so glad that I found you. What happened to the others? I only saw them for a moment, mostly the dragons fighting and then they vanished in that flash of light."

"How are you here?" she said slowly, not fully believing his story. *I have never seen his face before, how can I be sure this is really him?*

"How are you here?" he retorted. "How is any of this here? Where are we for that matter because this is not the Alakyne I remember!"

Groans came from the fallen men and Kioni turned to look at them before rubbing his still bleeding fist. A look of remorse was upon his face as he saw the damage he had caused.

"I don't know," Rosé muttered, and she walked over to them, meeting their gaze for a moment before looking back at Kioni. "I was with the others and Kyne was screaming and then I was here. Are you going to take me to the voice who wants me?"

"Not a chance," he said with a smile. "That's why I am glad I found you first."

"Take her away," hissed a feminine voice and they turned to see the mother still observing them. "Take her to Him. Give her so that we may be forgiven before her interference gets us all killed!"

"What is she talking about?" Kioni asked. "What happened?"

"She killed a sentinel trying to protect us," grunted Roco as he climbed to his feet, his arm clutching his abdomen as he took short quick breaths. "It wasn't her fault."

"It was every bit her fault!" spat the mother. "We were doing just fine until she killed him and now when we are caught, we will all be executed!"

Kioni caught his breath as he looked down at the small dragon, his brow furrowed. She held her head down, but movement nearby drew her attention and they turned to see Lioné helping his

327

father to his feet.

"She meant well," Lioné said. "She didn't know she is just a child."

"So, this sentinel she killed, is he someone important? Someone who could be linked to your family?"

"He was our escort, the one who allowed us to walk the streets of the city. They have already been looking for him and they will surely come back. I don't know what else we can do."

"Where is his body now? Is it still here?"

"No," Lioné muttered. "Thank God we were able to get it out when we had the chance. Threw it down into the sewer way so it shouldn't be found hopefully."

"Hopefully," muttered Roco not impressed. "I wouldn't like to bet my life on hope."

"Either way when the sentinels come, they are going to take us and interrogate us. It's only a matter of time," Lioné said. "We have done all that we can so now we just leave it to fate I guess."

Kioni looked over at Rosé and could see her shifting her stance, grief clearly across her face. He could see it plain as day, she cared about these people.

He sighed before speaking.

"I can help you. If I see his face, I can mimic it with aura. I can pretend to be him at least long enough to get the target off your back."

"How could you... How is that even possible?" Roco gasped. "There is no way!"

"Don't worry about how, just that I can. Now is there any way I can see his face or am I to go scour the sewers looking for his corpse?"

Rosé shook her head. "You are lying. There is no way that you could do that. I don't even know if Kyne could do it."

Kioni shrugged. "Well Kyne doesn't know everything. Where is this sewer?"

* * *

The wind was howling in Kioni's ears as he leapt quickly around a corner, just narrowly avoiding being seen by a jogging group of sentinels. Hundreds of them had begun to appear, their torches dotting the dark city as they went house to house. The constant banging of fists on wood followed by doors being knocked down and screams.

They really want to find her, he thought as he held his breath for a moment. *Something terrible has occurred here and I feel like it centers around Aaldra and the Dominion.*

Thoughts of his previous enemy coming back and undoing all their previous fighting flew through his mind, but he couldn't explain any of it. He wasn't sure how someone who was killed could do that. *Did Kyne really kill him or was he mistaken?*

He darted out from the shadows the moment the coast was clear, coming quickly to the iron bars that Lioné had told him about. The disgusting stench hit his nostrils immediately and he fought a gag as he fumbled in his cloak pocket.

He wasn't sure if it would work but he couldn't think of anything better. Placing the suicide stone against the bar, he activated it and watched as the iron bars started to disintegrate falling down into the darkness. The wave continued until it reached the stone where the bars met, disintegrating part of it before the mortar broke away. It continued a few inches before slowing and then stopping, the aura depleted. He took a breath through his mouth, not wanting to smell the sewer beneath.

The gaping hole was short, only a few feet tall but he couldn't make out any details beyond it. He needed to know how deep it was before he proceeded but he couldn't be caught. Back tracking a bit, he ran to the edge of the street, coming to an old broken box and with a quick jerk, broke off a piece of wood, the end splintering into many jagged points.

A nearby lantern hung, casting its light around the street and as fast as he could, he ran at it and held the wood in the flame. Every second he was exposed in the orange light made his stomach tighten up more as he waited for the wood to catch. He was majorly exposed, visible from all ends of the street and he wanted nothing more than to be back in the shadows. No sentinels were around yet but it wouldn't last for long.

A small flame caught and then with a jerk he managed to get some of the lantern's oil to splash up on the wood strengthening the

The Legend of Kyne: Chronocide

flame. He took off, dashing back to gaping hole no one still seen in the street. The flame dangerously wavered from his running, and he slowed a bit saving it before it extinguished.

Coming to the hole and holding the wooden plank out he could see that it was only a few feet deep. A slow-moving river of sludge and grime lay centered in the hole three feet wide that he was in line with as it vanished through a hole underneath his feet. On either side of the river was a small stone curb just over a foot wide.

The sewer river continued on under the road directly beneath him and vanished into a dark hole, hidden from his gaze. He gagged again as he saw human excrement floating in the river.

Am I really going to do this? he thought as he stared down at it. *There must be another way to save that family.*

But he knew there wasn't. His entire journey to the sewer from their house was spent brainstorming ideas and nothing was going to work. If the sentinel wasn't seen alive, they were going to be the number one culprit.

He gagged again and was scanning his mind for any other options when sounds of sentinels caught his attention. He was kneeling down, the torch still tucked into the hole. His light was partially obscured, but he was still going to be noticed. Without a second thought he jumped down, landing on the small edging that lined the river. He could feel his boots slide in the grime that coated it and hating every part of his life, dropped to his chest and started to crawl forward vanishing into the tunnel with the torch held high in front of him.

It was short, less than two feet tall and an awkward height so that he had to crawl low to the ground. Each movement forward made him shudder and he tried to think of anything else as he felt the slime between his fingers. Up ahead he could see objects lay across the river, broken branches and other strange things that somebody had thrown down their toilets.

Small paw prints of rats dotted the rivers edging through the sludge, but he saw none of them as he pressed on. The water was moving so slowly that it almost looked still. *It shouldn't be too far away,* and he continued on, his breathing shallow and each inhale making him cringe at the thought of the particles going into his body.

The Legend of Kyne: Chronocide

I really could just let them be found, he thought, the enduring pain he was going through fueling his angry thoughts. *They might survive, if there's no body found.* But he knew that wouldn't be the case and he despised that he could even think that with everything in his body. They had sheltered the young dragon and risked their lives for her safety. If they were found they would be tortured and then executed, there was no doubt about that.

Up ahead after nearly two minutes of crawling through the sewage he finally saw a dark mass in the water, and he sped up. The glimmer of bronze caught the light of the torch and he saw the pale deathly face of a man as he floated upon his back in the river.

His hair was matted with brown slime and crusty flecks covered his skin, but Kioni imprinted his features in his mind instantly. Long face with a sharp jaw and a dimpled chin forming two lobes. His eyes were cloudy, but he was certain they were green as all the Gaeilians were.

He was quick, ripping the pieces of armor from his body and awkwardly placing them upon his own body, the sizzle of the torch as it rested on the ground instilling fear of being cast into darkness.

He jerked it up just as the flame nearly went out and held it deathly still watching the flames reignite the remaining oil. He breathed a slow sigh of relief as the flames strengthened casting light around. It wouldn't last forever, and he needed to be quick.

As he managed the last piece of armor, the strange bronze skirt pulled up around his waist, he took one final look upon the sentinel, holding the features in his mind and making sure he could remember them well enough and then the agonizing return journey began. Unable to turn around, he started crawling backwards, the torch still clutched in his hand and the grime coating his knees. His back occasionally scraped the roof, and he could feel old cobwebs brush his face.

They better be grateful! he thought angrily as his hand slipped out from underneath him causing him to crash cheek first into the grime. Nearly half an inch thick and moist like the slime from a snail, he slid his hand back underneath himself and pushed back up to the most comfortable position he could manage.

"Better be damn grateful!" he hissed as he continued on.

The Legend of Kyne: Chronocide

He knew they would be, they all seemed like good people but then his mind rested on the mother and his stomach tightened. She was different, uncaring like the rest and dangerous. She could still very well give up Rosé in an instant.

He sped up, thinking about the sentinels still searching the homes and fearful that he might not make it in time. In less time than it took to reach the sentinel, his speed fueled with fear he felt the pressure of the ceiling on his back lift up signaling he was back at the entrance. Kneeling up, nearly striking his head upon the stone he could hear the globs of sludge fall back to the ground and he shuddered again, continuing to breathe through his mouth and avoiding all of the scents.

Torchlight was seen and with a quick toss, he dropped his own into the sewage where it hissed casting him in darkness. Kioni stayed there, still as stone as he watched a party of sentinels jog past him, the clanking of their boots echoing around. They were only a few feet away and he lowered his head down more for fear of being seen.

It took a few minutes before the coast was clear enough that he could remove himself and as fast as he could while keeping the clanging of his armor down, he made his way back towards their home. It wasn't far but more and more sentinels were starting to appear, and it was getting harder to stay hidden.

The grime covered him from head to toe and mistakenly he breathed through his nose causing a gag hard enough to induce vomit. Curling up against the wall of a building, Kioni vomited again, and he shuddered at the revolting state he was in. Never in his life had he ever been so disgusting, and he wanted nothing more than to clean himself with molten metal.

He rounded the final corner and caught his breath as he saw a sentinel a few doors down from the family's home. One stood outside a door while the other ransacked the other Kydrëans' home, tearing it apart searching for the hatchling dragon.

He was out of time!

Unable to sneak around them without being seen, he had no other option. Focusing upon the face, he felt his body shift and he grew a few inches, fitting into the armor more snuggly as he took the form of the sentinel.

The Legend of Kyne: Chronocide

Approaching the homes, he saw the other sentinel draw their sword at his sight for a moment before lowering it as he came more into view.

"What the hell," he muttered, and his face recoiled at his sight. "What are you covered in? Tayvel is that you?" and he cocked his head.

Kioni nodded.

"I haven't seen you for days, we thought you were dead or something."

"Nope, very much alive," Kioni said in an unfamiliar voice, and he held his arms out gesturing to himself. "Want to die right about now though."

"What happened to you? Where have you been?"

"Sleeping with women, having a merry time these last few days until that screaming. I was looking for the dragon when the home just next door was acting very suspicious. Those Kydrëans I'm always lugging around. I hate them! When I got near their waste system, they started acting funny, so I decided to look through it. The ground collapsed and I fell into their septic hole. Just disgusting!" he muttered, and he flicked some grime to the ground. "I lost my helm and obviously had to take it out on them."

"You lost your helm?" they gasped. "You are going to be in so much trouble."

"I am not going back to dig through that vile filth," Kioni replied.

"Did you find anything?" the sentinel said, cringing as more sludge dripped from Kioni's armor.

"Just some alcohol, some old fancy kind they kept hidden," Kioni muttered, thinking of the first thing that came to mind.

"And you took it obviously," said the sentinel, a sort of glee in his eye. "Drank it in front of the Kydrs as you beat them."

"Dumped it in the tank just to spite them. I was so pissed I didn't even think to drink it."

"Tayvel!" he cried out. "That was serious stupidity."

"What do you expect when you're covered in this," and he flicked even more grime off. "I'm beyond pissed."

"Go clean yourself off then. I am sure Captain Vira will understand your minor absence."

The Legend of Kyne: Chronocide

"I really doubt that," chuckled the other sentinel as he came to the doorway. "She is not an understanding person in the slightest. It would be best if she didn't find out at all. She's going to be so mad about your helm."

Kioni watched the man take off his own helm, his face covered in a thin fuzz of hair. He was young, younger than himself by a good margin of years with a big grin on his face.

"Nice to see you brought down a few pegs though. This is just a fantastic scene that I will be telling so many people about."

Kioni shook his head in annoyance and turned to walk away.

"Don't go to the barracks, your filth will make them disgusting. Go use the excess water we have for the animals. The well is just up the street."

Kioni nodded and started off. As he passed by the home that he knew contained the dragon, he stopped unsure if the other sentinels were still going to check it.

With a glance out of the corner of his eye to make sure the others were watching him, he took a breath and spit upon the door, coating the wood in grime. He turned and walked away, smiling slightly knowing that they wouldn't be checking that home, his current condition convincing them otherwise.

37. The Host of Windra

Kioni shuddered as he stepped quickly down the street, the vivid memories of the vile grime that coated his flesh still haunting him. He was much cleaner now, after a labor-intensive scrubbing in an animal trough. He got a few stares from passing sentinels but none seemed to bother him. A few stopped to gawk at him, jeering at his sullied skin and pride.

The sun had begun lighting up the early morning sky sending first shades of lightening blue followed by streaks of orange and gold through the hazy sky. He was a few streets away from the home when the two sentinels from before rounded a corner. He continued on at a quicker pace hoping to stay away from them, but his heart sank when he heard the name called that he knew to be the sentinel he was impersonating.

"Much cleaner Tayvel," one called with a laugh. "Can still smell you from here though."

He actually believed him though. He still reeked of defecation and decay, a combo that would be hard to get rid of completely. He needed real soap and something that could scrape his skin more intensely than his hands could. Molten metal was still in his mind, maybe it would do the trick.

As the sentinels approached, he could see quite obviously that there was no way he was going to get away from them without acting suspicious. Slowing his steps, he eventually came to a stop.

"Wow he really does reek Findel," the other sentinel said, his face expressing the smells he was enduring. "God you really need a bath."

"Just nasty," the first said chiming in. "The real showers are back up in the guardhouse, you're not going to just traipse through the rest of the day like that right?"

Kioni was silent, unsure of how he should act. The few things he had heard them say describing his persona was mostly that he was cruel.

"Speaking of which, why are you going back that way? Don't you remember that if we were not to find the target then we were to head back for further instruction at dawn?"

Kioni was still silent, his pulse quickening at the thought of them finding out. Even though he knew he was shielded he felt so incredibly exposed.

"I bet he's heading back to teach those Kydrëans another lesson, would expect nothing less from him," the second sentinel said.

"That's true Armon," and he turned back towards Kioni. "If you kill them, I won't tell."

"Wouldn't expect you to," Kioni muttered embracing the perceived persona. "But killing them ends the fun. I more of wanted to instill a bit of fear. Give them anxiety the rest of the day."

Before they could answer, a quick rumbling sounded and a massive nyloc dashed from the rooftops to the street nearby, a rider holding onto a saddle upon its back.

"First light, that was the orders," the rider called in a feminine voice before the creature darted around them rushing up the streets towards the citadel.

"Well, that ruins that fun for you," Findel muttered. "We better head back, don't want her getting all pissy."

Kioni's gaze lingered on the house for a long moment, the doorway tilted slightly from when he had busted it in earlier. Many of the other homes that were all connected down the line had items strewn about, doors broken to splinters and pieces of glass sparkling in the morning light.

I can't go back now, it would be too noticeable and even if I could get away, these two will know where I went drawing more attention to them. I will need to find a different way.

Turning away from the home, he reluctantly followed in step with them, slightly back and to the side keeping both of them in his vision at all times. Both wore a helmet but underneath he could see that each had dark brown hair and only Findel had a beard which was more fuzz than anything. They were both looking to be in their early twenties, younger than he was by a ways but each carried themselves with a confidence that could only be of someone who was a soldier.

"So, I still don't understand where you have been the last day," Armon said.

"Yeah, seems weird," Findel added.

"Like I said before, doing some personal business," Kioni said with a chuckle trying to keep up the charade.

"And your helm, I can't believe you lost it. You're out of uniform."

"I lost it looking for the dragon."

"She really won't like that," Armon muttered under his breath. "You know our orders. While we are stationed in this country every day is a working day in which we keep our armor on at all times. Only scheduled free days are different in the rarity that we have them. She is going to have your head."

"Perhaps," Kioni said shrugging. Inside he was beyond nervous but how he was acting seemed to be what these two sentinels were expecting. "I guess we will see."

"I guess so," Armon said, and they continued on, traveling up the street with other sentinels appearing around them. There were hundreds of them, all dressed in their armor, most of their features hidden beneath their helms but Kioni could tell he was getting strange looks as they all progressed up towards the citadel. Where the inner wall came together around the entrance to the courtyard a large building lay like a massive joint built into the wall.

The guards keep.

Kioni turned his head to say some smart remark back to Armon when he ran straight into something. Startled, he turned back to see a fist flying at his face and before he could move it struck him square on the cheek sending stars through his sight.

Staggering back, he clutched at his cheek, the metallic taste of blood filling his mouth from the split in his flesh from the impact of his teeth against his cheek. His assailant had left their arm held out from the strike for a moment, dark eyes piercing at him as they held a long stare.

The figure was dressed in golden armor, bracers covering their forearms, each wrapped tightly around the silky white sleeve of their shirt. The metal was thin, imprinted with swirls and other aesthetic patterns and the color reminiscent of heitrite. Similar greaves were noticed upon the figure's lower legs, bringing their baggier pants to a tight tapering before meeting their leather shoes.

Kioni couldn't make out many features, their mouth and nose obscured by a white silk mask while a white hood was concealed their hair before draping over their shoulder plating to a cape behind their back. Every piece of silky white fabric that covered them was edged with golden thread, even the front of the hood had been ornately stitched, attaching a thin sheet of golden armor plating at its front in an arrow point just over their forehead.

Kioni lowered his hand from his cheek, the raging pain dulling to a constant ache as he stared the figure down.

"Touch me again and you'll die Gaeilian," spoke a feminine voice as the figure stared at him, her dark eyes unblinking.

Kioni didn't speak and after a moment, she turned on her heel and walked away, her cape trailing after her.

"Smart move messing with the mercs," muttered Findel. "You really are not having a good day."

"Mercs?" Kioni repeated, the moment it left his lips his mind cursing at the stupid question. To his relief, however, Findel didn't seem to care much about it.

"Mercenaries of Windra. Keep getting loads of them daily. It looks like He really wants to continue pressing into the continent. More soldiers for his war machine. I really dislike it though, sure it's better than us Gaeilians dying in the battles. Send the mercenaries instead. It's when they start giving the mercenaries places of status by mixing them into our own ranks."

"Defeats the purpose of paid soldiers if they're not on the front lines." Armon muttered. "Doesn't sit right with me in the slightest."

The two sentinels continued their conversation with Kioni's mind wandering back to the figure from before. *Mercenaries being hired into the Dominion? If He is Aaldra then I wouldn't put it past him. Use foreign bodies to conquer your enemies.*

The thronging sentinels all pressed on, growing closer together as they shuffled through the archways before finally stepping out into a large room with a raised dais against the far wall. Sentinels filed in, separating into different rows in front of it as a few figures walked up its steps.

Drawing in line with the other sentinels, Kioni looked up and watched as someone approached the center of the dais. A man, jet black hair stretching down to where his neck met his shoulders and a trimmed beard that matched. His arms were tucked behind his back and his face carrying a cold and deadly confidence as he surveyed the sentinels with one piercing green eye, the other split by a large scar and faded to a milky white.

Shjilo, of course its freaking Shjilo. I thought I would never have to see his damned face again after Kyne and Ni'Bara dropped him.

"Where is the hatchling," he said calmly as he surveyed the few hundred sentinels in the room. The room was silent as he looked around for a long moment. "Don't all of you speak at once. I would believe that at least one of you would've found something, anything that could point us in the direction to find it?"

Again silence.

"So, no one then? Not one of you found a single scale, a fleeting mention of a dragon?" He turned his head looking at the others who stood behind him upon the dais before returning his gaze, a deep fire lit behind his eyes.

"Not one of you!" he roared. "Not a single one of you lousy sentinels found anything? And you wonder why He has invited the Host of Windra here with us. If you cannot complete this little task, then how do we expect to push our empire further inland? The eastern countries will not just lay down and be overtaken! I just..." his voice trailed off for a moment. "Get out! The lot of you, your captains will deal with you!" and without another word, he vanished through a doorway leaving the silent room behind.

"Dumb bastard," muttered Armon. "So sick of him, all he ever does is make our lives a living hell. It would be nice if he got transferred."

"Or murdered," chuckled Findel darkly.

Armon gasped at his words and Kioni snickered a smile at his words. Shjilo was a terrible person, and he felt the same way.

The Legend of Kyne: Chronocide

"Shh, they might hear you," Armon whispered.

"They won't hear me," Findel replied casually before gesturing around at the cacophony of sounds as sentinels all separated into their grouping. Some were being shuffled outside for more room while others had already started to be yelled at by their captains.

Armon took a deep breath, the look of panic still in his eyes but fading away as he surveyed the scene.

It was far too loud for anyone to hear him unless they were right there as they had been. Deep inside, Kioni despised these people, the horrors and chaos that they had caused but just for a fleeting moment he had a small liking for these two, especially because of their distaste with Shjilo.

"We should get moving," groaned Armon. "She will not take a liking to us being late."

"I wouldn't take a liking to her punishments," added Findel and the two started walking away, Kioni right behind them.

Hopefully I am part of their squad, he thought as he followed, pushing through the thronging crowd. *It would explain more why they seem to know me.*

The further on they went the more certain he was as they pushed past the dais towards an open door. A sentinel was there and as they passed, he nodded at each of them, staring at Kioni for a moment longer.

Does he know? There is no way...

"Where is your helm?" barked the sentinel grabbing Kioni's attention.

"I... I lost it," he stammered to which the sentinel rolled his green eyes in exasperation.

He didn't press on as Kioni walked through the doorway into a short hallway with a staircase at its end.

"You're an embarrassment," muttered Armon. "She is going to be so pissed."

"She might not notice," Findel added but Kioni remained silent as they all stepped up the staircase as it spiraled tightly leading them up to the top of the guards keep. Sconces lay, quenched of their flame but the thin windows that occasionally were seen on the north wall let in enough light to see.

The Legend of Kyne: Chronocide

Up ahead he could see more brightness and just as his legs started to burn from the ascent, he stepped out onto the flat expanse that covered the roof of Guard's Keep. The inner wall stretched out on either side with their battlements casting long shadows from the early morning rays.

Up ahead at the center of the square platform a group of sentinels were all lined up, facing away from them in two rows.

Kioni counted twelve including themselves as they drew into the back line of six, all of them facing the citadel with their captain in front.

She was a tall woman, not beautiful but not ugly with short hair that didn't even cover her ears. Her eyes bore a deep hate for everything this world contained, and Kioni could see them drill upon him immediately as he drew in line.

"Where the hell is your helm," she snarled, her voice carrying a malice that few could match.

"Told you she would notice," muttered Armon quietly.

"I lost it searching for the dragon."

"You lost it?" She repeated in a mix between a gasp of disbelief and a tone to mock a child.

Kioni nodded and without saying another word, the captain approached, flanking around the line and coming to him who stood at the end of the second row.

Drawing her face close to his she stared at him for a moment before her expression changed to that of disgust.

"You smell like..."

"Feces Ma'am," Kioni muttered, well aware of his scent.

"I would've said shit but sure, we can go with feces," and she took a step back. "Swimming in the swine pen it seems like?"

"Floor collapsed in a waste system while I was searching for the hatchling."

"So, your helm is in the toilet then?" she asked, her tone flat.

He nodded.

"She shook her head, her eyes flashing anger but her voice remained flat.

"You know the consequences for losing your helm Tayvel. I could have you executed for treason."

The Legend of Kyne: Chronocide

"Treason?" he asked in disbelief. "How is that treason?"

"Did I say you could speak!' She spat. "Treason because by taking off your helm while on duty it is perceived that your private life is more important than the Dominion. You more than took off your helm, you lost it which is magnitudes worse!"

"You can't be serious," Kioni argued, her flat tone irritating him. His anger had grown, and he could feel the tingles from the adrenaline of arguing with her flooding his abdomen.

"So, you continue to speak out of line and argue with a superior which is also known as insubordination. That could get you sent to the work camps for the remainder of your short life."

Kioni shook his head in annoyance which only seemed to anger her. He started to realize might actually be a good thing.

"I'm done," she hissed, and she spun on her heel. "Take him away, I think the mines in Loke' Ynen will be a good fit for him," and two sentinels spun around from the front line and two quick jabs to his stomach and cheek brought him gasping to his knees. His mind was hazy for a moment, but he felt himself jerked up to his feet before he was dragged away, not resisting in the slightest.

He was dragged down the stairs and as they reached the bottom a quick shove knocked him off balance and he crashed into the wall, the armor clanging all around.

"He reeks," muttered one of the sentinels.

"Move!" Ordered the other and he was forced on, moving through a few different winding halls before he was brought to an open area with a carriage. Two horses were attached by one sentinel while the other forced Kioni to undress into just his undergarments, the faded cloth stained a yellowy brown from the sewage. The sentinels face contorted with disgust and Kioni grinned at that.

The armor was left in a pile and once the horses were attached, the sentinel pushed Kioni up and into the open carriage where he took a seat. Two benches lined the sides of the carriage and Kioni sat on one while the sentinel sat on the other. The second sentinel sat at the head of the carriage and with a command guided the horses forward where they started to make their way down into the city heading for the archway that led in and out.

"The captain should've just killed you there for the

The Legend of Kyne: Chronocide

insubordination." spat the sentinel. "You'll be joining the other workers shortly and then you'll all be transported to the mines where you can live out the rest of your pitiful life."

Kioni shrugged which only seemed to anger him, but he didn't continue speaking. The carriage rumbled down the street, making its way down toward the wall where they passed out into the outer city. Shops lined the street, most nearly empty with the few Kydrëans selling goods, always accompanied by a sentinel.

He could see a few different shops selling ragged tunics and other forms of clothing. Adjusting in his seat, he knew he had to act soon.

The shops were decrepit little things, old rotting wood and grime coating what still stood. The Kydrëans didn't look to be doing much better, thin and sickly. Young men and women looked dozens of years older, their hair matted and greying from stress and undernourishment. Kioni watched as a sentinel came to a shop they were passing, taking a bite out of the bread before chuckling and dropping it. He then spit the piece in his mouth on the ground commenting on how it was too dry. The shopkeepers were shocked and angered but said nothing as they watched the bread smashed into the ground under his boot.

More groups of people were traveling on the road, mostly cargo carriages led by sentinels, but he did start to notice more and more of the Windra. All of them wore the same white hood adorned with golden accents and each had a long glaive. They spoke little, their accents thick when they talked. Looking around for any opening, he grit his teeth. He would have to act quickly. A group of Windra walked past led by a sentinel. By the looks of it they seemed to be new recruits, brought in to fuel their war machine.

An idea struck through Kioni's head, and he watched for a final opportunity.

There!

Without warning, he leapt out of the carriage to the cries of shock from his escorts. Dashing around a corner just out of view he grabbed a hold of some new clothing before taking off as fast as he could down an alleyway. A quick glance over his shoulder signaled they were after him, but he turned out of their line of sight just before they were able to fire their crossbows.

Stripping down to the nude, he plowed into a throng of people to their cries of shock at his sight and in the chaos managed to place on the trousers and shirt. Pushing through to the other side he ripped into another alleyway just as he used the Cloth of Concealment, changing his face to another Gaeilian he had seen in the city, not a sentinel but one of those who had moved to the new land.

Stopping his running, he fell in line with a group making their way towards the wall when his escorts burst forth, looks of confusion upon their face as they tried to search for him. He hid his panting as they swung their heads back and forth before continuing on leaving him far behind. A smile spread across his face.

Following the crowd, he migrated back up within the city walls, a few dozen feet behind the group of Windra. His mind was racing as he thought of different options on how to proceed.

He couldn't show his own face, something inside told him that would be a mistake. He contemplated taking the face of a Windra but the more he watched them the more he thought against it. He was familiar with the Gaeilian accent, able to mimic it easily but the Windra's was new, and it would prove very difficult.

He pressed on, making his way towards the home in which Rosé hid. He could figure it out later, in the meantime, he would see what things she knew and if they could piece any of the puzzle pieces together.

Shouting drew his attention, and he watched a flock of sentinels sprint past, their blades drawn and shouting. More were rushing after them and he could feel a panic rising in his chest at the thought of the young dragon being found. Taking a few steps as he accelerated, he suddenly came to a stop, noticing that none of them were running toward the home. They were all migrating up towards the streets around the citadel where he had arrived. She was hidden in the lower half of the city just a few streets over.

Something was happening!

* * *

38. Looking Over the Precipice

"Why can't you remember me!" screamed an elderly woman as she beat her hands upon the chest of an older man of similar age, each thump echoing across the street as she repeatedly struck him. His face was littered with a dazed confusion as he stared down upon the woman.

Her hair was undone, messy in white waves and tears were beginning to stream down her cheeks as she cried out again.

"I am your wife! What is wrong with you?"

Akami watched in intrigue as she and the other Kitsune guided their horses down the street past the couple. She couldn't draw her eyes away from it, looking beyond the curve of her hood as it tucked in around her face obscuring her from view. The woman dropped to her knees sobbing uncontrollably and the man, as if with no regards to anything in the whole world simply turned from her and walked away. Others in the street, a few children and other adults all were staring in shock at the scene that was unfolding.

The woman continued to sob for a moment before a passing child drew a little too close to her.

"Addi," she called out as if recognizing the boy. "Tell me you remember who I am?"

The child, a boy in his early teens leapt away from her in shock and fear. Calls from his mother nearby drew his attention and for a moment he turned back to face the woman kneeling upon the road.

"I don't know who you are, leave us alone!" and he ran away.

Akami let her gaze return back, tracing the road in its arc as it wound its way through the sea of buildings towards the citadel high up on the hill. She had seen this before, with others on their travels in Kydrëa. Loved ones forgetting family and other strange things.

The Legend of Kyne: Chronocide

Honestly, she didn't care much, didn't care at all for these Kydrëans that she was passing.

Each of them, from the youngest child to the oldest was an enemy to them, their existence threatening everything her people stood for. She could see it, the disgust upon her sister's face as she turned around to see her, her fiery red hair peeking through her hood for a moment before she averted her gaze.

Alakyne was in shambles with nearly no guards protecting the walls. They had heard rumors that the king had fled since the cataclysm had happened and Akami snickered at the thought. *A king who flees at the first sign of threat? It seems comical that someone like him could've truly fought back the Gaeilians. I find this whole country bothersome in the highest sense.*

Skirting around the splintered remains of an old caravan, its contents pillaged long before they arrived, the four Kitsune led the group, Akami bringing up the rear. She could see the faint haze, the trail that she knew to be her target Kioni as they had been following it for days now.

The sky was shattered, massive cracks spreading out all around them disrupting the very fabric of reality. Like a pane of glass, their world was unstable, and anything caught within the cracks was destroyed immediately.

She rounded a building with a jagged distortion coming into view. Its edges sharp as a knife and pulsating with unfamiliar power. It had pierced through the building, tearing through the walls before plunging into the ground where it vanished deep from sight. She could see through it, making out the other side in a rippling light as if looking up through the surface of a river into the sky. Wooden beams and a door had been caught in it, cutting clean through them leaving a smooth and flat surface up against the edge of the crack. She traced the line up through the building and into the sky where it joined other fractures before migrating up to the even larger ones.

It almost looks like a bolt of lightning frozen in time, she thought as she traced it even further. She could see the largest of the cracks all seemed to start high up in the sky, centering from the glowing column of power. She could feel the air, the energy that seemed to hover over the area and it made her skin crawl.

The Legend of Kyne: Chronocide

Shouting drew her attention back and she watched as a Kitsune by the name of Yu backhand some vagrant who had drawn too close to her horse. Her hood shifted over her face and a flash of the same scarlet hair was seen that matched her sisters. He stumbled back for but a moment before gasping at her sight and lifting a shaking finger up.

Akami could feel the aura before it happened and with a crack like the sound of a whip, the man was hurled backwards as if struck by the hand of a giant. Slamming into a wall, he slumped over unmoving, blood pooling down his neck onto his shoulders and his eyes glazed.

Akami furrowed her brow unimpressed with the whole ordeal. She watched as her sister guided her horse up towards Yu before a fierce exchange of words occurred. She could hear only bits and pieces but the more she heard the more irritated she became.

Nahonian words, not Kydrëan, she thought as they continued on for a moment. She had noticed people drawing into the street to watch their progress and she fiddled with her hood pulling it up tighter around her face.

Little good that'll do now that the whole city knows we are here, she thought, and she glared towards the Kitsune who led in front. The highest most skilled of her people and yet they could be so foolish. *Pathetic, it sickens me to even be seen with them. Our interests are the only thing keeping this alliance at all stable, the moment that's over it all comes crashing down.*

She slowed her horse as the others in front had done and came up to join them. She didn't say a word, just listened as Hayame spoke first.

"His trail leads off towards the citadel, but it looks to have come back this way, overlapping for a moment before continuing on." She pointed a finger towards the crumbling remains of a toppled building, the beam of energy stretching straight through it. "It looks like he went that way,"

"Obviously he went that way Hayame. Honestly, you act like we are children and it's getting old," one of the Kitsune said, a thin taller woman, her hair the same fox red. Her eyes were dark, almost lifeless and her voice carried the same monotonous tone that seemed to match. "We are only in this mess because of you. Don't forget that.

The Legend of Kyne: Chronocide

Kitsune is a way of life, don't think that just because you lead our tail of the order currently that we can't end your reign whenever we like."

Hayame's mouth seemed to drop open and Akami stifled a laugh.

"Is that a threat Mizu?" Hayame asked darkly.

"Only if it needs to be," Mizu replied cocking her head to the side and yawning. A strand of red hair dropped out from beneath her hood, and she seemed intrigued by it, her eyes darting over to the lock for a moment before returning her gaze back to Hayame. "You are no leader to me."

Hayame was silent for a moment before she urged her horse forward. Without a word, she trotted away heading towards the collapsed building. Yu followed with the other two Kitsune silent for a moment. Mizu groaned as she looked at Suka and then they followed with Akami bringing up the rear just as before. She was grinning under her hood, nearly laughing at what had occurred. The humiliation her sister was enduring was delightful and with it brought her own humility down a bit from her encounter with Kioni.

She for a moment almost forgot the look on his face as he rode away, her mouth dry and caked with dirt and the thumping of the hare's feet upon the road. She almost forgot the rage that had followed.

Almost.

Following along, Hayame led them towards the building, and they could all feel the strange sensation growing stronger. The stone building, built with bricks and mortar and cracked in many places, its walls falling apart into piles of grey rubble seemed to hardly be standing. Like an empty cracked eggshell, it lay delicately upon the ground waiting for the faintest breeze to finish the job.

Dismounting her own horse with the others, they tied them up nearby and scanned the area. More people, nearly a dozen were all looking at them. None seemed to be Kydrëan guards but that didn't mean that they couldn't do any harm. Turning back, she noticed Hayame was already pushing through the building, skirting around the broken walls as if she were walking around stalactites as she vanished from sight.

The crunching of stone upon stone was heard as Akami placed

The Legend of Kyne: Chronocide

her foot down gingerly, lightly stepping over the precipice of the building and cast into the shadows it held.

The building was lying on its side, large and littered with broken rooms. They made their way deeper into the building, pushing over broken debris. The doorway was horizontal and lifted off the ground from the angle of the building and with a light hop and a thrust of her arms, she launched herself over it to the other side.

She could smell it before she saw it, the putrid stench of a rotting corpse. Down underneath her feet and the stone, she could see the mottled grey arm and torso of a man, his body crushed from the weight of the building. Nearly flattened, she grimaced at the sight of him, turning away. She didn't feel sorry for him, not one bit. It was his problem why he was there in the first place, not hers. The only problem she had was the pain he was causing her with his disgusting stench. She continued on, stepping over him and following the others around the last wall before coming into sight of their target.

Ghostly white, glowing with an inner light, a massive white barrier of energy lay before them. The walls of the building reached it before vanishing into the light. It pulsated with power, strange magic that seemed to make her skin crawl.

Akami skirted around the others who were all staring at it intrigued. Her back pressed against the wall; she sidestepped not taking her eyes off of it. Making her way around, she darted her eyes back and forth looking for any sign of Kioni's trail. The white light made it hard to see but she could just make out the haze, hovering delicately in the air before it vanished into the beam.

"What is this," Akami said to herself under her breath as she delicately reached out a hand to touch its surface before hesitating. As she lowered her hand down movement nearby caught her attention and she turned to see Hayame had drawn up to the sphere.

It was large, nearly twenty feet in diameter as it carved its shape through the building's horizontal walls and cracking floors and its surface was covered in a swirly white glow. Akami watched as her sister mimicked what she had done, this time not hesitating but reaching out and touching it.

Her hand vanished into the light and for a moment, she feared the worst as her sister grew still. The other Kitsune joined her and with

The Legend of Kyne: Chronocide

a nod they all reached their hands up and touched it as she had done. As the final Kitsune's hand vanished into the light they all turned their gaze towards her and waited as if expecting her to join.

Reluctantly she reached her hand up. Her pulse quickened and she could feel her breath speed up as she gingerly reached out. She didn't want to touch it at all. If it was anything like the shattered cracks, then she could easily lose her hand but the others were quite comfortable and so she reached out.

Passing over the boundary, she watched her hand vanish beyond and then a strange sensation came over her. Almost as if her senses had been amplified, she wiggled her fingers and could feel everything from her joints grinding against their padded cushions deep inside to the muscle vibrations rushing up her fingers into her hand. The sensation intensified and all of them simultaneously stepped into the sphere vanishing from sight.

39. Welcome to the New World

A flash of light lit up her eyes for but a moment before it was gone, replaced by the grey of stone bricks. A wall lay spread out right in front of her, cast in a faint light from somewhere unseen. She could just make out the silhouettes of the other women who had joined her and she turned around. The barrier of light was gone, replaced by what she assumed to be the missing cylinder of the building it had carved out.

Shouting was heard before any of the others had even had a chance to speak and then she felt a rush of pain across her back as she was struck by a hard object knocking her down on the ground. Cries of pain tore from her mouth as she grasped at her shoulder before rolling to the side just as an iron bar was slammed into the ground next to her head.

More shouting and then a crash as aura was used, tearing a chunk out of the building wall and bright sunlight cut through the darkness. Flashes of bronze lit up around the figure in front of her and then she noticed his eyes beneath his helm. The splitting emerald green.

There were other attackers, three more all spread out around. Yu and Suka had been knocked to the ground as Mizu was with Hayame panting heavily.

Akami stared out into the sun strewn city. The pain in her back was intense, clouding her mind but she focused on the man who had struck her. He turned his gaze, his distraction fading away as he stared at her upon the ground. In his hand he clutched a metal rod nearly a foot and a half in length with a leather wrapped handle. Upon its end lay a small metallic sphere and from the pain in her back she could almost feel its imprint upon her flesh.

His face was flat, almost inhuman as he lingered his gaze upon her for a moment. She watched him trace her shape as she lay upon the floor before returning to her eyes, his nose turned up in disgust.

"Damn easterners," he cursed before swinging his mace, aiming straight for her head.

Akami's breath was caught in her throat, shocked at what was occurring. Her mind blank, unable to think straight as she watched his arms swing around, the rod rapidly approaching.

A rush of air suddenly tore past her ripping her hair around wildly as the man was lifted off his feet in a swirling mass. Twisting around as he increased in speed, she could see his arms struggling before stretching out wildly as he was unable to hold them back. The clang of metal sounded as the rod was torn from his grip and the wind intensified, speeding him up until his figure was but a blur. Muffled screams came from him, but most were lost to the wind as he twirled around.

Hayame was there, her hands up and her narrow eyes focused upon the spell as she thrashed his body around in a tornado of wind for another few seconds before lowering her arms and ending the spell. They met eyes for but a moment before Hayame looked away, returning to the other Kitsune who were fighting the other attackers. Flashes of light from aural attacks followed by screams as men in bronze armor were torn apart or crushed into globs of flesh rang around as Akami scrambled to her feet, her back aching and the tears on the edge of her eyes threatening to spill.

Her back screamed in pain, battered and bruised by the hard strike and each movement made her want to fall to the ground, but she pushed on as she approached the man who had struck her. She could feel her rage replace the pain and lifting her hand up she muttered "Kitala," causing the rod to rush towards the palm of her hand.

She imagined it, the absolute pain she would cause this man as she bashed him repeatedly. She would make him suffer for striking her.

For striking royalty! her mind roared as she took the final step before she raised her arm up. His face was dark purple, his eyes the red of blood and popped partially out of his skull in a glazed milky green. Mouth open and his tongue hanging limply between his teeth, she could see it bleeding and engorged with blood turning a sickly purple.

She was pissed beyond belief as she dropped the rod to the ground where it clattered loudly against the stone. The bastard was already dead, his brain probably turned to mush from the spinning force.

"Akami!"

Turning around, she watched Yu and Suka duck around a large blade before Suka kicked out colliding with the man's knee and Yu leapt up upon his chest. Hooking her legs around his neck she whipped her head around knocking him off balance as she twirled around in an arcing motion before diving down. Planting her hands upon the floor, she jerked him off his feet and sent him tumbling to the ground where his armor clanged loudly upon the stone ground. Two flashes of light followed and then he was still as more men began to clamber into the tight space.

Hayame was nearby, gesturing for Yu to join her and with a synchronized attack, they tore more of the building apart allowing more light and more space for fighting. The sky was not a beautiful azure but a disgusting haze that caused even nearby buildings to have their visual details muffled. The sun above seemed more of a darker orange as its light struggled to pierce through the veil.

The wall groaned and then pieces of stone started to rain down to the ground. The whole building shuddered as it struggled to remain in one piece, the only thing seeming to keep it in place was the wooden support beams that were starting to bend dangerously.

A crack sounded and dust fell down coating Akami's hair as the wood snapped. More wood started to snap and as fast as she could she dashed out of the crumbling building followed by her sister and the three others.

Any guards remaining in the building were gone from sight, enveloped in a cloud of stone and dust as the building was reduced to a large pile.

Akami spun around just as movement was heard and before she could even think she cried out "Kaiodin!"

A man in the same bronze armor was nearly upon her, blade

just inches from her neck and the veins bulging in his exposed forearms. His legs were adorned with an armored skirt that reached just past his knees and upon his breastplate lay a symbol that she had only seen in books. The angled double triangular shape of the Dominion of Gaeil.

"A sentinel!" she exclaimed as she looked upon the frozen man. "Erodath!" she spat, launching the sentinel back away from her as she whipped around launching another attack. The ball of aura smashed into the man less than a second after he collided with another sentinel engulfing them both in a flash of light followed by a deep boom that shook the ground.

Dozens more were approaching rapidly, crossbows drawn, and she watched as they all spread out taking cover and aiming at them. Yu and Hayame were distracted but the other two Kitsune were quick and in unison they both touched the ground with their hand using their aura to draw up a sheet of stone forming a wall just as the bolts flew.

Bursting through the other side, they watched as the broadheads pierced through it as the bolts were lodged halfway through the stone before stopping, covering the wall in hundreds of spines like the quills of a hedgehog.

"We have to get away from here!" shouted Hayame, gathering their attention. "There are too many of them to fight off like this. We can't risk it!"

"If we don't catch Kioni then we are all as good as dead!" screamed Mizu before she wrapped her arm around the edge of the wall launching an attempt of an attack towards the bowmen.

"If we die here, it won't matter anyways!" Hayame retorted. "Go! Now!"

Two sentinels had run around the corner with their blades sailing, catching Mizu off guard. She leapt out of the way of a strike before the second sentinel collided with her arm severing it off just below the elbow.

They all stared in shock as blood oozed from her stump for but a moment before the sentinel's sword clattered to the ground as he grabbed a hold of her shoulders. With a roar, the man heaved her up and slammed her back against the stone bolt covered wall as hard as he could.

The Legend of Kyne: Chronocide

Bolts burst through her chest littering her abdomen and breast with the bloodied tipped broadheads. She coughed hard as blood pooled in the cracks of her teeth; her fire red hair matted with forming clots.

The sentinel held her there for a long moment before withdrawing and to their horror, she hung there upon the wall, suspended by the six bolts that pierced through her.

Suka was upon him in an instant, and fueled with rage, she struck him down with a flash of lighting and then the other followed.

More coughing followed and a groan before the suspended Kitsune's head dropped down limply signaling her death. More flashes of light from flying attacks filled the air and Suka was soon breathing heavily, a pile of bodies around them.

"I think I got them," she panted heavily, a look of fatigued joy upon her face before her eyes widened and a blade burst from her chest. The world seemed to pause for a long moment as blood formed upon her mouth. She was tossed roughly to the ground, peeling from the blade with a sickening slurp and landing with a dull thud, a sentinel left smiling at them.

"Inferiority! Your people will soon feel our will easterners!"

"Come on!" screamed Hayame and she took off running with Yu.

Akami's stomach turned at the sight of Suka dying on the ground and Mizu suspended against the wall. Just as she turned to look away, a silvery glob of tar struck her in the foot, rooting her to the ground. Two more globs followed climbing up her leg before an intense electrifying pain racked through her body. She could feel her aura rapidly draining and more globs of tar flew, striking the others of her group stopping them mid stride. It swelled and churned, climbing and spreading over her body as it drained more of her power. She could feel it upon her neck and then her mouth. She couldn't breathe let alone cry out in pain as another pulse of pain racked her body.

The last thing she saw was the sight of a dark-haired man looking at her from a short distance away, a glob of tar in his hand before it was hurled at her covering her eyesight and casting her into darkness.

40. Let Us See If You Remember Who You Are

The sound of iron grinding upon iron rang around, rousing Akami from her dazed state. Her mind was foggy, overcast like a storm cloud covering the sun above. She groaned, rolling over on her side when she felt bindings grow tight around her wrists.

Her mind sharpened for a moment at the realization, and she tugged harder feeling them cinch tighter around her wrists. Looking down she noticed a fancy knot had been tied, binding her wrists together before reaching out and linking to the frame of the bed. She pulled again, this time slower and watched as the rope tightened through the knot putting more pressure upon her wrists and she stopped before it became too tight. As she released the tension, she didn't feel the rope loosen but rather it stayed tight.

Where am I, she thought and then she remembered the sound and jerked her head around to see a lone figure quietly observing her. He was of similar age; short golden hair lay flat against his head, and he was dressed in dark robes. His face was cast in shadow, silhouetted from the torchlight behind him but with a wave of his hand an aural light appeared showing her who he was.

She had seen his face before, studied it for years as her mother had instructed. The archmage of Kydrëa, the single most dangerous person who could stop their plans. Kyne.

She stared at him in shock as he seemed different than she had remembered him to be.

His skin was paler and his arms thin, as if he had never wielded a blade. The thing that was most striking to her however was his eyes, golden as she remembered but with a deep darkness behind

The Legend of Kyne: Chronocide

them that made her skin crawl.

"You're different than the others," he muttered as her figure was illuminated by his light.

Akami said nothing but instead readjusted herself on the bed, making sure to not pull upon her bindings for fear of tightening them. With success, she managed to sit up, guiding the length of rope between her feet where she noticed they had been similarly bound.

Unimpressed with her current situation, she went to use her aura to cut the bindings, but shock followed as she for some reason couldn't remember the words.

Kyne smirked as he watched her focusing on her bindings for a long moment before she turned back towards him. Her hair was a mess, knotted and ragged from her capture and she shook her head to the side swinging a few locks out of her face.

"No aural use for you easterner," he muttered when she met his gaze and his smirk lingered for a moment as a look of confusion spread across her face.

"How did you…"

"No concern of yours at the moment I'm afraid," he muttered waving his hand and her mouth clamped shut by his aura. "Your main concern should be doing whatever you can to remain alive. We have already killed two of you and the others… Well maybe you will be more reasonable than they were."

She struggled under his hold for a moment, her jaw quivering under the stress as it tried to open but his spell held fast for a long moment as he stared down at her.

"You resemble one of them," he muttered, and he took a step to the side, not lifting his gaze from her. "Family perhaps?"

The spell released and she gasped in relief.

"My sister," she replied slowly. "Is she alive?"

"For now," he said. "She needs to have some manners. All of you Kitsune are so… Irate."

"Just them not me. Not a Kitsune myself and I wonder, why they would be pissed? Perhaps being knocked unconscious? The others of our group brutally murdered perhaps?"

"Perhaps," he said slowly, his expression remaining flat. "You're Akami right? I saw it in their thoughts. Saw many things in fact, interesting and intriguing things. Why don't you let me know a little about where you came from Akami," he said drawing out the final word.

She shuddered under his deep gaze, the shadows beneath his golden eyes making her skin crawl.

"Their thoughts? You didn't... You couldn't..."

I could, whispered his voice in her head and she watched his lip curve up into a grin. *I can do anything I want here Akami. This world is mine.*

"Stop it! Get out of my head!" she screamed and then she went rigid, slamming back down on the bed stiff as a board. Her mouth clamped shut and her eyes darted around in terror as he continued.

Why don't you tell me how you came here, spoke his voice in her head and she struggled around, trying so hard to force him out but he remained like a pressing giant upon her thoughts. A single prod could crush her entire being and she started to shake from the strain of resisting him. *If you don't tell me I'll just have a look for myself then,* and the pressing mass ebbed closer, her mental wall bending from the strain. She tried to scream, tried to move but nothing and then he withdrew for a moment.

Final chance Akami of Iterasu.

I don't know how we got here! her mind screamed at him. *I don't even know where we are! We were pursuing someone, and they went through the distortion!*

I am now aware of him, he replied unimpressed. *Many have come through to my world but that one seems the most concerning as of now, other than you and your friends that is. Anything else you would like to tell me?*

I don't know anything else! Get out of my head!

He paused for a long moment, withdrawing his presence from her and she took a shuddering breath at the relief. She could barely see him, just on the edge of her vision but she could make out his face as he stood there still as stone. For a split second, as if the aural light had blinked, she saw his eyes go fully dark.

Like a tsunami, his mind reappeared, tearing her wall down without resistance and she screamed, her voice muffled as he tore through her mind, invading every crevice of memory she had.

She could feel her being fading away. Lost to the turbulent sea

The Legend of Kyne: Chronocide

of his raging thoughts and just as she closed her eyes, tears were felt on her cheeks and then blackness.

The streaming of sunlight through a window brought her awake and Akami groaned as she reached up and rubbed her temples. She was in an unfamiliar room, large and decorated with fancy pieces of furniture. Memories of what happened suddenly erupted in her brain and she nearly leapt out of bed, startled to see her clothes had been changed to a thin white dress. A breeze rolled through the open window, blowing her hair back and she looked around the room, terrified of what could happen but no one else was there.

She was alone.

"What happened," she groaned, her head aching and she began walking over to the door. Reaching out, she felt the metallic knob under her palm. Expecting it to be locked, she was shocked to find it swing open silently on its hinges revealing a long hallway. Dozens of tall windows lined the hall, illuminating it in the golden glow and she proceeded on, cautiously aware of anything that could conceal someone. At the end of the hallway, she saw it branch down to the sides, each going off to large rooms. She peered around the corners slowly, surprised to see no one else and chose one hall. Dashing down it as quietly as she could, she could feel the cool stone upon her bare feet, each step propelling her along.

She passed a few more rooms, each empty and void of all life, even the dining room was vacant. To her concern however she could see the plates piled high with delicious food.

"Something doesn't feel right," she said as she pressed on looking for answers. The further in she seemed to go, the more lost she became. Outside the golden light began to change to a faded blue and then a darker shade of indigo. She traveled down staircase after staircase looking for any way out.

This place is enormous, she thought as she rounded a corner entering yet another vacant and massive room. *I must be in the citadel, there is no other explanation.*

Movement caught her attention and she saw just the fleeting shape of a figure exit the room near the back.

She needed answers and knowing the risk, she took off in a

sprint after the figure. The door was left open, leading to a small darker staircase leading down and at its base she got a glimpse of the figure's feet before they vanished, hidden behind the stairwells ceiling.

Two steps at a time she flew down them, her breath calm and steady as she pressed on. Once at the base she scanned down the hallway but to her dismay saw no one.

"Where did they go?" she muttered swinging her head around as she looked for any sign of movement. The air was thicker down here in the dark corridor. Dark metallic sconces lined the walls with faint flickering orange flames. She shuddered, not liking this one bit and turning around she started up the steps when movement at the top caught her eye as a dark figure moved just out of sight.

She rushed up them, each step increasing as the eerie feeling behind her from the hall pressed forward and as she reached the top of the staircase she gasped in shock. The large room was gone, replaced by a long identical dark hallway stretching out of sight. A cloaked figure was a few dozen feet away holding still as they stared at her.

Akami felt her heart rate in her chest increase, each thump shaking her body as she took a step back. She had no idea where she was and every ounce of her being told her to get away.

Turning around, she took a fast step before she ran straight into the chest of the dark figure as they appeared in front of her. She cried out in shock and stumbled back just as their hood was lowered revealing a grinning Kyne. Dark shadows stretched behind him like wings, and she took another step back before turning around.

To her agonizing disbelief he was there again behind her, just as she had just seen him. His grin turned to a flat stare and then he spoke.

"Your mind is interesting. Much different than others I have found. You seem to have a decent defense to me but it's not going to save you."

"My mind?" she stuttered, taking a step back and then it became clear.

This wasn't real! She was trapped in her mind with this shadow sweeping through it. A massive headache tore through her brain, and she dropped to her knees crying out in pain.

"Maybe you might survive, I guess we will see," he chuckled

The Legend of Kyne: Chronocide

and just as the headache increased. She screamed again, the hallway trembling and then breaking apart revealing flashes of lightning and darkness. "Let us see if you remember who you are."

*   *   *

41. Cast to the Edge of Despair

Ni'Bara shuddered hard as the sensation of ripping into pieces racked his body. For a split second, the most intense pain he had ever felt surrounded him, tearing at his mind and body before ceasing a few moments later. The blinding flash of white suddenly ended and he could see the blue sky of mid-morning.

The sun caught his attention as it had not been near the horizon a few moments ago. Swinging his head around, he saw Auriel's figure upon his back with her arm outstretched as if she was reaching for something. Tears streamed down her face and her chest shuddered as she sobbed.

Then it hit him with a force like none other.

Kyne was not there!

He was nowhere as Ni'Bara searched for their connection, leaving only an empty hole in his mind. A gaping hole threatening to swallow him up. The flaps of his wings slowed, and he swayed in the air, disoriented and alone. So alone.

All around them stretched a world unknown to him. The ground far beneath them lay bare, not a single building or wall was seen. No trail curved up towards Alakyne nor farmhouses dotted the landscape. The city was gone, leaving only grassy plains with rolling hills in all directions.

Kol Faldîn lay further to the north, but nothing was recognizable about it. It was much further than it should be, so far it was merely a dark line tracing the horizon.

Ni'Bara swayed again as he dipped a few dozen feet in altitude. The feeling of utter powerlessness flooded through him, no possible way to undo what had been done.

The sobbing from his back was in his ears and the pain of their loss intensified.

He's gone? That can't be true though right? He was right here just moments ago. He couldn't have just vanished, could he?

"I can't stop it! It's much different this time!" Kyne's final words echoed in his mind. and then he felt that terrible pain and that flash of light.

That must've been what Kyne was feeling right before we were separated, the dragon realized with a sickening feeling. A thought started to creep into his mind, but he pushed it out. He couldn't think that, he wouldn't. Somewhere in his mind he felt as if he were to think those thoughts, to give them any form at all would make them truth and he refused. Kyne couldn't be gone for good, and he wouldn't think those thoughts.

Ni'Bara's thoughts went back a short time ago, to the exact moment when the aural attack was flying up towards them and he had swerved to avoid it. He bared his teeth in rage and self-loathing. If he hadn't been so abrupt, been so fast then Kyne wouldn't have fell and they would be with him right now!

An image popped in his mind for a moment of Kyne's body tearing into dust and his vision tunneled for a moment. Swaying hard, he veered to the right as he tried to push the image out of his mind. He was alive! He is alive!

The image crept back and no matter how hard he fought; he couldn't seem to get it away. It morphed from him turning to dust, to violently shredding to pieces, to going completely still as his mind was torn. Finally, the last image rested on Kyne lying face down on the ground so far down below them. His body broken and still as stone.

Ni'Bara swayed and then they began to plummet.

The wind roared around them and Auriel's screams were drowned out as Ni'Bara closed his eyes and shut his mind to the world. He wouldn't think of anything anymore and as they plummeted, his body rolled over, falling back first to the ground a few thousand feet below.

Cries from Auriel trailed with the wind and remained unheard by the dragon. Unknown spells struck him, trying to wake him from his trance but none seemed to work, and the ground rapidly approached. Only a few moments left.

Suddenly, Ni'Bara's body rapidly decelerated and Auriel leapt from his back just before he impacted the ground in a massive thump. She attempted to slow herself but tossed and turned overhead as she tumbled to a stop a short distance away.

There the two of them lay for a long time, both mourning in their own way. Auriel's mind racing for ways for them to get back to him and Ni'Bara's shut off from the world.

* * *

The sun continued its ascent for a few hours eventually reaching its peak high in the southern half of the sky before Auriel rose to her feet. The grey dragon was nearby, unmoving except for his rhythmic breathing.

Starting toward him, Auriel's sorrow had been clouded by a fierce rage. A rage at the world and a burning fury towards the dragon. "You coward!" she screamed as she raised her hand. Her aura shot out and struck him hard jerking him back a few feet. His body lay in a depression within the ground, as if the ground had turned to water the moment he had struck it and flowed away.

Another flash of aura struck him again and the dragon rumbled a long groan.

He was coming to.

"You think you can just leave me alone? Leave me after you were the one who cast him from your back and sent him to God knows where! You're pathetic Ni'Bara! Aerysil!" Another aural energy attack flew at him striking him across the side of the face leaving a smoking burn upon his scales.

Reaching him, she approached his head and grabbed firmly upon his eyelid and tore it up as if she was drawing the blinds up that covered a window. His eye was there, bright blue and radiating with a dim cyan flame.

"This is your fault! Why did you do it? You knew he was barely hanging on and you still tried to avoid the attack."

"I should've just let it hit me," he sighed as his pupil shifted and contracted. Lifting his head up, Auriel watched as a single dragon tear fell to the ground below sizzling as it struck the ground. "Even if I died, I should have let it."

Auriel's fury died immediately at that sight, and she stared in shock at the anguish that was apparent upon the dragon's face. She had taken it too far and had taken all of her anger out on him and she didn't realize that he was mourning him as well.

"Ni'Bara, I didn't mean..." she started as she realized the loss he had endured but he interrupted.

"It doesn't matter, you spoke the truth. I am the cause of this, all of this. If I hadn't avoided that attack, then..."

"Then you actually probably would have died along with both of us," Auriel said. "That attack was meant to kill not stun. That Kyne didn't want us captured, he wanted us all killed. Ni'Bara I am so sorry. You are not at fault for this, I don't know why I took all of my anger out on you. You are the only reason why both of us are even standing here."

"I felt him tearing apart."

"What?" Auriel furrowed her brow, dumbfounded and Ni'Bara's remark. A deep hole began to bore its way within her stomach.

"I felt his very being tearing apart as we were separated Auriel. It was the most painful thing I have ever felt, as if every part of me, physically and mentally was being shredded to pieces."

"What are you talking about?" she whispered. "Is he..."

"I don't know," the dragon started. "Our connection was cut off and then we were here, wherever we are."

"He's not dead," she said reassuringly, more to give herself hope than she would've let him believe. "He told us that's what it felt like when he warped. He probably is in a different time than us."

"Auriel, you don't understand. I felt what he was feeling."

"No, you don't understand! Kyne is not some weak child! He is the archmage of Tsora and the strongest person I know. He saved his people from a tyrant and killed a god! There is no way that he is dead! I refuse to believe that, and if you say it one more time, I will personally kick your ass so bad that you won't remember the last three days."

The dragon sighed as he stared at the fierce woman standing

The Legend of Kyne: Chronocide

before him. It was almost as if she too had been given the fire of a dragon and had its burning passion radiating throughout her.

"Understood," he said, her ferocity giving him a bit of hope. "Then we must do all we can to get back to him. Wherever, I mean whenever he is."

Auriel's heavy breathing began to slow, and she turned around, briskly wiping her eyes clear of the tears that had begun to form. She would not cry anymore. It wouldn't do them any good and wouldn't get them back home, back to Kyne and everyone else.

Digging a hole within the ground, she withdrew some water from her pack and filled it close to the rim. Little hope lay within her, but she tried anyways. Tried to scry her husband over and over again but the surface of the water remained blank and still. He really wasn't in their world.

"I have no idea when we are," she said as she swept her vision around. Thick white clouds dotted the sky and their rolling shapes slowly drifted across the sky. A light breeze ruffled the grass, bending their blades over in a synchronized bow.

"Alakyne is no longer here which means one of two things, either we are so far in the future that the city has crumbled to dust along with everything else that would've been left behind. The other much more likely scenario is that..."

"We are far in the past," Auriel finished.

42. A Lead

Auriel's words were shattering and as her voice drifted off, carried by the wind the two of them sat in silence. Neither of them uttered a single breath as they were frozen in place.

"The past," Auriel muttered to herself wishing it wasn't what she was saying. Every ounce of her being wishing it to not be so but deep down she knew that it was. There was no other explanation for where they were.

She stared up at the sky, at the large fluffy white clouds before returning her vision back to the sweeping grass covered plains.

How are we going to make it back? How are we going to travel through time? she began to panic. *We could spend our entire lives trying to find a way and it will be but a blink in the amount of time that still needs to pass.*

"Auriel?" asked Ni'Bara, snapping the Riel out of her panicked trance.

"I... I am fine. We just need to... Just need to..."

"We need to find out when we are first," Ni'Bara finished. "Before we are to formulate a plan, we must do that."

"How are we supposed to do that? I guess we could just ask one of the people that we have seen since we've arrived," she said sarcastically. "Even then are we to just ask them what the year is?" she snapped revealing her anger. "We don't even know what group of people live in this area and even if we find them who is to say that their calendar is even the same as our own? Ours is based upon Alakyne's life and I see no city that marks the beginning of our age. 1373 is the year we come from. Do you understand Ni'Bara? Do you understand the minimum time of how far back we have travelled?

"Watch yourself Auriel," rumbled the dragon as he raised his head up and stared at her. The air seemed to tingle from the anger growing within the dragon.

Auriel turned away from him and took a deep breath.

"I'm sorry, I don't know why I keep getting mad at you. I just don't know what else to do."

Ni'Bara was silent for a moment and then he lowered back down. "Like I said before, we need to try and find out when we are. I know some of the cities in Kydrëa are older than Alakyne. Our first bet should be one of those."

"Which ones are older?"

"I am quite confident one of the oldest cities is actually Tsora. Kyne has told me about it many times based on things he has read. Supposedly Tsora was around for a few hundred years before Alakyne even came around, back in the age of the beasts."

"Then let's go there, try and see if we can get any info we can. If there is nothing there then it means we are even further back in time."

Auriel leapt up onto Ni'Bara's saddle in a flash and within moments the two of them were airborne, climbing higher and higher into the sky. The loud thumping of Ni'Bara's wing beats was muffled by the rush of the wind as they climbed first hundreds, then thousands of feet up.

They soared around in a large banking turn, eyeing everything below them as they searched for anything familiar. The only thing that was even reminiscent of their own time was a large river nearby. It was big and like a silver ribbon, splitting the landscape and heading far off onto the horizon towards the dark line of trees. She knew that river, had lived near its source since she had arrived after she left her people.

Ni'Bara had spotted it as well and as if they were thinking the same thing began to follow its length from high above. Nearly scraping the bottoms of the clouds, they flew. The air was warm and the constant rush of wind drowned out any other sounds. Auriel could feel the sunlight upon her bare arms, and she looked down at the silver tattoo that graced her skin. Silver and swirly, she traced it with her eyes for a long moment before a wave of her hand caused it to ripple and change. Forming a distorted shape of a dragon's scale upon her arm, she smiled weakly as she pictured her husband.

The Legend of Kyne: Chronocide

A rumbling from Ni'Bara drew her from her thoughts and as the dragon stopped his movement, he hovered high above in air. His head swung back towards Auriel and then back out over the landscape.

"Do you see it?"

"Do I see what..." Auriel's voice trailed off as she recognized the dark haze of smoke near the river dozens of miles away. "Vly," she said and as her vision sharpened, she saw the thick billowing plumes of smoke rising from the edge of the large forest. It was still too far to make anything specific out.

"Go!" she shouted, and the dragon took off, using his height to gain speed as they rocketed down at an angle heading straight for the source of the smoke. It was far away but even a glimmer of hope that answers could be there drove them faster.

The ground below crept by as they continued to lose altitude, the dragon using every bit of it to his advantage to hold his blazing speed. They could see the forest more clearly now with the source of the flames coming from its outer edge. As they drew closer, they noticed the smoke seemed to trail deep into the forest, a lone line of burning trees.

The flames were large enough that they could see their orange flicker as the vegetation was consumed, belched into black smoke that filled the sky and burned the lungs of any who inhaled it. They were near it now; the end of the line being seen as a small village. Buildings were ablaze and charred as the forest burned nearby. A massive furrow had been carved straight through the village's heart, crushing anything beneath it before heading off into the trees. large trunks had been snapped like twigs and pushed to the side making way for whatever caused it, their branches charred and burning in an increasingly long line that led to the north.

Screams and crying was heard as they finally came to the village. They could see burning corpses, crushed from falling parts of buildings and the survivors running around trying to save what little they still could. A single woman lay sobbing on her knees near a black stain upon the ground and when Auriel understood what had happened, she nearly threw up. The shadow of a body lay branded upon the stone, its black soot marking its loss. It was but a mark left, the only thing that remained of whoever had been blown away.

The Legend of Kyne: Chronocide

She shuddered at its sight when more screaming brought her attention from it. The survivors were pointing up at them, shrieks of fear erupted and then they were all scattering around, leaving the deceased alone as they dashed into the homes that still stood or behind charred trees.

Ni'Bara circled slowly, looking for a place to land before he lightly touched down in the village center where the largest part of the furrow had been carved.

His whole body suddenly tensed, and his nostrils flared out as he sniffed the air, snaking his head from side to side. Auriel felt his back shudder and then the spines upon the ridges of his head flared out in an aggressive hood as he snarled, "It's an eldunaga!"

His words shocked Auriel and she looked around the village for what he had sensed but nothing was noticed except for the burning wood as a piece crashed to the ground below. She had heard about the eldunaga before but couldn't remember exactly what it was. Straining her memory, she recalled Kyne's voice saying the word and then it clicked and her blood chilled.

The eldercobra.

"Where!" she shouted but she already knew. It had slithered through this town, burning everything it touched before it had ventured off carving a scar through the forest.

The rage ebbing off of Ni'Bara was so thick that Auriel felt like she could feel it if she swiped her hand through the air.

"How is this even possible!" he snarled, and he brandished his fangs. "They should be gone!"

"Not in the past," Auriel reminded him. "We must be far enough back that we are when they roamed the land."

"So, then we are truly before the time of Alakyne then," murmured the dragon as his spines began to lay back against his neck.

"It seems so," she said, and she leapt from his back, landing light as a feather upon the ground. The scraping of her orichite foot wrappings upon the stone echoed around as she surveyed the scene before her. She could sense the hidden people around her. So far counting eight with more hidden further out of her senses.

"We do not wish to harm you!" she called out, holding her hands up in a peaceful gesture. "We just wish to talk."

The Legend of Kyne: Chronocide

No response came and more groans from the smoldering buildings sounded. Using her aura, she smothered the flames as best as she could, extinguishing them and preventing more destruction from proceeding.

"See," she said as she finished. "I only wish to talk."

Nearby she saw a flicker of movement as someone darted behind an overturned wagon. To her it looked like a young child, and she decided that was who she would approach first.

"I know you are there," she said directing her voice to the hidden figure and she started to walk slowly towards them. "I just want to talk to you."

More movement was noticed as the figure tried to tuck themselves in further out of view to no avail. Auriel was almost upon them as she repeated her question when suddenly the little boy, his age not much more than ten took off out from behind the cart. His clothes were torn to shreds and his short dark hair was covered in mud and ash.

Auriel took a few faster steps towards him but then came to a stop as she watched him run as fast as he could away from her underneath a charred building where he vanished behind some broken wooden beams. Nearby she heard a muffled scream that stopped just as it had started. The figure was within the home, hidden behind a shattered window. Broken pieces lay scattered upon the ground littering both it and the windowsill with the sparkling daggers.

More groaning from the crumbling buildings was heard and then a scream of terror caught her attention. Looking back to where the boy had hidden himself, she watched the building shudder and then it started to lean over in a slow-motion crumble.

He will be crushed! her mind raced and she dashed towards him as fast as she could, her aura guiding her steps. Suddenly a great crack sounded, and the building broke apart, falling towards the ground over top of the concealed and screaming child.

"Y'vinu!" screamed Auriel and just as her aura grasped hold of the boy, she tore him from the crumbling building a moment before it crashed to the ground in a puff of dust. The boy flew towards her where she stopped his momentum with one hand, and she took a deep breath trying to keep her composure before flashing a kind smile at him.

A look of terror spread across his face at the sight of her and he flailed around, scrambling to his feet and screaming and pointing at her as he backed away. movement was seen behind him as an older woman ran out into the street brandishing a wooden stick. She leapt in front of the boy, tucking him behind her and flailing the stick around madly.

She screamed in a foreign tongue, the words corrupted from the original Kydrëan language, older and thicker. The woman continued to scream, repeating the same phrases over and over again waving her hand.

"Linguas," Auriel whispered performing the spell over her and Ni'Bara. The warmth of her aura flooded through her mind, the woman's words clearing and becoming recognizable.

"Witch! You're a witch!" she screeched. "Get out! Go away! Go back with your demon creature of fire and leave us alone. You have already taken so many of us today!"

Auriel tried to calm the woman but was having no luck. She interrupted everything the Riel princess said, commenting on her devilish looks and evil magic. More figures had stepped out of the shadows of all ages and genders. Each of them bore the golden hair and eyes of a Kydrëan whether it be the children or the elderly. Most had weapons clutched in their hands, burning torches or pitchforks and anger strewn across their faces.

Ni'Bara swept his head around and watched as the mob began to approach Auriel.

"I think we should leave," he called out and Auriel nodded, slowly backing up as the group approached.

"Agreed," she mumbled. There was no hope getting through to these people. They were terrified and angry.

Cries of rage came from the villagers as they followed the backing up Auriel. She could hear taunting and jeers coming from them as their courage grew at the sight of her retreat.

"Leave us alone!"
"Witch!"
"Go back with those other witches who brought that beast upon us!"

The Legend of Kyne: Chronocide

"Demons!"

"Wait," Auriel said, and she stopped her movement. "Others who brought that demon? What do you mean?"

The mob stopped walking and more cries of anger came from them and the sight of her ceasing her retreat.

"Get out before we attack you!" threatened a man with a pitchfork and on that word Ni'Bara swung his massive mass towards them and snarled.

"Attack us!" he hissed. "You are lucky I don't burn you all alive for threatening her!" and his abdomen began to glow a bright cyan.

Their anger vanished immediately, replaced by fear and a few started to run away.

"Explain what you meant," Auriel called out. "What do you mean others? Are there others that can perform aura here? Sorcerers!"

"I am not telling you anything," stammered the man and he raised his pitchfork so that the prongs were facing her. "Leave!"

"I'll take care of this," muttered Ni'Bara and he swung his head down and met the man's eyes with his one. The air began to tingle, and Auriel watched as the man's arms started to lower down as he gazed into the dragon's eyes as if under a trance. The few Kydrëans who had still stood with him screamed in fear and all fled, scattering away into the ruins of their village. "Answer her question."

"I... I..." murmured the man as if he were intoxicated and not able to control himself. "I don't know what you mean by sorcerer and aura. They used magic, I know that. We welcomed them into our village and then they summoned the fire serpent before fleeing. So many of us were killed in the raid." his voice trailed off.

"Where did they go?" Auriel asked intrigued by the possibility of someone who knew aura.

"Down the river. They stole one of our rafts in the night and vanished. We thought they were friendly, they seemed innocent enough and just as they left, we were attacked. We knew it was them, we have all heard the stories but none of us truly believed them."

"What stories," rumbled Ni'Bara.

"Of those who are followed by monsters. The two roam the land whose presence is always followed by death."

Ni'Bara ended the trance and the man's eyes returned to

normal. A look of disbelief spread across his face before it was replaced by panic and he fled, dropping his pitchfork as he ran around a building out of view.

"Let's go," Auriel said, and she hopped up on top of Ni'Bara and a few flaps brought them airborne. He arced around, looking off into the distance, the line of burning trees stretching as far as they could see, a dark wall of smoke splitting the forest. As they soared up and away from the village, they discussed what had happened.

"They were terrified of our aura," she said. "If aura is so rare then maybe we need to seek out these two they mentioned."

"They could be dangerous."

"And if they are then we can either deal with them or leave. I am not worried about that. I think that we should try and find them. If they left by raft heading downriver late in the night, then they shouldn't be too far away. We could catch them if we try."

"I think it's a possibility they might have answers. They might even be sorcerers from Tsora. It still doesn't explain why they would summon and eldunaga, let alone how." The dragon banked in a curve and brought his figure over the silvery river. The smoke filled air was suffocating but after a moment they left its clutches. Behind them, the burning strip of forest had not stopped, hundreds of more trees catching fire and spreading, the wildfire only stoppable by a rainstorm that would not come for days.

They stayed low, skimming a few dozen feet over the water's surface as they traveled. The river was massive, one of the biggest in the country and as it gently curved around hills, the dragon stayed on a straight path. They traveled fast, passing over the marshy outskirts of the river and the little ponds that hid within the reeds and cattails. No sign of the boat had been seen yet and as they pushed on Auriel used her magic to summon aural trails.

Brightening into view, they traced dozens of paths all littering the surface of the water. They were thin and all identical signaling them to most likely be fish. A few had appeared crisscrossing the sky above the river and Auriel watched as a large heron darted out from the bank in front of them, fleeing from the dragon and leaving a faint trail. Then she spotted it. Two brighter trails near the edge of the river followed the slow moving current as it crossed the land. Following the lines with her gaze, the glare of the sun on the water making it hard to keep them in sight, she managed to lead Ni'Bara further on until they came to a spot where the path left the water and pushed into the marshy riverbank.

From above, as the dragon hovered in place, they could see the small wooden raft jammed into the vegetation, trapped and tangled. Thin, deep footprints lined the muddy bank and more aural trails had appeared, tying with the two in intricate knots. By the looks of it seemed to have been an altercation of some sorts and their targets had been dragged out of the river up into the grasslands.

Ni'Bara followed the trails, the scents of the humans easily distinguishable from the others he could smell. Following them, they found a road that mirrored the river on its course to the west. Hoofprints were left in the dusty ground and Auriel counted three human aural trails as well as the two she had initially been following, bringing their total to five.

Speeding up, they glided down the road for a quarter of an hour before they spotted their targets. Six horses were all trotting down the road with a small cart behind two of them. In the cart, two figures were tied up. Each of the horse riders were dressed in short light-colored shirts with sandals upon their feet. Auriel could see their tanned forearms even from this distance, the bronze color crafted from the sun's rays.

They rocketed overhead, screeching to a stop and landing, startling the party behind them. Auriel dismounted and held her hands up.

"We do not come in aggression. We just have some questions for you."

Upon hearing her voice, the men aboard the horses stopped their shouting and murmuring replaced it. Suddenly one guided their horse a little closer to her and the man began to chuckle.

"Well damn aren't you a pretty thing. I feel you would bring me quite the pleasurable accompaniment. Beautiful and riding this monster, just astonishing."

Auriel's lip twitched in irritation. She was not enjoying one moment of this man's compliments. She only wanted answers.

"I do not wish to speak to you," she continued. "I wish to

speak to the sorcerers that you have captured." and she gestured to the figures in the back of the cart. She realized that they had bags covering their heads and couldn't make out anything else about them.

"Nah," he chuckled, and he drew his sword, holding it lazily out, the tip drifting towards her. "How about you come with me, and we can talk about what to do with the giant flying lizard. You could even become one of my wives if you work hard enough. I guarantee you would easily be my favorite."

The Riel shuddered at his words and anger started to flood her body. "Your arrogance will get you in trouble," she spoke slowly. Drawing her own orichite blade, "Do not mock me or my companion. I won't ask you again."

The man chuckled again. "Such a spunky little thing. Hey guys," and he turned to the others who had all chuckled with him. "Don't you think I need a fiery wife? All the others are so boring and docile."

At his words, Auriel let her rage take a hold. In a flash, guided by her aura, she seemingly appeared in front of the man. With a leap, she brought herself up to his tall height where she spun around and kicked him straight in the chest. The man hurtled off the back of the horse, colliding with the ground in a yelp of pain. The other horses whinnied in fright, and they all started to thrash around before bolting away. The rumbling of the cart sounded, and Auriel watched the fearful horse run in a tight fast circle, veering away from Ni'Bara off the track where the cart started to lurch dangerously to the side. In slow motion she watched as it tipped to the side, dumping its contents upon the ground and knocking the horse over in a puff of dust.

Auriel sheathed her sword, still clean from the lack of bloodshed and she ran over to the two hooded figures who lay upon the ground. The horse nearby was thrashing with its rider pinned underneath it screaming in pain from the broken bones he had received. A wave of her hand and the horse's bindings snapped, allowing it to get up and gallop away, crushing the man beneath its hooves. She didn't have any care for these people and didn't feel bad about what happened. She could sense the deceit and treachery that they possessed.

Coming to the figures, she reached down and cautiously

removed their hoods. To her shock, they were but children, one girl and one boy. Easily siblings, the girl looked to be the oldest but not more than her mid-teens.

"Are you two alright?" she asked as their eyes widened at her sight.

"Are you here to rescue us," asked the little boy. His hair was the striking gold that matched his eyes and his skin coated in dirt and grime. She could tell that they were both very cute kids and with a nod, she hoisted them up to their feet. A quick spell broke their bindings and the two gasped in shock at her aura.

"You can do aura like the mages!" cried the boy in shock and wonder. "That's so cool!"

His sister grabbed his arm and gave him a stern look and his joy vanished completely.

"Who are you," she said, and her face hardened as she met Auriel's eyes.

"Someone looking for answers. I was hoping you two might be able to help me but..." her voice trailed off.

"What is that!" gasped the boy and she turned to see he was pointing at Ni'Bara who was sitting there looking at both of them.

"He's nice," Auriel said quickly in fear that they would run away at his sight.

"So cool!" the boy cried again. "Ouch!" he gasped as his sister clenched his arm again.

"Why did you rescue us?" said the girl again. "No one ever helps us."

"Well, I did. I am hoping you can tell me what year it is."

"What year?" they both gasped in shock. "What do you mean?"

Before she could answer, a cry of rage came from behind Auriel.

"How dare you mock me you witch!" screamed the male as he ran at her with his blade. "I'll kill you!"

Auriel swung towards him, her orichite blade already drawn when a grey blur appeared above the man. Fangs barred, Ni'Bara darted his head down upon the man, his torso vanishing into the depths of the dragon's mouth. Muffle screams were heard and then ceased as the dragon reared his head and flipped it back and forth with a sickening crunch. An object flew from his mouth crashing to the dirt road and Auriel averted her eyes as the severed bottom half of the man fell from Ni'Bara's fangs.

"He was warned," snarled the dragon as he dropped back down towards the three. "So, these are the supposed sorcerers we were looking for?"

"I think so," she muttered, sheathing her blade once again and turning at the cowering kids. "He won't hurt you."

"Unless you try and attack us," murmured the dragon and the two kids shook their heads wildly. "Never never," they repeated frantically. "Please don't eat us Mr. Lizard."

"Lizard," gasped the dragon. "Lizard?"

"He's not a lizard," laughed Auriel. "He's a dragon and his name is Ni'Bara."

"Dragon," they both repeated in wonder. "Like the legends! No one has seen any in thousands of years."

"Well now you have," said Ni'Bara and he puffed his chest out before bathing the sky in cyan flame. Expecting the children to scream in terror, he was surprised to see them staring in awe at him.

"What are your names," Auriel asked.

The two looked at each other for a moment before they said, Aya and Liam."

"Aya and Liam," she repeated, suspicious at the kid's strange behavior. She could tell this wasn't their true names but wouldn't pry for the time being. "Well Miss Aya and Mr. Liam, I have some questions if you don't mind my asking. First of all, do you two know what year it is?"

"Why do you keep asking what year it is?" Aya asked in confusion. "How do you not know?"

"That's not of your concern right now," she replied. "The year?"

"It should be 2689," she said.

"2689?" gasped Ni'Bara in disbelief. "How could it be 2689? that's nearly 1300 years in the future from our own time."

"Your own time?" asked Aya in shock. "What does that mean?"

Auriel gave the dragon a dark look, but he didn't notice, and he continued. "How could we be so far away? What happened to

Kydrëa and all of the people? Why are the eldercobras roaming the earth?"

"What's a Kydrëa," asked Liam.

"That's the country we are from," replied Auriel. "It once stood here a long time ago."

"I've never heard of it," responded Aya.

"How could you have not?" gasped Auriel. "It's an aural superpower. We just passed by where the capital once stood. I don't understand what could've happened to it."

"The only village is the one further up the river," Aya said gesturing to the distance. "I've never seen any ruins of a capital or anything. You people are strange."

"This doesn't make sense," Auriel said turning to Ni'Bara. "What could've happened to erase all of Kydrëa?"

"Kydrëa," muttered Liam to himself.

"Wait," the dragon said suddenly, and he dropped his head down closer to them. "What happened on the first year of your calendar?"

"The first year?" Liam asked. "I don't know. Aya, do you know?"

"Mother and Father taught me about it a long time ago. The first year marked the end of the great war. The war between monsters and man, the last time the dragons were ever seen supposedly."

"That's it!" gasped Ni'Bara. "Auriel, we are not in the future, we are in the past. Kydrëa hasn't been created yet, so the new era hasn't started yet. We are deep in the past."

"I don't understand you guys," said Aya. "You keep talking about the past and future like you've been there before but that's not possible right?"

"We didn't think so until it happened," replied Auriel. "Bad things happened to my husband, and we were sent here."

"Where is he?"

"We don't know," she said solemnly. "We were separated."

"I am sorry," said the young girl as she saw the Riel's face light up with sadness.

"We wanted to ask you guys because we heard that you could use aura. We wanted to find out the year and if the Sorcerers of Tsora would be able to help us."

"We don't know aura and they won't help you," she muttered. "They aren't very nice people. They only help for coin and mead, that's it. If you don't have any then you are on your own."

"You don't know aura?" Auriel asked and the kids shook their heads in confusion. "Well then where can I find them? Are they at Tsora itself?"

"Tsora's not a place," Aya nearly laughed. "Tsora is who they are. Tsora was the supposed first mage who created the order a long time ago. They don't really have a place they stay. They just roam the countryside slaying monsters for a living."

Auriel bit her lip in frustration at the responses she was getting. If the sorcerers weren't going to help, then what else were they to do?"

"Where can I find them?"

"Probably in one of the villages. They like to stay nearby them in hopes of monsters attacking. They have been getting more and more frequent, especially with the awakening of the three."

"Is that why you fled the village, because of the eldercobra?"

"The what?" Aya gasped. "An eldercobra this far from the mountains? That's impossible!"

"Well one just decimated that village up the river," Ni'Bara muttered, and the two kids looked at each other and tears formed in their eyes.

"Why does this keep happening!" Liam cried out. "They won't just leave us alone!"

His sister looked at him and beneath the crying exterior she saw a far deeper sorrow as she looked upon her brother.

"What do you mean," Auriel said softly, and she placed a hand on the boy's shoulders.

Between sobs he spoke, "It's like they won't leave us alone. They follow us constantly. Like we are monster magnets. They kill everyone we meet."

"We left that village last night to hopefully spare them and we thought it had worked. I guess not," Aya mumbled.

"Why do they follow you?" asked Ni'Bara.

"We don't know," Aya said quickly, dropping her eyes away

from theirs. "It just happens."

"You two should leave us before something bad happens to you," Liam said, his chest rocking as he fought his sobs. "I don't want anything to happen to you."

"We can take care of ourselves," she replied with a light smile to the dragon. "Don't worry about us. Worry about yourselves. Have you tried to get the sorcerers to help you? Maybe they can figure out the curse that seems to have been placed on you."

"We've tried!" wailed Liam. "So many times, but we don't have any money. We've tried to steal some so that we could pay but it never seems to be enough."

"And they won't help you anyways?" Auriel asked.

"No way," Aya said. "We were once trapped in a cave with a roc on the outside trying to get us for nineteen days. Sorcerers came near the beginning, speaking to us through the stone but when we said we couldn't pay they left us there. We only survived because of water dripping from the ceiling and the bugs we could find in the near blackness."

"How did you escape the roc?"

"On the final day the sorcerers returned and defeated the monster. We were so grateful and confused why they did but we soon found out. One of the nights when the roc had vanished for a time, but we were too scared to leave, it flew down to a settlement nearby. It killed and ate most of the people before returning. The sorcerers dealt with it only because the survivors of the town collected all their gold paid them to kill it. We just so happened to benefit as well."

"Despicable," snarled Ni'Bara. "To think that these humans can fell a roc but only do so for gold. Just despicable," the dragon shook his head in frustration.

"Do you two have any gold to pay them? If you do, they might help," said Liam. The sobbing had ceased, and his eyes had turned a puffy red.

"A little," said Auriel and she tapped the one of the few pouches that dangled from Ni'Bara's saddle. The jingle of coins sounded, and the kid's eyes widened with shock.

"If we find the sorcerers maybe we can convince them to help you as well," she said with a smile.

The Legend of Kyne: Chronocide

Aya and Liam looked both at each other and then back at her, their eyes wide with excitement. "You would really do that for us?" she gasped. "You just met us."

"And I like you," Auriel laughed, and she leapt up onto the saddle in a graceful jump. Staring in awe, they watched the Riel seemingly fly from the ground, aided by her aura. Her delicate toes, just visible between her foot wrappings slipped in one of the set of stirrups that were mounted onto the saddle, and she patted behind her. "Are you coming then?"

The kids threw a glance at one another before scrambling over to Ni'Bara seemingly racing as they climbed up his rough leg before sitting in the saddle.

"Hey, I wanted the front," whined Liam.

"Too slow," laughed his sister and she sat down directly behind Auriel. The Riel showed her the strap that she could hang onto, and the girl pulled it tight over her lap, locking her in place. Liam did the same behind her and once they were situated the dragon took off into the sky, their cries of excitement drowned out by the rush of the wind.

43. The Children of the Past

Auriel felt Aya's hands wrap tight around her, and she smiled as Ni'Bara rocketed off into the midday air. The rush of the wind drowned out most sounds, but she could just make out the excited calls and shouting from both Ava and Liam behind her. Ni'Bara flapped harder, pushing them further and further with each wing beat as they soared above the grassy fields below. Arcing in a large circle, he continued climbing until they passed through the clouds, casting everything in a temporary bright fog before erupting upon their crown.

Massive mountains of puffy white clouds rolled beneath them, great ridges falling to deep valleys. The dragon curved around a pillar and the green ground below came into view, piercing through the white veil like of verdant laced fissure.

Gasps came from the children and the dragon rumbled, ruffling his head before bathing the open sky below them in cyan flames.

The heat made the air shimmer in magnificent waves. The clouds parted and tossed around, guided by their rising columns of air and he rumbled again. Auriel looked back.

"You better hold on."

She felt Aya's grip tighten around her abdomen and saw Liam's hand fumble as he tried to tighten his own grip on the dragon. Suddenly a massive roar ripped from Ni'Bara's throat, and he dove down, his wings tucking tight as he dove like a falcon upon the hunt. Ripping into a tight twist, he wrapped like a corkscrew, his tail tight behind him, guiding his descent like a rudder through the air.

Three times they spun before his wings shot straight out to his sides and they straightened out, arcing back up and making their way above the clouds. The excited shrills continued behind Auriel and she smiled, shaking her head at Ni'Bara.

"You're quite the showoff," she muttered to herself.

As their flight calmed, the dragon's wings held still into a glide, the warm summer air flew through their hair as Auriel turned back around to face them. "Where do you think the sorcerers would be?"

They shook their heads and Aya shrugged her shoulders. "No idea," she said. "We have only seen them once. That was by a larger town far to the north in the mountains."

"Are there any large cities nearby that you know of?"

Aya shook her head again. "Once the monsters came most of the bigger cities were destroyed. If they had sorcerers, they might have been able to defend it, but I don't know."

"Where is the capital of Kydrëa then," Auriel started but right as she said it, she stopped herself. "Never mind, Kydrëa doesn't exist yet."

Behind his sister, Auriel heard Liam repeat, "Kydrëa," with a tone that signaled fondness of the name.

"Where would the capital of whatever this place is be? Do you even have a capital?" Aya shook her head again. "Ok, well then that's not a ton of help. Ni'Bara what do you think?"

The dragon turned his head revealing a single eye. "Cities usually follow water, whether it be rivers, lakes, or oceans. We should search there first."

Without waiting for a response, the dragon arced sharply to the left, guiding their flight to the west where the silver Ta'Gor river continued its march across the countryside.

Hours they flew, covering vast amounts of miles but below them no settlements were seen. Even the herds of animals that presumably wandered the fields below were not seen, either obscured by their height or not there at all.

Ni'Bara stayed above the clouds, hoping to keep unwanted visitors from noticing him and flying up to meet them. His eyes scanned continuously and tireless spotting for threats. He wouldn't be ambushed; an attack could be lethal to those who rode upon him.

Eventually the golden streaks of the sun nearing the horizon lit up their faces. Down below, the land had already been cast in the evening shadow but this high up allowed them a few more minutes of

The Legend of Kyne: Chronocide

its precious warmth. As it set, Ni'Bara slowed his flight to a glide and turned to face Auriel.

"We could continue on, I am capable. It could allow us a chance to possibly see the glow of firelight in the dark."

Auriel looked first down below them before scanning the horizon. The cool air touched her shoulder and she shivered slightly from its graze. Her skin bumped up causing the fine hairs upon her body to grow rigid. She glanced back at the kids and saw that Liam had slumped over; his head pressed into his sister's back sound asleep. Aya smiled weakly at Auriel and the princess could see the fatigue from riding visible upon her face.

She turned back to Ni'Bara and shook her head. A brief nod and the dragon dropped down into a gentle glide. Descending a few thousand feet, they made their way to a small group of trees that lined the banks of the river. Ni'Bara landed and to Auriel's shock the young boy had managed to stay asleep.

Watching Aya, she was impressed with the young girl as she gently unwrapped Liam from the saddle before looking around for how to get down. To Auriel it seemed like she was analyzing a way to carry him, and her thoughts rang true as she stood up before stooping down to grab onto him.

"Aya wait," said Auriel stopping the girl with a light touch on her arm. "I'll take care of it. You get down yourself, ok?"

Aya flashed a look of concern, but Auriel's smile comforted her, and she started the climb down. The moment she hit her feet she looked up to see her brother's body slowly levitating down towards her, Auriel had her hand aimed at him and her brow was furrowed in concentration.

Delicately, Aya caught him in her arms and kneeling down, laid him in the short grass that was near the edges of the trees. Auriel's footsteps caught her attention and then a blanket was first placed around her shoulders before a second was draped over her sleeping brother as he lay upon his side.

A wave of the Riel's hand and the nearby dry sticks rocketed together aided with her aura forming a pile which she ignited casting the orange glow all around. Ni'Bara slid his tail around them creating a large circle and he laid his head near Auriel before closing his eyes.

The Legend of Kyne: Chronocide

"Are you hungry," she asked touching his warm scales. A quick snort was his answer, and she withdrew her hand. "You should go hunt then. We will be alright."

"I looked for food the entire flight Auriel. I didn't see one animal large enough. I used to fly upon this land, and it would be littered with bison and other large animals. Now I see none."

"I was wondering that same thing," she muttered. "I looked too and didn't notice anything. I thought maybe it was because of the height. Do you think it is because of the monsters?"

"It would be my guess," he replied. "They are massive creatures who need fuel to live. Glutinous and wicked, they consume anything they can. The fact there were survivors in that first village shocked me."

"He's right," came Aya's voice and Auriel turned to see the young girl standing behind her. The blanket was still draped over her shoulders, and she held it tight against her chest. "They always eat everything they can. I have seen a hundred people torn apart by a single roc. Devoured and consumed, it ate and ate until there was nothing left."

"How did you escape?"

"We hid in a cave for nineteen days," she said reminding Auriel. "Either the snake didn't notice the people, or something distracted it."

Auriel clenched her lips in a puzzled look of thought. *What could've distracted it so much that it would've left the village?*

Reaching in her pack, Auriel tossed Aya a piece of dried meat which she caught, dropping the blanket to the ground. She scrambled upon the ground, bringing it back up across her shoulder before she looked first at the meat and then at the sleeping figure of her brother nearby. A guilty look spread across her face.

"I have more that we can give him when he awakens," Auriel said cheerfully, and she took a seat next to the fire followed shortly by Aya.

"Why are you being so nice to us?"

Between bites of food, Auriel laughed lightly. "Because I see two lost children trying to find their way. You are just like us. We just want to get back home."

"We don't have a home," Aya said as she swallowed a bite.

The Legend of Kyne: Chronocide

"Where are your parents?"

"Dead."

"Do you want to talk about it?"

"Not much to talk about. We were kicked out of our city a few years ago. A monster found us and killed our parents. Liam and I managed to escape."

"That's terrible," Auriel said, reaching out her hand and placing it upon Aya's. She had grown fond of the young girl in the short time that she had known her. She was kind and brave.

"It's just... It's..."

"It's what?"

"Never mind," she said shaking her head. "It's nothing."

"You can tell me; I can keep a secret."

The girl looked over to Ni'Bara and saw his eye was still closed. Auriel smiled and mouthed locking her mouth with a key. She knew the dragon was awake, but Aya didn't need to know it.

"The monsters follow us."

"You already told us that," Auriel said confused.

"Let me be more specific. They follow him," and she glanced at Liam's sleeping figure.

"Why him?"

"Ever since he was born strange things seemed to happen. He would have these weird tantrums like any child does and then monsters would appear. As he grew and his tantrums faded, he would have dreams. The dreams he could never remember but his eyes would glow white and then monsters followed. Eventually our village started to take notice and we were driven out."

"That doesn't make sense. What do you mean glowing eyes?"

"I don't know. His eyes would glow, and the air would tingle over my skin. It reminded me of the magic you do."

Auriel looked up to the darkening sky, the deep indigo and navy fading to black with silver dots coming into being.

"And they drove you out for that? Something that he has no control over?"

"My father tried to fight it, but he was hit with thrown stones. We all were, and we fled. Left our mountain village and finding ourselves alone in a dangerous world. My father knew a lot about

The Legend of Kyne: Chronocide

hunting, and we made do with what we could. Mother made our clothes and helped father hunt when she could." Her voice trailed off at the mention of her mother and Auriel saw tears from in her eyes. Out of instinct she wrapped her arm around her shoulder and brought her in tight. Her musky scent of mud and sweat touched Auriel's nose but she disregarded it. She could help clean them in the morning.

Aya whimpered for but a moment before regaining her composure enough to continue. "Then he was gone, taken by a monster. I don't even know which one got him and mother. We were tucked away in the small shelter they had made. We heard their screams and the thunderous steps of the beast as it plowed through the trees and then we were alone. We have been on the run since."

"Aya I am so sorry," Auriel said, and she brushed a tear from the young girl's face. "I didn't mean to upset you. I just... Maybe we can help you and Liam find a place to stay."

"Can we come with you?"

Her words caught Auriel off guard, and she thought hard for a moment. She could tell Aya wasn't asking to simply travel with them. It almost seemed like she was asking to go back to their time.

She brushed the girl's hair back and smiled weakly. "We will see Aya."

"Auriel," she said, brushing the rest of the tears from her eyes with the blanket. "I... I lied to you."

"Lied to me about what," Auriel said, caution in her voice and she withdrew her arm from the girl.

"My name's not Aya."

"I didn't think it was darling," and she smiled. "I could tell you were lying."

Her words made Aya's face light up. "You knew?"

"I had a feeling. What's your true name?"

"My name is Aria."

"That's a beautiful name," she said with a smile. The name cementing deep in her brain.

"And your brothers? I am guessing his name isn't Liam is it."

"His name is Alakyne."

* * *

The Legend of Kyne: Chronocide

44. Bitter Cold

The roar of the wind ripped through Kyne's ears as he fell back first. His vision was dark, and an intense pain rippled through his body as if it was struggling. Struggling to stay together and also rip itself apart simultaneously. He screamed out, in both pain and anguish. Not a word but more of a noise as he tumbled through the air.

His mind was blank, except for one thing. The sensation of his body tearing itself to pieces.

Another wave of pressure ripped through his body, and he cried out again, this time louder. He couldn't handle the pain; it was too much. To make it all end, that's all that he wanted. To be rid of this excruciating pain.

His body rocked again from the sensation, and he flailed his arms out, thrashing his body as it fell through the dark sky.

Then suddenly it stopped.

The roar of the wind continued in his ears as he struggled to focus. His mind was clearing but he was still disoriented. All he could see was darkness.

"Kaiodin," he muttered as he focused his thoughts.

Surprisingly his fall did not cease.

"Kaiodin," he said more firmly as he rolled over so his stomach was falling first. Once again nothing happened.

What is going on? he thought in disbelief as he started to notice snow falling around him, his body racing past the delicate flakes.

"Kaiodin!"

Nothing.

Suddenly, the view of the tops of trees came into sight and with a scream, His body smashed through the upper branches, snapping and breaking them until only silence as his body lay bleeding upon the snow-covered ground.

Kyne's eyes jerked open as he coughed hard, blood oozing out of the side of his mouth. He coughed again and a massive sharp pain was felt in his abdomen as his body recoiled. It was dark and frigid; the snowfall had ceased, and the edges of the clouds rolled by revealing the stars up above.

He coughed again as he tried to rise to his feet, but he stumbled over and fell upon his side. The snow was deep, nearly to his waist and it was so cold, cold unlike he had ever felt before.

"I have... I have to get up," he muttered, and he planted both hands upon the snow. Sinking deep down, Kyne winced as the icy top layer met his face and he lay there unmoving for a moment, his breath hard and heavy.

Pushing again, he managed to rise up and that's when he saw it. The dark red and warmth of blood as it oozed out of his abdomen. His hands reached down, and he could feel it. A tree branch had been thrust clear through, bursting out of his back just below his ribs. His vision swam and his mind grew foggy at the sight.

This... This can't be happening, he thought. He could feel his mind slipping away and his body growing heavy and cold.

"Asira," he said as he swayed, struggling to remain upright. "Asira!"

But no pull of aura was felt, and the wound remained, fresh and bleeding. His vision darkened for a moment and the next thing he knew; he was lying in the snow.

He needed to stop the bleeding, if he didn't then he would die. There was no sign of Auriel or Ni'Bara or anyone. It was just him, all alone in the dark and freezing snow.

"Asira," he whispered one last time, a single tear trailing down his cheek as he closed his eyes.

His eyes suddenly jerked open, as if he had been given new energy and he grunted as he rose to his feet. He would not die here! His family needed him!

Ripping his pack off his back, he grabbed a hold of the flap and said, "Otri!" A dark flash enveloped him and then he dropped to his knees on the cold stone ground. "Igathion!" Lights burst into life, and he smiled weakly. "At least the Ouroboros Bag works."

Staggering up, he walked himself agonizingly slowly towards the place where he stored his medicinal supplies.

They weren't far and after a short time he finally made it. Gathering what few things he could, he made his way to an open area and placed a water basin down. Pouring a few different ointments, silvery powders, and liquids, he finally tossed in a clean rag before he slumped down with his back against the wall. the branch lightly grazed the stone, and a sharp lightning bolt of pain tore through him, and he gritted his teeth. He had to get that thing out of him, but he was worried that if he did, he would bleed out.

He knew basic human anatomy from his lessons with Voron. Knew exactly where to stab someone to make them die fast. His wound was lucky. An inch or two higher and it could've hit his spleen, causing him to bleed out in minutes.

I don't think it hit anything super vital, he thought to himself more in hope than in confidence. He had to get the branch out, there was no other choice. Gripping it hard with both hands, he breathed out a few times rapidly as if getting the courage to pull. He could feel the smooth bark of the branch as he tightened his grip. It was large, big enough to grasp it with both hands.

With a jerk, he pulled hard, and the branch slid a few inches out before coming to a stop, a fresh new trickle of blood flowing from the wound staining his shirt. He grimaced in pain for a long moment before it subsided back to the long dull ache that he had felt for a time.

I can do this!

Screaming, he pulled as hard as he could and with a sickening slurp, the branch came free. Immediately he could breathe easier, and he gasped with relief. A gush of blood followed the branch, splashing onto his lap. He only had moments.

Rolling up the medicinal cloth, he grimaced and thrust it deep into his abdomen. A cry erupted from him, but he kept pushing until he could feel the edge of the wound with his wrist. Jerking his hand out, he flopped it down as the stinging intensified for a long moment before the first sign of relief was felt. The blood slowed to a trickle and then eventually stopped all together.

The Legend of Kyne: Chronocide

He was alive, at least for now.

The Legend of Kyne: Chronocide

45. Dwindling Aura

The lights within the bag flickered as if the flames upon the torches had been touched by a rough wind. Flickering heavily again, Kyne stared in shock as one by one the torches dimmed and then went out completely. Darkness quickly enveloped him, and a chilling breeze swept throughout the Ouroboros Bag.

"Igathion," Kyne called but the torches did not relight. Goosebumps crept across his skin as he staggered to his feet. He was weak and mildly lightheaded, but he managed to stand up and slide along the wall of the building. He needed warmer clothes as the air continued to chill.

After a few minutes, he had managed to find his way into the building and over to where he had his extra clothes that he had collected. Fumbling through the darkness, he felt the familiar thick coat that he once had carried and drew it up. No dust covered the material even though it had been years since it had been touched. The Ouroboros Bag prevented aging and other forms of decay with its strange magic.

Drawing the coat around him, he felt the relief of its silky warmth and sighed as he took a seat.

I'll rest here for a while, regain my strength, he thought to himself as he closed his eyes. His wound stung, but the pain was much more tolerable than dying and he sat there for a long moment. Just a little rest, that's all he wanted.

Suddenly he heard the sound of something falling over outside.

Panic raced through his mind, his eyes splitting open, and he reached for his sword as he staggered to his feet. Drawing it slowly, he crept towards the doorway with his hand outstretched. A dim light

The Legend of Kyne: Chronocide

shined from the sphere on the pommel of Aurora, and he could just make out the silhouette of his hand when more crashing was heard outside. Abruptly, the whole building shifted to the side, knocking him off balance and sending him crashing to the ground with the feather blade sliding away from him. Items fell all around, dimly lit shapes as they crashed upon the ground. The sound of glass shattering sounded nearby and then a hard object stuck his shoulder. The whole building lurched to the side again and a low groan sounded outside as it slid across the stone floor of the bag.

Kyne scrambled over to the glowing silhouette of Aurora and drew back up to his full height before making his way as quickly as he could to the door. Casting it open, he was met with a shocking sight.

Outside the building, he could see to his left the edge of the Ouroboros bags wall sliding in against the side of the building. The faint light from his blade was enough to let him see that other things had been caught in its slow movement and were steadily all being carried towards what he would assume to be the center of the bag where the silver serpent lay.

Sheathing his sword, he then lifted the scabbard up, to cast the fading light around while he watched as the nearby smelter and forge were overrun by a small food storage building, pinning it between the two and crushing it from the force as the slow-moving wall continued its journey.

The entire bag was shrinking but the objects inside were not!

He had to get out! If he didn't, he too would be caught in between something and crushed to death as everything within the bag imploded in on itself.

Stepping out of the building, Kyne started a quick jog, the fastest that he could manage as he headed towards the center of the bag. It was a few hundred feet away, much closer than it should be as the building had traveled a good distance but the moving walls were seeming to increase in speed. He pushed on but the wall that was slowly drifting behind him was beginning to catch up.

There! he thought as the light cast from his sword reflected off of the metallic serpent. Above it, he could just make out the opening less than a foot across and nearly thirty feet up casting a dim white light from outside.

The Legend of Kyne: Chronocide

His heart was thumping hard in his chest as each footstep shot pain through his abdomen, but he was almost there.

As his feet hit the serpent, he immediately jumped, expecting the rush up as he left the bag, but nothing happened, and he landed back upon the stone ground. Gathering his strength, he jumped as hard as he could, expecting the bag's aura to take him up towards the opening high above but he only lifted off a few feet before returning to the ground. Trying again, Kyne was dumbfounded as the bag's aura had seemingly vanished leaving him trapped as the bag continued towards him.

All around him, the buildings and objects that the bag contained pressed in as it all approached the center of the bag. He looked back up at the high opening and noticed that the ceiling above was descending. Hope appeared for but a moment before it vanished. The rate it was moving was not fast enough. The sides of the bag would crush him long before he could reach it!

There has to be a way out! Kyne panicked as he whipped his vision around. The light from the pommel was rapidly fading and the outside sky was barely any light at all. The silhouettes of the approaching objects were growing darker and their sounds growing louder.

He had one shot to get out. If he missed it, then it was all over.

Running off the platform, more of a hobble, he leapt as high as he could and managed to just grab the lip of the roof of the forge, its shingles cutting into his fingers from the rough stone. His abdomen screamed in protest, and he could feel his shirt growing wet as his wound was reopened. He pulled with all his might, ignoring the pain and the thought of bleeding out. The building trembled as it began to press into other buildings on its sides. Wood crunched and splintered but he just managed to make it up onto the roof.

He steadied himself, the feeling of walking on the deck of a ship caught in a storm the only way he would describe it. The hole was still too high but drawing nearer and he climbed up the splintering wood like a makeshift ladder, clambering onto a higher section of roof. The hole was nearly there, just out of reach and the crunching continued, causing the roof to shudder and sway as everything in the bag crushed in on itself.

The Legend of Kyne: Chronocide

Just as the roof collapsed, he pushed off as hard as he could and managed to catch the edge of bag. Pulling, he got up to his armpits when a pressure was felt on the bottom of his feet that lifted him up to the surface of the bag where he leapt out as a cloud of dust and broken wood burst from the opening.

He had made it!

Barely.

Loud groans sounded and more wood burst out of the opening of the bag for a long moment before growing still and silent. The bag remained upright, with a few splintered pieces of wood nearly a foot long and other items poking haphazardly out of the bag.

Breathing out a long sigh, Kyne watched as his breath turned to fog as it left his lips and he shuddered from the cold. It was a frigid cold; unlike anything he had felt in such a long time. The cold normally didn't bother him much anymore, but this was different.

Scanning his vision around, he saw the skeleton shapes of trees bare of all their leaves surrounding him. He could only see a few trees away before they faded in the fog like snow that was falling thickly around him. It was deep, nearly to his waist and burned as it slipped beneath his pant legs into his boots.

He had no idea where he was, let alone when he was. All he knew was that he was alone, trapped in a forgotten time.

He shivered hard as he made his way back over to the Ouroboros Bag, stooping down, he grabbed onto the black leather straps and pulled it so he could throw it over his back. The bag didn't budge an inch as if it had been anchored to the ground. He pulled again, this time with both hands but still the bag refused to move.

He was dumbfounded, no aura seemed to work, and it was as if the very Relics of Aute had lost their power as well.

"When the hell am I?"

Dropping the strap, Kyne sat down in the snow next to the pack for a long time, the black leather was slowly being covered with thick flakes of snow that quickly obscured the silver ouroboros.

"I'm sorry Voron," Kyne whispered. "I can't take it with me, it's too heavy. I will do my best to retrieve it when I can... If I can," he added.

He shivered again, hard, each muscle trembling from the

The Legend of Kyne: Chronocide

exertion. His abdomen screamed in protest, and he clutched it tight, holding it still as he fought the shivering. He rose up to his feet. He would freeze to death out here if he didn't find shelter from this cold. He had to get moving.

He had no idea where he was going but he had to try something. Choosing a direction that felt right to him, he started his journey, trudging through the deep snow. His thighs were burning immediately from the strain, but he pushed on, the activity keeping his blood moving and warming him up. His breath was quick, and he focused on drawing it in his mouth and out his nose, but soon his throat was dry and aching from the frigid air.

The snow seemed to intensify, and a powerful wind ripped through the trees, shaking their bare branches violently and almost knocking him over. Crouching down, his shoulders drawing nearly level with the snow, he pulled his hood up tightly over his head and hunched down even lower, pulling his arms in tight to his body. The wind continued for a minute or so before dying down to a cold breeze.

As he pushed on, the trees seemed to thicken, growing closer together and making it harder for him to navigate around them. Ducking low, He swept underneath a branch before immediately having to scramble over another branch. A sharp pain erupted upon his brow as he struck his head hard on a low-lying branch he hadn't noticed, and he winced for a moment while rubbing it violently.

He was pissed off at everything! At this icy world, at the lack of aura, at how his family was gone and he was all alone. Crying out in frustration, he punched his left arm deep into the snow and felt his knuckles reach the bottom in a firm thump. Pulling it up, he saw his dragon scales covered in snow, their grey gleam fading to a matte. Suddenly, a single scale fell off, drifting to the ground like an autumn leaf. Another one soon followed and beneath them, he could just make out the pale color of his human skin.

A wave of depression rolled over him as he lost his catalyst, each scale flaking off until his human hand was once more. He fought the urge to cry, to give up entirely. He had lost everything and was on the brink of death.

He couldn't do that; he couldn't do that to the others. They were out there somewhere waiting for him to return.

The Legend of Kyne: Chronocide

Shaking the remaining scales off his arm, he stared at them for a long moment, a burning feeling encroaching in his chest before he lifted his gaze and trudged on, focusing only on his breathing.

A few minutes later he found himself staring at a large crumbling stone wall. He finally knew where he was. He was outside of Alakyne.

The Legend of Kyne: Chronocide

46. Ruins of Alakyne

Kyne held his breath and tried to remain as still as possible, each muscle trembling slightly from the awkward position as he crouched down low against the wall. Two muffled voices were heard from up above him, possibly upon the rooftops as the windows would have changed the sounds of the voices. He couldn't make out any words, other than one.

"Hunt."

Kyne grunted as he grasped his abdomen, the pain from his stab wound burning like a hot iron had been thrust deep. His position was irritating it, that much he could tell and as he adjusted by slowly twisting on the balls of his feet and dropping to a knee. He felt some relief.

He had ventured into the city through a gaping hole in the crumbling wall, a shadow of its former glory. Archaic in sight, the city looked aged and worn, bricks crumbling to the ground in shabby piles the mortar flecking away. Snow littered the ground obscuring the streets in its thick blanket. It was thinner here, only to his shins but the cold was ever present.

Movement up ahead in the ruined street grabbed his attention and he watched as a dark figure dashed out from a hidden alcove and leapt into a pile of moldy and frozen hay and wooden splinters.

Cries of shock sounded as a small figure was ripped out of the hay and thrown to the ground by the figure. The cries were feminine and as Kyne squinted his eyes through the snowy air, he could just make out her long hair.

The girl was young, that much Kyne could tell, most likely in her early teenage years and her cries were silenced as the dark figure struck her across the face.

The Legend of Kyne: Chronocide

Rage flew from Kyne as he rose to his feet, gripping the hilt of his feather blade. He took a few steps, inching forward along the edge of the wall. He was in no shape to fight, let alone defeat this figure.

But he couldn't let anything happen to this child!

Taking a few more steps, he suddenly stopped still as two other figures leapt down from the roof of the building he was against. Landing on a small snowbank right in front of him. Kyne dropped low, praying that he hadn't been seen and to his relief the two hopped up to their feet and approached the other figure. The falling snow had thinned and the light from the partially obscured moons allowed Kyne to see the figures more clearly. The two who had their backs to him were most likely male with the other figure they were approaching a skinny and lanky younger man, around his own age.

"Gentlemen," called the first figure right before he kicked the girl in the back, sending her sprawling face forward in the snow. "You are more than welcome to watch, and once I'm done with her you can take your turn."

The two said nothing and continued their approach.

As they neared, roughly a dozen feet, the first figure drew a small blade and bent his knees down in a more offensive stance.

"I have been polite to both of you but if you have any interest in interfering with my play time then I'll kill you myself."

"We are here for you, for both of you," said one and he drew his own short sword.

"Your meat will feed us for the next few weeks."

Kyne's stomach turned at those words and the young girl screamed in terror.

Leaping forward, one of the cannibals struck wide, aiming for his head while the other dashed around, trying to flank him. A few more strikes were exchanged and seemingly to no one's notice, the young girl scrambled to her feet and disappeared running down a different street. The young man, with his dagger raised suddenly leapt forward, aiming straight for the other man's chest.

A twist of his shoulder followed by an arm lock and then there was silence as they stared at each other. Kyne could see it, the fear of eminent death in the young man's eyes as he was held pinned. Kyne could feel his heart thumping in his neck, his knuckles white as they clenched his blade. The other man suddenly stepped up behind and to Kyne's horror, bit down upon the man's neck.

A gurgled cry of pain and shock erupted from the young man as his throat was tore out. Blood oozed down in dark scarlet waves, staining his clothes and the icy snow beneath his feet leaving a growing pool.

The man released his grip and he fell to the ground, twitching and gurgling as blood continued to ooze from his neck and mouth, bubbles forming as he tried to breathe and his eyes growing hazy.

A loud spit sound followed as the man spat out the piece of neck from his mouth and he wiped his hand across his mouth, smearing the blood into his thick beard.

"We got us some good eating tonight," he erupted with joy as he lightly kicked the lifeless corpse upon the ground.

"So much wasted food," hissed the other and he stooped down and began to drink the still oozing blood from the man's neck. After a few moments, he raised his head up to the sky, gasping in satisfaction. "Such a warm a delicious treat!"

"Move," said the other and he shoved the first from the body as he too stooped down to consume the blood.

Kyne felt sick and he tried not to gag as he crept back along the wall away from the scene. shock and disgust were now quickly being replaced by panic as the thought of those two finding him and eating him flew through his mind. Once he was out of sight of those two, he took off in the fastest jog that he could, down the deserted streets of the ruined city of Alakyne.

47. Draconic

    Kyne's breath was heavy, each inhale and exhale flowing through his mouth. He was panting hard, exhausted and freezing as his footsteps crunched under the icy snow that lay upon the ground. The sky was beginning to brighten but still cast in a grey cloak of fog as he continued on as far away as he could get from the cannibals.

    The city was in ruin, buildings looking to have been abandoned for years and no sign of other humans. He was terrified, unsure if he was noticed by some unseen eyes within the shadows, but he carried on. He didn't know where he was going, all he knew was that he needed to find his family.

    They must've been cast here as well, he thought as he crept along the edge of a building approaching a small intersection in the streets. Behind him he could see the trail of his footprints and he cursed at not realizing it. His trail was completely visible to anyone who wanted to find him. The sharp edges of each indentation signaling the freshness of the trail. Scanning its length, he watched it fade to a foggy grey but saw no one, at least no one yet who was following him. He needed to get out of the snow, or somehow wipe away his tracks.

    Peeking around the corner, Kyne saw no one down the street and just as he took a step, he felt something crack under his foot. Glancing down, he saw something grey sticking out of the snow and as he brushed it away revealing the object, he recoiled back in disgust and horror.

    It was a human arm, bent funny with its flesh blue and in a frozen state of rot. Pieces had been bitten through the flesh revealing black muscle tissue beneath, covered in a white frost. It was almost shiny as it stuck out of the snow only a few inches, the purplish-blue fingernails drawing his attention. The snow was deep, but Kyne could

The Legend of Kyne: Chronocide

just make out the slight bump of what he assumed to be the body upon the surface of the snow. It was too hard to tell how long it had been there, but he was revolted at its sight.

Skirting around the corpse, Kyne looked around the city again, noticing the light was beginning to grow brighter as it was scattered through the thinning clouds. He knew Alakyne fairly well but in its destroyed state it was hard to tell exactly where he was. Looking further through the fog as it hung over the city, he started to notice strange jagged black marks upon some of the buildings, as if someone had splashed tar upon their surface. It was a light splatter, but all seemed to be upon just one side and as he placed his hand upon its cold surface, he felt it to be made of some kind of black glass.

Kyne touched it again, rubbing his left hand upon its surface and staring at the human features that had returned. His fingernails were long, not matching his other hand and his skin was paler as well from the shade it had experienced the last few years. He felt his chest tighten at its sight in sadness and anger and he let it drop limply to his side.

Further up ahead, he noticed the black glass that covered the buildings seemed to grow thicker and placing the rising sun on his right, began to venture further into the city. All of the northern edges of the buildings were covered in the stuff and the further he traveled the thicker it seemed to grow, forming great clumps that started to wrap around the corners of the buildings.

Footsteps were noticed in the snow, but they seemed old and partially filled in, so Kyne continued on cautiously the glass growing thicker and thicker. Far ahead as the snow stopped completely and the fog began to lift, he started to notice that the clumps had changed to jagged black spears that seemed to crawl around the sides of the building, their blade like surfaces reminding him of horizontal icicles as they stretched away from their source. Growing thicker and larger as he looked up the street, Kyne finally understood where they came from.

At the northern end of the city a massive mountain of black spikes radiated out from where the citadel once stood, the stone walls pierced and filleted into pieces by the barbs. The force that had caused them seemed to have blasted out from that very spot, spreading and covering all the sides of the buildings that faced it in glass. As it

The Legend of Kyne: Chronocide

wrapped around the buildings it formed identical spikes all pointing away from the center of it all.

The spiked mass was incredible, each black dagger stretching far through the walls of the citadel, their crumbling stone piled along the dark glass. The mass nearly doubled the immense size the citadel once had and had even pierced through the great wall that lay behind it.

What happened? Kyne thought and he continued on making his way towards the citadel. The closer he drew it became ever more dangerous as the barbs thickened and became more numerous. If he didn't pay attention, he could run straight into one impaling him and ending everything.

The slope of the city curved up as he neared the citadel and just as a light breeze drifted away, he noticed voices. Creeping along the edge of a building near the destroyed wall of the citadel he saw a few Dominion soldiers leading a cart around the spikes making their way towards it. Within the cart, partially covered by snow Kyne could see some strange glowing objects but he couldn't make out what they were.

More shouting came and he realized that the soldiers were yelling at the people who were pulling the cart. They were dressed in thin rags, their skin covered in snow and black sections covered their ears and fingers. They were freezing to death and Kyne watched as a sentinel whipped one across the back, barking orders to speed up as the slave screamed as he dragged the cart up the hill.

More whips cracked through the air as the sentinel struck the ground, each snap causing the slaves to flinch. Cries of fear erupted, and they pulled the cart harder climbing into the ruins of the citadel.

Kyne waited until the area was clear and then he pursued them, creeping across the snow as quietly as he could and entering. The courtyard was decimated, a hollow shell of what it once was, and he saw up ahead the slaves walking around the spikes heading towards a dark hole in the citadel's wall. Bodies ranging from fresh perfectly frozen bodies to nearly bones and every version of decomposition in between covered the hundreds of needle tipped points as if they had been thrust onto them to be displayed as trophies. Some were Kydrëans and others Gaeilian, but they all were very much dead.

Kyne skirted around one and saw their glassy frozen eyes, their

The Legend of Kyne: Chronocide

mouth locked in an immortal scream as they hung looking down at the black glass spike that had impaled them. It was a woman, nearly Kyne's own age and she looked to be perfectly preserved, eerily almost still alive, the humanity still visible across her face.

Shouting drew his attention, and he heard another crack of a whip from within the citadel and noticed the glow of orange torchlight. Dashing through the courtyard, he ventured into the citadel and found himself in a hallway, dozens of spikes piercing through the left side wall, some short with their deadly tips visible and others much thicker and puncturing completely through the other side of the hall out into the city beyond. The carts were out of sight, further into the darkness, and Kyne ducked under a glassy black crossbeam that was blocking his path.

Streams of faint light crept through the cracks in the crumbling walls allowing him to make out the silhouetted shapes of the black spears enough to avoid them as he pursued the sentinels. They traveled around the citadel, seemingly in a large circle as dozens of alternate paths had either been completely blocked by black glass quills or the halls had caved in from the floors above. Progressively they made their way higher and higher into the citadel and accompanying his quiet footsteps Kyne began to notice a slight muffled rumble. As they traveled on, the rumbling seemed to grow louder, a deep groan that made his bones quiver. It was not deafening but a constant background noise that made him uneasy as the hairs on the back of his neck rose up.

Rounding a corner, he caught his breath and dashed back, nearly being seen by the sentinels a few dozen feet away who had been stopped in front of a large ornate door. The King's Chambers lay beyond that, Kyne knew it and peeking around, he watched as one of the slaves was whipped for refusing an order. They were beaten mercilessly, each strike making Kyne wince, their screaming and pleading reduced to grunts and sobs.

A few more orders and the other slaves pushed the door open. They were ordered inside leaving the cart full of glowing objects in the hallway. The sentinels never stepped a foot inside, merely tossing the beaten slave inside, never crossing the precipice. They laughed as screams started before slamming the door shut.

The Legend of Kyne: Chronocide

More muffled screams followed, and Kyne cringed, trying to drive the sounds out of his head. Silence eventually came and hung in the air for a long while. The sentinels muttered something before the doors were reopened and they guided the cart inside.

Kyne ran down the hall and managed to stop the door from closing completely. Using one eye, he peaked inside but he could barely make out anything. The sentinel's backs blocked his view, but he could tell the source of the constant rumbling lay within the room.

The clicking of something upon the stone ground drew his attention and then a crunch as something shattered. More crunches and Kyne almost thought it sounded like chewing. He drew Aurora, imagining the calming relief the blade once had and pushed the door open further, allowing him to squeeze his body inside.

The sentinels had migrated further into the room, weaving around black spines that covered the floor that still remained, the back half of the room still torn apart. They were cautiously pushing the cart toward the center, the only place bare of the black glass in a perfect circle. Stretching around like a droplet frozen after it hit the surface of the water, the spikes were small, stretching across the floor but rapidly grew in size before the largest pierced through the walls on all sides of the room.

The rumbling intensified and something hideous shifted, making its way towards the barren center in a shuffling crawl. Upon all fours, it bore no tail but sickly grey skin with sores all over its body. Large in stature, it looked to be nearly seven feet tall if fully erect. No scales covered its hide nor hair and its face wasn't visible, obscure by the sentinels. More chewing was heard as Kyne shifted behind a black spear-like column, crouching and waiting, his heart thumping hard in his chest.

The creature shifted its stance as it continued to eat, sparks of the glowing items falling to the ground as it chewed, allowing Kyne a better look. Claws covered its hands and sprouting from its forearms looked to be the remnants of disfigured wings, never fully formed and torn into shreds. It was large, taller than Kyne by nearly a foot.

The creature trembled and the rumbling intensified, like that of a purring cat and Kyne felt the hairs on the back of his neck stand up as his anxiety increased.

The Legend of Kyne: Chronocide

It finally raised its head and Kyne caught his breath at the sight of a disgusting scaleless draconic features, its teeth covered in dried blood and glowing crystal as it chewed another mouthful. Cracked spines covered its head and it flicked it back, swallowing the meal it was consuming. Just as it stretched down for another bite, it paused, its back twitching and its nose flaring.

Opening its mouth, it clicked its jaw closed in a clapping sound as it jerked side to side erratically, its mouth salivating and dripping to the floor.

Then it spoke.

"I... I... I smell something!" it stammered in a breathy hiss. "It... It is familiar and brings a great hunger to me. I know you are... Are here! So many years it... It... It has been since we last met!" and the dragon's head suddenly jerked towards Kyne's direction. As they met their gaze, the scaleless beast's lip curled in a hideous sneer, its eyes a glassy white as it just stared for a long moment.

"I... I succeeded," it stammered, and it crawled around the sentinels who had drawn their swords upon the sight of Kyne. "Did you... Did you see, did you feel. It is gone... Gone... Gone! All of it, *aura* is gone from this world because of me," it said drawing out the last syllable in a hiss.

Kyne's skin crawled and he clenched tightly upon the hilt of his blade. He finally understood what this was, who this was.

"What happened to you Kyne," he said as he raised Aurora up and stepped completely around the black spike. "What have you become?"

"An evolution of you," it hissed. "D... D... Dragon aura has been imbued into my very soul exceeding what you once had. I am so... So... So glad that we finally meet once again, it has been far too long. Twenty years I have thirsted for your blood!"

Kyne reached up, grasping his blade firmly in both hands and taking a traditional stance. His abdomen throbbed but the adrenaline had taken over, a nauseating wave that made his whole-body quiver violently.

"You ruined the world," Kyne whispered.

"I saved it!"

A bloodcurdling screech erupted from the beast, and it dashed forward, knocking a sentinel to the ground and its claws raised. Kyne swung around the black spike just as the draconic monster collided with it in a crash, its claws screaming as they were ranked against it. Another screech as it scrambled around the pillar, after Kyne with an insatiable bloodlust.

Kyne dashed away but it was after him again, pursuing him as he leapt around the room. The exit was blocked by the incoming monster's mass as it hurtled towards him. The sentinels had momentarily watched the battle but had now decided to join, making their way after him and pushing him back towards the missing half of the room and the fall that would lead to his death.

As they stepped in between him and the monster, the air erupted in a roar followed by screams as the sentinels were torn apart, their bronze armor pierced by its claws and limbs ripped off. Blood splattered the room as it bit down upon their necks, its fangs sinking deep before tearing their throats out!

Kyne had to escape!

He was pressed up against the cliff-like edge, his heels hanging off and knocking a few loose rocks where they fell out of view. His heart was racing as he held up Aurora, his arms trembling in fear, actual fear.

The final sentinel sputtered on the ground, bubbles forming in the blood that littered his neck as he tried to breathe before he went limp, the draconic tossing him roughly to the ground. Blood drenched the beast's maw, coating the sickly grey skin in scarlet and rendering the white fangs red.

Its eyes were trained upon Kyne with a malice unlike anything he had ever felt, white and hollow.

Kyne was out of room; he wouldn't make it to the door and there weren't any forms of cover here. He swept his head back and forth as the monster approached, slowing as it crawled on all fours.

There!

He had one option and risking everything, he twisted and jumped, the draconic missing him as it leapt too. Kyne sailed through the air, falling over a dozen feet before he landed hard on the floor below, slamming into the wall and balancing narrowly on a small ledge. The bricks beneath his feet shuddered but held and he grimaced in

The Legend of Kyne: Chronocide

pain as his knees took the force.

A screech above came from the beast and Kyne dashed to the side right before it leapt down and collided with the wall, knocking it to pieces as it scrambled to stay balanced. It flailed for a moment, the ground giving out and then it fell, falling out of view.

Kyne caught his breath and looked around. This room was smaller, the doorway had been covered in fallen rubble trapping him inside. He could see a small crack in the broken wall where a large glassy spike had pierced through it with darkness beyond. He wasn't sure if he would even be able to fit through or how far it went but it seemed to be his only opportunity.

Looking back at the edge, he saw the draconic beast's hand stretch up into view, fumbling as it looked for a hand hold before digging its claws deep. A second later its head peered over, spotting Kyne instantly.

Kyne rocketed across the room as fast as he could. Each footstep was loud, and a louder pounding soon followed. He risked a glance back, knowing it was dangerous, but he needed to know. He was just in time, just in time to see the beast was nearly upon him, its jaw open lunging for the kill. Twisting over his shoulder, he slammed his back into the wall, its surface splattered with the blackened glass and raised his blade desperately.

The draconic was there, an arm lengths away and with a desperate swipe, Kyne sailed Aurora through the air where it collided will the draconic's outstretched arm. His jaws stopped inches from Kyne as a thud and a splatter of dark blood coated his face followed by screeches of pain and rage as the maddened dragon then flung his head around clutching his spewing stump.

His glassy eyes were wide with a crazed look and Kyne saw just on the edges of his mouth a flicker of heat almost like a mirage.

Kyne was close to him, close enough to end him right there! One final swing, that is all it would take, and he could possibly end the beast that had caused so much horror but something inside him screamed to flee, screamed that it would be a fatal mistake to fight him. A short inhalation and he ripped down the wall, dashing for the crack-like opening. At once a massive wave of heat struck him in the back and he twisted around just in time to see the place he had been standing covered in a pale, almost clear flame, the stone already bright red and oozing!

The stone started to slouch as it turned to putty and a swipe of the beast's only hand through it sent flecks of liquid stone flying in all directions.

If I had tried to attack him, I would have... Images of bubbling and charred flesh lit up in his mind and then he was there, the black spike protruding through the wall and a human sized crack upon its left side.

Turning to his side, he jammed his shoulders through the gap and with a cry, burst forth onto the other side just as the wall shuddered as the beast impacted it.

He was in a hallway, littered with more spears of black glass, Kyne finally recognized what they reminded him of as he bolted down the hall weaning in and out. It was the black diamonds that hovered above the seraph's islands back in the other world!

That's what they are! his thoughts screamed as a crash sounded behind him followed by more shrieks and falling stone. *They are virtually identical. He has done something nearly on the level of a god but what?*

Leaping down a flight of stairs, Kyne rolled over his shoulder on the impact and continued running, the adrenaline of the threat of imminent death shrouding the pain in his abdomen.

"I can smell you mortal!" screeched a draconic voice and then the hallway was engulfed in another jet of the nearly invisible flame.

Kyne could feel the heat rapidly approaching from behind him and without any other options he tucked around a jagged spine of glass that reminded him of a shark fin. A little wider than his shoulders, he tucked in the small space behind it just as the flames overcame it, ripping down the hallway another few dozen feet before slamming into the wall beyond.

The heat was more intense than Kyne could handle, and he felt his flesh screaming for relief as the black blade split the flames like a rudder in water. Another second that felt like an eternity passed and then the fire ceased.

He gasped at the immediate relief but out of the corner of his eye saw something glowing on his shoulder. Patting the flames that had ignited his clothes frantically, he revealed a scorched part of his shoulder and the red flesh underneath, burned but luckily not charred.

The Legend of Kyne: Chronocide

He had to escape this place but how? How was he to escape this monster?

Ragged coughs were sounded far behind him and then the clatter of something falling to the ground. More coughing and more clattering drew Kyne's attention and he peaked around his hiding place to see a ways away through the forest of glass blades to the bottom of the stairs. Sparkling objects were tumbling down the steps, casting faint glowing light around as they clattered down to its base where they came to a stop.

Suddenly a single warped arm came into view, sickly claws accented each fingertip and the shredded membranes of the imitation wings scraping against the floor. Another arm came into view and to Kyne's shock the beast put its full weight upon the bloodied stump, still dripping scarlet drops. Another cough erupted from the beast and more stones were belched from its mouth spewing to the ground in a dazzling rainbow.

The monster stumbled down the steps and came to the base, Kyne so intrigued with what was going on he seemed to be rooted to the spot. He had remained hidden behind the glass a few dozen feet down the hallway and hadn't been spotted yet. Another coughing fit and then the draconic Kyne started chewing the stones up again, flashes of light being seen between his teeth as they were crunched before being swallowed. Another mouthful and Kyne watched as the beast seemed to grow stronger, its posture increasing and the constant rumbling increasing in volume.

What are those things?

He had seen enough and wanted to get out of there. With a fleeting amount of hope that was immediately extinguished, he said a spell to no effect before he took off down the hall and flew around a corner leaving the monster far behind. The hallway was growing darker as they delved deeper into the ruins of the citadel, no longer streams of faint light illuminated his path and he collided with a few dark objects, each one jarring his body and shooting pain through his brain.

Crashes sounded behind him but they were more distant, and he pushed on, trying to get more separation between them. A few more corners were rounded, each time causing him more frustration as most of his pathways were increasingly blocked, the spikes growing more

The Legend of Kyne: Chronocide

numerous before suddenly he burst out into the snow-covered street, startling a small cluster of people down its edge next to a small fire.

Their surprise was not noticed by Kyne, and he skirted around them not paying much attention to if they were Kydrëan or Gaeilian. More crashes sounded and then a large thump and Kyne turned to see the beast had burst through the wall a few stories up and fallen to the ground on his side. There it stayed for a few moments before staggering up to all fours and sniffing the air.

Screams came from the people he passed by giving him a disgusting hope of escape as they were attacked by the monster which could allow Kyne to gain more distance. Each footstep was shin deep in the snow as he pushed on. The sky had lightened up quite a bit more with the grey clouds having risen up higher above the landscape releasing its foggy grip on those who lived below.

Kyne encountered no more people as he dashed down a street, trying to look for any place that he could hide but with a thought pressing deep in his mind.

He couldn't hide here. Getting into one of these buildings would be suicide, just waiting to be torn apart by that beast when it eventually found him. So, he pushed on, the black splattered glass thinning as he went, transitioning from the black splashes of glass to little clumps and then nothing.

Up ahead he could see the wall of Alakyne, crumbling and nearly completely destroyed but still a large distance away and approaching up the street, a lone horseman, a cape drawn over his back. He was large, way bigger than average and Kyne could feel that he was incredibly dangerous.

Skirting to the other side of the road, he continued on as they neared when he suddenly saw the man draw his blade and bring his horse to a stop. Kyne felt his stomach sink and he raised Aurora up to his challenge and then he noticed the man wasn't facing him but was looking down the road. A muffled sound was heard and then a rumbling before the beast flew into sight, running full speed at them nearly as fast as a horse.

This was it! This was how he died!

Turning around to face him, he took a few shaky steps back, the adrenaline finally wearing off enough to notice the throbbing pain in his abdomen from his injury. Clutching it for a moment, he noticed it was wet with blood. The wound had reopened from his actions and was slowly dripping out.

It wasn't life threatening at the moment and removing his hand, he placed it back upon Aurora's hilt smearing it with red streaks. Movement on the side of his vision caught his attention and out of his periphery he noticed while he had been backing up that the man had been inching forward until they had passed each other.

The monster was almost upon them!

Sweeping his cloak to the side, Kyne noticed a glimmer of a bright blue light and then the man was holding a similar glowing stone in his hand. Energy seemed to crawl up his arms, causing his veins to glow and swell and without a sound coming from him, a flash of electricity burst forth and tore down the street before colliding with the monster in a flash followed by a deafening boom of a thunderclap.

It screeched and stopped dead in its tracks, a smoldering patch visible upon his bare shoulder. Its body trembled and then it jerked its head towards this new opponent, a crazed rage in its eye as it took a few steps forward, its head swinging in erratic movements.

The stone was still glowing, but much fainter than before and suddenly another bolt flew out of it towards the beast.

It was aura! but how? screamed Kyne's thoughts and he spoke a similar spell to no avail. Just to his side, he saw the dark figure of the man's horse come into view and a thought came into his head. A thought that he hated more than anything but had to agree with.

That is how he could escape.

Another much dimmer flash came from the man and then grunts as he tried to deflect a swipe from the beast who was upon him. Without another look, Kyne dashed to the horse and leapt into the saddle to its shock. A loud whinny came from it in fright, but Kyne paid it no attention and pulled the reins to the side causing it to pivot around. A kick from his heel and they were off, dashing down the street at full speed.

Throwing a last glance back he watched as the man deflected another swipe before screaming in pain and dropping to the floor. The beast was nearby, its mouth open revealing its serrated teeth and Kyne could see the heatwave distorting the light in shimmers from the clear

The Legend of Kyne: Chronocide

flame as it swallowed the man.

The galloping sounds were all he could hear as he guided the horse through the gateway in the wall, their crunching echo reflecting all around and then he was gone, out of the city and flying over the open countryside leaving Alakyne behind in its ruined state.

*   *   *

48. The Curse of the Child

"Alakyne," Auriel gasped, and she heard the shuffling of Ni'Bara's head move upon the sound of the name. She threw her gaze at the sleeping boy and then back to Aria who was matching her look of shock.

"What's wrong?" Aria asked puzzled. "Why are you shocked at his name?"

"It..." stammered Auriel but before she could respond Ni'Bara interrupted.

"That's her husband's name," he said.

"His name is Alakyne?"

"Well kind of, it's just Kyne but he is named after Alakyne."

She seemed confused but Ni'Bara continued. "It's a family name given to him by his father. Such an odd coincidence they are virtually the same."

"Very odd," Auriel muttered initially taken aback with Ni'Bara's skirting around the situation. As she met his eye and his long stare, she understood why he had interrupted her.

They cannot know anything, it could corrupt the timeline, his eyes seemed to say to her. She nodded briefly as she understood his gaze before smiling at Aria.

"So, you are Aria and Alakyne. Nice to meet you."

The crackling of the fire sounded, and she turned to see a thick log had cracked in two halves, bending in the center where the bark glowed a deep orange. Along its edges she could see the dark patches aligned with the white of ash and with a sigh she stood up and tossed another log upon the fire.

"You should get some sleep young one," yawned Ni'Bara. "We have a long day ahead of us tomorrow."

"I can't yet," she said, and she eyed her brother. "Not until his curse is made seen."

"His curse?"

The Legend of Kyne: Chronocide

"When he dreams, he occasionally will enter into a strange trance like I was explaining before. I usually am able to stop it before anything happens by waking him up."

"And this happens every night?" Auriel gasped.

"Not everyone but most. It usually happens towards the beginning of his rest. He will go into the trance, speak weird things, and then I wake him up. He then goes back to sleep and in the morning, he has no recollection of what happened."

"Does he know?"

"No, he doesn't. I think he suspects it, but I have led him to believe we are both cursed for some reason."

Auriel was silent. She didn't know what to say to the young girl and she swung her gaze back to the fire. The sparks cracked as the flames licked up the new log, glowing embers rising up into the sky before burning away.

"I can watch him this night Aria," she said. "Why don't you get some rest. I will be fine and Ni'Bara doesn't sleep much either." The dragon snorted at her remark and returned his head back to the ground and he closed his eyes.

Aria stared at her for a moment before looking at the sleeping figure of Alakyne and then back to her. "Are you sure?"

"Of course."

Delight flashed across her face and then as if a curtain had been raised up, the fatigue appeared on the young girl's face. Laying her head down, she closed her eyes and Auriel sat and waited for a long time.

Aria's breathing slowed and after a deep inhalation, she knew that she was finally asleep. Climbing quietly to her feet, she made her way next to Ni'Bara's cheek and sat down, leaning her back against his dark scales.

"I can't believe it," she murmured.

"It shocks me too. Never in my life would I think we would actually meet Alakyne let alone have it be only a young boy. He doesn't seem any different than anyone else except this supposed curse."

"Do you believe her?" Auriel asked.

"I believe that she believes it. Before we learned his name, I was very skeptical but with it being Alakyne it makes me hesitate."

The Legend of Kyne: Chronocide

Auriel nodded. "I was thinking the same thing. We will have to wait and see if it happens."

They both looked at the kids for a long moment.

"So, are we to not say anything?" Auriel asked.

Ni'Bara rumbled deep in his throat like the purring of a cat. "I think it would be unwise. It could alter events like how Kyne caused this whole situation in the first place."

Auriel nodded again, agreeing with the dragon's wise words.

"Ok, we won't say anything. I hope what we have done now hasn't changed anything too significant."

A low moan came from Alakyne, and her skin began to crawl as she stared at him. She was waiting for the glowing eyes but with another groan, the boy rolled over onto his side and continued his sleep.

A sigh of relief came from Auriel, and she leaned her head back against Ni'Bara. She was exhausted too. She hadn't slept for what seemed like days, since she had been captured in the cell and she felt her eyes begin to grow heavy.

"You can sleep Auriel," whispered Ni'Bara. "If anything happens, I will wake you."

Auriel closed her eyes, the euphoric feeling of sleep filling her mind. Falling deep into her sleep, she was nearly there before she jerked her eyes open, and she sat up stiffer.

"No, no," she said, rubbing her eyes and slapping her cheeks lightly. "I told her I would watch him tonight. I can last a little longer."

The dragon snorted in amusement at her determination, and he felt her leave his cheek as she stood up. Walking away from the fire, Auriel left the orange glow and found the silent night air calming. The buzzing of insects made a scene of ambiance as she stared up at the stars. A streak of white flew across the sky and she smiled, closing her eyes and imagining Kyne. She missed him more than anything else in the world. The feeling of losing him brought the deepest feeling of emptiness that she could ever feel, and she tried to push it out. She had friends, others that she could interact with, but it wasn't even remotely similar. She wished the Light would visit her. Fix this whole situation and return her back home. She ran through all of the things she would give up. The first thing she thought of was her aura. She would give it up in a heartbeat to see her husband again. The skills that had been taught to her since birth, second nature to her, like walking and breathing, she would give it up. She would give up the pursuit to see her mother and sister again. To see her people meant nothing if she couldn't see Kyne.

Tears streamed down her cheeks, but her breathing remained calm. She let the waters flow, streaking down her face and dripping to the soft ground below.

There she stood in her silent mourning for such a long time, masking her fatigue better than anything else could. As she finally stopped, her tears drying up but the sorrow still present, she lowered her gaze down and turned back to the fire.

Movement caught her eye, and she gasped in shock as she saw the young Alakyne was climbing to his feet. His eyes were obscured by the orange glow of the fire but as the Riel darted towards him, she could tell something was off.

He stood there, still as stone for a moment as she approached and just before she touched him, he turned his head and spoke in a voice that caused her body to resonate with power.

"You are not meant to be here Riel."

Auriel's hand stopped inches from his shoulder, and she just stared at him.

"What do you mean Alakyne?"

"Your time calls and your husband waits for you. He who shares my name is the only one who can right the wrongs he has caused, but he cannot do it alone. You need to..." his voice was lost as cries of shock erupted from Aria.

"Auriel stop him!"

As if snapping out of a trance, the Riel grabbed hold of his shoulders and jerked him hard, waking the young boy from his dream.

Aria was upon him in a flash and the look she gave Auriel was a mixture of rage and confusion. "You said you would stop him!"

"I... I..." she stammered.

"We need to leave now! The monsters will be coming for us, coming for him!"

"Co... Coming for me?" murmured Alakyne and they both looked at him in shock.

The Legend of Kyne: Chronocide

"No... Not you, us," Aria quickly said but the young boy's eyes opened further, and he jerked away from her touch.

"What do you mean Aria? What are you saying? Am I the one who is cursed?"

"No, no it's not you Alakyne," she started but her brother took a step away.

"You're lying!" he screamed. His eyes were watery. "You're lying!"

"Alakyne I only..."

A screech tore through the night air.

"We need to go!" Aria said and Alakyne's fury had faded away. Running over to Ni'Bara who had risen to his feet, they all leapt onto the saddle and took off, the glow of the fire fading away down below them.

Another screech sounded far below and then the ground where they had been erupted in a flash of red flame as something sprayed it all around. Another beast erupted adding to the flame and as a third joined them, Auriel understood what they were.

Massive golden snakes, their hoods flared open, and their backs covered in flames slithered out of the ground, crushing trees and igniting them on contact as they spread out from one another. Red flames sprayed around bathing the remaining trees and countryside in fire, some flames even spreading across the surface of the river like a thick oil.

Another screech sounded and a dark shape collided with one eldunaga, knocking it to the ground. The moonlight was dim, but they could make out the silhouette of a massive bird as its talons sank into the snake, jerking it around and dodging the fangs at it struck. Finally releasing, the beasts roared at each other before the sky was lit ablaze in a blood red flame. The heat, even from the distance, was felt immediately and Auriel turned her gaze away.

More cries came and Ni'Bara guided them away from the beasts as the countryside was lit ablaze.

49. Those Who Wander the Roads of Kydrëa

It was Alakyne who spoke first, the young boy's voice shaky and upset. Auriel could feel him directly behind her as he turned to face his sister.

"You lied."

"I only did it to protect you!" she said, her voice raising in a desperate tone. "It was the only thing I felt like I could truly do for you."

"So, it was me who killed them then," he cried. "Mother and Father are dead because of me! That thing wouldn't have gotten them if I hadn't been born!"

Auriel was silent and the dragon was as they sat and listened. The air was constantly blowing in their ears as Ni'Bara cruised through the sky.

"Don't say that!" Aria screamed, her voice pushing past the wind. "Don't you ever say that again!"

"Why? Because it's the truth? You know it's true Aria! Don't you lie to me! You know that if I hadn't been born then you and them would still be alive back at home in Ysaroc. You would've never been driven out and you would be happy!"

Aria screamed in frustration and Auriel shuddered at the dark words the boy had said. She knew this fight wasn't hers and that she should keep her mouth shut but she couldn't let this continue any longer. The rift that could grow between them could spell disaster.

"She loves you Alakyne," she started. "She did it to protect you. Even from the short time I have known you I can see it as well as Ni'Bara. You are her entire world, and she would do anything to protect you. Even while you slept, she sat and watched you to make sure that you would be alright."

The Legend of Kyne: Chronocide

Alakyne turned to face her, and she saw his cheeks were flushed and the hot tears that streamed down his cheeks made them glisten like glass.

"She lied to me Auriel," he said softly, his chest heaving.

She placed a hand on his shoulder. "She is your sister, the only family that you have. Don't let this ruin that Alakyne."

Her words rang truth and as his eyes met her own, she nodded, signaling for him that it was ok. Turning in his seat, the two siblings met. Aria was crying now too and then they embraced, high up in the dark sky.

They really are just kids, Auriel thought as she watched them for a long time.

Far on the horizon, the glow of light began to creep up, revealing first the softening of the dark blue to a light azure and then the golden red streaks of dawn erupted across the landscape. The river down below them continued on its course cutting through the grasslands and fading away in the hazy blue horizon.

They could see the dirt road that followed its course upon the northern edge of the water and then Auriel felt Ni'Bara shudder, and he drifted slightly down.

"There are people along the path," he called. "I count four of them and they look to be heading the direction that we go. I don't think they have spotted us yet but that is a good sign that we are traveling the right way."

"Should we stop and talk to them?" Aria asked behind them. "They might know where the sorcerers are."

The two were silent as Ni'Bara held his wings in a glide. Lost in thought, the dragon held his position allowing Auriel to speak first.

"What do you think Ni'Bara? It shouldn't be too much of a danger to risk it."

"If you wish," was all he said, and he dropped down into a steep dive. The wind dried Auriel's eyes and she squinted, turning her head to the side to block as much of it as she could. Aria and Alakyne followed her movement, leaning forward and ducking their heads down.

Plummeting like a meteor, the dragon reached an incredible speed and in minutes, they were on the ground. Arcing up, the dragon straightened out a few hundred feet up, keeping most of his speed and hurtling across the landscape. The landscape below was but a blur, the grass a seamless mass of yellow green as they followed the road. Four black shapes were up ahead about a mile, but Ni'Bara was soon upon them. His nearly silent flight rocketing over their heads, startling their horses and their shouts of concern radiating from behind.

He banked in a large curve, slowing down as he angled his wings and just as the figures came back into view a distance away, Auriel saw the glow of something flying towards them.

"Vertai!" yelled Auriel and the ball of aura angled sharply away flying down into the ground with a deafening crash. The power contained in that single attack could've easily killed them all and mortally wounded the dragon. Thoughts of fear and panic wracked Auriel's brain as where the figures stood, she could see another massive glowing object coming into being. Suddenly it leapt forward, flying through the air at them where she deflected it again.

Another loud crash sounded and Ni'Bara started to claw at the air, wingbeats pushing them further into the sky. This was far more dangerous than they had expected and pulling up, they took off. The figures upon the road a few hundred feet away.

"Ahh!" cried Alakyne suddenly and out of the corner of her eye, Auriel saw his body hurtle off the saddle at a blinding speed rushing towards the horsemen.

Ni'Bara roared in rage and ripped to the side, pursuing the child who had already made it to them and had been forced to his knees upon the dirt road.

No more aural attacks approached them and with an earthshaking crash, the dragon landed, bellowing a roar and his abdomen glowing a menacing cyan. Flames licked the edges of his maw, clinging to the scales upon his cheeks.

"Stay," Auriel said firmly to Aria and before the girl could object, the Riel leapt off Ni'Bara's back, sailing two dozen feet and landing lightly upon the ground with her sword drawn.

Standing before her were four hooded figures, two aboard their horses and two standing on the ground in front of theirs. In front of those two knelt Alakyne whose eyes were wide with shock as he looked frantically from side to side.

The Legend of Kyne: Chronocide

The figures all had hoods drawn up over their heads and cloaks that grazed the ground they stood upon concealing any features. The only thing that Auriel could see that made her uneasy was each one of them carried a staff each adorned with a large colored crystal.

"Give him back!" she cried, raising her swords tip towards them. "Or else!"

"Or else what strange one," said one of them, the voice clearly feminine. Revealing a hand, she reached up and withdrew her hood. It was indeed a female, thin with ghostly pale skin. Her hair was black, long and pulled up tight, upon her face was a pair of glasses with dark cold eyes beneath them. Her nose was turned up at its tip, causing her nostrils to flare out and her mouth was pursed in a disapproving look.

"Or else you'll deal with me!"

The woman muttered a quick word and bumped the end of her staff upon the ground. Suddenly Auriel's blade was torn from her grip, hurtling in the air where it stopped, hovering delicately in the air directly in front of the woman.

Auriel was speechless as she watched her reach out a hand and nearly touch the blade before hesitating. As she sat there, her finger outstretched, she turned her head slightly resting her vision upon Auriel.

"Where are you from traveler? Dragons are thought to have been lost to this world thousands of years ago."

"Give him back!" screamed Aria and then she was on the ground, running towards them.

"Wait no stop!" cried Auriel.

Aria's arms suddenly bound at her side, and she flew forward, her feet dragging upon the ground. She tore past Auriel and landed next to Alakyne in a kneeling position. The other standing hooded figure had risen their staff up and the blue crystal in its apex was glowing brightly.

"Answer my question foreigner," ordered the female.

"I come from a faraway land," said Auriel taking a step forward. "Please give them back. We mean you no trouble."

"And yet you still had the boldness to approach us upon the back of your beast. What were we to expect?" she said, her voice carrying a bit of sass and she rolled her eyes slightly. "You could've attacked us."

"You attacked first!" snarled Auriel, rage feeding into her. "Don't you try and pin this on us!"

The woman sighed and tilted her head to the side, her long black ponytail swaying behind her head. Her gaze dropped down to the crying kids who knelt before them and then back at Auriel. Upon the edge of her nose where it met the side of her mouth Auriel saw the woman's face clench in a look of irritation. Lifting her free hand, she flicked it.

Alakyne and Aria were suddenly able to move and scrambling to their feet, they took off running towards Auriel. Dashing behind her, she raised a single arm up in a protective posture, her other reaching out towards the woman.

"My blade."

The woman turned her gaze to the still hovering sword, and she smiled a minute smile, hardly noticeable. "It's yours, come and take it."

Ni'Bara rumbled behind her, shaking the road with the warning sound and Auriel took a step forward. The kids behind her objected but she wasn't going to let these people keep her blade.

Dropping her arms, she continued her steps, her face determined and her posture confident. She marched down the road, towards the people as they all stared intensely at her.

She came to a stop five feet from them and held out her hand with a brief nod. "My blade."

"First. Your. Name," said the woman, drawing out each word in the sentence as if dissecting each syllable with her tongue.

"Auriel. Now my blade."

"Auriel where might you be from if I may ask."

"Far away, now give it back."

"You seem adequate with the use of aura girl," said the nearby hooded figure, this voice male. He removed his hood, and she met the gaze of an elderly balding man, his hair white and bending in a curve around his head. His skin was wrinkly and dark splotches covered his cheeks and his scalp. His eyes were blank of all emotion.

"Adequate?" asked Auriel in disbelief. "I am much more than adequate."

The Legend of Kyne: Chronocide

"With what you have displayed to us so far I would hesitate to say you much more than a novice girl," he responded. "Answer my companion's question." He thumped the end of his staff upon the ground and Auriel's mind grew hazy.

Swaying, she felt her vision tunnel and her ears grew numb to sound. She could feel her mouth open and the vibration of words in her throat, but nothing was heard.

Then it suddenly ceased.

"Aera, the land of the Riel. Interesting," the man muttered, and Auriel's mind began to race. Dashing forward, she grabbed her blade out of the air and leapt back but none of the figures moved an inch.

"What do you want!" she screamed, brandishing her blade to them.

"Knowledge, information, literature, scripture, tales, we want to learn everything there is to know about this world Auriel of Aera. We want to know about your land and of your people who have strange features like your own. Are there others like you who know aura? Know of its intricacies and its laws?"

Auriel was silent as she stared at the woman. She hated her with every ounce of her being. She could picture Kyne there, his power dwarfing them and she knew that she could as well. They had merely caught her off guard.

The man spoke, "Where have you gotten hold of this beast of yours? I would love to know so that I may obtain one myself."

"He's one of a kind!" she snapped. Her eyes meeting his own, cold and soulless.

"Then how much to purchase him?" he replied.

Ni'Bara snorted and took a step towards them, brandishing his fangs. "You disrespect me human!" he snarled. "Remember your place. You might think that you are powerful, but I promise you that you would not be able to stop me."

Upon hearing his voice, they all stared for a moment before the man spoke, his tone unchanged. "I believe you would be little more than a challenge dragon. We who kill the beasts of legend whose might could bring down a dragon would need little to defeat you."

"Beasts of legend that I have killed myself," hissed Ni'Bara.

The Legend of Kyne: Chronocide

"You underestimate my power!"

"Let us stop this," said the woman giving the man a look that he took very seriously. Ending his conversation, his mouth clamped shut and he held his staff as he observed them. "We do not wish to be enemies Auriel. We only wish to learn and grow. Dragon, I apologize for my companion's disrespect. We were not aware of the intelligence that the dragon's seemingly possess."

Ni'Bara snorted, sending jets of hot air across the ground.

"Then we will be going," Auriel said, and she took a step back.

The woman's hand raised up and Auriel stopped mid-stride. "Before you leave, why have you approached us?"

"We wanted to know where the nearest city was so that we could potentially find one of the Sorcerers of Tsora."

The woman's mouth formed a tight smile. "Well, it looks like you found them."

Auriel nodded, assuming this long ago. The arrogance of these sorcerers reminded her strangely of her brother. "I realized that."

"And why do you want one of us? Do you have a monster that you are not able to deal with?"

"Not a monster, more of a situation," replied Auriel darkly. "What do you know about time travel?"

"Time travel?" scoffed the male. "Not possible."

Auriel pursed her lips, pressing the thick tissue together as she contemplated his words. She had a feeling she would find a dead end. At least it was worth a shot.

Never mind," she called, turning her head. "It seems that you won't be able to help us after all."

"Wait one moment," the woman called, drawing her attention. "Time travel you say? To think someone so novice at aural manipulation would contemplate such an outlandish thing."

"Novice?" muttered Auriel, her anger returning. "You think me a novice sorcerer? Riel are trained in aura since we can speak. Do not question my knowledge."

The two sorcerers started to laugh wildly while the other two remained still as stone aboard their horses. The sun overhead beat down and Auriel felt a bead of sweat form on her brow.

"Riel? What is a Riel if I may ask," she jeered, jerking her stave around in an arc. "Never heard of you or your people. Your features are foreign, that's for certain but challenging a Tsoran sorcerer is quite impressive."

"Or foolish," added the male. "Our order runs this entire continent. Spread across like a blanket, we are above all, none are our equals."

"Until now," snorted Ni'Bara, the flames of his eyes burning, and she felt the air vibrate with his power.

"The dragon dares speak down to me? I gave you respect before but to offer yourself as superior makes my previous comment fallacy, Dragon. Watch yourself or you will end up just like any other beast that encounters us."

"Yet you only do it for coin," called out Aria to their shock and the girl stood next to Auriel. "Coin and mead as they say. The Tsorans are powerful but full of greed and gluttony. We have asked for your help in the past and yet you wouldn't. You would rather see people hurt and killed if it meant keeping your coin purses full."

"What did you need help with then girl?" hissed the female, her eyes growing dark at the mocking she had heard. "What big bad monster do you need dealing with? Did it hurt your baby brother? Hurt someone in your family perhaps? Maybe that's why you and the snot nosed brat travel alone, either your family left you or were too weak to fend for themselves in this big world."

Aria suddenly bolted forward, a cry of rage exploding from her mouth. The thumping of her feet was heard, a cloud of fine dust erupting from the road as she pushed towards them, the glimmer of a small dagger in her hand catching the light.

Moments before she reached them, her body suddenly went rigid and a cry from Alakyne behind them echoed around. The world was still for but a moment before the sorceress whipped her stave around in a fast twirl before colliding it hard against Aria's head with a crack sending the girl tumbling to the ground.

50. The Legend

The shadow of a cloud overcast the sun up above and a gentle breeze blew the tall grasses causing their slender stalks to wiggle. The only sound Auriel could hear was the hard thumping of her heart and the blood rushing in her ears as she stared at Aria's limp body, slumped over upon the ground. The female sorcerer smirked as she stared over her limp body, her stave held low at her side.

Thump... Thump... Thump...

All other sound was drowned out as a fit of rage formed in her mind. The savagery and assault that had just occurred to the young girl was unspeakable. Aiming her palm up, the Riel princess watched as her eyes met hers, a deathly stare as they faced each other.

She could feel the pull of the aura, the strain as she forced everything she could into her palm generating a pulsating silver sphere. She would kill them! Destroy them, leaving not a trace but a smear across the earth! She continued to fuel the attack, pushing everything she could into it. Time seemed to slow as they held their eye contact, what felt like minutes was less than a second. She felt the ground tremble as it reverberated from a roar of fury from Ni'Bara behind her. She could feel the heat of his flame touch her skin but paid it no attention.

Suddenly her sphere of aura dissolved away, particles of light shifting as they danced in front of her for but a moment before fading. An immense pressure ripped through the field and the sky overhead seemed to darken as if the sun itself were dimming.

"Watch yourself Tsoran!" roared a powerful voice and Alakyne's small figure stepped around Ni'Bara, his eyes glowing a bright white and his blond hair blowing wildly in the wind.

The sorcerers were speechless as they stared at the child, the boy not much older than ten years. Stepping towards them, Auriel watched as the very land seemed to bow to his power, the grasses bending away from his pressure. She could feel her legs giving in, struggling to remain upright from the immense pressure that pushed down upon her.

A flash of light flew through the air but inches before it collided with Alakyne, it turned to dust, vanishing around him in streams of glowing fog.

"My sister is not yours!"

With a swipe of his hand, the limp body of Aria jerked from the ground, flying toward them before landing at his feet delicately like a fallen feather.

He didn't look down, didn't acknowledge her, instead, he continued stepping towards the sorcerers, stepping around her limp body.

His eyes seemed to pulse, a white energy flowing just beyond them, swirling around the corners of his eyes as he continued his march towards them. Past Auriel he walked, a bombardment of attacks thrown at him and none reaching their mark.

Ni'Bara's roar was drowned out from the increasing gale that raged from the child.

Auriel couldn't make out anything the sorcerers were saying but could see the panic in their eyes as the two began to back up, approaching the others who were still on horseback. Another flurry of attacks flew but once again nothing touched Alakyne.

Auriel felt a flash of fear as she watched, fear of the power coming from him. It was unlike anything she had ever felt before, as if his aural reservoir was limitless, infinite in all of its power.

"You hurt her!" he screamed, the ground quaking and the pressure around them dramatically increased, slamming Auriel as well as the sorcerers to their knees. Behind her, Auriel heard the crash and from the corner of her eye could make out Ni'Bara's massive head pressed firmly into the earth.

The ground shook again, trembling from the power but this time it felt different. Compared to the constant power coming from Alakyne, the shaking was inconsistent, growing stronger as if something were approaching.

The Legend of Kyne: Chronocide

"Alakyne!" screamed Auriel suddenly as realization flooded her mind. "Alakyne stop! We need to get away before they..."

Before she could finish, the ground between Alakyne and the four sorcerers erupted in a scarlet flash, flames surged across the ground, bathing the dirt and grasses in their bloody red glow. The flash of gold caught their eye and then the hood opened as the eldunaga faced Alakyne.

The serpent of legend, golden in color, whose back was ablaze in flame flared its fangs, dripping with lust for death. Auriel could feel the malice in the air, she could feel the rage as it flowed across the land, filling her bones and she felt her own rage grow.

Insatiable, the fury of everything filled her soul as she looked upon the creature.

As if completely unaware, or uncaring, Alakyne continued his march towards the sorcerers who were now obscured by the massive golden serpent. It was but a moment before his figure was eclipsed by red flame, blasting upon him from above as the serpent covered everything in its breath.

Auriel could feel it as it flowed towards her but just in time, she said, "Etoch!" and it fanned around her aural shield leaving her unharmed.

Stretching the spell, she narrowly protected Ni'Bara, her instinct saving him from the flames as the onslaught continued for a few more moments.

Her mind was blank of everything but rage and fire, imagining the burnt corpses of the sorcerers turning to dust beneath her boot.

As they died down, Alakyne's figure came back into view, untouched and unmoving as he had stopped his approach. He was looking up now, the glowing eyes pulsating with power as he met the serpent's own. He was so small next to the serpent whose size matched Ni'Bara's, but Auriel could tell this fight wasn't going to be a fair one. Not for the cobra in the slightest.

Raising his hand, Alakyne merely swiped it to the side and as if the snake had been made of paper, its body was hurtled to the side hundreds of feet where it collided upon the slope of a hill, indenting it as its body sank into the soil.

The sorcerers were still there, having risen to their feet, Auriel could see the look of fear had grown. They were a few dozen feet from Alakyne, and the air seemed to hang in a stillness. The sounds of the serpent screeching in rage blocked out by the power that filled their souls.

A jet of flame suddenly slammed into Alakyne, scarlet like magma, it surrounded him but just as before, as it ceased, he remained untouched. The snake roared in rage; the others present not even in its gaze at its sole focus was upon the young boy.

A trembling began to shake the ground and in moments, it erupted directly beneath Alakyne, his figure obscured by the maw of a second eldunaga.

Rocketing out of the ground, the serpent snapped its mouth shut, swallowing Alakyne whole before lowering its gaze to the others.

Auriel felt the pressure holding her down vanish immediately and, in a panic, she leapt to her feet and dashed towards Ni'Bara. Aria's body began to stir, and the young woman groaned, coming back to consciousness as they faced the snake.

"Where did he go!" snarled Ni'Bara as he took a step, his winged hand blocking Auriel.

She didn't know, confused at what had transpired. His power was incredible and then it was just gone.

Behind the second snake, she noticed the two sorcerers who hadn't spoken were glowing, golden light flowing from their bodies and flowing towards the female who had her hands pressed together. An orb of aura began to form and as the first snake approached them, the ground it touched burning away, she released the attack.

Rocketing toward the snake, the same attack that had approached Ni'Bara earlier, they watched as it struck the snake, exploding in a bright flash of light and shaking the earth.

Auriel's clothes blew around wildly and her ears were ringing as the flash of light faded down revealing the golden snake flailing in pain. Where the attack had struck it lay a massive crater in the flesh, scorched and black. It screeched in pain and thrashed around wildly before a final screech came and it fell upon its back, twitching before it was still.

The remaining cobra looked upon the dead one for a moment before it swung its head towards the sorcerers, its fangs bared and the glimmer of flame in its throat. Its body, long and slender coiled around as it changed position before suddenly growing rigid. It began to shake violently and then in a flash of light, the snake split apart, raining blood and embers upon the ground. In the center, soaked in blood, stood Alakyne. His eyes were closed and for a moment he stood there, surrounded by death before he swayed and collapsed upon the ground.

In a flash, before Auriel and Ni'Bara could react, his body rocketed towards the sorcerers.

"What are you doing!" screamed Auriel and she took off in a sprint, her aura pushing each step faster and faster.

"He is coming with us!" she called and with a wave of her hand, a black bag flew from her horse landing in front of them. "His power is astounding and needs to be studied. Otri!"

All of the other sorcerers and their horses, as well as Alakyne vanished into the bag. The female sorcerer smiled at Auriel for but a moment before she said an inaudible spell and vanished into its depths following them. The bag trembled and then vanished in a speck of light.

51. The Sorceress of Tsora

Aria screamed. Screamed out her brother's name over and over as tears soaked her cheeks before dripping to the ground. Bright flames licked the grassland leaving a long-blackened scar upon the earth where burned husks remained. Unfortunate animals and plant life that had been caught in the wall of orange were consumed, the few birds and insects that could fly escaping the spreading flames that threatened everything they approached with pain and death.

Alakyne was gone, vanished with the sorcerers with not a trace. Auriel dropped to her knees, the smell of smoke filling the air and burning her lungs. Her chest trembled in sorrow at their failure. It had happened so fast, and, in a rage, she slapped her palm upon the ground. They had been distracted, the cobras drawing all of their attention allowing the sorcerers an upper hand. It was like a blink of an eye and then he was gone.

She slapped the ground again and cursed.

She knew exactly what had happened. The black bag she had just glimpsed could be but one thing and every moment that passed would be ages for those within its depths.

"Auriel!" snarled Ni'Bara snapping her back into focus. "Scry them! Scry the bag, something so that we may be able to find where they vanished to."

Without another word, the sobbing of Aria the only sound other than the crackling and sparking of the flames as they fanned away from them, she swiped her hand using her aura to carve into the ground how she had done many times. Another swipe and with no remorse withdrew the water from the still living grasses nearby, shriveling their stalks to a dry crisp. It formed a small sphere of crystal-clear water and allowing it to fall, it roughly splashed into her bowl, sending sparkling drops raining around its perimeter.

"Seioin!" and she pictured first Alakyne's face, but the water only turned a deep black. This was her confirmation that he still resided within the bag and focusing, she pictured it instead, its black shape and the silver serpent at its top igniting in her mind.

The water's surface changed, transforming into a sea of tall grasses with the laying perfectly hidden within. No marks had been left upon the ground. She cursed again as she tried to turn the image to give any other hint to where they had gone. It was only grasses all around, their blades raised far higher than the bag obscuring anything except for the sky above.

It was nearly a blank azure slate, a single small wisp of a cloud the only thing that hung above. Auriel looked at it with more focus for a moment, studying it and remembering as much as she could before she jerked her head up and swept it around. The sky was empty of all clouds but one single wisp nearly twenty miles to their south.

Leaping to her feet, she ran to Aria and grabbed onto the sides of the young girl's arms. She was still sobbing, all thoughts blank except for her loss and with a heave, Auriel hoisted her to her feet before embracing her for but a moment.

"Aria! We have a lead to where they took him, but we have to go as fast as possible. It's hard to explain but every second to us is minutes to him!"

She sniffled, rubbing her red eyes and Auriel directed her towards Ni'Bara who was waiting with his shoulder dropped to allow her upon his back.

A glance back at her pool and she said, "Sei'var." The water bolted to her hand where it hung in a glob, its flowing surface reflecting distorted images from all around.

Flowing it into an empty water skin, she too boarded Ni'Bara and then they were airborne, rocketing low over the grassland towards the lone cloud. She had been incredibly lucky that they managed to see that cloud and every second her stomach tightened more as its tingles of fear rocked her mind.

Ni'Bara's wing beats were powerful, and Auriel could feel the urgency coming from him as he pushed on. Everything was relying on his speed, and he couldn't, he *wouldn't* let them down.

The Legend of Kyne: Chronocide

A few minutes passed and they watched as the cloud drifted away, moving further to the east. Ni'Bara knew roughly where it had once been, targeting a specific area of the land with his vision and he continued on. As they approached, Auriel withdrew her water skin, turning around to block it from the wind with her body and she and Aria observed its surface as the Riel tried to scry them once again. The bag still remained where it had, alone in a field of grass but no clouds were above in the sky. They scanned it for a few more minutes, hoping to find any glimpse of Ni'Bara's figure but none were seen.

"It should be around here," Ni'Bara said suddenly, and he came to a stop, hovering a few hundred feet above the ground. "Auriel, do you know where it is?"

"We can't see much, it's just grass and sky. I just can't see anything else that would allow us to see where we are."

Ni'Bara's body pulled back, nearly knocking Auriel off the saddle before he suddenly bellowed out a torrent of cyan flame from his mouth. Flipping his head from side to side, the flames stretched out far before dropping, their glowing liquid like flames falling before finally fading away moments before touching the ground.

Auriel growled in frustration at the dragon's outburst of anger. Him freaking out didn't do much to help their situation. The dragon suddenly jerked up and they rose swiftly in the air, the delicate surface of the scry jerking and threatening to break. A minute of climbing in the sky followed before he stopped in a hover and blasted another wave of flame around.

"What are you doing?" Auriel called to him as he finished. "You are wasting time!"

"Can you spot my flame with your scry?" he roared, and another blast of fire flew around.

His words made her, and Aria gasp and they returned to the image, scanning the small visible section of sky and not noticing any fire. "No not yet," Aria called, and the dragon snorted in anger.

"I'll help," Auriel called and with a motion towards Aria to look into the sphere, she turned away. "Destikon!" she called and all around them the light seemed to fade, flowing towards Auriel and darkening everything. Aria cried in shock, but Auriel paid no mind and with a grunt, she hurled it away from them where it rocketed across the sky.

Light suddenly returned as it flew out of range, but they all watched in wonder as a dark ball of shadow many times the size of Ni'Bara hurtled away from them.

"Aria!" called the Riel as she noticed her not observing the scry. The girl nodded her head, realizing her mistake and quickly focused back on the scry. A few moments passed but she shook her head slowly, not seeing anything.

They tried again, Auriel launching a dark sphere and Ni'Bara spreading fire, but nothing was spotted. On their third attempt she threw it further to their side the opposite way the others had flown. A few moments passed and then Aria gasped and she looked at the scry. A dark fleck was moving across the sky from side to side before it vanished from view.

"That way!" she screamed and with a glance, the dragon turned around and pushed on. Bathing the sky in flame, they traveled on for a bit before the flash was finally seen on the scry. They continued on, using their aura and the image to guide them towards the bag. It was tedious, the grass a single monotonous tone beneath them with no bag in sight but they pushed on.

Lowering down, it took them another fifteen minutes before they managed to find the bag, delicately hidden in the grass.

"Aria you are staying here," Auriel called, and she leaped from Ni'Bara's back, crushing the tall grass beneath her. She was waist high in its light green shade with the bag a few feet away. "Ni'Bara you're coming with me."

The dragon nodded, lowering down to allow Aria off his back and without an objection she watched as Auriel and Ni'Bara vanished into the dark bag.

A rush of darkness and then the glow of torchlight caught her view as Auriel delicately landed upon the stone ground. The glimmer of a silver serpent lay beneath her feet just on the edges of her view. A crash sounded as Ni'Bara landed next to her, the glow of his abdomen casting light around.

The bag was completely different than what she remembered. No buildings lay scattered around and no fountain of water. It was

The Legend of Kyne: Chronocide

littered with wooden posts, burn marks across them and other strange objects. There were glass lenses, and floating spheres of energy that seemed to drift around high above them.

Far away, she could see the shapes of people and the glow of aural lights around them. They took off covering the distance in moments before they were there, able to make out the sight before them.

Alakyne was standing nearby looking at them in shock. Thick bags hung under his eyes and his face showed deep fatigue. He was dressed in a robe reminiscent of the four sorcerers who all stood nearby watching them as they approached.

Auriel felt her anger at his sight fly through her mind and she fought it, knowing full well the consequences she could reap if she acted in anger. She wanted to attack them with everything she could throw, destroy them in every possible way but at the sight of him unharmed she hesitated.

"What have you done with the child!" roared Ni'Bara, the flames of his dragonfire behind his white fangs.

"You found us much faster than anticipated," muttered the female, dropping her hood revealing her face. "One month was not enough to answer our questions."

"A month!" gasped Auriel not realizing how much they messed up. "You have been in here a month!"

"I thought you forgot about me," mumbled Alakyne as he stared at them. "After the first few days I thought you all just wanted to get rid of me. Get rid of my curse so that the monsters won't bother you anymore."

"A month and we have not been able to replicate what we witnessed!" cried the male in a rage. "This has been a waste of time Tira! The longer we waste our time with the child the more irritated I become."

The female sorceress turned towards him, and a flash of anger covered her face. "Watch your tongue Jurnen. You are not the one in charge!"

"I know what you are doing, it's obvious," he continued. "You hope that this child will be able to push Tiernyn out of command do you not? I know you are not a fan of him, but he *is* our Grand."

The Legend of Kyne: Chronocide

Tira growled low and her eyes flashed malice. She looked at Jurnen for a moment before swinging her head towards Auriel and Ni'Bara. "We have not harmed him. We have introduced the child to aura in hopes of drawing out his inner power, but we have not made much progress. He is no natural, incredibly unskilled. It shocks me that he was able to do what he did and the more time that passes the more I think my mind was playing tricks on me."

"Give him back to us," Auriel said, her hand reaching out towards him. "And we can forget this ever happened."

"That's not happening," Tira said. "Not until I fully understand what I saw. He has some strange power that I *must* understand."

"She wasn't asking," snarled Ni'Bara. "The young one is not yours to keep."

Tira sighed and looked at her companion Jurnen for a moment to see his disapproval. "You *were* expecting this," he muttered.

"A compromise then," she said finally. "You will take us so that we may speak with Tiernyn, our leader. We will remain in the bag and continue our training of the boy. What will take you a few days will give us months of time to continue our training."

"Not happening," Auriel said bluntly. "I don't care who you think you are, you're not taking away months of his life just to search for something that you won't find."

Footsteps were heard and then Aria suddenly dashed around Ni'Bara, running straight for her brother. She embraced him, knocking him back with her speed and then dropped to her knees looking up at him. Her face was littered with emotion, and she gently rubbed some dirt from his cheek.

"Are you alright?"

"I'm ok, I thought you left me."

She stood up and embraced him again tighter this time. "I will never leave you Alakyne. Don't ever say that again!"

As she withdrew, she guided Alakyne behind her and she faced the sorcerers who had been watching them unimpressed.

"Such an interesting family dynamic," muttered Tira. "I wonder if she carries the gift as well."

"She doesn't! Now leave them alone!" snapped Auriel. "If you don't let us leave, we will retaliate. We will fight!"

Tira shook her head side to side. "There is no need for fighting, all I want is for you to understand what I am trying to do. This boy has potential that could help everyone. *Everyone* Auriel. Do you not get it? His power could vanquish thousands of monsters allowing the humans to return back to how we once were. Mighty and prosperous."

"What do you plan on doing with him?" asked Aria softly.

"We just want to teach him to harness his powers, that is all," she replied, her gaze peering through her glasses softening.

"She wants to use him to overthrow her current leader," rumbled Ni'Bara. "He is nothing but a pawn to her."

"Do not worry about that right now," she continued. "Alakyne will make this world a better place. All I want to do is train him. We just want to train him while you take us to Tiernyn, is that so much to ask?"

"Absolutely it is too much to ask. I am not allowing you to corrupt a ten-year-old boy to become some weapon for you and your order. I do not know this Tiernyn, and I do not condone what you want."

"Will you be able to get rid of his curse?"

Aria's voice cut through their argument silencing everyone, and they all stared at her for a long moment.

"It is quite possible," Tira replied, pushing her glasses back higher upon the bridge of her nose. "If he learns to control his power then I suppose nothing would likely bother you anymore."

Aria looked first at her brother, their eyes holding for a long moment before she turned back.

"Then train him."

Shouts of concern flew from Auriel and Ni'Bara, but Aria shook her head and tears formed on the edges of her eyes. "I have to do what's best for him. Please don't fight this!"

Auriel grew silent and she looked at both of the children for a long moment. She could see that Alakyne had come to terms with it, his fear fading away and Aria had a stern look of confidence as she faced them.

"Auriel," murmured Ni'Bara. "It pains me to say it but, I think she is right. We are not from this world, and we cannot protect them forever. If we are to ever return home, then we will eventually have to leave them to fend for themselves."

Auriel bit her cheek, her frustration growing at the realization she had lost. She truly had lost the argument, but she wouldn't just sit idly by and watch.

"Alright then, as you wish. We will take you to this Tiernyn and you can train Alakyne *and* Aria," she said emphasizing the addition. "When we get there then you are done. No more training, understood?"

"Understood," Tira replied, and her face lit up in a grin.

Auriel left the bag with Ni'Bara and Tira followed shortly after. There they stood for a long moment in silence as the Riel looked upon the pale bald woman. Tira fidgeted with her glasses again before she suddenly spoke.

"I do not wish to be your enemy Auriel."

"You're making that very difficult," she replied. "You attack us, kidnap a child and then ask for help. You're on very thin ice Tira."

"You are indeed," rumbled Ni'Bara. "You may be powerful in your aura, but I promise you that you would not be able to stop me. If anything happens to those kids, then you will burn. All of you!"

Tira nodded, his words causing a flash of fear to appear in her eyes for but a moment.

"Tiernyn lies with a large accompaniment of sorcerers in Karstead."

"And where is this Karstead located?"

Tira's mouth opened in shock at Auriel's words. "You really must not be from around here. Karstead is the largest city on this side of the continent. The Lord of this land lies there."

"And this lord is Tiernyn?"

"No, it is not. To put it bluntly, Tiernyn is basically his bodyguard. He protects the city from any monster attacks alone or with his group of sorcerers."

"And why do you not like this Tiernyn?"

"To not like him is putting it mildly. He runs our order with his will as law. I know he thinks he means well but he is very arrogant, condescending, and I think he is corruptible. All I wish is for him to meet young Alakyne. The boy is someone I believe could help change our world for the better."

"And Tiernyn could make this happen?"

"He could," Tira said in a doubtful tone. "He also might not want to for fear it could take power from him. As I said, he is arrogant. The lord is in charge, but Tiernyn is the one who truly runs the city. He turns a blind eye to many horrors for a sizeable amount of coin. I do not wish him dead, but I do wish this situation would resolve itself. The beasts have awoken these last few years, and they threaten everything. We need to unite the people to stand up to them or they could extinguish our very existence."

Auriel looked at Ni'Bara, his eyes trained on her and for a long moment they stared as if they could hear each other's thoughts. "So where is this Karstead located?" she finally asked the sorceress, turning her gaze back to her. "Is it nearby?"

"Not nearby but not too far. A few days ride to the north along the other major river of this land. It lies just along the edge of the forest."

"It sounds like it's where Faldîn currently is," rumbled Ni'Bara quietly. "Perhaps the city bore a different name before."

"Tira," Auriel said as the sorceress turned to leave. "Do not think you have won, you have not. This is merely a simple allowance. I am *allowing* you to train the children for the time being. Only because she has wished it. I will be checking in on you frequently."

The woman turned her head, the sunlight flashing off of her glasses as she nodded and then she adjusted them, pushing them high up the bridge of her nose. "Otri," and the sorceress vanished into the bag leaving them alone once more.

"Auriel what are your thoughts telling you?"

"I don't know Ni'Bara," she said leaning against his side. "My instinct is to not trust these people one bit. They are quick to attack, and their arrogance is boundless."

"Your instinct matches my own," he replied, his deep voice causing her body to vibrate.

"I don't want to get caught up in these people's issues. Our goal is to return to our own time. So that we may find Kyne and Rosé. I foresee this could be a major distraction."

The Legend of Kyne: Chronocide

"Distraction or not, our lives have entangled with those children. If Alakyne is to become the legend that he is meant to be then we have possibly altered that course."

"But if we wouldn't have rescued them then they could've been killed," she said in exasperation.

"But we do not know that for certain. All we can do right now is let events unfold."

"And of the children? Am I to just let them be trained by these people?" She asked.

"It was Aria's wish and Alakyne needs to learn if he is to unite Kydrëa. I say allow it for now and we will travel to the predecessor of Faldîn. Peer in on their training from time to time. I will travel swiftly."

Auriel nodded and she vanished into the bag leaving Ni'Bara alone. The large dragon raised his head up and stared at the bright azure sky, a feeling of longing in his chest. He missed his companion, missed his best friend and he hoped beyond anything that he was alright.

Auriel appeared next to Ni'Bara a few moments later.

"They have already started their lessons. In the brief time that we spoke it's already been over an hour. Ni'Bara we should get moving."

The dragon nodded and as Auriel boarded his saddle, she felt her leg brush a hard object in one of the bags that was attached to it.

Paying it no mind, she sat down and then Ni'Bara was airborne. They flew for a few hours, Auriel peering into the bag every fifteen minutes or so. Each time she noticed the kids to be more haggard in appearance, but a new fire was burning in Aria's eyes.

The sky outside began to darken as the sun set and signaling, they needed to sleep, Ni'Bara dove down.

Auriel hated resting, each moment so much longer to the children but they needed it. She was exhausted and she could sense Ni'Bara was too. The dragon hadn't eaten in a long time, and she could sense it starting to have an effect on him.

"You should go hunt Ni'Bara," she said as she sat down next to a freshly made fire. "I know you need it." Ni'Bara rumbled in protest, his head resting upon the ground and his eyes remaining closed. "Just go look for a few hours. Use your dragonly senses to sniff

442

The Legend of Kyne: Chronocide

something out. This land can't be bare of everything."

"What about you?"

"I'll be fine," she said, and she unclipped a bag from his saddle. Withdrawing a piece of bread from it she waived it at him. "I have food and I am quite capable."

Silence for a long time before he spoke, "Are you sure?"

"Go hunt Ni'Bara."

His head lifted off of the ground and he opened his wings out, his neck stretching out like a long serpent. Taking two thunderous steps, the dragon pumped his wings and then he was off, gliding into the dark sky with the wind nearly knocking Auriel off balance.

The flames of her campfire flew all around, dying into embers before vanishing altogether leaving her alone in the dark with nothing but the moons and the stars to keep her company. Her eyes drifted up towards the planet she knew to be her people's birthplace and she stared at the dark grey and silver marks, tracing out possible continents and oceans. She knew her people weren't there, they were beneath them, cast in a strange spell that held them within the planet's center. But looking upon the moon did bring her a little comfort as it was the closest thing she could see.

She said a spell, her tattoos glowing brightly in the dark light and her fire was brought back together, Ni'Bara's damage undone as it caught and she sat down, watching the flames dance as they consumed the wood.

After a time, she paid the children one more visit. Aria had become quite the little sorceress in the time that had passed, not to Auriel's disbelief weeks had passed in the few hours.

Alakyne still struggled, able to form minor spells but his aural reservoir was shallow, unable to sustain anything for more than a moment. Auriel watched him, the child covered in grime and his face dripping with sweat as he tried to lift but a small book into the air with his aura.

The tingle of aura was felt upon Auriel's skin, and she watched as the book lifted a few inches off the ground. Trembling, it jerked up another inch before falling to the ground. Alakyne dropped to his knees, panting and sweat soaking the floor. Shouting was heard and Jurnen approached, his face littered with rage.

"Again!" he spat, striking the ground with the sole of his boot in a stomp. "Again!"

Alakyne struggled to his feet and began to raise his hand at the book when Auriel approached Jurnen. She said nothing but her gaze was all he needed. Seeing her displeasure, he turned on his heel and walked away muttering profanities under his breath.

"Here," Auriel said, and she used her aura to clean him up. Once his hair looked better and the grime had peeled away from his flesh, she gave him a bit of her own aura to help with his fatigue. As it flowed into him, she couldn't help but probe softly at his reservoir, feeling its shallowness. She hadn't seen someone so unlucky as him since she was but a child. A Riel who had been made fun of in her class.

She sighed and she withdrew.

"I'm just weak Auriel," the little boy said as he staggered to his feet. "I train everyday as hard as I can but no matter what I do my aura doesn't get stronger. I watch Aria improve day after day and I am ridiculed about my skill. I am an annoyance to them."

"Don't say that Alakyne," Auriel started but he cut her off.

"You know it's true though. They speak of me having this vast power but no matter what I do I cannot seem to find it."

Auriel was silent for a long moment. She swung her vision towards his sister who was performing impressive feats of magic for her short amount of training.

"I don't know Alakyne but I did see it for myself. You defeated an eldunaga and the sorcerers were afraid of you. Do not get frustrated, it will come to you in time."

"But I want it to come now! I don't want to wait for something that probably won't happen. They have tried Auriel. They have flooded me with aura, trying to expand this reservoir, break open a supposed dam that holds back my potential and they have failed. They have failed every time!"

Auriel left them shortly after, the young boy's anger fading to sorrow and then just a flat emptiness.

She didn't have answers for him.

She sighed as she leaned against a large rock, the orange flames of the fire scattering around the flattened grass that she lay hidden within. Far away from the road, she was certain no one would find them and if a beast appeared that she couldn't deal with, she could always summon the sorcerers to assist.

She clenched her fist at that thought and shook her head. She wouldn't ask for their help unless it was life or death.

Reaching into her pack she grabbed hold of another wedge of bread when her hand brushed a hard object. She withdrew the bread, setting it upon her lap before reaching back in and grabbing onto the object. As it came into view, she was puzzled for a long moment by its unfamiliarity.

It was small, a little larger than her fist. As a square is to a cube, this object was to pentagon. Every side of the object contained a five-sided shape as if it had become three dimensional.

She turned it over in her hand, the silvery color shimmering as she held it. Twisting it around in her grip as she eyed it, it finally came to her where it came from.

The depths under Alakyne, she thought as she sat it down on the ground next to her. *It was one of the items that I took from that strange altar.*

She eyed it again as she brought her bread to her mouth, setting the pentagon object down in a bed of flattened grass.

It was plain, bearing no markings that she could see nor any power that was felt. If it had been found anywhere else, then she would've assumed it to be a solid piece of metal. As she swallowed her last piece of bread, she picked up the object one last time, eyeing each side before she tossed it into her pack and laid her head down upon it.

Seeing it was a reminder of Kyne, a reminder of everything that had happened, and it made her body hurt, ache for his touch.

Stretching her legs out, trying to focus on something else, she felt the grass beneath her clothing when a thought came into her mind. Undressing, she used her aura to clean her clothes before cleaning her own body. She sighed at the fresh feeling as she stood alone bare in the grass. She hadn't been clean in a while, and this felt good. Not as good as a hot shower but still much better than nothing.

She put her clothes back on before laying down and closing her eyes. The flames nearby were dying down and little golden flickers began to flash in and out around her in the encroaching darkness. She

The Legend of Kyne: Chronocide

watched, mesmerized by the fireflies, whose light displays captivated her for a long time before her eyes drifted closed and she fell into a deep sleep.

She awoke to find the sun had just crept over the horizon, the dark red body of the flaming sphere casting its dawn rays upon the world heating it up. Nearby, she saw the sleeping figure of Ni'Bara, the grass he lay upon scorched from his hide.

"You are awake," he said, his eye opening lazily toward her and his large pupil contracting to a tight slit.

"You were very quiet," she replied, and he raised his head, yawning and revealing his fangs, stark white against his dark maw.

"I tried to be," he replied, and his tail raised up before slapping the ground with a loud crash, startling some nearby birds into flight. "I could've been more noisy."

"I appreciate it," she said, smiling briefly before all the thoughts and pains returned to her and she was reminded of everything that had happened. Her face grew solemn, and she looked towards the dark bag that lay nearby. The silver serpent stared back at her.

"Such a strange thing that we are to encounter this such a long time before Kyne has it," she said, and she started walking towards it. Stooping down, she traced the snake with her finger. "It truly is unchanged from our own time, indestructible just like the Light told him."

Ni'Bara watched her vanish. Their sleep had marked a long time since the children had been checked on and Auriel felt a bit worried before she saw them. Aria had cut her hair, shorter and straight across surprising Auriel, and Alakyne had seemed to grow a few inches from when she saw him last. After watching them for a while, she grew to learn that Aria had continued to progress at an astounding rate while Alakyne had been much more mild. He had finally shown some progress, able to form more complex spells and Auriel could tell his aural reservoir had grown a bit from their last encounter. Not by much but it had grown.

She smiled at him, but he just looked down, shame across his face. Aria bumped his shoulder and gave him a stern look to which he met Auriel's gaze and gave a weak smile.

The Legend of Kyne: Chronocide

They traveled that day just as they had before, the hours passing for them and the weeks for the children. Auriel watched them frequently, analyzing the sorcerers and learning the power they contained.

One visit, she watched as one of the two sorcerers who never spoke stood directly behind Tira as she charged an attack. His aura flowed into her forming the deadly sphere before she released it launching it across the multiple hundreds of yards long bag where it exploded with a flash of light.

Expecting the wall to be in ruin, Auriel was shocked to see it unharmed. Exclamations came from Aria at the sight and Tira smirked with cockiness.

"He is but a tool, an expansion to my own reservoir, she said, eyeing Auriel for but a moment. "He is mine and the other is Jurnen's. Their names were stripped from them and they were rendered mutes, their tongues torn out of their mouths years prior for crimes they committed. Once sorcerers themselves, they are now unable to utter the language of God to form spells. Thus, they are but tools for us, fueling our own aural spells."

"That's cruel!" exclaimed Aria.

"Cruel or fair Aria?" Tira asked slowly. "Do you want to know why he was punished? He as well as his brother were punished for wicked things done to innocent people such as yourself. Brutal and horrific murders and abuses too hard to speak let alone witness firsthand as I had to. Would you like me to explain further?"

Aria shook her head quickly at her words and Tira paused for a moment, eyeing each of them. Then she continued.

"They were to be tortured and killed but to waste such aural potential would've been a cruel punishment for all of humanity. They were stripped of their right to speak and allowed to live so that they may fuel our spells when necessary."

"What's to prevent them from just killing you while you sleep?" Auriel asked suddenly, eyeing the figure who stood motionless nearby, her skin crawling as she learned who he was.

"They wouldn't, aura has rendered it impossible. If they are to lay a hand upon me then the eternal spell keeping them alive would go out killing them instantly."

The Legend of Kyne: Chronocide

"Eternal spell keeping them alive?" asked Alakyne.

"Did I forget to mention that we tore their heart in two pieces, using our aura to fuse it back together. The fusion is but temporary, held in place by a link to each of us. If we die, they die, it's as simple as that."

*   *   *

The Legend of Kyne: Chronocide

52. A Cold Night

Kyne glanced back behind him again, still anxious and half expecting to see the pounding form of the draconic monster on the horizon, but he did not. He had pushed the horse into the fastest gallop it could, driving it though the snow and holding it there until Alakyne was obscured by sheer distance. Panting heavily, the horse finally slowed down to a trot, and they continued, Kyne unsure of where to go and just wanting to get as far away from there as he could.

No dragons were seen upon the sky and no silver haired woman came out of hiding to see him. He was alone and the more he continued on the more that feeling sunk in. He had been far away from them when it happened, not touching them and a thought came into his mind of them being left completely behind in the timeline.

If he succeeded in destroying aura, or whatever he did then does that mean... he shook his head, his lip beginning to tremble and tightness in his chest. He didn't want to think about it but no matter how hard he tried it kept coming right back. *If he succeeded, then what happened to them? they must've been...*

He shook his head before punching his palm as hard as he could, any distraction to smother the thought.

"He would've taunted me about it," he screamed out into the empty snow-covered field as the horse continued down the faint indentation that marked the road. "Auriel! Ni'Bara! Rosé," he said more softly as he remembered the young child. "He would've taunted me about it," he repeated, shifting his grip upon the reigns. "He is a wicked madman who wants to do nothing but kill and maim and hurt anything he can. He would've described what happened to them, would've said details that would make my stomach turn. If he didn't then maybe they didn't stay with him after all? Or they escaped, or even were cast somewhere else entirely. All I know is that I need to find them but where do I start looking? Alakyne would've been my first thought for answers but after seeing it I never want to step foot there again. Maybe Tsora?"

The thought of his school came into his head and then he realized that the school he had made was long gone, lost to the true timeline with this one still having the ruins of the original.

"I don't know what to do," he said and then he started sobbing, tears running down his face and his abdomen spasming. He was powerless to do anything. He had no idea what to do or where they could be.

"What is going on Light!" he screamed, his voice cracking as drips of his tears fell to his lap below. "How could you let this happen? Everything that we did just erased? I thought I was supposed to be the one in your prophecy who would stop the Darkness but that just seemed to ruin everything!"

His voice trailed away, and he waited, hoping that something would happen, a beautiful white bird would appear or be noticed watching him, but nothing did. Nothing appeared to lead him. He was alone and he continued on down the road. His sobbing faded away, replaced by anger and he punched his palm again.

"I should've killed that mockery of me instead of fleeing. Then none of this would've happened!" and he gestured all around. "He was strong in the mind, but I could've overwhelmed him physically and with my aura!"

Then thoughts of the crushing force of his mind came into being and a shadow of doubt drew in.

Would he have been able to win though?

That single thought kept him occupied as they traveled on with no direct trajectory guiding them. He argued in his mind that he could've won but the thought still lingered, and he knew deep down that he would've crushed him. Even with the help of the others that fight was unwinnable. He hated to admit it and continued arguing until the faint light far to the horizon signaled the day was coming to an end.

The bitter cold was going to grow much more intense, and he needed a shelter. He didn't have anything, no aura, no supplies, nothing but this horse and the blade upon his waist. He still had a little

The Legend of Kyne: Chronocide

bit of time and guiding his horse off the trail, he led it to a cluster of dead trees, not one baring any leaves at all as they had long been killed by the chilling temperatures. The snow was deep around the trees, coming to his knees as he dismounted, and he shivered as the icy pieces were jammed into his pant leg touching his skin.

Searching through them, he found some small ones and after tugging on their frost covered branches, he felt the satisfying snap and looked at their insides. A light tan signaled they were dry, and he began collecting as much as he could, making sure to not let any of them touch the ground. After his hands were full, he would tie them to the horse's saddle before he gathered more. He needed a lot if he were to go the entire night and two more times he gathered them, each pile progressively being loaded with thicker branches.

Finally, when he had concluded he had had enough, he started on digging a hole in the snow deep in the skeleton trees and eventually revealing the frozen ground beneath. His hands were cold, and he could feel the sensations fading away into numbness as he scraped again hard, his bare hands tucked into his sleeves in an attempt to protect them.

He wished he had his gloves, wished he had his pack and all of its contents, but he was on his own. Him and his blade. A simple human in a desolated world.

After a few feet had been exposed he started on the fire tower, stacking the thinner branches around in the best formation to catch the baby flames and fuel them to grow big and strong. Their life would save his own.

Drawing Aurora, he rubbed his finger against the razor-sharp barbs and with a grimace, tried to bend one to see the strength of the blade. Increasing his pressure slowly to minimize the damage he was soon putting all of his strength into bending a single barb similar in size to a blade of grass to no avail.

"It seems at least one thing has stayed the same," he chuckled solemnly. "They are still indestructible." Grasping a piece of wood, he started scraping it down his blade, peeling off thin coiling pieces where they fell slowly next to his tower making a pile of shavings. He continued for a few minutes, trying his best to make them as thin as possible and when he felt he had enough, he finally put the blade down. Scanning the small area he cleared, he looked with a fleeting effort for any flint like stone he could find. Anything that sparkled like a false crystal he knew could do it, but he found none.

Taking another branch, he carved some notches into it and then sat it aside, starting on another piece. The horse whinnied nearby as it brushed the snow with his mouth looking for food or water, either of which Kyne wasn't sure.

"That'll be the least of our problems," he muttered as he tore a strip of leather from the saddle. "A frozen corpse won't be eating much anyways."

Returning to his crafting, he tied both ends of the leather to a stick causing it to bow slightly before he twisted a second stick in the center of the leather strip. Placing it upright on a platform he made, he sprinkled some of the wood shavings at its base and with a rock, pushed down on the upright stick holding it firm. The fire bow was one of the only ways he had successfully made fire and he dreaded the effort he was going to need to use at this moment.

Thoughts of aura paraded his mind as he slid the bow back and forth spinning the stick at a blinding speed. Thoughts of confusion at how the man had used it and the strange glowing rocks that seemed to give the draconic beast power.

A short time later he added more wood shavings and continued on, drilling into the stone, the friction heating it up towards its combustion point. The sun was set now, he could tell as his breath drifted out of his mouth in a foggy cloud from his panting. A drip of sweat had formed on his brow and had migrated all the way down to the tip of his nose where it hung there for a long moment, threatening to freeze from the intense cold. As it finally dripped, Kyne's eyes watched in horror as it fell down towards his workspace and then in a miracle, it hit off to the side, just narrowly avoiding ruining everything and possibly killing him.

He needed to be more careful, and he leaned to the side as he continued, aiming his drips away from the wood. A short time later a little tiny bit of smoke began to drift up and he accelerated, forcing the bow back and forth spinning the stick rapidly. Quickly adding a few more shavings, he did a few more hard thrusts and then withdrew the stick. A tiny faint glow of an ember lay at its base and ever so delicately,

The Legend of Kyne: Chronocide

he placed the flame fetus in a pile of the thinnest shavings he had, reminiscent of grass clippings. A few breaths intensified the smoke and he struggled to remain calm, inhaling and blowing out smoothly causing it to grow more and more. A little flash and then the orange of flame came into sight, just a baby as it licked the wood.

Growing larger with every breath, Kyne delicately picked up the wooden platform it was on and guided it to his fire tower. Tucking it in and with a few more breaths and some added larger shavings, he watched with delight as the first of the sticks caught fire. A cool breeze threatened to blow the flame out and he knelt down over it, blocking it from the wind and allowing it to grow more and more. Soon most of the thinner branches were burning and he was able to add larger and larger branches.

The warmth quickly grew and even the horse seemed to notice, and it approached. Sweeping its face through the snow as if making a nest, Kyne's stomach dropped at the thought of it covering the fire, so he shifted his body in between it and the flames. It was his life that was on the line.

The bitter night continued to grow colder as the stars never became visible, obscured by the nearly ever-present blanket of clouds above. Fatigue was there but the cold was hindering his sleep. He added more wood and got the flames big before he managed to doze in and out of sleep, his body shivering as it tried to stay warm.

The following day Kyne guided the horse through the dead grove and back to the depression in the snow that showed the traveling road. The clouds had thinned more, allowing glimpses of blue sky but it was still so cold. He could see farther, with the city over a dozen miles away, just the tops of the crushed towers and the thin black spikes that pierced through the citadel roof were visible.

He had to find other people, people that wouldn't try to kill him, rob him, or eat him. People who could give him answers to what was going on. Remembering the map of Kydrëa, he knew where all the major cities were and also knew that dozens if not hundreds more dotted the landscape, not drawn on most maps due to their insignificant population and size.

One such town lay about a day's ride from Alakyne's west

453

The Legend of Kyne: Chronocide

along the Ta'Gor river. *At least if it's still there,* he thought as he led the horse down the road. He had lucked out and already been heading in that direction, so he didn't need to pass the dangerous city again with its demonic monster that resided there.

Already a good distance away, they traveled for half the day before they came to the town. Completely in ruins to his dismay, he led the horse down the center street of it, looking for any signs of life. Stone walls were crumbling in parts and coated in soot from fires long ago. No footprints were in the snow and as they passed through the small town that he didn't even know the name of, he continued on.

There are others, there have to be.

A few hundred feet past the city, Kyne stopped the horse, the thought too tempting and he ventured back, looking for a shelter in which they could rest through the night. If he could go without a fire, then all the better. Guiding the horse through a crumbling doorway into an abandoned home, Kyne dismounted and began searching for any place he could reside. Most rooms were stripped completely and only fragments of wooden furniture remained.

He went to another home, leaving his horse where it was in the first and then he went to another. Eventually noticing something odd about them, Kyne slowed his progress entering each one cautiously. A few of the homes had small areas that looked like people had been sleeping and as Kyne pushed open a door and stepped inside, he nearly cried out in shock as a shadow leapt towards him and he was met with a blunt object striking him across the arm.

Shouting in pain, he leapt back and drew his blade, watching as a thin man stepped into view grasping a wooden club. His hair was matted and partway down his back in length with his thick beard matching it. In his eyes was fear and sorrow.

"Get out!" he hissed. "Get out!"

"Ok ok," Kyne said releasing a hand from his blade and holding them both up in a non-threatening way. "I'm leaving."

"Get out!" the man shouted again, swinging his club around wildly.

Kyne felt his foot rise over the lip of the doorway as he backed out of the home slowly, his feet crunching in the snow. The man shouted again, swinging his club in a fevered rage. Kyne took a few more steps and when he was clear of the home, the man leapt forward and slammed the door shut casting him out in the cold.

Kyne was more cautious now, as he searched a few more of the homes. He found no supplies that were worth keeping, everything already plundered long ago. No other people were seen and as he trudged back through the snow towards his horse, he felt the sensation of being watched.

Looking towards where the man lived, he saw nothing, no sign of movement or peeking eyes.

I know he's there watching me, he thought, and he rubbed his arm where he had been struck, the pain dulling. With his other hand resting upon the pommel of his blade lightly, he trekked back. Entering through the gaping door, he saw the horse still standing in the main space. It snorted at his sight but didn't do much else other than continue standing.

A few of the other homes might've worked a little better than this one, either having more protection from the cold or a better view on his neighbor but this one would do, and he didn't want to try and move the horse. He had searched through the packs that had been stolen with the horse and had come across a blanket roll, some dried food, and a pendant from a time long past.

He curled up in the corner of the home as the wind outside began to pick up, situating himself into a position to keep as much warmth as he could. The ground was hard and cold, just dirt with the bricks of the home around him to block the wind. Frost had covered the ground but as he lay there, he could feel it melt away with his body heat. It was to be a frigid night, but he could already tell that he was much safer here in this home. With the horse lying nearby offering its own heat, the small room would suffice through the night.

Shouting outside woke Kyne up with a start and he fumbled for his blade, his eyes still groggy with sleep. The horse snorted in agitation, and he leapt to his feet, darting around the animal and peering through a hole in the wall.

Outside, across the street and down a ways a party stood in front of the neighbor's home. Bright torchlight cast shadows all around silhouetting their figures in the dark. Kyne could tell these people were not of the friendly type as the shining of steel glimmered in the orange light. More shouting was heard and then one of them thumped hard on the door, each strike causing the weakened wood to buckle.

They were dressed in thick fur pelts covering them from head to toe in the dark of night. Gloves were worn upon their hands and as they shuffled around in position Kyne counted four of them. Their horses were tied up nearby, more fur pelts draped over their backs reminiscent of Kyne's own steed.

A single word was barked and then the door was kicked in, the wood splintering in a loud crack. Rushing inside, screams of fright and more shouting was followed and he watched, his fingers gripping the edge of the hole, each turned a pale white from the strain. His stomach was churning, if they found him what would happen? He couldn't fend off four people at once, no one could.

Movement caught his eye, and he watched as two of the men exited, their torches still raised. When the third came into view he noticed that he was dragging something behind him. A moment later Kyne heard the screams of pain and saw that he was dragging the neighbor by his hair through the doorway before tossing him out into the snow. The fourth came into view with a small child not much older than five clutched in their arms. The child was screaming frantically, wailing and kicking at the captor but they didn't seem to notice and with a grunt, tossed the child into the snow next to presumably his father.

Kyne strained his ears, trying to hear what was going on but it was not feasible, a slight wind whistling through the hole masking their voices. A kick struck the man, launching him forward and more shouting followed swiftly by another kick. Screams came from the child and then a slap followed by silence as they both lay, cowering in the snow.

Crawling to his knees, the man pleaded at them, the glistening of tears illuminated by the torchlight upon his face showing his desperation. Suddenly, the man pointed towards Kyne's home, and they all turned to look at the gaping shell. Kyne ducked out of view, his pulse quickening and scanned the area for an escape route. The open doorway was his best bet but to escape them would be difficult if not impossible.

The Legend of Kyne: Chronocide

Slipping a single eye around the corner, he saw that two of the attackers had left the others, stepping cautiously towards his door. He had to leave, now!

Leaping onto the horse, he guided it towards the doorway and with a kick, it darted forward, galloping through the doorway out into the cold night, the fatigue gone, replaced by the rush of adrenaline. Shouting came from the attackers in shock at the sight of the horse as Kyne darted past them, heading towards the edge of the city.

The small pool of orange light that was cast upon the ground was replaced by the dark grey of snow as they passed them, up above, patches of the clouds were exposing the twinkling stars beyond whose light was faint as if seen through a thick pane of glass.

He spurred the horse faster.

Each hoof-beat pushed them further away from the shouting behind them. He wasn't sure if they were going to pursue and just as he turned to look, he felt his horse jerk underneath him. With a scream, the animal lurched forward, tossing them both to the ground, its massive body threatening to crush Kyne as they tumbled in the snow. Tucking his arms in, his mind flailing around trying to orient himself, he finally came to a stop, the icy cold snow scratching deep cuts upon his cheek and his breath ragged from the impact.

His abdomen throbbed from the unhealed wound and as he raised his arm up to hold it, felt the scream in his shoulder and its immobility signaling the dislocation. He climbed to his feet. Nearby, the deep furrow from the horse's body was noticed and then the horse who was thrashing around wildly, some roped object laced around its legs.

Drawing his blade with one arm, his other limply at his side, Kyne turned to meet the thundering hooves of two figures upon their steeds. Their torches were raised, and he could make out the features of thick beards and each one baring different eye colors. One that of crystal blue and the other a bright green.

"What have we here?" asked one as they came to him, guiding their horses to split around him, trapping him inside.

"I don't want any trouble," Kyne started, raising his blade up. "But I am not afraid to fight."

They chuckled at one another.

The Legend of Kyne: Chronocide

"Trouble? the only trouble you will be having is if you try and resist us boy," the gruff voice of a man was heard. The Gaeilian.

"I won't let you eat me!" spat Kyne, aiming his blade at him and shuffling slightly to the side for a better stance. "You are disgusting!"

"Eat you," gasped the Kydrëan appalled. "That is... Wow." He was silent for a moment as he looked at his companion.

"I have heard rumors of people doing that," said the Gaeilian. "We however have better more productive plans for you."

More hoof-beats were heard, and the other two fur clad figures joined them, both Gaeilian.

"So, it looks like we found some good meat then," said one cheerfully.

At those words the first two shot him a dark look at his wording before looking back at Kyne.

"Once more we are not going to eat you. You are going to bring us quite the lump of gold though."

The horse, who had been tied, screamed again and after more thrashing managed to get the wraps off of its legs where it jumped to its feet and bolted off down the road, vanishing into the darkness.

Its sight was disheartening as Kyne contemplated running after it. He could make it to the nearest building however. Using it as cover he could limit the fighting so that they would be forced a more one on one fight.

At the distraction of his horse drawing their attention, he bolted forward, each stride accelerating him as he dashed through the snow. He was close, twenty feet perhaps, and then something struck his legs, and he was falling down.

Striking the ground hard, he felt the blade narrowly slip from his grip but managed to hold on as he sank partially in the freezing snow. Something had bound him up and as he looked down to see it, noticed it was a cluster of ropes and steel balls, the same that had entrapped the horse.

Shouting sounded and then the orange of torchlight illuminated him as he fumbled with the ropes, slicing through them with ease with his blade.

"What an interesting weapon," said the Kydrëan as he peered

The Legend of Kyne: Chronocide

down upon him and then the others flanked his sides. Giving up on his bindings, Kyne sat down in the snow, his blade of light raised towards his attackers, the fear of death feeling his very being.

One lunged forward with their blade and Kyne deflected it. The moment he did, he realized their attack was never truly going to hit him, it had been a distraction. It was too late and unable to raise it back up fast enough, something struck him in the head making his mind grow foggy and he slumped over to the ground.

His vision swam in an out of focus as he was bound and tossed around, but the last thing he saw was them passing by the home of the man and child as they stared at them, both of their faces hard and lost of emotion.

53. Potatoes

The rumbling of wagon wheels upon rough ground drew Kyne from his daze. His head ached and he groaned quietly. The wagon lurched as it struck a rock and he was jerked around, slamming his shoulder into something.

His eyes were blurry, and he groaned again, wanting to reach up and rub them when he noticed the feeling of bindings around his wrists. His mind cleared more, and he noticed he had been bound up, his hands tied tightly behind his back. Other figures were nearby, most silent but one talking to someone that Kyne couldn't see.

His voice was quick and erratic, throwing glances from side to side as if paranoid. He whispered under his breath before shooting his head down, resting his head between his legs with a scream.

"Shut up!" shouted someone and Kyne watched a figure turn around, near the front of the cart. His vision was coming to, and he saw the figure stand up, a burly man of Gaeilian features. Walking towards the hunched over figure, his steps stabilizing him as the cart lurched over another rock. "Shut your mouth!" he growled, kicking the man lightly with his boot.

The man remained hunched over, rocking back and forth slightly, his voice a little louder than a whisper, quick and feverish.

"I said shut up!" roared the man and he gripped the man's hair and ripped him back up to a seated position, his eyes watering and his mouth continuing its needless rambling. A swift punch flew into his gut and then his hair was released, the Gaeilian walking back to his seat and turning his back to them.

The cart was small, two benches on either side with a third at the head where two men sat. There were four prisoners including himself. The crazed man whose skin bore scabs from constant picking

The Legend of Kyne: Chronocide

twisted in his seat, his hair thin and patchy. He looked to be an old man but something in Kyne told him he was not more than forty years.

Next to him was a large man, still as stone with a shorter beard. He was gruff, his age older but he was strong, a fieldworker by the looks of it. He stared at the floor of the cart with a flat affect and didn't seem to notice anything that had transpired. One arm was placed across his thigh and his other was but a sleeve, dangling partially before the end being tied up tight in a folded position where his elbow would've been.

The fourth and final prisoner sat next to Kyne. A younger man, Kyne presumed to be his own age who was of an athletic build and complexion. He was a handsome person with short trimmed blond hair who seemed cleaner than the average and held himself with quiet confidence.

"You're finally up," he muttered, noticing Kyne's movement after the ordeal had ceased.

Kyne nodded. "How long was I out?"

"A while, they brought you to us in the early morning, a limp sack of meat." He chuckled. "Thought you were dead if not for your slow breathing."

"Where is my blade," Kyne grunted, straightening his back and scanning around. The sun overhead was bright and hot on his skin as it beat down upon them and he realized suddenly. Looking outside the wagon, he found the sight of snow gone, replaced by a great expanse of yellowed plains and dead leafless trees.

"I wouldn't know," replied the prisoner, drawing Kyne back to his question. They have it or they left it where you were taken, the prior more likely as they can sell the blade."

He had to find it and looking around the wagon finally saw it, placed in its scabbard and leaning against the other captor's leg. "

Kyne looked down at his feet, rage setting in his chest. That was his! A gift that only he could receive. If his aura worked, he would strike them all down here and now!

"Give me my sword back!" his voice carried over the wagon and the Kydrëan captor coked his head to the side, slowly twisting back to meet his gaze, a smirk upon his face.

"Or what? You're in no position to give orders around here.

The Legend of Kyne: Chronocide

Sit back and shut up."

"I said give it back."

He turned fully around to face Kyne and held his hand up, twisting it over in the light. Kyne's heart sank at the sight and the captor noticed, his smirk growing. "Two rings and a sword were your gifts to me boy. Get over it, you will not be getting them back."

Kyne muttered a spell to kill under his breath as the captor turned back around.

Nothing happened and he gnashed his teeth. If his aura worked, then the blade would refuse to be wielded by anyone he didn't see as a friend. It would burn their hands and cause their minds to craze.

He had seen it before, when someone tried to take it when he was in a tavern. The poor bastard's hands were blistered, and he screamed about voices and creatures after him before he fled.

He looked back at his sword and then pictured his two rings, one from his parents and the other being Voron's. His mind grew fuzzy, and he looked around, disoriented at what was going on. He was a prisoner, one of four captured and taken by the people in the night, but where were the other two captors? He looked around again, shifting in the wooden seat. The road they traveled split the yellowed grass with the trees placed upon his right. Behind them nearly a hundred yards was another cart similar to his with a few people at its back.

The forest was bare of all leaves, their yellowed dry husks littering the floor. Not a single branch lay untouched by the beating sun above stripping all life from the area.

Where was the snow though, the frigid cold from the other night?

"Where are we," he said lowly directing it towards the young man to his side.

"Outskirts of Kol Faldîn. We passed around Alakyne a short time ago and across a boundary."

"Boundary?" Kyne muttered, confused at his wording. "Like the cities wall?"

"No, like a boundary," he said slowly, furrowing his brow, his dark brown eyes mirroring Kyne's confusion. "A boundary," he repeated but only receiving a blank stare from Kyne. "Separates the different areas, like the frozen one we had just been in to the hot and dry area we are in now."

It didn't make much sense what he was saying but Kyne nodded his head and looked away, towards the once beautiful forest. The heat was intense, the hottest day Kyne had felt in years and he felt perspiration drip down the side of his face. They were dangerously exposed here, signs of the sun's burning were already seen on the crazed man's arms, streaks of red with clear lines of white from areas that had been shielded.

Kyne couldn't adjust much, his coat that had been covering him gone, tucked underneath him by someone while he was unconscious. He couldn't move his arms to shield himself and so he sat there baking in the hot sun as it trailed across the sky before beginning its descent.

His back ached from the constant rumbling of the wagon, and he could feel his skin grow itchy as it slowly succumbed like the others. His companion who sat next to him remained mostly quiet, speaking occasionally to Kyne and making jokes about the others. He seemed friendly but Kyne knew that no one could be trusted, not in this world.

The crazed man, whom his new friend had nicknamed Rat, had tried rising to his feet a few times during the journey, each time being thrown down and struck by the captors. He snarled like a feral animal and spat thick globs of saliva at them which resulted in more beatings. He even tried to get a reaction from the armless man next to him but try as he might, the man didn't budge, just sat there still as stone.

Near the horizon, the sun hung low, red streaks lighting up the dried trees in a scarlet glow. The sky had an orange tint with not a cloud in sight. A few commands were shared, and the cart was pulled off the road where the captors leapt to the ground, talking to each other in a friendly manner. They each made their way to the back of the wagon and unlatched it before turning their attention to the prisoners. Their eyes turned dark, and threats were made, causing all four prisoners to one-by-one hop out. Kyne was first, his feet hitting the ground before a rough shove guided him to the side of the wagon where he was directed to sit. His companion soon followed and then Rat jumped off, landing upon the ground and collapsing in a tangled mess of limbs.

Shouting sounded and Rat was yanked to his feet before being thrown towards the others, stumbling and falling to the ground, his arms bound unable to catch him. Once they were all seated, each prisoner was given a small potato that was placed upon the ground in front of them. They gawked and jeered as the prisoners struggled to lean forward and pinch the vegetable in their mouths, their hands bound and unable to grab it.

Kyne chewed it raw, his stomach gurgling for food and was instantly sad after the final swallow. A water skin was passed around, each downing as much as they could before the captors sat and opened their own meals making each prisoner's mouth water at the sight.

The night enveloped the earth, casting its cooling shade around for instant relief from the daylight. Kyne's face was burned from the sun, he could feel the tight throbbing and the occasional feeling of freezing cold as a breeze would touch it. His neck was also burned but most of his skin had luckily been covered and his arms tucked behind him and blocked.

The sleeping was horrendous, laying on the ground in the dry prickly grass cut his skin and rocks dug into his ribs. As soon as he finally found sleep it seemed to end as they were jerked to their feet, the first streaks of dawn lighting up the sky. Then they were back in the wagon, rattling along the road.

Kyne asked the young man who was called Jaren where they were going but he didn't know either. They just traveled on, the sun rising into view and immediately the heat overtook them just like before, dousing them all in sweat. Rat continued to mutter to himself, gnawing at his shoulder through his clothes and drawing blood, screaming about wanting Flash.

Flash? Kyne thought as he watched the man who resembled a caged animal. *What is Flash?*

Down the road, far on the horizon, Kyne saw the dark color of storm clouds, seemingly frozen in the sky. They were to the east, ahead of their normal path but as they continued, Kyne never saw their dark masses move.

It was a low rumble as they neared, like the sound of a stream or the beating wings of a hummingbird. A wall of rain, nearly a straight

The Legend of Kyne: Chronocide

line blocked their path as the clouds above seemed to drop a torrent. The road was washed away, the rotting roots of the trees soggy with water. They were still dead, but not dry shells. Saturated, drowned plants black and wilted, with water covering their base in a rippling layer.

The water stretched over the boundary, into the dry area that they traveled and formed a thick river of water that flowed away from the forest, following the boundary line far out of view. Within, Kyne saw an occasional flash of lightning but nothing else, just a dark haze of rain.

It was chilling, soaking everything as they pushed into it, the wagons' wheels digging into the muddy earth. The splashing of water was heard as each horse slowed down, pulling the soon to be raft through the water that covered the ground. It was nearly half a foot deep and stretched as far as they could see.

Kyne was soon shivering, hating the thought of wanting the heat back as they were guided deeper into the wet. The wagon was drenched, soaking the wood to its core and filling their boots with a soggy mess. A small pond had formed at its base, the water filling up the wagon a few inches before finding cracks in the wood and flowing out.

The sun was obscured by the dark clouds and a few miles left the bright light so far behind them that it was lost to the foggy haze of rain. It never let up, never changed, just continued to pelt them as they traveled on through it. Kyne had no idea where the water seemed to come from, and it looked as if it would never end. And it didn't. It rained all day and when the night came, they could tell, utter darkness surrounding them, the rain still never ending. Kyne had struggled for nearly half an hour earlier in the day to get his jacket out from under the bench beneath him and had managed to drape it over his shoulders, offering a little bit of protection.

The captors had drawn some wooden shade over them keeping them dry and leaving the prisoners and horses to freeze and soak. They stopped the horses when it had become too dark to see, the orange glow of lanterns underneath their covering coming into being. More potatoes were tossed at them, landing in the soaking water in which Rat tried to steal two. The armless man struck him without warning across the face sending him tumbling to the side. Kyne grabbed his own potato and sat back on his soaking seat, eating it slower this time to try and savor it.

The night before was the best sleep ever compared to this. They sat, hunkered down in the rain the whole night, unable to lie down and unable to sleep. Frozen and wet, he felt his skin breaking down in his boots and was unable to do anything but deal with it.

The next day continued on, completely rain covered. Kyne felt an ache of sickness seeming to start and he coughed, his throat raw. The skin on his feet was blistered and so tender that he felt like he could pull the flesh off with his fingers.

Rat had tried speaking to him and Jaren a few times, his teeth chattering in between his words but they mostly ignored him. Kyne could tell that his incessant attempts at conversation were wearing on Jaren as his fingers were white from the tight fist he held.

No relief came from the rain and Kyne's coughing grew worse, his body aching and shivering. He was sick, for sure sick, and he feared it would only get worse. The night came and just as before, they were forced to endure.

It was dark and the fatigue had allowed Kyne to get a few moments of relief from the torture, lost to his own dark dreams when a clutter and thump sounded nearby waking him. It was dark, the lanterns extinguished and the captors seemingly asleep. To his right Jaren's figure was slumped over, his silhouette moving signaling slow breathing. More rumbling drew his attention across the wagon, and he could make out a dark shape kneeling down upon the floor.

"Hey what's going on?" groaned a captor, an orange light coming into being and the sight made Kyne gasp in shock. The armless man was kneeling down, his towering figure over Rat's flailing arms with his hand pressing Rat's face hard into the base of the wagon. The water was to Rat's ears and his flailing rapidly slowed and then stopped moments before the captors were upon him. He calmly stood up, releasing his hold upon the back of Rat's head and sat back down, the rain a constant background noise. The captors pulled Rat's limp body up, his eyes still open and his mouth dripping water.

He was murdered, the thought making Kyne's skin crawl. Drowned in the two inches of water that hugged the base of the wagon.

The Legend of Kyne: Chronocide

The night was over, the sleep gone as the captors beat the one-armed man bloody. Beat him so badly that it threatened his life, but he didn't resist. Just took each punch with a face as still as stone.

"We should drown him!" snarled the Gaeilian as they loomed over him laying at the base of the wagon. Grasping his hair between his fingers, he picked him partially off the ground before ramming him down hard against the wagon, crushing his nose and submerging him in the water with a splash.

The orange torchlight cast wicked shadows as it illuminated the scene in which Kyne and Jaren watched. Rat's corpse was nearby, still as stone as the captor held the man under the water.

Kyne held his breath as a long moment passed.

"We need him alive," spoke the Kydrëan captor calmly. "The gold he will give us... Is it worth killing him?"

"I think so!" hissed the other still holding him under.

"Then kill him," he replied flatly. "But the gold he would've given us you will owe me," and he climbed over the railing back underneath its covering and presumably back to sleep.

The Gaeilian cursed and then suddenly ripped the gasping man out of the water, throwing him to the side. "You are just a cripple," he spat, grasping the man's chin in his hand and bringing his face right next to his own. "But you will still get me something!" Looking over at Rat's corpse, he screamed in rage at his lost profit and with a cry, heaved him over the side of the wagon where he landed with a splash.

"They are going to sell us," Jaren muttered, understanding in his voice.

Kyne nodded, knowing the darkness obscuring his agreement. They were making these captors a whole heap of gold. Where were they being taken?

The night droned on, the captors returning to sleep while the prisoners remained exposed to the onslaught of rain. Kyne after a while looked over the edge of the wagon, expecting to see Rat's body but it was so dark that he couldn't see a thing. Jaren began coughing and their sounds were the only thing accompanying the rain.

As the sky went from black to grey, the captors awoke, and

The Legend of Kyne: Chronocide

they continued on. Kyne threw one glance down as they left and saw Rat's body, partially floating upon the ground, face down in the water.

A few hours passed and the glimmer of light on the horizon appeared. More miles and then they were out, back into the intense desert like heat leaving the monsoon behind. The trees nearby returned to their dry selves with a few remaining alive along the transition line.

Here they passed a few makeshift homes, just near the edge of the water and Gaeilians were seen. They spoke to the captors, coin was shared and then they continued on, the hot sun baking the water away.

They continued coughing, Kyne's throat raw from the effort and his abdomen hurt but the heat was welcoming as he felt his clothes begin to dry. He couldn't see his feet but could only imagine the pale wrinkly horror that they were.

The heat quickly dried everything and then they were sweating, traveling on along the forest edge.

Days passed, from desert that fried their skin to frigid cold, never-ending rain and even a constant hurricane like wind that threatened to flip the wagon. They traveled along the road, along the edge of dead trees, either fried to a crisp, frozen, or drowned, but all the same. Dead.

The windy area was one of the worst, most trees snapped and covered the road making it extremely difficult to traverse. The three prisoners were eventually forced to walk, allowing the wagon to climb over them easier. Small pieces of dirt and debris pelted their skin, inflicting painful stinging wounds but they pushed on, eventually turning into the forest and heading northeast.

The sun was but a faint smudge, obscured by the dust that hung in the air like a sandstorm in Otoruh but enshrouding a forest not the desert of Loke' Ynen. They continued on traveling, day in and day out. Venturing into more desert, this time the forest scorched from some previous fire that ate the dried and baked vegetation like a gluttonous snake who had found the den of a family of mice.

From the desert to a swamp and then frozen, Kyne's sickness seemed to grow worse, the guards laughed each time they forced them to eat the stale potatoes from the ground and Kyne could see his body shriveling from malnourishment.

More days passed and just as they came to a barrier separating

The Legend of Kyne: Chronocide

a frozen tundra from desert, Kyne saw they were upon the edge of the Riigar mountain range, their peaks bare of the once pristine glaciers. A camp had been set up along the transition line where the temperature seemed most manageable, and Kyne could see large open pit mines and hundreds of people dressed in rags.

Sentinels dotted the landscape, swords gleaming and the cracking of whips in the air. They were brought to a flat area at the base of the mine that covered a mountain's lower slope and ordered to exit. Sentinels approached and the captors were joined by the other two who had been pulling the wagon behind them. A conversation was started, and Kyne saw the glimmer of silver and gold shared between the captors. He coughed hard, doubling over, nausea in his gut.

A moment later the captors walked away, the Kydrëan with Aurora upon his hip vanishing into a building. Kyne's sadness intensified at its loss and then was replaced by anxiety as the sentinels approached, cracking whips and barking orders. The other wagon had three prisoners as theirs had and all six were led to a different covered building. The one-armed man hobbled after them, having caught the sickness and the beating he had received, he looked to be nearly dead, and Kyne expected it was quite a possibility.

They were shown to an empty area, flat blankets lay scattered around the floor. Through the windows Kyne saw some covered with frost and snow and others bare with bright sunlight streaming in as they straddled the barrier.

Each had their bindings removed and were ordered to strip down completely naked. There they stood, exposed to each other as the sentinels mocked their figures. Kyne could see his ribcage was more exposed, his thick muscled figure vanishing to that of a frail man.

He averted his eyes from the others, but he could see one of the six lick his lips as he stared at each of their exposed bodies one by one. Kyne didn't look but the sounds that soon followed made his gut retch.

He was thrown a clump of ragged clothes and he scrambled to get them on as fast as possible, giving him immediate comfort. They were also given a blanket and a small pouch of brown seeds they were told was currency. Kyne's wrists were caked with dried blood and scabs, and he rubbed them lightly, wincing at the pain the bindings had given

The Legend of Kyne: Chronocide

him. His coughing didn't cease and after a hard bout he managed to calm himself.

The day was early, but they were allowed to stay in the empty room, setting their blankets down upon the ground they scattered around the room, Kyne and Jaren getting as far away from the large creepy man who only met their eyes and smiled with glee at their disgust.

They remained there throughout the day, a sentinel occasionally entering the room to look at them before returning to their post. The day waned on and as evening fell, the room was soon flooded with other prisoners whom Kyne understood were actually slaves.

They stumbled in, exhausted and covered with filth, each placing a small cluster of the seeds into the pouch that was hidden on their person. Some had it draped around their neck like a pendant and others tucked it in their pants or in their shoes.

A short time later a sentinel entered, leading a small donkey who was pulling a cart ladened with potatoes, water pouches, bread balls, and other items of food, all of which looked stale or moldy. A line quickly formed, and items were exchanged for the small seeds.

Kyne watched for a moment when he felt his own stomach growl. Opening his pouch, he counted ten seeds and after watching, understood that he could afford one potato and a bread ball.

Noticing Jaren doing the same, he nodded to his new friend, and they made their way to the line. It was long but moving fast and every few seconds Kyne took a step forward making his way closer to his meal.

Suddenly a voice near his ear caught his attention and he saw a short bald and heavyset man eyeing him and muttering something.

"What?" Kyne asked confused at the man and then he took another step forward keeping up with the line.

"I said, do you want some Flash?"

"Flash?" Kyne mumbled remembering the word and he took another step forward. What he wanted was some food, not whatever the Flash was.

"No," he said flatly, and he continued on the line. The man asked again but Kyne declined to his obvious irritation. As he vanished

The Legend of Kyne: Chronocide

down the line, Kyne noticed other people huddled in corners and exchanging seeds for something he couldn't see. Every person who gave the seeds was skinny and frail, often covered with scabs and all having glee across their face as they returned to their blanket. Those who obtained the seeds often looked to be well fed, some even hefty.

"What was he asking you for?" asked Jaren.

"If I wanted some Flash."

"Isn't that the stuff Rat kept mumbling about?" Jaren pondered before stepping up and getting his rations.

Kyne followed and as they made their way back, he started to pay attention to what was happening. A huge portion of the slaves resembled Rat, thin and scabbed little wretches. Others looked normal, or at least as normal as a slave looked. All seemed to be dirty, with some covered in scars or fresh whipping marks. The ones who stood out were the heavier people who seemed to know exactly who to ask concerning the Flash.

54. Flash

The daylight came and the slaves were corralled outside, each receiving a pickax and shovel that they would return at the end of the day. Some were led up the mountain in the hot heat while others were guided into the tundra. Jaren and Kyne were separated almost immediately, and Kyne found himself in the heat, hacking away at the earth mining.

They were looking for aural stones that which Kyne quickly learned allowed the user to use a temporary amount of aura. He learned that they called the event that preceded this current state of the world was The Falling. The sky burned and massive meteors fell from the sky, glowing with the brilliance of gemstones and containing deadly power.

Aura faded almost immediately but those who found the stones were able to perform feats of aura. Each stone was different, some glowed red and other gold but they all did the same thing. Each gave a small amount of aura that could be utilized. The color indicated the amount of power the stone contained but Kyne didn't know which one was the best.

He found none the first day but watched as when one was found, the eager slave ran to the nearest sentinel brandishing it and receiving a fair pile of the seeds.

The day ended and as Kyne placed his tools down in the piles, he passed a sentinel and was given his own portion of seeds before he ventured inside. He spotted Jaren quickly and they exchanged updates on what happened.

The tundra was miserable, but he was able to find two stones and after brandishing the fat sack of seeds smiled at Kyne.

"Did you find any?"

The Legend of Kyne: Chronocide

Kyne shook his head and weakly smiled showing his own small lump.

"Here," said Jaren and he withdrew a pinch, handing them to Kyne.

"But they are yours," Kyne said in confusion.

"Now we can both have a good meal. Hopefully get back some of the muscle we lost," and he chuckled before gesturing to the food cart that had appeared.

Kyne had grown fond of Jaren. He was weird and quirky with things he said but he seemed genuine, even by his random act of kindness. Kyne wanted to trust him, and this would allow him a little, but he couldn't let his guard down. Not until he was absolutely sure.

More days passed, some with Jaren and Kyne in the same group, able to talk occasionally as they picked the ground for stones and other days they were separated. They bounced back and forth between the desert and the tundra and Kyne couldn't decide which he hated more.

His hands ached in the cold, but the work kept him warm where the heat was relentless as it tried to cook all the souls beneath its gaze.

It was exhausting work, each day threatening to take his life, but he pushed through, working through the hours and eating his fill. He found a few stones, very tempted to fight back with them but after watching a few slaves brutally tortured to death from trying, he decided too not. His sickness faded and his strength grew, filling out his frame slowly hiding the ribs below.

A few weeks passed when Jaren sat down next to him after a long day. They had been split the last three days and forced to work in alternate climates. Seeing his friend was welcoming and Kyne raised some food up, gesturing for him to join him.

He sat down quickly and smiled mischievously before looking around to see if he was being watched. Slowly, he withdrew a small pouch of dark purple paste and smiled again.

"What's that," Kyne said slowly, certain he knew what it was but not wanting to hear it.

"Flash."

"Why do you have it?"

The Legend of Kyne: Chronocide

"I was talking with the others, and I think I am going to try it."

Kyne was silent and he took another bite. He looked down at his human arm, bare of the dragon scales it once bore and flexed it for a moment.

"That sounds very dangerous. Have you forgotten Rat?"

"It's only dangerous to those who abuse it," Jaren justified. "If you use it right it can make everything so much better."

Kyne shook his head, disagreeing with his friend. He knew the threat it posed. He had heard about it, learned from the others who took it daily about its amazing time effects but still.

"It's too dangerous Jaren."

Jaren's cheerful demeanor grew dark, and he drew his lip back in a sneer. "Then I guess it's all for me then. Great friend you are," and he turned his back to Kyne and went to bed without eating.

The morning came and the two stood in line together, still not having spoken to each other since the night prior. They grabbed their things and were both ordered to the mountain slope covered in the never-ending heatwave.

Taking their place, they started to hack away at the earth and after a moment, Kyne noticed Jaren stop. He glanced over and saw his friend meet his eyes for a moment before he lifted his palm up, the purple paste spread across it. A swipe of his tongue and it was gone.

Kyne's stomach dropped and he watched as Jaren started to hack at the ground again, his jaw moving as he swallowed the paste. A few moments passed and then Jaren's body seemed to shudder, going rigid for a moment and then he started to hack away again.

His digging was different though, slow and constant, like he was possessed and after a moment of watching him, the crack of a whip drew Kyne back to his own work and he started hacking away. He would occasionally look at his friend, but he never got a response, even during their allotted bathroom breaks or when they drank water. He would shuffle to and from his job, his eyes glazed over and an expressionless look across his face.

It was late in the evening, nearly time to stop when Jaren's movement seemed to change, growing less methodical. Kyne looked over and saw his friend's face covered with shock. He gazed up first at the sky and then towards Kyne before a massive grin lit up across his

The Legend of Kyne: Chronocide

face.

"It was like I blinked and the day passed," Jaren was spouting to Kyne as they stood in line waiting for their rations. "I took it and a flash of white filled my vision. Next thing I know it's late evening and the sun is setting. My pouch is full of seeds from stones I guess I found, and I am mentally not drained from working all day."

Kyne stayed silent. He didn't know what to say. Yes, the flash seemed intriguing, to have painful suffering blip away seemingly sending him to the future sounded awesome, but also terrifying. He had seen other prisoners taken advantage of with it, bad things being done, abuse and robbery, even murder was not unheard of.

"It's too dangerous," Kyne repeated what he said the night before.

Jaren's face grew frustrated but before he could say anything someone got his attention. Turning around, Jaren saw the short fat man from earlier. His face was drenched with sweat, but a smile stretched from ear to ear.

"Did you like it?"

"Yes, it was incredible," Jaren said, Kyne fighting the urge to knock the bald man out.

They all stepped forward as the line progressed.

"I am glad," he replied, and he withdrew another parchment spread with paste. It shimmered and sparkled almost as if it had been made out of ground amethyst.

Jaren stretched his hand out towards it.

"Fifteen and its yours."

"Fifteen?" Gasped Jaren. "The other one was five."

"Fifteen," he repeated, swinging it lightly just out of reach of Jaren's outstretched hand. "The first is five, the rest is fifteen. If you don't want it, then I can find another buyer."

Jaren's hand dropped and he opened his bag revealing what Kyne counted to be sixteen seeds.

"If I buy it, I won't be able to eat," he muttered to himself and then he looked at the sparkling paste and then the seeds.

"What will it be?"

"I... I can't," stammered Jaren, defeat evident in his voice.

475

The Legend of Kyne: Chronocide

The man tucked the parchment back under his sleeve and said, "Very well, you know where to find me," and then he swept away, approaching another who nearly threw the seeds at him for the drug.

Jaren didn't look at Kyne, but Kyne didn't pressure him. He knew his friend was vulnerable and didn't want to start a fight.

They got their food and sat, silently eating it.

The next day they returned to their digging, neither of them finding anything. As the day finished, the bald man walked past them, not acknowledging either of them. He was just a few steps past when to Kyne's shock, Jaren whipped around and tapped the man's arm.

They met eyes, a nod was shared and then the exchange happened, Kyne watching the look of dependent glee lighting up across Jaren's face as he clutched the parchment tightly.

No words were shared and then the man was gone.

Jaren looked at the two seeds in his hand, looked at the cart, looked at the purple paste and nodded as if to agree with his decision. He met Kyne's eyes briefly before returning to his blanket and laying down.

Kyne got his food, only enough for a single potato and one bread ball. He returned and out of pity offered some to Jaren who declined. He ate in silence and as the torches were snuffed out and the chorus of voices declined, he too laid down and sleep found him.

55. A Friend or a Foe

Flash! That damned flash! Kyne's mind roared in anger as he stared at the faded form of his new friend, repeatedly striking the ground with his pickax. His face had a blank stare, his eyes unseeing as he continued working away. Kyne had tried to talk to him for a moment before a sentinel noticed and threatened the whip. He had tried to get any sort of response from him but there was nothing. Just an empty hollow shell.

The drug was strong, controlling more than half of the slaves and counting. Its power gripped them and made their suffering fly past in a blip and flash of light. He knew it was tempting, every day he suffered as he was worked to the brink of collapse. Sweat dripped off his skin and fell onto the bare dirt ground, steaming in moments after touching it.

He needed to escape, needed to get away from this place but couldn't think of a way that would really work. The sentinels were numerous, more fed than he was and wielding weapons of steel.

He missed his own blade, missed its brilliance and savagery that it contained. The Kydrëan slave trapper who had taken it had returned twice since he had been captured. Each time Kyne noticed him, his golden eyes dark from the lack of empathy and constant stream of death they had seen. Upon his hand lay Kyne's rings and upon his waist lay his scabbard, always there, always taunting him with it.

Commotion got his attention and he turned slowly to see sentinels running toward the tundra side of the encampment. Suddenly a flash of light and flame appeared followed by a slave running towards the stables where the horses were kept right on the border of the two desolate lands.

The Legend of Kyne: Chronocide

A sentinel tried to stop him and with a wave of his hand another jet of flame erupted drawing Kyne's interest even more. It was a new slave; one he didn't recognize as the shipment had come just yesterday. He was a young man, not more than sixteen with long lanky legs and dark hair. He was fast, covering a great distance in seconds and to Kyne's surprise seemed slightly proficient in aura.

More shouting and then the slave vanished into the stables. Kyne threw a look to see Jaren's reaction at the sight and immediately was disappointed as his friend was still working, still in his trance unfaltering.

Kyne looked back just in time to see the slave dash out aboard a horse. The thundering hooves upon the dirt caused butterflies in Kyne's stomach to appear. The thought of someone escaping actually might be possible. This slave knew some spells, but Kyne was the archmage.

If he can escape, then so can I.

Just as Kyne thought that an arrow flew toward the slave striking him in the back. The boy cried out in pain, hunching over but managing to stay on the horse as the distance continued to grow. He was nearing the hazy fog like wall of falling snow that would be his escape. Hidden from view, he could flee, traveling far away.

Another arrow struck him, the shaft quivering as it joined its companion. Then a third and the slave slumped to the side, falling off the horse and landing on the scorched earth a few dozen feet from the veil.

Kyne held his breath as he watched the sentinels so far away from him approach the slave. An idea came in his mind, and he looked around, seeing no sentinels anywhere nearby and a straight shot to the tundra where he could flee into the dead forest.

But even if I made it, he thought, turning his vision toward the frigid wall. *I am not dressed for the cold. Even if I was, I wouldn't last more than a night out there. I would freeze to death if I wasn't caught first. I don't have any aura to keep me warm and no weapon to defend myself.*

Barking drew his attention back towards the slave and he was surprised to see the young man had stumbled to his feet and continued his progress towards the cold, his horse standing right upon its edge just within reach.

The Legend of Kyne: Chronocide

The barking intensified and three large dogs bounded past the sentinels at high-speed heading right for their target. Just as they leapt upon him, Kyne turned away averting his eyes. The muffled screams made his stomach turn and his blood run cold.

He had forgotten about the dogs. He barely saw them. They stayed inside mostly, only coming out to relieve themselves or if a situation like this occurred.

They would smell him if he got away making his chance of escape all that more difficult. He would need a horse and that seemed virtually impossible.

A crack of a whip sounded, and he noticed it was directed at him. Quickly grabbing his pickax, he started to dig again, the small relief his muscles had received evaporating away as their chorus of protesting screams returned.

The day ended with no aural stones found, no one found any, and the sentinels were seething in rage. A single sentinel had entered the main room. A stubby man, not muscular or athletic in any sort of way. He was of middle age, bald except for a thick mustache and even thicker eyebrows above his green eyes.

"Not one stone found!" The commander of the group cried. "Not a single stone by any of you?"

The room was silent.

"No food!" he screeched suddenly waving his hands. "No food then if you can't work!"

Uproar erupted from the slaves and the cracking of whips sounded, corralling the slaves back into an obedient focus.

"I said no food," the commander stated, more calmly this time as he paced around the room eyeing the slaves. "If you are not to find what we search for then you are useless. If no stones are found, then no one gets fed. If you all die then we will just find more to replace you," and he spun on his heel and left the room.

The uproar immediately began again, and some slaves were whipped and beaten as they tried to defy the sentinels. Kyne watched, his stomach rumbling and his eyes heavy from the constant work and fatigue. The highlight of his day was the stale bread.

He had to get out.

Jaren and a few others stumbled into the room, their faces

The Legend of Kyne: Chronocide

displaying a dazed expression as if they had just woken from a long sleep. Kyne noticed him and they met eyes.

"What's happening?" Jaren mouthed.

"No stones, no food," Kyne mouthed, glad to have his friend back.

Jaren made his way toward him, a puzzled expression across his face. "No food? That ludicrous."

"That's what the commander just said. I guess not one stone was found today. He freaked out and said no food for anyone. If we can't find stones, then we starve."

Disbelief was across his face, shocked at what Kyne had said. Jaren sat down on his blanket and ran his hand through his hair.

"I think it might have something to do with that slave earlier today," said another slave nearby, not directly at them but more at the room.

"Slave?" Jaren asked.

"Someone tried to escape. Was killed."

"Oh," he responded, slightly having frustration in his voice. "I don't remember it happening."

"It's the Flash that's why," Kyne snapped. "You act like a zombie on it. You're not even a person anymore. You don't eat, you don't smile, you just take that purple paste and vanish, reappearing ages later slow witted like a demented elder."

Jaren was silent and looked down at his hand which was inside his pocket. Kyne knew that it gripped a small parchment coated in the drug. He slowly met Kyne's eyes and a look of sadness was deep within.

"It helps me through the suffering. If you just tried it..."

"I am not going to try it!" roared Kyne. "Don't ask me again!"

"I just..."

"You just what?" Kyne retorted.

"I just don't want to suffer. This is my escape. If you do not approve, then so be it. You are not my mother, and I am my own person. I can make my own choices." He stood up, grabbing his blanket and traversed through the large room, avoiding the other slaves' blankets before vanishing from Kyne's sight.

Kyne was angry and sad in so many ways. He had suffered for weeks here, away from his family, his best friend, his wife, and the

480

young one he was raising. He fought hard to be hopeful that they were alive and searching for him but a part of him was growing more and more full of despair.

Laying his head down on the rolled-up shape of his slave coat like a pillow, he tried to fall asleep, the chorus beginning to die down around him, and the torches being extinguished casting the room into complete darkness.

A hand jerked Kyne awake as it shook his shoulder roughly. The moment his eyes opened, another hand enveloped his mouth, and a whisper was heard in his ear.

"Shhh," it said, in a low drone.

It was dark, an inky blackness surrounding all sides. Kyne couldn't make out virtually anything, but a rough silhouette as faint light came from outside.

The hands were withdrawn, and he sat up sharply.

"I have a message from a friend," said a voice in a slurred and drunken manner. "I have a message from a friend."

Kyne shifted his seat, turning to face the figure better and as his eyes adjusted, he could see the faded out grey features of the slave who was speaking. It was an older man, nearly skin and bones whose skin bore scars from countless whippings and beatings. The thing that caught Kyne's notice more than anything was the strange, glazed look that stretched over his eyes.

"I have a message from a friend," the figure repeated again, the slur stretching out the final word.

"You said that," Kyne muttered.

A piece of parchment lay tucked in the man's collar, just in view and as the slave repeated the phrase again, Kyne reached up and took it. The darkness was too much to read it and the frustration was evident in Kyne's voice as he whispered, "You can go now."

As if under a spell, the slave rose to their feet and vanished out of view leaving Kyne alone with his note. He would read it first thing in the morning.

Faint sunlight began to stream in drawing Kyne from his restless sleep. Upon its sight, he tore the parchment out from its hiding

The Legend of Kyne: Chronocide

place in his waistband and scanned over the rough words.

> I know who you are, and I am here to help you escape. A friend or foe, you know not what I am, but I assure you a foe would not go to the lengths and the dangers to present this letter to you.
>
> The key to your escape lies with the stones and your aural prowess. Find them and hide them so that they can be used at a later time.
>
> I will be in contact and will give further instructions.

Kyne read it over twice more before he crumpled it up and stuffed it in his mouth, swallowing it to get rid of the evidence.

I can't hide the stones, he thought in frustration as he stood to his feet. He grabbed his coat after being assigned to the tundra and walked quickly outside into the blistering snow. *I have seen others try and they always fail, the sentinels always seem to notice when stones are found.*

Kyne started digging, sweeping the snow away before he attacked the frozen earth. He dug for a while, picking through the torn ground trying to formulate a plan. There wasn't anywhere he could really hide the stones.

Under the snow? he thought between strikes. *No, that wouldn't work. Even if I could get it tucked in, it would be covered and lost the following day. I can't carry them either. The sentinels check me before I enter the sleeping quarters.*

* * *

56. A Deal

Kioni sat in the back of the room, most of his clothes stripped off and he was scrubbing his skin vigorously with soap and steaming water. Rosé could see his skin was a bright red from either the steam or the scrubbing, she wasn't sure. All she knew was that the moment he stepped inside she nearly wanted to throw up.

He scrubbed for nearly half an hour, laboriously moving from arm to arm and then down each of his legs. The rest of the family mostly just sat doing their own things, their attention constantly being dragged back to him as he shifted his stance and the groan of the water bowl sliding a bit on the table.

Seri sat nearby, transfixed by his presence and the other two brothers were in a deep discussion, reviewing what he had told them earlier. Rosé could only make out bits and pieces as the sound from Kioni's scrubbing blocked most of it out. She could tell they weren't quite sure how he had done it and if he could be trusted.

"It just doesn't make any sense," Roco muttered. "Even if he could use the forbidden arts, even if he wasn't noticed he still shouldn't be able to shift faces so easily. They should surely know by now."

"I was thinking the same thing but for some reason he wasn't," Lioné replied. "This strange man could've easily killed any one of us, alerted any of the sentinels, or any number of things but he didn't. He dragged himself through the sewer to help us."

"Help her," Roco corrected, side-eying the small dragon who was looking right at him. Their gaze lingered for a minute, and she rolled her eyes at his comment before he continued discussing with Lioné.

I think he can be trusted, she thought to herself as she looked back at him. He had moved on to scrubbing his hair and face and was nearly done. *Kyne talked about him a lot back at home. He used to be his best friend.*

"So, Kioni," said the dragon drawing his attention from his scrubbing and she approached. Snaking her head up nearly to his eye level she said, "Do you know what's going on?"

He shook his head before returning to his cleaning, his hair was rinsed with cold water, and he ran a towel through it to dry it. Sliding one of Lioné's tunics over his head, he ruffled his hand through his damp hair and sighed at the relief before turning back to the dragon.

"I don't. It seems that somehow, wherever we came to, the Dominion here was never defeated. It seems that they have completely wiped out all Kydrëan resistance."

"I remember the stories about the sentinels, dozens of them that I was told but I wasn't sure if it really was them. The only thing I really remember is that bright light and then I was here."

"Kyne must've done something, or the Dominion did something to him. Either way it doesn't seem like they are satisfied with what they've done. I have seen mercenaries that are joining their military which means that they only want more."

"What's a mercenary?" asked Seri butting into their conversation.

"Isn't it someone who doesn't want to fight?" replied Rosé with a puzzled look trying to remember the word.

"No, a mercenary is someone who gets paid to join another country's military. Basically, they will fight for whoever pays them the most."

"But can't they die?" Seri gasped. "Why would they do that?"

"These mercenaries are from Windra, a large island to our south. I haven't heard much about them really at all, only that it's part of their country's history. They get most of their money fighting other nation's wars. I'm not familiar with many countries to our south but I know there have been many conflicts over the last few centuries. It would make sense that a nation would look for ways to get money, even taking part in it."

The two young girls didn't say much but Lioné and Roco seemed to have their attention caught.

The Legend of Kyne: Chronocide

"They have been here for a little more than a year," Lioné muttered. "More of them keep flocking in but we don't see much of them. They are usually kept up in the citadel or out in the military outposts that line the river."

"It's Aaldra right," Kioni muttered more to himself than anything. "He wants the whole world for himself."

"Don't say his name," hissed Roco. "You could get us all killed."

"By saying his name?"

"We aren't supposed too anymore. We are just supposed to refer to him as Him. Aaldra," Roco said as if the word caused physical strain. "Aaldra announced it a few years ago and anyone who is caught saying his name is executed."

"Same time that aura was outlawed as well. No one is even supposed to mention that it exists," Lioné added.

"He seems different than he used to be," muttered Kioni. "A powerful sorcerer banning aura is contradictory."

Rosé looked at Kioni for a long moment. She could see the look in his eyes, the look of a killer, but she could also see a deep kindness that reminded her of Kyne a lot.

Kioni didn't continue his talking but just sighed and walked past Rosé to the rest of his things. Stooping down, he picked up a belt and slipped some baggy pants over his undergarments. Just as he withdrew his kama sheath, Rosé watched as a shimmery silk cloth drifted out of his hand before landing on the ground nearby.

He hadn't seemed to notice but she felt intrigue as she stared at it, and she approached. It was bunched up in the corners like it had been tied together and just along the corner she could make out just part of a silver ring.

Just before she could touch it, he snatched it out from her reach and tied it quickly around his neck masking the strange symbol. His face bore an intense look of concern mixed with anger, but he said nothing. He continued putting his things on before he migrated towards the wall.

Rosé was startled by his response, but she could see that he was exhausted as he slumped down against the wall. She knew that he should rest. He closed his eyes and in moments he was asleep.

The Legend of Kyne: Chronocide

"How do you know him?" whispered Seri as she eyed the sleeping man.

"He was good friends with my brother and best friends with Kyne."

"You've said Kyne before, but I don't understand who that is," Seri replied.

"He's well... I guess he is kind of my dad."

"He seems like he means well," said Roco as he joined the two of them.

"I agree. I was skeptical at first, but it does seem like he does want to help you and in turn help us. Without him we would've been killed so we are forever in his debt."

"Don't celebrate just yet," hissed a voice and they looked over to see their mother peering around the corner before vanishing. "Don't celebrate until they are all gone."

Kioni awoke to the smell of food, and he could feel his mouth beginning to water. It was evening, the sunlight faint outside and he felt his abdomen ache from hunger, so he sat up and surveyed the house.

Everyone seemed to be doing something, the young girl Seri was talking with Rosé while the three men were setting the table, the eldest of the three, their father battered and bruised but moving well. Their mother was hidden from sight, only noticed by her occasional passings as she cooked some sort of stew.

A few minutes later Lioné brought both him and the two girls a bowl to a mild scoff from inside the kitchen. He heard nothing further, so he gratefully took it and began to eat.

It was warm, filling him up well as he gulped down the last bite. A few pieces of bread were shared but that was it, not quite enough to be full but enough to quench the gnawing hunger for a time. Glancing at the window and noticing the darkened sky, he furrowed his brow, irritated by how long he slept but an idea quickly came to mind.

This might be an opportunity to get some intel on what's going on. If I can sneak into the citadel, I might find some answers. Deep in his head a more pessimistic thought emerged. *You might get caught though, is it really worth it. Maybe you should just stay the night and try to figure out a way to escape the city. But if I escape, I might not truly know what's going on and*

The Legend of Kyne: Chronocide

where the others went. I need to find answers.

As the night waned and the family all took their different spots throughout the house, the two eldest brothers laid upon the floor offering him a bed to which he declined, giving it to Rosé instead. He took a spot on the floor with a thin blanket near the door and watched as the last lantern was extinguished, casting him into darkness. A few minutes later he heard scurry and was surprised to find Rosé had moved from the bed to the floor next to him, curling up like a pink cat.

He waited, staring at the ceiling for nearly two hours before he was certain everyone was asleep, focusing on their breathing and nearly gasping at the relief when Rosé's slowed and calmed.

She is relentless, he thought to himself as he slowly withdrew the covers. *I thought she would never fall asleep.*

He took a slow step, rising from his knees and nearly cursed as the wood groaned. He froze, his ears roaring from the blood rushing through them and he held his breath waiting. A long moment passed, everyone else's breathing remaining constant before he exhaled, progressing towards the door.

Slowly. Slowly, his mind repeated as he grabbed onto the metallic lock, gliding it over to allow the broken door open. Pulling it ajar, he slipped between the smallest crack possible out into the open street before guiding it back shut. Unable to lock it, he pulled it fully closed, the friction holding it in place and then he turned to survey the road.

No sentinels were nearby but he could just make out the faded orange lights a few streets over illuminating the higher buildings walls. No stars were seen, the air just a faint muggy grey scattering all of the light from above and below.

He took off as fast as he could, rushing down the street next to the building's edge. He didn't have any clothing that would mask him so that would be his first objective.

Alakyne was enormous, over a mile just to reach the citadel from his current position so he had time on his journey to find a target.

A sentinel will probably be the easiest, take their armor and use their face. They seem to always be in pairs though so that could be a bigger problem.

Trying to think of a plan, he pushed on trying to get a bit closer to the citadel. Thoughts of clanking up the long road in sentinel armor seemed incredibly unappealing to him. Ten minutes of quick dashes and moments of stillness to avoid sentinels brought him nearly to the inner wall. He could see up ahead two patrolling sentinels, their voices unheard.

I wish they were talking, he thought as he dashed after them. *It would probably help sneaking up on them.*

Then an interesting thought appeared in his mind, and he smiled wickedly as he recalled the image of Aaldra in his head from many years ago.

"Stop there," he called out, just loud enough for them to hear. His voice startled him for a moment, deep and thick, vibrating his throat with its tone.

The sentinels turned around in shock and their swords were drawn. Kioni was still concealed in darkness, but he waited as the sentinels approached. The moment they saw him their swords dropped, and they fell to their knees.

"Give me your armor," Kioni spoke, faking the confidence and authority.

"My lord, why... Why do you roam the streets at night? It is not safe for someone of your..."

"Not safe for me? The most powerful being in the world?" Kioni remarked, a bit of irritation lacing his voice as he mimicked Aaldra's arrogance. "Watch your tongue! Give me your armor as I asked."

Both sentinels scrambled to their feet, undressing as fast as they could. The clang of armor echoed through the empty street as they undressed down to their underwear and Aaldra's form watched. As they finished, he sized them up, figuring which one would fit his physique the most and after selecting it, he began placing the armor on.

The two sentinels stood dumbfounded as their lord, in the shadow of night dressed in their sentinel armor before turning to face them. In his hand clutched the helm. The other set of armor lay scattered on the street.

"Bring it and follow me," he muttered, and he started off at a brisk walk, the sound of their scrambling behind him making him grin which he hid with a turn of his head. He led them around a building to a long alleyway loaded with trash and other things. Starting down it, he

The Legend of Kyne: Chronocide

waited for them to come close behind him before he stopped and turned around.

"Wrong way," he muttered. "Go back," and just as they turned around, he leapt forward drawing his kamas from where they lay hidden beneath his clothing and in two strikes, gouged both men across the sides of their neck, killing them fast as they fell to the ground.

Stooping over them, he studied the sentinel's face, imagined it as his own and felt his physique change. The man's eyes lit up in horror at the sight of his own face looking down at him before he faded from the world.

Kioni slid their bodies to the side, spreading what he could around to cover them before he made his way out into the street, their deaths not a second thought to him. He had killed, killed dozens of people while he was in the Shades alone and he had sadly lost the part of his humanity that showed remorse. It had to be done, there was no feasible way to get rid of them without killing them. If they were to report what had happened it could prove to be his downfall.

He left the alley heading back into the streets towards the citadel. A few minutes was all it took before he was facing the inner wall, a set of stone steps leading up to the entryway. On either side at the base stood two sentinel guards. They sat still and watched as he approached, not stopping him as he passed. The only thing he noted was a short nod of acknowledgment.

The courtyard was barren except for two sentinels patrolling, circling the perimeter in alternating paths. Masking his fear, he pushed on, walking swiftly past the statue of Alakyne and entering the citadel's main hall. His face was concealed under the guise of the Gaeilian sentinel, but it still worried him that he would be noticed.

He glanced at his hands.

So different, he thought, and he turned his hand over inspecting the unfamiliar skin, the scars upon the knuckles, as well as the littering of freckles across the top. Even though he knew that underneath the concealing magic it was still him it still felt strange that he could change so easily.

This could be the most dangerous weapon on the entire planet, he thought as he pressed on, climbing up the familiar path towards rooms he thought could contain anything noteworthy. *No wonder Raptor said that I should keep it hidden. People really would kill for it.*

A few hours passed, Kioni scurrying from room to room as he searched. He found a few different documents, the only one he seemed interested in mentioning the moving of part of the military towards the northeastern edge of the country. A large armada seemed to be forming on the ocean, but he didn't read into it further.

Nothing that I need to worry about at the moment. I have to try and figure out what happened, and he placed the papers back into the envelope before laying it softly where he found it. He was in some high-ranking official's office high up near the top of the citadel, a window nearby with large curtains drawn concealing his faint lantern light.

Stepping outside of the room, he nearly gasped in shock as someone moved further down the hall, noticing him leaving. It was a female, her face concealed by the darkness but as she shifted, he saw her more clearly.

It's her!

Her dark black hair was loose, hanging over her shoulders and her narrowed eyes looked tired. She was wearing plain silk robes with her feet bare upon the stone.

Kioni stared for a long moment, meeting the easterner's eyes before she turned away continuing down the hall her gait slow and sluggish, as if intoxicated.

He dashed out of the citadel as fast as he could, only slowing when he passed other sentinels to not draw suspicion. It took him nearly a quarter of an hour to make it back to the house, his breath heavy and sweat covering his body. The armor was uncomfortable, heavy and awkward as he shifted his stance in the metallic skirt.

If the house is searched and they find the armor, then our cover is blown. I should try and store it nearby out of sight, he thought as he stood near their door. Swinging his head around, he spotted an alleyway littered with trash and broken wood pieces. A few minutes later he had stripped down back to the clothes Roco had lent him, the armor tucked away out of sight.

"Even if it is discovered it's far enough away to not draw unwanted attention," he said quietly on his way back. Down the street a short ways he could see a patrol walking, their backs turned so he slid around the corner, jogging to the home. A short quiet push of the door allowed it to open, and he slipped inside.

The morning followed, no one suspecting a thing as Kioni awoke to their voices. He said little, sitting up and rubbing his eyes. His head ached from the brief few hours of sleep he received but he knew he would have to get over it.

They ate a short breakfast of old, dried grain mashed and mixed with hot water. The grit caught in his teeth and a flash of real concern at chipping his teeth entered his mind. There wasn't much to do in the home. They weren't allowed to leave at all unless escorted by a sentinel, but none were coming, at least for a while. Lioné had told him that if a new escort even came today, it wouldn't be until the late afternoon when they would be able to head to the market.

A few swift knocks shocked everyone when they were heard just before noon. Two hard taps followed by a gruff voice.

"Open Kydrëans."

"Rosé hide!" hissed Kioni and the small dragon swung her head frantically around looking for a place. Two more slams on the door were repeated and, in a panic, she dove under the bed, sliding out of view to where it met the wall.

The door suddenly burst open, four sentinels flooding in with shouting and fists. Roco and Lioné both were the first to confront and the first to be brought to the ground, their faces battered, and their eyes glazed over, knocked completely out cold.

Kioni leapt to the side, avoiding a swing before landing his own just under the sentinel's armor upon his side. He hunched over from the blow and Kioni dodged another attack. A third, however, connected hard with him in his gut and he gasped for breath dropping to his knees.

"Where's the dragon," the sentinel spat in his face as he grabbed him by the hair causing Kioni to cry out in pain. Before he could respond his fist collided with Kioni's jaw knocking him to the ground spitting blood.

His mind was swimming, dozens of sentinels clouding his vision as they moved and shimmered. First there were four and then sixteen as he saw repeated copies appear. Darkness began appearing upon the edges of his sight and he felt something grab tight against his face lifting him up.

"I said where is the dragon!" roared the sentinel.

"I don't know," he mumbled through the sentinel's hand.

In a rage, the sentinel hurled him to the side, sending him sprawling to the ground just as a weird sensation of something being lifted from his face was felt. Staring up in horror, he saw the sentinel looming overhead, a silvery cloth clutched in his hand. He stared at it for a moment with his piercing green eyes before a feminine voice caught his attention. Turning towards the kitchen, he tossed it to the ground where it landed right next to the bed.

"It took you long enough," squealed the mother in delight as she stepped around the corner, Seri clutched under one arm as the young girl struggled in a fit of rage.

"How could you!" she screamed. "How could you betray her!"

"You can't betray someone who you were never loyal to Seri! Go to your room!" and she hurled the girl out of sight. "Now back to our deal," she said with a grin as she faced the sentinels who had just caught their breath.

"The deal is you give us the dragon," chuckled the sentinel.

"No, the deal is you take the little devil, and my family is left alone," she said in a strained voice. "We had a deal!"

"Ehh, maybe, I will have to think about it," he replied, his thick Gaeilian accent making it hard to understand the words. "I think the deal will be more of I take the dragon and you will owe me."

She shuddered at his words, shifting in her stance as he pressed forward, pushing her back up against the wall. A single hand was lifted and placed firmly next to her head, his breathing right in her face.

"Where is it!"

"You can't!" cried out Kioni as he struggled to his knees. "She's just a child!"

A swift strike dropped him to the ground again and his mind grew heavy and dark. He could just make out the mother pointing toward the bed and the sentinels reaching underneath it. His chest was heavy with utter terror, and he struggled to move but his body wouldn't. His vision swam again, and he heard arguing between the

The Legend of Kyne: Chronocide

sentinel and the mother before she was struck and dragged from the home.

Kioni groaned and rolled over, his vision laying upon the open doorway to the home. The final sentinel was just exiting, a struggling young girl was being dragged out by her arm. However, it was not Seri. She had a blanket thrown over her, covering her exposed skin, her hair a soft shade of pink and her skin baring a hint of the same tone. She was screaming his name, but he could barely hear it, the sound muffled and far away.

Just before the door slammed shut, she turned and met his eyes and he knew, the eyes of Rosé.

* * *

57. An Illusion of Alliance

Akami groaned as she rolled over in bed, the sheets being pulled up over her face to cover her eyes from the sunlight streaming in through the window. Her head ached, like a persistent pressure upon the inside of her skull and she wanted nothing more than to just lay in bed.

She closed her eyes tight and clenched her jaw, the pressure irritating her intensely for a few more minutes and then it started to ease, never fully fading away, however.

She felt her stomach growling and she finally withdrew the sheets observing the room she was in.

It was basic, nothing noteworthy except for a small table in the corner and the wooden bed that she lay upon. Outside she could just make out a large stone wall, golden figures walking along its apex.

"Oh yeah I am in Alakyne," she muttered, and she climbed out of bed, massaging her temples in an attempt to make the headache fade. "I had nearly forgotten."

She got dressed in the clothing that was laid out for her, a short black skirt and skintight shirt. A glance in the mirror made her shudder at her figure and she spent the next hour fixing her hair as best as she could.

When she felt like it was enough to maintain her appearance with the others, she ventured out of her room just to run face to face with a red haired Gaeilian.

"Akami perfect I was just looking for you," she said in a quick burst before trying to catch her breath. "You almost missed the meeting, we need to hurry," and before she could object the woman grabbed a hold of her hand and took off guiding her down the hallway.

Who is she? Akami thought as she followed along, her mind

cloudy. The woman bore a familiarity, but she wasn't sure if it was just the hair that matched her sister or something else. She wasn't a Kitsune that was for sure, her features not eastern in the slightest. Her eyes were green of a Gaeilian with her paler skin making the contradictory colors striking against one another. She looked to be similar in age, but Akami still couldn't remember, the thought almost there but just out of reach.

"You're late," muttered a dark-haired man as they rounded a corner. His arms were crossed over his dark black robes and his eyes matched hers in every aspect. It was obvious that they were related.

"Right on time actually," she replied with a bit of attitude before grinning at Akami.

"Your tardiness reflects on me just as much as yourself Voira," he said darkly. "Remember that."

"I don't have to remember when you tell me every day Ariov."

He remained silent and merely turned around, opening the door and allowing the two women to pass on into a large room. Over a dozen windows lay covering most of the far wall allowing one to look out over the city beyond. Criss crossing streets split the buildings as they stretched away toward the large wall that protected them from the outside. Above the sky was not a blue but a muted greyish yellow from the ever-present haze that hung around the city and the nearby river.

An oval table sat in the room's center, the polished wood glaring the reflected sunlight in dazzling beams upon the walls. Most of the seats were filled with older nobles, all of their eyes green of Gaeil. One cloaked figure dressed in white and gold was also present, their facial features obscured by a silk mask that covered their mouth and nose. To her shock she also saw Hayame as well as Yu present, the two Kitsune giving her flat stares.

"Let's sit over here," Voira murmured guiding Akami towards an empty set of chairs, the others were soon all filled leaving one. Ariov followed in after them and after taking the final seat they all turned to look at him.

"As most of you are aware, He has left, accompanied with the dragons, his son, and the two remaining Dark Princes Saathe and Alderiun. They have left in search of something but that is all that I have been told. They will only be gone for a few days but in their absence, I was left in charge to carry out duties involving the city."

The Legend of Kyne: Chronocide

"Preposterous!" exclaimed a man as he leapt to his feet. His jet-black hair shifted off his face revealing a jagged scar cutting through one of his eyes. "There is no possible way He would not have left the city in your hands when I am clearly the next in line."

"Next in line? The last time you were in charge those Kydrëan rebels nearly took the city and killed you. You have no place to take Shjilo, you are lucky to even still be here. Sit down before you…"

"Before I what?" he snapped back. "The rest of you can't keep agreeing with these… With these children? He is not even thirty years old and yet he acts like we should all bow down to him and his damned twin! First you two are brought here from the homeland and now we are enlisting foreigners into our ranks?"

A few glances were thrown around at the Windra mercenary as well as the easterners. The man's eyes lingered on Akami for a moment longer, malice and disgust present before he looked away.

"Final warning Shjilo," Ariov said darkly, his eyes narrowing in irritation. "If you keep going then I will have no choice," and with a wave of his hand two Windra soldiers walked through the doorway, their glaives drawn.

The color drained from his face, and he said nothing more returning to his seat and seething but he remained silent. Akami threw a sideways glance at Voira, and she rolled her eyes mouthing, "He's such a big baby."

Akami stifled a laugh before Ariov started to speak again.

"As I was saying before, in the meantime we are to not halt any of our war preparations. They will be returning soon, and I would like to have made at least a little progress."

An older woman, hair down to her hips and faded grey spoke next.

"If He felt that this quest was really that important then surely he would've taken more than just that small party."

Repeat what you just said Breyanne and actually listen to the words," he hissed. "Those in that small party are among the most dangerous things on the entire continent if not the world. Nothing stands a chance against multiple master sorcerers and the two dragons."

Breyanne nodded her head in agreement with her ignorance.

"We are still trying to recover from that attack from those

malicious copycats one of whom wore the young lord's face. We still do not know where they went but we need to stay vigilant."

Copycats? Akami thought, her brow furrowing but no one else seemed puzzled by the words as if they already knew what he was talking about.

"Part of the citadel was damaged greatly but repairs have been making fast progress. The most concerning part of the whole situation is the nearly fatal blow that Diahl, the Pale One received. He is still alive, or whatever *alive* would be for him," he muttered. "Anyways more young ones have been gathered to help his healing process but in this weakened state I fear if someone were to find him with ill intent…"

"Then use some of the Windra that we have received," spoke an older man who sat next to Shjilo. "Their combat skills are renowned. It would be a wise choice to take a few of them from the front lines to protect such a valuable asset."

"And yet none of them know the forbidden art," Ariov replied. "In a fight against someone trained then even the best combatants would be crushed."

"No one is to do that! It is heresy!" he screamed in shock.

"And yet just a few days ago two of the most dangerous users appeared right in our city's heart nearly destroying everything we have worked for. Do not preach gospel to me with your ignorance clouding your judgment. Just because aura is forbidden with death doesn't mean it is a lost art. Thinking like that could be your downfall."

"What about the easterners?" spoke another man, this one younger but the scars on his face showing years of wear and tear.

"That has crossed my mind," Ariov said. "The empress back east was kind enough to send her most talented to help in our alliance. I think it would actually prove quite useful as we welcome them into our Dominion."

Ariov continued talking but Akami's hearing faded as her mind drifted away back to her mother. Something just seemed off, she could recall the meeting she had with her as well as the Kitsune, how urgent it was for them to get to Kydrëa to solidify the alliance but the further she looked into her memories the more vague they became. Her thoughts became jumbled, unable to focus on the subject for longer than ten seconds and she had to keep bringing her thoughts back.

The Legend of Kyne: Chronocide

She looked at her sister, but she didn't get any response, the Kitsune focused intently upon Ariov and his speech.

I just don't remember even getting here, she thought. She did remember though, she remembered riding in and being greeted by Voira almost immediately, the red-haired woman at her side constantly. She could picture the first feast they had and when she was shown to her quarters, but something was just off. She couldn't tell exactly what it was, only that she was forgetting something so utterly important. She even remembered the night as she roamed the citadel halls, the stone cool beneath her feet and the strange sentinel that was staring at her.

"Is that alright with you Akami?" said Voira next to her snapping her attention back to reality.

"Oh yeah, uh sure," she mumbled as she saw everyone at the table focused upon her.

"Great," said Ariov as he continued. "Akami and Yu will be the ones to guard Diahl until he is back to his usual self. Hayame will be at my side as previously discussed and we will pull one of the Windra groups to be stationed as well.

Akami was shocked and annoyed that she didn't realize what she had agreed to, and only when she was standing outside of Diahl's chambers did it truly sink in.

"It's fine," Voira reassured her with a hand placed on her shoulder. Akami nearly shuddered from the touch but remained still. "You will only have to do it for a few days. We have new children we have gathered that will help bring him back. Just don't stand too close to him or your own life could be affected as well. I will visit when I can," and then she was gone leaving Akami alone in the room with two Windra guards stationed on either side of the door.

Sighing, she stepped forward and pushed the door open, the hinges swinging in silently revealing a well-lit room. Sconces lined the walls, unlit for the moment with enough light streaming in from a few windows. It was a set of rooms, large in scale and littered with books and scraps of food. She saw a few figures dart out of view, their height signaling they were most likely children, but she couldn't say for certain.

In the back of the room was a large flat wooden bed, the cushion long since flattened from age and upon it caught her attention.

The Legend of Kyne: Chronocide

A shimmering figure lay still as stone. His hair was long and paper white hovering a few inches off of the bed as if caught in a permanent breeze, his clothes mimicking it. Akami could make out odd shapes upon him and after shifting her position realized in disbelief that she was seeing the far wall and other objects, visible through his translucent body. His eyes were closed, and his features thin and frail like an old man.

Akami walked around the bed, her hand bracing against the post as she studied him. She heard the door shut behind her but paid it no mind, she was far more interested in Diahl than anything at the moment.

"Who are you?" muttered a voice and she turned to see a young boy staring at her. His face was thin and his eyes heavy. Upon his head she could see the strands had changed to a faded grey matching his skin tone.

Akami ignored him, turning back to the phantom before her. The boy repeated his question.

"It doesn't matter who I am," she mumbled turning back to face him, startled to find another child next to him, a girl of similar age.

"Are you here to rescue us?" she asked.

"Not in the slightest," Akami said, turning away from Diahl and taking a few steps. "I have the fantastic task of watching you while he recovers."

"You mean while he drains our life," spoke a third voice, another boy, this one older than the others in his early teens. "I know that's what he is doing."

Akami shrugged, "I don't know, nor do I care. I would like to have this headache go away and all of your talking isn't helping."

The younger children ran around the corner into the other room and the eldest gave her a dirty look before vanishing after them. Akami swung her gaze, her vision landing on a cushioned chair near the window. As she sat and glanced over the tiny fraction of the city she could see, she noticed the crisscrossing bars of iron caging them inside.

They really don't want these kids getting out. I really don't care either way, and she leaned back stretching her arms up above her head. *The faster he recovers the faster I can move on and get out of here.*

"You're kind of a jerk."

The Legend of Kyne: Chronocide

Akami turned her head in shock to see a young girl, a few years from ten years staring at her with a deep fire in her eyes. Her skin was pale as well as her hair but in the light from the window Akami was startled to see they both had a faint pink sheen to them. Her eyes matched as well, brighter and more ferocious as she stared her down.

"What's your name," Akami said coolly.

"Rosé"

"Well Rosé, you better watch yourself child," Akami muttered. "I wouldn't test me if I were you."

"Just you wait."

"Wait for what?" she retorted in a sarcastic tone.

"Wait until I am rescued, and he defeats you."

Akami laughed out loud. "I highly doubt that you will be rescued, but just to humor me, who will I be beating? Your brother? Your father?"

"My friend! His name is Kioni!"

Upon hearing those words, the feeling of a knife stabbing through her head grabbed a hold of Akami and she scrunched her eyes tight and brought her head down. The name continued to ring in her ears for a few more moments before it finally started to fade away.

"Ki... Kioni?" she whispered, her headache returning but not as viciously. The name was so familiar, as if he had meant a great deal to her but try as she could, she couldn't remember anything more. Raising her gaze back up, she saw that the little girl had left, moving back away from her and sitting alone next to the wall, her eyes still trained upon her.

The day wore on, the children avoiding Akami most of the time only occasionally venturing close, but the older boy always brought them away. The young girl with the pink hair occasionally shouted insults at Akami which annoyed her at first but as the day progressed, she started to enjoy the random vulgar words, some even impressing her with their savagery.

As the sunlight began to wane, Akami heard the door handle begin to turn and she rose to her feet, only to lose balance from a sudden weakness and she crashed to the floor. Embarrassment ripped through her and she clambered to her feet, her legs buckling but managing to hold. Walking inside was Voira and for a moment Akami felt a flicker of delight, someone who seemed friendly to her. She didn't really know her, but she came off as good intentioned.

"This is why we don't stay around Diahl very long," Voira muttered as she dashed to Akami's side and threw her arm around her shoulder. Leading her towards the door, Voira continued, "He drains everyone in his vicinity. That's why we usually keep our distance from him, but times are different right now."

As they passed through the doorway and out into the hall with the Windra guards, Akami immediately felt a huge relief, as if a heavy weight had been lifted off her shoulders. She hadn't even realized at the time, but he was draining her just as he was the others.

Outside she could see Yu was waiting, her face flat of all emotion and her eyes trained on the door. Without a single glance at Akami or Voira she walked inside, closing the door and cutting her off from view.

Voira let go of Akami, her strength returning enough to walk and with a nod to the guard led her up a flight of stairs back into a main area of the citadel. They walked around for a few minutes until they came to a large dining area littered with nobles and others of importance. Kydrëan servants were running to and from tables, carrying drinks and steaming food precariously balanced in their arms.

Hayame was seated nearby alone and without looking at Voira, turned towards her.

"Might be best to avoid," she heard Voira mutter behind her, but she ignored her. She could tell her sister didn't look too happy but she was used to that. It was one of her features that actually reminded her of her mother.

"Lady Hayame," said Voira with a slight bow. The fire redheaded easterner looked up at her with her dark eyes for but a moment before grunting in annoyance.

"And you wonder why people don't like you," replied Akami as she sat down nearby.

"Because everyone likes you?" Hayame responded sarcastically.

"I am adored," Akami said before taking a small bite of the food that was placed in front of her.

"Adored by none and feared by many," Hayame remarked. "They only praise you for fear of their lives."

"I am aware," Akami said flatly, and she took another bite. "I would still consider that adoration."

"And I would consider that denial."

"How has my brother treated you?" asked Voira, switching the conversation.

"Fine," she replied with a mouthful of food.

"I suspect he has you following him at nearly all times?" Voira asked.

Hayame nodded.

"So, we are tasked with babysitting," murmured Akami. "Such renowned work."

"It is what mother wanted of us. That is why we were sent here in the first place don't forget that sister."

Akami was silent, the memory of her final words with her mother replaying in her mind.

Lowering her voice, she said, "Do you by chance know a Kioni?"

Upon the name leaving her mouth she felt her headache return and Hayame went stiff. Voira gasped as she nearly inhaled food from her mouth at the sound of the name but managed a swallow.

"One of the children was talking about him and I thought it sounded familiar."

"Ariov was speaking to me today concerning the plans for our eastern forces eventually joining in the fray. They have just defeated the Otoruhns to the south, burned their final stand to the ground and have plans on moving more eastward. It will be a perfect opportunity for our people."

Akami was startled with Hayame's strange response, almost rehearsed in tone and her face blank of any emotion. She threw a glance at Voira who had taken a bite and was acting interested in Hayame's talking only concerning Akami more.

"Hayame did you not here me?" she asked.

She turned her head slowly, almost sluggishly towards Akami. Her eyes were empty of thought but to Akami's shock she watched as she seemed to slowly return.

"What?" she asked. "I guess I didn't hear you. What did you say?"

The Legend of Kyne: Chronocide

"I said do you know the name Kioni?"

Just as before Hayame's body grew rigid and her eyes seemed to glaze over. She started spouting something about Ariov, but Akami couldn't focus much on the words, her own head seeming to want to explode in pain.

The name seemed to fade from her mind, but she constantly thought about it, keeping it just within reach as the night wore on. Hayame finished first, vanishing out the door leaving the two alone at the table. Akami said nothing to Voira about how strange her sister was acting, and she didn't press. Akami could tell something was up and it made her concern all that much more noticeable.

All I know is this Kioni person must be someone of great importance.

* * *

58. A Little Friend

The smell of petrichor hung in the air, the humid fragrance enticing as Lily leapt from a rock. Just as her foot pushed off, she felt the grip of her sole give and then she was falling fast. Trying to grab a hold of the stalks of the reeds nearby, she felt them pass through her fingertips and then she was soaking wet, on her back in a small creek.

The water was cold, chilling her skin as she rolled over to her knees. Pushing off, she felt the silt of the creek's base sift in between her fingers as she heaved herself up.

She was drenched, soaking wet and her back felt bruised as she fought the urge to cry.

She hated falling, hated it more than anything else that she could think of and images of mean old Luke came into her mind. The mean boy who lived a few houses over, two years her age at an impressive eleven years old and whose height brought her to his chin.

They used to be friends, best of friends in fact as she remembered he was the one who had shown her this very spot in the creek to catch the biggest slimiest of frogs.

"But ever since he got bigger than me," she said as she took a step, her foot sinking deep into the banks mud covering the top of her foot as it collapsed in on the sides of the indent. "He started hanging out with those other kids and now he's just a big jerk!"

Her voice echoed around the creek, the continuous buzzing of insects returning, and a breeze blew the reeds in a brushing tone.

She loved this place, the isolation from everyone else. Hidden away in a think cluster of vegetation a few minutes outside her city, she could recall sneaking away from her mom, telling her she was going to play with her friends when she had really ventured out into the marshy riverside.

The Legend of Kyne: Chronocide

She knew she wasn't allowed, even with all of the monsters showing up more frequently, but she had been here dozens of times and hadn't seen any monsters before.

"Even if something showed up," she sniffed, pushing herself up out of the water and into the tall grasses, her clothes dripping. "The sorcerers would take care of it. I know they would."

A splash sounded, drawing her attention back to the small stream and trailing her footprints through the mud she watched another splash as a small object leapt in.

Her sadness vanished, replaced by intrigue as she watched another frog leap from the mud into the water. A low drone sounded, and she dropped low, scanning around intensely for the source. She knew it all too well and then she spotted it. Standing on a rock, a small frog was perched up. It was small enough to sit in the palm of her hand and she watched as its neck swelled out like a big sphere, vibrating and the low drone joined the others in their song.

She loved the sound, loved what it meant, and she watched for a moment crouched in the grasses.

The sun overhead was near the horizon, not much longer than an hour before sunset and she knew she should be heading home soon but she wanted to see if she could catch a frog.

Creeping low, she pushed through the grasses, staying up on the bank as she skirted towards the frog. The rock it was upon was only a foot from the shore. She would have to be fast if she was going to catch it.

Her breath grew quiet as she focused on each step through the grass, each sound causing her to grimace, expecting the frog to vanish but it remained where it lay upon the rock. The low drone continued to sound from it, and she hoped it was muffling her movement.

She was there now, in line with the frog and she pushed through the grass, leaning out over the muddy edge with her hand awkwardly tucked next to her. She had to be fast, like a snake!

Darting her hand out, she nearly had it when it leapt just out of her reach landing in the water with a little plop.

She sighed in frustration and stood up taller, her opportunity missed. She would have to try another day when she could sneak away.

Just before she turned around to start going home, movement

The Legend of Kyne: Chronocide

under the water caught her attention and she stooped down to see the awkward pudgy round body of a tadpole hovering just under the surface. Tiny little legs had just started to push out of its round body.

She loved watching them swim around, their tails flicking back and forth and their small limbs forming against their bodies. Thinking for a moment, the young girl reached into her pack and withdrew her waterskin, still full from when she had left. Looking first at it and then towards the tadpoles, she started to pour out the water, a thought in her head.

Guilt came as she watched the clean water fall into the creek and after a moment, she stopped her pour, her guilt too much. Placing it to her lips, she drank as much as she could, the warm water not the best tasting but the hydration welcoming. The last few drops were consumed and then she looked back down in the creek, the little cove in the dirt causing the water to slow allowing the tadpoles to swim in safety.

She saw one, then another, and soon she noticed tons of them, all in different stages of life from the smallest little dots with tails to basically frogs with only a stump left. They were fast and more agile than they seemed, darting around as they caught small insects that dotted the surface of the water. She wanted a big one, always wanted the biggest and stooping down, she held the waterskin face down and placed it into the water keeping it full of air. It grew harder to push down, fighting to jerk back up to the surface but she kept it still as she waited for a tadpole to swim by.

She had learned this trick from Luke, using the suction of the container to pull in the tadpoles. It worked more often than not, and she held still waiting for a tadpole to swim by.

There!

Twisting the waterskin down and driving the opening toward the amphibian, she felt water lurch inside as the air escaped but to her disappointment the tadpole evaded the suction, swimming away out into the faster stream. She tried again, failing but closer. She had to be quicker if she was going to catch one.

Her third attempt was on a massive tadpole, more like a frog and with a smile, she watched as the creature was slurped up into her container. With a cry of glee, Lily pulled it out of the water and smiled, half expecting someone to congratulate her but then she remembered she was alone.

    Her waterskin was dark, too dark to see the tadpole inside but she could feel it as it thumped against the container, fighting to get out. She felt partially bad about taking it but knew that she would raise it to be a big frog and would return it in a few weeks.

    She took a step through the water heading towards the shore when a dark shape darted out from underneath the vegetation drawing her attention. It was fast and small, like a tadpole but with two sets of flippers on its body. Its tail was longer than a tadpoles as well, but its face looked just like the others.

    She paused, watching it as it swam around for a moment before turning and seemingly staring at her in the water. She furrowed her brow, puzzled by the strange creature and then she eyed her waterskin. She had caught dozens of tadpoles before, but none have been this species before. She opened it and reluctantly poured the contents out, the dull thump as the tadpole fell into the creek before it swam away, fleeing for its life.

    The other tadpole just hovered there, staring at her. Its body rippled as the water flowed over it, causing it to almost shift in a dark bluish grey haze. It was very beautiful, mesmerizing in fact and she brought her waterskin up to her lips pumping it full of air. After it had swelled up, she brought it down in the same trick as before and ever so slowly, she inched it closer to the creature who remained still, only occasionally paddling its tail to keep the current from pulling it away.

    Quick as lightning, Lily flipped up her waterskin and with satisfaction, watched the little thing get sucked into its dark depths. No cry of glee escaped her lips this time, her excitement was too much. Her insides felt like they were going to fall out and as fast as she could, she pulled herself out of the creek, soaking wet and took off running through the tall grasses heading home.

*   *   *

59. Tiernyn of Tsora

"Land here," Tira said pointing down as she and Auriel lay perched upon Ni'Bara's saddle. "Here he will stay until we are able to allow safe passage into the city."

"And you are certain that we will not be harmed?" Auriel asked. "I remember all too well when we first met."

"That is why we need to approach this cautiously. If you were to be spotted, then yes you indeed would be harmed. Dozens of sorcerers of Tsora would be upon you in moments and I guarantee at least one of their strikes would find its mark."

Auriel looked at the woman as she pushed her glasses back tight upon the bridge of her nose. Her jet-black hair was pulled up slick and tight against her head, the wind not moving a single strand. Auriel was not fond of the woman. She was arrogant and entitled, expecting everything to be done for her before she even asked. The few days that she had known her were interesting as she had seemingly been checking in upon them nearly once a week.

The children had aged which surprised Auriel. Aria had grown more slender, in the midst of her pubescent years and quickly becoming a beautiful young woman. Her golden hair was still short, but it fit her new personality. Her attitude had changed, growing far more confident in her actions and how she spoke.

Tira had found a liking toward the girl, Auriel had noticed it, her always seeming to give her more attention than Alakyne. Towards the boy she was much more stern, more stressed and frustrated in his teaching.

Alakyne had grown a few inches over the time, still young with his baby face having no sign of adulthood in the near future. The only other thing that changed were his eyes, dull and tired.

He was still not exceptional at aural manipulation but over the year of his training he had become adequate. Auriel watched when she could, giving advice much to Jurnen's disapproval and Alakyne always seemed grateful. She knew that with the right teacher and approach, anyone could become a strong sorcerer.

As they landed, Tira took her Ouroboros Bag with the others still inside and Auriel accompanied her as they started on their trek toward the city. Ni'Bara remained behind, in the event he was needed and tucked himself low in the grassy hills hidden from view. Beyond the cluster of hills the area was relatively flat, with green vegetation that came to just below their waist. Each step had to be pulled up high to prevent the stalks from grabbing a hold of them and it quickly became an exhausting ordeal.

Nearly a mile of traveling like that took them to a flattened stretch of earth, beaten by frequent hooves and the wheels of carts. The road then took them in a winding path, crisscrossing a small creek a few times before rounding a hill revealing a city beyond. The creek met up with a thick dark blue river that led through the city, houses and other structures lining its sides growing thicker and closer together the further on. The road led right next to the river and as they entered the city, they watched as a small girl ran past them.

Her clothes were soaking wet, and, in her hand, she clutched a small waterskin as if it contained something precious inside. Just as she passed, she turned her head meeting Auriel's gaze for but a moment before she vanished, rounding a corner and heading deeper into the city.

"This way," Tira said following a branch of the road that led away from the river. Through the gaps in buildings, Auriel tried to make out everything that she could see, impressed with the size of the city. No wall lay upon its outside, instead dozens of towers, each adorned with a single figure upon their tops. They were hard to make out, but their hoods looked familiar enough to tell her they were sorcerers.

As they wove through the city, over a thousand years before her own time, she soon witnessed that at its center lay two large rectangular buildings. Each was three floors high with a long walkway stretching out between them over a courtyard. The area was decorated with dozens of people, walking along the different pathways or entering the buildings. The entire complex dwarfed the buildings nearby but was still nothing to the citadels she had seen in other cities.

The building's roof was slanted up to a shallow point, flat on both sides and decorated with various chimneys and other structures. It was made of wood with the walls being a mixture of both wood and stone. Brick steps led up to its entrance and as Tira led Auriel toward them she saw some figures come out to greet her.

It was two sorcerers, their faces obscured by their hoods concealing everything but their mouths. Both were female and when they spoke, she could almost taste the hostility in the air.

"Why have you returned Tira? Tiernyn will not be happy to see that you are back so suddenly."

"It is Tiernyn that I wish to see," she replied flatly.

"And who is the foreigner that accompanies you?" the other asked.

"Not of your concern. Go back to your meaningless task and do not stop me again if you know what is best for you."

Her dark words made the two opposing her grow rigid and Auriel saw both of their mouths tightened in fury. She was impressed at Tira and also appalled at her at the same time. Her confidence, no, her cockiness was unsettling.

Reluctantly, the two parted, allowing them passage and as she passed, Auriel saw them fumble in their cloaks, a flicker of a stave hidden within their robes. Tira led her down a few corridors, past rooms both empty and populated until they passed through a large room that looked to be a place of importance. Rows of benches lay all facing a long flat piece of stone with a single wooden chair at its apex. It lay empty and the braziers that lined the room lay cold and still, their light not needed as late afternoon sunlight filtered in through the windows high above.

Through the room they went to another side room connected near the apparent throne. The door was shut, but without hesitating, Tira opened it and stepped inside drawing the attention of someone seated at a desk within.

He wore no hood upon his head but light-colored robes upon his body. His skin was dark, tanned from his heritage and with his white hair, Auriel recognized him to be Otoruhn. He was handsome,

The Legend of Kyne: Chronocide

beautiful in fact with a short, trimmed beard whose color matched his hair. Decorated with beads, the hair upon his head was fairly long, braided into strands reminiscent of rope that lay draped over its side.

His face was immediately filled with displeasure upon the sight of Tira entering his room and with a drawn-out sigh, he rested his quill down upon the table before clasping his hands together and resting his chin upon them.

"Why Tira?"

His voice was rich and elegant, with a deep tone that resonated within the room. He didn't move, just kept his dark eyes drilled upon her, unaware or uncaring of Auriel's presence.

"Hello Tiernyn, it has been a while," she replied with a tone of sass.

"Not long enough it seems. Why have you returned? I told you when you left that Karstead is no longer your home. You and the fool Jurnen were to head elsewhere, finding work and spreading our teaching."

Tira pushed her glasses back up on her nose, a flash of irritation at his words. "You treat me like I was banished but that is not the case Tiernyn. Soriah is the lord of this city, and he finds me to be pleasant company."

The Otoruhn man shook his head, a flash of anger appearing for but a moment before vanishing back to his flatness. "Why are you here?"

"I found him, found the one we have been searching for."

"Who?" he said puzzled. "What do you mean?"

"The one spoken of in the texts left by Tsora himself. The one whose power will have no bounds. I found him."

Tiernyn's eyes widened in disbelief and then in mockery and he rose to his feet. "You are a fool Tira just like your companion Jurnen. That is but a story told to those in an effort to keep our order moving forward. The fact you think it to be true is..." he paused for a long moment, and he turned his back to them and looked out a window. "Well, it's embarrassing. Tira, of all people you were one of the last I would expect to think anything of this story to be true."

"This boy killed an eldunaga right in front of me," Tira exclaimed. "The power he possessed in that instant was unlike anything

I have ever felt before. Please see reason Tiernyn."

"And this is what brought you back here, accompanied by this..." and as he turned around his eyes met Auriel's and his demeanor shifted completely to that of intrigue. "Accompanied by this woman?"

"She was with the boy when he was found. She was with a dragon Tiernyn! An actual dragon! Can you not see? It all points to this child whom I believe can help save us all."

Her words trailed off as Tiernyn seemed uninterested in them. Instead, he was staring intently at Auriel, his dark eyes holding her own. She felt uncomfortable under his gaze, everything in her being wanting to avoid eye contact but she couldn't. She couldn't give into his intimidation. After what seemed like an eternity, he finally caved, swinging his vision back towards Tira and he sat back down in his chair.

"What is his name?"

"Alakyne," Tira responded.

"And this so called Alakyne is gifted in aura?"

"I have trained him for quite a while. His talents are mediocre but within him lies a dormant power unlike anything I have seen. It's like his aura is held back by some immense dam just waiting to be broken."

"I will meet with him as you insist," he said cooley, his eyes turning towards Auriel. "I would like you to be present as well Miss?"

"Auriel," she replied.

"Beautiful name," he muttered, and he looked down at his table for but a moment. "Auriel, I would like you to bring your dragon, I will alert the guardians, so they do not attack."

Tira nodded her head in a half bow and turned upon her heel heading for the doorway with Auriel at her side. Just as she pushed it open, a slight whine sounding upon the hinges, she stopped and turned back.

"He has a sister as well Tiernyn. A very gifted sister that I have trained as well. She will join us," and then they were gone, turning away from the doorway and heading out of the great hall.

Tira didn't speak until they had left the city, the final guardian tower far behind them.

"Such an arrogant prick!" she cursed. "Damn him and his

cunning. This is all just a waste of time."

"Why do you say that?" Auriel asked more out of sympathy than looking for answers.

"Well to start," she said, stopping mid-stride and turning to face Auriel. "The only reason we are even getting this introduction is because he is attracted to you!" she spat. "The sly beautiful man working his way with the ladies not giving a damn about anything that's important!"

"You gave a good argument," Auriel started but the flash of anger upon Tira's face made her stop.

"My argument was going to fail the moment he laid eyes upon me. I could've told him anything and he wouldn't have believed me. He has never liked me and now the consequences of my lack of caring about that are finally coming to bite me. I do not care what you do with Tiernyn after Auriel, I won't judge but for now, please try to avoid his advances for the time being."

"I am married Tira," Auriel said darkly. "Do not think I would betray my husband."

"I am aware Auriel," she replied, and she started walking once more. "All I will say is others that have met him have had partners as well."

They traveled in silence the rest of the way, Tira's words causing Auriel's mind to flare like a hot fire. *Betray Kyne! I would never in a thousand lifetimes. Tiernyn may be attractive but the thought of him...* her thoughts made her shudder and she focused on her steps as they left the road pushing through the grass, still flattened from their previous travels.

Ni'Bara was waiting for them as they rounded the hillside revealing his hulking mass. The sun was nearing the horizon, but they still had a few hours before dusk. Auriel explained what had happened while Tira entered her pack, presumably updating the others. A few moments later she returned, joined by the children and all of them climbed aboard Ni'Bara.

Traveling much quicker than on foot, he soared past the guardian towers, the sorcerers staring at him, but luckily no aural attacks were fired. He brought them over the city whose size Auriel truly didn't get to experience on the ground. It easily held twenty thousand people if not more and they could see the dark shapes of people darting out of their shelters to watch them soar above.

Ni'Bara brought them to the keep of the city, the large building that housed Tiernyn as well as other nobles and presumably the lord of the land whom they still haven't seen. Upon its rear lay a flat open courtyard decorated with ornate plant life and trees. There was enough space in which the dragon could land without damaging anything.

They dismounted, and after a moment in the back, Tira returned with Jurnen and their two tongueless attendants. Unsure of where they were to meet, they waited for a few minutes before a few figures approached from the keep. Tiernyn was in the lead, his strides graceful and uncaring as he approached. Upon his face was first annoyance but when he saw the dragon and Auriel it changed once again to intrigue.

"So, you were not lying about the dragon," he called, his voice booming around the area.

"Or about anything else," Tira muttered as they approached.

"So, Miss Auriel, you truly do have a steed unlike anything I have ever seen," he said, stepping toward her and reaching for her hand. Pulling it up to his mouth, he kissed it lightly to her shock before turning his gaze upward. Ni'Bara had lowered his head down, his spines fanning out in a hood, and he bared his fangs slightly.

"I am no steed!" he snarled lowly.

Tiernyn dropped Auriel's hand, eyes wide with shock. "It speaks!"

"Yes, he does," Auriel said, stepping away from the Otoruhn. She hadn't realized it earlier, but the man was very tall, towering over her with his robe obscuring everything but his hands. His shoulders were broader than an average man and Auriel felt uneasy as he looked back down towards her.

"Where is the child then?" he said.

"Alakyne," barked Tira and the young boy stepped out from behind Jurnen, his head held low and his eyes upon the floor.

Tiernyn's mouth pursed for a moment before he looked back at Tira with a look that seemed to scream, "Seriously this boy?"

Looking back at him, Tiernyn studied him for a moment, the

tingle of aura felt in the air. His look of annoyance suddenly changed to confusion, and he sat puzzled for a long time as he seemed to probe the boy with his aura. After a long moment, he spoke.

"Alakyne is it? Come here boy."

Alakyne shuffled forward before a rough shove from Jurnen sent him stumbling towards Tiernyn. The young boy met Tiernyn's eyes as he approached and when he was within a few feet he stopped.

Tiernyn suddenly grabbed at his own wrist, as if something was biting him and he fumbled with it, his cloak obscuring whatever was bothering him. After a moment he stopped, and he looked down upon him for a moment.

"It seems you have a gift then?"

"I would call it a curse," Alakyne replied solemnly, and he looked back at the ground. "It seems to get everyone killed."

Tiernyn was silent as his brow furrowed for a moment. Reaching out a hand, he nearly touched the boy before stopping and bringing it back to his other rubbing his wrist once again.

"He bears an immense power Tiernyn," Tira said. "I know you can feel it within him as have I."

He nodded and then he took a step back as if adjusting his stance to be more comfortable. "It is interesting," he replied and then he looked first towards Tira and then towards Alakyne."

"He is the one, I know it Tiernyn. He will be the one to rid us of these cursed monsters and become Tsora's true successor."

Her words seemed to make Tiernyn go rigid for a long moment, stiff as stone as he looked down upon the boy. A flash of disgust appeared for but a moment, hardly noticeable, and then he turned away obscuring his face.

"We will continue this at dinner. You will all be my guests, except the dragon as he cannot fit," and then he was gone, vanishing into the keep with the others who had followed him leaving them all alone.

"What a strange man," muttered Ni'Bara as he broke the silence. Within moments, Aria was the next to speak.

"He's gorgeous!"

Tira scowled and Jurnen furrowed his brow in annoyance.

"He makes me feel weird," whispered Alakyne. "All tingly and

515

The Legend of Kyne: Chronocide

odd. I don't like it."

"He's a bastard," Jurnen said. "Makes us all uncomfortable."

"You're just jealous because of his looks. He looks like a god, and you look like a slave," shouted Aria, seemingly upset by his rude comment about Tiernyn.

Her reaction startled Auriel but she knew how dangerous this man truly was. Powerful and beautiful, he was like a dark angel, able to persuade anyone to obtain what he wanted. She couldn't forget the look he had given towards Alakyne after Tira's remarks, and she walked towards the boy and put a hand on his shoulder. Out of instinct, he turned towards her and wrapped his arms around her waist in a long hug.

"Let's see what he has to say Alakyne," Auriel whispered. "Maybe this could be the home you and Aria have been searching for."

Movement drew their attention, and they looked up to see four servants rushing towards them, each pushing a wheelbarrow loaded with chunks of raw meat.

Once they had arrived, they dumped them quickly, never taking their eyes off of Ni'Bara before nearly running back around the keep to some obscured door. Another person arrived shortly after, dressed in more elegant clothing, a noble of this city. He told them to follow him for the feast that was being prepared and that the dragon would be fed graciously.

Auriel left Ni'Bara, nervous for his safety and him for hers. They didn't want to be separated but for this instant it was inevitable.

60. Feast and Suspicions

They were brought into the keep, Tira at the lead with the others on her heels. The braziers had been lit, alighting the stone and wood with their orange glow. They were led into a large room, a large square table with nearly a dozen seats around its perimeter. No others had arrived and after each picking their seats, Auriel found herself in between Aria to her right and Alakyne to her left. The others of their group sat on the other side of Aria leaving Alakyne upon the very edge.

After a few minutes, a few nobles entered the room followed by Tiernyn. They each took their seat with a thick older man dressed in sorcerer robes sat next to Alakyne. Upon the sight of the boy, he turned his nose up as if disgusted by him and he shuffled his seat over a few inches in an effort to make it noticeable of his disgust.

Auriel felt anger form, but she pushed it down, watching as Tiernyn welcomed them to Faldîn Keep.

"Sadly, our lord will not be joining us this evening so it will just be us."

Servants suddenly appeared, ladened with trays decorated with meats and fruits. Ornate cheeses flanked the sides of an entire roasted pig as it was placed in the center of the table and then a final servant brought a tray around placing a glass of dark red wine in front of each of them.

"None for the children," Auriel said waiving the servant away as one was placed in front of Aria. The young girl looked offended and started to protest when Tiernyn interrupted.

"It is customary for everyone to partake," he said, his voice sprinkled with a hint of anger. "They must drink, or it would be disrespectful."

Aria flashed a grin reaching toward the servant and grabbing the glass. The servant placed one in front of Auriel and with a twist, grabbed a glass placed upon the back of her tray and sat it in front of Alakyne.

Auriel looked first at it and then saw Tiernyn's eyes hover upon it momentarily before he met her gaze and flashed a smile. She felt an odd sensation in her gut. A sense of danger and her nausea increased as Tiernyn held his own glass up, delicately with the neck of it clutched between his fingers. Twirling it around, he brought his nose to the rim and inhaled deeply.

Setting it back down upon the table, he stood up, beckoning toward them all.

"I thank you again for joining me on this beautiful evening. We are to celebrate the discovery of Tsora's supposed heir," and he flashed a brief look toward Alakyne who was quiet and retreated in his seat.

As the sorcerer continued his toast, Auriel felt more and more like they were in danger, her eyes lingering on the dark liquid in Alakyne's glass. She watched as Tiernyn finished his toast and they all started to reach for their glasses. Alakyne nearly touched it when she couldn't wait any longer.

A quick spell was said under her breath and across the table, a tray slid off, clattering to the floor and sending food flying around. As everyone's attention was drawn, she focused hard, channeling her aura into the highly advanced spell.

"Aven igni."

Alakyne's wine glass and the man's next to him seemed to flicker for but a moment and then they were still. Auriel felt a massive drain of energy leave her and her vision started to darken for a moment, pressing in upon the edges. She tried to steady her breath, to keep the stress unnoticed focusing on each inhale and exhaling slowly and calmly. She had succeeded, just barely as she looked around, her spell going unnoticed. She had switched the two glasses!

"Anyways," Tiernyn said, raising his glass up. "A toast," and they all lifted their glass up. Bringing it to her lips, she tasted the bitter fruity flavor of the wine with just a sip before she placed it down, her eyes resting upon the man as he drank Alakyne's wine. Next to her, she heard Aria gag and cough, and she smiled a bit. Alakyne sipped his

The Legend of Kyne: Chronocide

without making a face and rested it down softly upon the table.

Time seemed to slow for a long moment as Auriel watched the man next to Alakyne down his glass in a few gulps, the red liquid staining the edges of his mouth. A deep sigh escaped his lips, and he placed the glass down, his mouth in a smirk as he eyed the other guests at the table. She watched for a long moment, half expecting him to start convulsing, foaming at the mouth by some unknown poison but the longer she waited the less it seemed to be so. They ate, stuffing themselves with good warm food well into the evening before Tiernyn ended the meal.

"Tomorrow Garet will assess you Alakyne," he said eyeing the thick man next to Alakyne. The man, food and crumbs covering his mouth and clothes looked at the boy with a dazed expression, the multiple glasses of wine apparently taking their toll. He grunted and then they were all dismissed. Tiernyn had a servant guide them to their arranged quarters. Auriel would sleep with the children.

Auriel made sure the two were fully asleep before she snuck out to Ni'Bara. The cool evening air and the sounds of chirping insects were around them, a pleasant blanket attempting to mask the treachery she was feeling.

"Tiernyn seems very dangerous," the dragon muttered picking something from between his teeth. "Even if he wasn't trying to poison Alakyne he seems to have some other intent planned for the boy. Be careful Auriel and watch him closely."

Auriel was soon back, lying upon a soft pillow with nothing but the starlight from the window illuminating the room. Just as she was nearly asleep, she heard a few quick and quiet strikes hit her door and her eyes jerked open. Her heart raced for a moment and as she stood, she tiptoed across the floor in an attempt to not wake the children. Pausing by the door, she looked back and could just make out their dark shapes still laying upon their beds, their breathing slow and rhythmic.

Opening the door, she was surprised to see Tira outside holding a lantern. She gestured for Auriel to step outside and she did, closing it quietly behind her.

"What do you need?" Auriel said with a yawn.

"Garet is going to either fail Alakyne or cause him great pain,"

The Legend of Kyne: Chronocide

Tira started. "He is the harshest sorcerer teacher that I know of. If Tiernyn wants to see Alakyne's power, then he will be the one to bring it out whether by hurting him outright or hurting Aria."

At those words the fatigue vanished from Auriel.

"What are you saying Tira?"

"I am saying to be wary of him. Watch Alakyne as close as possible these next few days. You might be able to stop unnecessary roughness. I will try as well but I can't promise anything. Tiernyn will certainly try to separate us."

As Tira left, her orange light vanishing down the dark corridor, Auriel was left with her mind racing. She couldn't let anything bad happen to these kids. They had become part of her life in the short amount of time that she had known them, and she had grown very fond of them.

Laying down upon the bed, she fell into a restless sleep, waking up multiple times throughout the night with thoughts of the horrors the morning would contain.

61. Trials and Temptations

Auriel rolled over in bed, stretching her hand up and she felt the touch of another body. Smiling, she drew in closer, wrapping her arms around Kyne's shoulders as she rested her head upon his bare chest. His breathing was calm and slow, and she just sat there, holding him.

His hands slid up her back, lightly touching her delicate skin with his fingertips as he made his way up to her hair where he interlaced them with her silvery locks. Calmly, he ran his hand through her hair, the tingling sensitive touch euphoric to her and she closed her eyes. She had been having the worst dream of her life, but everything was better now, and she pulled him in closer.

"Auriel?" he whispered in her ear, drawing her attention. She mumbled, acknowledging his words but he repeated it again. "Auriel?"

"Yes Kyne" she sighed, and she opened her eyes to see sunlight streaming in through the window and Aria looking at her with concern.

"Are you alright?" the young girl asked.

"I..." Auriel started, saddened by her dream and she sat up pushing her hair off of her face. "I am. What is it?"

"Alakyne is gone," she said.

"Gone!" she gasped, and Auriel leapt out of bed, nearly knocking Aria on her back and in a moment, her blade was upon her waist and her hair tied up with her aura. "Did you see anything?"

"Tira came and got him. I woke up just as they left. We might be able to catch them."

Auriel nodded and, in a flash, dashed towards the door, swinging it open and flying out into the hall. She looked in both directions, not seeing any figures but with a pointed finger from Aria signaling the direction they had gone, the two of them took off. Their feet were a constant thumping as they propelled themselves down the stone hall, Aria managing to keep up quite well with Auriel. They rounded a corner and up head they could see the doorway that led out to the courtyard beyond where Ni'Bara lay, the door slightly ajar.

  Coming to it, she pushed it open, terrified of what she was to see but she was shocked. Kneeling nearby, hidden from the dragon's gaze from a bush was Tira and Alakyne. The pale woman was kneeling upon her knees, nearly as tall as the boy and was holding his shoulders, telling him something of great importance. Auriel stopped Aria from calling out at his sight and they sat there quietly watching for a long moment.

  Tira eventually brought him in with an awkward embrace and when they separated, she turned to see Auriel and Aria observing. She nodded, briefly before standing up and straightening her clothes.

  They made their way down the short steps, Auriel nodding at Ni'Bara who had just noticed them before she reached the two. Aria grabbed Alakyne's hand and pulled him close to her, her mouth inching close to his ear as she spoke quickly and quietly. Auriel couldn't make out much but understood Aria's concern with Alakyne leaving and how he was to never do that again.

  Before Auriel could speak, Tira said, "Good morning. Today is going to be an intriguing day and I hope that he will be able to prove to the others what he has," and she looked towards Alakyne.

  "And if he can't?" Auriel asked, recalling Tira's words about the man who was going to test the boy and his savagery.

  "He will, I am certain of it. Confidence is what we need Auriel. Tiernyn is still in his chambers, but I expect that he will be wanting to observe the day's proceedings. Here," and she opened a small parcel of food and placed it upon a stand nearby. "Eat, all of you. You will need your strength and then she was off, walking quickly across the courtyard and back into the keep.

  Auriel looked at the food for a moment and felt her stomach growl at the sight. Spotting a stone bench placed against the back of the tall bush, she guided the children to sit. The stone was cool, cast in the early morning shade with dew still stuck to it. Taking a seat herself, they partook of the food, filling them up with fruits and vegetables that were

The Legend of Kyne: Chronocide

quite pleasant. As they finished, the children eating the last of the berries, Auriel stood up and made her way towards Ni'Bara who was still as stone, acting as if he were asleep.

The warm sun seemed to cause her light-colored clothes to glow, and its warmth was welcome as she traveled across the stone courtyard, skirting around ornate bushes and other forms of vegetation. Patches of trimmed grass lay between sections of stone and without touching it, she traveled around its perimeter until she was next to the dragon.

"How did you sleep," he mumbled, his eyes still closed and with each breath, Auriel could see the ripples of light rise from his nostrils from the heat.

"Fine," she said not wanting to recall her disappointing dream that was already fading from memory. "You?"

"It was adequate. Many people came to observe me through the night, but none seemed confident enough to approach me."

Auriel nodded and she glanced back towards the children, their figures obscured by the tall bush. "Tira warned me that this test today would be intense, painful even for him."

"I expected nothing less from these people Auriel. Do not be mistaken by their charm and intelligence. We mean little to them, do not forget that."

"I won't," she said. "I just want to help these kids the best I can."

"As do I. We need to make sure they are on the right trajectory, but we still are foreigners to this time. We mustn't forget that."

"It will never be forgotten Ni'Bara. Kyne and Rosé are out there somewhere. Our best choice of action right now I believe would be to observe Alakyne and see if Tiernyn or the others know of a way to hop through time."

The dragon snorted and his eye flickered open, his dark pupil contracting quickly in the sun to that of an elegant slit, who's top and bottom were barbed like that of an arrowhead. Cyan flames flickered within his iris, and he just stared at her for a long moment, her returning his gaze.

Calls drew her attention and she turned to see the kids coming towards them, the cloth from the food still clutched in Aria's hand.

Holding out her own, Auriel took them both and tucked them into a pocket, planning on disposing of it in due time. She was impressed with the kids, who had apparently cleaned up their mess after they were finished. She hadn't expected it and she smiled weakly at them.

They sat next to Ni'Bara upon the ground, cast in shade for a moment but as the minutes ticked by, the shade began to retreat closer and closer until they were exposed in the warm sun. Another long time passed before movement caught their attention and they say Tira approaching with her attendant trailing swiftly behind her.

"Where is Garet," asked Alakyne and he stood up. "How much longer do we have to wait?"

"Garet won't be joining us I am afraid," Tira said, and Auriel looked at her puzzled.

"Why is that?" she asked.

"It seems that he has fallen ill as of late last night. For today we are to continue our training as we have done in my bag," and she continued speaking to the kids with Auriel's thoughts drowning out her words.

Fallen ill? Garet has fallen ill? Could this mean... Could Tiernyn really have tried to poison Alakyne? It is seeming more and more likely that something foul is at work here.

Tira had directed the kids away from the dragon and as Auriel sat back down, she watched as the human sorceress ran them through some warmup drills, flexing and stretching their aura, each spell growing to a higher level.

They continued on for a few more minutes, caught in their work when movement near the keep drew Auriel's attention and she turned to see Tiernyn standing upon the steps, his brow furrowed as he stared at the two children. Auriel could've sworn she saw anger for but a moment but as soon as it had appeared, it was gone.

The Otoruhn turned his gaze towards her and when their eyes met, he flashed a brilliant white smile and reached up, pushing his rope-like hair across his head keeping each in pristine perfection. His robes still covered most of him, the only skin visible was that of his hands, his neck, and his head but as he strode towards her, it fanned out like a beautiful tail behind him.

"Auriel," he said, smiling again as he approached, looking at her for a long moment before flashing a glance at the children.

"Tiernyn," she said nodding her head and keeping her voice monotone.

"Such a beautiful morning to match someone as gorgeous as yourself I do say so. It brings me great pleasure to see you out and about, owning this keep as if it were your own."

His words made her skin crawl, and she fought the urge to flash him a disgusted face. She nodded her head in the only reply he deserved.

"Anyway," he continued. "I would love to give you a tour through my city if you would join me," and sweeping his hand from his robe, he reached out and delicately grabbed a hold of her own. His skin was warm, his hands large, dwarfing hers and she stared down at them touching for a long moment, unsure of what to do.

Withdrawing from his touch, she looked back up to him and flatly said, "I will stay with the children Tiernyn. They are my main concern."

"Oh, is that so?" he said, taken aback by her words. His look seemed almost hurt for a moment at her rejection. "The children are your main concern? I would think someone in your situation would put themselves in front. I have been told that you wanted information on skipping the pools of time?"

His voice darkened as his sentence ended, his eyes looking down upon her and Auriel took a step back.

"Who told you that," she murmured eyeing Tira who had not heard him and was continuing on with her training.

"Does it matter?" he said, a grin appearing upon his lips. "I might be persuaded to share some of my knowledge if you would repay me with your company."

Ni'Bara rumbled lowly, drawing their attention towards him and his gaze was locked upon Tiernyn's for a long moment.

"She is already taken Tsoran," he said lowly. "It would be in your best interest to leave her alone."

Tiernyn's gaze changed from shock to that of a smirk at the dragon's threat. Without saying another word, he spun around and started walking back towards the keep.

With a wave of his hand, he called back, "Taken or not Auriel, he is not here and I am. I will be available whenever you wish."

As he vanished within, Auriel released her anger in a fit of rage, clenching her jaw and shaking her hands. Turning towards Ni'Bara, she thumped the side of his hide in a strike of anger, the steel-like scales cutting the skin from her knuckles. She hadn't noticed and she struck him again, drawing blood.

"He's disgusting!" she snapped, turning around to see the kids staring at her in shock as blood dripped to the ground. Seeing their distress at her anger, she smiled weakly and waved them back to their training.

A quick but draining spell was said and she watched as the skin upon her knuckles grew back together tightly and the blood stopped. She itched it, the new skin sensitive and tender and then she sat down next to Ni'Bara leaning against him. The dragon angled his arm up, flaring the membrane between his long fingers so that it cast her in a nice shade, and they sat there for a long time, watching the children.

Tira tried her best to cause Alakyne to unleash his power. She was stern, almost outright mean to him and even struck him occasionally in what Auriel thought to be a sad attempt. Each strike caused Auriel to grow more and more angered, but she sat and observed, not stepping in unless it was absolutely necessary.

As the sun hit high noon, Tira sighed and ended their training, the two children sweating and panting as they lay upon their backs. They were drained but nothing had even seemed to hint at the boy's power.

Tira left them in a hurry, vanishing into the keep and as she left, Auriel approached the exhausted kids with a weak smile.

"You both did so great. Don't be discouraged."

"No matter what I do I can't seem to bring it out," Alakyne whined, and he sat up. "I have tried for months now, and nothing seems to work."

"I think it is a defense mechanism," Aria muttered, and she sat up too. "I didn't want to say anything, but it seems that it happens whenever you are in danger."

The Legend of Kyne: Chronocide

"But you said it happens when I dream though? I never remember my dreams, Aria."

"It used to," she said. "It hasn't happened since we met them, and she looked back at the keep for a moment. "I don't know if it's because of the training you have had or what, but I haven't noticed an event in a long time Alakyne."

"I was thinking the same thing," started Auriel. "Concerning the defensive part. It only happened when we were being attacked."

"I haven't said anything for fear of what they might do," Aria said, and she dropped her head down. "They might try to hurt him."

"Tira already knows that Aria," Auriel said. "She is not dumb. I guarantee she suspected it immediately and that is why she pushes you two so hard. Just keep doing what you are doing. We will keep working at it," and she reached her hands out, clasping them with the children's and pulling them up to their feet. "You two stink," she chuckled lightly. "We should go get you cleaned up."

Venturing into the keep, Auriel asked a few servants where the bath chambers were and were soon directed to a large circular room. A few large bowl shapes had been carved into the ground and near the walls were large wooden barrels full of water.

Each one of them found their own tub and releasing the water, Auriel gasped as its cold touched her skin. It filled the tub up, swiftly, obscuring her form and the other two followed suit. Gasps came from them at the water's touch and Auriel chuckled lightly.

"Varme," she said and using her aura, she warmed first her tub and then the others until it was almost too hot to bare. The children seemed grateful at that and all three of them sat in the hot stew, soaking in its warmth and enjoying a relaxing time.

As they finished, they climbed out, Auriel showing them how to clean their clothes with aura and they were all soon dressed, walking through the keep with their hair still damp. Auriel felt much better after her bath, and she could tell the kids did as well.

They returned outside with Ni'Bara and spent the rest of the afternoon in the courtyard. Tiernyn didn't return and Tira only showed her face when it was time to eat. No feast was set for them and without the children noticing, she used her aura to sense for any poisons of which she found none. They ate and then returned to their chamber, unsure of what the next day would bring.

Auriel changed into some more comfortable clothes, and she sat upon her bed, the strange pentagon object in her hands as she turned it over. She still wasn't quite sure what it was but fiddling with it helped ease her mind some.

"What's that?" asked Aria and she hopped off her own bed and jumped onto Auriel's.

"Something I found a while ago," she said turning it over one last time before reaching it towards Aria. The young girl took it, eyeing it in her hands for a moment before she started to pull at it. After a long moment of trying, she seemed to give up and handed it back to Auriel.

"It feels just like a solid piece of black stone," she said. "It's cool but..." and she shook her head as if unimpressed.

"What is it?" asked Alakyne and he lifted his head up from his pillow.

"Here," said Auriel and she lightly tossed it to him.

As his hands touched it, strange white lines spread rapidly across its surface forming intricate patterns. Auriel gasped and she hopped off the bed, coming to it and the three of them stared as more lines formed on its surface. As the final side started to fill with patterns, Alakyne turned it over to see it more closely and a silver serpent appeared biting its tail.

Auriel gasped again and she gingerly reached for the object to which Alakyne gave it to her. The lines remained and as Auriel touched it, she could feel something much more different from it. An aural power lay within it, commanding and powerful, it was foreign but also reminiscent of the power she had sensed from the Seraphs.

"It's a Relic," she whispered.

"What?" asked Aria.

"A Relic of Aute," she continued. "Something me and my family were searching for before we got separated."

"What does it do?" asked Aria but Auriel shook her head. She had no idea.

"Something is inside it," Alakyne muttered. "Something strange."

"What do you mean?" Auriel asked. "How can you tell?"

The Legend of Kyne: Chronocide

"I can just *feel* it. Something alive is inside it."

Auriel turned it over in her hand, inspecting each of its twelve sides before sighing, unsure of what to do with it.

Aria reached out and she was handed the object in which she too checked all of the sides. As she came to the final side, the one etched with the serpent, she used her finger and traced its body starting from its head around to where its tail vanished into its mouth. The snake suddenly started to glow and at its center a swirling vortex of white light erupted, launching a dark object out where it collapsed to the ground in a tangled mess.

* * *

62. A Chance of Escape

Kyne struck the ground again with his pickax, prying at the hardened dirt. His body was searching for aural stones, but his mind was trying to find any ideas of what he should do. He thought back to the note and its strangeness.

The key to your escape lies with the stones and your aural prowess, he thought as he recalled the strange line on the letter. *Aural prowess? How would they know that?*

He struck the ground again, tearing the iron tip of the pickax through the dirt and catching the lip of something hard. A flash of light caught his eye and he hit it again. *This is my chance*, he thought, excitement and nervousness sinking in deep. *I can truly test how well they are watching me.*

With the tip of his pickax, he peeled some more dirt up, dislodging the stone before flipping the end around and brushing the dirt back over it lightly. He had some ideas he wanted to test out.

Moving to a new spot a few feet away, he started hitting the ground again. Fourteen, fifteen, he counted in his head before he knelt down and grabbed onto a rock, grey in color that bore no aural powers.

Footsteps crunched through the snow, and he looked up to see a sentinel, displeasure on his face.

"Found something interesting?" he sneered the moment he saw Kyne holding the stone.

Kyne tensed for a moment, the thought of smashing the stone against the sentinel flashing through his mind momentarily before he tossed the stone away.

"Nope," he said, rising to his feet and grabbing his pickax again. A few strikes against the ground brought a snort of irritation from the sentinel and then the crunch of snow signaled his leave. Kyne glanced back through the corner of his eye, spotting where the sentinel stopped a few dozen feet away. A quick scan, fast as a blink came from Kyne as he whipped his head around, spotting all of the sentinels and the slaves in the near vicinity. The one who had approached was by far the closest with a few more slaves in his watch.

They are upon me in moments, he thought as he continued on. He had an idea forming but it wasn't finalized yet. If something were to happen and he got caught, then he would be killed for sure. He continued on, the freezing cold temperatures never letting up as the faint sun above illuminated his work field.

He found no other stones for hours as the other stayed hidden, a film of snow obscuring it. He had no idea how he was going to hide it, or where even he could but he had to think of something. Commotion drew his attention and he saw another slave crying in relief as he held up a faint glowing stone that he had found.

"At least we get to eat tonight," Kyne mumbled, and he felt the ache in his stomach. He had enough seeds for a meal and was almost sad at the prospect of not receiving more for the stone he was hiding.

Returning to his work, he picked at the ground, skirting around a tree for a moment out of view of the sentinel. A quick thwack against its bark by his pickax carved a descent mark into its surface before he stepped around and started excavating the base of it.

He would hide the stones here, at least for the time being. No other slaves ventured to this area, most opting to stay toward the barrier line where the trees were thinner as the slope of the mountain started.

How am I going to get the stone over here though?

He looked to where he knew it lay, a few steps away but under the gaze of the sentinels it could just as well be a hundred. He had to wait for an opportunity, some distraction or something, then a thought passed over his mind and he debated in his head if it were possible.

If I can do it fast enough, then I might stand a chance. But if I am seen its death. But it could work, it could even be the most useful tool I have.

His thoughts continued until he had finally convinced himself he would try it. It would be soon, the sun nearly setting. He was nearly out of time and with a quick glance spotting the sentinel's location, he traipsed back to where he had hidden the stone.

Smoothing the snow off it, he used the shovel to pry some dirt away revealing the glowing stone, a gem surrounded by mundane rocks.

The Legend of Kyne: Chronocide

His breath quickened and in one fluid motion, stooped down and touched the glowing rock with his hand.

Its surface was smooth and jagged, like a piece of shattered crystal. Glowing a deep amber, the power that it possessed was small but familiar as Kyne smiled at the aura within. His fingers wrapped around the stone whose size was not much larger than a grape.

"Did you find something this time," a voice said behind him.

Kyne's blood ran cold and out of the corner of his eye he saw the sentinel approaching. He was certain he hadn't seen the stone but if he hid it, he would surely be whipped for the second false stone.

Has he seen the stone yet? his mind raced. Time seemed to slow as he took a quick inhalation. The sound of footsteps behind him nearly there. *No, I don't think he has. He surely would have worded that differently. I can't lose this stone!*

"Altyne kin," he whispered as quietly as possible. Every part of his body assumed nothing would happen and then the feeling of aura touched his body. Directing the spell on the sentinel behind him and praying, he stood up holding two rocks nearly the same size and turned to face the sentinel.

He held his breath as the sentinel looked at them with a puzzled look. "You did find one then," he huffed and reached out and took one of the stones. He eyed the other one for a moment as if confused and started to turn away. Kyne dropped his hand, the stone in it quickly being tucked into his pocket before he said, "What about my seeds?"

The sentinel turned back, still with a look of dazed confusion on his face. He pulled out two bags, one he tossed in the glowing rock, Kyne half expecting it to clutter against the others, but he heard nothing. The other, the sentinel withdrew seeds from and handed them to Kyne.

Turning away, Kyne watched the sentinel return to his post and breathed out a shaky breath. He had done it, and he felt the lump of the aural stone against his hip. Taking his pickax, he skirted around the tree and the moment he was hidden from view, tucked the small stone within the notch he had carved into it. Tucked it right behind the layer of bark hiding it from the world and he started excavating nearby, as if nothing had changed.

The Legend of Kyne: Chronocide

But he bore a smile that he had not had for such a long time, each strike against the ground completely unnoticeable as his mind thought about the stone. He had used aura and was able to trick the sentinel into taking the false rock.

His grin widened at the thought of him removing the stones and being one short. He hoped the sentinel hadn't counted but knew that he for sure had. A panicked thought coursed through his mind of potential suspicion, but he pushed it out. There was no going back now.

They were led back a short time later, Kyne's eyes drilled upon the back of the sentinel's head as he directed them to where they could drop their fur coats and pickaxes before stepping inside. Each slave was then patted from head to toe, mouth ordered open, and their privacy evaporated as they were searched for hidden items before being allowed inside. As Kyne waited in line, the sentinel that he had tricked walked past the doorway, pausing near a small chest where he removed his pouch. Opening it up, he poured the stones into his hand, Kyne counted four.

The sentinel froze, his hand holding the four stones delicately as he stared at them again as if counting each one individually. All of them were the same orange amber glow as Kyne's was. He had seen others of different shades, but they were exceptionally rare.

The sentinel looked first at his hand, then out towards the path he had walked as if hoping to spot the missing stone and then back to his hand. Kyne was searched roughly by another sentinel as his gaze hovered upon the first. Just as he was ordered to open his mouth, the sentinel being momentarily obscured by moving bodies, Kyne sighed as he watched him drop the stones in and walk away.

That night Kyne sat on his blanket surrounded by other slaves but alone. His friend was not speaking to him, and Kyne hadn't seen him since the night before. He took a bite of food and laid his head down. The chorus of voices continued but Kyne closed his eyes as he took the final bite of his food, swallowing it and feeling his hunger satisfied as much as it was going to be.

More days passed, some with Kyne finding stones, others having none. The sentinels always seemed to be watching him, but he had managed to stow three more stones, each much easier than the

The Legend of Kyne: Chronocide

first. All were in different locations, one in the tundra's tree and the others in various places in the scorched earth of the lower mountain slope.

Kyne wasn't sure when he would be contacted next or how many he would need but he would continue. Each small amount adding to the potential jailbreak that he was going to attempt.

Nearly two weeks from his first letter came his second. He was sleeping when a figure awoke him, mumbling something about a word from his friend. He kept repeating it and after noticing the same glazed eyes as the first had, withdrew the parchment from his collar.

Well done, I count seven stones you have hidden. Unfortunately, I see you have them scattered around. Luckily, I was able to retrieve them. I have stowed them all in the tree that you first started with. I have arranged transportation for you the moment you can escape. Do not be seen, if you are, I won't be able to come in and save you. You will be on your own.

Three nights from now I will be waiting for you atop the mountain ridge.

Do not be seen.

Kyne crumpled it up and swallowed it as he had done with the first, the sunlight drifting in through the window signaling another nonstop day of slaving was to begin.

The day ended with no stones found upon the hot mountain slope. Jaren had been seen nearby but hadn't seemed to notice Kyne. Kyne could tell he was using Flash still as his movement signaled it. The young man had grown far thinner since Kyne had last seen him and even his hair seemed to have greyed.

Day two was also on the mountain slope under the scorching sun. Panic enveloped Kyne at the thought of not being able to retrieve the stones. He had to get into the tundra tomorrow or he was out of options.

The third day came and to Kyne's relief, he found himself in the tundra. Making his way to the tree, he glanced quickly and noticed they were there nestled in the tree bark just as promised. Sighing, he began working, nearby another slave joining him.

He was an unattractive man whose tall height was the only thing noteworthy about him. Eyes small and a large nose, he bore the face of a weasel who had managed to survive against all odds. He didn't speak while he worked, and Kyne started to notice that he wasn't trying very hard. Even the sentinel had noticed and after a few whips, the man had more gusto.

Kyne hovered near the tree, always seeming to keep right nearby but as the day progressed, the man seemed to migrate towards him. Was it just his imagination or was he getting closer to him? Kyne watched as the man struck the ground a few times before inching his foot behind him as if casually adjusting.

There! Kyne's thoughts roared as he saw him inch again. *Why is he coming closer to me?*

Then it clicked in his mind.

This must be the person sending the letters. It's this man.

Kyne watched him again shuffle closer towards him. He hadn't seen this man often, but he had seen him a few times over the weeks. *Why would he be risking everything to come contact me now? Is the plan off and he's going to tell me the bad news?*

Another long time passed and eventually they were nearly five feet apart, Kyne's eyes constantly drilled on the back of the man's head as they both labored on. The sun was high above, but its warmth was gone, the chilling air hanging tight around them.

How should I speak to him? he thought. *Should I say something, or should I wait for him to?*

Kyne didn't have to wait long before the man straightened up and turned to face him. In his eyes he bore only a cold flatness that Kyne didn't like. After a moment of staring, Kyne noticed that the man had positioned himself completely out of view from the sentinel, the tree blocking his path.

"What are you hiding boy?" he said, raising the pickax up and laying it upon his shoulder.

His comment was strange to Kyne, not making much sense in the context that he had perceived.

The Legend of Kyne: Chronocide

"I... I don't know what you mean," Kyne stammered, hoping the conversation would give him new insight.

"You seem to always hover by this tree whenever you are over here. I have noticed as well as others. It seems like you have something here that you want to keep your eyes on."

Kyne was silent. The idea of this being his letter writer evaporated away.

The man turned around and eyed the tree, looking for something. After only a few moments, he spotted the notch Kyne had carved. A grin spread across his face, and he reached into its depths.

He is going to ruin everything! "Are you the one who sent the letters?" Kyne asked, hoping his comment would distract the man.

He didn't look away but replied with, "What letters?"

That was all Kyne needed to know. Dashing toward the man, the moment an aural stone came into view, Kyne touched it, and they met eyes for a split second.

"Roke."

Kyne's voice was muffled with the snowfall and the resounding crack that followed made his skin rise in bumps. The man slumped forward, slamming his head into the bark of the tree before he slid down in an awkward pose. His neck had been broken and his eyes blank.

Kyne looked around to see if anyone had spotted him and to a quick relief, he saw he was still in the clear, at least for the moment. Using the rest of the aura in the stone, he managed to raise the snow up into a pile around the corpse.

The stones amber light faded away back to that of a mundane grey and he let it fall to the ground where it submerged beneath the white blanket. He was still hidden for the moment, but he could be found any second. Gathering the rest of the stones, he tucked them into his waistband just as the crunching of footsteps alerted him of someone approaching.

He was going to be caught!

Suddenly another slave walked around the tree, meeting Kyne's eyes for a moment before he continued on, choosing a spot nearby and he began to work the ground.

Kyne sighed a breath of relief and stepped away from the tree.

536

The Legend of Kyne: Chronocide

"No breaks!" snapped a far-off voice and he turned to see a sentinel pointing at him and then the menacing crack of a whip.

He scrambled for his pickax and started to work again, each strike slowly ebbing off the adrenaline rush. The day continued on and after some time he heard the thundering of far-off wagon wheels. Turning to look, he saw two approaching, thundering down the rocky road as it approached the complex from the south. He could see figures in the back of each wagon, more slaves.

He watched for a moment as they approached before an order to get to work drew him back to his duty. Out of the corner of his eye he watched as they approached and were all shuffled into the building. A few figures stayed outside speaking to the sentinels before they entered into a separate building where the sentinels lived.

Kyne strained his eyes, looking for the Kydrëan who had his sword but couldn't make anything out.

The day came to an end and Kyne was led back to the slave house with the others, all forming a tight line. The lumps in his inner pant lining were hidden by his clothes but the sentinels would feel it. He needed to trick them.

"Altyne vus," he breathed, and the moments the sentinel's hands touched him he morphed the spell. It was quick but just as he felt the sentinel touch the lumps, he was relieved to feel his hands move to a new location, seemingly not feeling them.

Kyne opened his mouth, showing it to be empty and then he was urged inside the loud room. He ate, spending the seeds he had on food, using them all. He ate alone, always looking for Jaren but not seeing his friend. Just as he swallowed his last bite, he finally saw him, moving slowly from the food cart to the blanket he had set up. He was nearby but Kyne could tell that the Flash was still in his system.

The day ended and as night overtook them, the talking diminished and then was snuffed out as they all fell asleep, resting for the continuing work the following day.

63. The Last Night

Kyne waited; his eyes open as he strained his ears for any sounds. It had been a few hours since they had ceased talking, long enough to hopefully have everyone asleep.

He sat up slowly, rising to his feet and he began sneaking over towards where Jaren was. He had thought about it for a long time but wanted to offer his friend an escape.

He found him and kneeling down, he placed one hand over his mouth and shook his hand, jarring the young man awake.

"It's me," Kyne whispered as Jaren began to flail and his movement slowed as he came to a realization. Kyne removed his hand.

"What are you doing," Jaren groaned, his voice slurred. "Go back to bed," and he lowered his head back down.

"I am leaving," Kyne said expecting Jaren to gasp in shock, but his friend did not. "You can join me."

Jaren was silent.

"Do you have nothing to say? I have obtained a sizeable group of aural stones and am going to break out. I have someone from the outside helping me. I will ask you again, do you wish to join me?"

Jaren mumbled something and he sat up again, his dark silhouette rubbing his eyes as he tried to see Kyne.

"Kyne is that you," he groaned. "Do you have some Flash?" and his hands fumbled for Kyne who easily knocked them away.

"No, I don't have Flash," Kyne hissed. "Did you not hear a word I said?"

"Give me some Flash," moaned the young man and he slumped over. Kyne jarred his arm but this time he didn't wake to it. For a long moment, Kyne stared down at the dark figure of Jaren's sleeping body. He was torn far more than he thought he should. This man wasn't much to him, but they had suffered together, and he believed him to be a friend. He didn't want to leave him behind, but he couldn't take him. There was no way that Jaren would be able to make it in this state.

"I am sorry my friend," and Kyne lightly touched the man's arm as his chest tightened. He stayed there for a long moment, grieving the loss of his friend and the torture and torment that he was leaving him in. "If I am to find a way back to my time maybe I can erase all of these horrors."

The beating of his heart thumped in his chest as he slowly rose up from Jaren's sleeping figure. The room was dark, the flames from the fires that were scattered around reduced to coals. The air was silent and still save for the snoring some of the slaves performed and an occasional cough from the sick. No moonlight streamed through the window illuminating his figure, probably exactly why his savior had selected this specific day.

He turned his head around, straining hard to see the shapes of bodies upon the hard floor and the sentinels that guarded the entrance to room. He counted two of them, their golden armor shining dully in ambient light.

There's usually three of them, he thought, looking around the room trying to find the other. *They always have three on duty. There,* and his eyes pinpointed on a moving shadow, slowly patrolling the rows of sleeping slaves. He was across the room and looked to have just started to roam.

Kyne's hand fumbled in his pocket, touching the aural stones and feeling their power. He had amassed a decent amount, but it was still finite. He could easily run out and had to use it as little as possible. This time though he had no other option.

"Altyne kin fel," he murmured casting the illusion spell over the sentinels standing guard. focusing on the image he wished for them to see. He pictured the patrolling sentinel turning and walking right to where he was. As the figure came next to Kyne, he morphed the image again, causing them to perceive Kyne as the guard while the other faded from sight.

Kyne knew it was all an illusion and their ignorance was what gave it power. If they knew something was off, then it would break the spell. Looking back, he saw the real guard had come to the end of the row and was starting to turn around and face him.

If he didn't act now, he could be seen!

Using the spell again, he made his image invisible to the patrolling guard, tricking both groups into seeing different things. One illusion spell was incredibly difficult to hold stable but two was nearly impossible. A single stray thought could cause something to fail and be noticed, and then the whole thing would fall apart.

Kyne's thoughts weren't even focused on the thought of failure, it was hard focused on what was happening right now. He pictured himself as the patrolling sentinel, walking around the sleeping bodies towards the others while the other was oblivious.

He was close now, could see the glimmer of their eyes under their helms. He nodded once, without stopping his stride and made his way directly in front of them before stopping and taking his stance.

They were all three in line, their backs towards a closed door that Kyne knew led down a hallway that led outside. In front of him he saw the patrolling guard continuing on, completely unaware of what was happening.

He could feel the energy from the stone draining quickly as he held the illusion for a moment. Keeping his figure to resemble the other sentinel while also hiding things from view.

"That was a short walk," muttered the sentinel next to him, catching him off guard and almost breaking his focus. He could feel it slipping away, the illusion shimmering but he managed to hold on, solidifying it and replying with a simple shoulder shrug. He had to end this quickly. After a second, he changed the spell, causing his true body to become invisible while leaving the ethereal form of the sentinel standing where he stood. Taking a step back so that he was behind the other two guards, he guided his apparition back into a walk, imagining each slow step as he painstakingly guided him over to where the real guard was patrolling.

With the figure only visible to the stationary guards and his own body obscured, he was able to end his work on the patrolling guard, causing a great relief from the drain. Eventually he lined his apparition up, the dark silhouette stepping in sync with the real sentinel and in one motion, he ended the spell leaving their attention onto the real guard who continued walking completely unaware.

To the standing guards, the only thing they had seen was the third, walk around, approach them, stand with them for a moment, and then return to his patrol.

Kyne inhaled slowly, he was still not in the clear yet as he stood behind the two, invisible but still there. The stone powering the spell was nearly depleted, but he had to continue.

Morphing the illusion spell, he muffled both his appearance and the sounds he caused so that none of the guards would notice as he cracked the door open behind and slipped through, the click of the door following.

His heart raced in his chest, and he swallowed a lump in his throat. Withdrawing the smooth crystal gem, he had used the aura from, he could see the pale and plain grey of a simple stone from the light of the braziers that lined the hallway.

He had completely drained one stone to get him out of the room. Illusion spells were not costly in aura and the shock of finding this out made his blood run cold.

If illusion spells drained this much aura, then battle spells would be a disaster! his mind raced at that thought and he leaned against the stone wall. He hadn't realized when he had started but the small store, he thought he had was many times smaller than that. One dragonrend would easily drain all of the stones and it probably wouldn't even be full powered.

"I just have to stay hidden," he whispered trying to calm himself. "It will only matter if I get caught."

He started down the hallway as quietly as possible. The heat from the faint flames in the braziers kept it a mild temperature and he shivered as he thought about the sub-zero temperatures outside the walls.

Rounding a corner, he came to two doors, the first to his right he knew led outside and the second straight ahead led to the barracks. He had never seen what was beyond it. Once he heard rumors of a slave running inside for some reason, but they were never heard from again. He assumed they were just rumors but the thought still stressed him out.

He pictured a majestic room lined with beds and all of the

sentinels each sleeping deeply upon their cushions. He imagined the warm blazing fire in the hearth and the scraps of meat from their meals still left on their plates or being gnawed upon by the dogs.

The dogs! Kyne's mind gasped in shock as his hand was mere inches from the door. He had forgotten about them. Masking a human from a human was easy, just vision and sight but with a dog he would have to mask his scent which he was confident he couldn't do. He could take the form of the guards, hell even all three if he wanted with the illusion spells cost being equal either way. It didn't matter the extent of the illusion but the amount of people it was cast upon.

He knew what he wanted, knew the risks of searching for them and pushing the door open, he was startled to see that it was not a fanciful room but just another long empty hallway. This one had more windows than the last, but the same braziers burned upon either side illuminating it. At its end he could see a few stone steps leading up to a shut wooden door, the panels bare of oil and paint. He took a few more steps when his stomach dropped at the groan of the door swinging upon its hinges.

"Altyne ulkin," Kyne said in a panic, casting the more powerful complete invisibility spell upon him and he pushed his back up against the wall in between two braziers.

Panting was heard and to his horror he saw three large dogs, brown in color with their ears cropped and standing straight up walking down the hallway followed by a Gaeilian male dressed in just his undergarments. His face bore fatigue and he rubbed his eyes as he stumbled after them.

Kyne held his breath as the dogs approached and to his despair, they all stopped directly in front of him. Their hair upon their backs started to rise, forming a long strip down its length as they turned their head towards him. He could see the beginnings of a snarl on their mouths and their noses twitched as they scented the air, sensing his presence before them.

Their snarl grew, all three showing their fangs and they turned their bodies to face him more head on.

His hand grasped the other stones, trying to figure out what to do. If they attacked, he had to deal with them, but it could be the end of everything. If he used up the stones then his best bet would be to make a break for it, leaving his blade behind and running as fast as he could through the night to the person he so dearly prayed was waiting for him.

"Go!" barked a gruff voice and the sentinel stepped into view, the orange flames dancing their light upon his face. He kicked one of the dogs, causing it to squeal in fright and all three seemed to forget he was there as they dashed down the hallway towards the door. "Go take your damn piss you mangy mutts," he mumbled, and he trailed after them. The door clicked signaling their leave and Kyne ended his spell.

"That was too close," he breathed as he turned to look at the door. He had nearly drained another stone in mere seconds from a freak coincidence. Was it really worth it to risk everything for Aurora and the rings?

The image of the silvery white feather blade appeared in his mind, and he pictured the Light when he had given it to him. *That blade is mine!* roared his thoughts and he felt a familiar dragonrage appear in his soul. He felt so much like his old self and as the rage diminished, he bit his lip. He knew the feeling was only because he was touching some aural source, but he missed it. Not the rage in particular but the power and gift that he once had.

Taking a deep breath, he dashed down the hallway, not sure of how much time he had before the sentinel would be back with the dogs. He had to hurry. Casting a spell to conceal his image and sound, he pushed the door open and was shocked to find the barracks much different than he had pictured.

They were plain, no ornate beds lined the walls and no hearth lit ablaze. What stood around the room were simple mats topped with shadowy figures that signaled sleeping sentinels. The fireplace was glowing brighter than the braziers, but the flames were winking in and out of existence as it tried to sustain itself. He didn't see any other dogs to his relief and after a few moments had managed to find the slave trappers sleeping on the edge of the room near a window.

The window was completely frosted over, looking west into the tundra with the dark bitter cold beyond. At its base he counted four of the trappers, each sleeping on the mats and fast asleep. He looked first for his scabbard and after he didn't see it started to examine each of the trappers.

These were the same ones that had captured him except one, one was new and the Kydrëan was not with them.

Kyne cursed under his breath, the thought of sending a dragonrend through the entire camp entering his mind as he felt a rage unlike anything he had felt in a while. His sword was not there, that was certain and that Kydrëan. *That damned Kydrëan traitor!*

Picking one of the trappers, he knelt down and risking everything, used his aura to bind the man's arms, legs and mouth. Slapping him hard across the face, the resounding crack hidden with his aura, Kyne smiled in satisfaction as the trapper's eyes shot open, their foreign green glowing in the orange light.

He didn't speak, more he couldn't speak as he stared at Kyne for a long moment before a look of realization and rage spread across his face.

"Where's the Kydrëan who was with you?"

The man started to struggle against Kyne's aural bindings and the archmage slapped him again, this time as hard as he could. Kyne watched the man's green eyes temporarily fade as his consciousness was threatened.

Kyne waited for a moment as the man's struggling stopped but it didn't return. The only thing that returned was the hatred that burned in the green irises.

"You speak you die," Kyne whispered, and he reached over, drawing the man's own dagger and placing it upon his neck. He released the binding spell only upon the man's mouth and watched it open. He expected a scream and had already muffled the sound it would cause but was shocked when the man spoke calmly.

"The Kydrëan you speak of is no longer associated with this mining camp. He has moved on and up in this cursed world we live in."

"Where is he?"

"How am I supposed to know that," he said flatly. "I don't keep tabs on him. We don't write letters and keep up on each other's day-to-day activities."

Kyne fought the urge to slap the man again and clenched his jaw.

"Where. Is. He."

The Legend of Kyne: Chronocide

The slave trapper was silent. Kyne could feel the aural stones draining even more. He had finished another off and was ebbing away at the next. His rage began to boil, and he raised his hand to strike the man again.

"I expect he would be closer to the sea in one of the big cities."

"What cities? Haakviid is vast. I am not searching the entire coastline!"

"If I were to guess it would be near Dawngôr. Shjavalk is possible but less likely and he's for sure not going to be further north than that."

Kyne lifted the dagger from the man's neck. "Why are you so eager to give up your comrade?"

The trapper laughed at those words. "Comrade? He is no comrade of mine. I hate him, every part of his loathsome little Kydrëan being. He's arrogant and cocky and vile in the things he says and does. I do some terrible things I'll admit it, but that man makes me look like a saint. Let alone the fact that we work with a damn Kydrëan. The inferior people we conquered giving me orders!"

Rage lit across the man's face as he remembered the other trapper. Kyne waited for a moment as the man's heavy breathing finally slowed and he regained his composure. "I tell you these things in the off chance you manage to find him and kill him. I know that will be folly though but either way it's a win win for me. Either you get away and kill him or you die, and I don't have to deal with your sorry ass."

"I'm not going to die," Kyne breathed into the man's ear as he leaned down. "I have my family I have to get back to. Kaiodin."

He watched as within seconds the man's eyes glazed over and his mouth hung ajar as he lost consciousness. Kyne held the spell, stopping the flow of blood to the man's brain for another dozen seconds before ending the spell. He hadn't killed him, but he did buy himself some getaway time.

The door nearby started to creak and fast as he could, he dashed to the window and pried at it, trying to force it open. The crunch of frost sounded as it resisted, and the panting of dogs and footsteps were heard behind him. It wasn't budging, the frost holding firm.

A quick glance, and he could see the dogs had stopped mid

stride and had risen their noses high up in the air. They were smelling him!

"Roke," Kyne said, and the frost shattered away allowing him to pull the window open, the frozen glass swinging out on a rusted hinge. A frigid wind rushed in but in a moment, he had leapt up and out of the window, swinging it closed behind him, hoping beyond hope his aura had kept it hidden.

Suddenly he was waist deep in freezing snow, the icy crystals cutting into his flesh. He immediately shivered hard as the rags that he wore did little to protect him from the cold. He was little more than naked as he plowed through the snow, his cracked boots littered with holes quickly frozen and full of snow.

He could feel his skin screaming in protest as he pushed each step, his shins being sliced from the ice. Behind him he could make out the glow of fire through the window and then the sudden barking of dogs was heard, muffled from the building.

He pushed harder, making his way around the perimeter of the building heading for the clear barrier where the snow seemed to stop as if it had been shoveled in a sharp line.

The barking intensified and then he could hear voices echoing from inside the building. He saw the glimmer of torchlight run past the windows, but he kept going. Turning his vision away from the building, he drove each step hard through the snow. He was almost there and in half a minute he burst out onto the barren dirt edge of the mountain slope. No vegetation blocked his path except for the skeleton trees the covered the hillside, long since fried from the baking sun.

The temperature change was immediate, far warmer than the icy cold he had just been in, more like a warm summer night but he still shivered, and he started a hasty jog up the slope. The dark silhouette of the mountain outlined by the faint stars above was imposing as it towered above him. He traced its edge, looking for the saddle not too far up its slope that was his destination.

"There!" he gasped; his breath already ragged from exhaustion. He could see it, to his left nearly a quarter mile away. It was a small ridge that flattened out before curving up and melding with the massive peak above.

He could make it!

The Legend of Kyne: Chronocide

Pushing on, his legs screaming and his skin still numb, he dashed through the trees while down below the shouting grew louder and then he stopped as he heard the rabid barking of dogs.

Turning around and looking down a few hundred yards, he saw people rush out of the building with torches in their hands. The dogs barking continued and from the sound of them he knew they had already picked up his scent.

Pushing on, he ran as fast as he could, the muscles in his legs growing sluggish and flimsily as he forced them further. He was close but the dog's barking was nearly upon him.

He had to use his aura.

Turning around, he waited, ears strained as he anticipated the hounds. In a few seconds they appeared, their dark shapes hurtling up the slope straight for him. He didn't have much aura, but he had to stop them.

"Mar'bi fos!" he said and the surface of earth in front of his turned to sand before he changed the spell rapidly solidifying it and stopping the dogs dead in their tracks. Their barking grew more enraged, and they screeched at him, but he couldn't waste any more time. He was out of aura, the last of it being drained away with that spell.

The saddle was nearly there, and he began a brisk walk towards it, his breath heaving in and out of his lungs. The dog's barking was loud, but he thought it seemed different, as if it were only two and not three.

Suddenly a massive sharp pain ripped through his leg, and he collapsed to the ground in a cry of pain. A figure behind him flailed its head, teeth wedged deep into his calf. The hot sticky feeling of blood was felt and Kyne screamed again, kicking at the attacking dog as hard as he could but it wouldn't let up. He kicked again, over and over striking it, but it was stuck fast, its teeth piercing his flesh and it flailed its head around back and forth throwing Kyne's leg around and threatening to tear a massive chunk off.

Kyne screamed again and then a flash of movement flew past him, a glimmer of silver and then the flailing stopped suddenly. The pain, however, didn't cease and he cried out again, scrambling back away from the beast.

The Legend of Kyne: Chronocide

A dark figure lay hunched nearby. They were motionless for a moment, as if staring off towards the incoming sentinels before they stood up and swept towards Kyne.

"I said to not be seen," said a gruff voice.

"You also said you wouldn't help me, and I would be on my own," Kyne replied, wincing in pain as his leg continued to bleed.

A grunt was the only reply that Kyne got, and he felt the figure grab his wounded leg before a piece of cloth was wrapped around and around tighter than Kyne liked.

"Up," ordered the figure whom Kyne assumed to be a man and Kyne was jerked to his feet. Putting weight on his wounded leg immediately caused him to cry out and he nearly collapsed, the figure managing to keep him upright.

"Dear God!" The man cursed and he jarred Kyne forward, helping him keep his balance as they stumbled up the hill a few dozen feet to the standing silhouettes of two horses.

"Who are you?" Kyne asked as he was helped up onto the saddle of the first horse.

"A friend," the man replied, and he leapt upon the other.

"What is your name friend," Kyne said more firmly, a feeling in his being not letting go. He could feel something strange about the man.

"Why do you always have to push the boundaries Kyne," the man replied. "It should be me asking the questions around here not you. What the hell did you do? The last time I saw you and the others you vanished in a flash of light."

The figure dropped his hood and Kyne gasped in shock for before him was the middle-aged face of Kioni.

64. To Finally Speak

"What? How? What?" Kyne gasped in shock. Kioni smirked at his look of disbelief, the dark shadows lining his cheeks contouring against his thick, ragged beard. "How are you..."

"Here? Still asking questions," Kioni sighed before turning away. "We should get moving."

Behind them Kyne could hear the shouting of sentinels in the far distance. The barking of the trapped dogs echoed around constantly, and Kyne shuddered at the thought of them breaking free as the first had. His leg ached in pain, and he leaned down and touched the cloth that had been bound around it. It was soaking with blood but seemed to have stopped the bleeding for now. He could feel pins and needles shooting down his leg but dismissed them.

Looking back up, he noticed Kioni had already guided his horse into a fast gallop away, vanishing into the shadows. A quick kick of his heel and Kyne was after him, the horse pounding across the dry dirt of the mountainside. Kioni's figure vanished past trees as he weaved the horse through them guiding it further along the saddle. The ridge was like a large road as it flattened out before climbing back up and curving to the east. They followed it, every few minutes Kyne glancing back and seeing the glimmering lights of the slave hold and the sentinels growing more distant.

A few torches had broken off from the pack and were further up the slope, probably aboard horses by the speed they had been traveling but Kyne's worry was fading as they continued to gain distance. The near pitch-black environment was the perfect escape for them, illuminated only by the faint starlight as Kyne tried to keep his gaze trained on both Kioni and incoming trees.

They continued up the ridge for another few minutes before

the horses slowed down to a fast trot, the slope growing steeper as they continued on. The hulking mass of the mountains above towered over them like giants of shadow and stone, their jagged peaks like fangs scrapping the meat from the sky.

Further and further, they traveled on, the horses eventually slowing to a walk as they guided them further up the slope. It had been over an hour now, the slave camp lost far below them, obscured by the dead forest. In the faint light with everything black and grey, Kyne looked out over the world and could see the striking line of snow cut straight along the edge of the mountains slope before curving further out into the forest vanishing in the shadows of the horizon.

The world was unstable, desolated from something and he had to know why. He wanted to ask Kioni, but a feeling of strange awkwardness kept looming between them. He still hadn't talked to his friend in a long time, since Ilana had died and even now, he could feel the tension in the air.

Another hour passed before they managed to reach the line where the trees thinned out, their bare trunks and branches like hairs among the mountainside. Other silhouetted peaks were now able to be seen as he followed the summit ridge of the mountain he was on, the ones further on even higher than these. Thousands of feet above the forest they towered.

The ice capped summits had long since melted away in the eternal drought this region had been forsaken too but with a glance behind him, he saw a few mountain massifs away, the stark white of snow. completely covered masking nearly every feature, the two regions seemed to be nearly opposites.

Far ahead in the direction they were traveling he could just make out the first lighter blue streaks signaling dawn and the horrors the day would bring.

"Kioni, the sun is almost up. Where are we going? We won't survive for very long upon the mountain so exposed and without water."

"We are almost there," he replied calmly, his horse still walking. "I am not ignorant of the dangers of this world Kyne. You have been here a few months. I have been here for years. Nearly twenty years surviving in this hellhole."

The Legend of Kyne: Chronocide

His reply silenced Kyne. He hadn't realized it had been that long. He had heard the draconic say something similar, but it hadn't really set in. Kioni looked older but he had thought it to be probably the beard.

Twenty years? I have been sent twenty years in the future?

"Do you know where Auriel and Ni'Bara went?"

Kioni shook his head, the growing light allowing Kyne to see the faint movement. "They vanished with you on that cursed night, the other version of you searched for them for a long time, searched for all of you."

Kyne took a deep shuddering breath, both happiness and sadness filling his being simultaneously. Rejoicing they were not left with the wicked version of himself, alone and having to fight him but also mourning the thought of where they could have gone.

Kyne thought of the potential scenarios of where they could go but then he realized something that didn't make sense. "Wait, how did you see us vanish? How were you able to see us?"

"We are here," Kioni replied not answering Kyne's question and he guided the horse around a boulder to reveal a fairly deep cave. Large enough for all of them, they entered, and Kyne noticed that it looked to be Kioni's home. Items were scattered around from a few beaten scrolls to a bedroll and even a sword. They dismounted and Kyne watched the man withdraw the kama sheath upon his waist, the strange crescent like design that held them delicately was placed on the ground next to his bedroll before Kioni stripped down into just his undergarments. As he sat upon the roll he sighed and stretched.

"Don't ignore my question. How did you see us vanish?"

"That's a very long story Kyne. All you need to know right now is that a few of us were able to make it through the portal you created and were transported to this new alternate world," and he gestured around. "I was there for but a moment before your fight caught my attention and I saw you flash away. Personally, I thought you had died and that I was trapped. So much happened and then the world fell apart. Dear friends were lost, and we ended up here. I spy upon the slaves down below from time to time. Robbing the trappers occasionally for food and provisions. And then one day I saw you of all people hacking away at the frozen ground. I couldn't believe my eyes. You

The Legend of Kyne: Chronocide

looked exactly how you had before but your arm was gone."

Kyne peered down at his human arm and a feeling of grief washed over him.

"It faded away just as soon as I arrived here," he replied, and he raised it up as if inspecting the flesh. Imagining the grey scales upon it, he turned his palm up and then over.

"I thought maybe it wasn't really you but that other Kyne, but you just acted different. After a few weeks of watching you I finally understood it had to be you. That's when I started sending those letters."

"You used the Flash," Kyne said more than asked.

"Smart boy. Used it to make them say and do whatever I wanted. Such a terrible but useful weapon."

"So addictive," Kyne muttered as he thought of his friend who he had left behind.

"Only for those who are unable to cope with the suffering. It is a release for the hell they endure. Do not mock them but pity them. It is their choice, and they are the ones who will have to deal with the consequences."

The beams of sunlight lit up across the entrance of the cave brightening everything in a nice golden glow. The warmth was nice, but Kyne knew it would soon become a nightmare.

Kioni stood up from his bedroll, made his way over to the entrance and drew a large piece of fabric from the cave mouth's top. Dropping it down, it shut the cave, blocking a good amount of the light from entering. He then walked over to a small pack, withdrew two potatoes and tossed one to Kyne who devoured it.

"It's not much but it's one of the few things that seems to be able to grow. You'll see eventually the farms that line the borders of the different lands. Only there where the desert sun meets the eternal rains that crops can grow."

"How many people are left," Kyne muttered between bites.

"Few," he replied flatly and took a bite of his own. The crunch of the raw potato being chewed was the only sound for a long moment. "Most died in the first few weeks, either freezing to death, drowning, lack of water, burning, etc. Every extreme environment is all that remains. I assume you have encountered most."

The Legend of Kyne: Chronocide

Kyne nodded. "Desert, frozen, windy, rain,' and he shuddered at the soaking horror he had endured.

"The lightning area," Kioni continued. "A strike hits the ground nearly every three seconds. No rain falls and it has caused fires that burned the landscape away. There is also the land where the temperature is mild, but the ground constantly trembles. Along the coast massive swaths have flooded as the ocean pressed in and enormous pits have swallowed hundreds of square miles."

"What happened?"

"It was you, well not really you but the other one. He did some spell not long after you all vanished. It was horrible. Killed a few innocent people and broke the world."

Kioni grew silent and Kyne saw him look away, his lip quivering under his beard. *Why is he so somber at that?* he thought as he watched his friend try to hide the sadness.

"What really happened Kioni? You're not telling me everything."

Kioni's expression dramatically changed, and his eyes went dark. "Don't think that after all of these years that I have forgiven you Kyne. I will not tell you everything, you are not someone that I can trust. You killed my sister, and you are responsible for the other losses I have also endured."

"Don't you even start," roared Kyne, anger flashing in his voice. "I did not kill your sister! I tried to save her!"

"And you failed!"

"How could you even say that? She was my friend too!"

"Your friend but my family!" Kioni shrieked. "She was my only family and you let her die!"

Kyne was silent as Kioni's words echoed around for a moment before they faded away. The older man had risen to his feet and was staring down at Kyne with such a hurt expression on his face that it made Kyne's stomach turn.

"You don't even know what happened," Kyne started.

"I know enough," he said, his lip quivering and the sparkle of tears in his eyes. "She was gone, and you vanished. Poof gone for so long. You weren't even the one who told me. I found out from some random sorcerer. You were gone for so long and then poof you were back with some new lady. It was like nothing had happened."

"I reached out to you the moment I returned from the Aera, and you evaded every single attempt to speak to you. Theo wouldn't help. I didn't even know where you were!"

Kioni was silent at that and the two stared at one another for a long time.

"I needed space."

"So, you blame me for giving it to you?" Kyne retorted. "Your argument has no warrant, Kioni. Get over it!"

As Kyne finished his word Kioni swung. It was a single strike, fast and hard, that struck Kyne right across the cheek.

The blow knocked Kyne's head to the side where he caught himself with one hand upon the ground. The blow dazed him for a moment, and he felt the taste of blood in his mouth from the split lip he had received.

He looked at Kioni and saw his friend with thick tears streaming down his face. The anger was gone, replaced by complete sadness.

Kyne slowly stood to his feet, his face already swelling and hot from the blow. He met Kioni's eyes and could feel his own sorrow at Ilana's death return. He had come to terms with it long ago but it resurfacing like this brought back terrible memories.

"I'm sorry," he whispered.

"I'm sorry," Kioni replied, his voice shuddering as he tried to speak between his sobs.

And the two embraced, holding each other like the best friends they once were. They had both lost a sister and had finally been able to speak about it.

"I'm sorry," Kyne whispered, tears streaming down his own face.

They sat there for a long moment before they finally separated, and the emotions faded away. Kyne could tell Kioni had forgiven him and when they met eyes, he finally saw his friend.

"This whole thing is all my fault," Kyne said, and he sat back down upon the dirt ground. Kioni sat next to him.

"What happened?"

And Kyne explained everything from the events after Ilana's

death to the defeat of the darkness. Meeting Auriel and their marriage as well as Rosé's growth. He spoke of the time distortions and their quest for the Relics of Aute.

"So, these Relics of Aute were gifts from God? You think that collecting them would stop the distortions?"

"That was what we thought," Kyne replied. "We had a few of them and knew the whereabouts of a few others."

"That's incredible!" he gasped. "These items must be immensely powerful."

"Very powerful. Xeono is one of them."

Kioni's mouth dropped open in shock and his eyes screamed in disbelief. "Xe... Xeono?"

"The one," Kyne replied. "We never got to it though before everything else went awry."

"How do you tell if it's a Relic? How did you know Xeono was?"

"The Light told me about Xeono, but they also bare his symbol. The silver serpent biting its tail."

Kioni's eyes widened as a thought of realization seemed to seep into his being. "Wait one second Kyne," and he leapt to his feet and dashed over to his mismatched items. Throwing a few pieces around, he eventually withdrew a small pouch and withdrew a simple matte cloth.

Returning he handed it to Kyne.

"Is this one?"

Kyne looked at it in confusion before turning it over and to his astonishment he saw the silver serpent upon the fabric. Its luster was gone, faded away.

"It is," gasped Kyne. "How did you... How did you find it?"

"I came across it while I was working with the shades. It was given..."

"The Shades!" interrupted Kyne. "You were part of them? How could... How did you manage that?"

"You're not the only talented one Kyne," smirked Kioni.

"I wasn't meaning that as a compliment," replied Kyne flatly. "Not a compliment at all. The Shades are nefarious and wild. Killing and murdering, most people think of them as a legend. Even I didn't know they actually were real."

"Not just murderers," said Kioni. "We protect our people from unseen threats."

Kyne shook his head. "Anyways, continue."

"I came across it working with the Shades," he said drawing out the final word and smirking. "It lets you change your form to whoever you wish it to be."

"So, like an illusion spell?"

"Without the use of aura and a more perfect form. It leaves no trace."

"That's a very dangerous weapon, could topple nations," muttered Kyne.

"Indeed, until it lost all of its power. It worked for a bit after The Falling but each time it struggled more and more until one day it just stopped working."

"Sounds like my bag. It used so much aura to hold the space it ran out in minutes."

"You can have it," Kioni gestured to the cloth. "It doesn't serve any purpose to me anyways."

Kyne dropped his gaze to the faded cloth and then back to his friend before he shook his head. "No, it is yours. I am no longer in need of the Relics, so you hold on to it, at least for now." He handed Kioni the cloth. "All I really want is my sword back."

"Do you have any idea where it could be?"

"The Gaeilian that I interrogated spoke of the man being sent towards the coast but..."

"But what?"

"I don't really know if I believe that. I couldn't feel any treachery from the man, but he also wasn't very confident. All he said was he would think Dawngôr would be his best bet."

"That's pretty far just for a blade Kyne, halfway across the country."

"Not just a blade Kioni," retorted Kyne. "A gift from the Light himself. That blade is the most prized possession I own, and it would dishonor him if I were to give up on it."

"You're talking about well over a thousand miles to get there. On a horse pushing it to its limit it would easily take at least a month.

The Legend of Kyne: Chronocide

That's assuming you have a good path to travel. I have most of the cataclysm zones mapped out," and he swung his body over the bedroll and pulled out a scroll. Unrolling it Kyne saw it to be an old map of Kydrëa with large colored swathes marked across its surface. Patches came together in curved oblong shapes and lines that almost resembled clouds. "See," and Kioni pointed to a spot on the map where the Riigar mountains touched the forest just north of the Tsoran mountain range.

Kyne looked at it for a moment, seeing an orange and white section coming together right where Kioni was touching. Following a straight line, he saw that they would cross a few different zones just to reach Alakyne which would be about the halfway mark. He shuddered as he saw the dark blue dotted area that he knew marked the never-ending rain.

"I know it will be long and hard but it's the only thing that I can do right now. All I want to do is get my blade and find a way to kill that draconic monster hidden within Alakyne's citadel."

"Oh, I see," muttered Kioni and he rolled the map up. "So, you've seen the abomination and think that your blade might actually be able to kill it?"

"It's worth a shot."

"That's a suicide mission."

"No one said you had to come," Kyne snorted. "I can get there on my own."

"You haven't changed in the slightest Kyne."

"It seems though that you have in your *aged* years."

"Ouch," Kioni said, mocking a hurt expression. "No, I have just grown more cautious. Learned after seeing people murdered and eaten to know to not go anywhere near Alakyne."

They were silent for a long time. Kyne could feel the cave's temperature had risen but was still comfortable enough that it wasn't inconvenient.

"Do you think killing him could undo all of this?" asked Kioni suddenly.

"No idea but it's the only thing I can think of doing."

"If there is even a remote chance then I'll come with you." Withdrawing the map again, he explained to Kyne the best possible route to get to Dawngôr. "Traversing along the barriers is usually the most feasible path except for when a frozen area meets water. That helps no one. Our best bet would be to travel south, following the border of the desert zone until we come to where the wind meets the snow. We can continue on this path further south until we eventually leave the forest. From there it will be switching back and forth a few times in an area where multiple zones meet before we get to the farmland. Thats where we will be able to replenish the provisions before continuing on past Alakyne and then to Dawngôr.

  Our best bet is to travel when it's safest. Desert travel is done at night, and we sleep during the day in the most secluded area we can find. We will plan on leaving tonight, if you can make it with your leg."

  Kyne looked down at the bloody rag across his calf. It had dried and had formed a thick clotted scab.

  "Here," and Kioni withdrew some medicinal ointment and another strip of cloth. After prying it off, to Kyne's annoyance and pain, it revealed the bruised and punctured flesh where the dog had bitten him. It oozed a bit of blood after the bandage had been removed but not much. Kioni globbed a chunk of ointment into each of the wounds which stung badly but Kyne didn't complain, he only winced. Kioni then wrapped it tightly before putting the ointment away.

  "Tonight, we leave."

  "Tonight," Kyne returned, and they laid down and tried to get some sleep.

65. Searching for the Dawn

They left that night, loading the horses up just as the sun set with all of Kioni's things and then they were off, traveling south. They skirted far around the slave camp, away from any scents the dogs could pick up before coming back to the barrier with the frozen wasteland. They traveled all day; Kioni's horses were very conditioned in travel and Kyne was pleased with the distance and endurance they had in them.

As the streaks of orange signaled the rising sun, they stopped under a denser section of the dead trees. Lining up some branches for more shade, eventually they had a spot large enough for both of them as well as the horses to lay beneath. One final thing before they slept, Kioni dug a large hole right on the border of the barrier and with a few sweeps of his arms pulled a large clump of snow into it. He did it a few times and then he returned to the shade just as the sun came over the horizon.

Kyne watched as the snowy piles quickly started to sweat and then he understood what Kioni was doing. Melting the snow so the horses could drink even a little before the next day.

Each night they traveled south, the barrier curving slightly west until they reached a different zone. The traveling was hard but manageable, each day managing to sleep away the hot sunny day. Once they made it to the wind though they tried to sleep when it was dark, traveling easier through the dust with a little light to see.

Nearly a week had passed by the time they made it out of the dead forest and into the farmland. It was littered with Kydrëan slaves, each tilling the fields or watering the crops as Dominion sentinels patrolled and whipped.

The field lined up right next to where the desert region met the rain. Great irrigation ditches had been carved, guiding the water onto the fields where the leafy green of vegetation grew. Even with the hot air, the constant supply of water kept the plants alive enough to grow, which in turn kept the humans alive. Even to Kyne's shock he saw a few animals along the border, darting between the live trees and vegetation that could survive there.

They hid along the outskirts, their horses out of view. In the evening when the slaves were corralled up and led back to their pen a distance away, they snuck into the field, uprooting dozens of potatoes and other root vegetables that had been grown. Collecting as much as they could, their packs filled to the brim, they trekked back towards their horses.

Kyne was walking much better, but his leg still hurt. Luckily the ointment Kioni had given him kept it from becoming infected and the bruising had yellowed. As he hooked the loaded pack upon the saddle, he saw Kioni do the same and as if they had thought the same thing, they traveled on, away from the farms for nearly an hour into dusk before they stopped to sleep.

It was frigid as they bundled up against the bitter chill of the wind. The water in their pouches had long since frozen and the fur on the pelts they wore were covered with frost. Kyne patted the horse beneath him and felt the crunch of ice against the blanket that was draped over the animal's body. They had tried their best to bundle them up and it seemed to be working well enough. The snow was nearly two feet deep, and it had greatly slowed their progress, but the walking seemed to keep the horses warm enough.

Alakyne's dark silhouette was on the horizon, partially obscured by foggy clouds. No snow fell currently but that did little to protect them from the eternal cold. Oh, how badly Kyne wanted to use the aural stones Kioni had amassed to warm himself, but he couldn't. There were a lot, but he could eat through them so fast. They had to use them for life or death only. The only time he had seen so far was to make the fires that kept them alive each night.

Kyne wanted so badly to go get the Ouroboros Bag. He could just make out the clump of trees where he knew it lay hidden, but it wouldn't do him any good. Its weight was inconceivable, and he couldn't do anything about it.

The Legend of Kyne: Chronocide

On they traveled, day by day, night by night. It took them thirty-six more days to make it to Dawngôr. They were exhausted, irritated, and hungry. The food they had would still last them a few days, but vegetables only helped so much. At one point Kioni nearly shot a bird they had found but it narrowly escaped.

Kyne's mouth watered at the thought of the bird that night as they sat next to the fire, the light obscured by the hills they laid between. They had followed the Ta'Gor river for days now and had finally come to Dawngôr. The river had long since either dried up or frozen completely creating long skinny lakes of ice or gorges of dried silt.

The city had remained mostly how it had once been, lying on Kydrëa's western coast, it had managed some luck as a desert area and a flooded one met right upon its outskirts. The city had nearly a foot of constant water flooding its lower streets and cellars, but the hot sun above kept everything else dry. Outside he had seen farmland being tilled by more slaves but now they were all asleep, the only thing that had been visible were the glowing torches illuminating the city before they had been obscured by the hills.

"If he is still a slave trapper then why would he be here if there are so many people?"

"No idea," murmured Kioni. "Might be trapping more slaves for the farms or to keep the city clean. If he's here though we shall find him. It's not every day that you see a Kydrëan working with Gaeilians."

The following morning, they left the horses behind, sneaking through the hills a few miles until they reached the farmland. They observed them for a few hours, looking at all the sentinels but eventually they gave up and continued on.

"Are you sure the horses will be ok?"

"They are very trained, and they are not dumb. They will stay near the barrier. It's the only place where they can get water and that the crops can grow."

Traveling low and hidden, they periodically saw glimpses of the city as it flashed between hills. It grew closer but it was nearly the end of the day by the time they had reached its walls.

"I think we should wait until the day and scout some more," said Kioni.

The Legend of Kyne: Chronocide

"I think we should capture a sentinel and interrogate him about the whereabouts of the Kydrëan."

"And then do what with him when we are done? Kill him?"

"If I need to."

"That would be unwise. His death would cause enough commotion to make our job harder," Kioni snorted. "You of all people should know that."

Kyne did and he said it more of a joke but was surprised to see Kioni had taken him seriously. He shook his head. "We can keep scouting." maybe we will see him."

And they did the following day. They hid near the entrance of the city, the main road raised up with wooden planks as the tide of water continued flowing. They kept eyeing everyone who passed but not one of them was the Kydrëan. Night soon found them, and Kyne was now beyond frustrated.

"We need to scout in the city," he argued. "That's where we will be able to find if he's there."

"That's suicide."

"You say everything is suicide," snapped Kyne. "I'll just go then."

"No, we go together," snapped Kioni back at him. "Let's scout a little longer. A few more days before we do anything hasty."

That night Kioni slept but Kyne did not. After a few hours, once the older man had started snoring Kyne crept away, dashing from their cover into the city beyond. In his pocket he clutched two ruby aural stones, much more powerful than the amber ones he had mined before. He needed to find Aurora and he was willing to risk them."

Dashing along the outer stone wall of the city, the grey mortar chipped between the bricks, he drew towards the entrance. He suddenly pinned up against the wall as voices were heard above him. A quick glance and he saw two patrolling sentinels above on the walkway, lanterns clutched in their hands.

He held his breath, hoping they wouldn't spot him and as their voices faded away, he relaxed a little. He didn't know Dawngôr well, having only been there a few times but he could picture the entrance to the city and the stone adornments near it that peaked off the wall.

The Legend of Kyne: Chronocide

He could use them!

Coming to them, he hooked his fingers upon the warm stone and began hauling himself up. Pushing himself further and further, he didn't look down, he just focused on what was in front of him. Soon he was near the top and peeking his head up, noticed the two patrolling guards from a few dozen feet away walking in a pool of orange light. Their backs were turned and with a quiet grunt, he hauled himself up and dashed down the walkway following after them.

It was mere wooden planks, four feet across and just large enough for two people to walk side by side. Below it he could only see the dark of the ground far below. The wall was much smaller than Alakyne's. No hallways that led to its depths and no ballistae had been mounted upon its towers.

He could see a spot that he could hide, up ahead where the support structure came out from below the walkway and arching up along the inner side of it. The sentinels ahead of him hadn't heard his steps or the faint creaking of the wood as he sprinted down its length heading towards the hiding spot.

Voices were heard up ahead and he noticed the patrolling guards had stopped their walking. Having come to the end of their patrol route, the duo began to turn around, returning the way they had come. Right into the path of Kyne!

He could try and fight them, but if they were heard, it would draw too much attention and ruin his chances permanently. He had no other choice!

Sliding to the ground, he swung his legs over the edge and jerked his body after it. He felt the panic of falling but just as his fingers came to the edge of the wooden planks, he felt them hold firm. There he hung, still as a sleeping bat as the lantern up above swung around as the guards began to walk back.

He looked down to see the thirty-foot drop to the ground below. The dark shapes of roofs nearby but far out of reach. He could hear their voices now as they had turned in his direction. Faint but growing stronger. They would see him just as they passed. He knew full well the human tendency to look down. He had to get underneath the walkway.

Nearly ten feet down the length he could make out the

support beam and a crevasse in which he could sit in. Scurrying as fast as he could, he shuffled his hands down the walkway as he hung. The sentinels were close but just before they cast him in the orange light, he swung his legs up and hooked them around the support beam. Releasing his grip, he brought his body underneath and held his breath as he lay perched between the joint in the wood. The y shaped structure was small, and he was cramped tight in the crook as he held his breath.

The creaking of wood sounded, and he felt a bit of dust fall on his face as the sentinel walked above him. The orange light peered through the cracks, streaking like ribbons as they flashed in and out of view.

Kyne leaned back, trying to make himself smaller, fearful that they might notice him through the separations in the wooden planks.

A loud crack sounded as a piece of the support beam peeled off under Kyne's weight. He nearly gasped and fumbled for a hold as his whole body threatened to fall backwards to the ground far below.

The sentinels stopped their walking immediately and Kyne saw the lantern light swing back towards his location.

"What was that?"

"Sounds like you broke something on the walkway. I've always said you were growing fat and now we have proof."

"Oh, shut up, I wasn't even by where it was, see look. The sound was over here," and the lanterns light blazed above Kyne. He felt his pulse begin to race and he fumbled for the small dagger at his waist as well as the aural stones. He might have to use them after all.

"Wait what's that? It looks like something underneath us," murmured the sentinel and Kyne watched a shadowy figure above begin to stoop down.

He had to use the aura. It was his only option.

Suddenly two grunts in quick succession were heard followed by thumps as the sentinel's bodies slumped to the ground. The walkway quivered from the blow, threatening to break the weakened structure.

"Get up here Kyne!" hissed Kioni's voice and in moments Kyne had swung around the beam and clambered up. A hooded figure crouched nearby two silhouetted bodies. The dark circle of blood spreading around them had begun to seep through the cracks and dripped to the ground far below.

The Legend of Kyne: Chronocide

"How did you find me?"

"I never was asleep. You still came even though I said not to."

Kyne tightened his lips together in irritation. "I told you I wanted to."

"And you risked everything."

"There's no going back now that you killed the guards. They will find them eventually."

"So now you are blaming me for this?" retorted Kioni. "You were the one about to be caught."

"I was going to conceal myself with aura."

"How was I supposed to know that?" Kioni sighed. "Still stubborn as always."

Kyne nodded. "Yep. Are you coming with me?"

Before Kioni could respond a gurgled cough sounded and a sentinel shuddered and writhed. The two were upon him in a flash, covering his mouth to prevent any sound from escaping.

"Wait," said Kyne, just as Kioni had risen his blood stained kamas. "Let's see if we can get him to tell us anything."

"He's not going to," Kioni snorted. "What's in it for him?"

Kyne eyed the man and could see his neck squirting blood from where Kioni had sliced clean through it.

"Where is the Kydrëan slave trapper," Kyne said as he grabbed the mouth of the man and turned so they were face to face. The sentinel was dying and could hardly focus on anything except that fact.

"If you tell me I'll save you."

The man's eyes were wide, as if he didn't understand. He coughed and sputtered again, his movements growing weaker. Kyne repeated himself more aggressively this time and the man seemed to understand, shaking his head as he clutched at his bleeding neck.

Touching the aural stone, Kyne used its power to mend the man's neck, just enough to stop the bleeding but not wasting the aura.

As the spurting ceased Kyne said his question to the man again.

"Where is the Kydrëan slave trapper?"

The sentinel spit blood from his mouth and he shuddered. His head began to drop back to the wood in a bouncing pattern signaling weakness and loss of consciousness.

The Legend of Kyne: Chronocide

"Tell me!" hissed Kyne and the man muttered one word. "Tavern."

Then he slumped over, unconscious or dead Kyne wasn't sure but with the amount of blood that soaked the ground Kyne assumed either way he would be dead eventually.

Standing up, he took a step away and felt the sticky suction of the blood on his boot accompanied by the slurp as it was raised.

"Tavern," Kyne repeated, and he looked at Kioni.

"Don't look at me, I don't know of any tavern. I haven't been here in decades."

Kyne scanned the city around him, the orange torchlight of patrolling sentinels scattered around. It would take at least an hour before the other guards would switch shifts. Then they would find the bodies. They had to move quickly.

Out in the city, Kyne noticed a few different areas spaced around with more lights than the rest. To him they looked to be places that had something happening.

Pointing to the nearest one, Kioni nodded at Kyne, and they ran down the walkway coming towards a ladder. The wooden rungs were warm under Kyne's hands as he descended. No splinters of wood pierced his hand for they were smooth and worn from years of thousands of climbs.

The ground felt solid as Kyne leapt the short distance, the impact jarring his knees more than he liked. He was so much weaker than he once was, returned back to a simple human. A thump next to him signaled Kioni and they were off through the city streets. Most were completely deserted and void of life. Occasionally a stray cat was seen but its dark shape was easy to miss as it vanished in the shadows of an alley.

Lights nearby caught his attention, and they watched as a group of sentinels without their armor walked out of a building. Their speech was slurred and their walking uncoordinated as they stumbled through the streets. There were three of them, but none looked like the Kydrëan.

As they ventured on, Smells of meat drifted in the air and voices were heard. Kyne peaked through a window to see a few more people in the building, drinks spread out across the bar and scraps of

The Legend of Kyne: Chronocide

food still left on plates. In the corner, he could make out two females sitting upon the lap of someone and then Kyne saw it. The golden eyes and the face of the Kydrëan he wanted.

His blood began to boil as he searched madly with his eyes, spotting his sword hidden beneath one of the girls upon the man's waist. The black leather was his, he was certain.

Their giggling drew Kyne's gaze back up and he watched as one girl held some fruit up by a vine in which the other girl as well as the Kydrëan male took a bite. As they chewed, more giggling came from the girls and then the Kydrëan kissed both girls, one right after another to Kyne's disgust.

He shuddered at the thought but to his satisfaction saw the man gesture for the girls to get off him.

"I need to take a piss darlings," he muttered, his voice slightly slurred. "Don't wait for me though," and he chuckled as he made his way towards the doorway.

Kyne slid over out of sight with Kioni following him and watched as the door opened up and the man stepped outside.

This will be easy with a two on one, Kyne sneered in his mind. Suddenly more voices were heard, and another larger man stepped out after the Kydrëan. This man was enormous, towering easily a head over both Kyne and Kioni and brandishing a long steel war hammer.

"Master Emrys," the man called to which the Kydrëan grunted without looking at him. He had already managed to pull down his pants and was relieving himself on the side of the building. "You pay me to protect you, so I am doing that. Those girls wish to rob you."

"Obviously," he muttered as he finished. "That's why I robbed them first," and he chuckled lifting up his hand revealing a small silver bracelet."

"Well done," replied the man. "Are we to return to our quarters then?"

"Indeed," Emrys replied calmly, his voice more stable. "After we figure out why some unwanted visitors are spying on us."

As if on cue, the large behemoth of a man swung his hammer straight for the wooden boxes the two were hiding behind. A massive crash and splinters rained down upon the ground as they narrowly avoided the strike.

The Legend of Kyne: Chronocide

"I thought I could sense someone there," muttered Emrys and he turned to face them, the larger man stepping in front of him. "Why do you spy upon me?"

"Because I want what you stole!" roared Kyne.

The man gave a confused flabbergasted look and threw a side glance at his companion before returning his gaze to Kyne.

"Boy, I steal a lot of things. You'll have to be more specific. Was it some jewelry, or a horse, maybe even a girl?"

"It was my sword!" Kyne fumed and he pointed at the blade. "Give it back and I will let you live."

Emrys looked first at the blade and then back up at Kyne. He squinted for a moment, trying to discern features in the dark and then his eyes widened, and a grin spread across his face.

"How did you get here boy? I do remember you. Easy enough to take out, I thought you would still be in that mining camp I left you at."

"Give me my sword!"

"That is not going to happen," and he sighed as he reached down and drew the blade. The silvery feather sparkling in the dim light. "I have grown fond of it, and I do not wish to part. It is no longer your sword so you can beat it if you know what's best for you."

Kyne took a step forward, withdrawing his hand from his pocket, a ruby red aural stone clutched tightly in his grip. "I'll ask you one last time."

"Take him out," Emrys ordered and fast as lightning the massive man leapt forward, swinging his hammer over his head. In a flash he brought it down upon the ground causing the stone to crack just as Kyne narrowly dodged it.

Kioni met the man with his kamas, and a fierce duel erupted as he evaded swings before clawing towards the man. Unable to shorten the distance, they clashed again and again.

A flash of aura flew from Kyne, rocketing towards Emrys but just before it hit him, he flicked his hand and it arced away. Chuckling the Kydrëan withdrew a sapphire blue aural stone and smiled again.

"I am surprised that you know aura boy. Well, not really actually. That explains how you managed to escape. I, however, have spent years training in aura as I trapped countless Kydrëans. You might be proficient, but I am sheer talent."

A golden flash came from the man and Kyne twisted over his shoulder. The hum of aura whizzed past his ear, and it made his skin tingle from the force.

This man was proving to be more difficult that Kyne had initially expected. He didn't want to use all of his aura dealing with him. He needed help.

A quick glance towards Kioni and then the ground speared up underneath the large man as Kyne forced his aura into the earth. A cry of pain came from the man as it slammed into his chest, knocking him off balance before Kioni was upon him.

Another flash of gold came from the Kydrëan and this one scraped Kyne's arm. Burning fire flew through his mind at contact with the aura and he gritted his teeth. Turning around, he was expecting another attack, but his opponent was frozen.

Emrys was staring at the dead bodyguard and then looked back on Kyne with rage.

A soundless spell came from the man's lips and then Kyne felt his body go rigid as he was bound by the aura. He fought hard but it was too strong, and he could feel the aura from his stones fading fast.

Emrys had begun running towards him, Aurora clutched in his hand. The spell was too strong, and Kyne knew Emrys's own stone had much more stored aura than the two he held. Kioni was too far away; he wouldn't be able to help him.

Images of Auriel flashed in his mind, her beautiful smile and piercing eyes, eyes he would never again get to see.

Emrys stopped just before Kyne with the feather blade held an inch from his neck. The cold smile that spread across his face sent chills down Kyne's spine. A smile of someone who cared about nothing. "I am going to kill you first, then I'll kill your friend. Then I am going to go back in the tavern with those girls and enjoy the rest of my night. You mean nothing to me boy. Just a cocky arrogant slave who learned one too many magic words and thought they could rule the world.

Kyne felt Aurora touch his skin. The blade like barbs of the feather drew blood immediately as it was held there for a long moment. Tears were in Kyne's eyes.

A strange tingle was felt from his aural stones and without any other thought, he let it flow. The power was fast, flowing up through his bound body to his neck where it touched the feather blade.

Immediately the silver feather began to glow a soft white light as its energy was returned and then Kyne smiled back at the man as he realized what was going to happen.

"What have you... Ahh!" he screamed, and the blade was dropped to the floor. The spell binding Kyne ended, and he watched as the man's hand blistered, and he screamed again and again about shadowy monster around him. Stumbling backwards, batting the air wildly, he started to claw violently at his pretty face. Carving thick bloody fissures into its surface with his long nails. Dropping to his knees, he continued to claw, drawing more and more blood before he finally started to slam his head upon the stone ground. It took three hard hits before he slowed and then two more. Then he slumped over, dead.

"What happened?" gasped Kioni as he came upon Kyne, his breath heavy and blood dripping from his kamas.

Kyne stooped down and grabbed his sword, feeling the immediate calming it had upon him. "Don't touch my sword. Anyone I deem not an ally will be driven insane."

*   *   *

66. The Fourth

Auriel shuddered as the thing coughed violently as it lay upon the floor. Its pale skin was littered with blisters and scars exposed to the air except for a few thin pieces of dark cloth tied upon its waist. Its fingers were sickly and dark, as if stained from blood and tar and adorned with fingernails that came to a point more like claws.

It convulsed, coughing again before it struggled to its knees, then with a shaking stand it rose. Its back was turned to them, hairless and disgusting, Auriel pulled the kids behind her, and she drew her emerald orichite blade. The dark sky outside the window was void of movement and as a breeze rolled through the crack in the opening, it seemed to whistle and almost laugh at them.

A deep pressure was felt around them, depressing their emotions and Auriel could feel nausea forming in her abdomen as the creature shifted its stance, tracing its gaze upon the stone wall. It hadn't noticed them yet, but she had a feeling she knew what it was.

The orange light from the lantern at the bedside table flickered and as if on cue, a low groaning drone came from the creature as it turned towards them. It bore no hair upon its face, bald as an old decrepit man. Its eyes were dark and black and as they rested upon them, it formed a hideous grin. Its mouth was adorned with yellowed teeth, each sharp as a human canine tooth and stained dark.

It groaned again, this time rising in pitch as it turned to more of a shriek and then it dashed forward towards Auriel, arms outstretched.

Swinging her blade up and twisting towards the side, she brought it through the wraith's wrists, severing its hands off. In one fluid motion, Auriel twisted around as the creature stumbled forward and with her aura, ripped it off its feet, pulling it rapidly back and slamming it into the wall where it slumped over.

The Legend of Kyne: Chronocide

The children cried out in shock, but Auriel waved them off, turning towards the creature and to no shock, she watched it twitch and crawl to its feet. Its wrists dripped thick globs of blood to the ground where they pooled in a sticky mess. Taking a few steps forward, the wraith left red prints of its bare feet, the blood slurping with each step as it was pulled up in sticky strands.

It screeched again and ran towards them, but Auriel held firm, using her aura to bind the creature, freezing it in place. She could feel its strength, feel the lust for her aura and for her soul as it clapped its jaws at her.

"The Relic!" she called, not keeping her eyes off the creature for fear of it breaking loose and in moments, Aria was next to her holding it.

"What do I do?" she screamed in fright as she stared at the wraith as it fought against Auriel's hold. The princess could feel her aura rapidly draining and she gritted her teeth shaking her head. She had no idea what to do with it.

"Touch it to the thing!" shouted Alakyne but Aria hesitated, staring at the wraith with eyes full of fear. She looked back at Alakyne whose eyes were wide at her. He seemed to be shouting but all sound was drowned out as she looked back at the wraith. Her fear was impeding her movements, hovering over her like a dark cloud as she stared the beast down. Time seemed to slow, and she could feel each heartbeat thumping in her neck. In her hand, she clenched the Relic tightly and then she glanced at Auriel who was focused upon her task. Beads of sweat rolled down the Riel's cheeks and she looked to be exhausted from holding it back.

Taking a staggering step forward, Aria watched the wraith's eyes dart towards her, and it started to shake violently as it tried to force against Auriel's spell with everything it had.

"Aria do it!"

Alakyne's voice erupted behind her and before she knew what she was doing, she was approaching the wraith, the Relic outstretched in her hand. Bringing it to the creature, she touched it to the ouroboros that lay emblazoned upon its surface and in a bright white flash, the creature vanished, leaving the Relic back in its dormant and darkened state.

The Legend of Kyne: Chronocide

Auriel gasped as the spell was ended and she slumped over, sitting upon the bed. Her hands were placed upon her knees as she held her body up and she panted deeply.

"Are you ok?" Aria asked and she ran toward her.

"I'm fine, just tired," she chuckled softly. "Holding it like that was much more difficult than I thought it would be."

"What was it?" whispered Alakyne and he stood next to his sister.

"I think it was a wraith," Auriel sighed. "One of the great calamities of our world."

"Wraith?" they both asked simultaneously.

"It's what was fought long ago by all the races. Decrepit things that suck souls out of people. Somehow one was trapped in that thing."

"How did you know how to use it Alakyne?" asked Aria, turning towards him.

"I just felt it," he stammered taking a step back as the two women stared at him in shock. "It just seemed to be the right thing to do."

"Do you know what it is?" Auriel asked and she reached out and Aria placed it in her hand. Turning it over, she eyed all the sides, each void of the strange markings.

"I think it traps things inside," he started but Aria gasped in annoyance.

"Obviously it does that," she said furrowing her brow.

"But I think it could trap them permanently inside. I don't know how else to explain it, but I think that thing has been trapped in there for a very long time, lifetimes long Aria."

"If it's a Relic I would expect nothing less, a Relic of Containment," Auriel muttered. "That bag you two were in for your training is also a Relic. In my time my husband owns the bag."

They both stayed silent, looking first at her and then at the object.

"So, you think time might flow differently in the container then?" whispered Aria.

"Maybe?" Auriel thought. "But there is no way to know. I don't want to let that thing out again it's much too dangerous."

As she put the Relic of Containment down upon the

The Legend of Kyne: Chronocide

nightstand and the minutes waned on, they all started to feel a little calmer. Some keep guards came and checked on them soon after due to the commotion, but Auriel waved them away saying they had been training.

"What is going to happen? How long are we going to stay here?" asked Aria as they all lay upon their beds, the lantern extinguished and the room dark.

"I don't know," Auriel responded. "I really don't know."

67. The Sweetness of a Pastry

"How many Relics are there?" asked Alakyne as they all walked through the courtyard the following morning. They had just been out to see Ni'Bara who just returned from a hunt and his concern for the interaction with the wraith had been nearly catastrophic.

"Well twelve," Auriel started recalling what she had been told. "In my time there is a thirteenth that is given but that is all I can say."

"Given by who?" Alakyne asked.

"The Light, the god of our world," Auriel said without breaking her stride. She wanted to teach them the least amount of lore possible, but this knowledge contained nothing of the future, so she thought it to be alright. "He gifted twelve relics of immense power to each of the different races to further their growth."

She could tell he was not satisfied with her answer, but she said no more. He asked about the races to which she explained it, briefly flashing her ears and they nodded, having noticed them when they first met.

She led them to the feasting hall where they were to eat the first meal of the day. Tiernyn had sent a messenger to them indicating this and that Alakyne was to be tested by him later that day. She had read the letter twice over, analyzing its contents before they had made their way here. A few other residents of the keep were present, eating their meals, but it remained mostly empty.

Auriel was on edge; she had been since she had first stepped foot in this place, and it only seemed to worsen the longer she stayed. Without letting them notice, she used her aura to sense their food for poison as she had before and when she was satisfied, began to eat herself.

As they finished, Tira soon joined them, the woman's black hair pulled up in a tight bun revealing her ears with her glasses tucked tight behind them. Her face bore a look of concern but before Auriel could ask, she started.

"Garet is dead. He was found this morning in his room, stiff as a board."

"What caused it?" Auriel asked, knowing the answer herself.

"I'm not certain but to me it seemed almost like he had been poisoned. I had heard of a recent illness erupting out in the city, people falling gravely ill as if a plague has begun and I initially assumed him to be part of that, that is why he was quarantined. I do not think that to be the case now however."

Clattering of dishes sounded, and they all looked to see trays of deserts being placed upon a table for all of those in the room to partake. Alakyne eyed them with a devilish grin, but his sister turned back towards Tira, intrigued with what she was saying.

Before she could continue, Auriel gestured for them to leave which Alakyne leapt up, dashing towards the pastries and cakes. Aria hesitated but the look she received made her moan and she turned around, following her brother.

"He was poisoned," Auriel said as they were out of earshot.

"How do you know? Wait did you..."

"No, it wasn't me, well not directly," Auriel started and Tira showed a look of concern. "At the dinner the other night when we first arrived, how weird they were being about the wine. I felt off so without anyone noticing I switched Alakyne's and Garet's."

"They were trying to poison Alakyne!" she gasped, and Auriel placed a finger to her lips signaling her to be quieter. "You're certain?" she whispered feverishly, and she leaned in closer.

"I am quite certain. What you have just told me screams validity."

"Why didn't you tell me this sooner?" asked Tira.

"I wasn't sure you could be trusted either. Remember, it was not that long ago that you tried to kill me and kidnapped the children."

Tira paused for a moment, a look of hurt flashing into sight before vanishing. "I see your reasoning. If I were you, I probably would've done the same thing Auriel. Now what else do you know about this?"

"Only that someone doesn't want Alakyne to live but I have a feeling I know who it is."

"Tiernyn?"

Auriel nodded and Tira pursed her lips in a look of thought. "If this is true then it might be wise for us to leave. We can return here in a few years once Alakyne is able to defend himself more properly."

Auriel nodded, the thought intriguing to her. She had come to this city in hopes of finding a way home but the longer they stayed the further that hope seemed to sink into the ground. Ni'Bara didn't like it much either. He wasn't able to even walk through the city and explore what this time had to offer. He was nearly trapped in that courtyard, sleeping the days away.

"When should we leave?" the Riel asked quickly, noticing the children were on their way back to the table, plates loaded high with desserts.

"I think tomorrow," Tira stated. "I want to see what Tiernyn has to say about him. Once that is done, we can leave early on before dawn."

Alakyne sat down, already his mouth was stuffed full of food, sugary syrup lacing his lips. Auriel was petrified when she saw the boy but luckily she sensed no poisons within them and they all ate. Auriel wasn't that hungry but after tasting the delicate sweetness, she tore at it. Fruity juices erupted in her mouth causing her eyes to roll in delight and she scarfed the pastry down in seconds.

Eyeing the children, Aria seemingly distracted by the delicious deserts and forgetting their conversation earlier, Auriel smiled. She felt better knowing that they were going to leave soon. Knowing that the kids would be safer made it easier for her and Ni'Bara to eventually leave them behind in hopes of finding a way back home.

Tira left them shortly after, vanishing deeper into the keep and Auriel ventured down the halls in hopes of exploring a bit more. Rounding a corner, they were shocked to see Tiernyn approaching, two sorcerers on either side and all three speaking quickly to one another.

Upon seeing Auriel, Tiernyn's face alighted with a smile, and he waved the sorcerers away. As they passed, Auriel looked to her side, noticing one of the sorcerers eyeing Alakyne through the opening in his hood.

"My sweet Auriel," he boomed drawing her attention back to him. "The morning beauty reminded me such of yours that I hoped to see you. If I may ask," he started but Auriel cut him off.

"Once again Tiernyn I am taken. Please stop your advances."

"Oh Auriel," he chuckled. "I am afraid I cannot do that. I am captivated by your beauty, and it is my goal in this life to make you mine."

"It's not going to happen," she replied flatly.

"And yet your husband is not here," he replied in a darker tone. Eyeing the children for a moment, he reached up and rubbed his wrist.

"And if he was here, you probably wouldn't be alive," Auriel said menacingly.

Her words took Tiernyn aback for a moment and then he chuckled, his laughter booming down the hallway. Standing taller, he looked down upon her for a long moment.

"I think you forget who I am Auriel. This world has no equal to me, not you, not your dragon, and certainly not your so-called husband."

The air seemed to tremble as he flexed his aura, allowing Auriel to feel the hint of his power. She was indeed shocked, her hairs tingling upon the back of her neck as bumps formed upon her skin. He seemed to glow as he emanated his presence upon them for a long moment before it ceased, and he took a step back.

"You are indeed powerful," Auriel said, and her words seemed to satisfy Tiernyn causing his dark look to return to a much more pleasant one. She didn't press on, nervous of what his rage would lead to.

"How about I take you upon a tour of the keep," he said lightly to which she shook her head. "I insist," he said in a darker tone and Auriel could sense the danger in his voice. Eyeing the kids for a moment, she could feel their fear at his words. She knew she couldn't turn him down again, for fear of retaliation. At least his way she would be able to watch him more closely and keep an eye on the children at the same time.

The Legend of Kyne: Chronocide

"Alright," she said.

His composure dramatically shifted as he got his way, and he flashed another smile turning upon his heel. "We shall begin here, near to my own study," and he started off in a brisk walk followed shortly by the three of them.

He led them down a few hallways, showing different rooms and speaking about the history of the keep before he finally came to a double door. "This is my study," he started, and he eyed Auriel with a grin. "It is where I personally reside and where I sleep," he said without taking his eyes off of her. The tension in his stare was uncomfortable but Auriel held firm and he pushed the door open revealing a great room inside.

A table sat on one side adorned with scrolls and other objects of interest. Another room lay at its back and Auriel could just make out the edge of an ornate bed with posts and a high canopy.

He showed them a few things, items of aural importance but none were noteworthy to Auriel. To her he seemed to just be showing off in hopes of intriguing her.

"Your room is huge," gasped Alakyne causing Tiernyn to stop his movement and he turned slowly towards the boy.

"Indeed," he said with a smile that looked strained. "Biggest in the whole keep."

"Shouldn't the lord have the largest room?" Aria asked. "Speaking of which I haven't even seen him."

"He stays in his room most days, high up on the top floor. He leaves the day-to-day things run by me," Tiernyn said, and he put the object in his hand back down upon the table. "Shall we continue," and he walked out of the room, pausing in the doorway until the others had exited. Waving his hand, it shut softly, and he smiled at Auriel.

He led them down the hallway towards another room and as they entered, they were shocked to find the kitchens, littered with dozens of servants all tending large pots or rolling out dough. Flames lay in different holes dug into the ground heating up the contents of the pots that lay above them as steam rose up in great plumes.

Alakyne was intrigued by each and every item of food that was being made. Auriel could tell in his face that he yearned for it, the taste of everything.

The Legend of Kyne: Chronocide

As Tiernyn led them on, Alakyne lingered for a moment and then was called back coming reluctantly. Two more rooms were entered with the final one being a place for aura. Sorcerers were scattered around, scribbling on notes or forming different objects with their aura. The room was large, similar to Tiernyn's own and its walls were lined with tapestries and maps of many different regions. Upon seeing them accompanied by Tiernyn, the half dozen sorcerers that were present seemed to stop and stare in disbelief. A long awkward moment of silence followed, and Auriel saw Tiernyn smiling wickedly at them all. Her skin crawled at his grin and as she looked back towards the sorcerers as they traveled on, she saw them start to return to what they were doing.

What is he up to? she thought as he led them through the room, eyeing each thing individually. *At first, I thought he was showing off but now I wonder if he is more likely showing us the power he holds.* They continued on for a few minutes before a loud boom sounded shaking the keep.

Whipping around, to her horror, Auriel saw the children were gone and her heart began to race.

Dashing out of the room, she took off down the hallway toward the source of the explosion. Another soon followed and she could see it was coming from the kitchen. Ripping around the corner, she gasped at the sight before her. Aria stood, facing down a sorcerer. Flames had been spilled around, setting the room ablaze. Alakyne stood behind her, a pastry clutched tightly in his hand.

Auriel's first thought was that the children had done something wrong, angering the sorcerer but the look upon Aria's face screamed something else.

"Stay away from him!" Aria suddenly screamed throwing a blast of aura at him to which the sorcerer blocked it easily. Scanning the room again, Auriel noticed that more damage had been done than previously noticed, as if Aria herself had been blocking attacks from the sorcerer.

"What is going on?"

"They are trying to get Alakyne!" Aria screamed when she noticed Auriel and the Riel's blood ran cold. The sorcerer threw a look at her and as he looked back at Aria, he swiped his hand launching the

The Legend of Kyne: Chronocide

young girl to the side exposing the cowering Alakyne. Cocking his hand back, Auriel saw the glimmer of steel and with a flick, a dagger was thrown.

Time seemed to slow as Auriel propelled herself forward, stretching her aura out to stop the dagger. It was too fast and before she could, it struck and Aria hit the floor.

Alakyne cried out in shock at the sight of his sister falling in front of him and he dropped to his knees next to her, blood already pooling out of the wound.

Tiernyn was suddenly next to Auriel, a look of disbelief at what was happening and then Alakyne screamed!

His roar shook the very earth and a massive pressure erupted around, bringing everyone roughly to their knees. The sorcerer who had thrown the dagger suddenly cried out as Alakyne lifted him off of the ground with his aura. Attacks were thrown but they all dissipated and with his eyes glowing pure white. Alakyne killed the sorcerer, rending him in twain and casting the pieces across the room. Dropping to his knees, the glowing light from his eyes faded and as the pressure lifted, Auriel dashed forward to Aria, already forming the healing spell.

She removed the dagger and with all of her power, forced the wound to close. So much blood littered the ground and Alakyne began sobbing.

Then the ground began to tremble.

* * *

68. Mr. Tadpole

Sunlight streamed through the opening in the windows curtains and Lily awoke to the sound of her mother calling. It was hard to make it out and as the little girl groaned, she stretched her arms and rubbed her eyes. Suddenly images of her little friend popped into her mind, and she leapt out of bed. Her mother had stopped calling but she knew she would be there soon. She had to hurry.

Pulling the small box out from under her bed, she withdrew the wooden lid revealing a small glass jar filled nearly to the rim with water. A small creature lay at the bottom and as she lifted it up to her eyes, it began to swim around frantically as if excited to see her.

"Good morning, Mr. Tadpole," she giggled, and she withdrew the lid of the jar. Dipping her hand inside, she felt the slimy touch of the tadpole brush against her, and she giggled again.

It had grown in the last two days that she had kept it hidden under her bed. She had tried to feed it many different things from small vegetables to fruit but it didn't seem to take any of those. Even insects that she found outside stuck to the house or under rocks didn't really interest the tadpole. It was when she grew desperate and put a piece of beef from her dinner into the jar that it tore at it ravenously.

It had changed shape too, its tail much longer and more streamlined and its head had started to grow narrower forming a pointed muzzle. Upon its sides lay only two stubby limbs, more of arms than legs and no fingers had formed yet.

She smiled as she placed the jar back in the box as her mother shouted from down below again.

"I'm up!" she called back while placing the lid onto the box, casting the tadpole in darkness before sliding it far under her bed, making sure to get it to the other side next to the wall. Changing out of

The Legend of Kyne: Chronocide

her nightgown into some soft wool pants and a shirt, she ran her fingers through her hair in a failed attempt to untangle it before she dashed out of her room closing the door behind her.

Immediately outside her room lay a staircase to her right that led to the front door and just as she reached the top, she watched as the door swung open and a man walked inside.

"Daddy!" she cried, and she took off down the steps two at a time. Just as she reached the bottom, he had set something down upon the ground and turned to face her. His eyes were met with dark bags underneath from exhaustion, but they still bore a cheerful look as he stooped down and embraced his daughter.

"You didn't come home last night," spoke a voice behind her and as she separated from her father, she turned to see her mother standing nearby, arms folded and a look of frustration upon her face.

"I'm sorry Darling," he said reaching down and picking up the package he had placed upon the floor. "I was stuck at the keep. The new visitors are causing quite the commotion."

"They can't keep you there all night every night," she said, her look changing to that of concern, and she stepped forward, embracing him tightly. "We need you here too."

"I know," he said as Lily looked up at her two parents for a long time. She hated that her dad worked so much, being some builder for the keep kept him busy. He was there constantly, and she wished he could stay home.

"Are you going to be home the rest of the day?" she asked him, and the two adults turned to face her.

"Yep, all day. I don't have to be back until tomorrow morning."

She laughed in delight and ran at him, hugging him hard against his leg and almost knocking him over.

"He should get some sleep though Liliana," her mother said. "He was up all night remember?"

"Oh," she said, and she backed up, letting go and looking up at them. Her mother was pretty and young, fair skinned and lighter hair almost red to a degree. Her father, however, was not much taller with a dark short beard and hair that matched. He wasn't built thick, but a thinner man more suited to the sciences and architecture in which he had been great at.

"I have some things I need to do anyways Lily," he said cheerfully waving her sadness away. "I'll just go to sleep tonight when you and Mom do."

"What things," her mother said.

"I have to go to the market remember. We are running low on grains, and I need to get some payment for some work I did a few weeks ago."

"I could've done that for you," she started but he waived her off. "You shouldn't be doing anything. You should be resting to give the little one growing inside you a fighting chance. You know when Lily was born how hard it was on both of you."

"I know," she said. "It's just..."

"It's just you can't sit still," he chuckled, and he grabbed her hand. Bringing it to his lips, he kissed it lightly before lowering it down. "Let me do these things and then we can spend the rest of the day together."

Reaching down he rubbed Lily's head and said, "Ready to go?"

She nodded and with a smile to his wife, the two of them left the home and went out into the morning sun. Walking down their street, they passed some of the other houses, all of which had been designed by her father. She grinned as she looked at them and then back at her own admiring how beautiful they all were but more importantly how hers was the biggest on her street. They lived in a wealthier part of the town closer to the Faldîn Keep and with it came the safety of the patrolling guards. She felt safe walking around outside but knew that the further into the city she went the closer she needed to stay with her dad. She had heard stories of children going missing.

"What are the new people like Daddy?" she said as she skipped next to him matching his large strides.

"Odd," he said without stopping. "Very odd indeed."

"What do you mean?"

"Well, the big creature they came in upon..."

"The dragon," she exclaimed. "It's huge and so scary. I heard it ate some of the sorcerers."

"He didn't eat the sorcerers," he laughed, and he patted her back. "Even if he tried Tiernyn would have destroyed him in an instant.

The Legend of Kyne: Chronocide

It's surprising but he actually talks."

"He does?" she gasped, and she stopped walking with her mouth wide open. "How can he talk?"

"Lily, we need to keep going," he said gesturing for her to follow after him and as she caught up, he continued. "Yes, he can talk, seems pretty intelligent to me actually. The others who came with them were two kids, not much older than you and some strange woman with silver hair and funny ears."

"Is she pretty?" asked Lily.

"Very pretty," he replied.

"Prettier than Momma?"

"No, my dear," he laughed. "No one is prettier than your mother. Now why would you ask such a thing?"

"Because Luke said his mom is prettier than Momma."

"Well, that Luke is not very nice is he," he said with a look of concern, and he stopped walking, turning to face her. "I thought you two used to be friends?"

"I did too," she said looking down. "Now he's just a big fat jerk."

Her father looked up for a moment and down the street as if eyeing something. Lily knew he was looking at Luke's house but as she turned to look, she saw no one outside. She almost wanted to see him there, wanted to see his big ugly face and brag about how her dad was better than his. Then she remembered his father's injury and retracted that thought thinking it too mean. Instead, as her father turned back and began walking, she stuck her tongue out towards the home as if insulting the young boy with all her might.

Her father led them to the market square where he bought a few different bags of grain and then came to a butcher. She could feel her mouth drooling at the sight of the chopped meats and was glad that they could afford it. Excited for what he was going to buy, she was disappointed when after speaking with the owner, he was given a small coin purse and a cheerful farewell.

They left and returned home, heading up the street. As she passed Luke's house, she still didn't see movement inside. Up ahead, standing at the front of her home was her mother, arms folded and her foot tapping as if impatient.

The Legend of Kyne: Chronocide

"Lilianna," she said her brow furrowing. "What is that thing you have hiding under your bed?"

She stopped her steps suddenly and her blood ran cold. Her stomach tightened and she could tell by her mother's look she was in big trouble.

"It's Mr. Tadpole Momma. He's my friend."

"He's down the toilet," she replied and Lily's heart broke. "What?" she cried, and her eyes began to well up."

"I told you to stop bringing animals into our home. After the cat ate that last frog and got really sick, I... I can't do it anymore Lilianna. I have already told you this before."

"But he was so cool," she wailed, and she took off running, pushing past her mother and up the stairs to her room. Without looking at the empty spot under her bed, she dove upon the mattress and buried her face in it. She sobbed for a long time, upset in losing Mr. Tadpole and upset over Luke being such a meany.

A few minutes later her father came into the room, sitting next to her and placing a soft hand upon her back. He said nothing, but just sat there for a long time and his presence was all she needed. Sniffling, her nose running, she sat up and rubbed her red eyes.

"Why did she throw him down the toilet?" she said imagining the dark sewage hole that lay outside their home. The opening led straight down to an underground river where everyone in the upper classes' waist floated away from the city. "He will die in that gunk!"

"I didn't actually put him in the toilet," her mother said, appearing in the doorway and holding the glass jar with the tadpole inside.

"Mr. Tadpole!" she screamed in delight, and she bolted towards her, only to be stopped by a wave of her mother's hand.

"You can't keep him Lilianna," and she started coughing hard. When she finished, she wiped her mouth and continued. "He has to go away. He's ugly anyways. Are you even sure it's a tadpole?"

"It's a new type of tadpole that I found," Lily started but her mother began coughing hard again causing her to show a look of concern. Before she could say anything, her father was up and next to her mother.

"Are you ok?" he asked with worry. "You sound sick."

586

The Legend of Kyne: Chronocide

"I think I might be. A whole bunch of the city has fallen ill these last couple days and I guess it's just my time to get it," she said weakly, and her face was much paler than before. "I'll be fine. Lilianna I just want you to take it away please."

"But Momma..." she started but her mother interrupted.

"No buts," and then she coughed violently for a short time. "I can't with you right now Lilianna. Please just take it away. I want the ugly thing out of my house now!"

Handing the jar to the young girl, her mother turned and walked further down the hall vanishing into her own room. As the door closed, more coughing was heard.

Lily stood there for a long moment, looking at the little creature with sadness.

"He is quite odd looking," her father said softly, and he brought his eye next to the jar. "Are you sure it's a tadpole?"

"I think so," she said pulling the jar to her chest. "I found him with all the other tadpoles. He's special and different just like me."

"Indeed, he is," he chuckled. "Shall we return him to his home?"

"Are you coming with me?" she said in shock.

"If you'll have me."

She leapt around in shock and glee, her sadness momentarily gone as she sloshed the jar around. She had never been able to show her father the little creek and she was so excited! Walking down the stairs followed by her father, they left their home and started their way down towards the road that led out of the city. The sun was still far to one side, still late in the morning with a few hours before midday and they were quick, making their way down the streets and out of the city. Down the road they traveled for but a moment before Lily veered to the side, bringing them closer to the large river that flanked their city. Following it, the grass knee high, they traipsed for a long while before coming to thicker vegetation. Here a second small stream wound its way towards the large river and after pushing the cattails and reeds away, they both stood on the bank.

Down below them lay the small cove in the river where the frogs and tadpoles were and after a moment of looking, she spotted one of the tadpoles. Looking at her jar, she was really shocked at how different hers really was. It truly didn't look much like a tadpole at all.

A feeling of sadness at the loss of her special friend was felt in her chest and her eyes began to water up. Kneeling down, she removed the lid and hovered the jar out over the water's surface for a long moment. She wouldn't cry, she had to be tough now, but she was still so sad. Her eyes glistened with tears as she looked back at her father for reassurance and as he nodded with a weak smile, she turned back and began to tilt the jar spilling water into the stream.

A moment passed and just as the tadpole was nearly out, her father said, "Wait."

Tilting the jar back immediately, Lily felt her heart begin to quicken and she looked at her father with hope.

"If you really like him that much and you promise to take care of it, I'll talk to mother and I'll try and convince her to let you keep him."

She screamed in glee and raising the jar up to her eye she said, "You hear that Mr. Tadpole! You get to come home with me!" Sticking her finger in it again, she rubbed the little slimy thing for a moment before clamping the lid back on and climbing back away from the bank.

The water sloshed harder in the jar as it was more than half empty so holding it steady, she walked as carefully as she could as her father led them back to the road and towards their city. Passing the gates, she noticed that tons of people were looking as if they had fallen ill, coughing violently and pale with sweat glistened skin.

The more they saw the quicker her father's pace grew. "We should get home; this illness seems much worse than your mother led on. With your tendency to have worse reactions than the average person I really don't want you to catch it, Lily."

Trying hard to keep up without shaking the tadpole to death she said, "I feel fine though. I don't think I'm sick."

"But you can still get it if you are near those who are ill. When we get home, we might need to keep you and Momma separated for a while."

They nearly ran, passing more and more sick people. It seemed to affect people of all social status from the poor vagrant on the side of the road to the rich noble who strode from his home. The only people who didn't seem affected were those closest to the palace, but it seemed to be getting closer to them.

As they entered the home, they came to the main room to see her mother there, a look of shock at the sight of the jar in her hand. Before she said anything, her father held his hands out in a calm gesture and said,

"She was very sad dear."

"And you're a softy," she replied flatly. "So, she's keeping it then?"

"If it's alright with you," he replied with a weak smile. She held her flat gaze for a long moment before it broke, and she sighed.

"Whatever, keep the little thing. Just don't come crying to me when it dies."

Lily looked at her dad and the two smiled for but a moment before a massive force ripped through the home causing everything to tremble violently. Lily could feel her bones quivering and unable to fight it, she was forced to her knees, dropping the jar to the ground where it landed and, on its side, began to bounce violently from the shaking house. Her father dropped to his knees and her mother followed soon after, the force threatening to push them all face down into the ground.

It was unlike anything she had felt, making it hard to breathe and hard to think. The power caused everything to quake as if in fear of what was causing it. But as soon as it started, it suddenly ended, the force easing up and allowing them to rise to their feet. Cries of shock erupted from both her parents and as they scrambled through the house, making sure everything was alright, Lily stooped down and picked up her jar to see Mr. Tadpole stiff as a board.

"Momma," she called out drawing her parents' attention and they all peered intently at the small creature as it lay suspended in the water.

"It looks like it might be dead," she muttered but just as her words left her mouth, the creature began to tremble violently. Its body shifted and swelled, forming strange shapes and as it reached the jar's capacity, Lily dropped it where it collided with the floor, this time shattering into dozens of pieces. There the creature writhed upon the ground, its body growing in waves before it opened its mouth and screeched a deafening tone!

The Legend of Kyne: Chronocide

* * *

69. Pestilence

The ground trembled and a massive roar ripped through the keep as Auriel knelt down next to Aria and Alakyne. The young boy had not stopped his sobbing and the screech had seemed to draw Aria out of her daze. The ground trembled and then shook again followed by massive crashes as an explosion erupted outside.

Leaping to her feet, she helped Aria up and together with Alakyne they began to head towards the doorway. Tiernyn was still there, his eyes drilled upon the wall towards the sound and as they passed, Auriel spoke, "We will deal with you after this."

Rounding the corner, more crashes were heard, and they quickened their pace coming to the outside courtyard in moments. Ni'Bara was already there, his head reared up in a snarl and his spines flared out. His gaze was directed towards the city where an immense writhing mass lay.

Helping Aria upon the dragon's back they were all soon airborne, Ni'Bara's sides quivering in a prolonged snarl. Below them the massive creature thrashed, dozens of buildings, mostly homes of the upper district lay crushed beneath its mass. Its size was unlike anything, dwarfing a dragon, a roc, and even the seraph by a large margin. Its size was in comparison that if Ni'Bara was but small dog, the creature was a bear!

It's head alone was as large as the dragon, brought to a point with its mouth full of thick teeth longer than sabers. As its body flailed, crushing more buildings, Auriel spotted a single set of fins near its front, enormous and flat. Its body was long and slender, not quite serpentine but close and coming to a paddle shaped tail. Flashes of light flew at it from a sorcerer and as if merely irritated, the creature flipped its tail up before bringing it down in a swipe smashing everything in its paths and plastering the sorcerer's corpse across the city like a red coat of paint.

Another screech erupted from the beast as it spotted Ni'Bara's hovering mass and as it opened its mouth, a massive plume of purple and black smoke erupted towards them rapidly. As if a toxic pyroclastic flow, the wave spread up bathing the sky. Auriel could feel a nauseating pain in her abdomen the closer it got, and she knew they had to avoid it at all costs.

Ni'Bara twisted around, dropping into a tight dive before straightening out and rocketing under the plume, only a few feet from it. The beast continued belting the smoke, flailing its head around trailing after them but was too slow and Ni'Bara managed to jet away flying high out of reach.

The further they got from the creature, the more that they all started to feel better, as if the sickness was being lifted from them. Down below, they stared in horror while the creature smashed more buildings as it struggled to travel through the city. Like ants, the human corpses littered the streets with more fleeing as it thrashed about. Partially averting her eyes, Auriel witnessed a fleeing family crushed like bugs, flattened against the stone ground as if they were nothing.

Rage enveloped her and with a cry she screamed, "Rik'tar!"

A bolt of electricity leapt from her hand, arcing through the air in a blinding flash before colliding with the top of the creature's body. A scream of pain erupted from the beast just as the thunderclap followed and its head swung around towards them. Looking up, it stretched its neck high, as if reaching towards them. Its maw opened revealing the inky darkness and then another plume of smoke blasted up towards them, this time much more aggressive than before.

Even with their height, it rapidly approached and Ni'Bara narrowly avoided it, arcing around before diving at a steep angle. The trailing of cyan flames was seen upon the edges of his face and with a roar, he unleashed a torrent of inferno upon the beast as they flew over it. More screams erupted and Auriel turned her head to see it thrashing violently around as if in pain.

The sky above had rapidly grown overcast, thick grey clouds seemingly appearing out of nowhere and dropping lower and lower towards the ground. A flash of lightning erupted within and then the rain started. Ignoring it at first, they turned around for another assault when behind her Alakyne started to cough violently. Suddenly Auriel started coughing as well and then a wave of fatigue followed by nausea erupted through her being. The sound of vomiting was heard, and she could just make out Aria attempting to cast it over Ni'Bara's flank, bathing him in the disgusting sludge.

She felt her mouth begin to water and knew very well what was to follow. Leaning her own head over, she felt her stomach retch, tightening in a violent and painful contortion as her throat was forced open. Another retch followed, this time launching the contents of her stomach forcefully from her body in a liquid blast. She tried her hardest to avoid Ni'Bara but with the wind she watched as some of it flipped upwards, coating her leg as well as his side. She retched again hurling more contents out into the air where they mixed with the rain falling in disgusting drops.

The dragon swayed in his flight, dropping dangerously and nearly throwing them off his back. Auriel could tell something was wrong and as she struggled to speak to him, she vomited again, this time nothing leaving her but just a dry heave.

The dragon swayed again and then they were diving at a steep angle down towards the city with the thrashing beast. The wind roared in their ears and the tingly knot of falling was felt in her stomach followed by panic at the rapidly approaching ground. Ni'Bara's head was curled towards the side as if in extreme pain.

At the last moment, he stretched his wings out and with a massive crash, they glided into the courtyard of the keep, flattening dozens of ornate plants and stone benches. The impact jarred them all, nearly launching them from his back and as they came to a stop, Auriel ripped the bindings holding her in place on the saddle. Sliding down his side as her feet hit the ground, she collapsed, slamming her knees into the stone and bruising them instantly. Her nausea had not gone away, and she began coughing hard, each belt rocking her chest. Aria and Alakyne joined her on the ground, each coughing as hard as she was and then the sound of a torrent of fluid struck the ground. To her shock, Auriel turned to see Ni'Bara vomiting, the contents colliding with the stone ground and sizzling as if covered by lava itself. The dragon heaved again, spewing more out and as the sludge pooled and flowed, she moved away just in time to avoid it running over her leg.

A massive crash sounded, and she turned in horror to see the ineffable beast had made its way to the keep, tearing the wall of the courtyard down in one sweep as it struggled to reach them. Its beady eyes were drilled upon Ni'Bara, and she could see drool dripping from its fangs as it snapped its jaws towards them.

She could hardly move, let alone stand. Her nausea and fatigue made that impossible. She brushed her wet hair from her face, her forehead covered in sweat and then she noticed a strange scent. Breathing in, she realized it was coming from the falling water. Looking up into the clouds, she could see the rain had not ceased in the lightest and the clouds had even grown darker as more of the remaining smoke from the beast had risen up.

The rain! her mind roared, and she caught a small pool in her hand and brought it to her nose. The moment it was there, she recoiled, the scent nearly causing her to vomit again. It was like a sewer, like the scent of plague if it were to have one, pungent and toxic in every possible way.

She could hardly think, her mind swimming but with all of her might, she managed to say the intricate spell, "Sei'var kaiodin!"

Immediately, the water striking around the immediate vicinity stopped falling, forming a bubble around them and every second more water joined making the bubble more like a wall of tainted water. Another wave of her hand to finish the spell and all of the water clinging to her hair and clothes as well as the other three was peeled away from them, forming a sizable blob after which she launched far away. The instant the water was gone, she felt immediate relief, and her strength began to return. She stumbled to her feet, continuously holding the bubble of rain above preventing it from reaching them and all four of them turned to face the creature who had stopped its movement.

A look of rage had appeared across its face, and it bellowed out a massive screech followed by a wave of purple and black smoke. Auriel couldn't hold the rain and stop the attack at the same time; it was too much for her aura to handle especially in this weakened state. Ni'Bara's roar was drowned out by the sound of the beast, and they all stared death in the face.

The Legend of Kyne: Chronocide

Suddenly a gale of wind ripped around them directing the smoke away at a sharp angle. Another gale was thrown upward carrying most of the rain from Auriel's bubble away lightening her load significantly.

Turning around in shock, she watched as Tiernyn approached, his cloak blowing wildly in the wind. His hair was dry and as the rain tried to reach him, it stopped mere inches from his skin before falling away and colliding with the ground. The air began to vibrate with power as the sorcerer approached, his face displaying a look of rage. His dark brown eyes began to glow a deep gold and then to their shock a flicker of lightning began to form upon their edges.

Raising his hand, the sorcerer pulled his sleeve up revealing his dark skin adorned with a golden bracelet whose surface was etched with glowing markings.

"Xeono," Auriel whispered in shock and then with a cry, Tiernyn hurled a spear-like bolt of lightning toward the creature where it buried deep into its flesh for but a moment before exploding in a violent blast. The creature screeched in pain and attempted to fire another projectile attack but before the smoke even left its mouth a second bolt was embedded into the roof of its mouth.

A blinding flash of light erupted from the beast's eyes as the bolt exploded and it writhed around in agony. Suddenly its body began to shrink rapidly, its flesh boiling and contorting as it was obscured from sight with the wreckage. The rain above abruptly stopped, the clouds dissipating. Tiernyn's voice rang out loud and clear.

"The leviathan is attempting to escape. Block the waterways!"

A few sorcerers appeared, Tira among them sprinting towards the location while they sat and watched. Auriel ended her spell, sending the remaining plague-like water away in a splash and felt the immediate relief. Her mind was racing and with a look from Ni'Bara could understand he was feeling the same way.

"Leviathan!" they both spoke simultaneously, and they turned to watch as the sorcerers came to the spot it had been.

"It's gone!" one of them cried out. "It vanished down one of the sewage drains!"

Tiernyn cursed and then he strode past them, his glowing eyes continuing to burn. His face was irate, fueled with anger at the

The Legend of Kyne: Chronocide

destruction of his city and as he came to the hole that marked the entrance to where it had fled, he held his hand out above his head. A golden bolt of energy materialized and without a sound, he threw it down, launching it out of view into the network of tunnels flooding them with power.

Only a moment followed, a mere two seconds before a small explosion was heard further down in the city followed by a massive crash as the creature returned, erupting from the ground and swelling in size, thrashing about in pain and agony. Without hesitating, Tiernyn hurled three more bolts, each colliding with the creature and just as the last one met its mark, it stopped moving, only twitching here and there.

The leviathan was dead.

70. Under the Veil of Beauty

"Aria!" gasped Alakyne drawing Auriel and Ni'Bara's attention away from the dead leviathan to see her collapse to the ground. Her skin was pale and her eyes foggy as if struggling to focus. Holding her head, Alakyne was wrought with grief looking at his older sister, the one who had protected him for so long on the verge of death.

"What's wrong!" said Ni'Bara as he swung his head around just as Auriel was upon them. Feeling around her abdomen where she had been struck, she found only the solid clot that had formed within the cloth. No fresh blood was noticed, and Auriel wasn't sure what was wrong.

"Is it from the rain," wailed Alakyne. "Is that why she is sick?"

"I am not sure," Auriel said, and she placed a hand upon the girl's mouth. "Kitala tainted water," she said, and a few drops of water came out of the girl's mouth, hardly noticeable. Aria's eyes rolled back in her head, and she went limp just as Tira came upon them, her eyes full of worry.

"Something is wrong with her," Auriel said as she met the woman's eyes. "It's not the rain though, she was struck by a blade earlier."

"A blade!" gasped Tira in shock and she dropped to her knees. Her look of concern for the safety of this girl was shocking to Auriel and as she watched her delicately push the hairs from the girl's face, Auriel could see the true passion she had for her.

"It was another attempt on Alakyne," Auriel continued. "Some sorcerer trapped them in the kitchens. Aria tried fighting them off, but he threw a dagger. It struck her but I stopped the bleeding. She lost a lot of blood but that doesn't explain all of this."

The Legend of Kyne: Chronocide

"Where did it hit her!" shouted Tira but she had already found the dark stain on her clothes. Biting the edge of the fabric with her teeth, she grasped it in both hands and tore it up, shredding her shirt in two pieces. She was exposed, her skin pale and upon the side of her abdomen just below her left breast was a dark mark, the stab wound with dark shadows spreading from its center.

Auriel gasped at the sight, not realizing at first that the dagger had been poisoned. "When was she struck?" ordered the sorceress.

"About fifteen minutes ago roughly."

"Right before that pressure was felt. I am assuming that was Alakyne. It would also explain the triggering and revealing of the leviathan."

"Kitala poison," said Auriel holding her hand over the wound but no substance came out from it.

"I doubt that will work. If it's what I think it is, then aura won't have much of an effect on it. Its venom from the lurdoc, a small bat-like creature. The venom is incredibly hard to deal with let alone use aura on. The creature it came from uses aura and it very essence repels it."

"How do we get it out of her!" cried Alakyne and he held his sister tightly.

"I am afraid we don't," Tira said softly. "There is treatment for it, but the venom is fast. By the time we get it she will have already been too far gone."

"She can't die," he wailed again, and the ground began to tremble. Auriel could feel the pressure beginning and she grabbed a hold of him holding him tight in an attempt to calm him down. The pressure softened and then faded, and he started to sob.

"I am sorry," Tira whispered. "If I could save her then I would in a heartbeat. If I could stop time, then I would."

Auriel held tightly onto both of the kids, her own eyes welling up with tears and she saw Ni'Bara reach down towards them. His eyes were filled with sorrow and as the two held their gaze for a long while, he suddenly twitched.

Rearing up, his eyes widened and then he jerked his head down towards them. "You asked if you could freeze time Tira? Well Auriel can. The Relic Auriel! The Relic of Containment!"

The Legend of Kyne: Chronocide

His voice shook the ground and as the last word was said, Auriel was already upon her feet. Using her aura, she took off, nearly flying over the ground in a blur. Tearing through the doorway of the keep, she blasted down the hallway and into her room. There it was, sitting right where she had left it. Grasping the strange object, she was back near the others in moments, her breath quick and her hair wild.

Holding it out, she looked at Alakyne as if awaiting instructions, but the young boy just stared at her blankly. She gestured as if he knew how to activate it, but he shook his head.

"I don't know how to work it," he stammered. "Last time I just touched it, and it started glowing. If we open it up again won't that thing come out?"

"I don't know," Auriel muttered but she reached it towards the boy. "If so then I'll kill it. It needs to come out anyway. I don't want her trapped inside with it."

Aria groaned and her eyes fluttered open. She was mumbling something that was hard to make out.

"What was that Aria," Tira said leaning in.

"Just... Let me go. That thing," and she coughed hard. "That wraith is too dangerous to be set free."

"Don't worry about the wraith Aria," rumbled Ni'Bara. "I'll take care of it."

She coughed again and Alakyne touched the relic. The white lines spread across its dark surface rapidly and just as soon as the ouroboros became visible, Auriel touched it. A flash of white and then the wraith was there, upon the floor. Tira yelped in shock at its hideous sight but just as it began to move, Ni'Bara snatched it in his jaws. With a flick, he launched it up above him and then engulfed the tumbling body in a flash of dragonfire. Nothing struck the ground as it was reduced to mere ashes.

"We will do all we can Aria," whispered Auriel and she brought the cube against the girl's forehead. A flash of light and then she was gone, the Relic losing its bright markings.

A fit of rage tore through Auriel and she scanned the courtyard looking for the one she knew to be responsible. Then her eyes finally rested upon the Otoruhn sorcerer, standing a few dozen feet away. His hands were tucked behind his robes and his handsome face was flat of all emotion.

"This is your fault!" she screamed, and she took off towards him. He held his ground, unmoving and just before she was there, she watched the tip of Ni'Bara's tail come between her and Tiernyn. Running smack into the tail, she nearly had the wind knocked out of her from the rock-hard limb and she whipped her head around to see Ni'Bara's look. His spines upon the edges of his face were flared out and his lip drew into a snarl. Turning back towards Tiernyn, she was startled to see the man in a hideous smirk. His beautiful face revealing the sinister beast underneath.

"Smart creature," and he brought his hands out from behind his back. The glow of a blade of lightning clutched between his hands. Taking a few steps towards her so that they were an arm lengths away. "The fact you are still alive is a testament to your tenacity Auriel. If you had drawn even a few steps closer to me then you would be a corpse." Flecks of spit struck the ground and she turned away disgusted with him.

"You tried to have Alakyne killed!" she seethed. Her rage increasing and she wanted so badly to push Ni'Bara's tail out of the way!

"Not as hard as I should have, I am afraid," he replied, the bolt of lightning fizzling away and he cocked his head to the side. "It seems it's a lot harder to kill a ten-year-old than I thought it to be. Too bad the girl had to fall as well, she seemed like she had some potential."

"She's not dead yet!" Auriel hissed and her hand reached for her blade. Just as her fingers connected with it, Ni'Bara pulled his tail back, yanking her away from the sorcerer.

"You are just afraid of his power!" she cried as she was brought back to the others, Tiernyn a fair distance away.

He raised his hands out to his sides as if challenging her.

"Afraid," he laughed. "I am afraid of nothing. Even after witnessing what occurred earlier, I no longer feel threatened by the boy. I should cast you out, let you fend for yourselves until the beasts overtake you."

"You wouldn't!" screamed Tira taking a few steps towards him. "You wouldn't dare!"

"Don't try me," he hissed. "Whatever connection this boy

The Legend of Kyne: Chronocide

seems to have to the beasts is disturbing in the least. I honestly would be shocked if no other nearby monsters were not upon the city gates by the end of the day."

"All we want is the antidote to the lurdoc venom Tiernyn!" screamed Auriel. "Give it and we will go peacefully."

"And if I don't?"

"Then we will take it from you!" Auriel's voice echoed around, drawing everyone in a gasp. Nearby sorcerers who had been eavesdropping stopped what they were doing and had turned fully to face them. All wielding staves, the crystals upon their ends glowing dangerously as their aura was charged.

Tiernyn folded his arms, leaning upon one leg more than the other as he cocked his hip. His mouth contorted in a look of deep thought. After a long moment, the clouds above finally dissipating and streaks of sunlight reaching the ground in golden pools, he sighed.

"Oh my Auriel, the one who evades my advances now proceeds to threaten me? Auriel, that is a fight I promise you will not win. Have you wondered where the lord of the city is? Held up in his room unaware of anything that happens. He is but a puppet, someone to hold in the palm of my hand. I am in control of everything you can see. I am a god!"

"Then today a god falls!" snarled Ni'Bara and flames appeared between his fangs.

Tiernyn seemed unimpressed by his remark, and he shook his head. "A fight here would not be wise, just leave, get out of my city while you still can walk."

"Not without the antidote!" Auriel yelled.

"I don't have the damn antidote!" he roared back. "Why in the hell would I keep it here if I was using the venom to assassinate people?"

His words made her skin crawl, and her anger was slowly replaced with fear.

"You lie Tiernyn!" called Tira interjecting. "I know you are not that stupid. What would happen if you were struck by the venom?"

"That's where you are completely outclassed oh sweet Tira, the constant thorn in my side. Why you couldn't stay away still irritates me to my very core. I wouldn't be stupid enough to get struck with my own

The Legend of Kyne: Chronocide

venom."

"Arrogance will be your downfall Tiernyn," Tira said. Dropping her voice, she muttered so only they could hear. "We should escape while we can Auriel. He is far too dangerous. We can try and get the antidote after we are safe."

Auriel gritted her teeth knowing full well that Tira was right. A look from Ni'Bara out of the corner of his eye and he nodded a short movement signaling he agreed. Turning back to face Tiernyn who was smirking, she was beyond frustrated at her apparent failure and reluctantly she joined the others as they rapidly climbed upon Ni'Bara's back. Without taking her eyes off him, Auriel watched him stay completely still, only turning his head slightly as they flew away from the desolated city.

Down below she could hear the screams of mourning as families had been destroyed and loved ones killed beneath the terror. The leviathan's corpse lay completely still, unmoving as its long body lay strewn through part of the city.

She half expected a flash of lighting from Xeono to approach but it never did. Tiernyn just watched them as they flew away into the late afternoon.

* * *

71. Removing Thorns

"No!"

Rosé's voice echoed around the small chamber startling Akami from her fierceness. She was taken aback for a moment before she scowled, furrowing her brow. This little girl was irritating her more and more the longer she was around her.

"How about this then," Akami said waving her hand around and Rosé's body grew rigid before lifting off the ground a few inches. She was slow and methodical as she guided Rosé up towards the ceiling, pinning her against the wooden beams. Akami smiled wickedly at the child, "I don't take no for an answer, not from my people, not from my servants, and certainly not from little girls. Don't test me! Tell me who he is now before I let my anger cloud the rest of my judgment."

The young girl glared in anger, every fiber of her being tense under Akami's hold but she finally broke.

"He is a friend, someone I just met."

"Then why does his name cause me pain, the very thought of it causing me to want to split my head open with an ax. I don't remember anything, as if the memories are just out of reach!"

"Are you from the other place then?" Rosé asked as she was lowered back to the ground. Her hair had already begun to pale like the other children's, her cheekbones visible now as the flesh sunk in and her eyes had dark bags underneath them. Her words startled Akami, and she paused for a long moment.

"Other place? What do you mean?"

"The other Kydrëa where these bad people were sent away. I don't know much about it, only what I was taught but these people shouldn't be here."

Akami turned around, her head spinning at the thought. She waved away Rosé before walking over to her seat by the windowsill and she brought her knees up close, bathing in the faint light and looking out on the small speck of outside she could see. Rosé didn't say anything else, vanishing to the far side of the room while Akami lay lost in her thoughts.

What is she talking about other Kydrëa? That doesn't make any sense. Mother sent us here to create an alliance, the Dominion has been here for over a decade now, right? A flicker of doubt entered her mind as she recalled the memories. *This place, these thoughts don't fit in right. I remember it but they are all so faint and hazy, haloed by a shimmering veil that almost seems fabricated.*

The day waned on, one boy trying to escape as the guard opened the door to bring food and he was swiftly brought down to the ground before being dragged back inside. Another younger boy, this one just old enough to walk, was brought in shortly after, crying about his mother and where she went.

His screeches were insistent and the longer it continued the more riled up Akami got until finally she snapped, locking his mouth shut with her aura.

"Your mother isn't here, and she won't ever be coming," she hissed. "Your voice is driving me insane, and I cannot deal with it anymore!"

Standing up, she grabbed hold of his arm, wet tears and snot dripping down his face. She launched him over towards the adjoining room and as he ran through the doorway, she slammed it shut.

"You really are nasty," muttered the oldest boy as he sat in the corner, hunched near another child. "Even if he wasn't going to see his mother again you could've at least lied to him about it."

"And what would that solve," she replied.

"A little bit of comfort for a small child."

"Comfort is for the weak. In the real world no one is there to comfort you. Only the strongest survive hence why you are there, and I am here."

The children said no more leaving the room silent.

"Mother always taught me that, that the strongest are the ones who survive," she muttered quietly. "It is why we were able to return back to our home after taking it back from my stupid uncle. These children have no idea of the hardships of the real world. The illusion of that is what brought them here in the first place."

"What brought them here was these people abducted them from their families," said Rosé. Akami turned to see the girl standing next to her, her eyes full of defiance. "You spout this nonsense that only the strongest survives but I think that is just a shield you use to justify your actions."

Akami rolled her eyes. "You are but a child, a strange child but still just a child. Don't lecture me about my actions, I am of royal blood, and I can do anything I want."

"Royal blood means nothing to me. You are just a mean person who wants to hurt others. Don't you ever forget that. Don't you ever forget our faces when we are gone, killed to fuel that monster who sleeps behind you!"

Her words startled Akami. Her fire and passion burning deeply inside causing for but a moment a glimpse of sorrow. She was starting to like her; this feisty girl reminded her a little bit of her own self.

Swinging her legs up onto the windowsill and taking a seat, she shooed the girl away without continuing the conversation, the rest of the children remaining silent and keeping their distance. Akami thought about it the rest of the day, her thoughts flickering from the young ones around her and then back to her own childhood. She grew up in royalty, given everything she had ever wanted, compared to these children who had grown up in poverty. Born with a pretty face that only grew in attractiveness as she aged, she was blessed from the very beginning whereas some of them did not get that same fate.

But the longer she thought about it the more her thoughts lingered on how all of them were so hopeful that their parents would come and rescue them. Come save them from the nightmarish hell they were enduring being drained of their very life force.

Mother would never save me that's for sure, she thought, and she leaned her head onto her hand, balancing the weight on her elbow. *She would sooner see me dead than bother herself with any sort of inconvenience.*

She tried to recall a single loving moment shared with her mother, but nothing was brought to mind, only fleeting memories of her father before he passed when she was barely able to talk. She could just make out his figure, his face faded from memory, and she felt a tightness appearing in her chest and to her shock her eyes had filled with tears.

She brushed them quickly away, the wetness leaving streaks upon her sleeve just as the door swung open, Yu stepping inside. Without a word, Akami left, the euphoric feeling of the pressure being released filling her body and distracting her from her moment of sorrow. She ate a quick meal and then went to bed, hoping the next day would be one of the last.

The day repeated just like the last, however one of the children, a young girl coughed the whole time as she lay near the wall, refusing to eat or drink anything. Rosé didn't talk to Akami once and neither did any of the other kids. They all just sat for the whole day in silence before her shift was up. Diahl was slowly recovering, the mark on his transparent abdomen shrinking by the day but he remained still, lost in a form of stasis as he tried to recover.

The following morning as Akami walked down the hallway towards Diahl's room she was startled to see two sentinels exiting the room, a small board being carried between them. Upon it she could see a small figure concealed by a cloth and for a split second, a thought of panic flew through her mind as she nearly ran towards it. Pulling the cloth up, she noticed it was the young sickly girl from the previous day, her body pale and cold.

She pulled the sheet down, strange feelings flowing through her. Feeling of relief and also sorrow filled her mind as she pushed the door open to see the children. None of them were saying much, Rosé was seated against the wall, her pink hair nearly grey and her eyes drooping.

She realized just as she saw her, the relief she was feeling that the little one who had passed was not Rosé and that shocked her more than anything.

Why should I care if she dies? she thought throughout the day as she watched them. She didn't know why whether it be because she reminded her of herself or something else, she didn't know. But one of these days she would be gone and there wasn't anything she could do about it.

A few hours passed before surprisingly the door swung open and Voira stepped inside, a big grin upon her face.

"Come with me, I have a surprise."

The Legend of Kyne: Chronocide

She followed her out into the hall, past the Windra guards and up a few flights of stairs before Voira stopped and turned to look at her.

"You are going to love this," she said with a big smile. "Should be around here, ah yes. Found her. Look down there," and she pointed out one of the hallway windows towards the courtyard where a small figure was seen dashing around an ornate bush before crouching low. From this far away Akami couldn't make out any details, only that they were female.

"Who is it?" she said in a bored tone.

"Just wait," she giggled. "This is so funny to me that I wanted to have you see what happens."

The figure vanished behind a wall and Voira turned quickly, running down the stairs with Akami hot on her heels. She had no idea what was going on, but this was far more interesting than being locked up in that stupid room all day. She needed this more than she realized.

They migrated down a few levels until Voira found her, the woman obviously Kydrëan skirting around two sentinels who were making their rounds.

Voira giggled again, mouthing, "Impressive skills," to Akami which brought a grin to her face. The Kydrëan woman was not fast and not agile in the slightest and mocking her seemed to be quite pleasurable. The Kydrëan ducked low, not realizing that the two were watching her from above as they peered through a gap in the railing that lined the courtyard walkway. They watched her pull out some piece of parchment and after a quick moment she took off again, heading underneath them and deeper into the citadel.

The midday light was bright and wishing she could be in it a little longer, she reluctantly followed after Voira, this time at a much more leisurely stroll.

"Did you notice anything?" Voira asked.

"About the Kydrëan woman not really."

"More along the lines of how she made it so far inside without being caught. Even with her mad skills of stealth she shouldn't have made it this far, no one could."

"Then how did she..."

Voira laughed interrupting her. "There're basically no

sentinels here! We are letting her sneak in for amusement."

Voira's words shocked her and Akami pulled a strange face of confusion before her face lit up in a smile.

"Where is she going then? Do we even know?"

"I know exactly where she is going, and it will be even better once she gets there. It's as if the fates have aligned for all the things to happen just at the perfect time."

They continued on making their way back to the hallway that Diahl's room lay in and to Akami's shock she noticed the Windra guards were no longer there, the hallway empty of any souls. Voira led her to a separate doorway that led to an empty room and leaving the door cracked slightly they waited, their eyes peering at Diahl's door.

A few moments later they heard footsteps and watched as the woman ran right past their door heading towards where the children lay hidden. Thoughts of realization began to hit and then Voira said something quietly. A yelp came from the woman and then they walked out into the hallway. The Kydrëan was sinking into the stone ground of the hallway right in front of the door, the rock flowing like putty as it consumed her. She was already at her knees and sinking fast. Her eyes were full of panic as she screamed at them.

"My daughter! Give me back my daughter!"

"And why should we do that," Voira taunted. "You are the one who broke into my home to steal my property. I do find it awfully rude of you."

"Your property? How dare you!" she screamed. "Give her back to me! You stole her from her mother!"

"Oh, my apologies," Voira said in a dark mocking tone. "Do tell me her name so that I might be able to help you locate her. We do have a lot of children as you might be aware."

"Her name is Jezzi. Her name is Jezzi!"

"Oh..." Voira said drawing out the word. "Well shoot, that was what I was actually afraid of."

Her tone was condescending as she stepped around the woman who was now past her waist and nearly to her shoulders in the ground.

Akami could feel her own amusement rapidly fading away as she watched the lady screaming. It wasn't funny anymore.

The Legend of Kyne: Chronocide

"What do you mean?" the woman cried out.

"Well, I hate to break it to you, but she actually isn't here with the others. But don't you worry. I am here to help you out with all my power. In fact," and she paused for a long moment, her eerily cheery mask slowly transitioning to a malicious dark and twisted grin. "In fact, I'll send you to her right now," and with a wave of her hand the ground opened up dropping the woman down to the floor below where she crashed hard.

There was a long moment of silence as Akami looked first at Voira before a blood curdling shriek rang up from below followed by sobs of anguish.

A pit forming in her stomach, Akami leaned over the hole and looked down to see the woman kneeling next to the deceased child who had been taken from the room just a few hours ago.

"She only died this morning," Voira called. "If only you had been a little sooner. Anyways, thanks for feeding my nylocs. You actually spared some cattle today," and just as the ground sealed back over Akami heard the beginnings of a scream.

"One of my favorite things in this entire world," Voira said with a big grin, and she stretched her arms out to the sides. "So funny how much they try to get their children back. I feel like it's almost a weekly occurrence."

Akami was disgusted with what had occurred, her stomach churning hard, and she looked away. She was feeling things that she had never felt before, coming in massive waves as she pictured the child's dead face. *And the other children*, her thoughts rested on Rosé and then she imagined her dead and her skin cold.

"Are you alright Akami?" Voira said with a hint of concern. She felt her hand placed upon her shoulder and with everything she could muster, the skills she had honed throughout the years, she turned back with a big smile and laughed out loud, faking joy from witnessing the horrors she had just seen. She would play Voira, trick her with all her might into believing her. At least that could maybe give her some time to think things through.

"Right! So funny. I knew you would love it! You easterners are just as brutal as we have heard." Movement down the hall caught their attention and they saw the two Windra guards returning to their posts.

609

The Legend of Kyne: Chronocide

"Anyways, you do have to return but if another shows up then I'll come get you if you want."

"Of course, I would want that," she replied, and she turned and walked past the guards back into the room, her face reflecting joy and her insides crawling with turmoil.

She sat there as the sun progressed its way across the sky. Her gaze seemed to linger on Rosé, and she noticed that she was moving less and less. The night came and Akami was relieved of her duty. Leaving the room and the children behind she returned to her own quarters. Her mind kept resting on the small pink-haired girl, how weak she had seemed and how she hadn't moved from her spot the entire day.

She is nearing the point that child, Jezzi was at. She will be gone soon if I don't do something, she thought as she ate a piece of bread. *I don't know what to do though. Why do I even care what happens to her? I have never cared before so what makes her so special.*

She still didn't have an answer but as the night progressed and her eyes began to droop, she had finally decided what to do.

"If I can save her then maybe I can undo at least some of the wrongs that I have caused."

72. To Risk Everything for a Child

Akami dashed through the cracked door to her room, her bare feet upon the stone absent of sound. She was running quickly, evading sight as she made her way down the hall. Her hair was pulled up tight against her head in a bun and her robes trailing behind her. Dark in color, she was nearly invisible in the shadowed hallway, only coming into sight occasionally as she passed by the lit sconces.

Her footsteps were light as she leapt around the pool of flickering orange light, landing back into the cover of darkness just as other footsteps caught her attention. Up ahead she could hear them growing closer, from the sounds of it they were likely just patrolling sentinels.

If I am seen I could just play it off like I am wandering around. I already have a little authority with the alliance and all.

She took a step forward; her tanned skin being lit up to a copper color with the orange light and she waited a few moments just as the sentinels rounded the corner coming into view.

Suddenly, she dashed back out of sight an instant before she was noticed, tucking into a small alcove near a window. Her pulse was thumping hard, the feeling in her neck as she took a deep breath realizing how dangerous of a move that actually was.

If I am seen and events play out as planned, then I will absolutely be the prime suspect. A strange easterner wandering the citadel late at night might be a little suspicious.

She stayed out of view as they passed, taking a deep breath only after they were out of sight.

Is this really worth it? she thought as she continued on. *Is it really worth jeopardizing everything for a stupid kid?*

It wasn't even rescuing a child that was what drove her though, it was rescuing *that* child. The one who for some reason seemed connected to her and her strange memories that didn't fit just right. *It all stems from him, the one whose thoughts provoke pain as if I am not supposed to remember. Saving her might lead me to him and that might get me some answers.*

Evading the sentinels in the citadel was fairly trivial, most of them more lazily patrolling than they probably should be. To Akami it looked to be that they were quite confident no one was getting inside the citadel, they weren't expecting someone to already be inside.

Diahl's room was up ahead, just coming into view when she nearly gasped in shock, her speed increasing. One Windra guard lay dead, leaning back against the wall, a massive streak of blood stretching down its surface. His throat had been slit and he looked to have been run through with a large, bladed weapon.

The other Windra guard was nowhere to be seen.

Am I too late? she thought with a panicked thought, and she threw the door open running inside. To her shock she saw the children all cowering in the corner, crying in fear as two people wrestled in the middle of the floor. One was the Windra guard, his mask pulled up covering his features and his arms wrapped tight around Yu's neck. The Kitsune's face was a dark shade of purple, the vessels in her eyes bursting red as they were nearly thrust out of their sockets.

"Erodath!"

Akami slammed the Windra guard with a strike of aura breaking his grip upon the Kitsune and knocking him back a few feet. He was fast, scrambling to his feet and in a blink, he had grabbed onto the glaive that was nearby.

Akami slammed him again before he could move, launching him off his feet where he crashed into the wooden post of the bedframe snapping it in two and causing the whole thing to shift to its side launching Diahl to its edge.

The phantom hung there for a moment before he continued to slide, nearly falling upon the Windra who just narrowly slid out of the way as he crashed to the floor.

The guard was on his feet again, this time with no weapon and he was throwing his head around as if looking for something.

His eyes rested upon Rosé and then he pounced towards her like lightning.

The Legend of Kyne: Chronocide

"Not a chance! Kaiodin!" Akami screamed and just before he reached the cowering girl he froze in place.

Holding the spell, Akami dashed to the Kitsune who lay coughing heavily on the ground, her neck bruised but the color of her face slowly changing from purple to a bright red. She was breathing heavily, and her eyes had nearly no white left, replaced by a blood red.

"What happened?" Akami said lifting her up to her feet where she swayed for a moment before catching her balance. She coughed again, doubling over and gagging.

"He snuck in and ambushed me," she whispered, her voice nearly absent and she coughed again. "Got to me before I could even say any words."

Akami turned her gaze back to the Windra who was still frozen, and her eyes narrowed in anger. She could feel her aura fading but she would hold him for a bit longer.

Yu was able to stand and the longer she went the more she seemed to recover. Her throat was a deep purple from the vice-like grip his arm had been in around her neck and she gingerly touched it wincing.

Taking a few steps towards him, Akami had a great idea. Twisting on her toe, she hurtled her shin towards his abdomen in a fast roundhouse kick, ending the spell an instant before it collided allowing her full force to slam into him with no protection.

She could feel her shin slip underneath his ribcage, digging deep into the delicate organs that lay nestled there and immediately he collapsed to the ground gasping for breath.

"Stop," called out a strained and faint voice and she turned to see Yu approaching, her gait slow but her eyes full of fury. "He's mine!"

Barely able to speak, she snapped her hand to the side launching him into the wall with a crack. She did not let up, launching him back across the room to the other side where he struck a wooden cabinet smashing it to pieces and causing the children to cry out in fear.

He coughed hard and rolled onto his back, heaving for air as Yu approached, her red hair draping over her shoulders in ratted knots. A swift kick to his abdomen was thrown then another strike from her elbow collided with the side of his face knocking him on all fours.

"I'll kill you Windra!" she hissed. "Orus!" and he lifted off the ground, bound by her spell. He squirmed, trying to fight against it but she held him awkwardly up just out of reach of the ground and unable to break the spell.

She walked over and struck him again with her fist hard into his abdomen before ripping his hood off. His hair was back and Akami could just make out the odd color of blue in his eyes.

"Piece of filth, laying your hands upon me!" and she shoved the side of his head over roughly before her other hand slapped him hard across the cheek. "Let's see your ugly face before you die, shall we?" and she grabbed hold of the white cloth that covered his mouth and nose. The golden laced cloth was torn away and the moment Akami saw his face her head nearly imploded, and she dropped to her knees in pain.

She could hear a deep and powerful voice shaking her mind. "Forget Kioni! Forget how you came here! You are Akami, daughter of the empress of Iterasu, sent here for a planned alliance! Kioni is no longer of your concern!"

Akami gasped in pain and scrunched her eyes, wishing it would stop. The voice continued on, repeating over and over, each time growing more powerful and shaking her very being. She could hardly think, hardly move but she fought as much as she could, fighting against the imposing pressure. It was too powerful, like a hurricane bearing down upon her and her very mind was threatened to blow away.

She strained to open her eyes, see him again as thoughts and memories of him flew by. She could just make out Yu as she walked over towards his glaive, grasping it and slowly approaching, the thick bladed tip aimed straight at his chest.

Akami tried to call out, tried to push past the thoughts that were threatening to crush her mind, but she couldn't utter a single sound as she watched the vision of Yu approaching fade in and out. She was almost gone, nearly lost to the tempest but one thought persisted above all else.

She needed Kioni alive!

Unable to focus on anything, she found out that suddenly she was on her feet. A shaky step followed, and the storm seemed to lighten a bit. She took another step, and it followed suit as she fought against it with every part of her being.

"Stop," she called out weakly as she raised her hand out, Yu paying no attention to it. "Stop," she called again.

"He is to die," Yu hissed, her voice wicked and full of hate.

"We need him!" Akami screamed, taking another step forcing the winds in her mind to split around her.

"He is to die. We do not need him! What are you talking about Akami?"

The Kitsune took another step, only a few feet away from Kioni. The glaive glistened wickedly.

"Something happened here, something to our minds Yu don't you understand? Kioni can help us find out what's going on!"

Yu said nothing and only froze momentarily at the mention of his name before she shuddered and looked at her for a long moment. Nothing was said and she took another slow step forward. Akami was out of options as her head swirled, the storm fighting against her and pressing in causing her to grimace in pain.

She had to stop her, no matter the cost!

With a cry, she ran forward, her legs heavy and the world seemed to slow down as her hands met Yu's torso. The next thing she knew, Yu was crashing to the floor, Akami's push knocking her back where she collided directly on Diahl's transparent figure.

Her body grew rigid like a board before arching back in an awkward posturing. Her mouth drew open in a voiceless scream and then she thrashed hard. Akami panted heavily before she saw the room sway and then she crashed into something firm.

Her head was spinning, and she blinked a few times as the storm ebbed away from her mind. She looked up to see Kioni's face looking down at her with shock, her face resting firmly against his chest.

She cried out in shock, ripping her head back and taking a few steps before shuddering hard in disgust. He held still for a moment before a cry of joy came from nearby and Akami turned to see the young pink haired girl staggering towards him, her eyes full of joy.

"You came!"

"You really are still a little human girl."

"It's because of your thing, it changed me, and I was too scared

The Legend of Kyne: Chronocide

of being caught to take it off," she muttered as she came to him, his arms wrapping around her in a tight embrace.

"It's ok Rosé, I am here now," he said tucking her head tight against his body. Akami watched them for a moment before turning back to Yu with a look of shock appearing on her face. The Kitsune's hair had turned grey just like her skin and every passing moment she shriveled up more and more like a dried corpse.

Kioni spoke behind her just as Diahl started to move.

"We need to kill him before he kills all of us," and without another word or objection from anyone, Kioni grabbed the ghostly blade from his hilt. Just as Diahl's eyes started to stir Kioni thrust it straight through his chest.

Diahl shuddered hard, his eyes darting open for a moment as he looked at Kioni in shock and then he faded into a ghostly fog leaving a grey stain upon the ground.

Instantly Akami felt the draining weight lift off of her and she looked over to the children, noticing that they could feel it too. Their skin gained a little more color just as their hair did and they all started to climb up to their feet.

"We should go," Kioni said grabbing onto Rosé and taking a few steps towards the door.

"Not yet," Akami said lowly, and he stopped mid-step.

"I am not dealing with you today," Kioni said flatly. "You already beat me up pretty bad," and his hand drifted to his abdomen. Akami could see the forming of a bruise appearing upon his swollen cheek.

"You're not leaving until I get answers," she hissed. "Don't test me, Kioni!"

"What do you even want," he said turning his head around to her. She watched his dark hair flick off his forehead and his blue eyes burned into her own.

"What happened to me! Someone corrupted my memories, invaded my mind! It was him I know it that archmage friend of yours!"

"It's not him," Kioni muttered. "I am certain of that. I don't have many answers but what I found out the last few days as I infiltrated the Windra mercenaries is that in this world Kydrëa never defeated the Dominion. Their leader Aaldra is still at large and just as powerful and for some reason he has taken this world's version of Kyne as his son. Aaldra is incredibly dangerous, I guarantee he was who attacked your mind and messed with your memories."

"It wasn't Aaldra," she said shaking her head in frustration. "It wasn't him; I remember it. I was in a cell, and some golden-haired man came to me. I am no idiot, Kioni! I have studied your people for years. I know who the archmage is and what he looks like. He attacked me without mercy, pushing into my head. I..." and her voice trailed off.

"My Kyne wouldn't do that," Rosé said, and she grabbed onto Akami's hand. "He wouldn't."

"Well, this one did," Akami said, pulling her hand away. "I have been violated to the highest degree."

"If he truly did that then he is more dangerous than I ever could have imagined. We should get out of here before he comes back," Kioni started. "Someone is going to find us."

Akami looked around the room for a moment, the remaining children, five including Rosé all staring at her with scared eyes.

"Avenseiose," and a swirling of aural trails appeared around. She moved her hands, and they watched as multiple trails vanished and moved, altering the webbing. She continued for a few more moments before finally stopping. "There, now they won't be able to find us, at least as easily as before. We should get out of here; do you know how we can get back to our world?"

Kioni shook his head and took a few steps away.

Akami nodded, the idea she knew to be fleeting at best. She had no idea how to return either and the more she thought about how she got here the harder it was to recall the memories. But at least they were returning.

Akami gathered the other children and just as they made it to the doorway, he turned back towards her.

"Thank you."

She nodded, a slight smile appearing on her mouth before she made it vanish.

"You know my name, but I don't know yours," he said. "May I ask what it is?"

"It's Akami."

"Akami, well, I guess for the moment we will be allies," he

said, as he turned towards Rosé. "May I have my cloth back?"

The young girl nodded, and she reached her hand up towards her mouth, pulling a silver cloth away as it materialized in her hand. Immediately her physique shifted, her skin rippling with metallic scales appearing and her clothes ripping off.

Akami gasped in shock as the rose gold dragon returned.

* * *

73. Divine Connections

"I think he fears Alakyne because of his connection to the Relics," muttered Tira in the late evening as they lay in a clearing far within the reaches of Kol Faldîn.

"Why do you say that?" Auriel replied, her mouth full of dried bread muffling her voice. Nearby Ni'Bara lay intently listening. Alakyne was sitting next to the fire, the boy hadn't spoken a word since they left.

"These Relics of Aute as you have explained are gifts from God, yes? And they seem to activate near Alakyne's presence?"

"The container did," Auriel said, and she looked towards her pack where she knew the object lay hidden.

"I think Xeono did as well," Tira said. "Remember when we first met Tiernyn. He was fine, his usual smooth-talking self until he came upon Alakyne."

Auriel furrowed her brow, not recalling much of it. The only thing she remembered was his insistent stare as if he were undressing her with his eyes.

"He kept messing with his wrist. That's where that gold bracelet is that you call Xeono. As far as I am aware no one even knew that was the source of his power. We all believed he was some chosen prophet as he led us to."

"Seems like he is just a cunning man who with his good looks acquired a powerful item. Xeono is legendary to this land. Able to cause war and decimate kingdoms," Auriel muttered.

"You seem pretty familiar with it Auriel," Tira muttered. "Oddly familiar."

"My husband fought someone just like Tiernyn a few years before I met him. I have heard the stories of its power."

"So, you really are from a different era then," she muttered, eyeing the young boy. "I honestly didn't believe you. But this makes more sense."

"I cannot tell you anything more for fear of it altering the future," but Tira was already shaking her head.

"Nor do I want to know about your problems. The problems then, whenever they are, don't mean much to me. Your time is yours alone, what matters to me is the things currently happening. We need to get the anti-venom so that we can save Aria. I fear that Tiernyn is not going to let us just roam this land much longer. If it comes to that we might have to leave completely. I know the land stretches far to the south and east, so we have a few options."

"Once again we are driven out from the home, we thought we had found," spoke Alakyne softly. "No matter what we do we seem to be cursed. From the moment I was carried in my mother it seems I was destined to cause suffering."

"Don't say that Alakyne," Auriel said. "You are not cursed; you are blessed with an incredible gift. Why would you say that?"

"Because monsters follow us, kill people, my parents, those villagers, and now my sister are all dead because of me."

"Aria is not dead!" Auriel replied sternly.

"Not yet. Mother should have just let me die when I was still within her. Maybe that would've spared everyone."

"What happened Alakyne?" Tira asked. "Why do you keep saying that you were not supposed to survive?"

"Mother was great with Aria's birth. I heard from the elders how strong she was, not uttering a peep of a cry. Aria herself was a strong baby too. Vigorous and full of life. When I was made and still in her belly, however Mother grew so ill.

Healers came trying to save her, but nothing seemed to work. Eventually it had come to a moment when they weren't sure if either of us were going to make it. One day a massive storm threatened Ysaroc, my village in the mountains. Threatened to tear our homes up from the earth and wash away the people down the mountain slopes. Mother was bedridden, sick as can be, and Father was trying his hardest to save what he could of the farm. Animals were lost, swept away by the water and when the storm reached its peak, pieces of our roof were torn off."

"That sounds awful Alakyne," muttered Tira and the woman sat next to him draping her long arm over his shoulder. Her glasses reflected the flashes of orange light from the flames and for a moment there was a long pause of silence before he continued.

The Legend of Kyne: Chronocide

"And then the storm finally ended, the rain stopped, and the clouds parted. Father had been trapped by the flooding out in the barn with the remaining animals and when he managed to get back to the home, he told me that he thought she had surely passed away.

But she hadn't. He found her lying curled up in the center of the room. The floor had sagged, forming a pool around her and she was lying in it, nearly covering her entire face. I guess just moments before he got to her some sound came from above and perched on our roof looking down through the hole was a large white bird. It sang a beautiful song stopping him in his tracks before it flew away. He told me that a small piece of down, the fluffy under-feathers of the bird drifted down and landed right on my mother's belly.

She woke up and after that moment everything seemed better; until I was born, and the monsters began to show up."

"A strange white bird," muttered Tira and Auriel looked at Ni'Bara, her chest quivering at the knowledge she had just received. Ni'Bara shook his head ever so softly and she agreed in not letting them in on any more information about that. They would let them speculate.

"I think it was a devil," Alakyne said. "A devil who cursed me to summon monsters."

"Or an angel," replied Tira. "You think of your gift as a curse but the power you have could be so much more. I have witnessed the destruction you can cause all on your own, but it is always because someone you love is in harm's way. It is you who defends them Alakyne. You are the one who stopped the eldercobra and nearly killed me for striking your sister. You destroyed the sorcerer who hit her with his blade, and I know you will continue to protect her once we get her back."

"Not if I just hurt her myself."

"Stop it Alakyne," snapped Auriel. "We have told you this before. We all agree you are not cursed so stop acting like you are. The monsters are drawn to you not because they are like you but because they want your power. It is like a drug to them."

His head turned away from the fire and met her eyes, a glimmer of hope in them.

"They want my power?"

"Of course they do. You are the thing that can destroy them.

They want it so that they can continue ravaging the land unobstructed."

"Tiernyn fears your power too Alakyne, that's why he tried to hurt you. He is an even bigger threat that I thought but with you we could potentially take care of him."

"How's that?" he asked.

"I'll let you know after we get the antidote. I think I know where we can find some. The lurdocs like to live in caves along the coastline. If we find one, I think I can make some myself. The only problem is it will need to be with my equipment in my bag, which is still in Faldîn Keep."

Her words caused a pit to form in Auriel's stomach and she looked into the fire.

"So, we will be returning there?" she said.

"Indeed, we will have to. I can try myself so that you all are not put in danger."

"No, I will come with you," said Auriel and her words caused Tira's eyes to light up.

"You... You would do that for me? I thought you despised me."

"I used to but the more I get to know you the more I see that you truly want to help the children."

Tira looked down at Alakyne and lifted her hand from his shoulder and ran it through his hair. She didn't have to say words. Auriel could tell just from her look. She didn't have children, but she had seemed to make it her mission to adopt these children as if they were her own.

The evening faded to night, and they slept, the three adults taking watches for fear of attack from unwanted monsters, but none arrived.

The following day they traveled southwest, heading for the coast where the small mountains met the water. Intricate caves lined it and Tira was certain it would contain at least one lurdoc. They flew all day, just reaching the coast as the sky was darkening to black. They set up camp and planned to search the following morning.

74. Mist and Seafoam

The wind was harsh, ripping through Auriel's hair and nearly toppling the young boy as they stood perched upon a rock. The great sea of Haakviid stretched out before them, its waves rough and dark as the gust continued. The sky was an ominous grey with deep tendrils of blue clouds stretched between. A flash of lightning was noticed upon the horizon and Auriel shivered.

Tira was nearby investigating something on the stone, perhaps guano but she wasn't sure. Flecks of white powdery substance was lifted up by a stick and Tira brought it near her face before nodding.

It is for sure guano, Auriel shuddered, imagining the sour stench that it had. Piles and piles of the droppings lay scattered around making it hard to avoid stepping upon it. From seabirds and lurdocs alike, the cliff-side was covered in it.

Large boulders were strewn about, peeled off of the cliffs above them and tumbling down to the sea below. No sandy beach lay here, no relaxing place to sit in the sun. The waves were harsh, carving deep gullies within the rocks and wearing them down, cracking them to pieces before they met the icy water.

Alakyne nearly slipped and Auriel managed to stop his fall, narrowly falling herself as she struggled for balance. The rocks were covered in a wet slime from the constant sea mist and each step was precarious as they trudged on further down the cliff.

Ni'Bara had dropped them off high above, allowing them a difficult climb down the cliff-side to the base before they traveled on. At first, they contemplated dropping them off in the water, but it proved far too dangerous. She could have used her aura but unsure of Tira's skill in movement spells and Alakyne's lack in experience she agreed on the decision.

They had traveled down the cliffs for a few miles, looking for any sign of the lurdocs. A few small caves were noticed but nothing seemed to stir in their dark depths. She had never heard of a lurdoc before other than Kyne mentioning parts of them used for aural catalysts.

Tira had described them as similar to bats but incredibly foul to look at with little arms and long tails. Their venom was dangerous, but a single bite wouldn't kill any of them. What she warned them about is once you were bitten once, you were marked and either by scent or by something else the other non-aggressive lurdocs would all swarm you.

"So, are we just going to try and catch one?" Auriel asked through a panted breath as she leapt over to another boulder. Resting her hand against the cliff wall, she turned to see Alakyne following behind her at a much slower pace.

"Indeed," the sorceress replied, and she fixed her hair, tucking the loose strands up with the rest that had been pulled up tight in a knot. Her glasses were partially foggy from the sea foam or her own body heat, Auriel wasn't certain.

She said a spell and the fog vanished, the crystal-clear lenses reflecting the scene out to their left. The turbulent ocean had not ceased, in fact it seemed to be growing more chaotic and the wind was picking up. Movement in her glasses was noticed first and then as Tira turned her head, Auriel followed to see Ni'Bara swooping down towards them.

"The weather is growing worse," he said as he struggled to hover nearby, his voice nearly being lost to the wind.

Auriel nodded. "We haven't found them yet. Watch for my signal for you to return alright?"

The dragon hovered for a moment, his look stern. "Be safe then," and gliding up, he vanished over the cliff above them a few hundred feet.

They were nearing where they had spotted the small caves and pushing on, they eventually found them. They were small, the largest barely able to house Alakyne standing up straight and the smallest more of a burrow for a badger in the stone. Following Tira, they all stepped inside, the two adults crouching down low and waiting for Alakyne to join them.

The Legend of Kyne: Chronocide

The wind outside howled but the moment they were inside, everything seemed to grow muffled, their breaths echoing around. They staggered through awkwardly a little farther before Tira conjured a light, the small orb showing them what they had entered.

The cave was long and narrow, straight like an arrow but to her despair, Auriel traced the ceiling noticing it didn't seem to grow any taller. It continued on for a few dozen feet before the light was lost. Nothing seemed to move in the cave, and they moved deeper, their eyes peeled for any sign of movement. She wasn't sure how big they were, Tira only said not too big, and Auriel shook her head in frustration.

A lot of help that description is.

Expecting a large bat like creature, she was shocked when Tira stopped and pointed at something small dangling from the ceiling. It was tiny, able to fit in the palm of her hand and as she took a quivery breath, she struggled to make out what she was seeing.

It was small and dark, wrapped up in a tight little ball with its head hidden. A long tail stretched up, connecting with the ceiling in a silky white glob. The sight reminded Auriel almost of if she had thrown a chunk of mud at the ceiling and it had splatted.

The lurdoc wasn't moving at all, still as stone and Tira turned around in her awkward crouch and began fumbling in her small pack. Auriel felt her legs beginning to shake and her muscles screamed for relief as she dropped to her knees, shifting her weight off of them.

Tira had soon withdrew a woven sack and ever so slowly, she brought the sack up and around the lurdoc. Bringing the lip of the bag to the ceiling, she brought it closed and with a final swipe of her hand, pulled it off the ceiling and cinched it up trapping the animal within.

The bag violently flailed around as it tried to escape, pushing against the fabric and forcing it to stretch outward. A muffled shriek came from the bag, but Tira lowered it and with a smile, nodded to leave. They all turned around and started their journey out, only a few dozen feet to the entrance.

The bag continued to thrash around, Tira holding it tight as she brought up the rear with Auriel next and Alakyne in front. The boy hadn't said much, only bearing a flat and saddened face. More screeches were heard but they disregarded them.

Just as Alakyne stepped out into the open, Tira shouted in

pain and Auriel turned to see her slap some dark shape from her neck where it slammed into the wall before falling at her feet. It reared up and Auriel recoiled, finally understanding what it truly looked like.

It was not black but a deep dark green. Small, it bore a set of bat-like wings and a long slender tail. It had no legs but only arms, each adorned with two dark claws as it lay grasping at the dirt ground. The animal screeched again in rage and its face was horrendous. Coming to a point, more like that of a lizard, its bottom jaw was cleft, splitting into two triangular shapes littered with many small, jagged fangs.

Tira took a step and with a swift kick, knocked the creature past Auriel where it tumbled down between the rocks. Her hand was clutching her neck, and a small stream of blood was starting to ooze from between her hands.

Auriel's look of worry was dismissed by a wave of her hand.

"I'll be fine, but more will be coming now!" and more screeches were quickly heard further within the cave.

With the sack clutched in her hand, the blood slowing its flow as it clotted on her neck, Tira joined the other two outside the cave and they took off over the boulders as fast as they could. The storm was beginning to rain, thick drops pelting their skin stinging with every strike.

Alakyne slipped hard, slamming his shin into the rock as he fell, and Auriel stopped to look. His shin had a large chunk of flesh torn clean off, already oozing blood and the boy's eyes were watery as he fought back tears.

Heaving him to his feet, Auriel guided him forward, holding onto him as he limped around a rock. The rain was making the situation even more dangerous and with a realizing thought, she launched a blazing orb of light straight into the air signaling Ni'Bara.

"He can't get to us here," Tira panted turning around to face her. "The wind is too strong."

"We can just use our aura. Going at this rate someone will surely break an ankle or worse," Auriel said, and she looked back towards the mouth of the cave. A few dark shapes had flown out into the rain, flying erratically as they tried to find Tira.

A few had started to near and as a bunch more came, they eventually seemed to find their target.

The Legend of Kyne: Chronocide

"Oo'nar!" shouted Auriel directing the wind towards the approaching lurdocs and as it struck them, she watched as they all flailed around caught in the gale. In mere moments, they had all dove down landing upon the rocks and to her shock, used their tails as anchors as their bodies flew like kites in the wind.

She held the spell for a few moments longer but the moment the wind stopped they all took off in flight again towards her. She tried the spell again but just as before, they cemented themselves to the rocks with their sticky white goo as when they had found them hanging in the caves, and as the wind stopped, they bolted towards them.

"Erodath!" Tira yelled and like a giant smacking a bird from the sky, a few of the lurdocs were launched back tumbling into the pile of boulders and lost from view.

Auriel looked at her in shock and saw her beaming in pride, her hair wild and sweat upon her brow.

"Oh, you have to be kidding me," she muttered, and Auriel turned back to see the lurdocs were back, flying quickly towards her.

She didn't want to kill them; they were animals defending their home but at this rate they were eventually going to make it to her.

"Aira tar," she said with a soft whisper, saddened by the consequences and an orb of light rocketed towards the incoming lurdocs. Just as it reached them, she clenched her fist tight, causing it to explode and launching dozens of arcing bolts of electricity, striking nearly all of them simultaneously.

Those it struck fell from the sky immediately, their bodies still as stone and she shook her head, frustrated by the needless deaths. More soon took their place and as she launched another attack, she heard a scream from Alakyne followed by a sharp pain on her shoulder. Turning her head, she watched as the face of a lurdoc withdrew its maw, its fangs covered with blood, and it screeched right at her face.

With her arm, she struck it away and immediately felt the hot sticky ooze of blood spread down her shoulder.

How did it evade my attack? I am sure I stopped all of the ones closest to us.

Another cry from Alakyne brought her attention back to him and she turned to see right next to her, the boy with three lurdocs spread from across his back and one upon his leg. He was flailing wildly but they all seemed to be holding fast as they bit harder, pumping their venom into his body.

"Erodath!" Auriel cried in rage, and she struck all of them away, watching them slam the cliff-side and laying still for but a moment before stirring.

Alakyne was crying and Tira was battling more that had come from above, hidden within unknown crevasses far above them. They were surrounded with more and more coming and just as she charged another arcing spell, she saw Ni'Bara's dark figure launch off the cliff flying towards them.

Diving fast, Auriel grabbed onto Alakyne and with a nod to Tira they both said, "Orus!"

Their vision darkened as the spell ripped them airborne where they hovered for a moment as Ni'Bara's mass dove beneath them, coming to an abrupt stop just in time to catch them. The aural strain on Auriel was intense and with a look at Tira she could tell she was feeling the same. As the lurdocs approached, more and more flying into the heavy rain, Ni'Bara took off climbing up into the sky and arcing up over the cliffs face. The beasts pursued but were quickly left behind.

The land was dark and foggy with rain obscuring everything from view, but he continued on, quickly tearing the rain from his scales as he carried them away from danger.

Auriel touched her shoulder and was pleased to see the bleeding had already stopped. Assessing Alakyne's wounds, she smiled noticing his were all superficial as well. He was still crying but as the minutes tolled on, he started to simmer down.

"We will all be fine," Tira chuckled weakly. "Not enough bites to do much harm other than annoy us honestly. But this," and she raised the bag that had stopped shaking as the creature within had ceased moving. "This is quite a success."

The dragon flew quickly, escaping the harsher clutches of the storm and the further on they went, the clearer the sky became. To the north, cast in the light shining through the thinning clouds, they could see the lumbering shapes of small mountains. Covered from base to summit in verdant trees, they were tall but not even half the size of the Riigar Mountains. No glaciers touched their slopes, and their summits still held the touch of vegetation as if unknowing of the barren summits further inland.

They stopped shortly after, dressing their wounds as best as they could. Auriel only sustained one bite whereas Alakyne had four and Tira had gotten two. They stung and she could tell they had been laced with venom, but she was still puzzled why it wasn't killing them.

"They don't have a lot that they inject at once. The blade that struck Aria likely had been dipped in pure venom, probably from a few hundred. The venom is much more lethal in high quantities. A true assassins attack," and she shook her head in frustration. "Once we get my pack then we can surely make an antidote for her."

"But how are we to get your pack," Auriel asked, the thought having bothered her for a long time. "Tiernyn will surely notice us returning. I bet Ni'Bara would be hit before we could even land."

The dragon scoffed nearby, clearly irritated with her words. "Struck before I even land? I would like to see him..." His voice died off as Auriel flashed a look.

"Come on, don't be arrogant. You know just as well as I do the power Xeono has. Tiernyn even seems more dangerous with it than Aaldra. He killed that leviathan in no time at all. We were all there, sick and nearly dead and he struck it down."

Ni'Bara turned away, his eyes flashing a hint of anger, but Tira spoke next. "Tiernyn is the single most dangerous thing that I know. I would surely rather fight off hordes of beasts than fight him one on one. Dragon, you know this to be true, don't be foolish."

"I could've taken the leviathan," he muttered, a puff of heat blasting up from his nostrils as he turned his gaze back to them, ripples in the air signaling its blazing temperature.

"Really?" Auriel furrowed her brow giving an exaggerated look towards him and she watched as he slowly gave in.

"Fine, maybe I couldn't have taken it. If we all didn't magically get sick from the tainted rain, then it would've been a different story. I have slain both an eldercobra and a roc."

"But that is what makes the leviathan so deadly," Tira said. "It is the embodiment of pestilence as the roc is to famine and the eldercobra is to war. They all embody a bane of humanity Ni'Bara. It's what makes them even more dangerous than just their physical strength."

"What do you mean?" asked Auriel confused.

"I suspect that's the reason the city was growing sick. The leviathan had made its way into the city, either through the sewers or maybe caught in a fishing haul. Spreading its pestilence around until Alakyne made it snap."

They looked towards him and saw the boy avert his eyes to the ground. They knew it bothered him to talk about his so-called curse, but they needed to.

"What if we use that to our advantage then," Ni'Bara said as he swept his tail around in a big arc. The whoosh of air blowing the grass over in a dangerous bend.

"We can't," Auriel started but Tira raised her hand out as if asking for a moment of speech.

"I think that might be the ticket," she said. Removing her glasses from her face, she rubbed the bridge of her nose for a moment as if contemplating the idea. "If we can get one to attack the city, we could use that as the distraction to get to the pack."

"I can't do it," Alakyne nearly screamed. He had risen to his feet and his face was contorted in anger and grief.

"But you can," Tira replied, her voice calm and genuine. "I have seen it before Alakyne, I know you can."

"You're wrong!" he screamed even louder. "I can't do it!" The air began to tremble, vibrating in a deep hum.

Auriel and Tira took a slight step back as they watched the boy, tears began streaming down his cheeks and to their shock, his hair started to rise as if he were falling. The trembling intensified and his eyes flickered, a pale white emanating from deep within as the boy cried out in pain.

"Auriel we should get away!" rumbled Ni'Bara and without taking her eyes off of Alakyne, she leapt back towards the dragon.

To her shock, she watched as Tira, instead of joining her, walked forward, dropping to her knees in front of the boy and wrapping her arms around in in a tight embrace.

The trembling intensified and then the pressure was felt, the force as if gravity was increasing tenfold drove the Riel to her knees and she watched as Ni'Bara struggled to fight it as well. Panic was flowing through her as she watched the bright white of his eyes fully take over, a strange misty fog emanating from them like an angelic breath.

Tira was speaking, unheard by the others, as she struggled to hold on to the boy. Her hair, still tied up in a bun had begun to rise and thrash around, unraveling in the turbulent wind that was rising.

Auriel tried to call out, but her voice didn't make it, the pressure forcing her breath out and the wind changing to a gale. Alakyne's mouth slowly opened, as if in a slow-motion wail and to her shock and horror, the boy began to rise up in the air, his feet dangling as they left the earth.

Tira still clung to him, holding him tight as she fought the pressure pushing him down.

And then time seemed to grow utterly still.

The wind stopped suddenly, and the pressure began to weaken, relenting upon them as Tira held the boy close, whispering softly in his ear. Slowly he lowered back down to the ground, his eyes returning to normal.

Reaching his arms up, he wrapped them around Tira and the two held themselves for a long moment, his sobs intensifying as they echoed around over the field. Rising to her feet, Auriel smiled weakly at them as they withdrew, knowing that Tira had saved them all.

She truly does care for him.

"We can find another way then Alakyne," Tira said as she withdrew from him. "I know that you are a strong young man and if you don't want to, I won't make you."

"I... I..." he stammered.

"It's ok, there will be another way," Auriel said.

"I can try," he squeaked out, his voice cracking and they all laughed lightly at the sound.

"Are you sure," Tira said, reaching out and moving a strand of hair from across his face. "You don't have to."

"I will try. I will try for Aria."

75. Aute

"We should move," Ni'Bara said, eyeing the sky and the small mountains far behind them. "I feel very exposed out here."

The two women nodded, and the boy followed as they all climbed onto the saddle. A leap and a large powerful flap sent them skyward, leaving the site behind. They climbed high for a few minutes before Ni'Bara arced around and jerked his head as if signaling below them.

Far below and a few miles back, they watched as two enormous birds stood where they had just previously been. Dark in color with their striking white heads, Auriel knew they could be only one thing.

"Arpri, the primal eagle of death, or known in the common tongue, the roc," Tira murmured as she watched the two birds walk around the land below, their heads low as they slammed their beaks into the ground searching for Alakyne.

"Disgusting wretched things," rumbled Ni'Bara and he accelerated, his abdomen tightening with each wingbeat. Auriel could feel the urgency with each flap and as he accelerated faster and faster, she fought the urge to fall back into Tira. Alakyne was in front of her and leaning over him, she forced him down low, holding him securely in place as the dragon rocketed away.

Once they had gotten up to speed, the feeling of being launched back fading allowed Auriel to glance back towards the birds where they were proceeding to brawl with one another. She watched as one jumped forward, talons outstretched, and wings flared as it collided with the other's breast. Even the few miles that had grown between them, from their sheer size she could still easily see what they were doing.

If they start heading towards us, I can hide us with my aura, she thought as she contemplated options. *I could hide us or even lure them away. It depends.*

But as Ni'Bara pushed onward at the fastest speed he could hold, the arpri as Tira had called them faded away beyond the horizon. On all sides, they could just see utter expanse of grassland turning to a pale shade of blue as it was lost from sight. They continued to gain height and eventually Ni'Bara slowed, hanging into a glide as he allowed his muscles to rest.

They traveled on, passing far above little villages and homes dotting the landscape. It was the farmlands that Auriel noticed first. A deep verdant that lay like a delicate emerald upon a sea of peridot. Clusters of trees lay in tight little copses that dotted the landscape and as they strained their eyes, they could just make out the homes nestled in like eggs in a bird's nest.

A short distance away lay a small blue river, thin and narrow as it wound its way over the landscape. Little canals had been carved near its edge, directing water towards each set of farmland. They were far too high to see any people down below but to her relief, it seemed like the people were doing well. No attacks had been made by beasts or other raids by marauders.

They had passed over this river recently but not having been over this specific village. Alakyne was leaning over as he stared down at the multi thousand-foot drop below. The wind was loud, and his golden hair was blowing wildly. She could see just the side of his face but could see the thrill there, a faint forgetting of the horrors that would come to meet them on the land.

The night came as they nestled upon the ground, as before each took a turn for watch except for the child who slept restlessly. Murmuring was heard, muffled by his head, twisted over and nuzzled into his pack. It intensified as he turned over, his eyes closed but his mouth moving fast. It was hard to hear as Auriel leaned in and with a wave of her hand, she cast a muffling spell over Tira in an effort to keep her asleep. Ni'Bara had left them a short time ago, his glittering underside adorned with small flecks of white mirrored the stars as he glided over the campsite vanishing beyond the light of the fire. He was off to hunt something to eat, having not eaten in days.

Auriel leaned in closer, trying to make out the words he said. Most were jumbled mumbles, no specific words but more sounds and moans. His breath suddenly quickened.

He jerked to the side before calling out Aria's name. Crystal clear, his words rang all around and Auriel looked over towards Tira before remembering she couldn't hear him. More mumbling came and then he called out her name again, this time rolling over in his restless sleep.

"Cligen sweet one," the Riel whispered as she directed the spell upon the boy in an effort to soothe his nightmare and almost immediately, he seemed to relax. A deep sigh came from him and then his breathing slowed back to a rhythmic pattern.

She returned to her seat, awaiting the dragon's return. The sky dazzled above, twinkling glimmering stars shining above them, and she leaned back on her hands looking up remembering a cold chilly night where they sat just like this.

She felt a tightness well up in her upper chest as she thought about her husband. She missed him more than anything else, drowning out all the sorrow of losing her people. She wanted him there with her, to feel his warmth upon her skin and pull him close, his breath in her ear. She closed her eyes, imagining his scent and she smiled weakly.

"I still haven't found a way to reach you my love," she whispered. "I think about it every day. I think about you and my dear little Rosé. I pray to the Light and to any other unknown gods that might exist that she is safe and that I will be able to return to you soon."

"The arpri the primal eagle of death, the alamere, the alpha of the sea, and the eldunaga, the eldest of the wicked flame," Tira said as they sat by the cool remains of the fire. The sun had risen up casting glittering flecks of light from the dew that lined the vegetation.

"So, is that what they are really called?" asked Auriel as she ate what little food they still had. The dry bread lodging in her throat was discomforting and she forced a swallow.

"Well sort of," she sighed. "They have many names but that's their name in the old language. We usually just refer to them in their names in the common tongue."

Auriel nodded and took another dry bite. "And you really think that the distraction will be enough? Tiernyn seems to be an intelligent man."

"Well, that is the biggest understatement I have heard in a long time," she laughed out loud. "I would bet nearly everything I have on the notion he is the most intelligent person on the continent. He is cunning and ruthless."

"Indeed, he is," and Auriel sighed. "He won't be so easily tricked."

"I don't think he would assume us to be imbeciles, returning to his city so soon. He would expect something more designed from us."

"If you say so," Auriel sighed, and she rose to her feet. "What if we encounter Jurnen or your mute?"

"I don't know, I haven't really thought about it."

"He did seem to not care when you were exiled," Ni'Bara said. "He just sat there and observed. The tongueless seemed to do the same."

"Jurnen is an asshole, and I would expect nothing else from my mute," she said quickly as if offended that it had been brought up. "They are merely tools to the sorcerers. Mine was assigned and now that I am gone, he will surely be with another."

Tira looked away and Auriel could tell she was annoyed and bothered. Even if they were just tools to them, their crimes they committed stripping them of all of their rights. They were still a tool that was with them constantly in a similar way to a blade, and she looked down at the single edged orichite blade at her hip.

If this were to be taken from me and given to another I would be hurt too.

"We will reach the city later today Alakyne," spoke Tira, more authority in her voice and she pushed her glasses up tight. "Then it will be up to you."

"I'll try my best," he muttered and without saying another word he climbed up Ni'Bara's leg and positioned himself on the dragon's saddle.

The other two flashed looks of concern at one another and they too followed his lead, each taking their seat. Ni'Bara rose to his full height and swung his head around to look at them. "Where are we going to do this then?"

The Legend of Kyne: Chronocide

"Just get us above the city as high as you can, we will conceal you. We can take it from there."

They flew for a few hours, the dragon continuing to gain height at a calm pace. Far on the horizon they could just make out a smudge of dark, like a line tracing the edge of the earth. It was the forest and nestled near the edge of the river was the city. Faldîn, or how it was currently named Karstead was enormous.

It still shocks me that this is the ancient home of Kyne's family. I still haven't seen it in my own time, but I really hope I get to see it. I wonder how different it truly is.

Tira behind her started muttering something and a fierce tingling wrapped around her, stretching over her skin and underneath her across Ni'Bara's flank. As it faded away, the tingling still hovered, just barely noticeable and the Riel glanced back noticing Tira in a deep focus.

She looked away.

Tira's focus was what was keeping them alive and as if on cue, the dragon shuddered before accelerating, arcing toward the city directly. Like a slow-moving scene, the city crawled towards them until eventually it lay spread out beneath.

Coming to a stop, the dragon flapped its wings hard, repeatedly trying to hold his position high up in the sky. Auriel grabbed onto the saddle and for a moment, leaned dangerously towards the side looking down upon it. She could just make out the roof of Faldîn Keep, their target.

"Alakyne, it's up to you," Tira said, her hand not leaving Ni'Bara's side, but she awkwardly turned to face him. The young boy looked down over the side for a moment before meeting her own gaze.

"You can do it," she said, with a reassuring nod. Auriel mimicked her and smiled trying to boost his confidence.

The boy seemed to respond to their praise and taking a deep breath, he put both hands on his thighs and furrowed his brow, his face contorting in a strained focus. He held it there for a long time before gasping for breath.

"I believe in you," Auriel said, and she nodded repeating her gesture.

The Legend of Kyne: Chronocide

He tried again, focusing on drawing out his inner power, but try as he might, he couldn't seem to touch its source. His face strained, turning a deep crimson and he gasped for breath again.

He cried in frustration and struck his leg with the side of his fist. He hit it again, two more times in repeated succession before raising his gaze and a look of desperation upon his face.

"I don't think I can do it," he whispered.

"You can Alakyne. It's not just for us, it's for Aria. Without you we have no chance of getting her treatment," Tira said. "I can't help you."

And her words hovered in the air for a long time mimicking the dragon as his wings continued to flap. Auriel could tell he was starting to show fatigue and knew they had to do something, or they would have to retreat.

"Alakyne, let me try and help you," she said, a thought coming to her mind. Climbing from the saddle to a standing position, her legs flexing as she maintained her balance like a boat upon a rough sea. A quick light step around, her orichite foot-wrappings providing enough grip upon the saddle to keep her secure and soon she was seated behind him. She could feel the edge of the saddle digging into her lower back and with a gesture of her hand, the other two slid forward, allowing her some more space.

"Let's try this again," she said. "Try to find that feeling you had the last time. All I am going to do is feel what you do with my aura."

Alakyne nodded and as she placed her hand upon his back, she felt him go rigid as he tried to bring out his power.

She closed her eyes, stretching her aura forward into his own where she was able to feel the small source of power. She could feel it, tossing and turning as if the sea were amidst a hurricane's gale. Straining harder, she felt the boy begin to shake as he seemed to squeeze his face. In response the power within seemed to lose its turbidity, slowing down and growing calmer until he gasped for breath.

"Again."

He repeated the exercise and to her surprise, the more he strained to unleash his potential, the softer his reservoir became. It only swelled the moment he started.

"This time I want you to try something different," she said

drawing his attention. "Instead of forcing your power out, I want you to simply try to touch what you have. Sense it and touch it."

"But how do I do that?"

"The same way you perform any spell. Feel the pull deep within you. Turn your sight inward and swim in the power you possess."

Ni'Bara turned his head around, looking towards her for a moment. She could tell he was getting close to his breaking point. They had only a short time left before he would need to land. Hovering was incredibly exhausting compared to open flying.

"Let's try again," she said, and she gestured for him to turn around in his seat so that they were facing one another. Tira remained stationary, focusing on maintaining their spell that was keeping them hidden. Reaching out her hands, Auriel grabbed onto Alakyne's and motioned for him to close his eyes. For a moment just after they were closed, she observed him. His messy golden hair similar to her husband's and his pale skin but his warm hands clasped in her own.

Closing her eyes, she was met with darkness and immediately stretched her aura out towards his. Deep within, she could feel it like a crystal clear and still pond, free of all disturbances.

"Ok Alakyne," she said, and she squeezed his hands. "This time I want you to touch your aura, reach deep within and just feel it."

"I'm trying," he responded. "It's hard though, every time I get close it seems to run away from me."

"Don't stretch out to it, merely be present and bring it towards you," she said feeling the boy's aura remaining utterly still. A long moment of silence followed and then to her surprise, she felt a single ripple as if someone had placed a finger right into the center of the pond.

"Beautiful," she said with happiness evident in her voice.

"You can see it?" he whispered. "It feels so strange."

"Yes, I can," she replied. "In due time if you train long enough you actually can bring it out of your body in its pure form just like you can feel right now. My brother was incredibly good at it."

"I bet that took him a long time."

"Many many years of hard training and look at you. Already you have touched it which is a feat in itself. Now, we need to bring your true power out."

"How do we do that?" he asked, and she felt his hands pull away from hers. Opening her eyes, she saw him staring at her with confusion. "How am I supposed to bring forth a power I don't know."

"I think you do know," Auriel said, and she grabbed his hands again. "I think this power you possess is masked by the love you have for your sister. Focus on her. Focus on the danger she is in and how you must protect her."

They closed their eyes.

Auriel soon felt the same touch as before, the surface shimmering in a single ripple as the boy felt his aura. There they sat for a long time, but nothing seemed to change.

"Think of Aria," Auriel whispered and the moment her voice said the name, the aura began to shiver. It lasted for a moment before growing still. "Aria needs you."

The pond trembled again as if vibrating and this time it didn't stop. Auriel felt the boy's hands tighten and the aura within him began to shake more, each moment growing more and more vigorous. She could feel something strange within him swelling and suddenly, the small pond of aura she was touching was flooded by a tsunami of power. It flowed all around, threatening to tear her apart as she struggled to remain where she was as a bystander.

She could feel a deep pressure around, a power that made the air tremble and as she opened her eyes, she could see through the boy's closed eyelids, the glow of white and the thin fog rising from the corners. She held on, expecting the massive pressure to push her down but it never did, they just sat there, his power flowing all around them like a veil.

"You did it," she whispered, and she watched as his eyes opened up revealing the light within.

"I... I feel strange," he mumbled, his voice distorted, powerful and deep, unlike the young boy from before. "I feel like I know you, I can see you like the others but you and Ni'Bara seem different. You seem off like the parts that make up your body aren't supposed to be here."

Auriel's eyes widened with shock, and she met Tira's gaze. She could tell the sorceress was shocked as well at the words from the boy but before they could speak, he continued.

"I sense things down below. Things that seem to speak to me in tongues I cannot speak but yet I understand. One lies with us as well in your pack Auriel."

"Do you mean the Relics of Aute?" she said as she watched him peer down to the ground far below.

"Aute," he repeated, sounding out the word. "Aute" he said again. "Yes, that is it. Aute sounds too familiar, as if I am Aute and Aute is me. I cannot explain it but I just…"

Suddenly the light from his eyes faded and his pupils contracted tight as he was brought out of his enlightened state. Leaning forward, Auriel caught him on her shoulder, allowing him a moment to recover before he was able to right himself.

"What happened?" he murmured. "I feel funny."

"You did it," Tira said. "And it looks like you have invited some friends to party."

To the southwest, closer to the ground there were two large shapes darting across the land. Wings spread wide casting the land in a deep shadow as they tore through the air. As they drew upon the outer farmland, their flight causing the crops to yellow, they watched as aural attacks rocketed towards them from the city's towers.

"We should go," Auriel called and noticing the approaching rocs, Ni'Bara tucked his wings tight and they plummeted. A sickening feeling pulled through Auriel's abdomen for a moment as her hair began to blow wildly. Leaning forward, all three held on as tight as they could as the dragon darted out of the sky like a concealed meteor.

The flying aural attacks missed the rocs and as each of them flew over the final stretch of farmland, they watched as a massive flap of their wings uprooted trees and homes alike.

76. Xeono

Screams rang up from the ground, the piercing sounds striking Auriel's ears like a knife to her brain. The wind tore around them, the dragon plummeting towards the rapidly approaching city but she could still make out their horrendous screams. Buildings below shuddered as two dark shadows ripped over their roofs, shingles torn up in a furious wind.

Ni'Bara stretched his wings out only partially, guiding them in a gradual curve to their left, away from the eagles and towards the city's keep. Flashes of light flew up from the ground, a few striking the rocs but most didn't seem to do anything to them.

The ground was near and with a jarring motion, Ni'Bara spread his wings dramatically slowing their descent and causing his riders to hunch forward under the force. Auriel could feel her vision darken upon its edges and for a moment as it pressed in swallowing her sight, she thought she was going to pass out. As the dragon came to a stop, landing upon the ground as softly as he could, Auriel felt her mind begin to clear.

The scene was flashing in and out of focus, partially distorted from the forces but as she took a deep breath, she felt her sight grow more stationary. Behind her she felt Tira lurch to the side and with a leap she crashed to the ground. Falling in a drunken roll, she managed to get to her knees before she retched, heaving up her stomach contents upon the stone ground.

Auriel felt her own stomach lurch and she fought the urge to throw up, but as soon as it began, it started to edge away. Alakyne in front of her had leaned forward, his head resting against Ni'Bara's back.

He is unconscious? she panicked and reaching her hand forward she put it underneath his nose. The warm humid air confirmed his breathing just as Tira vomited again. Turning to face her, Auriel looked down from the saddle and saw the woman had already risen to her feet. Brushing her mouth with her sleeve, she noticed her gaze and straightened her back to a better posture.

Auriel could tell she was embarrassed.

"Watch him closely," Auriel said, and the dragon rumbled while swinging his head around eyeing the few humans who were running away. They had surely been noticed by now, but they only needed but a moment to retrieve the pack.

Suddenly a powerful force rocketed overhead, a pulsating ball of aura that shimmered like a comet before it collided with the breast of one of the rocs. A flash of light followed by a deafening boom sounded. It took only a few moments before the bird collided with the ground. Houses were crushed under its mass as it slid to a stop. Its beak lay partially open, and a screech of pain erupted from it.

Nearby, just out of view Auriel could hear shouting and smaller aural attacks flew towards the bird. Flaming balls and electrical arcs surrounded it, bombarding it in a furious attack. It screeched more fiercely this time shaking their bones with its high-pitched squeal. Auriel clamped her hands over her ears in an attempt to lessen the noise and watched as it stumbled up to its feet. Its wing was bent at an awkward angle and upon its breast lay a scorched mark of burned feathers and the red of blood.

The roc took off, pushing around buildings in an attempt to flee but another massive force was felt, and a second attack flew at it. An explosion blew apart the immediate vicinity, flattening trees and ripping roofs from homes as the roc was struck again launching it forward onto its front with a crash.

More shouting and the attacking sorcerers ran in view. For a split-second Auriel feared they would be spotted, and their attack could be lethal if they were struck by one of them. A tingle was suddenly felt, and she watched as everything from her own arms to the saddle and Ni'Bara all faded from sight.

Auriel turned to see Tira, still visible nearby, but she had turned her back to the sorcerers and had managed to throw her hood up in an attempt to remain unnoticed.

"Stay hidden."

The party continued on its way, unaware of their presence and they watched as a group of five cloaked figures ran into view towards the roc. Three more followed at a slower but still brisk pace and Auriel felt her mouth open in shock. It was Jurnen with both of the mutes on his heels. Another massive attack was being charged, their aura flowing into him and without a sound the sorcerer launched it up into the air towards the second roc.

It narrowly missed, rocketing past for a few seconds before exploding in a massive flash of light. Jurnen staggered forward, trying to keep his balance and Auriel could tell he was exhausted. The two who followed behind him also swayed and one took a knee as they tried to catch their breath.

That attack is incredible, but it uses far too much power. A missed attack is far too dangerous the risk.

She felt movement in front of her and blindly reached her hand out searching for Alakyne's invisible figure. She touched his clothes and directing her hand to his shoulder, pulled him in close just as he started to say, "What happened?"

"Be quiet Alakyne," she muttered. "Tira concealed us, but we can still be heard."

She felt him shift around as she assumed he was surveying the scene and she heard him gasp. "Is that a roc?" he whispered.

"A dead one," she replied. "They struck it down in two attacks. We have to remain hidden, so they don't see us."

"Auriel," called Tira nearby and she turned to see the sorceress had drawn close.

"Here," she replied and removing herself from the saddle, she jumped to the ground. Even unable to see her legs, she managed to land delicately right next to Tira and the spell upon her ended revealing her beautiful figure.

"Ni'Bara keep Alakyne safe. We will be back in a few minutes."

With a nod to one another, the two women took off in a sprint towards the stairway that led into the keep. Pushing the door open, they bolted down the hall, heading for Tira's quarters.

"I didn't see Tiernyn, we should be in the clear at least for the moment," Tira panted as she pushed on.

Shouting was heard as nobles fled to the lower levels underground in an attempt to protect themselves from the outside, but none were seen until they rounded a corner running face to face with a sorcerer escorting some woman.

Upon seeing them, the sorcerer paused for a moment before a look of realization lit up across his face. He started to shout something but before he could finish his first word Auriel was upon him, her orichite blade thrust deep through his abdomen and piercing out his back, the green blade covered in sticky hot blood.

A yelp of shock came from Tira at the sight followed by a scream of fear from the woman who bolted away down the hall.

"Erodath," she muttered, and a force smashed into the woman's back just as she came to the end of the hallway and turned toward a door. The force struck her launching her hard into the wall where a loud crack was heard, and she slumped over unmoving.

Tira was in shock, staring at her with eyes wide open as Auriel used her aura to flick the blood from her blade before sheathing it. Looking down at the sorcerer she had slain, she could still see the look of shock upon his face adorned with his glassy eyes.

"You stabbed him," Tira stammered. "With a sword... You stabbed him."

"What's the difference in using a blade or my aura?" the Riel asked, the response from Tira irritating her as if the sorceress was full of judgment.

"It's just... We never use swords. Physical attacks seem so barbaric."

"And tearing apart people with aura isn't? It seems to me that killing with my blade would be on par with my aura. My people have always been trained in physical combat. Focusing solely on aura is limiting in so many ways."

Understanding came across Tira's face after those words and fiddling with her glasses for a moment, she then lightly stepped over the corpse and started guiding her towards their destination.

Flying up a set of stairs, at the summit lay a door and pushing it open she heard Tira sigh in relief. Darting over to the bed, she withdrew a black leather pack adorned with a silver serpent. She threw it over her back and without a word, they darted through the door on their way back.

As they came to the base of the stairs, before they could even react, they noticed Tiernyn at the base looking up at them.

"Y'vinu."

The spell from the man jerked them forward, knocking them off balance and sending them tumbling down the staircase in a bruised and battered pile. Auriel felt a hard pain across her leg and as they finally came to a stop she clutched her thigh, tears in her eyes as the muscle spasmed.

Tiernyn was looking down upon them, his face littered with disgust and a swift kick to first Tira and the Auriel's ribs sent them both hunching over gasping in pain.

"I knew you would be back for that damn pack," he hissed before kicking Tira again hard in the back and sending her sprawling forward. "The moment I felt his power and the arpri showed up I knew you were planning something!"

Auriel tried to crawl away but with an unheard spell she was launched back towards the stairs slamming against them and shooting pain through her back. She coughed out hard and felt her mind swim as he looked down upon her.

"Trying to run now Auriel? That doesn't seem like you at all. The Auriel I know, the one who turned me down would never try to run," and he mocked her, talking in the voice of a child as he smiled wickedly. "You could've been with me, but you chose her and those children."

Auriel coughed and she clutched her ribs, bruised but not broken. Tiernyn studied her for a long moment, Tira lay unmoving nearby and then his eyes lit up as he gained an incredible idea.

"That thing you used to trap the girl. Where is it?"

"Not here!" she spat, and she struggled to her knees.

"Somehow I don't believe that," he chuckled and with another light kick of his foot, pushed her over to her side where she curled up in pain. "Kitala container," and as his voice was heard, Auriel felt the hidden pocket in her undergarments begin to thrash around violently as the Relic within struggled to escape like a caged animal. The thrashing intensified and the moment Tiernyn noticed it he ended the spell.

Coming to her, he knelt down and touched her leg, his hands gentle for but a moment as he felt for the item. Whipping out a knife,

645

The Legend of Kyne: Chronocide

he thrust it through the fabric and tore it apart revealing her exposed leg from the top of her knee nearly to the bottom of her hip.

Auriel thrashed around, trying to throw him off but before she could utter a spell, she suddenly grew rigid as he forced his aura to bind her. She fought, thrashing as hard as she could as he tore more of her pant-leg off before running his hand briefly up her thigh. His touch made her shudder in rage and disgust, and he could see it upon her face.

Smiling, he brought his face inches from her own and closed his eyes before inhaling deeply. "Your breath is so sweet, like a freshly open flower on a warm spring day. I wish we could take this so much farther but," a tearing sound was heard, and he lifted the hexagonal relic up from her with a gleam in his eye.

"Come with me you two," he laughed as he rose to his feet and turning on his heel, he walked away for but a moment before Auriel and Tira were jerked forward. Being dragged feet first and bound by his unrelenting aura, they struggled to resist, to drain his power so that they might be able to break free.

But try as they might, his aura didn't seem to have an end and he continued on through the keep in a pleasant stroll with the women being dragged on behind him. Rounding the final corner and coming to the top of the stairs that led out to the courtyard, he waved his hand launching them past him down the steps and upon the ground where they tumbled for a moment before coming to a stop.

Auriel wanted to cry out in pain, scream in rage at what was happening, but she couldn't breathe, and she struggled to gasp as her vision swayed from her beating. Nearby she could make out the shape of Tira as she stirred and then she noticed the woman's arm snapped clean in two and hanging limply, the only thing seeming to keep her hand attached being her muscles and skin.

Ni'Bara stop him! Auriel's mind tried to scream as her lungs struggled to let out even a gasp.

The dragon's figure phased into being as the illusion spell ended, his face littered with dragonrage and his mouth dripping with cyan flame. No words were spoken by him, and he engulfed Tiernyn in the hottest dragonfire that Auriel had even seen. The stone steps seemed to turn to goo and the walls of the keep sagged, the rock melting and the wood turning to ash from the blaze.

He didn't cease his attack and with a shimmering haze around his tail, he whipped it around before slamming it down upon Tiernyn's obscured form. The ground quaked from the attack and as the flames subsided, she was in disbelief as Tiernyn remained standing. His hair was matted, not in its pretty braids and beads of sweat lay upon his face. He was kneeling down, in a circle of unmelted stone.

As he stood up, she could hear Ni'Bara inhaling for another blast, but a flash of light stopped him and to their horror, Aria slumped into view falling to the ground in a limp heap. Cries of shock came from Alakyne and Tiernyn seemed to smile as he drew himself up to his full height.

"You burn me you burn her," he laughed. "It's over. You have lost, all of you."

"Tiernyn you bastard!" screamed Tira. "Let her go! She will die if she stays outside of that for too long!"

"Obviously she will die you complete an utter excuse of a sorcerer! All of you will not be leaving this city." The Otoruhn's dark eyes started to glow a deep gold and the flash of electricity was seen radiating from his wrist. Auriel felt panic in her mind thinking of anything that could stop him, but nothing came to thought. They had truly lost.

"The only one who will be dying today is you Tiernyn," snarled the dragon and his spines quivered as he turned his gaze upon the sorcerer.

Auriel watched in shock as Tiernyn slowly lowered his arm, the electricity fading away as the dragon locked him in a trance-like state. Before Auriel even had a chance to say anything, Ni'Bara's tail slammed into his side, launching him like a ragdoll across the courtyard where he flew out into the city lost from view.

Alakyne screamed, drawing Auriel's attention towards him and she watched as he leapt to the ground running towards his sister. Aria had begun coughing intensely, white foam appearing upon the edges of her mouth.

"The container!" screamed Tira and Auriel looked frantically around trying to find it and then she realized where it was. Taking off in a sprint as fast as she could, ignoring the intense pain in her leg and

The Legend of Kyne: Chronocide

aided by her aura, the Riel princess rocketed across the courtyard and out into the ravaged city. Dashing down the crumbling streets and evading any people she encountered, she quickly found the body of Tiernyn, still as stone and broken beyond repair.

His eyes were glassed over, and blood gurgled out of his mouth as his body spasmed the last few blinks of energy it had. One leg was twisted awkwardly around and the other had his femur protruding out of his skin and through his cloak in a jagged bloody spear.

She knelt down and felt around his cloak looking for the Relic and as she came to his pelvis, felt the crunch of bone and she recoiled. The man was broken, like a shattered window he lay in a pool of his own blood as it clotted upon the stone ground. A lump in the end of his cloak drew her attention and to her relief she pulled out the Relic. Turning on her heel, she took a single step before a massive force tore through the city, pushing her down to the ground and threatening to crush her.

It was unlike anything she had ever felt and as she lay there, struggling to resist, she realized truly what had just happened.

Tears streamed down her face as she sobbed, her cheek pressed hard into the ground as the pressure intensified. The only explanation for this was Aria was gone, and she screamed again in sorrow at the young girl who was unable to be saved. The earth shuddered from the loss and the sky above swirled, clouds forming out of nothing. The wind intensified and flashes of lightning were seen.

She could hardly breathe, the pressure upon her lungs making it nearly impossible to inhale and as the ground trembled again, she felt it quake.

Fissures spread around and the flash of red flame lit up and down the city streets. She could hardly see but what she could make out seemed to be dozens of them approaching. More continued to erupt from the ground and dark shadows were seen darting out of the clouds above.

A deep roar came from the north, and she watched as large shapes rapidly appeared above the roofs of the buildings. All of the beasts, the eldercobras, the rocs, and the leviathans all seemed to be centering on Alakyne.

She suddenly felt a strange tingling in her hand and struggling to turn her head, she felt the Relic of Containment begin to lift off of the ground. As it continued to rise, she felt the pressure seem to lighten off her and she clung to it as tightly as she could. Next to her she watched as Tiernyn's limp corpse was lifting off of the ground just as she was, his hand raised up above him.

They lifted off of the ground, first five, then ten, then twenty feet into the air. The tops of the buildings passed her vision revealing the hell that lay before her. There were hundreds of them, some already in the city with more approaching from all sides. The river nearby was flooded, the land washed away in a deep inland sea. Massive bodies of leviathan thrashed around crushing everything in their way and spreading their wicked miasma of disease. Like circling vultures, demonic eagles circled above in multiple rings, progressively curving lower and lower as they approached.

Auriel felt the Relic jerk and then she was rapidly rushing towards the keep, the mass of Ni'Bara coming into view. His head was rearing back and forth, fear in his eyes. Tira was standing next to Alakyne as the boy hovered a few inches off of the ground, his eyes glowing angelic white.

Auriel and Tiernyn were brought nearby, and she let go dropping to the ground where she collapsed to her knees, her legs buckling from injury and fatigue. Tiernyn and the Relic continued on gliding towards Alakyne before stopping in front of him.

He was still as stone as the limp body and the Relic of Containment hovered in front of him. Auriel was trying to grasp what had happened but Ni'Bara's shuddering body drew her attention to the approaching masses of beasts.

"I can't stop them," the dragon shivered. "Maybe one or two but this... Auriel I think we are going to die."

His words made her blood run cold and she looked at Alakyne who was still hovering in place unmoving. Tira was sobbing hard kneeling next to Aria's body.

"But I thought Alakyne was the one who stopped them, that is what the Priloc said," she started. "He can stop them."

"We have changed things too much Auriel. Events have been altered by our presence here."

"But Alakyne is supposed to use the power of Xeono to destroy them," she whispered. "He can do it."

"He is supposed to be joined with a legion of dragons do you not remember? With the aid of them he vanquished the tyrant beasts."

"But..." she started but Ni'Bara swung his head around to face her, a fierce panicked level of fear across his face.

"But nothing! The dragons are supposed to be with him when it happens. If they aren't here, then he isn't supposed to fight them yet. He is just a boy, maybe in ten or twenty years they might reveal themselves and they could unite. He is just a boy, and we are alone!"

"You are not alone dragon," spoke a deep resonating voice. Drawing their attention, they looked to see Alakyne had stopped floating and was standing upon the ground, his eyes still glowing. A halo of white aura seemed to flow around him, and he spoke again. "You claim that a legion of dragons were to destroy these beasts? I see no legion but only one."

"Can you stop them?" Auriel asked.

"With help possibly," the powerful voice said. "The vessel within that contains my consciousness yearns for his sister. His grief will give us the strength that is needed!"

A pulse of power shook the ground and reaching out his hand, Alakyne touched Xeono as it lay exposed against Tiernyn's wrist.

Golden bands of light and symbols blazed into being and the Otoruhn's body turned to dust fading away and leaving the band clutched in the boy's hand. Slipping it upon his wrist, his face absent of emotion, he turned and gazed upon his sister for a long moment. Auriel was nervous, intimidated by this incredible presence that lay in front of her.

"So, who are you if you are not Alakyne," she said drawing his attention towards her.

"I do not understand," he said.

"Who are you?" said Tira as she stood up and stood next to Auriel. "What is your name?"

"You are mistaken Human Riel and Dragon. I am Alakyne and he is me. Aute is my deeper consciousness brought to the surface by the traumas of today. Now," and he turned to face Ni'Bara directly. "It will be you and I who will vanquish these corrupted souls."

Ni'Bara took a step forward and looked up at the approaching

The Legend of Kyne: Chronocide

rocs above before lowering his gaze towards the serpents and leviathans that pushed the ever increasing sea further into the city. Flame, water, and wind all met at this single point and with a roar the glittering grey dragon leapt up into the air, the flicker of flame visible leaving a trail like a comet.

Ni'Bara ascended higher and higher, approaching the hoard of rocs that had stopped their circling, hovering as he came to meet them. He could feel the power of Alakyne and the strange feeling of familiarity that reminded him of the seraphs flowing around him. The boy possessed something beyond comprehension, and he had to try. He had to try for Auriel, for Rosé, and for his best friend!

He had to try for Kyne!

Roaring, he jerked forward, the eagles returning with their revolting screech before they flew towards him. Down below Auriel watched in horror as the dragon, enormous in stature but dwarfed by the approaching rocs rushed them. Each nearly twice his size and the hundreds of them resembling a cloud of mosquitoes as they rapidly drew nearer.

Another pulse of power came from Alakyne, and his white halo grew more intense. Raising a single hand upwards toward the dragon, a beam of light erupted from his palm, engulfing Ni'Bara in its power and obscuring him from view. The rocs stopped mid-flight, confused by what was happening and then to Auriel's utter disbelief, hundreds of dragons erupted from the beam of light. Each resembling Ni'Bara in every way, shape, and form. Flashes of cyan flame lit up the sky as the War of the Primordial Immortals began.

Alakyne turned his attention towards the approaching hordes of beasts and a golden light began to erupt from Xeono. Auriel could just make out the ouroboros glowing intensely as a blade of lightning was formed.

With a grunt, Alakyne hurled it toward the nearest eldunaga, striking it straight in the head and tearing it completely off in a golden flash of light. The snake collapsed to the ground in writhing mass while the others roared in rage and scarlet flame was laid upon the land. Another bolt struck, then another but even with the incredible power Auriel watched as the serpents pushed closer towards them. The city burned with large billowing clouds of black smoke rising up into the

The Legend of Kyne: Chronocide

sky.

The dragons continued their bombardment and soon eagles were falling plummeting to the ground where craters were made in large crashes.

"Alakyne it's not enough!" screamed Tira stopping him mid-throw. "They are too legion. There are hundreds of them. We should escape while we can."

Alakyne shook his head, his golden blond hair blowing wildly, and the halo of energy brightened again flowing into the spear of lightning he hadn't thrown. The shimmering gold changed, turning to a bright white and as its brightness grew Auriel had to shield her eyes.

With a cry, the young boy, the legend of humanity, hurled it straight up where it continued on its path hundreds of feet into the air before exploding in a flash of golden light. Thousands of thunderbolts fell upon the earth like rain upon a blazing fire, extinguishing the beasts as they were battered by the blades, tearing them apart.

*   *   *

77. To Bloom in the Wind

Blood dripped down the tip of the glaive clutched in Kioni's hands; the blade thrust partway through a Dominion sentinel's chest. The steel glinted faintly in the torchlight, the orange glow scattering around as the sentinel dropped his arms to his sides, his eyes wide with shock.

Muffled cries of shock sounded from the children behind him.

"Here," Akami whispered as she peered through a doorway into an empty room.

Kioni removed the glaive and in one sweeping motion, hooked the staff behind the man's back and hurtled forward into a ragged stumble guiding him just through the open door before he collapsed to the ground spurting blood from his mouth.

Akami muttered a spell, smearing their aural trail and wiping the blood drips away as they continued on. Rosé brought up the rear, her head snaking back and forth as she scented the air alerting them of possible threats.

Akami had been quite taken aback by the sight of the dragon but with the current events that had taken place she had just decided to go along with it. Running behind Kioni, she had her cloak drawn up over her head just as he used his Windra garb in an attempt to conceal their faces.

"Another two are up here," Rosé muttered from behind. "I think they are walking away."

"Do we wait until they pass?" Kioni slowed to a stop as he turned to look at Akami.

"If we do we risk more time in the citadel. The moment someone is found the whole place will be littered with them. I don't think we should."

The Legend of Kyne: Chronocide

Kioni nodded, her thoughts agreeing with his own and quick-footed, he darted around the corner with her steps hot on his heels. They were about thirty feet away and his footsteps hadn't alerted them yet. The hallway was dark, with no windows to the outside as it delved deeper into the citadel.

Running the first sentinel through the middle of his back with the glaive, Kioni jerked it out just as the second turned in confusion. With a twist over his shoulder, he whipped the long staff around, striking him across the side of his face. A sound was heard a moment after as their bodies hit the floor, Akami sweeping away the bloody marks and moving their bodies away.

Kioni's face was covered but Akami could see the drip of sweat forming upon the olive skin of his brow. He turned away, his staff returning to both hands and he took off again. She was impressed with his savagery and lack of hesitation. Without remorse he slaughtered these sentinels no question and she was intrigued.

They continued on through the citadel a few more floors down before they had made it to the courtyard. More sentinels were noticed but they evaded sight, passing through the inner wall to the stairway that led down into the city.

Altyne ulkin," the easterner muttered, masking them all as they darted right in between the guards, their bodies invisible and their sounds hidden. It took them another short time before they managed to get far enough into the city to take a short break. The children were exhausted, their breath heavy and they looked as if they were nearly going to collapse.

"Go," Kioni motioned towards them. "Go find your families, flee this city if you must but do not get caught. There will be no mercy from the Dominion if you are found."

They all nodded and separated, the last to leave was the eldest boy who looked at Kioni. "Thank you, thank both of you," and he glanced at Akami before vanishing down an alleyway out of sight.

Akami looked away as Kioni eyed her and he could see just the tiny edges of her mouth smile. He was so confused by what had happened. Before she would've killed him without hesitation and now, she was helping him escape?

He shook his head before turning towards Rosé trying to

return his focus to the task at hand. "We need to get out of this city. I haven't been able to find anything else about where the others have gone, and I don't think they know. Leaving is our top priority before Aaldra and that other Kyne return."

She nodded. "Do you know how we can get home?"

"No, I don't. I have tried to find a way but as of now I think we are trapped. We should focus on staying alive for right now and once we get away, we can start searching for a way back."

The dragon nodded again, her affect showing sorrow. She said nothing more but followed along as Kioni and Akami dashed away towards the entrance to Alakyne a little over a mile away. They arrived quickly, and after evading the guards had managed to sneak through the wall's interior to a smaller entrance meant for the sentinels. The iron bars that barred their way were cool as Kioni grasped them lightly, his gaze peering through the square gaps as he looked into the outer city. He felt an iron rivet brush his cheek and then he turned away looking for a way to open the bars.

"Here," Akami muttered before he could even step and the bars shuddered before swinging open, the easterner gripping a small lever. The faint moonlight from the crescent moons above glanced off her face and Kioni froze for a moment. For an instant the two held a gaze, not one of malice but of magnetism. It was only a moment but then they both awkwardly looked away, him stepping through the bars first.

Rosé followed, seemingly unaware of the new tension in the air and Akami was the last through. Kioni dashed down the edge of the massive wall for a few steps before turning to look back, his hand reaching up to gesture for them to follow when a look of concern appeared on his face.

Akami had turned around and was walking back through the doorway, her gait slow and methodical.

He ran back to her, reaching out and grabbing hold of her arm lightly drawing her attention.

"What are you doing? We need to keep moving."

She turned to look at him, her eyes glazed over but she said nothing and continued walking through the entrance. He felt her slip from his light grasp, and he watched for a moment as her steps slowed and then she turned back to face him with a look of confusion on her face.

"What just happened?" she asked rubbing her head as if she had a headache. "I feel like I was drugged."

"Come on," he shook his head and held out his arm. "We need to get moving. The sun will be rising soon, and I want to be out of the city before dawn."

She nodded and grabbed his hand stepping back towards the doorway but just as before, the moment she passed through it she grew rigid and her eyes blank. She pulled away, turning back towards the inside as before and in a few moments, she was on the far side of the room, her gait not slowing this time.

Kioni dashed after her, grabbing a hold again much firmer and his touch seemed to snap her out of it as she turned back towards him, her eyes showing her mind returning.

"What... What happened?" she mumbled.

"I don't think you can leave," he replied slowly. "Something seems to be drawing you back inside."

"What do you mean?" she said, her voice showing more concern and she pushed past him, running outside but a few steps beyond the border and she slowed to a stop.

Kioni followed her just as she began to walk back and he grabbed onto her, guiding her further away from the wall. She fought for a few steps, each moment growing more strained as she was pulled away until she started shouting that she needed to get back.

The woman clawed and thrashed, her voice rising as she struggled out of his grip, trying to force her way back into the interior of the wall. Kioni cringed as her voice echoed around, cutting through the dead of night and he reluctantly let go, allowing her to run back to the wall where she passed beyond the border and out of view.

Far distant shouting was heard and high above him he watched the orange glow of flame dangle over the edge as a torch was raised, the sentinels looking for the source of the scream. More torches ignited and shifted in the outer city, a few streets over but they were heading their way.

"What do we do?" he asked softly, more to himself, but Rosé answered.

The Legend of Kyne: Chronocide

"I don't think that she can leave Kioni. Whatever they did to her is holding her back. We can't let her stay though."

"I think we might have to," he whispered, and he stepped after her, stopping her methodical walk through the hall.

"Akami, I have to go," he said as she looked at him with blank eyes. "If I take you with us, you will get us caught with your yelling. I am sorry."

She just stared at him with her drunken look for a long moment before turning away. She said nothing more and continued walking through the wall out of sight leaving Kioni standing in the doorway.

* * *

Akami awoke with a start as Hayame's voice rang through her door. She groaned as she sat up, her eyes crusty and her head pounding. Before she could say anything, the door burst open and her sister ran in, her hair flashing a fiery red and her eyes full of rage.

"They killed Yu!"

"Who did what?" she yawned, her thoughts a jumbled mess in her head. She didn't understand a thing, the words did not carry any meaning to her. She yawned again.

"Yu! Yu was killed, I don't know who, but someone did it! Someone broke in and killed her and Diahl and all of the children are missing."

Akami grew more interested, the fatigue vanishing from her in an instant. "You can't be serious," she said in her own language. "There is no way. It's too fortified. She's too powerful to be…"

"She is dead!"

Hayame's voice pierced through Akami's head, and she caught her breath in shock as the reality of the words sank in. She didn't really care for Yu, none of the others really but since they had come to Kydrëa they had lost nearly all of them, only Hayame and herself remaining.

She leapt to her feet, her robes bunching up awkwardly, but she paid no mind. "Have you traced them? Followed their trail surely that would…" but Hayame's look made her voice trail off.

The Legend of Kyne: Chronocide

"Of course I did!" she hissed. "Do you think I am an idiot? That was the first thing I did and what I found was even more concerning. Your trail was littered all over the room and the others were smeared around as if someone had tampered with it."

"You can't be... There is no way I would..." Akami stammered confusion filling her head. *I didn't do anything; I have been sleeping all night.*

"Well, you had to have something to do with it," Hayame snapped. "Why else would your trail be there?"

Akami's mind started to race. She had thought about wanting to take the little girl, but she hadn't actually done anything about it. *I got back to my room last night, had a glass of wine and went to bed. Surely, I didn't...*

"I know you did it," Hayame cried out. "I knew there had to be some reason mother sent you with us on this damned mission to ally with the Dominion. I knew she despised us but this, this is beyond it."

"I didn't do it!" Akami snapped back. "Why would I kill one of my own people when I am in a foreign land? Surely you aren't stupid enough to actually think that."

"It's more that I am not stupid enough to fall for your deception!" a flash of aura appeared in her hand, and she clenched the muscles in her arm.

"I didn't Hayame! But if you don't believe me then so be it."

The aura leapt through the air just as her sentence finished, narrowly avoiding her as she twisted over her shoulder. The words were quick, a hiss of a whisper as she forced her aura into the ground and in an instant, it jerked up right beneath Hayame's feet. She launched straight up into the ceiling where she slammed her upper back hard before crashing to the ground. Akami was already speaking her next words, striking her rapidly from all angles with aural strikes. Two swift blows struck her in the abdomen and just as she gasped out a word, Akami muttered, "Oo'nar," pulling the air out of her lungs and making her gasp.

Hayame was on the floor, the whole ordeal lasting less than ten seconds. She was panting heavily, her chest heaving as she tried to reinflate her lungs and Akami leaned down right next to her face.

"I told you I didn't do it," she hissed, and she touched her sister's temple. A bright glow flooded through her as she passed the memories from her night to her sister and as her panting slowed, Akami straightened back up. Brushing her robe back down and flicking her hair over her shoulder so that it draped down her back, she waited, ready for an attack from Hayame to come. But it never did, the Kitsune merely sat up and stared at her with irritation.

"If it wasn't you then who would it be?" she muttered.

"How the hell would I know?" Akami turned around and walked towards her things. Dropping her robe to the ground, uncaring that her sister could see her, she grabbed her day clothes, a short white kimono adorned with pink cherry blossoms sewn into the fabric. As she finished tying the matching pink sash around her waist, she looked back to see her sister had left, the door still cracked.

Angry little thing, she thought, her mind still racked about what she had just heard. *I couldn't really have done any of that right? It was just a dream, right? That strange man and the dragon?*

*   *   *

Kioni sat against the wall of a small room; the young dragon curled up nearby. A single window, the glass broken and jagged lay above him streaming in faint sunlight illuminating the dirt floor. A few hours had passed, and they had made it out of the city and down to an old, abandoned farmhouse, the land barren of crops, dead and dry.

His mind was still focused on the easterner, and he couldn't think of anything else.

Why do I keep thinking about her? She has caused me nothing but trouble. She has tried to kill me, and I know that is why she is here. She must've followed me through the strange distortion. If so, then why do I feel like I abandoned her?

He pictured her blank stare as she turned away from him and vanished into the dark city.

Should I really have risked everything just to try and get her to come with us? She would've screamed just as she had done. That one scream nearly got us caught. I had to kill that young sentinel who came looking which was more difficult than it should've been. He rubbed his hands, the knuckles scrapped and bruised.

The Legend of Kyne: Chronocide

The dragon twitched, her tail shifting around her body before resting back down.

Rosé seemed sad about leaving her, which also confuses me. Why would she even seem attached to her? Unless she was... and his mind thought back to Akami bursting through the door interrupting his chokehold. *Was she coming to free the children? There is no way, right?*

As his thoughts rested upon that fact, the guilt began to increase about abandoning her. He couldn't shake it and he fought an intense battle in his brain, thinking of all the possibilities and risks for what he was about to do.

The evening came and as Rosé slept, he gathered his things, leaving behind the glaive and placing the kamas sheath upon his waist. Slipping the mask over his face, he pictured the features of a Windra, his face changing as he approached the door.

"Are you going to get her?"

Rosé's squeaky young voice called from across the room. Kioni looked towards her and nodded. The dragon nodded back and then he was gone, dashing through the night, the white Windra cloak trailing behind him.

78. Out of Sight but Not Out of Mind

An hour later, he was running through the citadel, a few dead sentinels left along the way. He had seen only one Windra and they had been walking through the halls as if patrolling so with that as an idea, he slowed down and began to march.

Under his cloak, the sticky blood that had been wiped upon his pants dried and cracked, a constant reminder of his sins.

He passed by the Windra, a brief nod was the only thing shared and then he was alone again, traveling through the citadel. He dashed up a flight of stairs, two at a time and came to their apex quietly like a cat. Movement ahead caught his attention, and he watched as two sentinels rounded the corner coming into view. More and more had been seen throughout the city from the events of the previous night. It had brought unwanted attention to potential intruders making Kioni's quest much more difficult.

He continued walking towards them, his pace slow and his posture relaxed and confident but his mind racing.

"Windra," snapped on of the sentinels and they both stopped a short distance away. Their hands were placed upon the pommels of their swords, but they had not been drawn.

Kioni remained silent.

"Why do you roam the halls alone in the dead of night."

Kioni swallowed the lump in his throat and took a deep breath. "Same as you sentinel of Gaeil," he said slowly, his tongue stretching in awkward positions as he tried to mimic the thick Windra accent.

"And yet I don't recall Ariov appointing single Windra

mercenaries to roam around the citadel alone at night. We are to always be in pairs."

"And I know that to be a lie," Kioni spoke defiantly as he thought about the individual Windra he had seen. "Mind your place Gaeilian before you overstep your boundaries."

"Why you..." the sentinel hissed and just as he began to draw his sword, the other placed a hand upon his arm stopping him. He said nothing but gave a look and then they were gone, walking past Kioni.

He took a slow breath before he continued on. He had narrowly avoided a dangerous situation, even if it was just sentinels trying to start a fight.

She wasn't in the cells, and I haven't seen anything mentioning her execution. Maybe she hasn't been traced to Diahl which means... Maybe she could be in her quarters?

Kioni thought about it for a moment, more of a fleeting hope but he had no other idea where she could be. Dashing up another stairway, he began to search the rooms of nobles. Quietly he picked dozens of locks, peering inside but she wasn't in any of the rooms.

A few hours had passed, and he was just about to give up when the lock clicked, and he swept quietly into the room, closing it softly behind him. Upon the bed he could see a figure, the white sheets that hung from the bed canopy obscuring any identifying details.

He reached out and gently grabbed the edge of the fabric, pulling it back to see Akami, sleeping still and silently. She was dressed in a simple nightgown, a silk shirt pulled up revealing a small glimpse of her navel. Her shorts were low, her smooth legs mostly obscured by the blanket as it bunched up and around her like a nest. Her hair was spread out over her pillow keeping the upper part of her chest visible.

He stepped lightly towards her; his footsteps guided by his Shade training. He could barely see in the darkness but was certain it was her, her beauty quite visible and for a long moment he stared at her, admiring her as her chest slowly rose up and down in a rhythmic fashion from her breathing. She was gorgeous, beautiful in so many ways and her awkward position made him smile as he thought of her tossing around in the bed in her sleep.

Reaching out, he softly grabbed her arm, holding it down firmly at the same moment he clamped his hand upon her mouth. She

The Legend of Kyne: Chronocide

was awake in an instant, her eyes full of terror and then rapidly narrowing in rage.

Intense pain ripped through his hand as she bit hard, drawing blood but he was just fast enough to reach up and grab a hold of her collar as she tried to launch him across the room with her aura. The force ripped him from his feet, tearing the fabric diagonally but he managed to hold on and stay close enough to her. Before she could say another word, he pulled his own mask down, revealing his face.

"Akami it's me! Stop!" he hissed.

She stared at him, her mouth wide open in shock and then she doubled over, her hands on her head as she moaned in agony. He reached out tentatively and placed a hand on her shoulder, but she shoved him away, grimacing from pain for a long moment before she could recover enough to look at him.

"What happened?" she murmured.

"It seems like you forgot me," he replied. "I came back for you."

"Kioni?" she muttered as she recalled the name, her hands clenching, the fists pressed against her head, and she winced.

"Yeah, it's me, don't ask me why I came back for you but..."

"But you did," she said slowly. "You actually came back for me. It... It's so strange. I had actually forgotten everything that happened. Just returned right back to my usual routine. You could've left me and been leagues away and I wouldn't have even noticed a thing."

Kioni shrugged awkwardly and then looked down at his hand, fresh blood still oozing out of the bite. Looking around for something to bandage it, he was startled when Akami was faster, tearing a piece of her sheet off and handing it to him.

"Sorry," she muttered.

"It was my fault. I shouldn't have woken you up like that. I had no idea you would be so ferocious."

She grinned. Flicking her hair over her shoulder she looked at him for a moment before she glanced towards the dresser and was up quickly to her feet. Light steps skimmed the ground as she darted to her things. She paused for a moment before turning around at him and furrowing her brow.

"Turn around."

The Legend of Kyne: Chronocide

"What?" he said confused. "Why would I..." then he realized she was clutching her clothes in her hand, her other arm balancing the shredded nightgown on her shoulder preventing it from falling. He spun on his heel immediately, dropping his eyes down in an awkward stare. He could hear the rustling of silk as it hit the floor and he felt his pulse quicken. Thinking of anything to distract himself, he noticed he was still clutching the fabric, a small collection of blood drops growing upon the floor.

He was quick, tying a slip knot before placing it over his palm covering the bite marks. A quick tug tightened it firmly and then he wrapped it around a few more times, careful as to not secure it too tight. A quick wiggle of his fingers made him nod his head in satisfaction.

"Ok, I am ready," she muttered, and he turned around nearly catching his breath in his throat.

Her hair was still down, draped over her shoulders and her eyes looked away as if she was embarrassed by her appearance. Upon her chest lay interwoven pieces of leather and golden rivets coming up to flared shoulder guards. Her waist was wrapped in a silk cloth, tight and formfitting as it tapered to her rib following the natural curve of her body.

Only her feet were exposed, the rest of her legs obscured by a flowing silk cloth as it guided its shimmering form around each of her legs like a pair of light pants. He could see her katana, sheathed at her side, the dangerous blade hidden in its scabbard.

It took him a long moment to realize his mouth had slightly grown ajar, his eyes tracing up and down her figure. As they rose to her eyes, he saw she was also staring, the slight rosy tint of a blush appearing and then she looked away.

He swallowed a lump in his throat, his breath threatening to overwhelm him, and he looked away. He could feel his pulse throbbing in his neck and each beat of his heart seemed to shake his whole body; anxiety flooding thorough him at the thought of her able to hear it.

"We should get going," Akami said quickly, and she headed towards the door.

"Your... your shoes?" Kioni stumbled over the words.

"My shoes?"

The Legend of Kyne: Chronocide

"Don't you need them before we leave?"

The moment the words left his lips he nearly cringed at the idiocy and random comment. He was embarrassed and she seemed to notice as she turned, raising her arm and showing a small pair clutched in her grip.

He merely nodded quickly, not wanting to continue further on the subject and then they were gone, dashing through the citadel. With her aura they were able to avoid most of the patrols, Kioni wincing with every step as they ran along the side of two patrolling sentinels, expecting them to notice but they didn't.

Incredible, he thought as he trailed after Akami, the petite woman fast and agile as she leapt down a flight of stairs in three steps before nearly leaving Kioni behind. *I really should practice my aura more. If I could learn these sort of spells then that would change a lot of things for the Shades.* The moment the thought entered his mind he felt his stomach tighten. *If I ever get home that is. I may never even see them again.*

"Over here," Akami mouthed as she came to a stop, interrupting his thoughts. She was standing near a window and with a jerk managed to open it, the large pane of glass swinging out a few inches before coming to a stop. With a quick glance down, Kioni saw they were still dozens of feet above the ground, sections of roofing lying to their right at a dangerously steep angle and the dark hazy night sky beyond.

It was open just enough and without hesitating, Akami squeezed through the gap, swinging out to the side and balancing next to the wall. Kioni followed her motion climbing out dangerously high above the ground, a single step spelling certain death. His feet were situated on a small ledge, a little more than the width of his feet causing him to lean forward to balance, the pressure firmly upon on the balls of his feet. His hands were tucked to his sides awkwardly as he touched the stone wall with his chest. His heart rate was ramping up again and slowly turning his head in an effort to not knock his balance backwards, he saw that Akami had already walked the length of the ledge and was just stepping off onto the steep roof beyond.

Kioni took a deep breath and focusing on each step, shuffled his body along the edge until after ten seconds he could see the roofing. It was steep as it stretched up a short way before coming to another wall. Another look up and the roofing continued on like a giant angled set of stairs. The rim met up with ledge he was standing on and inching a few more steps he guided himself onto the steep angle. Akami was already on her way, a few steps up the slope and a ways away guiding herself along its length.

"Where is she going," he muttered, thoughts of her actually going to push him off the roof entered his mind for a moment, but he brushed them out. He traced the roofing, following its length until it came to another wall. It was dark and hard to make out but as he neared it, he saw an identical ledge as before was poking out of the stone, fragments chipped from weathering.

Akami said nothing but waited until he was there before she scrambled onto the ledge, positioning herself at nearly a diagonal allowing her to walk much faster. Kioni recoiled at her, thoughts of the eastern woman slipping and falling flooding his mind at her recklessness but then she was gone, around the corner and out of sight.

He sighed before continuing on, unable to mimic her and returning to his awkward shuffle. He could see glimmering orange light dotting the citadel gardens below and more covering the city beyond the inner wall.

That's it! he thought as he realized where she was taking him.

He accelerated, rounding the corner onto another section of roof with Akami a few yards away. The inner wall wrapped around the citadel, joining with the main wall at the back above a set of cliffs preventing a back attack. Right where they were, he could see the wall was nearly underneath them, still nearly twenty feet of straight fall.

Sentinels were walking along its length as he traced the curve as it stretched away from the citadel in a large arc. It was wide, adorned with dozens of structures along its top. He could make out weapons of war in the dim light cast from their torches, positioned out over the city like wicked sentries.

Akami motioned down to the wall, and he gave her a look, in his mind screaming, "That is a massively far drop!"

She shook her head and, to his shock, leapt off without a moment of hesitation. She sailed through the hair, her jet-black hair stretching out above her and her silk robes flapping madly threatening to alert the sentinels with their sound.

The Legend of Kyne: Chronocide

An instant before she landed, the ground seemed to rise up to meet her guiding her to a quick stop, her knees not buckling once from the strain. Kioni rubbed his eyes, confused with what he thought he saw.

There is no way she just did that.

Down below he saw her gesture for him to follow and then she was gone dashing a few dozen feet before tucking herself around the edge of one of the box-like stone structures that decorated the top. He could see pools of orange light on either side, and he watched as she seemed to vanish just as the lights met showing two sentinels patrolling, skirting on either side of the structure. They continued on, passing nearly under Kioni and following the curve of the wall to his right. Akami was suddenly back, a dark shape as she stood next to the strange building and Kioni eyed the wall again.

He had jumped from places of similar height, but he has always landed on things softer than solid stone. This actually instilled a bit of fear with thoughts of his ankles breaking on the impact.

She couldn't be trying to get me injured right? he thought. *Does she think a normal person could actually do this?*

He looked down again, imagining the fall and tracing the angle of the roll he would perform. He needed momentum first of all. Guiding his body horizontally while he fell would allow him a more efficient roll and maybe saving him some broken bones.

The only place he could go was up the steep slope and slowly he backed up, his boots pointing his toes down as they tried to keep as much grip as possible.

He looked back towards Akami and saw her dark shape was no longer there. Panic started to flood him again, his eyes rushing down the length of wall looking for her dark figure. More sentinels were approaching but they were still a few minutes of patrolling away.

"Damn it," he muttered, and he looked back towards where he was going. He could hardly see the wall, the lip of the roof blocking his view, but it was now or never.

Dashing forward, *One... Two... Three...* and then he was flying out in open air, his stomach tightening with adrenaline as the top of the wall rapidly approached. He angled his torso forwards with the momentum preparing for the impact when a split second before he hit,

The Legend of Kyne: Chronocide

he saw Akami come into view nearby, her hand outstretched.

Nearly losing his focus, he brought it back just in time, landing first his feet and then collapsing down to slow his momentum into a roll. A puff of sand exploded around him and then he was back on his feet, more sand sliding off his white Windra robes.

Akami waved her hand and Kioni saw for just a moment the ground ripple and then it was back to the stone.

"Thank you," he breathed out as he realized what she had done. She nodded before taking off, him following her fast behind. They rounded the structure and came to a door. It wasn't locked and then they were flying down a stone spiral stair.

It was black as pitch inside and he couldn't see anything, only managing to use his hands to prevent striking the wall as he rushed after Akami, her footsteps signaling her speed.

They spun around and around as they descended when suddenly a glare of orange, Akami's figure slamming into his chest, and his momentum launching them both into a sentinel all happened nearly simultaneously.

A cry of shock came from the sentinel and then another shout sounded from behind him with a second coming into view. The two nearly lost their footing but Akami managed to launch herself back just as she dropped low. Kioni was drawing his kamas and then a flash of steel and red as she sliced across the sentinel's abdomen. The world seemed to freeze for a moment as Kioni met the sentinel's eyes and then he was moving on, shoving the falling man over and driving his kamas towards the second sentinel.

The clang of metal sounded as his adversary twisted, glancing the kama strikes off his shoulder plate but Kioni was quick, taking a few steps down the stairs as he passed him before spinning around and driving the curved blade of his kama straight into the man's exposed thigh.

Just as he grunted in pain a spurt of blood struck Kioni in the face, and he watched as the sentinel slumped over, his neck split open from a blade that hung right next to Kioni's face. Akami held it out there for a moment, the two frozen in place and then Kioni felt his back slam into the wall as Akami rushed him, her hands prying the Windra mask down before her lips slammed hard against his own. He

668

The Legend of Kyne: Chronocide

staggered back for a moment gathering his balance and then his hands were in her hair, his lips guiding across hers, the taste of her tongue in his mouth. He didn't know what or why this was happening but the lust he was feeling was unlike anything else he had ever felt before.

* * *

Akami dashed through the city streets, Kioni a bit in front of her. She could still taste him in her mouth and her heart nearly skipped out of her chest at the thought.

Why did I do that, she thought. *Was it just the moment or something else? Just recently I wanted to kill this man and now it seems I can't control myself around him.*

Kioni glanced back at her for a moment, his hood draped over his shoulders and his dark hair brushed to the side of his face, his mask gone. She shook her head and continued on, trying to push the thought out of her mind. *No matter how good that kiss was there is no way this could ever work. My people and his people are sworn enemies.*

The city continued on, sloping at a slight angle as they made their way towards the main wall. The upper district roads were wider, nicer built with each stone fitting together nicely in the roadways but the further on they went into the lower district the more jumbled they became. Pieces jutted out at odd angles, and she caught her foot on one sending her sprawling forward, nearly slamming her chest into the ground, only stopping herself with her aura.

She was on her feet in an instant, Kioni had barely turned to look at her confused with what had happened. She shooed him forward and after a few more steps, came to a dead stop. She was frozen in place, her head roaring with an incredible voice that overtook everything else.

"It is time!"

Then darkness enveloped as her mind seemed to collapse upon itself. Massive pain racked her body and glimpses of images appeared momentarily before vanishing. She saw Kioni, confused as he was bound up, ropes tied around and sentinels surrounding him. She caught sounds, children screaming, buildings crashing, and then a flash of metallic pink before an unconscious dragon lay at her feet.

The Legend of Kyne: Chronocide

She tried to call out, scream, do anything but she couldn't. She couldn't move as if her very own body was controlling itself. She felt a heavy presence push into her mind and then it was as if she was staring at herself in a mirror, her twin smiling at her. She spoke but her voice was not her own but that of the one who had invaded her mind.

"No matter how far you run I will always be a part of you Akami of Iterasu. Thank you for finding my prize. I should be indebted to you, but... But how could a god be in debt?"

* * *

79. A Boy or a God

Like rain the spears of golden light fell upon the land, cutting through each beast without mercy. Their bodies, torn to pieces thrashed upon the ground in their final moments. Flames spurted out in red puffs before ceasing and the final smear of fog was shredded from the air. Rocs fell like fallen angels, tumbling out of the sky as the hundreds of Ni'Bara's tore them from their domain.

Like a single being, their claws tore the rocs from the sky and their fangs ripped the remaining leviathans from the cursed inland sea that had formed. Burning their corpses in dragonfire, the primordial immortals were slain.

Auriel and Tira watched in wonder as streaks of sunlight pierced through the clouds illuminating the freed land in its golden glow. Dark smoke from the raging fires had begun to lighten to grey as the remaining humans fought to put them out. The water from the river receded, flowing back along its original path and one by one the dragons vanished from the sky until only one remained.

Hundreds of people flocked to the glowing boy, surrounding him in the masses and dropping to their knees. Their heads were bowed, and Auriel could hear the murmuring, like a single chorus all chanting one word.

"God."

"Auriel," murmured Alakyne drawing her attention as the halo of light faded away from him. The foggy mist drifting away from his eyes revealing the golden originals laced with tears. She was over to him in an instant, her hands wrapped tightly around his body, and she pulled him into a tight hug. "Is she... Is Aria really gone?"

Auriel nodded her head as she tightened her grip around him, and she felt his body rock as he began to sob uncontrollably. Hot tears streamed down his cheeks, and she quickly joined him. As soon as it had started, they both felt the touch of Tira as she grabbed onto both of them joining in their mourning. Ni'Bara circled above, bellowing out a lamentation of sorrow that caused the earth itself to shudder as if it too felt the loss of her life.

They sat there for a long time, the boy unaware of the growing mass of people that had begun to surround him. It seemed like the entire city, from the oldest grandparent to the youngest child just able to walk had all migrated to the courtyard of Faldîn Keep. Bowing down, their heads upon the stone ground, they all murmured the constant hum of one word.

"God."

As the murmuring grew, it drew their attention and they separated, each wiping their eyes, red and puffy from the tears. Alakyne was afraid, she could see it upon his face as he quickly rushed towards Aria's still figure and knelt down as if to protect her.

"I don't think they want to hurt you," Auriel said as she came to him, Ni'Bara finally landing upon the ground. "I don't think they want to take her either."

"Why do they keep chanting like that," he cried, beckoning towards the crowd who had begun to grow silent. "Why do they keep calling me a god?"

"Because you saved all of us with powers not even Tiernyn could control," said one who had risen to their feet. A woman, middle aged with wrinkles forming upon the sides of her eyes and skin that had spots dotted across it as it had been touched by the sun. "A god walks amongst us mortals, freeing us from the torment of those monsters."

"I am no god!" he screamed. "I am cursed don't you see! Everyone around me gets hurt and will eventually die! Even her," and he looked down upon the pale face of his sister. "I couldn't even protect her," he whispered softly.

"But she protected you," Auriel said drawing his gaze up. "She didn't die in vain Alakyne. She died protecting you! If she hadn't taken that blade, then you would have, and you would've died in her place. Those monsters would've still roamed the land and millions more would die under their power."

He was silent.

The Legend of Kyne: Chronocide

"Without you this world would have fallen Alakyne," Ni'Bara rumbled deeply. "Auriel and I promised to not speak of the future for fear that it would alter it, but I believe there is something we can now speak of. There are legends of a man, wrapped in a golden light who brought the heavens down and defeated those very monsters. His name was Alakyne."

His eyes widened in shock and Tira mimicked him.

"You can't mean... Surely it isn't..." Tira stumbled her words trying to find out what to say.

"It's true Alakyne. Remember my husband, his name Kyne is not a family name but a derivative of yours. He was named in honor of the legend that you are. You were destined to defeat those creatures. If Aria hadn't saved you then everything would be different."

"Do you mean..."

"Yes, you saved us all Alakyne, but Aria saving you saved the world."

Auriel's voice trailed off and Alakyne's eyes looked down on his older sister for a long moment. Her face was pale, but a look of peace lay upon it. Lifting his gaze back up, he looked out over the mass of people and then back to the others who stood by him.

"What am I to do now?" he whispered. "I don't have her anymore to help guide me."

"I will do my best," Tira said with a smile.

Auriel nodded her head. "And so will we. All three of us will help you become the leader that you are meant to be."

"But what about getting home to your own time," he said. "You have people waiting for you."

Auriel was silent for a long time, and she looked at Ni'Bara. "We will be fine," she said. "It may be impossible for us to return home anyways. In the meantime, I think we will be alright."

"I think I know of a way," Tira said softly drawing everyone's attention.

"What do you mean?" asked Ni'Bara. "How would we get back over a thousand years in the future?"

"I have been thinking about it for such a long time. The answer is right here," and she beckoned around her. "Two items brought together through time. Your Relic of Containment could hold you inside the Ouroboros Bag until you reach your own time."

Auriel gasped in shock and a flicker of hope tore through her gut for a moment and she looked towards Ni'Bara. Immediately her hope vanished as she saw his look of sorrow.

"And how would anyone know to release us at the time that we need to? We could be released in a few decades or ten thousand years in the future overshooting our time completely. There is no way to stop that."

His voice caught Tira off guard and as he finished, Auriel could see the realization spread across her face. "But... But there has to be some way... Any way to possibly get..."

"It won't work," Ni'Bara said. "There is no guarantee."

"What if we pass it on through the sorcerers. Our duty is sacred, you even mentioned that our order still exists in the..."

"Because my husband reformed it after all the sorcerers were murdered," Auriel interrupted. "No one would be able to release us anyways. We surely would be lost to time."

"There must be a way," Tira said. "Somehow."

"I think that we might just have to remain here," Ni'Bara said slowly, his voice causing Auriel's heart to crack. "Maybe we are destined to raise..."

"I can do it."

They all turned in shock to see Alakyne looking at them with a fierce fire in his eyes.

"What do you mean?" Auriel asked.

"I can alert someone from your time to release you. I don't know how to explain it, but I can sense your times are different. I will call to them, and they will listen."

Auriel and Ni'Bara were shocked beyond disbelief. The young boy before them held himself differently than he had before. His fearful look of suspicion and nervousness had been replaced by a deep confidence and a wisdom that made Auriel understand why the legends were as they were.

"You can do that?" she whispered.

"I will, for you, and for Ni'Bara. You two have brought me from out of the deepest pit of despair imaginable. Constantly on the run, fearful for what the day might bring. I have lost more than I could

The Legend of Kyne: Chronocide

imagine today but your words have given me new light."

"What do you think?" Auriel asked Ni'Bara. The dragon looked at her for a long time and then she saw a flicker of hope appear deep within his eye.

"If we have a chance, no matter how slim it is with him. I think we should take it."

Auriel turned back to see Tira had already grabbed the Relic and had placed it in Alakyne's hands. With the symbols glowing brightly, the young boy looked upon his two friends with happiness and sorrow.

"I wish I could have met your husband, Auriel. Kyne seems like an incredible man and even though he is named after me, I will do all I can to live up to his name."

She smiled and as he held out the strange object and its surface touched her, her body vanished in a flash of light leaving Ni'Bara behind.

"Thank you," the dragon said as Alakyne approached.

"No thank you," he said. "You have done more than you could ever imagine."

Ni'Bara closed his eyes and as he felt the object touch his snout. Moments before the bright light enveloped him, he heard a strange roar that seemed to erupt from the little boy shattering all of time and space. The scream shook his very soul, tearing through all fabrics of reality as it stretched through time.

"Your family lies within the bag!"

*   *   *

The Legend of Kyne: Chronocide

80. A Harrowing Revelation

Kyne staggered back, catching himself on a frozen tree, the icy bark scraping against his palm. His mind screamed, screamed and submitted as a powerful voice shook his very soul. It seemed to burn the words in his mind, like a hot brand pushing into his flesh, excruciating pain searing through his memory as it locked itself in place.

Kyne slid down the tree, dropping to his knees thrusting them into the deep snow.

"Kyne are you alright," Kioni's voice sounded near his ear, and he felt a hand as it was placed upon his shoulder.

The voice was fading away, an echo as the burning ebbed after it. He opened his eyes, looking upon the frozen landscape in confusion. Turning his head, he saw Kioni, a look of concern upon his face staring at him. He shuddered from the cold and pulled his cloak up tighter over his shoulders while his friend helped him to his feet.

"Did you hear it?"

"Did I hear what?" Kioni replied. "All I hear is the sound of our footsteps upon the snow."

"It... It was someone's voice, calling out, more like screaming. I felt the earth tremble, everything was shaking from its power."

Kioni shook his head and furrowed his brow, "There were no voices, Kyne."

He could hear it clear as day, the power it contained was insurmountable. "Are you certain? It was there I promise."

"I don't doubt you," Kioni replied with a shrug. "I have seen much stranger things in my life than someone hearing voices. Do you think it could be that *thing?*"

Kyne turned his head towards the faint outline of Alakyne a

few leagues away. They had traveled from Dawngôr heading towards it completely against Kioni's wishes. They had argued for days about preparing more or going there immediately. But as they traveled Kyne's mind had already been made up. If there was only one thing left in this world that he could do, he would kill that monster.

"I don't think so," and he reached down and grabbed the horse's reigns that he had dropped before he started walking again, pushing through the bright snow that glared the sunlight. The sky was absent of clouds, the cascading sunlight ricocheting off the snow in a blinding glare. "It didn't sound like him, and I didn't sense any malice, only a power that seemed absolute."

Kioni came up to his side, the crunching of snow constant as they followed the divot in the surface that signaled the road beneath, leading the horses on their trek. They had ran them as far as they could, nearly to complete exhaustion and now they were walking them at a slower pace as they regained their energy.

"What did they say?"

"It said, your family lies within the bag."

"What? That's very strange," he muttered. "Are you certain that's what it said? Your family lies within the bag?" Kyne nodded. "Do you think it was meaning the Ouroboros Bag?"

"That's the only bag I could even think of that makes sense," Kyne sighed. "It just doesn't add up though, how could *my family* be in the bag when it has been hidden for the last few months absent of any power. There is no possible way they could be there."

Kioni stayed quiet leaving Kyne to his thoughts.

There is no way, right? They couldn't be there; it doesn't make any sense. Even if they had been trapped inside when I was sent here, I would've sensed them.

His mind stayed under turmoil as they traveled on, the sun passing overhead before beginning its descent. Alakyne's mass loomed ahead, taking over most of his eyesight with its size. The large stone wall, broken and crumbling from the rapid freezing and chaos that had ensued those many years ago, obscured much of the city. They turned away, leading the horses in a large skirting path as they kept their distance from the massive barrier.

They had seen a few travelers on the road and had avoided

The Legend of Kyne: Chronocide

them all. None were to be trusted and walking into Alakyne in the broad daylight would be just as dangerous. The cluster of trees that coated the western wall were coming into view, their branches void of leaves and icy snow clinging to the tops of their branches.

Kioni came to a stop, catching Kyne's attention and he turned to look at his friend, a look of sorrow had appeared upon his face.

"What's wrong," Kyne said coming to a stop himself. "We are almost there."

"I don't like being here."

"I know, its creepy and I can already feel the evil that looms here. We will be quick."

"No Kyne, you don't get it. I don't want to be here. I haven't been here since that day and I just..." his voice trailed off.

"You've already told me this. The world broke and all of that stuff. Why are you acting weird now that we have gotten here? I thought you wanted that thing dead."

"That was before we got back here."

"Tell me what happened."

"Kyne I..."

"Kioni tell me what happened now damn it! I am sick of you avoiding the question!"

"I lost her!" he screamed. "I lost both of them to that, that damned beast. He killed her in his weird sacrifice, pulled her soul right out of her and collided it with the others. It all happened so fast but... But the bastard made me watch. You made me watch Kyne!" he paused for a moment tears streaming down his eyes.

"Kioni it wasn't..."

"I know it wasn't really you Kyne, but you look so freaking similar, it makes my skin crawl. The only thing that was different was his eyes, the deep darkness within them beyond anything I have ever seen. They looked like Aaldra's eyes Kyne! Remember when he ambushed us? Remember his eyes!"

Kyne nodded, knowing full well the wickedness that had been contained within them. He had seen them firsthand himself not too long ago. He could remember the evil pressure before they erupted in a golden light upon the volcano's summit.

He could see Kioni was distraught, his eyes drippy and his

The Legend of Kyne: Chronocide

chest shuddering as he tried in vain to remain under control, his gaze constantly avoiding his own. But he still hadn't answered everything. Kyne had to press on even if it hurt his friend, he had too.

"You can tell me Kioni, I promise I can take it," he said softly.

"I don't think you can Kyne. I don't think you can," he repeated, his voice trembling and icy tears fell to the ground, catching in the sunlight.

"Just tell me."

"It... It was Rosé."

The Legend of Kyne: Chronocide

81. Back to Where He Started

Kyne's mouth dropped open and his stomach churned up in a tight knot, threatening to expel all of its contents onto the snowy ground. His mind was swimming and a fierce panic had taken a hold of him.

"No... No... You can't be serious. Not her, not Rosé!"

"I am sorry," Kioni whispered. "I couldn't stop it. I was bound up and I couldn't break free. I tried Kyne, I tried as hard as I could and every damn day, I think about the look that little girl gave me before she was... before she was..."

"Murdered," Kyne said softly. "She was murdered by that monster."

"He used their souls, brought them together in some weird ritual and then everything seemed to break. I don't know much else about what happened. I escaped in the chaos just barely with my life."

Kyne was silent for a long time, his chest quivering from the shock and sorrow that filled his being. His little girl was gone? *That can't be right, right? She never even reached the alternate timeline; how did he even find her?* But deep down he knew that she had travelled there with them. He could deny it all he wanted but deep down he knew she was there.

I should've searched for her. I could've found her and avoided all of this if I hadn't tried to get all my things. If I hadn't tried to fight that corrupted version of myself!

He dropped to his knees, tears welling in his eyes, and he sobbed softly at her loss. He couldn't do anything, he was powerless. No matter how much he wanted, he couldn't travel through time anymore, there was no possible way for him to undo it. She was truly lost.

The wind began to pick up and the horses began to whinny, drawing their eyes up towards them. He wiped away the tears, his chest still tight and burning and met Kioni's eyes. His best friend had tried to save her and failed. *I guess the world has its own humor in some wicked irony. I couldn't save Ilana and he couldn't save Rosé.*

"Kyne we should get out of the open," Kioni said with a deep breath before guiding the horse into a trot. "I don't like being this close to the city so exposed."

Kyne nodded and wiped his eyes again as he stood up. Noticing the reins on the ground, he knelt down and grabbed them before he followed after Kioni. He wouldn't forget her, he never could but for now he needed to focus on the task at hand. If there was any chance that the others might be in the Ouroboros Bag, then he would have to take it.

The wind began to pick up but within a few minutes they had stepped off the trail and were approaching the trees. Each step closer to the trees blocked the wind more and more until they were finally enclosed in the frozen wood. The branches high up swayed and rustled but down on the ground there was hardly a breeze or a zephyr.

"Where is the bag Kyne," Kioni called out as he rounded a tree studying the ground.

"I don't know, it was dark, and I was injured."

"You have got to be kidding me," Kioni muttered. "We are going to be searching here forever, aren't we?"

"I came to a broken piece in the wall, that's how I got into the city. If we find that I might be able to retrace my steps."

Kioni turned to his right, traveling through the trees. Up above, through the bare branches they could see the hulking mass of the wall baring down upon them. It was enormous but seemed almost fragile as large chunks were missing, and big cracks split the stone.

They came to the wall and after a short walk down its length he started to recognize things.

"Here," he gestured at a sizable crack. "This is where I was. The bag shouldn't be too far this way," and he turned away from the wall trudging through the snow and trees. Nothing seemed familiar but by gauging the distance traveled, eventually he came to a stop.

"Around here then?" asked Kioni. Kyne nodded and they both tied their horses up nearby. Starting off on either side of their tracks, they began to trudge through the snow, searching for a lump buried underneath it. Hours passed and Kyne could feel his throat dry and cold. A quick swig of his drink and he returned to his search. The sunlight was dropping low when Kioni finally called out to Kyne's delight.

"I found it!"

Kyne dashed through the snow, each step pushing through the heavy sheet as he raced towards Kioni. His friend was actually near the wall, the stone structure only a few trees away. He was kneeling in the snow, brushing chunks away from some object. When he saw Kyne, he pointed up towards the trees.

The branches above were snapped, pieces missing or dangling loosely from the few fibers that remained.

"Rough entry?" Kioni muttered.

"Honestly it sucked pretty bad," Kyne tapped his abdomen where the scar was. He pushed on and after helping Kioni brush more snow away, he sighed as he stared at the bag.

It was there, perfectly undamaged with pieces of wood jutting out awkwardly from its opening in jagged splinters. The leather was untouched, pristine just as it always was and that at least made Kyne a little happy. *At least it wasn't damaged.* He grasped the leather cord and with a jerk, felt the bag hold firm, unmoving as if it was anchored to the ground itself. He pulled again, this time more aggressively but it still held fast.

"Let me try," Kioni said, and Kyne handed him the straps, smirking when he couldn't get it to budge an inch.

"How many aural stones do we have left?" Kyne asked.

"Not enough to waste in an attempt to get this bag to move," he replied sharply. "You should've thought this through more before we wasted our time trying to get it.

"I have thought about it for months Kioni. I have tried to think of anything that would work but that's the only idea I have come up with. Maybe refilling some of its energy will help it regain its power."

"And if you're wrong?"

"I'll take that risk."

"You'll take the risk by using the stones that I have collected. Brilliant reasoning Kyne, just astounding."

Kyne shook his head from Kioni's sarcasm and held his hand out, waiting as Kioni drew a single aural stone out, ruby in color just like the ones from before.

"You get one," he said. "That leaves one left."

"Only one?"

"Unfortunately, yes. We drained the others on our journey here with all of our fires and getting water."

"I hadn't realized," Kyne started. "I thought we had more. If that's really the case, then I don't want to waste..."

"It's alright Kyne," Kioni said interrupting him. "If you think it will work then we can risk it."

Kyne paused as he held the glowing red gem in his hand before his vision focused on the bag. He had no idea if it would work. Even if it did would this small gem be enough aura to fill it for a bit?

If you are watching Light, and you have grown tired with my struggles I would truly appreciate some intervention, he thought in his head and he paused for a moment, a small fleeting hope that rapidly faded as nothing happened.

Stooping down, he held the gem out, touching it to the bag's silver serpent. The glowing energy swirled immediately, flooding into the bag and to his shock and slight relief, he watched as the wooden splinters began to recede back into the dark depths.

Reaching onto the strap, he pulled, expecting it to still not move but to his shock and happiness, it lifted off the ground.

"Kioni, I can't believe it. It worked!" he gasped.

"I can't believe it either. If that worked, then maybe the voice you heard..."

A massive crash sounded as the nearby wall of Alakyne exploded. Chunks of stone rained to the ground, burrowing deep into the snow. They both leapt to their feet, their blades raised up towards whatever had happened. Kyne swung the bag onto his back as he shifted Aurora, the barbs sparkling.

Streaks of red sunlight spread around from the setting sun, illuminating the draconic beast as it crawled out of the rubble, more

The Legend of Kyne: Chronocide

stone crashing to the ground threatening the whole wall's stability.

"You!" the scaleless dragon roared. "I knew you would return! I could smell you the moment you arrived back in my city. I have waited so long to repay the favor!" he lifted the stump of his arm up and his lip furled in a snarl!

82. Ethereal Flame

"Kioni watch out!" Kyne screamed as he leapt around a tree, avoiding a blast of wicked heat from the beast's open maw. The frozen trees ignited immediately to Kioni's shock, and he only managed to duck out of the way just as the draconic swung its head around bathing the woodland in its nearly invisible flame.

"You shall all burn!" it roared, its voice distorting to more of a shriek. "Burn to ashes that will rest at my feet!"

Kyne glanced up and saw the branches high above his head dancing with orange flames that leapt higher into the sky matching the setting sun.

I have to get closer! his mind furiously roared as he darted out from his cover, leaping behind another tree just as it was bathed in fire.

He peeked around the corner as the onslaught ended to see the draconic had turned away from him, focused on Kioni who was dashing away through the trees, each footstep sinking to his knees in the snow slowing him way down.

"I know you," it hissed as it snaked its head following his movement. "I... I remember you from long ago. To be blessed with two is... is... Delicious!"

Two bounds brought the creature to the tree Kioni was behind and with a snap, it brought its jaws around it nearly grasping Kioni in its jagged fangs. It was larger than most men, nearly seven feet tall with pale sickly grey skin and absent of all scales. Shredded remnants of a wings lay from its remaining forearm, the other but an ugly stump that matched what should be a tail protruding a few inches from its backside.

It screeched again and Kyne saw a flash of silver as Kioni's kamas slashed through the air carving a deep slice across its face. The

The Legend of Kyne: Chronocide

draconic recoiled, stumbling back a few steps and clutching at its face. Blood streamed from a large slice that etched its way across his face just narrowly avoiding its eye.

"Mortal injuring a god!" it roared and then it was upon Kioni in a blur, slamming its claws right towards him. The ringing of metal sounded and then one kama was flying through the air before embedding itself in the snow.

Kyne could think of nothing else but one thing, he had to get over there as fast as possible!

Using what little aura he could, he significantly lightened his weight and dashed across the surface of the snow as fast as he could. He could see them a short distance away. Kioni was swinging his final kama around wildly back and forth as he backed up. His right arm was dangling at his side, large pieces of flesh torn from the bone and blood oozing all over the snow coating it in a thick film.

The draconic was approaching him slowly, matching his steps, but just before Kyne reached them, it turned as if noticing him and blasted a wave of hollow dragonfire.

Kyne had no cover, no way to stop his momentum and with a quick thought, dropped to his back, ending the spell and allowing him to sink through the snow just as the flames washed over him. He winced, the heat searing his face, but it only lasted a moment before it stopped, and another screech was heard.

Darting back to his feet, Kyne watched the draconic pull at the second kama from his shoulder, the pommel blade wedged deep into the flesh with its barbs locking it in place. Another quick jerk brought it free, and crimson blood burst free, oozing down its stump of an arm.

Kyne felt the aural reserves in his stone and knew it was already nearly depleted. He was running out of time and Kioni was in imminent danger!

I have to draw his attention on me, Kioni won't last much longer without a weapon and his arm, God his arm! And Kyne's eyes watched his friend take another step, the shredded meat of his arm threatening to tear completely off as it rained more blood. His skin was already growing pale as he lost countless amounts of blood to the frozen ground.

"You failed!" Kyne screamed, trying to get the beast's

attention. "You failed at stopping aura and look at yourself! Your very existence is based on aura fueling your power. The hypocrisy is..."

"Completely obsolete mortal!" it hissed, and it turned back towards him with malice in its eyes. "Sacrifices were made to get what I want."

"So, you sacrificed most of the world to fuel some revenge against aura? Who do you think you are?"

"I... I... I am you Kyne," it stuttered, coughing afterwards and it took a few steps towards him. "I am everything you couldn't become!"

"An embarrassment?" Kyne roared back and his response seemed to catch the draconic beast off guard for a moment before his lip curled in a snarl.

Kyne darted away, using what little aura he could to guide his body over the snow and away from Kioni. Each footstep pushed him forward as he darted towards a toppled tree. Three steps up its angled trunk and then he was airborne leaping towards a high up branch.

A swift strike collided with him and then he was falling, his mind twirling around and then icy darkness as he was thrust deep into a snow embankment. Each breath heaved out of his lungs, causing raking pain to fly through his mind from his ribs. He could hardly breathe, each inhalation causing excruciating pain and he cried out before gritting his teeth.

He couldn't feel Aurora in his grip and with a trembling push, he managed to lift himself up awkwardly on all fours to see the draconic stirring a distance away.

"He caught me so fast," he gasped, and he pushed himself all the way up to his feet, his knees buckling but holding for now.

"He can't escape!" screeched the draconic as it clambered up, pushing its stump hark into the ground as it heaved its body back up to its two legs. "Maybe he will return if I kill him!"

"Who will return?" Kyne called out, trying to distract him while his eyes feverishly searched the snow for Aurora. He seemed to not listen, rather he stood and looked up into the darkening sky, the final streaks of red fading as evening fell.

"You said we would be able to rule together, to fix the wrongdoings of him but then..." he paused as his eyes dropped down towards Kyne. "Then you left me!"

He dashed towards him, but Kyne swept his sword. He was quick, just out of reach of the blade as he skirted around before leaping up onto a tree and scurrying up its branches. Kyne could just make out its shape, high above him. Smoke was filling the sky, and he could see the glow of flames spreading through the trees as the woodland began to burn.

"Burn! Burn! Burn!" it screamed before it breathed out more ethereal flame igniting dozens of surrounding trees. "Burn the mortals!"

"Roke," Kyne muttered, and he snapped the base of the tree in two, the wood fracturing in a jagged scar. It swayed for a moment, a cry of shock erupted from up above and then the tree toppled over, falling fast before it collided with the wall of Alakyne in a crash.

Stone fragments toppled to the ground as the wood lodged itself in place and Kyne watched as the draconic fell forty feet from above before embedding itself into the ground hard.

"Kitala Aurora!" Kyne called, using nearly the rest of the stone as his sword rocketed towards him from beneath the snow.

The beast was close but Kyne, risking everything ran as fast as he could, his sword raised.

With a cry he brought it down, aiming straight for its neck but at the last second, it stirred, twisting around and kicking at Kyne's leg toppling him over. The world twisted around and with a final flick of his wrist, he aligned the blade as he fell, the feather slicing straight through the draconic's remaining arm severing it completely off.

Blood splattered all around, covering Kyne's coat in the scarlet mess. It screamed in pain while it staggered backwards, armless and manic.

"You left me!" it screamed at the sky. "Left me in this hollow world cursed like this! How could you leave me Elucia!"

As the word rang around, the world seemed to shudder.

"Kyne, you have to stop this!" the real Kyne said as he stood up and faced him. "We can help you!"

"Help me?" it hissed. "Why would I ever stoop so low as to ask for help from you? I have spent my life trying to undo the wrongs of this world and I will not stop until all of it is extinguished!"

The monster leapt forward, its mouth open and Kyne recoiled, raising his sword up in a feeble attempt to block it. The blow knocked him back onto his back, his hand placed upon the flat of his blade and the draconic's mouth clamped down hard across the barbs. Blood dripped from where the blade cut into his gums, but he seemed to not care, forcing harder as he pushed down bringing his fangs dangerously close to Kyne's chest.

The stench of rotting flesh filled his nostrils and Kyne struggled to breathe as the draconic forced itself upon him. Kyne could feel it, the pull of aura flowing through the air, and he watched as deep within the bowels of his maw, a shimmering haze was approaching.

Ethereal flames poured around the blade Aurora as it was still clutched in its fangs, engulfing Kyne in their inferno.

Etoch! Kyne's mind roared and he felt the final bit of aura from his stone flood through him morphing into a shield.

The flames poured over him, eating away through his stone's power. It seemed never ending, the shimmering haze distorting everything from view. He was running out of aura!

Twisting to his side while releasing a hand off of Aurora, the blade was forced down, jamming into the snowy ground right in front of his face. At the same moment he slammed his elbow as hard as he could into the draconic's head.

The rampant pain exploded in his elbow, but it was soon shattered by a headache unlike anything he had ever felt. Unbounded pain tore through his mind, contorting his vision and thoughts into a tight knot as it bore down harder and harder.

He couldn't think let alone react as the draconic turned its head back towards him, eyes filled with a burning hatred.

He wouldn't notice the beast's mouth open as it prepared another attack, the haunting veil of power emerging from within its depths.

He didn't foresee what would happen as a figure slammed into the draconic, knocking it off of him and them both tumbling to the ground.

Kyne's head warped and stretched thin, threatening to break from the strain and he tried to call out, his voice corrupting into a vile scream as he writhed on the floor. Bright white was flooding the edges of his vision pushing in upon its center.

The Legend of Kyne: Chronocide

He could just make out the figures nearby through his distorted gaze, struggling for a moment before the draconic clamped its mouth around Kioni's neck, the scarlet blood seeping down his shoulders. His face was pale and his eyes open in a glassy gaze before he smiled weakly at Kyne. Kyne tried to scream out but just as the sound left his mouth, he was gone.

83. Family

Rosé
Rosé
Rosé
Kyne's thoughts continually repeated as he struggled to maintain consciousness, his entire being threatening to tear itself apart. He could feel an almost euphoric feeling as he rushed through a strange world filled with every sight possible and also a deep nothingness that he couldn't quite understand.

Everything in his mind was focused on one thing. Getting to the hatchling, getting to the one he needed to prevent from dying.

A buzzing filled his mind, increasing in sound and pressure until it was deafening. He wanted to cry out, scream in pain but he couldn't lose focus on her, on Rosé.

Just as fast as it started, it was over. He was face down on the hard ground. He could hardly breathe as if the air had been knocked out of him. He twisted his head around and could see he was still in the woodland, the sun blazing up above, red through the deep haze.

A roar shook the earth and two dragons circled overhead, emerging from the haze before vanishing beyond the city wall.

Did I really...

He pushed up to his hands and knees, startled and eternally grateful for his blade that was still clutched in his one hand. The glow had returned, and its calmness was stronger than ever, helping clear his mind of the traumas he had endured. He had watched Kioni's final moments, the image burned into his mind, but maybe they could be undone.

A thought of realization and he grasped at the strap on his pack, each moment the movement growing more frantic as he tore it off his back and threw open the flap of the bag.

"Otri!"

A blur of darkness and then with another spell, the torches around ignited casting the inner depths of the Ouroboros Bag in light. It was perfectly how it once was, as if all the damage had been undone. Nothing had seemed to be moved or damaged in any sort of fashion. He could see the many structures inside from the forge to the dwellings and even the food storage all seemed to be in order.

But no Auriel or Ni'Bara.

He called out each of their names, as loud as he could and waited, his voice echoing around the massive room for a long moment before he tried once more. He could feel panic rising up in his chest, the pressure threatening to consume all thought.

"The voice said they were here!" he screamed out loud. "It said my family lies within the bag! Where are they! Auriel! Ni'Bara!"

Nothing responded.

"Kitala Auriel!"

Nothing.

Hysteria began to set in, and he ran, ran around the inside of the bag, the hundreds of feet that its diameter was, but he couldn't find them. Minutes passed as he finally came to a stop, breathing heavily and his heart broken. He sat outside the dwelling, his back pressed against the wall and his knees locked against his chest, he could feel the tears forming in his eyes.

He took a deep shuddering breath, trying to maintain his composure as he looked out across the bag. He could see the fountain nearby, powered by the bag's aura and flowing crystal clear. He could see the collection of trinkets he had received as well as the location he had placed Voron's own items after he died, not wanting to go through them.

His eyes darted back to that spot. He hadn't searched there but they couldn't be there, right? A last-ditch effort, he stood, walking somberly towards the small building in which he had arranged Voron's things. He had tried to set them up as well as he could, keeping everything visible and when he walked in, he surveyed the single room.

It wasn't very large, ten feet long on each of the four walls and with a spell, he lit the lights inside illuminating everything. He could see scrolls and other things that he had read as well as clothing items. A few artifacts lay there and as he studied each of them, his eyes rested on a strange three-dimensional hexagon.

He had seen it before, the familiarity was uncanny and as he got closer, he raced through his thoughts trying to remember why it was sticking out to him. Just as he reached out for it, he remembered; his arm reaching out identically towards Auriel's open hand in which it was placed, moments before they were separated.

"How is it here if she never..." he reached out and picked it up, turning the strange object over in his hands. It seemed normal, like a black stone object whose weight matched what he felt like it should weigh.

Turning it over again, he could feel a tingle appearing in his hand and pushing towards it, flooding the object with aura, watching it begin to glow. Symbols appeared, white and etched across its surface and he turned it over again, eyeing each one of them.

He turned and walked out of the building, continuously turning the item over in his hand until he saw something that made his pulse quicken and he stopped mid-stride.

A silver serpent biting its tail.

A trembling finger reached up to trace the ouroboros and just as it connected, a flash of white and a crash as a massive dragon seemingly appeared and a humanoid figure followed. They collapsed to the ground, unmoving for a moment as Kyne stared awestruck before one began to stir. Raising her head and looking around in a daze for a moment, her eyes rested on Kyne's, and she smiled.

"You found us."

Kyne was in her arms in an instant, tears flooding his eyes. He kissed her intensely and pulled her in closer, the warmth of her skin as her body pressed up against his. He held her there for a long moment, breathing in the scent of her air and tracing the curve of her body. Tears rolled down his face and as he opened them up, he saw Ni'Bara looking down at him.

It's been a while, Kyne thought, but there was no response and then he realized it. Stepping away from his wife, he looked down at his arm and saw the human skin.

Ni'Bara's eyes widened, and Auriel cried out in shock as they

The Legend of Kyne: Chronocide

noticed it. He smiled weakly at both of them before he said, "A lot of things happened."

"It seems like it," muttered the dragon.

"It's alright my friend," Kyne sighed.

"At least now I don't have your constant annoying thoughts about Auriel's attractiveness and the things you would do," muttered Ni'Bara in a joke but Kyne could tell his friend was hurting. He walked towards the large grey dragon. Reaching out his hand, he placed it upon his friend's snout and immediately felt his skin begin to burn and peel.

He cried out, recoiling in pain and to his wonder, watched as the flesh melted away, revealing grey scales that covered his entire left arm, crawling up before vanishing under his shirt sleeve.

It itched and burned but he ignored it, pure happiness flooding his thoughts.

Can you hear me? he asked gingerly.

Ni'Bara nodded.

Kyne, Auriel, and Ni'Bara ravenously ate the stored food in the bag as they described everything that happened to them. The stories of Alakyne shocked Kyne, filling his mind with thoughts of wonder and jealousy. After they had finished, he explained his world, knowing the information he was to share would cause immense grief and as he spoke the words, he watched the color drain from Auriel's face.

"He didn't... He couldn't..." she stammered.

"She is but a hatchling!" roared Ni'Bara and his chest began to glow a bright cyan.

"We need to stop him," Kyne started. "We will stop him. I saw the other dragons flying outside. I don't even know what time this is, but aura still exists, so he hasn't done anything yet."

"We need to go now!" Ni'Bara roared.

"We have time," Kyne said still sitting down. "The bag alters time remember. We need to figure out what is going on before we just rush in. We can't be ignorant Ni'Bara."

"But..." the dragon started before he grew silent, the flames subsiding.

"I'll scry her," Auriel said quickly, and she reached for a jug of water.

Kyne shook his head, "It doesn't work in here. We will have to leave the bag."

Auriel's eyes widened as she realized her mistake and in less than a minute they were outside the bag. Kyne placed the summoned water into a bowl, and they all stared down as she performed the spell, the returning verdant trees concealing them from prying eyes.

The surface swirled and contorted for a moment before an image appeared of the young dragon in a cage, a muzzle placed upon her maw. Two guards dressed in white stood in front of her and Kyne recognized them immediately.

"Windra!" he snarled. "Why the hell are they here? Did he seriously recruit them into his Dominion?"

"Who are they?" asked Auriel.

"Mercenaries from down south. They are ruthless and exceptional killers. I can't believe he would even think about doing that. Not even Aaldra enlisted them for their volatile nature was too reckless."

"Where is she," Ni'Bara said as he leaned in over them.

"Looks like the citadel, and by the looks of the stone somewhere high up, but I don't see any windows so I can't be sure."

"We should go and get her then!" the dragon snarled. "I will tear the building apart!" but Kyne shook his head, standing up.

"If you are seen then it could..." he paused for a moment as a thought entered his mind.

It could work, he said to Ni'Bara as he showed him.

"It might," he replied.

"What might?" Auriel asked, annoyed as she realized they had been talking without her. Kyne explained and then they were off, the bag back upon his back, running towards the wall of Alakyne.

84. One Final Step

Kyne's foot pushed hard, his toes curling through his shoes as he balanced on the thin lip of the brick, leaping up to the next and then the next in rapid succession. The wind blew in his hair, the smell of soot burning in his nose and the blur of the wall as he ran up the vertical face aided by his aura. Auriel was to his side, mimicking his steps as they flew up the hundred-foot wall.

The final push brought his hands just to the edge and grabbing it hard, he clung there followed a second later by Auriel.

Taking a deep breath, he pulled himself up slowly, his muscles in his back contracting as he guided his body up allowing his head to peek up over the edge. They were on the western side of the city, the girth of the wall blocking most of the city. He counted six sentinels, all of them nearby as they patrolled, their bronze armor striking against the monotone background.

"Altyne ulkin," he muttered, casting the invisibility spell over himself and his wife, masking their figures from all those in the nearby vicinity. He gestured up, catching her attention and she followed as they clambered up onto the top of the wall.

Each of the stone bricks fit perfectly together forming a mesh of rectangular shapes as his feet struck them. He held out a hand, helping Auriel down off the battlements and he looked south towards the entrance of the city. The wall was massive, over thirty feet wide from side to side as it stretched around the city, adorned with cube structures every so often that led deep into its bowels. Battlements lined either side with ballistae spread around, their heitrite tipped bolts aimed out over the landscape in a deadly show of force.

Kyne traced the curve of the wall, its arcing shape coming to a point before stretching across the southern side where it came to another point a few miles away. Continuing his gaze, he swept it over the city until the massive citadel came into view, the final point of the triangular wall hidden behind it.

The second inner wall lay separating the citadel from the city. *The royalty and the commoners,* he thought. Similar in structure, just not as big, he could see the glinting shapes of the sentinels that patrolled its length as well.

"Kyne," Auriel whispered drawing his gaze and he looked to see a party of sentinels emerge from one of the structures. Marching in unison, their feet raising and falling in rhythm, they marched on right past the two of them, completely unaware as Kyne stepped to the side allowing them to pass.

He could feel the drain as more people stepped into his spell, but it was fine for now. He would describe it as wearing a pack that constantly has a weight and every person who approaches adds a little more weight to the pack.

He was strong and his shoulders would hold.

They were fast, running along the wall's length, careful to avoid sentinels when possible. Each and every battlement that flew past blurred into a hazy line and Kyne felt a bead of sweat appear upon his brow. He could feel Aurora secured to his waist, the blade moving and swaying with each step perfectly in rhythm with him and hardly noticeable.

More sentinels were covering the walls, slowing their progress and they had to slow down, returning to a fast walk as they wove their way through the throng.

"What's going on," whispered Auriel in his ear and he shrugged, unsure of why.

"No idea."

More pushed on, filling the wall's walkway and forcing Kyne and Auriel nearly to the edge, stopping their run. He peered out of one of the battlements, down into the city below and could see sentinels and Windra patrolling down there.

"This is getting annoying," he muttered, climbing onto the battlement. His aural strain was increasing by the second and he wanted the release.

"Very annoying," Auriel agreed, and they took off, every other step sailing them over a battlement gap. The citadel loomed ahead as they went on, passing the growing crowd until it was only the stragglers who began to approach. They stepped back down onto the main walkway and Kyne shuffled to the side just as a Windra passed by him.

Kyne shuddered, a strange feeling coming from the foreigner and to his shock, the Windra stopped.

"I sense you Sneak!" he snarled, and, in a blur, he ripped his glaive out in a circular path nearly taking Kyne's head off as he leapt back out of the way.

The swinging blade was tucked in tight towards the attacker's body and with a grunt, he lunged forward, the tip aimed straight for Kyne's hidden chest.

How does he know where I am?

Kyne twisted, the blade missing him, but another strike followed, this one too close to dodge. He reached for his blade, knowing it wouldn't be fast enough but then the Windra was gone, a fading shout as his body hurtled off the wall where it fell out of view.

Kyne panted hard as he looked around in disbelief, noticing Auriel lowering her palm and shaking her head.

"That would be your luck. Killed before we even get to the real enemy."

"Thanks," he said, looking away from her, his hand pushing the half-drawn feather blade back down into the scabbard.

"Be more careful," she added, and he felt her shoulder bump his playfully. He turned to see her looking at him with a weak smile that showed more worry than anything else.

"I will be," he whispered, and he wrapped his arm around her shoulder pulling her in close and he felt her head lean into him. No other words were said, they just held each other as they looked towards the citadel. He was hers and she was his.

Shouting broke their moment and they turned to see sentinels looking out over the edge, presumably to where the Windra had fell to his death outside the wall. Other Windra were appearing and as they swung their heads around, as if scenting the air, they turned towards them and Kyne knew in his heart, they had been spotted.

More shouting and as the two took off with the illusion spell fading away, they heard a massive horn call!

The Legend of Kyne: Chronocide

*   *   *

Kioni looked out over the city from high up in the citadel. His hands were bound behind his back by iron cuffs and dark bruises covered his arms and face. He couldn't see much, the glass warped and foggy from grime, but he could still hear it, the echoing of a horn as it rang throughout the city.

"What was that?" he called out to the sentinels who stood guard outside his room. They held their stance, unmoving for a long moment before the rattling of armor was heard and another sentinel, this one a captain, appeared. Kioni couldn't make out anything of what was said, but it must've been important because the sentinels immediately entered the room, the iron bars swinging in silently.

"What was that!" he cried again, this time leaping to his feet. They said nothing and a few strikes were thrown, Kioni taking a few with his arms before one connected with his jaw, knocking him into a daze and then he was dragged out of the room.

He could hear the brushing of leather on stone as he came to, the sentinels were pulling him forward, each of them having an arm interlocked with his as his feet dragged behind. He groaned and stared at the ground as the stones passed by underneath him.

He was brought up a flight of stairs, down a few corridors and then they pushed open a door guiding him inside. The sunlight was bright, casting around and he could feel a breeze which startled him. Lifting his head up, he saw they were in a large room, the back of which had been completely torn apart revealing the outer wall of Alakyne and the ground far below. He traced its edge as he was brought closer, following it down as many floors came into view, each having the same massive gouge that carved its way through the citadel before ending in a pile of rubble at the bottom.

He was tossed to the ground, his knee striking the stone hard, and he felt a sharp pain rip through it, a small yelp leaving his lips.

Movement nearby finally grabbed his attention, and he expected a strike but when none followed, he looked up to see Akami's beautiful face looking down upon him. It was blank of expression, her eyes hollow. She said nothing but just looked down at him.

The Legend of Kyne: Chronocide

"Akami," he panted, scrambling to his knees awkwardly, unaided by his bound hands. "Get me out of here!"

"She can't hear you," hissed a voice and he felt his skin crawl as he slowly turned his head to see a cloaked figure standing nearby. His head was bald, tattoos etched into the flesh and his eyes were almost white, an icy blue.

"Akami," Kioni whispered as he stared at Saathe, an intense fear ripping through him.

Saathe flicked a finger and Kioni's face was jerked to the side as if struck by a club. He grunted, blood filling his mouth as his lip split. He spit, the blood splattering over the ground and he looked first at Akami who was unchanged and then back at Saathe.

"I know she is in there!"

"She isn't," Saathe muttered in annoyance, and he brought his finger down in a flick, the aura slamming Kioni's face hard into the ground and holding him fast. "I assure you that!"

Kioni grunted, the pressure bruising his face as it forced him hard into the ground. He struggled against it, managing to twist his head to the side. Out of the corner of his eye, he could see Akami, and she had turned her gaze, averting her eyes from him.

Kioni was released.

He gasped, not realizing he had been holding his breath and managed to sit up, his chest heaving. Saathe had turned away, looming over someone who was being held nearby that Kioni hadn't noticed before. They were mostly obscured from view behind a few sentinels but as Saathe stooped forward, his hand lifting her chin up she cried, her skin frosting where he touched it and then Kioni saw it, the aspen shaped ears and silvery hair.

She looks like... Is she a Riel?

Footsteps were heard as more people entered. The redheaded woman Voira and her dark-haired twin Ariov as well as two sentinels dragging something.

"Rosé!"

The young dragon was bound, iron cuffs locked around her wrists and chains binding her wings tight to her forearms. Her tail had been awkwardly wrapped up against her side and fastened to another binding that held it tight. Across her mouth was a muzzle, the metallic

The Legend of Kyne: Chronocide

clamp locked around her mouth preventing her from opening it at all.

The dragon turned her head awkwardly to see Kioni and as the two met, he saw her eyes well up and she looked away.

A deep rage tore through him and he leapt to his feet, his eyes set on her. He took a single step before he was suddenly brought back down on the ground, the back of his knee throbbing as a sentinel slammed their boot hard against it driving his knee into the stone.

"Don't even think about it Kydrëan," he spat and before Kioni could utter a sarcastic response, a swift strike struck him in the jaw knocking him all the way down.

His head was spinning, the taste of iron in his mouth and nose. He groaned and turned back towards Akami seeing that she was looking down through the many floors avoiding looking at what was going on.

I know she is in there he thought, and he moved his jaw, the joint popping and aching intensely. *I know it!*

More Windra were coming in and then he caught his breath in his throat as Lord Aaldra came in. His beard was its familiar trimmed length, dark and clean and his golden Kydrëan eyes bore a deep narcissist with them.

His robes were dark, the satin silk shiny and pristine as he strode around, looking first at the hatchling, then at Kioni, and finally the Riel.

Another figure suddenly entered the room, and everyone seemed to go rigid as if they all had an invisible blade pressed up against their spines. He could feel it, the malefic and malicious presence pressing in all around as the figure came into view making him clench his jaw.

It's Kyne, he thought, not in a question but matter of fact. He had a feeling this would happen. The voice rang over the city when the other vanished. He knew it was him, he just didn't understand why.

Kyne strolled in, his skin pale and his hair short. He was confident and so similar.

He wore a dark black tunic. The strings lining his chest interwoven and laced with ornate beads as they dangled nearly a foot down. His sleeves were long and baggy, concealing his hands but even his frame carried significant muscle mass from the width and roundness of his shoulders. The sight made Kioni very uncomfortable. He could feel power emanating from him unlike anything he had felt in a long time.

Kyne met his eyes and Kioni shuddered uncontrollably as a deep and wicked darkness was held within, nearly hidden behind the golden iris.

He grinned at Kioni for a moment, holding his gaze for a long time until he finally twisted away, his baggy tunic ruffling as he walked towards Saathe who was kneeling. He passed him, not acknowledging him at all but instead came to the Riel in which he stared down at the young woman.

She frantically started to writhe around in her bindings, struggling to get out but the sentinels held her firm, and Kyne merely looked down with disgust.

The Riel started to speak frantically in an unfamiliar language and after a few repeated cries, Kyne raised his hand up and her voice was cut short.

"Ugly things aren't they," he muttered semi to himself but also to the rest of the room who remained silent. "Cocky and strange, I can't believe the other one would actually find one attractive, let alone marry it! To think a people whose lives are solely bent on aura is beyond me."

"They were formidable," Lord Aaldra said drawing his attention. "Do you not recall how difficult it was..."

"Do you not recall that interrupting me is heresy!" he hissed and Aaldra grew silent. "Don't forget your place, Father. I let you live that day only because you could be useful for me, a figurehead. Haven't you wondered why no one speaks your name, only referring to you as He?"

"I understand," Aaldra said bowing his head.

"I don't think you do," Kyne said turning away from the Riel and walking around Aaldra.

"I do..." Aaldra started and then he suddenly began screaming, clutching at his head before tearing large cuts into his cheeks as his nails dug deep.

"Do you though?" Kyne continued as Aaldra writhed on the ground.

The Legend of Kyne: Chronocide

His cries rang around for another few seconds before Kyne broke his gaze and Aaldra was seemingly released from his grip, panting and moaning in despair. Blood dripped down his face and his perfect hair had grown disheveled.

"Why don't you do something useful and kill the intruders before they interrupt me. I am already irritated beyond comprehension that I am being rushed. This was supposed to be a magnificent and world changing event, one I wanted all the nations to witness!"

"I... I already sent Alderiun to intercept them." Aaldra stammered. "He took the..."

"I know what he took," Kyne muttered interrupting him. "I am the one who created it after all."

"Alderiun will stop him. He is one of the Dark Princes."

"That he defeated not once but twice. Alderiun will die and you will have to deal with the consequences Father."

"I... What..." Aaldra stammered. "What is your plan? Why did you go to all this work just to get these three?"

"These three will help me liberate the world from the tyranny of aura. With them I will finally be able to destroy it!"

*   *   *

Kyne swept low, ducking out of a swing of a glaive while simultaneously hurtling Aurora in line with a sentinel's leg, severing it just below the knee. The hallway clattered with the ringing of armor as the Gaeilian collapsed to the floor screaming in pain.

Auriel's orichite blade danced between different strikes and parries, her speed much faster than theirs as she twirled around before batting a strike away. Rebounding from her block, she guided her blade straight towards the sentinel's side, cutting straight through the gap in his armor. A flash of red and then he joined the collection of corpses that littered the floor.

Kyne could feel sweat dripping down his back as he fought off the final Windra, the mercenary's glaive deadly as it was thrust around before swiping across nearly cutting Kyne's leg.

They were armor less, the only thing being Auriel's orichite shirt but that would be very minor protection here. How badly he wished he had his armor. It had been left behind, lost when he was sent to the future and captured by the trappers.

He leapt back, narrowly avoiding another swing of the glaive and watched as the bladed staff was ripped around over the Windra's head in a big circle before coming towards him again.

I'm done with this, he thought as he leapt back again, pushing his back up against the wall of the corridor. No where else to go.

"Ilumace!" he shouted, directing the erupting light straight at the Windra, blinding him temporarily. He staggered back, rubbing his eyes vigorously and Kyne could see the upper part of his cheeks, where the skin was visible above the face covering contorting in pain.

"Roke," he muttered, snapping the glaive in two and with a final swipe, brought his feather blade across the man's chest, slicing through the fabric and the thin armor underneath. The flesh held for a moment as the Windra's hands dropped from his eyes, his gaze staring at Kyne in shock before a line of blood appeared. The flesh suddenly separated, revealing the muscle striations underneath before they were covered by copious amounts of blood. He swayed for a moment, staggering back into the wall where he slowly slid to a seated position, his hands feebly prodding at the massive laceration.

The corridor was quiet, the only sound being the two of them panting. Kyne flicked his blade, the blood coming off it instantly as if it resisted being dirty before he placed it back into his scabbard. Auriel did the same, wiping hers across one of the Windra's white cloaks staining a long red strip.

"These guys are insistent," she muttered as she looked down upon him, the cloak still pulled up tight and with his face covering, only his eyes visible.

"It's part of their culture," Kyne replied, stepping over a corpse and making their way down the hall. No more sentinels or Windra were coming which was odd, but he needed the break. "They make money fighting other people's wars, which is about the extent of my knowledge about them. I know they are vicious, ruthless in their execution but that's about it."

"It doesn't seem like they know aura," she muttered as she followed him.

"No idea, but it does seem that way. Or they only sent their foot-soldiers here and any aural users are back in their homeland. Maybe my twin didn't want to pay for the more expensive soldiers."

Auriel laughed out loud at that, the morbid joke amusing as they rounded a corner, Kyne peeking around first before stepping making sure it was clear.

"Either way they do seem to know how to sense for it which makes things much more difficult."

Auriel nodded, the Windra much more annoying to fight than the sentinels. They were almost there, only another length of hallway decorated with windows to his left before a flight of stairs. The King's Chambers were there and that was where Rosé was!

Kyne began running down the hall, the excitement and fear taking over. He didn't notice when Auriel had stopped running next to him, nor did he hear her shouts from behind telling him to stop.

He took another bounding step and a flash of pain ripped across his leg. Suddenly, his body stopped dead, his momentum ceasing. He could just move his eyes and he could see red, the feeling of blood dripping down his leg. The hallway was still empty, nothing in sight.

His body was rapidly pulled backwards coming to Auriel and he winced as he looked down at his leg. A perfect half circle had been carved across the outside of his lower leg, nearly a quarter inch in diameter. It was small, but perfect as if a master sculptor had carved it out of his leg like it was made of clay.

It still bled, the blood soaking his pant-leg, turning the light fabric dark and wet. He used a small amount of aura to fuse the vessels together stopping the bleeding. He would live but it would leave an interesting scar.

"So close," called out a voice and they looked down the hall to see someone coming down the stairs, their boots coming into view followed by the flowing grey robes. "If only you had kept going Kyne," laughed Alderiun and he came to the bottom of the stairs.

"What did you do to him!" cried out Auriel but he didn't answer. Instead, he stretched both hands forward before pulling them back towards himself.

A massive force tore both of them off their feet, rapidly dragging their bodies down the hall towards him, right towards the

The Legend of Kyne: Chronocide

trap!

"Kaiodin!" Kyne screamed and they felt everything stop. They were nearly upon it, the puddle of blood from earlier only a few feet in front of them.

Kyne could feel the aural drain from fighting Alderiun's spell hold for a moment before it ceased, the necromancer sighing. Dragonrage was filling Kyne's mind, the overwhelming desire to destroy spreading throughout him. He hated it but loved it at the same time, the raw power, uncontrollable lust for destruction fueling his body and with a swipe, he hurled an arcing blade of aura towards Alderiun.

It flew past the blood puddle and then suddenly dozens of flashes of light filled the hall as cyan sparks erupted all around. It tore at the blade, ripping holes from it as it traveled on with more and more sparks raining around in all directions as if from a meteor shower. Each spark continued spreading around, embedding themselves into the stone ground, the wall, and through the glass shattering it into fine dust before it finally dissipated a few yards from Alderiun.

"Understand it yet?" chuckled the necromancer and as his laughing increased, a dark haze of aura began to flow out from beneath him, surging forward and filling the hall with its miasma.

It pushed forward, flowing over the invisible blades, and Kyne watched as all around, just as his attack had done, small streams of dark aura appeared like dots throughout the hall. The haze poured out of them like small waterfalls before rejoining the rest as it pushed forward.

The attack was speeding up and the two drew closer together. In unison they cast the shield spell, "Etoch," and they watched as it flowed around them, traveling on down the hall.

It hung in the air for a long time, not pressing in upon their shield but merely flowing around it before it eventually started to fade away.

"What is he doing," Auriel muttered quietly.

"Necromancy," Kyne breathed in response and as if on cue, they could hear clambering of metal. Turning around, they watched as the previously slain Windra and sentinels rounded the corner. Their walking was slow and awkward, more of a stumble and the color had faded from their skin, ashen in color. They clutched their weapons as they once had, the broken glaive blade held like a massive dagger as it stumbled forward.

"Disgusting," Auriel raged looking back at the necromancer. A swipe of her aura and the deceased walking corpses were ripped from their feet, rushing down the hall right past the two of them and through the trap.

Dark blood splattered the hall as they were shredded apart, flashes of red and pieces of flesh falling around from random spots as if it had been teleported directly from their bodies.

"Thu'mar," Kyne said quietly, forcing his aura into the stone ground beneath him. He could feel each of the interwoven bricks that lined the floor and the right wall as he stretched his grip toward Alderiun. Passing by the necromancer, he grasped a hold of the very staircase and with a grunt, tore it forward.

A massive piece broke off, shaking the ground from the force and rocketed towards Alderiun's back but just as it touched him, it seemed to pass around him, flowing like water before it continued on through the hallway shedding apart to rubble.

The broken stones covered the fallen sentinels and Windra, but they began to stir, crawling to their knees slowly. Copious amounts of holes and slashes covered their flesh, some directly over the bones of their legs making them buckle and break sending them back to the floor.

Kyne could feel the tingle of aura the instant before it hit him and with his earth spell still active and not needing to utter the words, he brought his gaze to their feet, flowing the stone up around them and locking them in place as Alderiun pulled much harder this time.

The force nearly broke their ankles as the stone held them firm, their bodies jerking forward violently from the pull, but it held.

"Are you going to try and come get me?" taunted Alderiun beckoning for them to come. "We have the dragon, even have your friend too. Come with me and I can show you to them." He laughed out loud, his voice filling the room and the two glared fiercely at him. "No, you don't want to join me? Oh well, I guess I'll be going then. I will give your regards to them, actually," and he paused. "Maybe if you're still down here I can just bring them to you. I mean, they might be a little different, paler and not as much *spirit*." He laughed again drawing rage from both of them at the thought.

The Legend of Kyne: Chronocide

"Kyne do it!" Auriel cried out her words catching him off guard for a second but he did the first thing that came to mind and hurled another dragonrend towards him, this one bigger and stronger.

"Again, with that," muttered Alderiun. "I mean you can waste your aura, that's fine with me."

The attack struck the trap, shredding it apart as it raced forward engulfing some of the undead and small flashes of aura rained around randomly just as before. It was drawing closer to Alderiun, but Kyne knew it wouldn't do anything, he had to think of something else.

Next to him, he heard Auriel mutter something and as the final flash of light sounded, Kyne gasped in shock. Alderiun was there, just as before, but Kyne could see a wooden stick near his chest.

He coughed, violently and looked down at the stick for a moment before grabbing onto it and pulling, revealing the broken glaive's blade and a fatal wound upon his chest. Blood oozed for a moment as he just stared at them before he collapsed to the ground.

The remaining undead immediately crashed to the floor, the aura powering them gone.

"What did you..."

"Used your attack as a distraction," laughed Auriel.

Kyne smiled and looked back down the mess of the hall. Blood and debris covered everything, but they still had to press on.

"How are we going to get past the trap," Auriel muttered.

"I think I know what it is and if so, it's disgusting and messed up but..." he paused. "I think I can beat it. Thu'mar," and he took a chunk of stone from the wall, morphing it into a large rectangle a little taller and wider than both of them. "Come on," and he began walking forward pushing it on ahead of them.

The grinding of the sliding stone wall filled the room, followed by the occasion gurgle as it squished a corpse, pressing it hard against the contact point of the wall and the ground shredding it like ground beef.

A long smear of blood followed the wall, but they ignored it, stepping on until suddenly small pea sized holes began to appear as they cut through it. As if on cue, pea sized cylinders rained down from all over, appearing out of seemingly nowhere throughout the space of the hall.

The Legend of Kyne: Chronocide

"I thought so," Kyne muttered.

"What is it?"

"He made a ton of portal spells and lined the hall just making them small enough to not be seen." He looked at where one was and could just make out the hazy image of the hall but from a different angle as if peering through a tiny window. "You walk through it and whatever touches the portal goes through the portal, carving a perfect hole right through you."

Auriel's face contorted in disgust, and she watched as Kyne stayed right next to the slowly moving wall, guiding his body around each hole as it appeared. She understood his plan and followed along. Each foot more holes burrowed their way through the stone, but it gave them something to see, and they could contort their bodies around the spaces pressing on.

As they came to the end, Alderiun's corpse nearby, he slid the wall away, the thing so littered with holes it looked like a block of cheese. The hall behind was covered in a fine assortment of cylindrical stones, each cut perfectly from Kyne's wall, but none had touched them. *Except for the first one,* Kyne thought, and he looked down at his torn pant leg and the wound beneath that still burned intensely.

The stairs were long, the left side still more windows than walls overlooking the city beyond. The sky was a yellow haze, the light from the sun above scattered but he could see the chaos outside. Thousands of sentinels were throughout the streets and covering both the inner and outer wall. He could see each of them easily with their golden colored bronze armor shining against the bleak background. They looked like they were gathering.

Gathering for us.

They came to the top of the staircase and just a few feet away, turning to their right were the King's chambers, the door left slightly ajar as if welcoming them.

85. A Sorcerer's Symphony

Kyne gasped as he pushed the door open, revealing the broken room as it was before they had all been separated. It was large, nearly big enough to house a dragon with the back wall completely gone, revealing the outside. A breeze rolled through the room as he looked at everyone present.

He first noticed Rosé, her shining scales catching his eye and his pulse quickened as he saw her bound up, the reaper Saathe behind her, hovering like he had claimed her as his own. He then noticed Kioni, restrained and beaten, an eastern woman directly behind him which shocked him immensely.

Others were present too, the siblings that had been their captors Voira and Ariov as well as a few sentinels. Finally shifting his gaze over he saw that there was another easterner, this one with red hair right next to Lord Aaldra and his imitator, the one who bore his face.

"Welcome Kyne," he called out, rising from his throne, his large tunic ruffling as he took a step off the dais.

"Give me back my family Kyne!" the real Kyne called out loudly. "Stop this before any more people get hurt."

"Why would I stop when I am so close to succeeding," he replied and he took a few steps to the side, stepping past the red-haired easterner and Aaldra.

"Because I have seen what you do, what damage you cause. You ruin the world!"

"I save the world," he countered. "Whatever you saw must have been glorious!"

"It was anything but," Kyne replied. "It was complete desolation, chaos, and pain. Nothing could be worse than what you did."

The Legend of Kyne: Chronocide

"You speak lies," he retorted. "Do not try and convince me, I have spent my life searching for an answer and I have finally been given one. I will not waste this opportunity."

"Son," said Aaldra suddenly. "I think you should listen to him."

"I am not your son!" he spat. "That facade has long since evaporated. Do not think that because you can call me , that it means anything. You are but my slave Aaldra!"

"Please..." he started.

He waved his hand and Aaldra's eyes grew glassy, and his posture stiffened. His mouth relaxed and he stood, frozen in place.

"Better," muttered the twin. "So annoying. Now where was I? Oh yes, I remember. Kyne I will not..." he paused for a moment. "This is getting obnoxious having two Kyne's isn't it. Soon there will be one, and you will not be the one remaining, but for now you can call me..." his voiced trailed for a moment as his expression seemed to be lost in thought. "How about Enyk. Yeah, that sounds good. Enyk, its Kyne but reversed. Just how we both are. Opposites in almost every way."

Kyne gritted his teeth in frustration, and he felt Auriel's hand touch his.

"Look," she whispered, her voice trembling. He followed her gesture and then finally noticed the third figure, bound up and surrounded by sentinels.

"A Riel," he breathed as he noticed the features and his eyes widened. "You couldn't! You wouldn't dare!"

"Oh, I would," Enyk laughed. "I did have your memories after all. Such an interesting thing, this Darkness."

Kyne screamed and out of sheer instinct, unleashed the most powerful dragonfire he could muster right towards him.

The roar of the cyan flames shook the room as it collided with Enyk in a massive flash. His figure was lost from sight as Kyne poured more power into the attack, the stone wall beyond turning a bright red and beginning to ooze like sludge.

He held the attack for a long moment before it slowly faded away, to his shock revealing Enyk holding both his hands outstretched. Kyne could see it, just barely visible. The pearly white claws adorning his fingertips.

The Legend of Kyne: Chronocide

Enyk smiled as he reached up, grabbing the collar of his tunic. With a jerk, he shredded the fabric allowing it to fall to the ground revealing someone far different from the first time they fought.

Both of his arms were adorned with scales, one grey and one copper in color as they crawled up to his shoulders and spread partway onto his chest. Single individual scales continued across the rest of his chest and dotted his abdomen.

He was no longer frail and weak but incredibly muscled, veins spreading up across his abdomen and covering his upper chest like spiderwebs. Each muscle seemed to be chiseled like a statue, hard and defined as Enyk straightened up, popping his chest a few times as he noticed Kyne's gaze.

"Many things have changed since you vanished Kyne," he sneered. "I took what you had to the fullest extent!"

"And I have seen what you become!" Kyne roared back in challenge and with a swipe, hurled a dragonrend towards him. The arc was deflected to the side before Enyk returned the attack, the blazing orange blade of aura slicing through the air right towards him and Auriel.

He could feel the power, he understood its might and the danger that it contained and with a cry, he tackled Auriel to the ground just as it sailed overhead, cutting through the wall and shifting the whole citadel on its foundation.

Dust rained from the ceiling and Kyne coughed as he helped Auriel to his feet. The others in the room all seemed to have grown stiff, as if frozen by Enyk.

Enyk stared at Kyne, his golden eyes swirling in their depths and a flash of dark power came into being behind them threatening to extinguish the gold.

"What have you done?" Kyne whispered and he climbed to his feet.

"Not what I have, but what I will," he said, and he leered, his smile haunting. His eyes flashed and everyone in the room seemed to be released, gasping for breath and relaxing their posture. "Saathe, if you will."

Kyne whipped his head around to see the reaper strike the Riel down with his scythe, the blade splitting her flesh open wide before she dropped to the ground. Auriel cried out in shock but her voice was drowned as the Riel began to shudder and heave with breath. A sickening gasp came from her throat and then a moment later a glowing white wisp left her lips as she lay still upon the floor.

Saathe grinned, his tongue licking his lips as he stretched his hand out to his side, right above Rosé.

She suddenly began to shudder and gasp intensely, her body contorting as the power took hold of her. He raised his scythe up, preparing to strike the dragon down.

Auriel screamed out and Kyne felt hysteria sync in. It was now or never!

"Ni'Bara!" he screamed and withdrawing the Relic of Containment from his pocket, a flash of white filled the room.

* * *

Kioni cried in shock as the massive figure of Ni'Bara appeared, rearing up and slamming his head into the ceiling, tearing it apart and revealing the sky above. Pieces of stone and wood rained down all around while cries of shock erupted from everyone present. The dragon roared, shaking everything and the ground buckled, the stone cracking under his weight.

A flash of aura struck the dragon in the side, and he could see Ariov running at him, another attack already leaving his palm.

Ni'Bara roared again, raising his arm up as he shifted his stance, the ground buckling again. He brought it swiftly down, directly upon Ariov, crushing him flat from the blow before the room was ablaze with dragonfire, bathing the sentinels in an inferno.

Kioni shielded his face, tucking it away as the heat threatened to char his skin. He could see Akami shifting nearby, her own hand raised and an attack forming.

The blast struck Ni'Bara in the leg, burning a chunk of scales and his roar signaled it hurt. His gaze swung towards the easterner and Kioni could feel the dragonrage flood the air.

His maw opened, the glow of cyan forming upon his abdomen but a golden glow nearby caught his attention. Turning away from Akami, the dragon looked upon Aaldra who was forming a golden

The Legend of Kyne: Chronocide

spear of lighting in his hand.

The two Kyne's were fighting, aural attacks leaping between them.

Aaldra cocked his arm back to fire but as Ni'Bara's gaze rested upon him, he seemed to freeze, as if in a trance. Ni'Bara's tail sailed through the air, right over Kioni and Akami's heads, carving through the walls before it struck Aaldra flat in the chest, slamming him into the wall and sending Xeono's attack hurtling up against the ceiling where it exploded raining golden sparks all around.

The citadel buckled one last time, the ground collapsing and Ni'Bara roared as he twisted, leaping out the large hole before he was engulfed in the falling rock and spreading his wings as he sailed out over the city wall.

Kioni watched as the stone ground fell beneath their feet, pieces raining to the floors below and continuing on breaking floor after floor as the citadel fell apart. He could feel the whole building sway.

Akami was nearby, staring blankly at the encroaching wave of falling rock peeling away beneath their feet.

"Akami!" Kioni cried out and as fast as he could, he leapt towards her, colliding with her hard and knocking them both against the wall.

She cried out in shock, her sound drowned out by the room as most of the floor fell away, only areas against the walls remaining. Kioni glimpsed Kyne and Enyk, dashing among the falling debris, flashes of light and then they were gone, somewhere down below.

Akami grunted again and Kioni lifted himself up, staring at her eyes as he tried to find anything that signaled she was still there.

"I know you are in their Akami!" he said, and he pressed his forehead against hers. "I will find you!"

He didn't know much about aura, really nothing at all but he knew that somehow Enyk had corrupted her mind. *If he could do it, then I can too!*

Concentrating as hard as he could, focusing on their contact, he tried to imagine his mind stretching out, reaching forward. He could feel a wall blocking him, holding him back but centering his focus, he felt it give, his own aural mind wall falling allowing him forward where

The Legend of Kyne: Chronocide

he collided with a raging storm.

He was lying on his back, rain battering his face and the wind howling in his ears. The sky above was dark with storm clouds, flashes of lightning decorated his vision and he gasped for breath.

Rolling onto his hands and knees, his hand pressing hard into the muddy ground, he pushed himself up to his feet.

Hazy mountain silhouettes dotted the landscape all around as he realized he was tucked in a tight mountain valley. Fir trees covered the landscape, surrounding him in a dark foreboding forest. He was in a clearing, surrounded by trees and dark wet vegetation as more flashes of lighting lit up the scene.

Between their flashes, he saw a small building, far off in the distance. No light lay within it, but he knew that was where he needed to go. Taking off, as fast as he could, he ran through the muddy ground, the water soaking him with its frigid grip. Each footstep splashed hard, sending up muddy water all around soaking the grasses and other vegetation but he pushed on, entering the forest line, the building still far away.

He persisted, running as fast along a stone path that led to the building, a home. Long wooden panel walls had been slid shut, blocking everything inside from view. The few windows were still dark, but he approached the home anyways. Reaching out, he grabbed a hold of the panel wall and pulled it hard to the side, but it held fast.

This isn't real! he thought fiercely. *It's all in our minds. I can open it if I just focus...* the door suddenly slid open to the side revealing a dark and dry dwelling.

Mats had been spread across the floor, a few pairs of shoes sitting right by the entrance and dead plants lay in pots along the wall. More sliding panels made up the walls, separating one large room into four. The next room was empty, similar to the first and the following room was a space for eating, a wooden table low to the ground and cushions around it. Dust lay coating it thickly and the dark lighting made it hard to see anything else.

He came to the final room, a simple bedroll lay against one wall, a small chest next to it with paintings upon its top. Sniffling was heard and Kioni turned to the side, along the slid panel in the corner

The Legend of Kyne: Chronocide

lay a young eastern child, her knees tucked up tight to her chest.

"Akami," he said softly, and he approached.

The child tucked her head down, hiding her face.

He moved closer, placing a hand on her knee.

"Go away!" she cried out and she shifted, turning to the side a bit and keeping her head down.

"Akami, I am here to help you. It's me Kioni."

"I don't care! I want to be alone! The storm is too much, if I go out, I will die!"

"No, you won't," he whispered. "The storm is what keeps you trapped. He put it there to frighten you. Akami, trust me."

"How can I trust you? I hardly know you," she said raising her head up.

"You know me enough," he said with a weak smile. "Come," and he stood up, grabbing her hand but she stayed seated. "Akami, we need to go."

"I don't think I can Kioni, outside is too much. In here I am protected."

"In here you are trapped," he said, stooping back down to the child. "In here he maintains his grip on you. You have to fight it. The Akami I know would never be pushed around like this."

"The Akami you know?" she laughed weakly. "You don't know the true me Kioni. You don't know the horrible things I have done."

"I know you wanted to kill me but instead helped me escape. I know you found friendship with Rosé and risked everything to save her. Even if you have done horrible things, I know you can make up for it. I know deep down you are a good person."

"I..." she said before stopping. She looked down for a moment but as she raised her gaze, her figure changed back from a child to her adult form.

"I will help you," he whispered, and he leaned in, pressing his lips softly against hers.

They held it for a long moment, the rain outside seeming to slow its chorus of pelting before finally stopping. He withdrew, a smile on both of their faces and as he stood, he pulled her up to her feet. His wet clothes were now dry as he led her through the house to the doorway. As they stepped outside, streams of sunlight split the storm-clouds, a rainbow hovering in the air and the chorus of birds beginning to sing.

Kioni opened his eyes, meeting Akami's own as he realized their lips were still locked. He could feel her lips move, drawing him in closer as her tongue brushed his own. He wanted her so badly, but they couldn't. Not now.

He broke away, looking out over the destruction. Nearby he could see Voira, the red-haired woman screaming as she knelt over her brother, Auriel nearby watching unfazed.

Voira looked up, tears and hate in her eyes and with a scream, she ran at Auriel, a dagger in her hand.

"I'll kill you! I'll kill you all!"

Auriel twisted, easily dodging the blade before swiftly kicking her in the leg. Voira cried out, dropping the dagger where it clanged against the ground. A swift punch struck from Auriel, colliding with Voira's nose, crushing it under the force and sending blood flowing out of both nostrils. She coughed hard, splattering blood around as she fell to her knees wailing.

"You creep," Auriel muttered, turning away from her. A flash of light caught her eye, and she whipped back, narrowly deflecting the attack from Voira sending it against the wall where it exploded.

"Kitala blade!" she screamed, and the small dagger flew from the floor to her hand. Stepping forward, she thrust it right into Voira's neck, embedding the silver blade deep.

Voira gasped as her airway was cut off. Her eyes were full of confusion and then panic as she struggled to breathe, blood pooling down the embedded blade. She stumbled back, the dagger sliding out of her neck still clutched in Auriel's hand. Taking another step in a daze her foot hit the edge of the broken floor, sending her falling out of view.

Auriel sighed, turning away from Voira when suddenly another red-haired woman was in her face, her eastern features full of anger. She felt the blade in her hand jerk around and before she could react, Hayame had rammed it hard into her side.

* * *

The Legend of Kyne: Chronocide

Orange and cyan flames enveloped the sky, swirling together as the two dragons rushed after the hurtling figure of Ni'Bara who was diving towards the ground. He twisted hard, his head struggling to remain stable from the force as he rapidly decelerated and banked left, the two pursuing hurtling past him. Their flames ceased as they arced along the ground narrowly crashing into the city below, their wind ripping the roofs off in droves.

He continued his bank, finishing in a spiral as he rose before turning to face them. His leg screamed in pain, burned by one of their flames from earlier and he could feel the flesh crack and bleed from his movements. Down below he could see his own scorch marks upon their hides, each having received major damage in return.

Their flight was fast, closing the distance in second. They were suddenly too close, only a few tail lengths away now, each flanking with a trail of fire and smoke falling behind them. Ni'Bara suddenly dropped, tucking his wings tight just as two blasts of fire collided overhead. Twisting around, he focused all of his aura onto a single point on his tail and with a flick, collided it with Ky'Ren's chest. A deafening boom sounded as the dragon's bones were cracked under the powerful force and he was hurled away in a roar of pain.

Ni'Bara went for another swipe of his tail, but his twin dodged it, blinding him with his leathery wings before his tail collided with Ni'Bara's side knocking him off balance. He was dazed, hurt and trying to hold his flight when his twin was suddenly upon him driving his fangs into his back.

Ni'Bara broke free a fraction of a second before the twin was able to clamp down fully, narrowly avoiding death and ripping around grabbing a hold of him. Digging the claws upon his feet deep into his mirror's abdomen, Ni'Bara held on tight as they fell, twirling dangerously in the air. His mirror screeched in pain, bathing the air in fire before snapping his jaws towards him, biting down onto his shoulder.

Hot blood bathed the grey dragon's scales, oozing out from between the gaps in the mirror's fangs before rising up in globs as they tumbled towards the approaching ground. The swirling mass of stone and wooden buildings filling their field of view as the two fell, locked

The Legend of Kyne: Chronocide

together in a death spiral.

Flames licked Ni'Bara's mouth as he inhaled, his focus bent on rendering the copy into a pile of ash but before he could breathe out, his twin flailed around like a feral dog, threatening to tear his arm off.

Pain consumed Ni'Bara's thoughts, pushing in as his body was thrashed around, his shoulder nearly dislocating from the force. He could feel the flesh, the muscles tearing and shredding and as the pain grew, so did his dragonrage, enveloping every part of his being. He could feel it, flowing through him and across his body.

All thought was lost by the rage that enveloped him!

Flaring the spines that covered his head, Ni'Bara whipped around, slamming into the thrashing beast and embedding them deep into his muzzle. Another slam of his head caused the dragon to release his hold upon his shoulder. The mirror was in a daze as they continued to fall, blood coating the side of his face from countless puncture wounds.

Ni'Bara could see his opening as his mirror's neck became fully exposed. The soft flesh of his neck waiting for the kill.

Time seemed to slow as he lunged forward but just as he started to move, he hesitated. The ground was nearly upon them! It was too late to pull up, there wasn't enough time! With a quick thought, he clamped his claws deep holding his twin firm and jerked him around. Spreading his wings, he pulled their momentum to an angle before his twin's body slammed into buildings carving a trail of destruction behind them. Ni'Bara clung tight to him, using the copy's body to soften the collisions as they plowed through countless Kydrëan homes and businesses, crushing dozens of people and filling the city streets with screams and destruction.

As they came to a stop, his twin unmoving, the dragon's neck bent at a funny angle. His back had been shredded apart, the scales torn off from the collisions and the bloodied muscle revealed beneath.

Ni'Bara snorted in triumph, the glow of flames appearing between the scales of his chest. He wanted to finish this, burn the wretched thing to ashes!

A flash of light stopped his attack and Ni'Bara leapt up out of the way just as Ky'Ren's own flame engulfed the ground, casting the twin Ni'Bara from view. A second later he slammed into the ground,

The Legend of Kyne: Chronocide

cracking it under the force.

A Dominion sentinel screamed in fright, exiting a building, and running away but with a flick of his tail, Ky'Ren smacked the man, turning him into paste within his armor as he was cast through a wall.

Ni'Bara through a glance back as he leapt into the air, his wings beating for the sky. Ky'Ren was looking upon the deceased dragon before turning away. His face contorted in rage and then he was off, flying after Ni'Bara each wingbeat pushing their ascent further.

Ni'Bara was slow, his arm injured from the bite and he hadn't gotten very far ahead. The haze that hung over the city quickly faded the ground from sight, obscuring his figure as he arced away in an attempt to have a moment to rest.

That bastard! his mind snarled as his eyes darted towards the vicious wound upon his shoulder. The flesh had been shredded into pieces, blood oozing out in a thick scarlet wave. *I can hardly fly! I have to end this. Now!*

A roar cut through the air and Ni'Bara twisted to the side just as Ky'Ren rocketed past him, narrowly missing him. The screech of his wings filled Ni'Bara ears as he righted himself, following Ky'Ren as he curved around before coming to a stop nearby.

"You won't last much longer," hissed Ky'Ren. "You can hardly fly."

"Even two against one you can't beat me!" he replied with a snarl, a silvery haze tracing along the outline of his body. "It brings me joy to kill you again!"

*   *   *

Akami watched Auriel collapse to the floor, her sister looming over her, disgust upon her face. Kioni next to her cried out in shock scrambling towards Auriel.

Akami watched Hayame's gaze flick towards him and with a sweep of her hand, an attack was launched at him. Akami stretched her aura, grabbing onto Kioni in less than a second and tearing him back to her just before the strike narrowly missed him, saving his life. His eyes were full of shock as he watched her step forward, her hand telling him to stop.

The Legend of Kyne: Chronocide

"I'll take care of her."

"This has been a long time coming Akami," Hayame called out, stepping around Auriel who laid curled up. The remaining flooring of the room was small, nearly a dozen feet wide and situated near the doorway, the back half of the room completely gone.

"You don't have to do this Hayame," she called out as she approached. "I can help you force him out of your head."

"That's where you are wrong. I like him here. I always have. He gives me strength, much more than anything Mother did. I would rather stay here, fight and die for him than return home to that wretched woman. Return home with you just to have you continue to embarrass and humiliate me.

"It wouldn't be that way!" Akami cried out. "We can be sisters once more!"

Hayame laughed. "Sisters? We haven't been sisters in a long time Akami. A very long time."

"But I thought..."

"Thought that I had forgiven you? That we were going to capture Kioni and return him to Mother together? I was going to be the one to return him. It was *always* going to be me. You would have been on the journey."

"You were going to betray me?"

"Obviously! I haven't forgotten anything like I led you to believe. I should've killed you the other day when I accused you of killing Yu. It was clearly you! We all knew! I could've easily snuck into your room and slit your throat. But..."

"But you couldn't kill your sister when you were finally presented about it," Akami replied.

"Not in the slightest," Hayame snapped. "I was told by Him to keep you alive while he was gone, that is the only reason! You were to be a sacrifice!"

A flash of lightning flew through the air and Akami dashed out of the way, sliding to her side and hurtling two attacks in quick succession.

Another bolt of lightning flew but Akami redirected it, colliding it with the stone in a flash of sparks.

"I don't want to do this!" Akami cried out. "I don't want to kill you!"

"You won't have to," Hayame sneered. "I'll kill you first!"

An aural arrow hurtled towards Akami at a blinding speed, slicing across her abdomen cutting through her clothes and side. The burning fire tore through her and she swayed, maintaining her balance.

"I am sorry," she whispered. Using her aura, she launched a single stone towards Hayame who stepped to the side, easily dodging it and laughing. Just as she went to take another step, Akami muttered, "Kaiodin."

The spell momentarily froze a single foot, just for an instant but enough to knock Hayame off balance and as she stumbled forward Akami unleashed two more aural attacks. Hayame blocked the first with a cry but the second missed her block, colliding hard with her chest and launching her far across the room where she collided with the wall.

Her chest was scorched, and blood pooled out of her mouth as she coughed a weak laugh.

"Looks like you finally beat me for the last time," She coughed again hard, blood flicking across her clothes.

"I can heal you," Akami said softly. "I can save you, my sister."

"We were never truly sisters Akami. Never," and she sighed, her body growing limp as her last breath left her body.

Akami felt a heaviness form in her chest for a long moment as she looked at her sister. She felt sorrow but also like a heavy weight had been lifted from her spirit.

"Auriel!" shouting was heard, and she turned to see Kioni kneeling down next to her shaking her hard. Leaving her sister behind, she approached and was startled when Auriel groaned, her eyes opening up.

"Ouch," she muttered," clutching her side and as she sat up, Akami noticed no blood.

"How did you..." Kioni started and Akami lifted up her torn shirt, revealing the orichite undershirt perfectly fine. She lifted that one up revealing a nasty bruise on her side but no stab wound.

She met Akami's eyes and mouthed, "Thank you."

Akami nodded, knowing that Auriel had allowed their duel to happen. Smiling herself she turned to look at Kioni. "We should get

The Legend of Kyne: Chronocide

out of here soon; the building won't last much..."

A golden glow nearby caught her attention, and she didn't finish her words, turning instead to see Aaldra had stood up, his eyes glowing and electricity erupting from them. His face was contorted in rage, blood dripping from a laceration on his scalp and lifting both hands, he brought them together.

Akami was violently jerked to the side, Auriel mirroring her, and the two women collided hard, dropping to the ground in pain. Kioni was then torn off his feet, his neck coming right to Aaldra's grasp, and he held him off the floor for a long moment as he looked at him.

Then he was gone, gliding out of the building down towards the courtyard where the two imbued with dragon aura fought.

*   *   *

86. Dragonsoul

Kyne dashed off the falling block, hurtling through the air just as an orange arc of power sailed beneath him, severing everything in its path apart. His feet planted upon another piece of debris, the ground still far below as they fell before launching off, sending his own dragonrend up towards Enyk who had twisted out of the way.

Do you think you can actually beat me? taunted Enyk's voice in Kyne's mind as he tried to focus on what he was doing. He could feel the unbounded pressure hovering just outside his defensive wall, close but not entering.

I have to! Kyne screamed back, hurtling another attack before dashing through the air to another falling chunk of stone.

Enyk could completely overwhelm his mind, Kyne knew that and right now, he had to end the fight before he tried.

They dashed among the falling debris, propelling off back and forth as it all fell, each moment moving in slow motion as they used their aura to increase their agility. One final push brought Kyne far to the side just as the majority of the rubble crashed to the ground in a cloud of smoke. His feet slid hard against the courtyard's stone pavement, but his stance held.

The citadel above swayed, Ni'Bara far above weaving in and out of attacks from two other dragons as he led them high and away.

Enyk alighted gracefully upon the ground, his shoulders relaxed with his head raised up, as if he were looking down upon Kyne.

Why do you try to resist?

Why are you an asshole?

Enyk chuckled in Kyne's mind before he started to walk slowly to the side, moments later more pieces of the citadel crashed down where he had been standing. *I could crush your mind you know. Squish it between my fingers like a tiny insect! It would be easy!*

The Legend of Kyne: Chronocide

Then why don't you do it? Kyne replied, a thought entering his mind. He pushed on, *if you are a god like you say you are then this fight shouldn't even have to happen right?*

Enyk stopped his walking, turning towards Kyne and a look of rage alighted upon his face, his nose scrunching up in a snarl.

I would rather kill you with my bare hands!

Then let us see who is really the one worthy of this power, Kyne said, and he tore his own cloak off, revealing a similar muscular build. The scales upon his arm glowed a faint cyan and he could feel the power flowing through his body. Directing it around him, he could feel it etch its way across his skin, carving into his cells as he imbued them with the dragon aura.

It itched and burned intensely for a moment as they changed and then it was gone, his white skin gone, replaced by a greyish hide reflective of Ni'Bara's own. It covered everything, stretching up his neck before ending right underneath his jaw. It bore no scales but would protect him more than anything else really could.

Dragonskin.

Kyne hated using it, it was a massive and constant drain of aura, but it was needed.

He watched as Enyk sighed, stretching his hands out to the sides, and his own skin began to warp and change, patches of grey and coppery orange flowing in swirls as it covered him. He smiled, mocking in every which way.

They suddenly sprinted at each other, each footstep accelerating them until the world was but a blur. With a roar, the two collided forearms, the blow shaking the air and for a moment, they hovered a few feet above the ground as if stuck together.

Their feet alighted and immediately Enyk swiped at Kyne, his claws sailing towards his abdomen. He twisted out of the way, his own strike colliding with Enyk across his cheek. The blow was astoundingly hard, but Enyk whipped back as if not injured at all, his cheek covered with the dragon skin before it crept back down to his neck.

Kyne threw another punch, this one parried away before a swift jab impacted his abdomen. He could feel the pressure, the pain minute as it impacted but he blocked it out, twisting around and swinging his leg in a roundhouse kick towards him.

The Legend of Kyne: Chronocide

Enyk blocked it with his own raised knee before darting forward, two punches striking fast. Kyne blocked them with his palms, pushing them to his side. In a blur, Enyk had tucked his leg up and dashing forward, slammed his foot into Kyne's abdomen as hard as he could, launching him far back, the breath bursting from his lungs.

Kyne gasped as he felt his feet slide across the ground, his balance was off, and he could see a glow coming from Enyk.

A massive ball of dragonfire erupted out of his mouth, hurtling towards Kyne like a meteor of swirling cyan and orange.

He screamed, in pain, in fear, in anger, in a need, and he raised his palm, the fireball colliding hard with him, jarring his shoulder back. He could feel the power, the intense vicious energy raging within it. He pushed as hard as he could, struggling to hold it back. He could feel the scales upon his palm burning, the pain ripping through him, and he shuddered as his feet slid back upon the ground.

It's too much! he screamed in his mind, raising his other hand draped in aura and held both hands back, the fireball continuing to press on.

He slid back more.

You can do this! roared Ni'Bara's thoughts in his mind. *He is but an imitation. You were the one who saved your country, you were the one who saved the world from the Darkness! The Deathsbane, the Kingkiller, the Godslayer!*

Kyne roared, his voice mutating as he raised his hands, directing the flaming ball over his head where it launched high into the sky. A flash of light followed by a deafening explosion that shook the ground.

He panted hard, sweat covering his face. He could see the burns upon his palms, the scales charred black. He thought of Ni'Bara, the dragon's words giving him new energy. He couldn't give up!

His eyes focused and alarm ripped through him as Enyk was already there, dashing low, his claws outstretched as he brought them up, slicing across Kyne's chest carving out four streaks of blood.

He staggered back, narrowly avoiding a second strike and weakly parried a punch aimed at his face.

Enyk's face was a brutal look of cool confidence as he let fly two quick jabs, each colliding with Kyne's abdomen before a swift hook-punch flew, colliding with his jaw.

Pain split his mind as his head ripped to the side. Blood pooled in his mouth as his cheek split against his teeth and his head was spinning while he tried to look back at Enyk.

"All of the training you have ever had, all the countless hours spent pushing your body and mind to the limit, I remember it," and he tapped his head with his finger lightly. "All those memories, the memories *you* gave me, I embraced them! I analyzed them while you shied away, hid from mine. Too terrified to see the atrocities I have committed."

"It doesn't matter," Kyne coughed, twisting back to face him and straightening up, blood dripping down his face. "Even if you know the things, you haven't executed them in practice. Nothing would compare to the countless hours *I* spent pushing my body and mind!"

Enyk chuckled darkly and Kyne watched as the skin upon his chest began to flake away revealing more scales beneath it. His hand suddenly began to glow with an aural haze. It stretched and flowed around the surface of his arm, silhouetting it with an otherworldly halo.

"And yet it was me who pushed the limits. Hours spent training and it was I who unlocked new things, things that you haven't even discovered yet."

Enyk reached forward, a single finger outstretched and lightly touched Kyne in the middle of his chest.

Dragonforce.

Kyne felt his chest cave in from a blow unlike anything he had ever felt and then he was flying through the air. A crash and then darkness.

He was stuck. Pressed into the inner wall of Alakyne, like a human ceramic mold he hung there. His chest screaming in pain and his head swimming. He had been nearly killed, the only thing saving his life was the dragonskin upon his flesh and he felt it waver, the grey hide flickering in and out of existence.

Ni'Bara, he thought weakly, defeat filling his mind. *Ni'Bara I can't, he is too powerful. I can't do it.*

There was no reply this time and he glanced up, the dragons out of sight, beyond the clouds and the haze that hung around the city.

The Legend of Kyne: Chronocide

Everything hurt, his body, his mind, even his heart hurt as he looked at the citadel as more rubble broke off of it. Flashes of light high up within signaled somebody was fighting an aural battle and his mind drifted to his wife.

Auriel.

Rosé.

Ni'Bara.

And even Kioni.

I put you all in this mess. He exists only because I created him. If I had told them what was happening sooner, or just vanished away never to come back... the grim thought hovered in his mind as he saw Enyk slowly approaching him. *If I didn't exist...*

Then we would all have died! roared Ni'Bara's thoughts and the dragon's burst through the clouds, fire bathing the sky. *Defeat him!*

Enyk dashed forward, his steps increasing in length as his speed rapidly accelerated.

Kyne could feel his body, bruised and battered but he had to move. He had to!

Peeling away from the wall, his legs buckling hard but holding, he leapt to the side just as Enyk sailed through the air feet first, impacting the wall and the stone cracked, spreading rapidly up and to the side along the wall before pieces started to break away. He could hear shouting of people above, trying to escape as it shuddered before it began to fall.

Using his aura, he pulled himself away just as the wall collapsed on top of Enyk, engulfing him in a cloud of dust and stone.

Kyne tumbled on his back, rolling hard for a few moments until his momentum slowed and he came to a stop. His dragonskin flickered again but was holding for the moment.

Enyk suddenly appeared, walking out of the dust, completely unscathed. Both arms were outstretched to his sides, as he laughed loudly.

"Rik'tar," Kyne muttered, and the flash of lightning leapt from his palm heading straight for Enyk who deflected it easily sending it to the side with a loud thunderclap.

Kyne tried again; it was redirected with a flick.

Forcing his aura into his palm, he created a massive spear of

The Legend of Kyne: Chronocide

glowing cyan blue.

"Sen sytori!" he screamed hurtling the dragon killing attack straight at Enyk.

It collided hard with his outstretched palm, shaking the vicinity with its power and the world seemed to hold still as he held it back before the power eventually faded away and is disintegrated.

"To think that someone of your reputation would actually prove to be so weak!" Enyk called out. "I took your idea and decided to make two catalysts! Hence why I insanely outclass you."

"Two is forbidden," Kyne coughed, blood oozing out of his insides before being forcefully ejected onto the ground. "Two is corruptible!"

"They made that rule to create control and order," he called back as he stepped forward, every second shortening the distance.

"It corrupts the user, distorts everything about them. I have seen what it does to you, the wretched monster that you become!"

"I do what I must to succeed," he said darkly. "Now," and he came to a stop a dozen feet from Kyne. "Let me sing you a lullaby so that you may go to sleep!"

His eyes turned to slits and more skin flecked off revealing more scales.

Kyne returned the song and with a roar, the two collided their aura, their Dragonsong upon each other.

The earth seemed to shake and quiver as the power was unleashed. Kyne could feel his body violently trembling, pain tearing through him, but he pressed on, forcing the roar as hard as he could upon Enyk. He could feel wetness upon his mouth and cheeks, and he realized what it was as he saw Enyk's own face pouring blood out of his eyes and nose.

He forced more, holding the spell and he felt his mind darkening upon the edges. His shaking intensified and he felt as if his body was being torn apart.

If you don't stop then we both die! rang Enyk's voice in his head.

Then we both die!

His attack continued, the darkening haze tunneling his vision. He could feel his legs growing weak, his sight stretching away as if his very presence was being dragged away from his body.

The Legend of Kyne: Chronocide

A roar suddenly cut through his mind and a massive crash sounded right next to them, breaking the spell and they both gasped for breath.

Blood dripped upon the floor and Kyne tried to wipe it away, the scarlet liquid smearing upon the skin of his arm. His dragonskin was long gone, his aura nearly depleted.

He heaved hard trying to catch his breath and to his satisfaction, he saw Enyk doing the same thing. They breathed for a few moments before Enyk turned slowly to see what had happened drawing Kyne's attention.

Ky'Ren was laying at an awkward angle, his arm broken and scorch-marks upon his hide. A roar of triumph echoed above as Ni'Bara climbed up over the city wall heading for the other mirrored Ni'Bara who had begun to flee.

"Damn it!" Enyk roared in rage, swinging his gaze around the dragon who groaned in pain as his life started to ebb away. "You embarrassing piece of... Argh!" he screamed out loud, punching the dragon's hide.

He ran his hand through his hair in frustration as he turned back towards Kyne and as he pulled his hand away, clumps of hair were clutched between his fingers.

"It will consume you," Kyne murmured. "It will drive you mad."

"It doesn't matter!" he spit, and he tossed the hair to the ground. "Nothing matters but my mission! The mission I was tasked with! Do not confuse..."

A flash of gold towards the citadel caught his attention and they turned to see Aaldra flying through the air towards them, someone clutched in his hand. As he alighted next to Enyk, Kyne's heart sank as he dropped Kioni's limp figure to the ground. His eyes were glowing wildly with golden energy that hummed and buzzed as he looked upon Kyne with annoyance.

"My son, I will take care of him," and he took a few steps towards Kyne. The Lord of the Dominion, blood dripping from his scalp made the air vibrate with power as a spear of lighting formed from Xeono.

Enyk's face changed from confusion to a contorted rage and

The Legend of Kyne: Chronocide

with a scream he drew his hand back before launching a dragonrend straight for Aaldra's turned back.

It cut straight through him and collided into the ground directly in front of Kyne launching him back from the force in a heap of dust.

Kyne coughed hard, his mind swaying with disorientation and confusion at what had just happened, but he managed to roll to his hands and knees. Enyk was looking down upon Aaldra's torn body, his eyes full of hate. He was mouthing something unheard to him and Kyne saw blood bubbling from Aaldra's lips.

Saathe was nearby, standing next to Ky'Ren and with shock, Kyne watched as a silvery wisp was drawn from the dragon's mouth. Holding it out to Enyk, he withdrew a second wisp and started to walk towards Kioni.

Kyne tried to scream, his voice cracking and he collapsed onto his forearms. He could hardly move, let alone stand but he had to do something!

"It will be but a moment my lord," Saathe hissed as he lifted Kioni up by the neck, the point where he touched his skin freezing a sickly blue. Kioni screamed and kicked hard but then suddenly started gasping as Saathe opened his mouth.

"Wait," Enyk said suddenly, the wisp of Kioni's soul just within the confines of his lips. "Use him instead."

Saathe dropped Kioni to the ground who began to violently cough. Turning to Enyk, Saathe looked for a moment with hesitation at what he was asking. Enyk's face contorted. "Now!"

Saathe's face went flat, and he swept down picking up the broken body of Aaldra. Blood coated his robes, a massive slice nearly severing him in two, but he still groaned. He was still alive.

"See Father, at least you will be able to do one thing for me. You will help me unlock the gate, unlock the bindings that hold our world!"

Saathe breathed in, a silvery wisp leaving Aaldra's lips and brought it to the others that hovered above Enyk's outstretched palm.

Each wisp was different, and as they drew around each other they began to pulse and react, swirling faster and faster.

"This is the end Kyne, when I come back, we will have a chat!"

The Legend of Kyne: Chronocide

and he laughed as he brought the souls together in a glowing orb. It began to swell, swirling around him as it grew in size.

Panic ripped through Kyne. He could hardly move; he didn't have the strength to stop him.

You have to Kyne, spoke Ni'Bara's thoughts.
It will probably kill me and create a fell region.
You have to.

"Aven igni!"

Kyne forced his aura, every ounce of it into the spell, morphing the world around his body. He could feel his energy rapidly draining, darkness flooding in but just before it snuffed him out, he felt his body contort and twist and then it was colliding with Enyk.

He had to focus, his head swimming as he formed the words of the spell, the spell that would kill both of them but the moment he touched Enyk, his mind stretched, and he felt his body scream in pain as it began to distort. He could feel his atoms pulling apart, dozens and hundreds of him and Enyk trailing around them as their time threatened to split.

He was too weak to care, too weak to scream. All he could do was wait as the distortion intensified beyond anything he had ever experienced, the swirling sphere of souls engulfing both of them in their power. His body tore apart, Enyk's as well, and they seemed to swirl together, creating ungodly mixtures as their thoughts intertwined and as they were dragged away, what followed was silence.

87. The Caretaker

Kyne awoke, face first upon smooth white marble, his ears ringing. He groaned, his head and body throbbed and ached, but the feeling was fading away. He pushed up to his knees, rubbing his eyes briefly as if in an attempt to clear his head.

His hands no longer hurt, the scorch marks long gone, faded away replaced by scales on his left and human skin upon his right. His fatigue was also gone, as if he had been completely replenished.

He looked around, confused with what he was seeing. It was a massive room and upon further inspection it seemed to have no end, stretching to a blurred line. Beautiful ornate oak pillars spread around with bookshelves linking between them nearly twenty feet high, the ceiling another twenty feet above their tops. From his angle, he could only make out the single long corridor like stretch between two bookshelves that he lay in between.

He stood up.

Light shined from glowing orbs high above tucked against the ceiling as if they were little stars, illuminating everything in their reach. The space was vast, turning to both sides, he traced his gaze down the bookshelf noticing a junction not too far away. Hoping for answers, he began a brisk walk, his feet silent upon the marble.

Coming to the end of his row, he peered around the corner and to his shock noticed hundreds more towering bookshelves, all in parallel as they came to the crossroad as it itself stretched out of view. He was completely surrounded, aisle upon aisle, the library never ending as it stretched all around him.

He swung his head around, looking at the ceiling and then back down from where he came, the stretch of books constant. None of them seemed to be missing, with each having a small inscription of unfamiliar symbols upon them written in a language he did not know. Some were thin, only a few pages, while others were monstrous in size as wide as his outstretched hand was long.

He reached out to grab one when movement caught his attention, stopping his hand inches from the book. A man, deep wrinkles etched into his face and his body thin, and delicate stood nearby, his arm outstretched above him as he slid a book into place before reaching for another.

Kyne's pulse leapt to full speed, and he fumbled to grab onto his blade, but the man seemed to not notice or care. He withdrew a book, flipped through a few pages before swinging a thin strip of cloth in like a bookmark. As he shut the book, the part of the book behind the marker vanished.

He nodded as if satisfied and then placed the book back before reaching for another.

"Where are we?" Kyne asked, taking a step towards the man.

The man remained silent, drawing another book and performing the same action, this one shrinking dramatically leaving it only a few pages thick.

"Where are we?" Kyne said again, more forcefully.

"Hmm," mumbled the old man and he turned towards Kyne as if just noticing him.

Dressed in white robes, covering everything down to the ground, the old man stood with an apparent hunch. His hair and beard were both long, white in color just like his robe and his face was littered with splotches and weathering, deep fissures carved into the skin. But his eyes. His eyes looked young and full of authority.

He mumbled again before turning to look at Kyne.

"You shouldn't be here you know."

"And where should I be?" Kyne replied, letting go of his blade.

"The other one was supposed to win, kill you in battle before you could stop him. Ahh, he is with you I see," he sighed, looking to his side as a confused Enyk stepped into view. He was puzzled, looking around in shock but as their eyes met, his brow narrowed, and he drew his hand back.

He screamed and swept his arm through the air, Kyne raising his own hands to block it but no dragonrend appeared cutting the

The Legend of Kyne: Chronocide

bookshelves to pieces. Just his echo as it faded away around the hall of books.

Enyk tried again, swiping his arms repeatedly but nothing seemed to happen. He spoke no words, just emitted pure rage as he took off running at full speed toward Kyne.

Kyne matched him, rushing forward, his hand upon his blade's hilt. He knew Enyk had no weapon of his own, this was his chance to strike him down!

Suddenly the bookshelves began to vibrate softly and then everything changed, the shelves moving and shifting around, the floor dragging both of them apart before cutting them off as more shelves shifted into position. The vibrating intensified and then they all started to flicker and vanish, the marble floor turning to a rich and earthy brown adorned with long grasses and flowers.

Kyne could see hundreds of small rivers cutting across the landscape. Their silver serpentine shape carved around the area forming the making of a healthy marshland. Some came together with smaller streams jutting out of their joining and trailing away, growing in size before joining another. It was like a net, each fiber a river as it wound its way over the land, meeting and joining others in intricate patterns. Some were dammed off, the water pooling up but never overflowing.

The trickle of water was a constant rumble as Kyne swept his gaze around, the glare from the sun above making it hard to see. After a moment he noticed that the old man gone. A short distance away, he watched a middle-aged woman come into view, rounding a small bush and walking through a stream. Her hands were covered with mud and as if on cue, she knelt down, drawing muddy earth up creating a dam blocking off the water.

Expecting the water to continue flowing over the embankment, topping it over, Kyne was surprised to see it seem to stop in place, as if the water had stopped flowing down that stream all together.

"And yet you are still here," she said as she stood up. "You feel so much like the other one. Tell me, how did you get here?"

"I don't know," Kyne started. "I don't even know where I am."

"You are in the In Between," she chuckled as she crawled out of the stream, traipsing over the grassy embankment and entering another one. She continued walking away from Kyne a short distance before she knelt down, starting work on another dam.

"Who are you?" Kyne asked as he approached.

"I am merely the Caretaker, the mender of lines if you must. I tend to these fields, controlling the flow of water when necessary."

"And where is Enyk?"

She gestured to the side and Kyne turned to see Enyk a far distance away speaking with another figure, whose back was to him. They turned, revealing an identical woman to the one he was speaking to and as she gestured towards him, Kyne watched as his twin noticed, as if they were looking through a mirror. Without hesitation, Enyk took off running, mud and grass tore up as he bolted straight for Kyne, his far-off scream carried by the light breeze.

"No matter how many times I encounter this man, he never seems to change," muttered the woman and she swept her hand. The ground shuddered and changed, the sky and grass and dirt all vanishing into a long building. The roofing was glass, allowing bright sunlight to stream in. Along each of the walls was a wall of plants, ivy and different vines creeping up, stretching for more surface to grow.

A young girl, perhaps fourteen in age was nearby, a pair of shears in her hand as she untangled a messy knot of competing vines before cutting one. The instant it was cut, the plant shuddered and then seemed to harden into stone.

Scanning the wall Kyne noticed dozens and hundreds of plants had been changed to stone, some long, some short. At the end of what Kyne decided was a sort of greenhouse he could see through doorway into another rectangular room, identical to this one.

The young girl began to walk away.

"Wait, please explain!" Kyne said causing her to stop mid-stride. As she turned around, Kyne could see the same eyes that the previous two incarnations had but her brow was furrowed.

"Explain what? Explain how your insistent meddling has created nearly unfathomable knots in the strings of reality? How did you, a simple mortal human, manage to cause so much damage in such a short time? In all of my existence... In all of existence, I have never had to do this!" and she gestured to the wall, more vines being noticed that were all entangled together. "It's never ending!"

"I didn't mean..."

"Mean to what?" she replied, her voice carrying intense annoyance. "Mean to disrupt the natural order of things? This stems from him," and she shook her head. "His meddling in his family affairs affected more than he could realize."

Kyne was confused and then suddenly he realized who she was talking about. "You mean the Light?"

She nodded, her lip twitching and pursing in annoyance.

"So, it was killing the Darkness that knocked the timeline off balance?"

She nodded again and as she turned away, the scene changed again. The ground and sky turned an opaque white. The plants vanished and a few wells began to appear, stone grey very different than the white of everything else.

Kyne looked around for the girl, but she was gone. Enyk and the other were also nowhere to be seen.

A well was nearby and as Kyne drew closer, someone seemed to phase into being, a young man, similar in age to himself. His arms were outstretched above the well, picking at something unseen.

As Kyne cautiously approached, he watched as strange strings came into view, stretching up through the wells opening and reaching far up into the air out of view. Each string was incredibly thin, like spider silk and he watched as the Caretaker delicately plucked the strings apart, untangling them before withdrawing a thin blade and cutting a few.

"What is this?" Kyne muttered as he stepped up, his hand reaching towards the strings. As his fingers brushed them, he suddenly got intense images of hundreds of people, all different ages and different times at the final moment of their death. Children dying from illness, men dying in war and women in childbirth. Some were elderly, dying upon their deathbeds and others were young, infants not even taking their first breath.

He recoiled, his mind racing with horrific thoughts.

"The lines of every human that has ever or ever will live," the Caretaker replied. He withdrew a tangle of knots and held it out to Kyne. "Your meddling, your *mistake* is what caused this," and he shook

The Legend of Kyne: Chronocide

the knot at him. "Wwhat caused him," and then he gestured to the other side of the well where Enyk had appeared with an elderly woman.

Kyne met his gaze, but Enyk no longer ran, he just stared in an intense anger, his eyes carrying hate and they watched as the two caretakers walked together, phasing into one, the young man remaining.

"I could just erase you," he muttered, reaching up and grabbing a string. As he pulled it out, Kyne noticed it was different than the rest, splitting in two like a split river. "I could cut you back when you were a child, ending your life before any of this could happen."

"You couldn't!" gasped Kyne, fear striking through his voice. "If that happens... Then everything, everything I have done will be..."

"Undone," the caretaker chuckled. "Severing the knots that you caused would be far easier than trying to untangle the disaster the two of you have created. The fact that you made it here at all is astonishing."

"He interfered," Enyk hissed. "Interrupted my endeavor, my goal to free the world!"

The Caretaker listened as if interested before nodding his head. "Yes, he did I'm afraid. Interrupted what damage you caused quite spectacularly. He leapt through time, more like forced his way through it. He wasn't supposed to make it back to your time you know. He was supposed to be sent *elsewhere*, somewhere far off in the distant past, unable to ever return. It's quite puzzling though. How did you manage that young Kyne?"

Kyne shrugged. "I focused on where I wanted to go, on getting to Rosé. Once I heard what *he* did to her I knew I couldn't let that happen."

"Interesting," the Caretaker murmured, releasing the string and letting it fall back into the darkness of the well.

"I can fix this," Kyne said suddenly. "Send me back and I can fix it."

"Absolutely not!" roared Enyk and he bolted towards Kyne, his claws reaching for his throat.

The Caretaker tapped his foot and Enyk grew rigid, his eyes frozen.

"What did you do to him?" asked Kyne, gasping in shock.

The Legend of Kyne: Chronocide

"Gave him some time to think," the Caretaker chuckled. "Every second, each one that you experience will be perceived in his mind as twenty-five years. Unable to move as his body is still feeling the real time. Unable to sleep, unable to even turn his eyes for to do so would take him years of concentration for such a minuscule task."

He waved his hand, Enyk gasping and collapsing onto the ground. He curled up into a fetal position and wailed out loud a blood curdling hysterical screech.

"Ten seconds, that's all we felt but what did he feel Kyne?"

"Two hundred and fifty years," he said slowly, his body shuddering at the horrific thought. *Two hundred and fifty years of staring at the same point, unable to move and only left with your thoughts.*

"Indeed," he chuckled. "Now, your offer intrigues me. I will give you one chance to undo this mess, but if you fail, I will gift you with the experience I gave him... Forever."

He swept his hand and Kyne suddenly felt like he was falling, falling through darkness until he landed on his abdomen in cool sand.

Gasping for breath, he lifted his head up, orange torchlight lit up a large cavern. Massive columns of human skulls stretched up to the roof, the light causing their shadows to shift and dance like an ethereal play.

I... I am back?

A swirl of energy began to form nearby, and he watched as his past self-came into being.

Kyne's eyes widened, realizing how fast he had to move.

"Oo'nar!" he cried, ripping a gale up and sending sand flying all around obscuring both of their figures. The past Kyne turned in shock and met his gaze for a moment before Kyne screamed, "Erodath!"

A force slammed into the past Kyne's body, launching him far out into the water where he landed with a loud splash.

Cries of shock rang through the sandstorm as the two reapers searched for the source but just as Kyne noticed their figures appearing in the wall of sand, their approach eminent, he was suddenly falling again, the world swirling and turning white before he landed, dropping to his knees panting hard.

"Well done," the Caretaker said with a light clapping of his hands.

"Did I do it?"

"That you did. The timeline will now be able to be mended. He will however need to be dealt with," and he looked over at the still wailing Enyk."

"What about my skipping through time? Won't this just happen again?"

"I have mended that for now. I will keep you stable."

"Why is this happening?" Kyne asked.

"Because we are off balance," he replied, and he turned away from the well looking off to the distance as a strange building began to form. It contained no walls, just many columns that held up a flat roof, all carved out of pristine marble. Situated on a small, raised platform, the structure was an elegant but simple masterpiece.

The caretaker gestured for Kyne to follow, and they walked up towards it, their steps eerily silent. As they passed inside, the columns began to shift and morph, swirling into strange shapes. The Caretaker pointed at one and Kyne watched it change from a column to a beautiful white bird.

Realization filled his mind and as they looked at the column next to it, Kyne noticed it had been broken into three large pieces. It shifted, an identical black bird appearing, broken and fragmented as it lay upon the ground. Above the roof teetered, pieces of marble cracking and falling to the floor like snowfall.

Kyne looked around, seeing more columns shifting, beings coming into view. A twin headed serpent with the body of a man was one, and a single twisted double helix was another. He wanted to study all of them, understand what they meant but the Caretaker spoke catching his attention.

"They were but children, still are children," he corrected himself. "Able to do so many things but still just children. The Light as you call him didn't truly grasp the consequences of his actions, what destroying his brother would truly do to all of the others, and he gestured at the remaining columns.

"So, there are more?" Kyne whispered.

"The Light and Dark are but only a small part of the Omni, the All. The primal gods that shape the fabric of reality. Your Light, the creator did many great things, your existence is evident, but it is still but a part of the great whole."

"And with the Dark's death everything is off balance?"

He nodded. "The Destroyer provided balance, everything in the All needs to have balance for without it we unravel."

"What do we do?" Kyne walked over to the dark bird statue, picking up one of the three pieces, light as a feather. He could feel the power, the utter chaos within and he shuddered.

"Nothing can be done."

"Why though?" Kyne said, turning the fragment over in his hand. "Why can't we just put the pieces back together? Form a support without actually bringing him back?"

The caretaker paused for a long moment. "I have never thought about that. Bring the Destroyer back but only in body not in mind? I do not know but maybe... Maybe that just might work."

"Let's try then," Kyne said reaching for another piece, but the Caretaker stopped him.

"I will consult with the others. We are all one, we decide things as one."

Kyne nodded and he placed the other piece gently back down. He wanted to ask about the Light, if he could see him but something inside his heart told him that he wouldn't, and it wasn't the place to ask. If the Light wanted to see him, he would've done so by now.

They walked out of the building back down to the well, Kyne looked around and noticed a few others nearby. Each was a simple stone well with millions of thin strands stretching up from their depths.

"So, are those the Dragon's and the Riel's timelines?"

The Caretaker nodded.

"And what is that one?" he said pointing at a fourth nearby.

Before he could answer, Enyk had risen, his eyes wild with madness.

"I will kill you! I will kill you all!"

The Caretaker shook his head. "The timeline has been fixed I'm afraid. Your timeline no longer exists which means that you should no longer exist." Raising a hand to the twin he held it out as if offering a hand to him.

"I can't! I won't! I have to complete my task!" he screamed, his voice manic and wild.

"Unfortunately, you will not be doing that. The atrocities you have committed are unforgivable. The millions killed and tortured. Kyne, son of Aaldra, you who disowned your birthright, went against everything you were taught as a child and desecrated the world with your rage, you will spend the rest of existence in that perpetual stasis that I gave you a taste of. Eternal time to reflect upon your wrongdoings."

Enyk's face contorted into a look of fear, and he took a few steps back, "No! No! I can't go back, I can't! Please!"

"No," the caretaker said softly. "Judgment has been decided."

"I will not go back!" a mutated voice roared from Enyk. "I will destroy all of you!"

Suddenly a black shadow poured out of his eyes, gliding through the air in a swirling mass of dark wings. Oily black skin covered its body, stretching upon thick root like tendrils that spread behind it like dozens of tails. With eyes flat and white, it screeched before darting up towards the building of the All.

Kyne's skin crawled as he realized what it was, the power, the pressure, the feeling could only be one thing.

"It's a seraph!" he gasped.

"Once but no longer, reduced to a fiend," muttered the Caretaker. "I wondered if that's where he had gone. The pieces of mystery are beginning to fall into place."

The fiend glided up, sweeping over the statue of the Dark and then was hurtling back towards them, the three pieces clutched in its clawed grip.

The Caretaker waved his hand as if he had grown tired of what was transpiring and a beam of energy flew towards the seraph, but it evaded it, weaving around a well of strings before heading towards Kyne.

Another beam flew towards it causing it to swerve out of the way gliding up at a steep angle. Arcing around, a roar screeched from its jaw, and it breathed a wave of black angelic flame, swallowing the Caretaker in its fury and causing him to scream in pain as he was consumed.

It came to a stop, hovering near Kyne. It was much smaller

The Legend of Kyne: Chronocide

than the others, as big as he was but he could feel the power flooding from it, just the same as the others.

"So, you must be Elucia," Kyne muttered.

"No longer Elucia!" it snarled. "I am Marok, do not mistake me! I have renounced the Light, forsaken my siblings for something far more that only Dark could've given me!

Kyne drew his blade, the feather catching the fiend's eye.

"How is it that a mortal is allowed to hold a piece of a god?" he hissed in astonishment. Marok drifted around, never taking his eyes away from Kyne.

"Given to a mortal from a god," Kyne replied, and he pulled back, taking a stance of challenge towards the beast. "A mortal who with it has slain a god!"

"The Dark is eternal Kyne of Kydrëa. I know who you are, I have seen your thoughts as your twin has. I know your aura does not work here; do not think it will save you from me. I will be the one to get revenge upon you and restore the cosmos back to the way it was. Empty!" Black fire started to pour out of his mouth, falling softly to the ground and spreading around as he glided slowly forward pressing Kyne back until he was up against the well.

"I don't need my aura; I can kill you with…"

Suddenly a beam of energy collided with the fallen seraph's side, tearing part of its body apart and leaving pieces hanging in the air like oil suspended in water. It screeched whipping around before darting away, another attack flying from the Caretaker who had crawled to his feet.

The fiend swept around flying away but suddenly stopped mid-flight before rocketing back, the creature being dragged back by the Caretakers power. The young man's calm face had changed to that of rage, his skin burned partially away revealing strange lights within.

Kyne could feel the power, the power only comparable to a god pouring from the Caretaker and it scared him more than nearly anything else. He could feel the primal force tearing the seraph back, dragging it as if it were nothing but a child. Marok flailed in rage and fear, the sound piercing Kyne's ears as it writhed, twisting and turning while spewing dark fire all around. Suddenly it jerked to the side, colliding with another well's tangled web of strings.

The Legend of Kyne: Chronocide

It screamed and bathed the air again in black fire when suddenly it broke free from the Caretaker's hold. Like an animal trapped in a net, it flailed around, slamming into the ground and then into the well cracking the stone with the force. Another bellow of flame erupted and then a sickening snap as thousands of strings tore apart.

The fiend darted away, pulling hard against its bindings and stretching them out as it approached Kyne, its momentum slowing until it was but a few feet away.

Kyne could see it, the look of pure evil within its eyes as they met and for but a brief moment, the world seemed to freeze.

A crash and then the entire well was torn apart, releasing the hold upon the fiend where it tackled Kyne in its tangled web of strings launching them both back into Humanities well in a flash of light!

Kyne awoke, laying upon his back in the courtyard of Alakyne. The citadel was untouched, the morning sun stretching up over the wall casting its light upon the towers and beautiful windows.

He groaned, his head pounding, and he rolled over, noticing to his relief Auriel and the others all next to him. He grabbed her shoulder, drawing her awake and then Ni'Bara rumbled.

Even Kioni and the eastern woman Akami were there, and on his other side he saw Rosé.

He smiled, not knowing what had happened but grateful that everything was back to normal.

The moment lasted for but a few seconds and then the world shuddered, their bodies distorting and stretching apart, threatening to tear.

They cried out in pain, all of them writhing upon the stone ground as it seemed to swell, expanding and morphing as if the very land was changing. The distortions intensified, tearing at their bodies with more force and Kyne screamed, his voice filling the sky. Massive hovering islands came into being, miles above them and appearing over the landscape.

He twisted his head, fighting the pain and watching as far to the east a mountain unlike anything he had ever seen came into view, crawling up into the sky and crushing the earth beneath its weight.

Dozens of more islands appeared, many miles in size with one

744

materializing directly overhead. The world groaned and everything vibrated, buildings spreading apart and walls cracking from the strain. The land swelled, stretching as new stone and earth took form, splitting everything apart.

The distortion slowed, the trembling quieting and their pain receded. All were gasping upon the ground, sweat dripping down their noses. Kyne could see Auriel's hand next to his and he placed his hand over hers.

Rosé cried out in shock and Auriel flipped her hand up, clenching onto Kyne's hand, her finger interlocking tightly with his. Kioni grabbed a hold of Akami, hoisting them both up and Ni'Bara swept his tail around them like a protective shield.

The citadel behind shuddered as towers fell, the wall of Alakyne splitting into pieces and then dark figures began to fall from the islands far to the ground below where they landed on all fours.

"What's going on?" screamed Auriel as she drew her blade, releasing her hand from Kyne.

He had no idea, he just watched as hundreds of wraiths crawled to their feet, their mouths agape revealing a deep darkness that craved one thing more than anything else.

Souls.

The Legend of Kyne: Chronocide

The World of Kyne

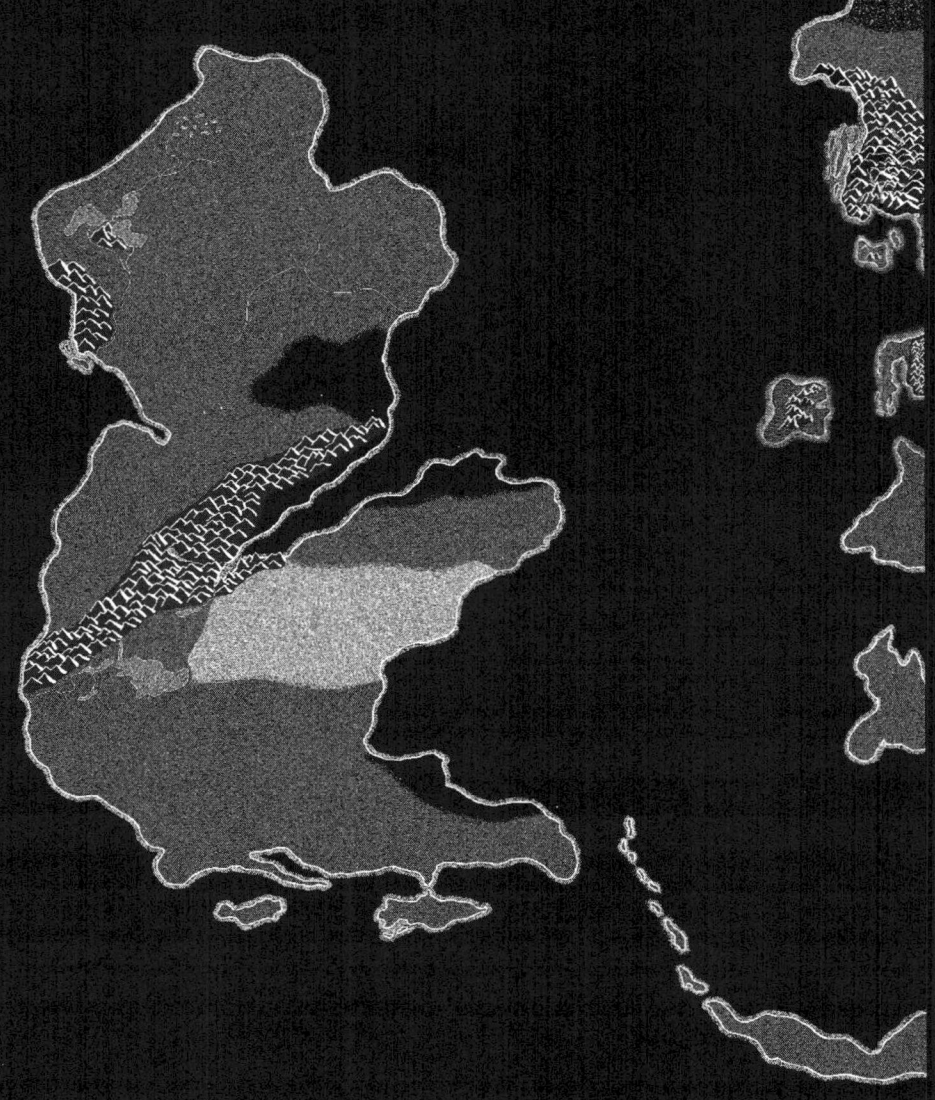

The Legend of Kyne: Chronocide

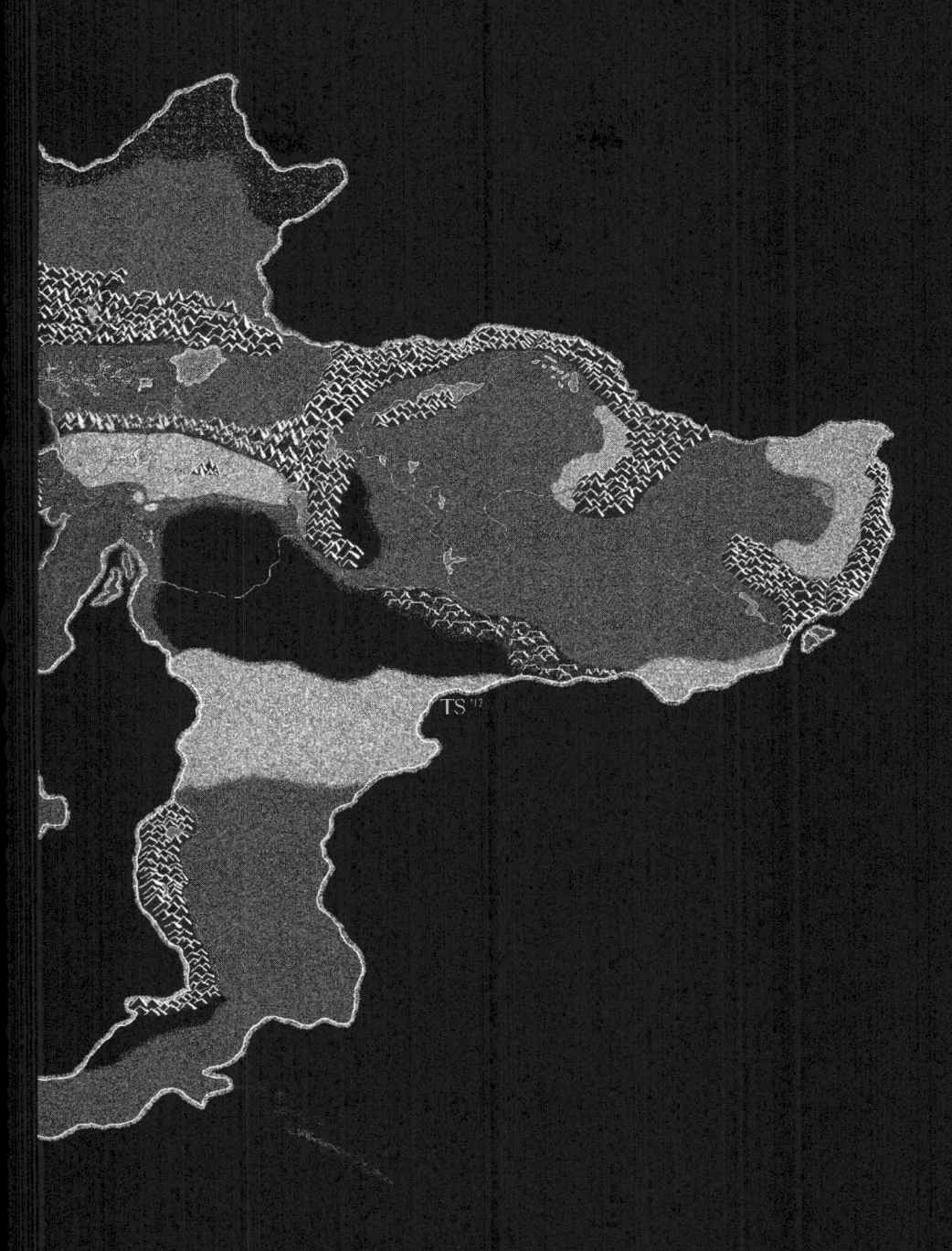

The Legend of Kyne: Chronocide

The Legend of Kyne: Chronocide

The adventure continues:

The Legend of Kyne
Omnicide